A.W. Mykel is the author of
The Windchime Legacy and
The Salamandra Glass,
both published by Corgi.
He lives in San Antonio, Texas.

THE LUXUS

A.W. Mykel

CORGI BOOKS

THE LUXUS

A CORGI BOOK 055 2 13871 1

First publication in Great Britain

PRINTING HISTORY

Corgi edition published 1992

This book is set in 9½/10½ pt Cheltenham Roman
by Colset Private Limited, Singapore.

Corgi Books are published by Transworld Publishers Ltd, 61–63
Uxbridge Road, London W5 5SA, in Australia by Transworld
Publishers (Australia) Pty Ltd, 15–23 Helles Avenue, Moorebank,
NSW 2170, and in New Zealand by Transworld Publishers (NZ)
Ltd, 3 William Pickering Drive, Albany, Auckland.

Made and printed in Great Britain by
BPCC Hazells Ltd
Member of BPCC Ltd

For Carl

I'll miss the nights at the Wiggy; shuffleboard at the Terrace Tavern until we'd close the place down; bowling at 2.00 a.m., too drunk to see the pins; and the nights we spent telling the same old stories and laughing until our sides ached.

I am grateful for those memories, and for a thousand more that visit me more these days. I'm grateful for the friendship we shared.

I knew no man more generous, sincere, and utterly dependable. I was proud to call him my friend . . . and my brother. I will miss him.

Prologue

PONT L' EVEQUE., FRANCE: The damp, changeable weather had a distinct English quality to it. Indeed, the countryside, with its gentle hills broken by hedgerows into a patchwork of small, brilliantly green fields and pastures, reminded him more of the pastoral south of England than of the north of France. It was a quiet and timeless place where nothing had changed in the past hundred years except the generations who worked the land. For Rafael Sonterra it was a place of frequent refuge.

The sounds of a sturdy door moving on old hinges broke the morning stillness. Sonterra's eyes shifted to the familiar half-timbered farmhouse across a narrow pasture and to the figure stepping along the walkway and into the ankle-high ground cover.

He liked watching Greta. He had from the first moment he saw her, nearly six years earlier. She had seemed back then almost waiflike, all eyes and innocence. But it wasn't innocence that had led her to the place of their first meeting. She had come to hear his words, to learn the ways of revolution. And it was his words that had captured her – his words and the dark, penetrating eyes staring out at her from behind the kaffiyeh he wore to conceal his appearance.

Her beauty had intrigued him, and he watched her for long periods of time from a distance as her training progressed. There were times when she felt his gaze on her and turned to find him staring. His magnificent eyes spoke the chemistry that destined them to be lovers.

It wasn't until a year later that they met again, in private and at his choosing. He wore no kaffiyeh this time; the name Rafael Sonterra provided not even a clue to the man

7

standing before her. But she knew, the moment she saw those dark eyes and felt them looking clear through her to her naked soul, that they were the eyes of the great fighter she had heard speak. And they became lovers that night.

Sonterra watched as Greta high-stepped through the dew-laden growth, her breath wisps of quickly vanishing vapor in the brisk morning air. She crossed the narrow brook between them, stepping on two flat rocks rising above the water. She nearly slipped on the second as she pushed off. It made him smile.

His fingers completed a final corkscrew twist in the paper matchstick, giving it the precise symmetry of a drill bit. He let it slip from his fingers to the grass beside him to join several others, all exactly alike, victims of this small, unconscious habit.

Greta trudged up the steep slope to where he was sitting, and plopped down on her knees in front of him. Her nose was pink from the cold air and she was short of breath. She was wrapped in a fluffy down blanket, and from beneath it she produced a small bottle of Calvados, the delicious apple brandy for which lower Normandy was famous.

'You left the house early this morning,' she said, handing the open bottle to him.

'Yes, the morning was beautiful,' he said in his low, nearly monotonal way of speaking, a trace of Spanish accenting his English.

'You missed a wonderful breakfast. Madame Morvan prepared an *omelette Mère Poulard*. She knows how much you like it.'

'I wasn't hungry,' he returned. He shifted his position so that she could sit between his legs and lean back against his chest. He wrapped his arms around her, his left hand sliding in under the blanket to rest on her belly. He had learned just two weeks ago, when she had joined him at the safe house, that she was expecting his child. She was in her fourth month and just beginning to show. He liked to feel the bulge, to have contact with his son.

8

'Madame Morvan says it will be a boy,' Greta announced, taking the bottle from his hand and setting it down so both his hands would be free. 'The way she fusses and beams, you'd think it was her grandchild. She's very fond of you, you know. So is her husband.'

'I know that,' he said. 'They're good and trusted friends. I've always been generous with them, and they with me. We go back many years to a time when there were few friends.'

Just then his hand felt a tiny kick, the very first.

Greta sat erect, her hand going to his. 'Did you feel that?' she asked, her voice jumping with excitement.

There was another feeble stirring.

'Meet your little Rafael,' she said, looking back into his face. What she saw was almost unbelievable. There was a smile . . . and what almost looked like tears welling up in his eyes.

He kissed her cheek tenderly, then tightened his embrace to bring her closer.

'Are you happy?' she asked.

'Yes, very,' he replied, pressing his cheek against hers. 'You've given me the greatest gift.'

There was little in the life of Rafael Sonterra that brought happiness. There were moments of triumph and mad exhilaration that followed his victories, but none that brought *happiness*. One did not do the things that Rafael Sonterra did to derive happiness from them.

They sat for a time in silence, caught by the wonder of the moment.

'I'll gain weight, you know. I'll . . . get ugly,' Greta said. 'Will you still love me when I'm ugly?'

He put his hand to her face and kissed her gently. 'You'll never be ugly to me,' he told her.

'I'm just beginning to show. You won't say that when I look like a melon.'

'You'll be a beautiful melon,' he said, then coaxed her gently, hinting that it was time to return to the house.

They rose to their feet, exchanged a short kiss, and began negotiating their way back toward the house.

'When does Kammal arrive?' she asked.

'Today. Before dark.'

She paused for a moment before asking the next question, because she knew the answer was one she didn't want to hear. 'And when will we leave Pont l'Eveque?'

'Tomorrow. You and Kammal will leave very early, before the Morvans rise. I will leave sometime later,' he answered.

'So soon,' she whispered. 'Then we'll have this one night together,' she said, taking him around the waist. One night to tap all of the passion within them. One night to celebrate life and the new happiness they shared.

It was after dark when Kammal arrived. The car moved slowly along the narrow lane and pulled into the open barn.

Sonterra stood well back in the darkest shadows as Kammal got out of the car. Just a precaution to be sure that it was, in fact, Kammal and not an enemy.

Kammal was late. That displeased Sonterra, who placed high value on precision in both timing and execution. But what displeased him even more was the car, a Mercedes 300 SL. Cars like that were noticed, and attention was the last thing they needed. Kammal's tastes were expensive, especially when it came to cars and women. If he wasn't careful, it would get him killed someday.

Sonterra slid silently out of the darkness as his friend closed the car door.

'You're late! What happened?' he asked.

Kammal jumped at the sound of the unexpected voice. He spun, his eyes straining to see into the darkness. 'You could have caused me a heart attack,' he said excitedly toward the figure he could not yet see, but whose voice he had immediately recognized. 'Worse yet, I could have been armed and shot you dead in blind reaction.'

'You would have missed,' the voice said from a new location, behind him now.

He turned to face Sonterra, and felt a finger tap his forehead.

'Bang, bang. You lose.'

Kammal shook his head and smiled in defeat. He never could beat Sonterra at anything.

'You're two hours late. What happened?' Sonterra asked, his irritation diminished by the little game.

'It was a longer drive than anticipated. I needed to stop for a short rest,' Kammal replied.

'Well, you're here now, and you're safe. That's the important thing, my brother,' Sonterra said, extending his open arms.

They embraced tightly, exchanging kisses of greeting on the cheeks. Sonterra pounded his friend's back affectionately, two things coming to his immediate attention. There was the distinct smell of a woman's perfume, and his friend had lost even more weight since the last time he had seen him.

'When have I ever let you down?' Kammal asked, their faces close in the darkness.

'Never,' Sonterra replied. The smell of liquor on Kammal's breath was unmistakable.

'How is Greta?' Kammal inquired.

'She's well. And expecting my child,' Sonterra announced.

Kammal was silent for a moment, trying to gauge the feelings behind the words. He had already learned this news from Greta. Both had been uncertain how Sonterra would react to the development. It seemed clear that he was pleased.

'Does this change anything?' Kammal asked, his voice a bit tentative.

Sonterra shook his head slowly. 'No, we go on as planned. But I want her safe. Should anything go wrong, I want her and the child away from danger.'

'I understand,' Kammal told him. 'She'll be half a world away, in complete safety,' he said with assurance.

'Come, let's go inside. Say hello to Greta and eat

11

something. You must be hungry. Then we'll talk,' Sonterra said, taking Kammal around the shoulders as they left the barn.

The reunion was a joyous one. Madame Morvan had prepared a delicious meal for the expected guest, and her husband had brought out his finest wine to celebrate the coming together of friends. The Morvans retired soon after the dinner was completed, to leave their guests in privacy. The old couple knew the routine and never asked questions.

Sonterra's concern for Kammal grew even deeper through dinner. He had watched the food pushed aside in favor of the excellent wine. They had been through a great deal together, and there was no other man alive whom he trusted more completely. Perhaps the strain of the past years had finally caught up with his friend, or perhaps the weakness had always been there and he had just refused to recognize it. Whichever was the case, he needed one last effort from this man whom he loved like a brother.

Time passed quickly and the hour grew late. Greta quietly excused herself, knowing that Sonterra would join her when he and Kammal had finished with their business.

The two men left the house and walked in the chilly darkness along the narrow, winding brook that meandered across the lower pastures. They walked for a time without speaking. Finally they stopped. Sonterra looked up into a clear night sky brilliantly speckled with stars. He stared upward as though in some prolonged prayer.

'I've waited so long for this,' he said at length, almost as if speaking to himself. 'This one great battle. I've lived for this moment, Kammal. It has been the whole purpose of my existence. Everything up to now has been but a prelude.'

'Yes, I know. And I understand,' Kammal said.

'No, you can't understand,' Sonterra replied, shaking his head ever so slightly. 'To want something so long and so badly, and then to get the chance ... *one* chance. It must be perfect.'

'It will be. Everything is ready.'

12

'Everything. Have we thought of *everything*?' he wondered out loud.

'It isn't possible to think of everything, my brother,' Kammal replied. 'Nothing would get done if we waited to satisfy every objection, to think out every alternative. We have thought of *enough* to make it work. A time comes when the plan must be trusted, or the planning goes on forever.'

Sonterra looked into his friend's face. 'Sometimes you sound just like your father.'

'I am my father's son. He was my teacher, too, or have you forgotten?'

Sonterra shook his head. 'I haven't forgotten.' Nor would he ever forget Abu Hassan Nasir, his greatest teacher, his 'father', the greatest man he had ever known. Abu Hassan had brought purpose into the life of Rafael Sonterra; had taught him wisdom and guile and the meaning of strength; had taught him patience and judgement; had developed within him the humility and confidence to become a true leader in whom the fire of leadership burned brightly, warming all who would follow. Abu Hassan Nasir had brought Rafael Sonterra to life in a world that thought him dead.

'You're right. We are ready . . . I feel it. And we *will* succeed. We *must* succeed.'

Sonterra looked at his watch. 'It's late, and you must leave before dawn. We had better go back so that you can rest.'

The two men turned and began their walk back to the house.

'The new codes, have you learned them?' Sonterra asked.

'By heart,' Kammal answered, the lie a little one. He knew most of the codes, but his memory wasn't what it used to be, grown dull from the alcohol and drugs that had invaded his life. He had been in the game for so very long, too long. And the longer it went on, the greater the price it extracted. Kammal Nasir did not have the strength of

13

Rafael Sonterra, and had never had the superior abilities of his 'brother'. He made up for those weaknesses by applying boundless effort. He drew his strength and courage from Sonterra's presence and leadership. But too often the men were apart – a separation of necessity in a world of danger. He needed the presence of Rafael Sonterra. In his absence, he buoyed himself with his high life-style, the cars, the women, the alcohol, and the drugs. He was just careful enough and fast enough to stay out of the path of oblivion. The chances that he took were, in fact, greater risks than he realized. He had come dangerously close to using up his share of luck.

The two men reviewed the details of their plan one last time. Kammal seemed very well prepared, which eased Sonterra's concern. If all went well for the next two months the plan would be in motion, unstoppable. Then he could take Kammal and Greta to safety and care for them.

'And when it's over, where will we go?' Kammal asked, sounding almost like a small child posing the question to his father.

'Anywhere that you wish,' Sonterra answered. 'Anywhere in the world.'

'Together?'

'When it has ended I'll have drawn all accounts even. Then it will be our time to live. You, Greta, my son, and I.'

'Together,' Kammal whispered.

'Together,' Sonterra repeated. 'In a better place.'

Greta's teeth bit into her lower lip as she fought back the sounds of her passion. She moved rhythmically as she sat astride her Rafael, perspiration glistening on both of their bodies. The goosedown quilt had been kicked aside, the heat of their lovemaking defeating the coolness of the room.

Being pregnant had changed Greta. Perhaps it had been the fear of becoming pregnant that had kept her passive and quiet in their past lovemaking. There was no longer any fear. It was fact, and it was wonderful. She was free to

14

express her love, to seek its pleasures. It was like rebirth. She aggressively sought everything she had missed before, and now hungered for new heights of satisfaction.

She was insatiable, every part moving and feeling and giving off fire. Her rhythm broke for a moment, her fingers digging into the tops of his shoulders as his hands gently kneaded her breasts. Her pelvis jerked, stopped, jerked again, then held still. He could feel her tighten on him, her face filled with euphoric tension, her eyes half closed and rolling upward. She held a moment longer, then began a slow rhythm again, her breathing coming in gasps. Her first of what would be many orgasms.

The tempo picked up again, the movements stronger now to bring Rafael to his climax. Just as he could feel her changing levels, she could feel his. She worked smoothly, picking up the rhythm to a faster and faster pace as she brought him nearer to climax.

Her pace was frantic now, as she built to another orgasm of her own. She could no longer fight back her gasps, and the sighs, which came softly at first, grew louder, matching her movements exactly until she gave out with what was nearly a scream, her body shuddering with convulsive ecstasy. At exactly the same moment Rafael's hands gripped her buttocks tightly, his own fulfillment coming in almost explosive spasms. They gasped and thrust forcefully against one another several more times, and then collapsed in spent satisfaction. Their breathing remained heavy for a few moments, then began a slow return to normalcy. They were totally entwined, in complete contact with one another, the wetness of their bodies enhancing their sense of closeness.

Greta kissed his face and his lips over and over, while her pelvis shifted to keep him inside her.

'I love you,' she said in a breathless whisper.

He smiled and held her tightly. They remained silent for a long time, caressing one another softly.

'It will soon be time for you to leave,' he said into her ear.

15

She tightened every part of herself against him. 'I don't want to leave you,' she said.

'You must. You know that.'

She let out a short breath, as if to protest. But she didn't, for she knew better.

'You know that,' he repeated.

'Yes, I know,' she said in a whisper.

'It won't be for very long.'

She nodded, her face tight against his neck.

'And above all, you must do what Kammal asks of you. Without question.'

She nodded again, silent tears in her eyes, wetting her cheeks and his neck.

'And our son must grow inside your body. He must be strong and healthy.'

'He will be,' she replied. 'And his father must come home to him,' she said after a short silence.

Sonterra smiled. 'I always do,' he said.

'There can always be a first time,' she said, her hand tracing the small scars that spanned his entire left side.

His left hand brushed away the hair from her face, and their eyes met. 'I *always* do,' he repeated.

Her right hand rose to catch his left. She looked at the scars that covered it. There had been one time, before she knew him, when he nearly didn't return. Once when some miracle spared him and not the others with him.

'It's time,' he said.

'Just one minute longer,' she pleaded.

At any other time he would have insisted that she move now to prepare for her departure. But he, too, wanted that one last minute together. So he held her, savoring every passing second.

She didn't have to be told again. She rose from the bed in complete silence and put on her clothes. She dressed quickly, without turning to look back at him. A soft knock sounded on the door as she finished the last buttons of her blouse.

She walked to the door and hesitated a moment, her

back still toward him. 'Until later, my love. Go safely,' she said, then opened the door and walked out.

A few moments later, Sonterra heard the faint sounds of the car doors, then the engine starting. The car revved smoothly, then pulled out of the barn and drove away from the safe house.

Sonterra remained in the bed for a few moments, looking out of the window. The sunrise was about an hour and a half away. The Morvans would be rising soon to start their daily routines.

He rose from the bed, dressed quickly, and left the room. He made his way quietly down the hallway toward the bedroom of his kindly hosts. In near-perfect silence he opened their door and slid into their room. He approached the side of their bed.

Madame Morvan was sleeping soundly under the protection of her partial deafness. Her husband rustled slightly, then settled, his face turned straight up toward the ceiling.

Sonterra leaned forward and placed his silenced Beretta on the pillow beside the old man's temple. He kissed the old man's forehead.

'Good-bye, my old friend,' he whispered.

The old man's eyes opened and blinked wearily, trying to focus on the face above his own.

Thud! Thud! The silenced weapon coughed.

'No more pain, and no more fear, old man,' Sonterra whispered. 'You go to a better life.'

Sonterra straightened up and shifted his aim to the old woman and, without remorse or hesitation, fired again.

1

MEDELLÍN, COLOMBIA: The rain was unending. The large white panel van was a stark contrast to the deep green of the forest through which it passed. Rock music blared loudly from bad speakers, and the windshield wipers scraped a noisy, uncoordinated rhythm. The driver's eyes were intent on the rain-soaked road, while the man in the seat beside him studied the map in his hands.

'This is the last bend,' the passenger said. 'It should be just ahead.'

The van rounded the bend into a final straightaway. Ahead of them lay the huge fenced compound of the Skyco Research Institute and the manned security entrance. The man beside the driver folded his map as the van coasted to a stop at the gate.

The guard looked out from the dry security shelter. The face behind the wheel of the uniform-service van was a new one. He stepped out of the small building and tucked the clipboard with the entry log under his arm to protect it from the rain. He went to the front of the van and made the routine entries, recording the registration tag number and the time of day, then approached the driver's window. He looked in.

The driver's face was not the only new one. So was the one belonging to the man in the passenger seat.

'Where's Costa today?' he asked, stretching his neck to make a closer inspection.

'Vacation,' the driver responded, holding out his employee badge.

The guard compared the picture on the badge to the face, noted the number on the log, then looked past

18

the driver to the second occupant, who also held out his badge so that it could be examined.

'So, Costa is on vacation,' the guard began. 'And where is Valdez?' he asked, lowering the clipboard.

'Sick, I suppose. He didn't show up for work today,' the driver replied.

The guard made a closer inspection of the side of the van. There was what looked to be a bullet hole in the door, just below the handle. He had seen this same van every week for the past two years, and there had never been a bullet hole in it before.

The guard stared without expression into the face of the driver. He peered into the driver's window, trying to see into the back of the van, but the inner panel door was drawn closed.

'Please step out,' the guard said, and backed away enough for the door to open.

'Is there some problem?' the driver asked.

'Please turn off your engine and step out,' the guard repeated, his tone quite serious. The clipboard went to his side in his left hand, while the right hand came to rest on the butt of his handgun.

'If you insist,' the driver replied. He shut off the engine and eased the door open.

The silenced weapon came into view at the same moment the driver cleared the door. The shot came through the open window from the passenger seat, hitting the guard in the throat.

The guard retched, and his hands clutched involuntarily at the wound. He dropped to his knees, a look of horrified disbelief on his face. He doubled over, almost to the ground.

The passenger moved over to the driver's seat and put another well-aimed shot into the top of the guard's head. The rear door of the van flew open following the second dull report of the weapon. The man who exited the van was wearing a uniform identical to the guard's. He took the guard's body under the arms and dragged it back into the security hut and activated the electric sliding gate.

The driver got back into the van and started the engine.

'No one is to enter,' he said. 'Wait twenty minutes, then disable the gate and head for the pickup area.'

The man nodded.

The engine revved and the van pulled through the gate and into the compound. The gate closed behind the vehicle.

The van moved slowly, observing the posted speed limit, and progressed into the compound proper. It zigzagged its way unerringly to the rear of the employees' building, which housed the locker rooms and the cafeteria. It backed up to the building and stopped. The driver killed the engine.

The two men got out of their seats and opened the interior sliding door leading back to the uniform bins. They stepped into the rear compartment, then closed the door behind them.

The driver's companion looked into the five anxious faces that had been concealed in the rear of the panel truck. He unfolded a sketch of the compound and laid it across one of the bins, checking it quickly to make certain of his bearings. He tapped the outline of Building Two.

'Quickly. There is no time to lose.'

One of the men handed him a subcompact Ingram with two staggered ammunition clips taped together. He inserted the clip and snapped the arming bolt. 'Let's go,' he commanded.

The back doors of the van opened and the seven men exited rapidly, moving with quiet precision away from the employees' building. They walked swiftly between two buildings and across a stretch of manicured lawn toward Building Two.

Ernesto Delgado, head of Medellín Research Institute security, rounded the bend in the road on the approach to the Institute. He brought his car to a stop at the gate and reached for his security badge. He didn't really take notice of the face in the security hut, his attention going to the knob of his radio to lower the volume. He reached for his hand-held radio and pressed the transmit button.

'This is Delgado. I'm at the main gate. I hope you boys have the coffee on,' he said into it.

'There's a full pot on, boss,' came an immediate reply.

That didn't mean a thing to Delgado. The pot was always empty by the time he got to it, which meant he had to make the next pot. His men seemed dedicated to keeping that tradition unbroken. 'There had better be *one* cup left in that pot when I get there,' he threatened. The threat, like the empty pot, was part of the tradition. One day they'd fool him and there would be a cup waiting. Maybe for his birthday, he thought.

Inside the compound, the intruders moved swiftly to the rear of Building Two, going directly to an emergency exit. The door was locked, designed to open only from the inside.

The driver produced a stout lock-pulling tool and screwed the bit deftly into the key slot. He locked the jaws on the doorknob and shoved the weighted grip down the shaft to the knob, then pulled it forcefully toward him. There was a sharp metallic crunch, and the lock came out cleanly.

The door was opened and the seven men filed in quickly. The last man in stayed at the emergency door, a second at the first landing, a half-flight up. The others moved rapidly up the stairwell.

The soft alarm at the central security console was immediate. The security officer's eyes went to the glowing light on the panel and he hit the switch just below it. Four video monitors responded instantly, showing the inside of the emergency exit area and the entire stairwell. He saw the armed intruders plainly as they scampered toward the floors above. The security officer tripped the alert switch, calling out the affected building and the entrance number into the microphone. The morning quiet of the compound was shattered by the wail of the alarm.

The sudden sound of the alarm stopped the intruders for a brief moment.

'*Go! Go!*' the leader shouted to get them moving again.

Delgado had only begun to feel his annoyance at the

slow response of the guard at the entrance when the sudden clamor of the alarm sounded.

He rolled down the window and stuck his head out.

'Open the gate, you idiot!' he shouted.

At the same instant he saw the face in the window and his eyes widened.

The guard came through the door quickly, gun in hand, and fired a deafening shot at the security chief. The bullet struck the roof post just beside Delgado's head. Delgado ducked quickly out of the line of fire and drew his weapon, then sprang back up.

The next shot was Delgado's, and was better aimed. The man in the guard uniform took the shot in the chest and was knocked back into the hut.

Delgado stamped down on the gas pedal and crashed through the gate.

He snatched up his radio. 'Report! Report! What's going on?' he screamed into it as he raced into the compound.

The assailants moved quickly and deliberately up the staircase. A third man stayed at the second-floor landing, with the rest continuing on. At the third floor a fourth man positioned himself at the landing, while the lock-pulling tool went into use again on the door to the third floor. In a matter of seconds the door was open.

The remaining three intruders burst through the door and ran straight into two female technicians.

The automatic weapons opened up in deafening unison, dropping the surprised technicians with devastating effect.

The three gunmen advanced down the hallway, adrenaline pumping full in their veins from the first ear-splitting discharges of their weapons and the relentless clamor of the alarm.

Ernesto Delgado sped through the compound at top speed, his radio held up to his ear with his free hand.

'Armed intruders have forced entry into Building Two through the west emergency stairwell,' a frantic voice screamed after a maddening delay.

'Converge on Building Two,' Delgado commanded as he

raced on. 'All internal units converge on the stairwell. Seal off the hallways to all laboratory wings. Get the helicopter ready, I'll meet the crew at the pad. Protect all security areas,' he commanded.

He pushed the accelerator to the floor and raced for the helipad, which had just come into view.

The intruders advanced farther down the hallway. Three technicians appeared from one of the labs to investigate the disturbance. The weapons opened up again, killing one of them. The other two ducked quickly back into the lab. The weapons kept firing in short staccato bursts to keep the hallway clear of the curious.

The gunmen raced to the lab where the technicians had retreated. One of the assailants tossed in a grenade; this action was followed shortly by the thump of the explosion and the sound of shattering glass.

Skyco security responded quickly to Delgado's orders. Heavily armed personnel converged rapidly on the violated emergency exit from the outside. Internally, armed personnel moved with military precision toward the affected stairwell on the lower levels to contain the attack.

The intruder positioned at the ground-level emergency exit opened fire on the forces approaching from the outside, dropping the nearest two.

Skyco security poured withering return fire at the doorway, driving the intruder to cover. Two grenades sailed through the air at the doorway, the first hitting the doorframe and bouncing away. The second was dead on, deflecting off the door and into the stairwell. The outside explosion was harmless to all but the building. The grenade in the stairwell, however, ended all armed resistance from that position with sudden and brutal punctuation.

A second later, elements of Skyco security, moving through the building, burst through the door at level one, spraying what was left of the two intruders at the lowest level with automatic weapons fire. Then they redirected a ferocious volley upward toward the second-floor landing at the intruder they knew to be there.

The man holding the second-floor landing tossed a surprise of his own in the form of a grenade. But the real surprise came when it failed to go off – a dud.

The intruder was caught between security personnel from below and those just coming through the door at the second level. The crossfire was murderous, taking him quickly. Two Skyco security men fell to wounds from ricochets – one to the leg, the other to the face.

The trio of gunmen on the third floor advanced toward the biogenetics wing. They were met just short of their objective by two security guards firing automatic weapons from behind good cover. The driver died instantly in the first exchange. A second intruder went down in the same volley, crying out from wounds to both legs. The advance toward the biogenetics wing stopped there, with all hope of further progress plainly ended. There was nowhere to go but back the way they had come.

The leader of the assault sprayed the hallway with a final flourish from his last clip, then picked up his wounded comrade in a fireman's carry, and began a swift retreat.

He discarded the empty Ingram and pulled his handgun, firing at anything that moved. He heard the ferocious sounds of conflict from the stairwell where his compatriot was holding off security forces approaching from below.

He reached the stairwell with additional Skyco security forces closing swiftly behind him. There was only one way to go, and the remaining three intruders took it, heading up the stairs toward the roof.

Skyco security pursued up the stairwell and unleashed a murderous volley of gunfire that caught the group just short of the steel fire door to the roof. All three went down in the concentrated firepower.

The leader rolled to his side, gasping from wounds to his leg and lower back. His men were dead and he was beyond all fear of dying. He picked up his partner's Ingram and discharged the last of the clip down the stairwell, then clawed his way to the fire door, pushed it open, and fell through the opening to the roof. The door had barely closed, muting the sounds in the stairwell, when he heard the helicopter.

He struggled to his feet and looked up to the hovering craft and the unclear figure of a man hanging out. He squinted into the driving rain and saw the rifle. The impact of the first shot knocked him back against the steel door, and his hip exploded with pain. A second shot tore through his left collarbone, crumpling him to the black and gritty roof surface.

He lay facedown and dazed, his nose and mouth filling with blood from the massive shoulder wound. He turned his head away from the spreading crimson pool and coughed. He fought the pain to keep himself conscious.

His neck and eyes strained as he looked up one more time at the helicopter. There was no escape, and no surrender. With all the strength he could muster, he dragged his right arm upward toward his chest and set the muzzle of his handgun under his chin. He hesitated just long enough to spit a vile curse at the hovering death above. Then he pulled the trigger.

SAN ANTONIO, TEXAS: The imposing estate of Asher Sky, set on four thousand acres of prime hill country north of San Antonio, was one of the most lavishly maintained personal residences and grounds in the country. The house was palatial, built entirely from native limestone; its garages, stables, and security and servant quarters all possessed equal charm. Beautiful gardens abounded all across the estate. There were three large swimming pools: the first, for staff members, was situated adjacent to their compound of buildings; the second, Olympic-sized, was for the guests, who often occupied the cabana-like apartments surrounding it; and the third, smaller than the others, was close to the house, in soft seclusion, for private use by the family.

There were four tennis courts, two with compound surfaces and two with grass. Beyond them were two croquet lawns and an eighteen-hole corporate golf course so well designed and maintained it would have been the envy of any country club.

The house, in addition to being Asher Sky's principal residence, had an entire wing from which every aspect of his varied business interests could be run. He used it on the infrequent days when he didn't feel like traveling the ten miles to the Skyco World Headquarters complex situated on four hundred acres off of the 1604 loop, north of the city. There weren't many days when he didn't go into the office, whether it was the one in San Antonio, Los Angeles, New York, London, Paris, or aboard his 747. But for Asher Sky, every day and all day were business hours. And at eighty-seven, the man was a dynamo in tune with every aspect of his empire, one of the largest privately controlled corporations in the world. He looked and acted sixty, but had the wisdom of a man who had done and seen more in one lifetime than any other ten men, and had an undying belief in tomorrow and man's ability to do *anything* he set his mind and will to do.

Asher Sky sat quietly beside his private pool, a large glass of iced tea in his hand, listening to the report being given by Tom Danziger, the head of Skyco's Department of Corporate Policy. This was an innocuous title giving cover to Skyco's corporate intelligence arm, whose capabilities rivaled that of a small nation-state. It utilized the latest in computer technology and high-tech snoop systems, and employed a number of experts with world-class experience. Business was war, and it was conducted with no less intensity.

Danziger carefully laid out every known detail of the attack on the Skyco Research Institute in Medellín. Sky didn't interrupt once, his spongelike mind absorbing every fact.

When Danziger had finished, Sky placed his half-empty glass on the table beside his chair and brought his finger-tips to his forehead, as if to shield his eyes from the sun.

'Seven of our people dead and three wounded,' he said

in a tone of painful disbelief. He held a long, pensive silence, which Danziger did not break.

'Who was responsible?' Sky asked at last.

'Unknown this soon. They carried no identification except for employee badges of the firm holding the linen contract. They turned out to be phonies.'

'It would have been helpful to take one alive,' Sky suggested.

'Yes, it would have been. But Delgado's men have been well trained, and in view of the situation, they responded with full force to protect the facility. We can't fault them,' Danziger replied.

'Can the attackers be identified?' Sky asked.

'I'm sure they can. We've already begun efforts. It shouldn't take long as far as the men are concerned, but as for who they represented, that could take some time.'

'So, we have no clue?'

'Nothing. But we know with reasonable certainty what they were after,' Danziger said.

'Building Two, third floor, biogenetics wing. The Luxus,' Sky said as if speaking to himself.

Danziger's silence affirmed Sky's assessment.

The Luxus project was one of Skyco's most closely kept secrets. Few people in the United States were even aware of it. There were fifteen at most in Colombia, all intimately involved with the project in one capacity or another.

Every precaution had been taken, security clearances checked and double-checked. The project had even been moved out of the United States to the more remote Research Institute in Medellín. But nothing was theft-proof, as Sky knew only too well. He had made a string of fortunes by 'acquiring' various protected technologies from England and Germany in his earlier days. Thieves were always smarter than inventors. And Asher Sky was a bit of both.

The soft swish of terrace doors opening caught the attention of the two men at poolside. Sky's majordomo escorted two people to the terrace. The first was Sky's daughter, Alexandra, president and chief operating officer of Skyco, and the other was Dr Tunis (Tim) de Roode, vice-president of Science and Technology.

Sky rose to his feet as they approached. He greeted his daughter with a warm hug and extended his hand to de Roode.

'Tim has been filling me in on the details,' Alexandra told her father, a look of worried concern on her attractive face.

Dr de Roode had been briefed earlier upon Sky's instructions. Not as much had been known at the time, but it was enough to paint a clear picture of the threat presented.

Sky gestured for them to be seated, and dismissed the majordomo with a nod of his head.

'It could have been a great deal worse had Delgado's security force not acted so swiftly and decisively,' Sky told his daughter.

'The attack was stopped well short of the biogenetics wing,' Danziger assured the new arrivals.

'I'll see to it personally that Delgado and his men are commended for their performance,' Alexandra said.

'What was the extent of the damage?' de Roode asked, his narrow features drawn tense with worry.

'The structural damage at the point of entry is quite severe, with moderate damage to the third floor. One lab was totally destroyed, and the hallway leading to the biogenetics wing was shot up rather badly. There was no damage to the biogenetics wing itself,' Danziger replied.

'And the casualties?' Alexandra asked.

'Four technicians dead, one wounded, with three security fatalities and two wounded. We'll have the names within the hour,' Danziger answered.

Sky's mind skipped quickly over the facts he had been given by Danziger earlier. Certain aspects of the event were curious and raised serious questions.

'Tell me, Tom, as plans go, how would you rate the attack on the Institute?' he asked.

Danziger thought for a moment. 'Well timed, but poorly conceived. Early morning was a good time to stage it, and using the uniform van gets high marks. But they went about the rest of it all wrong.'

'I think the obvious assumption that the Luxus was their objective is a correct one,' Sky said. 'But based on the facts, what do you suppose they intended to do with it, or *to* it?'

Danziger considered his response carefully. 'They obviously knew where it was, so they had somehow obtained good information. They deployed themselves in a manner that suggested withdrawal back the way they had come, except that the van was too far away to make that practical. We can rule out a suicide mission aimed at destruction of the wing and the Luxus because they simply didn't have enough firepower and explosives to carry it out. And most certainly they would have advanced as a group, protecting their rear as they moved. The party attempting penetration of the biogenetics wing broke and retreated at the first sign of stiff resistance. They had survival on their minds.

'Weighing all the facts, I'd say they intended to steal the Luxus, or what portions of it they could, possibly destroying the rest.'

Sky turned to de Roode. 'Was the project far enough along that any of the Luxus could have survived outside the laboratory environment?'

The scientist nodded. 'We produced the first quantities capable of survival only last week,' he replied.

'How much?' Sky asked.

'Not much. Enough to be transported in a single case.'

'Enough to carry,' Sky said, a statement more than a question.

De Roode frowned. 'Yes, enough for one man to carry easily.'

Sky looked back at Danziger, the implications clear.

'Then we have *two* problems. The attack itself being the first, and the fact that highly sensitive information was passed out of our control being the second – and the more serious.'

'We can protect the Luxus,' Danziger said. 'And we'll

29

find the source of the security breach,' he assured the others.

'How long will that take?' Sky asked.

Danziger shook his head. 'I can't be sure. A week, two weeks.'

'Or a month?' Sky asked.

'It's quite possible.'

Sky turned back to de Roode and Alexandra. 'I don't have to tell you what the Luxus means to this company. It is potentially one of the most revolutionary developments in the history of man. Somewhere in that facility is a serious security risk that endangers the entire future of the project – and possibly of this company. There has been one attempt to steal the project already, and who knows when another one will be made? We don't know *who* is behind all of this, or what the scope of the next attempt might be.

'Delgado's security notwithstanding, there is the serious threat of further attempts. I want suggestions,' Sky said.

'Can't we beef up security and go on round-the-clock alert status?' Alexandra asked.

'We could do that,' Danziger responded. 'But the entire Institute could be laid flat and incinerated with napalm or rockets in just minutes if destruction *was* the aim and the people behind it were motivated enough.'

'I think the Luxus must be moved,' de Roode said, 'and it must be done immediately and secretly. We must try to bring what can be moved to safety here in the United States and destroy the rest. We can start up the project again under a new project code.'

'We took the Luxus research out of this country to escape regulatory controls placed on recombinant DNA experimentation,' Alexandra objected. 'The red tape in the States will halt all further progress.'

'Or we could move it until our security problem is resolved,' de Roode suggested. 'We can start up again in another country. In the meantime, we can protect it better here.'

30

'I agree with Tim,' Sky said. 'It should be moved immediately.'

Sky turned back to Danziger. 'Tom, I want you and Tim to work out the details. Get the Luxus out of Medellín within twenty-four hours. Do it without fanfare, as unobtrusively as possible. Let's bring it home until we can make a new place for it. Then I want that leak in Medellín found and plugged.'

2

COLOMBIA: The twin-engine Cessna coughed and sputtered as it strained over jagged, mist-shrouded Andean ridges. Its engines were losing power due to carburetor ice buildup, a peril known to all fliers.

Sweat rolled down the face of Harry Gill as he squinted through the heavy mist at the occasional blur of tropical forest below. He had seen the mists this heavy only a handful of times in all the fifteen years he had been flying these mountains.

The engines sputtered again and hesitated briefly, causing a great deal of apprehension in his passenger.

'Something is wrong with this plane. We're going to crash! I know it!' the passenger cried, unable to hold back his fear.

Gill made a few deft adjustments, recycling carburetor heat back through the air intake. The racket was terrible as the carburetor ice dislodged and passed through the engine cylinders, sounding like a handful of bolts in a garbage can. It was music to Gill's ears.

'What's that? Now what's happening to the engines?' the frightened passenger asked.

'Just take it easy. I'm clearing the carburetor ice. It'll be peachy keen in just a minute,' Gill replied, a trace of annoyance in his voice. A moment later the engines smoothed out and surged with renewed power.

Gill's face and body were drenched in sweat. But it wasn't so much from fear of being lost. He turned his head, casting a quick glance at his anxious passenger, then turned back to his control panel. His stomach was rolling over like a tumble dryer from the building nervousness. *Why the fuck did I wait?* he wondered. *I'm only making this a lot harder on myself.*

Gill reached for the bottle on the copilot's seat beside him, opened it, and took a long pull of Jack Daniel's. His passenger gaped in disbelief.

'What are you doing? Stop that! You're going to get us both killed,' the bespectacled man said sternly.

'Shut the fuck up,' Gill returned sharply, glaring at the man, whose face had turned apprehensive and pale. He felt suddenly sorry for him.

Stop this shit now, his brain scolded. *Don't think about it, just do it.*

But Gill looked away again, his stomach knotting even tighter.

The passenger pressed his face to the window and caught a glimpse of the sun through a tiny break in the cloud cover above. 'What in the—' he began in puzzlement. He leaned forward in his seat and strained to see over Gill's shoulder. He searched the control panel for the compass. He found it and confirmed his suspicion.

'You idiot! We're going the wrong way!' the passenger yelled.

Do it! Gill's brain shouted.

'You're drunk, and we're going to crash.'

Do it now!

'If we get out of this I'll see that you never fly again,' the man screamed. 'I'll go straight to the authorities—'

'You go straight to hell,' Gill interrupted, turning back toward the complaining passenger. His right hand came up quickly toward the man's face.

The man blinked and pulled his head back in a reflexive

32

response, the eyes focusing on the barrel of the gun in Gill's hand.

The .22 automatic barked twice sharply, sounding like a small firecracker.

The passenger's head kicked back slightly, then leveled back at Gill. His eyes were locked in disbelief, the mouth open in a silent gasp.

Gill couldn't believe it. The man was still alive. Both shots had been in the face, and the fucker wasn't dead. He was just staring back at him.

Crack! Crack! Crack! Gill fired again without thought.

The placement was more deliberate this time. Another to the face, through the left spectacle; the last two to the head.

The passenger's head stayed back this time, his eyes still open, staring up to the cabin ceiling. At least the eyes weren't looking at him anymore.

Gill turned away quickly and dropped the gun in his lap. He picked up the bottle again and took another long swallow. His heart pounded as if it were going to explode in his chest.

Shit! He had never killed a man before. He looked back over his shoulder at the man who had been alive just moments before. *Don't think about it*, he told himself and turned away.

In reality, the actual deed wasn't the hard part. Once the first shot had been fired, the rest followed somewhat easily. It was thinking about it that was torture – summoning up the guts to point the gun and squeeze off the first round.

That wasn't so bad, he told himself, swallowing dryly and trying to calm himself. *It wasn't so bad.* Then he took another drink and almost couldn't swallow it. His chest heaved and his hands shook as he set the bottle between his legs and squeezed the steering controls. He fought an urge to get sick and forced his attention back to his flying and the next part of his job.

A few minutes later, Gill spotted a high ridge through

33

the mist to his left. He was exactly on course. He hit the two switches on the control panel, which opened the butterfly valves in his modified fuel tanks, dumping the contents. The gauges dropped immediately. The plane was now flying on reserve fuel.

He wiped the back of his hand across his stinging eyes to take away the perspiration. He now had ten minutes of flying time left to thread a needle.

Gill bolstered himself with another swallow of Jack Daniel's, then squinted into the heavy mists for landmark sightings. A good pilot would never touch booze in the cockpit, and Gill was a good pilot. But at times like these, he was a better pilot drunk.

Mists were not uncommon over the Chocó, one of the wettest spots on earth. The mists today, however, besides being unusually dense, were at a much higher ceiling than normal, concealing what was normally visible at his present altitude and speed. And today he needed those peaks desperately to cross-fix his location.

Gill dropped altitude, and the vague peaks disappeared altogether. The real danger now was that he'd run out of fuel before finding his destination, or that he'd fly straight into one of the hidden peaks, putting a rather unpleasant end to his day.

Gill flew as much by instinct as by instruments, picking a course like a blind man. Every now and then he'd catch sight of a familiar ridge and make an adjustment.

The gauges fell to dead empty as the minutes sped by. He knew from past experience that he still had a squeeze left in each tank. He'd lose the starboard engine first. About a minute later he'd lose the port, then he'd glide her to the end of her string.

He caught sight of a jagged peak as he skimmed barely above the razor-backed ridges of some of the world's most awesome terrain. That one point of recognition was enough, and he banked sharply to the right and dropped his altitude in a controlled dive. He plunged into the mist and into total blindness.

The starboard engine coughed, then cut out as he leveled off and eased down through the mist. Suddenly the dark green of the forest unrolled beneath him and the mist was a solid blanket above.

He followed a winding gorge, then banked again sharply to the right. A long, green valley unfolded before him. The port engine coughed, but didn't quit.

His eyes strained ahead to a narrow break in the forest. It wasn't exactly a clearing, but it was the eye of the needle that he was looking for.

He pulled once again on the bottle, then capped it and set it on the copilot's seat. The port engine coughed again and this time cut out for good, the throaty sound of its power replaced by the softer rush of air.

Gill glided the Cessna toward the break, praying he'd have the airspeed to make it.

The break in the forest was about five hundred feet long. It was heavily shrubbed, with skinny young trees scattered about, but nothing that should turn a controlled crash landing into a funeral.

He dead-sticked in just over the last of the taller treetops at about sixty miles per hour, with his flaps full to slow the approach, then pulled the nose up to drop the tail. The plane reached stalling speed and fell tailfirst into the break. The tail wheel hit and the nose came down hard, and the Cessna became a land sled, crashing through the light cover.

The ride was anything but gentle, and the trees did heavier damage to the plane than he had estimated. Every nerve in Gill's body screamed toward panic as the plane tore its way through the break, closing rapidly on the taller trees at the end of the clearing. He could do nothing but watch and hang on.

The plane veered to the left, then back to the right, sliding a bit sideways before it stopped abruptly, not more than twenty feet from the heavy forest line.

Gill let out a long breath and took a quick inventory of his body parts. Everything was still there and working without pain. It hadn't been a pretty landing, but any landing he could walk away from was a good one.

Gill wasted no time. He quickly unbelted himself and deactivated the emergency homing beacon, which had gone on automatically during the controlled crash. There would be no signal to help in the location of this plane. He grabbed the Jack Daniel's and went aft. Taking a last look at his dead passenger, he felt sudden elation over his accomplishment and the fact that he was walking away from it in one piece. He picked up the metal case the scientist had carried aboard, grabbed a backpack he had stowed, and pulled a stout machete from a storage compartment. Then he opened the side hatch and climbed out.

The path cut by the plane was fairly straight and narrow. It would be visible from the air for a week or two, until the rapid growth of vegetation reclaimed it. The plane had held together surprisingly well, leaving behind only a few pieces of tail section and a small bit of wingtip in its wake. It had settled nicely into the rightmost edge of the break, which would make it difficult to spot from the air without flying directly over the opening at a lower altitude than most pilots would dare. The usual mists would keep it hidden from anything higher. He congratulated himself on a damn good job.

Gill slipped into the backpack, took a compass reading, and headed off into the thick tropical forest. He had two days in which to make his rendezvous. It should be a piece of cake.

Some men would do anything for money. Harry Gill just had. And he had made himself a very rich man.

SAN ANTONIO, TEXAS: Tom Danziger had a sense for situations, and everything about this one smelled bad. He reread the threadbare facts collected about the loss of the plane carrying the Luxus and one of Skyco's top scientists. He had seen situations deteriorate in the past, but few as rapidly as this one. The fact that there was so little information made it worse.

36

Danziger had spent the better part of his life dealing with information – obtaining it, analyzing it, making recommendations. The more challenging and interesting the obstacles became, the better he performed. And just about now he was getting very interested.

It was his reputation for solving just such problems that had caught the attention of Asher Sky eight years ago. Sky had some background studies done on the man and his performance for the Central Intelligence Agency. Danziger was solid, possessed numerous contacts in the right places, and had a knack for distilling what was worthwhile from seemingly useless information. His was an instinct that couldn't be taught. He was just the type of man Asher Sky wanted to run his corporate intelligence operation.

The courtship was short and direct. Alexandra handled the details for her father. It was hard to say no to a beautiful woman who talked as sweet as she looked – and who made a six-figure offer.

Like most major international corporations, Skyco Inc. had an urgent need for a top-notch intelligence capability. To be sure, it had always had one, but the need was made more acute by volatile world conditions. Knowing what the competition was doing was always a necessity. But the real interest was in what the *world* was doing. Overseas investments needed protection. Economic, political, and social trends had to be studied constantly. Political risk analyses had to be made daily to improve corporate decision-making capabilities. Trade secrets had to be protected, and stolen when possible. Skyco needed constant updating on special technological developments, sociopolitical issues, potentials for violence from terrorism or the overthrow of friendly governments. Anything that could affect Skyco's corporate policy domestically or across the globe had to be studied quickly and accurately. The job grew more difficult as the world grew more complex.

News of the plane's disappearance triggered immediate action. The corporate crisis team was assembled. It consisted of Sky as CEO, Alexandra as COO, Danziger, Dr de Roode, and a special team of advisers selected personally by Sky and consisting of trained scholars and former highly influential politicians. Their job as a group would be to review the known facts, to evaluate this information and to speculate on options presented to friends and potential enemies alike. For this purpose they had been gathered not at Skyco World Headquarters, but at Sky's residence, where their comings and goings could be kept as secret as possible.

Danziger had prepared to address the group together with Sky, Alexandra, and de Roode, in order to present the facts as accurately as they were known. He sat in Sky's personal study waiting to be called into the conference room where the committee had been convened.

The door opened and Asher Sky stepped in for a short conference with Danziger before the briefing.

'Any word from the Colombian office?' Sky asked.

Danziger shook his head. 'We've begun low-profile search efforts between Medellín and Bogotá. So far, nothing has been sighted. The plane is still missing.'

'Do you think there's a chance that the plane has put down somewhere safely?'

'Not likely.'

'Foul play?'

'A possibility, but again not likely. At least based upon the precautions taken, it shouldn't have been possible. Only Dr Stillings and Delgado were aware of the removal of the Luxus. Their files are solid. We just don't see either of them as our problem,' Danziger replied.

'And here? Who was involved?'

'Dr de Roode and I were the only ones aware of the details.'

'This pilot . . . Gill? What about his background?'

'Certainly the least reliable of the bunch. But he had no idea of what or whom he was carrying. He was simply contracted to fly a cargo to Bogotá.'

'Then you're reasonably certain that the attempt to

move the Luxus strain to safety was a well-guarded secret?' Sky asked.

'Yes, I am.'

'We have to find that plane, Tom. What are our chances?'

'Difficult at best. The terrain is mountainous, with heavy tropical forest below the treeline. There's no emergency beacon to home in on via satellite. There were no Mayday signals received, so whatever happened probably took place quickly. If we're lucky, we'll make a sighting and be able to get to the wreckage by helicopter. The Luxus could have survived the crash in the transport container. There's a lot of area to cover, and the longer it takes, the more attention we'll draw, unless we're lucky and spot it quickly.'

'What about the possibility of survivors?' Sky asked, knowing the hope was a slim one.

'There's always a possibility, of course. But knowing what lies between Medellín and Bogotá, I'd say the chances aren't very good.'

'Damn it,' Sky hissed. 'Maybe we were trying to be too smart.'

'Don't think that way, boss. We did the right thing. Chances of losing the plane were too small to be considered a real risk. At the Institute anything could have happened,' Danziger said consolingly.

'Has the rest of the Luxus been destroyed?'

'No, we were able to stop it in time. We at least took the precaution of waiting until the Luxus was here in our hands before destroying what's left in Medellín. The remaining material can't survive outside the laboratory environment, and we've set up heavy security to protect it from further attempts. We should be able to generate enough to transport again before final destruction,' Danziger replied.

'I want that started immediately,' Sky said. 'In the meantime, we have to find the plane and recover our property before whoever made the attempt learns that it's missing.

39

Once they're aware of that fact, they stand as good a chance of recovering it as we do. I don't have to tell you what that will mean if they do,' Sky said.

'We'll find it,' Danziger said.

'We had better. All right, let's get this briefing over with. We have a lot of work to do, and every minute is important.'

The two men left the office and went into the conference room. All conversation ceased as they entered. Sky walked briskly to the head of the conference table. Danziger took a seat at the far end of the table. Undivided attention went to the short, stocky figure of Asher Sky, who remained standing when he reached his place.

Sky activated a small control console built into the table, and dimmed the lights. A moment later a large wall panel behind him lit up, with a map of Colombia projected onto it. A heavy silence descended over the room.

'For the past three years we have been conducting highly sensitive research at our Medellín Institute,' Sky began, tapping the spot on the map with a pointer. 'The exact nature of that research is known to a select number of people within Skyco, both here in the States and actively involved in the project in Colombia.

'Two days ago the Medellín Institute was attacked by a small invasive force, numbering eight.'

Low murmurs rose at this announcement.

'The attack was handled efficiently by security personnel after overcoming the initial surprise and swiftness of the strike. The attacking force was completely neutralized, but not before gaining entry to Building Two, the area where our most highly sensitive research is carried out. There were casualties among Institute personnel.' Sky looked to Danziger for help on the exact toll.

'Three security personnel were killed and two wounded, with four technicians killed and another injured,' Danziger reported from the far end of the table. 'Penetration into Building Two was stopped at the secondary security checkpoint,' he clarified.

'Who were these people?' a voice asked. The question

came from Phillip Cleland, former Secretary of State and one of Sky's closest friends.

'We're still working on the identities,' Danziger replied. 'There were no survivors for questioning, and none of the attackers carried meaningful identification.'

'Can we assume their ultimate objective was this particular research just described?' Cleland asked.

'That's what we're assuming.'

'And exactly what is the nature of this research that made it so important to these people?' Cleland went on.

Sky didn't answer the question himself. Instead he deferred to Dr de Roode, the brain behind the project. 'Tim, I'll let you field that one.'

Dr de Roode rose slowly from his chair. He was a tall, thin man with a permanent air of seriousness about him. The dark features were crammed into a frown, the eyes behind the glasses intense, like a chess player concentrating twenty moves ahead. And like a chess player, he was a deliberate man; a quick thinker but slow talker whose words never ran ahead of his mind, or his alternatives.

'They were after a dream,' de Roode said, then paused in his usual style to formulate his explanation.

Alexandra Sky didn't have the patience for de Roode that her father had. Perhaps she didn't appreciate the depth of his intelligence, which often stayed a level or two above that of anyone he spoke to. She let out a quiet sigh and sat back, resigned to what she knew would follow.

'The Philosopher's Stone, gentlemen. The dream of the ages,' he continued, confusing everyone in the room. 'It has been the dream of scientists since the earliest of times to discover that one magical substance, or element, believed to have the power of transmuting baser metals into gold. The ancient alchemists devoted their lives to it.'

Asher Sky looked on, always amused by de Roode's unique approaches to explanations. Always the riddle to trap you, then the meaning. The benefit was that you never forgot what he said.

'They were after our Philosopher's Stone. The Luxus.'

'What the hell is he talking about?' Cleland asked, posing the question directly to Sky.

'I'm talking about what will amount to one of the greatest discoveries of mankind when the work is completed,' de Roode answered. 'The ability to make gold from rock. I'm talking about *black* gold, of course. Oil.'

'I still don't get it,' Cleland complained. 'Can't someone put what he's saying in simple English?'

'Recombinant DNA,' Alexandra replied. 'Our research at the Medellín Institute has to do with the genetic restructuring of very simple microorganisms to produce new strains capable of acting like tiny, living processing plants able to extract oil from any place it exists.'

De Roode's face tightened with Alexandra's explanation. He didn't appreciate her rude interruption, or her lack of patience. She did this to him constantly.

'One of our greatest resources of petroleum lies trapped within rock, shale, and coal,' she went on before de Roode could regain their attention. 'Only a very small percentage of this is capable of being removed by conventional methods. Even our underground retort methods, which were pioneered over ten years ago and seemed to hold the promise of the future, yield paltry amounts when compared to what this new technology will produce. Our spent wells, for instance, no longer capable of producing even one barrel from existing techniques, are conservatively holding in excess of two hundred billion barrels of oil in the United States alone,' Alexandra explained. 'Retorting the deep shale beds is expensive, complicated, and very time-consuming. We have to *burn* fuel to *make* fuel, not to mention the environmental considerations of pollutants that would be generated, possibly contaminating groundwater as it percolates through burned retort sites. These sites also have to be filled with injections of grout. The work and expense are staggering.

'By comparison, the same retort site that might cover many square miles underground and produce perhaps one hundred and ninety thousand barrels a day can produce five times that much oil at only ten per cent of the cost of retorting, using five per cent of the manpower, while leaving behind zero pollution.'

'Are you saying that we have the means to do this now?' another voice asked. This question was from Dr Marcus Lent, the youngest member of the advisory team, a specialist in political science from Stanford University.

'Not exactly,' de Roode answered before Alexandra could reply. 'But we've opened the door to that possibility. At the most, we're one year away. The Luxus is an organism that will function in soil, rock, and shale formations to produce oil.

'What we have done, in very simple terms, is to take a common organism and redesign it genetically, enabling it to loosen soil, survive high temperatures and pressures, withstand high salt concentrations, and function both aerobically and anaerobically – that is, with and without the presence of oxygen. Its by-product is petroleum, and when its work is done it dies, leaving behind no trace of harmful pollution,' de Roode explained.

'That's a miracle,' Lent said, amazed.

'No, that's the product of scientific research,' Alexandra corrected him. 'Its value cannot be estimated until all of its potential has been explored.'

'Give them the bad news, Tim,' Sky said.

'The bad news is that our Luxus is not yet perfected. What has been described to you is what *will be* a year from now, if our research goes on without interruption. As our Luxus strain exists now, improperly used it is capable of destroying existing oil reserves. It digests oil faster than it produces it. Seeded into a reserve, it would digest oil at a rate that defies imagination. Until we perfect a way to shut off several enzymatic systems, we have a threat to our oil reserves that cannot be answered.'

'You mean that it *can't* be stopped?' Cleland asked.

'That's correct.'

'Give them the rest of it,' Sky said.

'There's more?' Cleland exclaimed.

'And . . . our total supply of Luxus is missing.'

'I thought you said that the attempt at the Institute was successfully stopped?' This question was from Byron Moore, a member of the National Security Council during the preceding administration.

'It was,' Sky answered. 'But out of concern to protect the strain from further potential danger, we elected to remove it and bring it here to the United States. The plane it was on is missing. It went down in Colombia, somewhere between Medellín and Bogotá, this morning.'

'This is a matter of critical intelligence,' Moore responded immediately, clearly indicating that the development posed an urgent threat to the security of the United States. Matters of this magnitude warranted immediate transmission at the highest priority to the President and other national decision-making officials to make them aware of the possible threat of its use against the nation's oil reserves.

'Not until an intelligence estimate has been made,' Danziger put in quickly. 'We must determine what actual degree of danger exists in the event that we cannot retrieve our lost property.'

'I disagree,' Moore returned.

'Only the people in this room are aware that the Luxus is missing, or what it is capable of,' Danziger responded.

'Someone tried to take it,' Moore said bluntly. 'Obviously, someone knows *something*. This matter must be reported,' he insisted.

'We know only that someone attacked the Institute. We don't know what they knew, or, in fact, that it *was* their intent to take the Luxus,' Sky said.

'Let's not get into a game of semantics, Asher,' Moore returned. 'The fact is that the potential exists to do this nation great harm, and that the means to do that harm is out of our control. Now you tell me that that doesn't constitute a direct threat.'

'Only if the strain survived,' Danziger interjected. 'The odds are high that it didn't survive the crash.'

'But you have no proof of that.'

'We need time to make the intelligence estimate.'

'Time, young man, is a luxury we don't have. Unless you can guarantee that the Luxus has either been destroyed or that all of it is safely in our hands, you have no choice but to notify the White House,' Moore shot back point-blank.

'You know I can't make that guarantee. But there *is* one I can make, Mr Moore,' Danziger returned. 'Twenty-four hours after you notify national security interests in Washington of the problem, that information will be big news in Moscow Center. Then we'll have a problem whose magnitude goes well beyond our "potential" problem as it sits now. What we don't need is a race for the goods. We need a quiet effort that will draw as little attention as possible. Now, if you can tell me that I'm wrong, I'll make the call to the President myself.'

Moore stared blankly at Danziger, like an opponent who had been checkmated with a surprise move.

'We do have national security well in focus, Byron,' Sky said. 'That was one of the reasons the work was moved out of the United States to begin with. The Luxus is not, and never will be, intended for use as a weapon. We need time to finish our work on the Luxus to make it a safe and beneficial contribution to mankind. We're very close to that now. We just need time.'

'What's being done to locate the plane?' asked a heretofore silent member of the advisory team. This was Dr Christopher Bunch, a socioeconomist from Cornell University.

'Everything possible is being done, short of notifying the Colombian authorities,' Sky replied.

'Why not notify them to enlist their assistance, informing them only that one of our planes is missing?' Bunch asked.

'For the same reasons,' Moore replied. 'What they know, the Soviets could know. It's a juicy bit of intelligence data that could get red hot in a flash if news of the attack on the Institute has gotten out.'

'So would it be to whoever made the attempt on the Institute,' Danziger added. 'It wouldn't take a genius to figure out the possibilities. There's also the fact that it wasn't a Skyco plane. We contracted a private source for the job, specifically to prevent that connection from being made.'

'That cinches it, then,' Lent broke in. 'Whoever owns the plane knows, or will know soon, that it's missing. They'll tell the authorities.'

'The plane was owned by the pilot,' Danziger began. 'He's a one-man shop. American, been living in Colombia for the past fifteen years. He's a loner, no family, no real friends to miss him. It won't get out that quickly. This pilot flies odd cargo in and out regularly, so his being there wouldn't have caused undue suspicion. He had no knowledge of what he was flying, or why. He's a bit of a rogue. Takes jobs that no one else would want. He's a good flier, does things his own way. He's quiet and efficient.'

'Let's assume, as I think we must, that this plane has crashed somewhere between Medellín and Bogotá,' Cleland began. 'What if you're wrong about his being missed, and it becomes an issue?'

'If he is missed before we find the wreckage, and if he is connected to our moving the Luxus out of Medellín, then we'll have a real problem. The strain would be up for grabs. The first to find it would own it,' Danziger answered.

'So, what happens next?' Cleland asked.

There was no immediate response, though Asher Sky knew very well what he intended to do. 'What would you do, Phil?' he asked his old friend.

Without hesitation Cleland replied, 'I'd get help. The best I could find.'

'Marcus?' Sky said, looking to Lent.

Lent shrugged. 'I have to agree.'

'Byron?'

Moore nodded. 'Assuming the worst-case scenario, meaning involvement by outside agencies competing for

46

possession of the Luxus, I'll get help. Good help. It's possible that action outside the limits of the law will be required. You'll want to protect Skyco to the greatest extent possible. That means getting somebody capable enough to deal with any situation . . . somebody in a position to do whatever is necessary at every level, and who can run the risk of unlawful activities without endangering Skyco's international position. You will need to carefully limit your own involvement.'

Sky looked at his daughter. 'Alex?'

'There's a saying that while one lingers to consider where to begin, it becomes too late. I say we contact our friends at Intel-Trace, explain our situation, and ask for their help.'

A faint smile crossed Sky's face. It was exactly what he'd have said, and what he had already decided to do. There was no lost pride in recognizing when help was needed and going to the right place for it.

'It seems that we're all in agreement, then,' Sky concluded. 'We can't underestimate the scope of our problem or ignore the fact that our own actions may be limited.

'Necessity requires no decision, gentlemen. I agree with Alex. Intel-Trace's capabilities far outclass our own. We've used them before, and we're one of their major financial backers. There's no question of their integrity and their ability to get results. One phone call will get immediate action on a scale larger than we can hope to achieve. They're also far better equipped to handle our adversary, whoever that may prove to be, on their own terms. The call will be made tonight.

'They'll want a complete background on everything that's happened from the moment the Institute was attacked,' Sky said, looking at Danziger. 'Pull every scrap of information, every report, Tom. Contact your people in Medellín and get the latest update. Every fact. Nothing is too small to be overlooked.'

Sky looked at his watch. 'I want everything on my desk

within two hours, Tom, Intel-Trace is to coordinate its efforts through you. Are there any questions?'

There were none.

'Thank you, gentlemen. I'll be contacting you with progress reports as events develop. Please stay available to meet again on short notice.'

Without further conversation, everyone rose. The four board members filed out of the room. Alex and Danziger remained behind.

'Tim, I'd like you to stay behind for a moment,' Sky said, catching de Roode just as he reached the door.

When the four were alone in the room, Sky addressed the scientist. 'I want you to prepare a comprehensive background on our Luxus project. Our friends at Intel-Trace will have to know exactly what's at stake. Also, I want you to pull the files on everyone involved in the project. And I mean everyone, from Dr Stillings to the janitorial staff responsible for Building Two maintenance. I want any staff here in the States included. Any questions?'

'None. I'll have it on your desk by morning,' de Roode told his boss, then left the boardroom.

'I want you close on all of this, Alex,' Sky said to his daughter.

'How much do we tell Intel-Trace?' Alexandra asked.

'They get everything they need to know. Everything. I don't have to tell you what this could do to Skyco, should that strain end up in the wrong hands.'

'I know.'

'I know you do. We're so close to great things. We can't lose it now.'

'I'll have everything ready in two hours,' Danziger said, checking the time on his watch. 'I'll call Martin Trace directly over the sterile security line at the Center.'

'Do you want company when you make the call?' Sky asked.

Danziger thought for a moment.

'I think not, Chief. Byron Moore made a good point

48

earlier about limiting your exposure in the interests of protecting Skyco's legal position – as well as your own. It's probably best this early on to keep you "informally" apprised of the details of any communications with Intel-Trace. I'll make sure that any formal record of communications is properly sanitized,' Danziger replied.

Sky understood what Danziger was telling him clearly enough, and chose not to pursue it further.

'Just between us, Tom, what *are* our chances?' Alexandra asked.

Danziger assessed her level gaze.

'I can't give you percentages, Alex,' he began. 'I've known Martin Trace for over twenty years, and I can guarantee he'll provide the best help available anywhere in the world. He has connections with every intelligence organization across the globe. If we're successful in keeping the news of the missing Luxus under our control, then our chances should be very good.'

'And if we're not?' she asked.

'We'll still have the best chance possible.'

She would have liked a stronger assurance, but she appreciated his frankness. That was one of the things she admired about Tom Danziger. He didn't tell you something you wanted to hear, unless it was the truth.

'How soon will Intel-Trace get on the problem?' Sky asked.

'If I know Martin Trace, and I do, he'll be working on it before he hangs up the phone,' Danziger replied.

'Then it appears we're wasting valuable time,' Sky said. 'Make your call, Tom, and let's get started.'

3

NEW YORK CITY: Bob Elias toweled himself off quickly after stepping from the shower. He dried his hair briskly, then stood, studying himself in the mirror. He didn't feel forty-eight, but was beginning to look it. It wasn't the body; he had always kept himself in reasonably good shape. It wasn't the hair, either. It was still full and dark, with only an accent of gray at the temples, but he had had that for years. He stared hard at the face and neck. It was the skin, he decided. Especially around the sharp blue eyes. When had the wrinkles started, he wondered. Not a lot of them, but enough. He shook his head and draped the towel across his neck.

He applied some deodorant and reached for the aerosol can of shaving cream. He turned on the hot tap water and had begun wetting the stubble on his face when the phone rang in the bedroom.

Elias shut off the faucet and walked to the phone, reaching it on the fourth ring.

'Elias,' he said into the mouthpiece.

'Please hold for line check,' a male voice said. There was a pause while the line was electronically scanned for taps.

'Please state your identification code and clearance,' the voice said.

'Triple Jack, five-nine-three. Clearance Alpha-Scramble,' he responded, his eyes going to the clock radio. It was five-forty-five in the morning.

The customary wait followed as the computer completed its cross-check of clearance codes and voiceprint.

'Accepted,' the voice said. 'Call Jack Tar on scrambled line three. One minute,' the voice announced, then the line went dead.

Elias checked his watch, then left the bedroom immediately and walked across the large penthouse apartment to a locked office. He punched a five-number code into the security lock, then entered.

The office was fairly large, like all of the other rooms in the apartment. It was swept twice weekly for electronic debugging. This room was certifiably 'sterile'. He walked across it to a desk situated in front of a large wall library with a built-in credenza. He sat behind the desk and spun the chair to face the credenza and the three phones on it. He picked up the center phone, checked his watch again, and waited.

The special scrambled line in the penthouse office was there only for emergency use. Normally such calls went through security lines at the Intel-Trace office, which Elias typically opened at seven. Whatever this call was about, it couldn't wait.

The one-minute mark passed, and Elias tapped in a three-digit speed-dial code, got a single tone and two quick beeps, then tapped in his identification code.

There was a single ring, and a new voice answered.

'Please hold,' the voice said.

The short delay was for another line check for security integrity.

'Good morning, Bob,' a mellow voice greeted him. It was the voice of Martin Trace. The boss didn't call often. When he did, it usually meant top priority – drop all else.

'Good morning, Martin,' Elias returned.

'Sorry to disturb you so early, but we have a matter of some urgency,' Trace said.

'It's not a problem. I was up. Go ahead.'

'We received a call late last night through the Alpha security line from one of our clients with a potentially nasty problem. They've asked for our services.'

'Go ahead, I'm listening,' Elias said, already touching his pencil to the large notepad on the desk.

'The client is Skyco, headquartered in San Antonio, Texas,' Trace began as Elias wrote quickly.

Elias knew Skyco well, as did everyone in the business world. It was one of the world's largest privately held corporations with widely diversified interests, its primary holdings being in oil.

'The call was placed by Tom Danziger, Head of their Corporate Policy Department. I've known Tom personally for a long time, and he wouldn't call me directly unless their need was desperate.'

Elias scribbled the name and dropped the pencil. He turned back to his desk, propped the phone between his shoulder and ear, and turned on the computer terminal in front of him. He gained access to the data files and keyed in the name Skyco. He followed quickly with the name Tom Danziger. The screen came to life almost immediately with a brief profile on Danziger.

'As I'm sure you are aware, Skyco is a company deeply committed to scientific research. One area of great importance to the company is recombinant DNA. They have a principal site on the outskirts of Medellín, Colombia, where highly secretive work is conducted.'

'Hold just one second, Martin,' Elias said, keying in Medellín.

The screen filled with summary details of the Research Institute in Medellín.

'Got it. Go ahead.'

'Three days ago this facility was attacked by unknown parties, who successfully gained entry to the compound in a laundry-service van and mounted an armed assault against the most highly secured laboratory section, referred to as Building Two,' Trace continued. 'The assailants penetrated the building and inflicted considerable damage before being stopped by resident security forces. The attacking force, numbering eight, was completely annihilated, with no survivors for interrogation.'

Elias worked the keyboard deftly, calling up data on the security force. 'Security in Medellín is headed by Ernesto Delgado. According to the file, they have pretty stout capabilities down there. Any Skyco casualties?'

'There were ten reported,' Trace answered.

'Were there any secondary attempts?'

'None.'

'Was Skyco able to determine their objective?' Elias asked.

'They are reasonably certain the attempt was made either to destroy or take a highly secret strain of microorganism under development. Danziger referred to it as "the Luxus",' Trace replied.

Elias keyed in the word *Luxus*, but the file contained no data on it.

'The file is empty on Luxus,' Elias said. 'Did Danziger use any other name referencing this genetic strain?' he asked.

'No, Luxus was the only name used.'

'Well, either it's a new project or they've kept this secret extremely well,' Elias remarked.

'I'd say that the latter is the case. Tom did say that the project had been moved to Colombia almost three years ago.'

'Three years, and we don't know *anything* about it? Interesting. A well-kept secret like that, and the attack . . .' Elias began, nodding his head slowly. 'There was inside help.'

'Skyco headquarters was notified immediately. A corporate decision was made to remove the Luxus strain to safety by airlift to Bogotá, then to the States. The plane carrying the Luxus and the director of the Institute never reached Bogotá, and is presumed lost somewhere between Medellín and El Dorado International Airport. A private, low-profile search has so far come up empty,' Trace explained.

'Is the organism potentially dangerous to human life?'

'We've been told that it is not.'

'If my knowledge of Colombian geography is correct, the area in question is pretty rugged terrain,' Elias said. 'A violent crash with a potentially dangerous organism could be a nightmare.'

'Your recollections of the geography are quite correct. The area is mountainous, with heavy tropical forest cover below the treeline.'

'Were any Mayday signals picked up?'

'None,' Trace said.

'We can assume that since their search efforts were

unsuccessful, there was also no homing beacon on the craft,' Elias said, more to himself than to Trace. 'I presume they'll want us to locate the wreckage as quickly and quietly as possible.'

'Exactly. We've begun close-up satellite scans, but don't really have sufficient daylight yet to be effective. We have to find the plane and possible survivors, then recover the Luxus, arousing as little attention as possible. With no homing signals to scan for, the contact will have to be visual, with on-site confirmation. That means highly specialized search teams, with at least one expert recovery team.'

'I've got just the man to lead the recovery team. Go ahead,' Elias said.

'Should word of the loss get out, we can expect rather determined competition to reach the strain. It could get complicated.'

'The man I have in mind can handle it,' Elias told his boss.

Trace was silent for a long moment.

'I guess I'm curious. Who are you thinking of?' he inquired.

'Michael Quinn,' Elias replied, expecting a reaction. He wasn't disappointed.

'Quinn?' Trace repeated. There was another long silence.

Elias was tempted not to wait out the silence and to begin an immediate defense of his choice. But he chose not to. It was better if any objections came right to the surface and were met with thoughtful justifications. Fast talk didn't work with a man like Trace. Logic did.

'I guess I'm going to ask why you've selected Quinn,' Trace said. 'He's so far down on everyone's list right now, you'd have to be on your belly to notice him.'

'He knows rain forests,' Elias began, unfazed. 'Three tours in Vietnam: one year recon, one year Special Ops, the rest Black Angel Ops. Five years CIA after that, including three penetration assignments in Cuba. He had a

54

good background before we recruited him. Spent one year Panama, ten months Nicaragua, and fifteen months Colombia for us before being reassigned to duty in Europe. He's fluent in six languages and has a lot of mental horsepower. There was a time when we considered him one of our best.'

'Before the Dieter incident in Helsinki, I'd have agreed with you,' Trace said.

'Perhaps we'd better talk about it,' Elias suggested.

'I'd rather you made another choice.'

'I could do that. But anyone else would be a second choice. There's no-one, and I mean no-one, better than Quinn in a situation like this,' Elias began in defense of his selection. 'Helsinki was nine months ago, for Christ's sake, Martin. He's been kept on the shelf ever since.'

'It was almost an international incident,' Trace reminded Elias.

'Dieter needed killing. He was on our list. Right near the top, as I remember.'

'That's not the point I'm making, Bob,' Trace said in quick response. 'The point is that it wasn't his sanction. It wasn't an Intel-Trace operation. He was acting independently, without authorization from us.'

'Dieter killed his sister, Martin. He killed her because of an operation that Quinn ran against him two years ago in West Germany. Dieter lost a shipment of drugs to the authorities, and a fortune in cash that was never recovered. The girl was only nineteen years old. She was a nice kid. Clean, bright, and beautiful. Mike was really proud of her. They abducted her, tortured her, and then killed her with a "hot shot" of heroin. But not before they violated every orifice of her body. There was no mystery involved. Just a strict payback for the job that Quinn did on Dieter. And he did that job for us, Martin.'

'The fact remains that he took matters into his own hands, without clearance from us. There was also a high-ranking KGB official killed in the deal, or did you forget that?'

'I know exactly what happened,' Elias said coolly, holding back the frustration that was beginning to build.

'You might also remember that the KGB official in question was the subject of a major investigation being conducted by the Soviet GRU.'

'I remember. But I also remember learning about that well after the incident.'

'The fact remains that Quinn acted without authorization. He's undisciplined.'

'I'll admit he has his own way of doing things. But that's precisely what makes him successful. He's unpredictable.'

'Not unpredictable. More like out of control,' Trace countered.

'Label it any way you want, Martin. He was a highly effective agent. He belongs in the field, not on the shelf.'

'There was also the matter of the money, Bob,' Trace added. 'And not just the missing money from the Dieter affair in West Germany. The word that got back to us somewhat indirectly from Moscow was that the Soviet was carrying two million dollars in cash for an apparent deal with Dieter. As I remember, there was never any mention of cash in the debriefing that followed.'

'Its existence was never proven,' Elias replied. 'Quinn has rather substantial wealth through an inheritance. He didn't need that money.'

'Perhaps not, but it was never found.'

'Money wasn't his motive, Martin.'

'Of course not. It was revenge. And he used Intel-Trace resources to get his intelligence on Dieter.'

'He used his initiative,' Elias countered quickly.

'*He used our resources*,' Trace repeated.

'He used *his* network of contacts. And I didn't discourage him, especially with Dieter's status in our files.'

'The Soviet had no such status.'

Elias let out a breath into the receiver. 'I can't argue with that. And I can't argue with the fact that it's strictly against our policy to kill innocents, though Tomarev can hardly be classified as an innocent. It was an unfortunate mistake, the fact that he was dirty notwithstanding. Under any other circumstances I believe Mike would have let him go. The fact remains, however, that Tomarev drew a weapon and would have used it. He was no longer an innocent from the moment he took his weapon in hand.

'We could debate the issue further, Martin, but there's really no point. If you insist, I'll make another choice for the assignment, but it's still my opinion that if you want the ideal man for the job, he's the one.'

There was another long silence.

'All right,' Trace said at last, his reluctance perhaps overshadowed by the urgent need. 'He's been unassigned since Helsinki. Are you sure he'll accept the job?'

'I think he will,' Elias replied.

'Then you have clearance to make the contact and the offer. But this one has to be by the book.'

'I understand.'

'How soon can you talk to him?'

'He's in Paris,' Elias said, looking at his watch. 'I can take the first available Concorde over and have an answer today. In the meantime, there are some things I'll need.'

'OK. What can I do?'

'I'd like to have complete details of the attack. With backgrounds of everyone at the Institute, especially peripheral personnel even remotely involved in the project. If there are insiders working for the other side, they'll probably be in this fringe group. I'd also like a complete book on the aircraft and the pilot – maintenance records and repair history in particular. And on the Skyco personnel, I'd like detailed information on their financial backgrounds. Maybe someone's spending more money than he or she makes or has debt problems. Anything like that can give us insight into possible motivations. I want you to include in that the backgrounds on the casualties as well. Because they're dead or wounded doesn't mean they couldn't have been a party to it.'

'You'll get everything you need. Anything else?'

'Yes, I want Christopher Wadelaw in Colombia waiting

for our arrival in Bogotá. He's the best damn helicopter pilot alive over the forests. I'm sure I'll need more when I've done some initial research. I'll contact you in the usual way.'

'Fine. We'll start collecting the information you requested immediately.'

'You'll hear from me today concerning Quinn,' Elias said.

'Good luck. We'll talk later,' Trace said, then the Alpha line went dead. Elias wasted no time. He secured the office, then finished his morning rituals. A flash of energy and excitement coursed through him as he walked back through the apartment. A slight smile broke across his face. This wouldn't be just another day at the office.

4

PARIS: Bob Elias walked casually along the River Seine on the Quai des Grands Augustins. A light but steady rain was falling, which suited Elias just fine. Less than pleasant weather meant that fewer people would be on the streets.

Elias stopped at the Pont Neuf, the oldest bridge in Paris spanning the Seine to the Ile de la Cité, the largest of the islands in the Seine and the site of the Palais de Justice and the Cathedral of Notre Dame. He turned on to the bridge and began walking across it to the island, stopping once midway to look over the edge into the dark, moving water. He checked his watch, then scanned the banks of the river from where he had just come and those parts of the Cité that he could readily see. He could feel the eyes watching him as surely as he felt the rain, and wondered how many were watching and for how many different reasons. He knew one pair belonged to Michael Quinn, and took some comfort from knowing that they were the eyes of a friend.

He hadn't seen Michael since the final day of debriefing after the Dieter affair in Helsinki. Inwardly he supported what Michael had done. Dieter was a real shitball who had deserved to die. Had the sanction been authorized, Quinn would have come home to a hero's welcome. But he was no hero on that day, and Elias had to represent the agency's position.

Elias had given behind-the-scenes support, taking ultimate responsibility for making the Intel-Trace resources available to Quinn that had enabled him to track down Dieter. But there was nothing Elias could do for him when the 'missing' money became an issue. Quinn simply clammed up and did little to defend himself. The existence of the money was never proved, and it had effectively ended the career of the man who had been Elias's best agent.

Elias lingered a few moments longer, then continued across the bridge. He had told Martin Trace that Quinn would help on this assignment, and he wondered, as he walked toward his rendezvous, whether he had spoken too soon. There had to be some bitterness in Quinn for the way he had been treated by the internal-affairs people of Intel-Trace. They hadn't cut him any slack at all, despite the record of service he had compiled. There was always the chance that Quinn would tell Elias to go take a dive off the bridge he was walking across. In any event, he was in Paris to learn the answer to that question, and he knew that he'd have his answer before very long.

Elias came to the large equestrian statue of Henri IV, paused a moment to scan the area, then walked around the statue and descended a stairway to the tree-lined Square du Vert Galant. It was the farthest point of the Cité and could be approached only from the direction in which he had traveled.

He stopped at the base of the steps and looked toward the end of the square. It wasn't a square, actually, but more like an elongated triangle, with wooden benches running at intervals along the perimeter to the tip of the island. All of the benches were empty except for the very last one. He shoved his hands into his pockets and approached the solitary figure sitting there in the rain and appearing to read a magazine. Elias stopped directly in front of him.

'Hello, Mike,' he said.

Quinn shut the magazine, a French *Batman* comic book, and looked up without speaking. The sharp, slate-gray eyes squinted and locked on to the face of his longtime control.

Michael rolled the comic book and raised it. 'Do you believe they actually sell this shit?' he asked.

'Sure. As long as there's assholes like you to buy them,' Elias replied. 'How've you been, Mike?'

'Does anyone really care?'

'I do. You know that.'

'God, it's great to have a fan club. I'm doing fine, Bob,' Michael replied. 'What's on your mind?'

'I've got a job I thought you'd be interested in.'

Michael shifted in his seat and turned to look behind him, then to the right and to the left. 'There's no-one else around, so you must be talking to me,' he said.

Elias nodded slowly. 'That's right.'

'Must be a suicide mission. I don't think I'm interested.'

'Actually, it's pretty hot,' Elias said. 'Are you interested?'

Michael stretched out his legs to full length and leaned back on the bench. He was a big man, six feet four inches tall, with an angular, athletic build. There was a look of puzzlement across his dark features as his mind wrestled with whether to trust this old friend. He looked almost oriental when he squinted; his hair, drawn back tightly in a short pony tail, added to the illusion.

'Why are you coming to me, Bob?'

'I figured if I didn't get your ass back into the field, you'd get fat and old before your time.'

'Me, fat and old? When was the last time you looked at yourself in the mirror? You look like you've been working too hard, Bob. You need to slow down and enjoy your life a little more.'

60

'Hard work is what I do for enjoyment.'

'Cut the shit. Why me?' Michael repeated.

'OK. Two reasons. First, it's time you came off the shelf. I never lost faith in you, Mike. You were my best operative and I need you back. Second, this job has your name all over it. Nobody else even comes close.'

Michael studied his shoes for a moment, then looked up into Elias's face. 'Thank you. It means a lot to hear that, especially from you. You've got my attention. Tell me about the job.'

'Recovery of a lost plane. Maybe some survivors. And a valuable cargo, about the size of a fat briefcase,' Elias said, offering no more until questions were asked.

'I hope that briefcase ain't filled with money. Because if it is, you definitely came to the wrong guy,' Quinn said dryly.

Elias smiled. 'No money this time. I can promise you that.'

'Where?'

'Colombia. Somewhere between Medellín and Bogotá.'

Michael frowned. 'Pretty rough country. Has the plane been located yet?'

Elias shook his head.

'What kind is it?'

'Twin-engine Cessna,' Elias replied. 'Pilot and one passenger,' he added, anticipating the next question.

'Small plane, bad terrain. You might never find it, especially if it cleared the mountains and went down in the tropical forests.'

Elias smiled. 'That's why I'm here, Mike. There's a good possibility it went down in the trees somewhere. We've had air-search activity over the mountains already, and eight hours of intensive satellite search since we were called in. Everything has come up empty so far.'

'Those are awfully big mountains. Deep ravines, jagged peaks, a million places a small plane could just disappear into. I don't think the satellites will help,' Michael said.

'We know.'

'The forests are just as bad. In some places the terrain isn't a lot better. And where it is, the tropical growth is so thick that a *big* plane could be hard to find without a major burn.'

'Like I said, that's why I'm here. If it did go down in the bush, we'll need expert help getting to it fast. That's why I came to you,' Elias said.

'What's the cargo?' Michael asked, ignoring the compliment.

'It's biological,' Elias replied.

Michael squinted pensively for several long moments.

'Everything about this one . . .'

'I know, I know,' Mike interrupted. 'Everything about this one says "Michael Quinn". But I'm not the most popular guy in Intel-Trace circles these days.'

'I can't deny it,' Elias returned. 'But Helsinki is in the past, Mike. The question is, are you ready to move back into the present?'

'A few months ago I couldn't have answered that,' Michael confessed. He felt a brief flash of pain again over the loss of his sister. Her death had devastated him. It was only his anger and hatred that had driven him in the relentless pursuit of Dieter.

'And now?'

'And now . . .' Michael repeated, his voice trailing off. 'All I have left is hatred . . . and a memory of an innocent kid who never had a chance to live. She was smart and pretty and had enough money and spirit to be happy for the rest of her life. Then some piece of slime decided it was time to get back at me . . .

'Killing Dieter wasn't enough, Bob. It was too fast, too easy for him. I wish I could have killed him in small pieces, over and over again. And that still wouldn't have been enough. The world is filled with scum like Dieter.'

Quinn's face took on a rigid, tight set, and he nodded slowly. 'Yeah, I'm ready,' he said, continuing to nod. 'I'm ready, all right.'

'I thought you would be,' Elias said softly.

'I'll agree to help you,' Michael began. 'But I'll need some answers.'

Elias felt relief flood into him, and knew instinctively that Intel-Trace's chances of succeeding had just improved by no small measure. 'I'll do whatever I can,' he said.

'From your description of the case, I'd say we're probably talking microbiological here, right?'

'Yes', Elias answered.

'Is it dangerous?'

'From everything we've been told, it poses no threat to life,' Elias replied.

'Besides the first person to find it, who does it belong to?' Michael asked.

'Skyco. It was being transported from their Research Institute in Medellín,' Elias told him.

Michael nodded. 'I've heard of the Research Institute there. How much do you know about the situation?'

'Not a great deal. And next to nothing on the organism.

'This is genetically engineered stuff. Top secret, worth a bundle to Skyco, and bad news in the wrong hands. Somebody else wanted the strain, too, which the Skyco people call the Luxus. The Institute was attacked by a small hostile band the day before it was put on that plane. The attempt was crushed by Skyco security. But it tells us something very important. Somebody *knows* about this top-secret project, where it was kept, and probably just what it can do for them if they get their hands on it. How does that translate?' Elias asked.

Michael thought for a moment. 'Skyco is diversified, but their main interests are in oil. They've pioneered some interesting techniques in drilling, oil recovery, and extraction of fuel from shale. I'd give pretty high odds that we're talking about something to do with oil,' Michael suggested. 'When it comes to genetic engineering, though, the possibilities are unlimited. There's no telling what their scientists could have discovered . . . or created. They haven't shared any more in the way of details with you?'

'Just what I've told you. But whatever it is, they don't

have it anymore,' Elias said. 'It was new enough that there wasn't much of it. Everything they had was on that plane.'

'I don't think *everything*,' Michael said, then went on. 'You have to understand how these things work. They could have transported all they had that was capable of life outside a laboratory environment. The rest, if they haven't destroyed it, would be useless to someone else outside of that environment.'

'Does that mean Skyco could make more?' Elias asked.

'It *should* mean that, but doesn't necessarily,' Michael replied. 'Without knowing more about what they've developed, I can't really answer that. There are too many factors.'

'Can I assume that tomorrow morning will be soon enough to leave?' Michael asked. 'I have some business to conclude here in Paris.'

Elias nodded. 'Until the plane is located, there's little we can do from your side of things.'

Michael knew that *his* side of things was small compared to what Intel-Trace would already be doing to tap its vast investigative resources. 'I'd like to make one suggestion, if I may,' he said.

'Sure. What is it?'

'I have a very good friend in Colombia. His name is Carlos Trevino. He's a deputy administrator of the National Parks Department in the Ministry of Agriculture. He's had a lot of experience locating downed aircraft in heavy rain forests. I'd like to contract his help. I think we could use his experience.'

'If you recommend him, then he's fine with me. How do we reach him?'

'I'll place a call to Carlos to alert him. He can meet us in Bogotá. We'll also need a good bush jockey,' Michael said.

'I'll have one of the best waiting for us. We'll coordinate the search from the Institute. We'll need to get an early start tomorrow.'

Michael nodded. 'I'll be ready before daylight.'

'Good. We'll arrange for a car to meet you at six,' said

Elias. He pushed his hands into his pockets again and turned to go. When he had ascended the stairs back up to the bridge, Michael Quinn rose slowly to his feet and traced his control's steps. He could already feel a change inside, as though some source of energy had been infused into him. A part of him was coming back to life. He hadn't felt that way in a very long time. Elias was right. It was time to come back into the present. He had been away too long.

5

COLOMBIA: The spritely little Hughes 500M darted like a dragonfly as it skimmed jagged peaks, plunged steeply into rapids-choked gorges, and knifed with the agility of a jack rabbit through twisting ravines. Christopher Wadelaw was an impressive pilot who handled the nimble helicopter as if it were wired to his nerves.

Bob Elias stared down in wonder at the razor-backed ridges of the Andean peaks. He had spent a lot of time in helicopters in 'Nam, but nothing, except perhaps intense enemy ground fire, had ever charged him so highly. It was like a kid's first roller-coaster ride, with no end in sight.

Less taken by the beauty below, Michael Quinn and Carlos Trevino studied every possible bit of rocky surface and deep-green-covered slope for signs of wreckage. They were on a course between Bogotá and Medellín, and after an hour and fifteen minutes in the air, they were coming up with nothing. When they came within sight of the Institute, Michael leaned toward Wadelaw and asked him to circle the compound several times before setting down. He carefully compared the layout with the diagram supplied by Elias, making several brief notations of his observations.

Elias knew exactly what Michael was doing. He was looking for escape routes the Building Two attack force might have intended to use. One thing was clear from the report: they could not have gone out the way they came in. There could be more valuable clues awaiting them on the ground.

With the air surveillance completed, the helicopter put down on the Skyco landing strip. The four men were met by Ernesto Delgado, head of security at the Skyco Research Institute.

'Welcome to Medellín,' Delgado said in greeting. 'You made good time from Bogotá. My name is Ernesto Delgado, but please call me Ernesto,' he said, offering his hand first to Elias.

Quick introductions followed, and the small group climbed into a Jeep Cherokee for the short ride to the headquarters building.

Delgado led the entourage through a tight security checkpoint where the visitors were issued badges bearing bright red codings. They were led down impressive hallways, drawing the curious stares of busy Institute staff members.

Delgado pushed his way through a set of heavy redwood doors, the group close behind. They came into a sumptuously appointed conference room, well lit and with thick, dark green carpeting. Standing at the far end of the long, highly polished conference table – also of redwood – were two people whom Elias and Michael recognized immediately from the Skyco files provided by Intel-Trace.

Tom Danziger stepped forward to greet them; Alexandra Sky remained at the head of the table.

'Gentlemen, may I introduce Mr Tom Danziger?' Delgado began in introduction.

Elias was the first to extend his hand. 'Bob Elias, Intel-Trace,' he said.

Danziger assessed him with the respect due a long-awaited opponent. 'Mr Elias. Yes, I had been given your name.'

'Just Bob is fine,' Elias said, smiling.

'OK, Bob.'

'And I'd like to introduce Michael Quinn,' Elias began, making the introductions of his team.

'Mr Quinn . . . I know, first names. Hi, Mike,' Danziger said, again extending his hand.

Michael nodded and took the extended hand in a firm handshake.

Danziger registered the name permanently in his memory. Later he would make one phone call to unlock the file on this man to whom they were entrusting so much.

'Carlos Trevino,' the Colombian said in self-introduction before Elias could speak his name.

'Mr Trevino. Ministry of Agriculture, isn't it?' Danziger asked, to Carlos's amazement.

Carlos nodded with a small but proud smile.

'I have known your boss for many years,' Danziger said. 'How is Enrique?'

'Well. Very well, thank you. I shall convey your kind inquiry.'

'Please do.'

'And this is Christopher Wadelaw,' Elias continued.

'Chris. My pleasure to meet you.'

'Likewise,' Wadelaw returned, not a man of many words.

'Gentlemen, I'd like to introduce Ms Alexandra Sky, president of Skyco, Incorporated,' Danziger said, turning with the group toward her as she approached.

Alexandra Sky was no stranger to anyone who followed world events. She was a frequent subject of leading news magazines and tabloids.

Elias was impressed by this tall and attractive woman. With great poise she voiced her greetings, calling each man by name as she shook his hand. She had the unmistakable air of a Sky about her. He also noticed the way her eyes had returned to Michael following the introductions. She was obviously intrigued by him. Elias noted that Quinn had always seemed to affect women in that way. In a gathering of any size half of the female eyes within watching distance would be locked on to him. He had a presence that commanded attention. It was almost magnetic in nature. Not being a member of the opposite sex, Elias couldn't quite put his finger on what it was. Maybe it was everything. Michael was a handsome man, big and athletic, his dark features having a quality of mystery to them. Yet there was something . . . in the eyes . . . a vulnerability, perhaps.

'Why don't we make ourselves comfortable at the table, gentlemen,' Alexandra said, breaking into Elias's musings.

The group complied, settling quickly around the table.

'By now you've no doubt been apprised of our situation here,' Danziger began. 'In front of each of you is a summary of such facts as we now possess. Bob, at your request I've also compiled comprehensive backgrounds on certain specific personnel. These files are confidential, gentlemen, as will be any findings resulting from the subsequent investigation.'

'I take it that our special-investigations team is already here on the job?' Elias asked. It was their job to isolate the affected areas of Building Two in order to gather as much evidence as possible.

'Yes, they've been working almost nonstop since yesterday afternoon,' Delgado responded. 'Building Two has been closed down except for essential personnel in the biogenetics wing.'

'That's fine. I'll meet with the team later today for a progress report,' Elias remarked. 'I'll be glad to give you duplicate reports of all pertinent findings,' he said to Danziger, who would doubtless be Skyco's authority on site during this phase of the investigation.

'Yes, thank you,' Danziger returned.

'The first thing I'd like to do is to inspect the site,' Michael said.

'We expected you would,' Danziger responded. 'Ernesto will accompany you and give a verbal summary of what's in the reports.'

'Have you identified any of the attack team yet?' Elias asked.

'Inquiries are still under way. We're probably a few days away from anything positive. We haven't gone through official channels here in Colombia for obvious reasons, so the process is slow.'

'Let us have what you've got so far,' Elias began. 'We have considerable resources for matters like these.'

'Gladly,' Danziger said without reservation.

Danziger's apparent attitude pleased Elias. He didn't seem to have ego hangups like some security chiefs. There was none of the uneasy chemistry that often developed when outside help was called in. Danziger was obviously secure in his abilities and didn't feel threatened by Intel-Trace's presence. He would be a cooperative conduit to Sky.

'When will you begin?' Alexandra asked.

'Immediately,' Elias responded. 'We'd like to walk through the entire event, starting with their entry into the compound. While Mike is doing that, Chris and Carlos can review the air-search procedures undertaken so far and begin working out our search patterns.'

Elias turned to Michael. 'While you're going over the grounds, Tom and I can review these confidential personnel files.'

Michael looked to Danziger. 'Perhaps a little later you can give me a brief workup on the Luxus. Details about the transport case, the vials, whether we're talking cryogenics or desiccated stock here. We'll need to know how to handle it when we find it,' he said. 'There will undoubtedly have been some environmental stress, even if the transport case survived the crash.'

Danziger liked what he heard. This man seemed to understand the nature of their missing prize. His early impressions were bearing out.

'Ernesto, see that these gentlemen get what they need,' Alexandra said. 'I'd like you to personally walk Mr Quinn through the attack. Take all the time that's needed.

'You will find very comprehensive charts of our search efforts,' she said, directing her attention to Wadelaw and Carlos. 'We've brought in two of the most knowledgeable region experts in the country. Both are highly educated Guajiro Indians. No-one will know the region better then they.'

'Very well, gentlemen. Let's begin,' Danziger said, rising to his feet. Time was a precious commodity with the stakes so high, and he intended to waste very little of it.

Michael's inspection of Building Two was quick but thorough. After going through the affected areas he took a solo walk along the perimeter of the compound in the general area of Building Two. Since it was clear to him that the attack force must have planned a secondary escape route, he was looking for anything that would let him know how that withdrawal was intended. Perhaps not all the attacking force had entered the compound. One or more could have been positioned at the compound perimeter, besides the one at the main gate, or they may have relied on inside help that never materialized once it was clear the attack would fail.

Michael returned to the conference room when he had finished. Elias, Danziger, Alexandra, and Delgado were there ahead of him.

'Any opinions, Mr Quinn?' Alexandra asked.

'It wasn't much of a plan,' Michael began. 'Either these men were amateurs or this plan was never intended to succeed.'

'Explain,' Elias said.

'There was no way out. According to all the reports, they started shooting the place all to hell as soon as they reached the third floor of Building Two. The van was too far away to be useful in the escape. There are no signs along the perimeter of the compound to indicate a preplanned point of exit, unless there was outside help that didn't stick around when things heated up. The only way I see to have gotten out was to go up, which is exactly what they tried.'

'Up?' Alexandra asked, puzzled.

'To the roof of Building Two, where a helicopter could lift them out,' Michael explained.

'There was a helicopter, but it was ours,' Delgado said. 'There were no other helicopters spotted.'

'That doesn't mean that one wasn't a part of the plan. They failed to penetrate the biogenetics wing and, therefore, had no prize. They could have simply been abandoned.'

'A helicopter would have had to hover for quite some time to lift that many men. Certainly it would have made too good a target to make that practical,' Alexandra commented.

'Ms Sky—'

'Please, I prefer Alex.'

'Alex,' Michael began with a polite nod, 'I've been in helicopters that could knock this whole compound flat in minutes and thoroughly neutralize any ground force. This compound and its security force – no disrespect intended – would have been child's play for the right pilot and ship.'

'Well, then, why didn't it come in?' she asked.

'The plan fell apart too quickly, and, as I said before, they didn't get what they came for. The risk wasn't worth it, there was nothing to gain. And, if I'm right, these men were expendable.'

'*If* there was a helicopter,' Alexandra clarified.

'That's right. *If* there was one. It's only speculation on my part.'

'How did they get their information?' Alexandra asked. 'They obviously knew where to go. That information was not common knowledge.'

'There's a very strong possibility of inside help,' Elias replied.

'A spy?'

'Not necessarily. A source of information would be more likely. This could have been an unknowing party who was played very well by the adversary,' Elias explained. 'It'll take a while for me to finish going through these personnel files to develop a list of possible suspects. I can get my people working on any leads quickly. A few days will get us a lot closer to those answers.'

'How much is known about the pilot of the plane?' Michael asked.

'According to his file, he's pretty reliable,' Danziger answered. 'Been flying in and out of here for several years. Has a good record of performance.'

'Does he come in on a regular schedule?' Michael asked.

Danziger flipped through some pages. 'Yeah, pretty regular. Couple of times a month, at least.'

'And was he scheduled in the day after the attack?'

'Yes. He brought in a shipment of maintenance parts.'

'I can see where you're leading,' Alexandra said. 'But you're losing sight of one fact. The decision to fly the Luxus out was made in San Antonio. Harry Gill could have had no previous knowledge of that, nor could he know that he'd be asked to fly it out.'

'Yes, the decision to remove the strain was made in San Antonio, but that decision was communicated to the Institute the evening before the Luxus was flown out, was it not?' Michael countered.

'Yes, but directly to Dr Stillings, the director of the Institute,' Alexandra replied.

'And where is Dr Stillings now?'

Alexandra's brow wrinkled. 'I see your point,' she conceded.

'Which brings up the possibility that perhaps the plane never went down at all,' Elias suggested.

'Exactly,' Michael said. 'It could have landed anywhere, or gone down anywhere. I suggest we widen our search area, not necessarily concentrating on the sector between Medellín and Bogotá.'

'We'll check out every known landing strip within range of that plane,' Elias said. 'If it landed, it'll turn up. We'll check out Panama and Ecuador as well.'

'In the meantime we'll continue searching under the assumption that it did go down,' Michael said. 'We'll widen the search area and get everything into the air that we can.'

Elias looked at his watch. 'There isn't much we can do from the air today. We'll start at first light in the morning. I'll get the airstrip check started immediately. Is there a secure phone that I can use to contact my people?' he asked Danziger.

'Yes, you can use the phone in our security office here,' Danziger replied. 'We can arrange to have any special lines you need brought in.'

'That'll be fine. We've got a big day ahead of us tomorrow,' Elias said, picking up the thick bundle of personnel files.

'Well, thank you very much, gentlemen,' Alexandra said. 'This has been very enlightening. Everything you need will be at your disposal. We've arranged quarters for you here on the Institute grounds. You'll be quite comfortable. Please don't hesitate to ask for anything at all. Until morning, then. Rest well.'

Following the meeting, Elias and his team were led to their quarters. He was hanging his shirt in the closet when a knock sounded on his door. He went to it and opened it. Michael was standing there, and the look on his face told Elias he had business to discuss.

'What is it, Mike?' Elias asked.

Michael entered the room and closed the door behind him.

'I'm convinced that the roof was the pickup point, Bob,' he began.

'What you theorized earlier about the roof made pretty good sense. What makes you so positive now?' Elias asked.

'The attacking force wasn't carrying radios. That fact wasn't included in the report filed by Delgado's men,' Michael explained.

'Are you sure? Maybe it was just omitted.'

'I checked through the recovered effects before returning to the meeting. There weren't any there. And they weren't carrying any kind of flare devices. That means either a preplanned pickup or a retreat back the way they came. And we've already ruled that one out.'

'They could have planned their escape through the perimeter fence outside of Building Two,' Elias offered.

'I don't think so. There weren't any signs of outside support along the perimeter there. I'd have found signs of presence if someone had been outside that fence. Also, from that point on the perimeter, it's three-quarters of a mile to the main road. Skyco's security could easily have beaten them to any planned rendezvous. It had to be the roof,' Michael said.

'What do you suggest?' Elias asked.

'Dig hard on Delgado's staff. I think our source might be there. They used a helicopter, and it *was* in position,' Michael responded.

'Delgado was on that helicopter himself,' Elias said, recalling details from the report supplied by Danziger.

'That's right. But it was a matter of timing, more than anything else, that put him there. He had just barely arrived when the attack began. After surviving the attack on his life, he began directing the defense efforts. The helicopter was already mustering when he got to it. And the fact that he was on it may have been the reason it wasn't used.'

'That's an excellent point, Mike. There were three other men on the helicopter with Delgado. It'll be one of them,' Elias said.

'Or all of them,' Michael added. 'We'll have to determine that.'

'Damn,' Elias said, clenching his fists. 'This is going to complicate things. We'll have to keep Delgado out of the main loop of information. Anything he knows can be leaked to whoever is behind this. He'll start getting suspicious if he's not a part of what's going on here. We need his cooperation too much at this point to risk that.'

'Maybe we should tell him what we suspect,' Michael suggested.

Elias shook his head. 'Not this early. This is still speculation, as good as it sounds. I need to get some hard data first. We'll keep him involved when it's unavoidable, and shelter the rest of our information. When we have proof, we'll bring him into it.'

'OK, agreed.'

'I'll get right on the crew of the helicopter.'

Michael nodded and turned to go. 'See you in the morning, Chief.'

Elias watched as Michael left the room and walked down the hallway. He was glad now that he had held his ground against Martin Trace on bringing Michael in on the assignment. He had a lot of confidence in Michael, and he had never lost faith in him. He was surer now than ever before that his choice would pay off before this job was finished.

The better part of the night was used to good advantage. Elias searched relentlessly through the files, looking for anything that might lead to the inside contact. He put into motion the investigation on Delgado's security staff. Everyone at the Institute was suspect, even at office and maintenance levels.

Michael, Carlos, and Wadelaw spent their time carefully mapping out new sectors for intensive air search. The sectors between Medellín and Bogotá would still get the heaviest attention, as the complicity of the pilot or the missing scientist was still mere conjecture.

Intel-Trace's team of crime-scene investigation specialists would continue to examine and analyze what evidence could be uncovered and made useful. They would also begin their own efforts into uncovering the identities of the attackers.

It took three days of intensive effort before the first clues broke. These led to the identities of three of the unknown attackers. All were small-time hoods, second-rate mercenaries who had never been associated with major terrorist or criminal groups. They had been well armed, however, which meant they had support from some substantial source.

It was also on the third day that the single most meaningful discovery was made.

The air-search efforts to this point had been fruitless. Twenty-two planes and helicopters had run endless patterns, crisscrossing the mapped sectors over and over again, calling in two finds, but of the wrong type of aircraft. The efforts didn't stop for these other lost sorties, though their locations were charted for later investigation and reporting to the authorities.

It was on a late-afternoon run through the Chocó, a primitive region of jungled hills and mountains about 140 miles south-southwest of Medellín, that the find was made. The region, which was usually cloaked in thick mists, was brilliant and clear owing to unusually high wind activity. One of the pilots was making his final runs through the winding gorges when his eye caught a narrow strip of what appeared from a distance to be a clearing. He checked his fuel gauges, and decided that although the levels were low, his fuel was sufficient to make at least one good pass over the area.

He came in low and dead-center through the narrow valley, eyes fixed sharply on the clearing, which proved not to be a clearing at all – or at least one that had not been used for some time, as it was interrupted by enough young tree growth to prevent any landings, even by helicopter. It was just as he began to pull up over the high growth and low ridges near the end of the clearing that he saw a flash of something white to his right. He had gone by too quickly to see it clearly, so he increased his altitude and circled back to try again from the opposite direction and along the far side of the gorge.

He throttled down and came in slower the second time. There was no mistake. It was a plane. And it was a Cessna. He pulled up again and made a wide sweep, coming in as low as possible on the third pass. He concentrated on the center of the clearing, and released an electronic homing beacon as he passed over the site. He circled once more at high altitude, tuning his receiver. The signal was strong and clear. He radioed in his find, using a predetermined code giving the frequency setting of the homing signal, then headed for home.

76

Within minutes the satellite locked on to the signal and began close-up photographic surveillance of the clearing, sending its signals back to the Intel-Trace satellite control center in the United States. The signals were processed in microseconds and relayed to Bogotá in scrambled sequence, where they were reassembled and sent on to Medellín.

The pictures were remarkably clear. They showed the unmistakable figure of a Cessna 310 sitting partly under cover at the far edge of the clearing. Three of its registration numbers were visible. They matched numbers on Harry Gill's plane.

Word of the find was not broadcast to the operational aircraft, on the chance that their communications were being monitored. The search efforts had even been continued to the normal quitting time. All efforts would resume in the morning, with only the recovery team of Michael, Carlos, and Wadelaw knowing that the siting was a confirmed find. Even the pilot who had made the find would be back in the air in a new sector, unaware that he had made the critical discovery. They were taking no chances of alerting a possible adversary to their success.

Elias's team was informed upon their return to the command center established at the Institute. The group scrutinized the pictures with great patience.

'What do you think?' Michael asked Carlos and Wadelaw as they examined the collage of enlarged satellite photos showing the entire clearing.

Wadelaw leaned his lanky, six-foot frame close to the pictures with a magnifying glass. 'I gotta hand it to him,' he began. 'He put that baby down like a real pro. Minimal breakup.'

'Could there be survivors?' Elias asked.

Wadelaw zeroed in on the aircraft with the magnifying glass. 'I'm certain of it. The hatch looks partly open, like someone got out of the plane,' he replied.

The glass moved to the only visible wing and its engine. 'From what I can make of the port-side prop, it looks like he made an unpowered landing. See here?' he said, touching the area with a pencil point. 'The blade above the wing is straight. If it had been spinning, it would be bent back.'

'Any idea where he was heading?' Elias asked from in front of a large wall map of Colombia.

Wadelaw walked over to the map and studied it for a few moments. 'Tuluá and Cali are out of the question. They're on the other side of the mountain range. I'd bet he was making for airstrips in either Buenaventura or Tumaco. Probably Tumaco. It has more possibilities. It's a busy port. It's also very close to the Ecuadorian border. One thing's for sure, though. He wasn't heading for Bogotá.'

'You don't think there's any way he could have been off course?' Danziger asked.

'Not a chance,' Wadelaw replied. 'He's ninety degrees and two mountain ranges in the wrong direction. A pilot with a seeing-eye dog wouldn't be that far off.'

'Can you get in there with a helicopter?' Alexandra asked.

Wadelaw went back to the photos. 'I can't be sure. There are a lot of trees down there.'

'We can clear out what you need, just like for the medevacs in 'Nam,' Michael told him. 'Carlos and I can rappel down without any difficulty.'

'Yeah, I don't see a problem,' the pilot said.

'OK, then, we go with first light,' Elias told his team.

'I want you to take some special equipment,' he said, pulling a long duffel bag from under the table. He took a moment opening it, then began removing the gear.

'For starters, you're to wear these,' he said, tossing flak jackets on to the table. 'We're going to assume the worst.'

He dug in again, pulling out two weapons, the first a Ruger Mini-30 rifle equipped with a folding stock and pistol grip. The second was a Franchi SPAS-12 assault shotgun, a remarkable weapon well suited to the heavy bush. It could be fired in either pump or semiauto mode with the depression of a selector button below the forestock. It, too, had a short folding stock and pistol grip. 'Just in case the worst turns out to be just that.'

Michael looked to his friend Carlos for reaction. There had been no mention of possible violence.

'Your part in this is done, Carlos. Chris and I can handle this,' Michael said.

'You will still need me,' the Colombian replied. 'I'll go in with you.'

'You're not obligated beyond finding—'

'I'll go in, Michael,' Carlos interrupted. 'I know how to use these weapons. I've been in the army and have dealt with rebels before.' The matter was settled.

Elias handed each man a compact radio and an ultra-light headset. 'These are your communication sets. Keep in constant contact with me. I want a play-by-play of everything you see, as you see it. If there are survivors, you're to bring them out, with the strain.

'This little device is in case I have to communicate visual data to you,' Elias said, holding out what looked like an ordinary digital watch. 'It has a high-resolution LCD screen. The signal will be satellite-relayed in a very tight beam to prevent interception. The unit has a built-in homing signal on to which our communications satellite can lock. It's also capable of serving as a backup to your radio if there's a malfunction.

'The rest of your gear is routine. A backup Smith & Wesson Airweight is in the bag for you as well, Mike.'

'What about the Browning High Power?' Michael asked, inquiring about his favorite sidearm.

'I knew you'd ask,' Elias returned. 'What I have for you, instead, is this,' he said, holding out an unusual-looking handgun. 'I think you'll like it.'

'Glock seventeen,' Michael said. 'Never fired one, but I've heard good things about it.'

'The frame is constructed entirely of a tough feather-weight polymer. The magazine is a staggered seventeen-round clip to give you considerably more firepower than the Browning. The entire piece weighs in at under twenty-eight ounces fully loaded.'

Michael accepted the piece and looked it over carefully.

'It is light. That's a lot of firepower.' He held it in firing position. It felt very comfortable in his hand and was well balanced.

'Nine-millimeter. Same as the Browning, but with less recoil and a faster action,' Elias added.

'It'll do nicely. Thanks.'

'I think that's everything. Let's get some dinner, then plenty of rest,' Elias told his people. They were a day's work away from finishing what they had come to Colombia to do – unless, that is, Elias's fears became reality.

The helicopter ride in took less than an hour. The winds had returned to their usual pattern and the soggy Chocó was again shrouded in mist. The helicopter was pelted soundly by large hailstones at nine thousand feet, just west of Manzinales as they came in over the last of the treacherous ranges. The poor visibility did little to hamper their progress as they keyed in on the target homing signal.

Wadelaw skirted a few low ridges, then plunged straight down through the mist, the lush valley opening up below them. They followed the bends in the gorge to the clearing, then hovered for a few moments over the site. There were no signs of human life below.

Michael and Carlos readied themselves quickly, then rappelled swiftly and smoothly to the ground.

'We're down,' Michael announced into the voice-actuated microphone attached to the ultralight headset.

'What do you see?' came Elias's voice from the Institute, the communications directed through the narrow satellite band.

'The plane looks a little worse from ground level than it did in the satellite photos,' Michael responded. 'No visible signs of survivors. My nose tells me we might not find any, either,' he said. His sharp senses had quickly detected the smell of death.

The two men moved directly toward the Cessna, their movements swift but cautious.

'The door is ajar and without signs of damage,' Michael

described as he drew nearer the plane. 'I'd say that Chris was right. It was probably opened from the inside.'

They circled the plane once, then went for the door.

Michael raised the Franchi to the door and opened it slowly. It swung up freely. The Franchi poked into the opening, followed cautiously by Michael's head. He saw the body immediately. It was in advanced stages of decomposition, but he could clearly make out that it was what was left of Stillings. He stepped up into the fuselage.

'Got one body here. Badly decomposed. It's Stillings,' he announced.

'What about the pilot?' Elias asked.

'*Nada, Compadre*,' Michael replied. 'We know who made it out.'

He turned to give the body a closer inspection, and saw the bullet holes in the face and head. They were surrounded by flash and powder burns. 'Stillings is dead from gunshot wounds to the head. Small-caliber, at close range.'

'Great,' Elias said, the worst quickly becoming the reality. 'What about the strain?' he asked, already knowing the answer.

'Nowhere in sight.'

'Can you get the helicopter down?' Elias asked.

'Yes, but we'll have to clear a landing area. The trees are young. It should only take a few minutes.'

Michael left the plane. Carlos approached after having given the plane a closer inspection.

'The landing was planned,' Carlos began. 'The fuel tanks are empty. They are modified for dumping their loads. Gill probably jettisoned his fuel a good while before coming in, to remove any risk of explosion. There's not a drop left in the reserve. That explains the unpowered landing.'

'Looks like he executed it perfectly. You were right, Chris. The guy's a pro.'

'Clear me some space. I'll set her down,' Wadelaw said from above.

Michael and Carlos went to work immediately, taking down the young trees with their machetes. Within a few minutes, enough ground was cleared for the helicopter to put down without danger to its rotors.

Wadelaw was out of the helicopter instantly. He inspected the plane and confirmed Carlos's assessment.

Michael had gone to the edge of the clearing while Wadelaw made his inspection of the craft. He returned to the plane at about the same time that Wadelaw was finishing up.

'Gill headed out to the west. Left an easy trail,' Michael said. 'He might have been a pro as an air jockey, but when it comes to ground movement through the thick forest, he's a real rookie. His trail is trackable even after six days' growth.'

'What's our next step?' Elias asked.

'There's only one option,' Michael began. 'We track Gill out. There's no way we'll catch him, unless he got himself hopelessly lost. I wouldn't bet on it, though. All he needs is a compass, and he'll get himself to some kind of help somewhere.'

'Well, we know he's armed and dangerous now, so proceed with care, Mike,' Elias said.

'Yeah, don't worry about the careful part, anyway.'

Wadelaw went to the helicopter and returned with a body bag. It was an unpleasant job, but they got Stillings packed away for the trip back to Medellín.

'Chris, can you leave me one of your sector charts?' Michael asked. 'It may provide some clues to Gill's likely destination.'

'Sure, no problem. I'll take a swing to the northwest and give you an idea of what lies ahead, too. What about a rendezvous?'

'You may as well return to the Institute. I'll call you later with instructions on a meeting site.'

'How long will you be in the bush? I can drop you supplies,' Wadelaw offered.

Michael grinned. 'This place is a supermarket,' he said. 'I won't need a thing.'

'We'll be fine,' Carlos said to the pilot.

'Uh-uh, pal,' Michael said to his friend. 'You've done your

job. I'll go on alone. Taking risks wasn't part of your job description.'

'Just the same, I'll stay with you. I know the forests, too. You know that.'

'I know you do. But there's a hostile out there with nothing better to do than kill people. I'd feel better with you back at the Institute. Chris can bring you back in if I need you,' Michael said.

'Four eyes are better than two, my friend. Let me come with you . . . please.'

Michael weighed the risks. Their chances of actually catching up to Gill with a six-day lead were realistically nonexistent. And he knew Carlos was completely at home in the forests. The company wouldn't hurt, either.

'OK. But if there's any trouble, you hit the ground and stay there. Clear? That's unconditional.'

Carlos smiled and nodded.

'Looks like you get to solo it home, Chris.'

'No problem. I'll tell my life story to the stiff. Remember, I can get to you in a hurry if you need me.'

'We're going on, Bob,' Michael told Elias. 'I suggest you work on identifying that inside source. Looks like Skyco's got one for sure.'

'I'll handle it. You just be careful,' Elias said.

'Don't worry about us. It's just a walk in the woods.'

It wasn't the 'walk in the woods' that worried Elias. He knew Michael's jungle training and experience in Vietnam made him eminently qualified to survive in that environment. There weren't many men anywhere who paralleled his abilities in the forests. What bothered Elias was the fact that Gill wasn't expert in the forests. That left clear possibilities of a rendezvous with a party, or parties, who did possess that ability. An encounter with them *could* be a major risk.

Michael checked his watch. 'I'll contact you in two hours, unless we find something unusual before that,' he said into the radio.

'Negative, Mike,' Elias replied. 'Every hour on the hour.

If you find something even remotely suspicious, turn it on and leave it on. I want constant communication if things begin to heat up. Understood?'

'You got it, Chief,' Michael said, looking at Carlos with a broad smile.

The Colombian returned the smile and nodded. 'Just like old times for you, isn't it?'

'Yeah,' Michael returned. 'Just like old times. Let's go find this jungle boy before he hurts himself.'

6

CHOCÓ RAIN FOREST, COLOMBIA: The forests were his element. In them, the two sides of Michael Quinn found a strange and peaceful coexistence. He moved through them with the natural ease of a wild creature, charting the sounds, sights, and smells, scanning for signs of the danger he knew to be out there, ever-vigilant, ready to react, ready and trained to take a life so quickly that even the time necessary for the recognition of danger was too long a delay for the adversary.

Rain in the Chocó was a daily event. The region typically received twenty-five feet of precipitation annually, and when it wasn't raining, it was a virtual hothouse with a relative humidity seldom below ninety-five per cent. At the moment, however, there was rain – a lashing, thick downpour that brought a temporary refreshing coolness to the trackers as they followed the trail of Harry Gill.

Gill had set out on a westerly course, which he held quite accurately. If their location was correct, they were between the San Juan and Tadosito rivers, moving directly for the point at which they merged. Both rivers were large and wild in places, but navigable in the direction of flow by means of a sturdy but simply constructed balsa raft. The materials were available everywhere, and all that was needed were a machete and a passing knowledge of knot-tying. Once they were on the river, the destination could be any one of the many small villages on its banks, or any trail heading away into a new region of forest. The odds of finding Gill weren't good, but his trail was all they had, so they worked it as best they could.

To be sure, their going was easier than Gill's had been. He had headed straight through the thickest parts of this tropical green hell of wildly tangled palms and hardwoods, vines and thornbushes stout enough to stop heavy machinery. The only way through was to hack at the obstructions. Hacking was an art in itself. The experienced hand let the tool – the machete – do the work, delivering almost effortless blows at practiced angles. But it was clear that Gill was no artist – not even in the vaguest sense. The blows he delivered were poorly aimed, and badly angled, requiring a good deal of force and exertion. They could spot quite easily the places Gill had stopped to rest. They were even predictable by simple observation of the pattern of his tired blows. Michael guessed from the distance between resting points that Gill was a strong man with a great deal of endurance. He would have to be, to withstand the physical strain and the unavoidable biological hazards, namely insects, that would find him an appealing source of nutrition.

During the absence of rain the mosquitoes were fierce. Periodically they would encounter the *manta blanca*. This was a dreaded white veil of minute sticky bugs in dense swarms. Inadvertent inhalation of these tiny pests was an awful experience. Biting ants and stinging caterpillars were another abundant nuisance, not to mention the snakes and their dangerous venoms. But to Gill's credit he had pushed on, defeating the obstacles.

Darkness began to set in rapidly beneath the mists, and the two men set about gathering food. A few minutes of scouting resulted in an armful of ripe mangos and fat, buttery avocados. A snare returned a quick profit of a paca, a jungle rodent of rather good size and good-tasting meat.

The jungle sounds changed as darkness set in, the symphony of varied bird calls being replaced by the nighttime chorus of insect sounds. Water was everywhere in the plant life surrounding them. A few rapid chops with the machete produced thick bamboo-like shafts from which pleasant-tasting water trickled as though from a faucet left open just a crack.

They ate to their content and rested their fatigued bodies. Michael felt a good deal more soreness than he wanted to admit. Although he had always kept himself in reasonably good shape, his body had forty-three years on it, and was beginning to show the wear and tear of the mileage. His shoulders and back ached considerably, though his legs still felt strong, which was a good sign. What he really wanted was a long shower and a soak in a hot tub. But for tonight, at least, he'd have to settle for a secure spot in a tree.

At night the activity in a rain forest moves upward, for two basic reasons. The first is to seek rest and nourishment. The second is to avoid becoming the meal of some larger ground predator. And so, too, Michael and Carlos moved upward into the trees to sleep in safety.

Michael's experience in Vietnam had taught him to sleep soundly with his body totally relaxed. But the ears never slept. It was a skill learned of necessity. He was safe in this element, surrounded by a million of nature's sentries. How simple life seemed to him in this complex environment. How natural it was to feel safe in this world. The reason he had come back to it didn't matter, he loved being back.

The east glowed amber as the first light of morning made its way through the topmost layers of the forest canopy. Michael had been awake before the first gray light pressed through the cloud tendrils that touched the forest crown. The first rain wouldn't fall for about four hours, so the trackers used the time to cover as much of Gill's trail as possible, eating a breakfast of mangos and wild bananas on the go.

From the information they had been given about the strain, they knew the metallized case would weigh about eighteen pounds and would probably be carried in some kind of a back harness. Inside were twenty-four metal vials, each containing a desiccated consignment of the Luxus strain. It was dormant and relatively safe from environmental stress as long as the case and the individual vials maintained their watertight integrity. Alexandra had confirmed that the organism posed no threat to life. No more information was given them, nor was it needed.

It was just as the heavy rains began to fall again that Michael and Carlos came across the second trail. This one was rather well used and bore signs of age. Gill had obviously camped here for a night.

Before they could theorize that he had taken one direction or another Carlos picked up Gill's trail fifty yards to the north as it continued due west. Gill had simply slid north a bit to use the trail as cover. The markings were unmistakable. Gill had pushed on, his markings as evident as a thumbprint.

They had tracked the new trail for almost half a day when they made another discovery. The markings changed, though they continued on in the same westerly direction. This part of the trail was *not* cut by Gill. The hand that had cut this trail was experienced. Gill had met up with someone, which raised a big question.

Michael contacted Elias immediately.

'Go ahead, Mike,' Elias said.

'We've got a problem here. Gill has crossed another well-used trail. Carlos picked him up again a little north on the same westerly heading. We're about a half-day into the trail change, and it's clear that Gill is no longer cutting his own trail,' Michael told him.

'Sounds like he rendezvoused with someone. Any way to tell how many are moving on the trail now?' Elias asked.

'Carlos is backtracking to look for signs. From this point

on, it looks to me like *one* person going west. It's not Gill, unless he followed his new partner very, very carefully.'

'Any opinions?'

'Could be that his new partner followed him carefully, then went on alone. That would leave Gill free to go back to the second trail. He could have gone north or south on it. There's no telling, with the condition of that trail and the rain.'

'And there's no telling which of the trails the Luxus moved on,' Elias added. 'Gill could have kept it or turned it over to his contact.'

'That's right. If this trail stays on its current heading, it should run into the San Juan River very soon. We'll lose it completely from there.'

'What do you suggest?' Elias asked.

'I'm not sure. But if I were Gill, I'd want to keep the strain in my possession until I got paid. A payoff in the middle of a tropical forest wouldn't leave me feeling too secure. I say we go for Gill. Problem is that we don't know which direction he took on the other trail. We also don't know who uses this trail. Carlos suspects it's used for drugs or some other contraband, which makes it very dangerous. Carlos and I could split up and head in opposite directions to see if Gill cut off the main trail at another location. I don't mind the risk to myself, but I'm concerned about exposing Carlos any further.'

'Will he go on?'

'I'm sure of it.'

'You can keep in contact with your radios. I don't see that we have any other choice. We have to pick up Gill again,' Elias said.

'I think you're right, Bob, but I don't like it. I'll head back to rejoin Carlos, then you get a fix on our coordinates. That will locate the second trail for you. You might be able to learn something about it, like maybe where it begins and ends, possibly even who uses it.'

'OK, head back and contact me as soon as you get there.'

'Right. I should make contact in about three or four hours.'

'I'll be waiting.'

The rain that day was punishing, falling straight down in huge, stinging drops. The only sounds were the roar of the rain on the foliage and the occasional earpiece crackle of radio communication between Michael and Carlos as they worked their way back to the main trail. They made very good time on the trail they had established.

'I don't know how we missed some of these signs,' Carlos radioed from his position about thirty minutes ahead of Michael. 'They're clear to me now. Someone headed back along this trail,' he continued, speaking in his native Spanish.

'Maybe they were too easy, Carlos. The obvious is often the hardest to see.'

'I think you're right, my friend. I'm nearing the other trail. Shall I wait for you here, or do you want me to begin tracking north?' Carlos asked.

'We'll have to split up anyway. You go ahead to the north. I'll head south. We'll check in with each other on the hour and half hour,' Michael told his friend. 'I don't want you to take any chances, Carlos. If you spot trouble, or even suspect it, I want you out of there in a hurry. Head back in my direction as fast as you can. Got that?'

Michael moved smoothly through the widened trail, waiting for Carlos's response. But there was only silence.

'Carlos, did you get a copy on my instructions?'

There was still no response.

Michael unclipped the wet radio from his belt and shook it.

'Carlos, did you get a copy?' he repeated more urgently.

There was only silence.

'Goddamn radio,' Michael muttered. 'You'd think they could make these things waterproof. Quinn to base,' he tried, to check his transmission. 'Come in, Elias. Do you read?'

'Ten-four, Mike. We have you loud and clear. A little water won't hurt that gear,' Elias replied.

'I'm receiving you clear, too. I think Carlos is having problems with his set. Try raising him.'

Michael listened to Elias's attempts to raise Carlos. There was still no response.

'He's not responding, Mike,' Elias said. 'He might have inadvertently switched his set off. I'll keep trying. If we can't reach him, you'll have to trail north after him, just in case his set has failed. We wouldn't want to lose him on a potentially hostile trail. How far behind him are you?'

'Maybe thirty minutes. I'll pick up my speed. I should catch up to him in about an hour. I can move pretty quickly if I don't have to cut a trail.'

Michael picked up the pace considerably. The last thing he wanted was to have his friend stranded without communications. If the set was dead, even the homing signal wouldn't function. Carlos could probably figure out that his set had failed on the approaching half hour when the next communication was scheduled – that is, if he had received the transmission.

Michael's pace, though swift through the unrelenting rain, was not without caution. He kept his vigil sharp for signs of danger. It wasn't long before the first sign turned up.

He was about fifty yards off the contraband trail when he spotted the handle of a machete near the far edge of the smaller trail he was backtracking. He stopped immediately and crouched low to conceal himself. He edged forward toward the machete. It was Carlos's. There were also signs of a struggle. Deep furrows cut into the soft ground from the powerful scuffling of feet gave Michael a clear sign.

He listened intently, but the sounds of the rain were all he heard.

He switched off his radio and removed his backpack and let all nonessential gear fall quietly to the jungle floor. He turned the SPAS-12 upside down, depressed the selector button beneath the slide grip, and pushed the grip forward, locking the weapon in the semiauto action. Then he slid silently into the thick bush away from the path. He moved in a wide arc to the south.

Within minutes he came in sight of the contraband trail. His eyes strained into the distance ahead, and what he saw tripped the switch to the dark side. Carlos stood unnaturally upright against a tree. A bright splash of crimson, originating below his chin, spread down and across his chest. The face was twisted and blue, the limbs limp. He was not standing at all, Michael realized. A wire was strung tightly around his neck and to the tree. It was all that held the lifeless body up. Michael gritted his teeth in seething anger.

Then he saw the first man hiding low in the forest growth, holding a sawed-off, double-barreled shotgun raised at the decoy trail he had been traveling. Michael squinted into the rain and looked for others. There were two more. They knew he was near. They must have heard his communications over Carlos's radio. He turned and looked back down the main trail. He caught a flicker of movement – the ear of an animal. A burro. There were two others, all heavily laden with cargo. Drug runners, he was sure.

In ghostlike silence he moved deeper into the forest, then toward the animals. He saw one man, squatting low, a World War II-vintage M-1 carbine in hand, guarding the contraband.

Michael circled deeper and to the rear of the animals, then moved in. The sounds of the rain provided additional cover to his movements.

The man was nervous, the hands gripping the weapon tightly. He never heard the movement behind him.

Michael's left hand caught the man's face and chin from behind, and twisted the head violently to the left. At the same instant the Ka-Bar fighting knife struck upward with forceful precision to the base of the skull, severing the spinal cord, then drove farther upward. A sharp twist of the blade scrambled the lower brain stem and ended the man's life in complete silence.

Michael let the body slide soundlessly to the jungle floor,

then he crossed the trail. He widened his arc and moved deeper into the forest to come in from behind the concealed enemy. He approached the two men farthest from the trail with the SPAS-12 in ready firing position. The knife would be useless, since the two men were no more than six feet apart. Taking one without alerting the other would be impossible. He would have to take both quickly with the SPAS-12 and redirect his fire at the fourth man rapidly enough to take him by surprise as well, before he could return fire.

Michael moved in as close as possible, to improve his chances of taking the nearest two in a short, rapid burst. He took one step too many, the last causing a loud snap beneath his foot.

All three heads turned at once, and his chances for complete surprise were past.

Michael opened up without hesitation on the two men nearest him. Three loud blasts erupted from the SPAS-12 in less than a second. The double-O shot shredded through the first two targets.

The fourth man swung his AK-47 toward Michael, but the SPAS-12 spoke again, brutally. The AK-47 discharged harmlessly as the man doubled over and disappeared, the force of the blasts knocking him back through the heavy shrub.

It was then that another man whom Michael had not seen opened up with automatic fire, shredding the forest growth around him. A second short burst erupted, this one better aimed, and Michael went down as a series of heavy blows struck his chest and the SPAS-12.

He lay stunned and motionless, the SPAS-12 uselessly out of reach.

There was a short silence, then the sounds of rapid movement through the heavy brush. The man appeared and stood cautiously over Michael's body, the weapon ready in his hands.

His last volley had been true and well aimed. He had heard the thudding of the bullets striking his target. He regarded the motionless body for a moment, then turned to inspect his fallen comrades.

The Glock 17 was up and aimed the moment his head swung to the side. A single shot ripped through the side of his head, and he fell heavily through a tangle of shrub and vines.

Michael winced and grunted as he sat up. The Kevlar flak jacket had stopped the bullets, but not without pain from the force of the impacts. He felt as though he had been kicked in the chest. Elias's foresight had saved his life.

His senses rallied and his eyes searched frantically for signs of more attackers, but there were none. He raised himself to one knee, the Glock 17 poised and scanning his fallen enemy with deadly menace. His jaws were clenched, his hand tight on the weapon, his rage looking to be spent further.

Secure, his brain signaled.

Michael rose to his feet, made a short inspection of the bodies to confirm their demise, then moved quickly toward the lifeless Carlos. He untied the wire, which had bitten deeply into Carlos's flesh, and caught his friend's limp form as it fell away from the tree. He lowered him gently to the ground and knelt beside him, checking for a pulse, though he knew there would be none. He cursed and wanted to cry out in rage over the senseless death of his friend.

Why this gentle, good man? he wondered. And he admonished himself for allowing Carlos to come along against his own better judgment.

Michael switched on his radio.

'Elias, come in,' he said into it.

'Where've you been, Mike?' came the familiar voice. 'You've had us worried.'

Michael was silent for a moment. He placed his hand on Carlos's chest.

'We have a problem here,' he responded.

'Go ahead.'

'Carlos is dead.'

'What happened?' Elias asked, his voice suddenly tense.

'There's been a small close-quarters skirmish here. There were five in all. The situation is secure.'

'Jesus! Who were they?'

'Looks like drug runners. This must be a proprietary trail,' Michael explained.

'And Gill?'

'He wasn't one of them.'

Elias was silent for a moment, his brain racing through alternatives. 'We're taking you out,' he said at last.

Michael did not object to the decision.

'We'll have to arrange a pickup,' Elias said.

'OK. Can Wadelaw zero in on my homing signal well enough to locate me?'

'Yes,' Elias replied.

'All right,' Michael said. 'I'll clear out of this area. There's a spot about ten klicks from here where the terrain is flat and elevated. I can clear an area large enough for him to land. It should take me about three hours to get there.'

'He'll be there. Is there anything I can do in the meantime?'

'Find out who runs this trail.'

'We're already working on it. I suggest you clear out of the area immediately. There may be more company coming along.'

'Roger that, Chief. I'll be out of here in a hurry,' Michael returned. 'I have just one little thing to attend to,' he said, reaching for the Ka-Bar.

What had started as a simple search-and-recover operation had just become a great deal more to Michael Quinn. The killing of his friend had tripped a switch inside of him. The dark side had taken over and gone into action, and it wasn't about to let go. This wasn't a job anymore. It was a war.

THE MEDELLÍN INSTITUTE: A single bank of recessed lights provided modest illumination on the sector maps used in the aerial search. The rest of the large conference room was in near darkness.

The maps bore trackings of the orderly patterns being used in the search. As a precaution against giving away news of the discovery of the Cessna, there were no marks to indicate that any wreckage had been found in the object sector. For the same reason, the search procedures were still ongoing. The pilot who had made the find had called in the coordinates in code. These were simply changed when decoded to designate an area twenty miles to the south of the actual sighting. The find was labeled 'negative contact'.

Michael sat at the far end of the table, out of the halo of light from the head of the room. He sat silently, watching the other three men in the room reading the transcript of his verbal report.

Prominently missing from the group was Alexandra Sky. Her involvement has ended the moment the strain was confirmed missing by the recovery team. The reasons were obvious: to ensure that Skyco Corporation would have no knowledge of subsequent actions that might go beyond the limits of the law. Her prior knowledge of such events could implicate Skyco, as well as her personally, quite possibly damaging the corporation's international position. This was precisely one of the reasons why Intel-Trace had been enlisted, to take the brunt of any such eventuality. It was Intel-Trace's job to assume such risks for its clients.

Alexandra would, in fact, be leaving Medellín on the first plane to Bogotá in the morning. From there she'd head straight to San Antonio. News of significant events would still reach her and her father, but only secondhand, through Danziger, or at later debriefing sessions with Elias.

Bob Elias was an amazingly quick reader. He had read the report twice already, and he waited patiently for Danziger and Delgado to finish.

Danziger finished and set the sheets neatly before him, a look of grave concern across his face. Delgado finished a few moments later, relit his cold cigar, then sat back and waited for either of the other two to begin.

'He makes it sound simple,' Danziger said, tipping his head toward Michael. 'It's hard to believe they could have done it so cleanly. We never had a chance. Their information was good, their timing flawless, and they got away with the prize. There's no question that they had help from the inside. There's no other way it could have worked. Question is, was it Dr Stillings himself, and did they remove him to clear their trail? Or was it someone else inside, in which case Stillings was just a poor sonofabitch who was in the way?'

'I've been through Stillings's file, and I doubt very strongly that he was involved,' Elias said. 'You have almost a hundred fifty people working here. I can narrow the possibles down to about thirty. Of those, I can rate fifteen as suspects, based upon the exposure they have to sensitive information. All fifteen are being thoroughly investigated right now.'

'Even if you find the right person, that may not take us very far. We may gain a possible contact on the outside. We've both played the game long enough to know those odds.'

'The odds don't worry me,' Elias returned. 'It's all in how much effort we're willing to put into this.'

'There's more,' Michael said from the darkness.

All heads turned toward him.

'We have the trail that Gill doubled back to.'

'Certainly he's long gone by now. We may never find him,' Delgado said.

'Men like Gill don't hide well long-term. The people who hired him know that. He's probably already dead, or will be soon, unless they want to buy time by leaving him out there for us to chase,' Michael said. 'But finding Gill isn't what I meant. An item with the value of the Luxus won't stay at a courier level for long. It'll move up fast into important hands. Gill's contact was most likely already in that category.

'That trail is well used. The people Carlos and I encountered were drug runners. There were about three hundred kilos of very pure cocaine on the pack animals. I don't have to tell you how valuable that is. It was just bad timing that put us in the same place at the same time. But trails like that are proprietary. This one connects a source – probably a processing lab – and a primary distribution point. Being caught on that trail means death to anyone who doesn't belong there. I don't think Gill would have used it unless he was intended to.'

Danziger caught the drift immediately. 'The first important "hands". A secure trail that no one would dare come close to, with a distribution network at the other end. Only this time they pass another form of contraband with far more potential value than a load of drugs. Fast money for fast and easy work.'

'Exactly,' Michael replied. 'A simple contract to transport and deliver merchandise.'

'And maybe knock off Gill along the way, leaving him under a pile of jungle rot to feed the worms,' Danziger added. He liked the reasoning.

'Bob, can you run a make on the trail and its owner?' Michael asked.

Elias nodded. 'Routine stuff. I should have it within twenty-four hours,' he said confidently. 'In the meantime we'll work to develop the insider angle to use as a back door. Despite the difficulties involved here, this could provide us with another lead to follow. Depending upon who's behind this whole thing, that pyramid may not be a very tall one, unless we're up against a major intelligence agency of an interested country . . . which must be considered a possibility.'

'That's all we'd need,' Danziger mumbled.

'Gentlemen,' Elias said, tossing his notes on to the table, 'give me twenty-four hours on the trail, and we'll intensify our efforts on the fifteen names. We'll convene again tomorrow at oh-seven-hundred.'

Without further conversation, the four men rose to their feet. Delgado and Danziger were the first to leave. Elias caught Michael by the arm before he reached the door.

'You've fulfilled your obligations, Mike,' he said. 'I defined a search-and-recover objective. What comes after this is my problem. You've done your job. Now it's up to us to complete the assignment.'

'Maybe to you I have,' Mike said. 'But I have a definite interest in this now, and I don't intend to walk away from it.'

'I hear you,' Elias said softly. 'I'm very, very sorry it turned out the way it did for Carlos, Mike.'

Michael placed a hand on his friend's shoulder. 'I know you are. But what happened wasn't your fault. Like I said before, it was just bad timing. It's just that I can't – I *won't* – let it end like this. Carlos was my friend.'

It was that, but it was also more, Elias knew. To Michael Quinn, there was no room in this world for Dieters and Tomarevs and the likes of the man or men behind this. He had reached the saturation point, and there wasn't room enough for a single drop of indifference. Something *had* to be done. *Someone* had to do it. He had lost too much in his life to be the one to walk away.

'We'll do it any way you want, Mike,' Elias told him.

Michael nodded. 'Then let's get to work. We both have a lot to do.'

PARIS: The top edge of the daily edition of *L'Humanité* lowered about an inch, enough for the dark eyes to peer discreetly at the clock on the wall in the lobby of the Hotel Duminy. Thirty minutes remained in the two-hour time window established for communications. Yesterday's window had been missed, or wasn't needed, at the Hotel Delavigne. The time windows in this early phase of the plan were very wide because of the delays frequently experienced with overseas communications from certain parts of South America. For the same reason, every communication schedule allowed for three windows over three consecutive days, each at a different location.

Rafael Sonterra went back to his paper, casting innocuous glances periodically at the people in the lobby. He could spot a watcher in a moment. He went back to the article he was reading, a stinging column criticizing US President Culland Brice's snub of the latest Soviet challenge to reduce nuclear armaments in matching numbers with the United States.

The dark eyes looked up again a few minutes later, in time to see the desk clerk give a message to a page. The boy began an immediate circuit of the lobby, calling the name Rossini. When the boy had left the lobby to take the page to the lounge, Sonterra rose and left in the same direction. He waited outside the lounge until the boy appeared once again.

'Excuse me, young man,' Sonterra said in very good French. 'Were you paging the name Rossini?'

'Yes, Monsieur,' the boy returned politely.

'I am Rossini,' Sonterra said.

The boy held out a brass tray with a small white envelope on it. Sonterra took the envelope and dropped a tip on to the tray.

The page thanked him and left.

Sonterra opened the envelope. His overseas call had arrived. Booth number two, operator 219. He went quickly to the booth, reached the operator, and waited.

The connection was a good one.

'Rossini, are you there?' the voice of Kammal said from across the ocean.

'This is Rossini,' Sonterra replied.

'At last, my good friend. I have received your cabled letter of credit and the deal is progressing well. We have just one small detail to work out in our final negotiations, however. Nothing to worry about. The agent is asking for a product-liability waiver. Do you have any difficulties with that?' Kammal said, his codes perfect.

There was trouble, though not serious for the moment. The code told Sonterra that the movement of the strain had gone according to plan. The negotiations hangup meant, however, that the operation had not gone as cleanly as hoped. 'The agent' meant that a serious investigation had been started and that meaningful progress had been made. The investigation had been expected, but the progress had not. 'Product-liability waiver' told Sonterra that, in Kammal's opinion, a 'housecleaning' was needed to eliminate further risk to the security of the operation.

'I have no problem with the waiver,' Sonterra replied, giving the go-ahead. 'I would like all transactions concluded as rapidly as possible. Do you foresee any further delays?'

'No, the remaining details should be routine. I think we can do this in a single day. Two at the most,' Kammal replied.

'Do you feel that the agent is reliable?' Sonterra asked, requesting information on the level of the investigation. The phone rested between his shoulder and ear. His fingers began the unconscious corkscrew-like twisting of a paper match as he concentrated on Kammal's words.

'This is a new agent, aggressive, perhaps overly concerned with detail. But I don't foresee any problems,' Kammal told him.

'Very well, then. Grant the waiver, but get back to me if any new concessions are requested.'

'Yes, I will, my friend. Rest easy.'

'I shall. Thank you for your fine efforts on my firm's behalf. Go safely.'

Sonterra broke the connection, then sat for a few moments in the booth.

An outside agency had been called in by Skyco. Kammal was wise to request a housecleaning. If it was accomplished quickly enough, it would be impossible to take the investigation beyond Medellín. Sonterra was pleased with the progress so far, and with Kammal's steady performance. If the next few days went smoothly enough, he'd have pulled off a clean theft of a most valuable prize – one that would increase greatly in value every day that he held it. A prize that was the key to the success of a plan he had waited a lifetime to fulfill.

The Hotel Duminy sat on a quiet street running parallel to the Rue de Rivoli, and was convenient to the Louvre and the Tuileries. Sonterra felt good, but needed to think. He left the hotel to lose himself in the quiet immensity of the Louvre. There, amid the most inspiring works of man, he would contemplate and refine his own greatest plan.

THE MEDELLÍN INSTITUTE: The knock sounded softly on the door to Bob Elias's quarters. He went to the door, checked the peephole, then undid the lock. He opened the door to Tom Danziger, who stood there looking past Elias into the small but comfortable room. Michael had arrived minutes before. Danziger nodded in greeting and walked in.

'So, what's up? Why the secret meeting?' Danziger asked.

'We have some information we'd like to share with you,' Elias replied. Danziger stared at him, waiting.

'We think we've just found our insider,' Elias announced. He held out a photograph.

Danziger looked at the picture, which showed an attractive woman accompanied by a handsome escort.

'Her name is Teresa Comalinas. Your Medellín operation uses a secretarial pool system, of which she's a part. She's been filling in as a replacement for Stillings's secretary, who's on maternity leave. She's been in place for a little over two months now,' Elias explained.

'Who's the guy with her?'

'We believe he's her contact. His name is Angel Solis. They've been seeing one another for about two months. They're not living together, but they see one another almost daily, with a lot of overnights,' Elias said.

'As Stillings's secretary, she'd have access to a lot of information – the kind you'd want to protect,' Michael said.

'And that's not all of it,' Elias picked up. 'We've also just learned that she's been having an affair with Delgado for about the last four or five weeks.'

'Delgado?' Danziger said, openly surprised.

'It appears that your security chief has a weak spot for the ladies, especially Institute employees. Over the past four years he's had affairs with four that we know of, including Comalinas,' Elias said. 'He's a security risk.'

'Are you sure about his involvement in this?' Danziger asked.

'Yes, but it would seem he's only an unknowing source of information. She probably got enough about the security of this place to allow the band that attacked the Institute to get themselves in, as well as supplying them with the info on where the strain was kept. I'm sure she also picked up the details about the strain being transported out of Colombia, though we're not sure whether she got that from Stillings or Delgado. She's been pretty busy with Delgado. There's no telling how much she's learned and passed on about our involvement so far in this investigation, but we'll have to assume the worst. She and Delgado spent part of the night together last night. She's in town tonight, though, with this Solis character. He's probably our link to the next level of our adversary's network,' Elias said.

'What do we do about Delgado?' Danziger asked.

'We use him,' Elias replied. 'Now that we know their information source, we can feed them whatever we want to. The information will be trusted.'

'How long do we let them run?' Danziger asked.

'Until we track Solis to his contact. He's under close surveillance now.'

'Is she in it for money?' Danziger asked.

'I'm sure there's money involved. But it appears she's in it mostly for Solis. Apparently the ladies think he's got a lot of style. That is, if they can overlook his bad temper. He cut up one of his lady friends once. Didn't kill her, but he didn't leave her too pretty, either.'

'Well, at least we've gained one advantage,' Danziger said. 'We can control what they learn from this source from now on. Wouldn't it be nice, though, to be able to track the line of communication all the way to the top?'

'I don't think we'll get that lucky,' Elias commented.

'We also have the drug runner's trail,' Michael said.

'What have you learned about it?' Danziger asked.

'The operation belongs to Hector Cantú. He's a major mover in Colombia. The DEA has a book on him a yard wide. He's untouchable here. No one will mess with Cantú. The DEA tried once. Lost six good agents in the process. Even the Colombian government won't touch him. He has a lot of influence both with the government and with the army. Even the recent crackdown on drugs doesn't come close to hurting Cantú. He's too powerful.

'The trail connects one of his largest processing labs to his primary distribution center outside of Bajo Baudó. This center runs most of its cocaine through Panama. He's got other networks all throughout Colombia,' Elias explained.

'It'll be risky trying to run through Cantú,' Danziger said.

'I'll handle that part of it,' Michael assured him.

'The lab?' Danziger guessed.

Michael nodded. 'I'm sure I can get his attention easily enough. The rest will be tricky, but I think we can learn something useful.'

'These are *very* nasty people, Mike,' Danziger warned. 'An entire government hasn't been able to touch him.'

'I'm aware of that. But I can talk his language,' Michael told him. The meaning was plain enough to Danziger.

'As for our meeting tomorrow morning, we'll exclude all of these details,' Elias advised. 'We can keep Delgado busy checking into the names on our list. We'll remove Comalinas's name, to avoid any suspicions on his part.'

'Then we'll meet as planned?'

'Yes, at oh-seven-hundred.'

Danziger nodded his agreement. 'In the morning, then.'

'Don't report any of this back to San Antonio yet. Give us at least forty-eight hours to get our operation rolling on Cantú. Then we can report back through our secured communications system. Is that agreeable?' Elias asked.

Danziger nodded once again.

'See you in the morning, Tom.'

Danziger rose and left the room.

'Cantú will be tough, Mike. I can get some field operatives in to give you a hand,' Elias offered.

'I won't need them,' Michael said. 'Wadelaw and I can handle it. He was a pretty hot jockey in 'Nam.'

Michael handed Elias a sheet of paper with a shopping list on it. 'Can you get that stuff by tomorrow?' he asked.

Elias scanned the list. 'Looks like you're planning on going to war.'

Michael smiled. 'I'm just going to give him a little tickle. Can you get it?'

'I'll have to call in some markers to get the big item, but I can manage that. I've done enough favors for the right people. I can have it by . . . say, ten o'clock tomorrow night. Is that OK?'

'Fine.'

'I don't suppose you want it here, though.'

'Right. Collect it all somewhere remote, just outside of Bogotá. Chris and I will take it from there.'

'Have you talked to Chris about this yet?'

'No, but I have a strong feeling he'd give anything to get back into that kind of gear.'

Elias nodded. 'You'll have it all. I might be able to improve on a few of these for you.'

'That's fine, as long as it's not so new that I don't know how to use it. I've been out of this line of work for a while.'

'It'll be what you need,' Elias guaranteed.

'Fine. We'll see how Cantú responds to some rather direct stimulus.'

Michael stood motionless in the shower, the hot stream of water concentrated directly on his head. He was thinking about Carlos, who was on a cold slab in the compound hospital. He wished desperately that he had been more insistent that Carlos leave the crash site with Wadelaw. He knew he wasn't responsible for what had happened, but he felt he could have prevented it. The image of his friend strung up against the tree just wouldn't leave his mind. He had the same sick feeling that had followed the news of the death of his sister. It only served to fuel the hatred burning inside of him.

He lingered a moment longer, then turned off the shower. He was just beginning to towel himself off when a knock sounded at his door. He wrapped the towel around his waist and went to answer it.

He was surprised to see Alexandra standing there when the door opened. She hadn't expected to see him practically naked, and her surprised eyes dropped quickly to the towel, then moved up along the hard, tanned body. She hadn't imagined him to be so well muscled when they first met. She nearly flushed at the sight of him, in a purely physical arousal response – a feeling she hadn't experienced in a very long time from the sheer sight of a man.

'I'm . . . sorry,' she began, embarrassed. 'I can come back later.'

'It's all right. Come on in. I'll get something on,' he said.

He turned away from the open door and walked across the room to the small closet. Her eyes took immediate notice of the scars on his right side, thigh, and forearm. She had never seen scars from bullet wounds before. There was a great deal more to this man than her first impressions had suggested. She walked into the room and closed the door behind her.

'I'll be leaving first thing in the morning,' she began as Michael found the provided bathrobe and slipped it over his powerful shoulders. 'I just wanted to tell you how sorry I am about Carlos.'

'Thank you,' Michael replied.

There was a brief moment of awkward silence.

Alexandra Sky was a beautiful woman. She was as tall

and willowy as a model, and didn't look her forty years. Her hair was long and wavy, not quite blonde, her eyes honey brown and soft.

'You couldn't have planned for what happened,' she said, then fell silent.

'We shouldn't be talking about this, for your sake, and for Skyco's,' Michael told her.

'I know. But I couldn't leave without telling you how sorry I am.'

Michael nodded. 'I do appreciate it.'

'Yes . . . well, is there anything I can do?'

'Just keep yourself a safe distance from Medellín and this entire investigation,' he said quietly.

Alexandra started to turn toward the door, but hesitated. 'Can we talk off the record?' she asked.

'Sure. You were never here.'

'They're withholding most of the information from me, for legal reasons, but I want to know . . . we have very serious trouble, haven't we?'

Michael nodded his reply.

'Do we have a chance of recovering the Luxus?'

'I don't know,' he replied. 'We have some leads. They're not good ones, but as long as we have something to work with, there's always a chance.'

She liked his use of 'we' in his response. This was also Intel-Trace's problem, and this man's, as well as Skyco's.

'I won't ask for details,' she said.

'Good, because I'd be embarrassed by having to refuse them to you,' he returned. 'I can only tell you that Intel-Trace is a very capable agency. I'd never bet against them at any odds.'

His words were reassuring.

There was really little else to say, but she didn't want to leave. She was curious about Michael Quinn.

'May I ask you a personal question?' she went on after a short pause.

Michael stared into her eyes. He didn't say no.

'How did you come to be involved with Intel-Trace?'

106

He didn't answer right away. It made her feel somewhat ill at ease, he could see that. But it didn't change his mind about not offering an answer to her question.

'It's a long story,' he said finally. It wasn't the kind of question he liked to answer, no matter who asked it.

She caught the message and simply nodded.

'Well, I guess I'd better be going,' she said smoothly, extending her hand. 'Good luck, Michael. We have a lot of confidence in you and your associates. Perhaps when all of this is behind us, you'll come visit us in San Antonio.'

'Perhaps,' he returned, taking the hand.

It wasn't a handshake, really. Their hands touched gently and maintained contact. Her eyes met his, and for a brief instant she became nearly lost in them. There was something that captured her. It was strength and intensity, but also a vulnerability, and almost childlike innocence. They seemed to show qualities of ruthlessness and sensitivity at the same time. There was something very different about this man.

'Yes, I hope you will,' Alexandra said.

Their hands parted and she turned toward the door. Michael followed her to it.

She opened it and turned to face him, searching for an answer behind those dark, intense eyes.

'Well . . . good-bye,' she said at last with a smile.

She turned and walked away from the room, feeling a little surprised at herself – and a bit embarrassed. Men didn't usually affect her. But somehow this one had. What was it, she wondered. Was it the mystery behind those scars and those eyes? Was it his quiet, commanding presence? Or was it the sheer sense of power and masculinity that emanated from him? She shook her head at her own silliness and went to finish packing.

8

MEDELLÍN, COLOMBIA: The marijuana cigarette glowed in the darkness, then dimmed like a streaking firefly as it was passed. Angel Solis held the deeply inhaled smoke as Teresa Comalinas accepted the joint from him. She inhaled long and steadily, then held it, a catlike smile across her contented face. Sex was always better with marijuana.

Solis closed his eyes and laid his head back on the pillow. His heart was pounding a wild rhythm. But it was not from the excitement of their sexual play. He had, in fact, not performed very well earlier, and for the same reason.

He looked at Teresa, beautiful in her nakedness. She had been a very exciting sexual partner these past months, with a rapacious appetite and a great deal of stamina. She was totally uninhibited and would try anything to get or give pleasure. What a true waste, he thought, to have to kill her.

Solis had killed before – always people he had wanted to kill, and who, in his estimation, had deserved to die. They had been people who had seriously crossed him, or had killed his friends or members of his family. He had never killed for hire. But he would today. And it would be someone he did not want to kill.

He had questioned the order at first when it was given. He had even asked why. Two mistakes, and he knew it. The contact, whom he knew only as Ramón, didn't answer either question, reminding him, instead, of the sum of money he had been paid to obtain information for the principal. It had been a great deal of money, and there was an equal amount still due.

There weren't many men that Solis was afraid of. But the look that had crossed Ramón's face at his initial hesitation clearly indicated that he would be among these men.

'You will do this little thing, yes?' Ramón had coaxed, his hand on Solis's shoulder. 'Perhaps for an added bonus?'

Solis nodded, his gut tight with fear. 'Of course. You can

count on me,' he had replied, trying to sound nonchalant. He knew he would have to complete this deed. He also knew that he had better disappear after the final payment, more to avoid further contact with Ramón than from fear of the authorities.

'Something is bothering you,' Teresa said, her hand fondling his limp penis, trying to coax an erection from it.

'Not really, my love,' Solis replied, the tone unconvincing.

She transferred her grip to his testicles, giving a gentle squeeze. 'Tell me . . . or else,' she said playfully.

His mind was blank and her grip tight. 'I . . . I just . . .' His mind raced. 'I can't stand the thought of you being with him,' he improvised quickly. 'I don't like that pig Delgado touching you,' he lied.

She released his testicles and took his penis again, beginning a rhythmic stroking. 'He is nothing to me but a means to our happiness,' she said. 'I would do anything for you. Anything.'

'Yes, I know. And I love you,' he lied with practiced ease. 'I'll try not to let it bother me again.'

She took a last drag on the marijuana and handed it back to him. Then she slid down and began kissing his chest. Her kisses went lower to his stomach and thighs, then her tongue began a playful teasing.

He dragged hard on the marijuana, then dropped it into the ashtray. His hands went to her head, his fingers entwined in her hair as her mouth accepted his erect penis. She began a skillful, rhythmic motion that defeated his anxiety.

She brought him to the edge of orgasm, then slid up along his body, kissing him hotly.

Solis rolled to his side, then on top of her as her hand guided him inside her. Her sighs of passion began immediately as he thrust into her with mounting urgency. Her sounds made her level of passion easy to read. He thrust harder and faster, but began to lose his erection again. The thought of what was ahead was too heavy to permit sustained concentration.

His left hand went around her raised leg and his fingers gripped the base of his penis, squeezing to keep the erection alive as his right hand reached upward under the pillow to the stilettolike knife.

Her passion during their lovemaking was wild. She didn't notice either movement.

The left hand maintained the erection as she neared her explosive orgasm. The right hand tightened on the weapon.

Her wild panting stopped as she shuddered with orgasmic pleasure. At the same moment he released his penis and raised himself as if to get deeper penetration. Then, in a swift motion, his left hand came up and covered her face. Solis leaned his weight forward, pushing her head back into the pillow. The knife struck quickly to the throat as her arms rose in a defensive reflex.

A horrible retching sound emanated from her as he drove the knife deeply and twisted.

Her arms and legs flailed wildly, her fists beating at his head and chest. He twisted again forcefully, the left hand covering her nose and mouth to silence her.

He kept his full weight forward, fighting awkwardly to keep his balance as she thrashed wildly for what seemed the longest minute of his life. He worked the knife again and again, trying to force the life from her.

Her resistance weakened and her arms fell limply to the bed, and all movement finally stopped. Solis pushed himself up to his knees and took his bloodied hand away from her face. The expression on her face was locked in pain and horror, her lifeless eyes staring accusingly upward to his face.

Solis gasped for air and felt suddenly ill at the realization of her blood covering his hands, arms, and chest. The sight of it was terrible enough, but to feel the warmth of the life it had once fed became overwhelming. He had always killed at a distance, never up close and with his hands, never covered with the warm blood of his victim.

He fought back an urge to vomit, then removed himself from the bed. Fear gripped him.

He washed off the blood and dressed quickly, gathering

up any traces of his presence. He couldn't help taking another look at her lying lifeless on the bed, covered with her own blood. He paused at the door, the nausea building again. This time he couldn't hold it back.

He threw up on the floor, nearly going to his knees from the involuntary retching that followed. He finished, feeling weak in the legs, but forced himself into action. He opened the door and walked out into the semidark hallway, then left as quickly as his weakened legs would allow.

He left the hotel and moved up the block to his parked car. As he pulled away, a second car started its engine. One man exited the car and entered the hotel. Then the car pulled away from the curb to follow him.

Danziger and Michael arrived in the conference room just minutes after Elias's call. The look on Elias's face reflected the urgency of the new development.

'What is it? What's happened?' Danziger asked immediately.

'Teresa Comalinas has been murdered,' Elias said.

'Solis?' Michael asked.

Elias nodded. 'Not more than twenty minutes ago. We heard the whole thing over the bug in the room.'

'Shit!' Danziger hissed.

'Where is he now?' Michael asked.

'We've still got him under surveillance. He went straight back to his apartment. He's there now, but I don't expect him to stay there long.'

'Do we take him?' Michael asked.

'No,' Elias replied, shaking his head. 'We're going to let him run. We'll stay with him in case a contact is made. He'll have to report to somebody, and with any luck at all, it will be face-to-face. We'll mark the contact and trail him.'

'If it's face-to-face, the contact will certainly kill him,' Danziger said.

'You're right. At least they'll try to kill him. But it's the contact we want. That's the most we'd get from him, in any case.'

111

'If we take him, we may be able to discover just how much they've learned,' Michael suggested.

'Perhaps. But we'd lose the contact for sure. We have to have the contact to lead us closer to the person who stands behind this,' Elias said.

'Delgado,' Danziger said. 'Perhaps we can determine how much they might have learned from him. He was one of their sources. They'll know that. They could have it in their minds to try for him, too.'

'I've already dispatched a team to get him into protective custody. We'll get Delgado in here where we can hold him safely,' Elias said. 'How long will you need to set up things on your end, Mike?'

Michael thought for a moment, then replied, 'Two days ought to do it.'

Elias nodded. 'OK, you and Chris leave for Bogotá tonight. Your gear will be ready by late tomorrow morning. You can leave any time you're ready. What about the details?'

'I haven't worked everything out yet. I'll need to check out the cocaine lab location first. I can relay my information to you through Chris,' he answered.

'All right, you and Chris get moving. Tom and I will run the contact angle from here for as long as we can. We'll keep you advised as to where we are when we have to move. Be careful, Mike. You're running a high risk with Cantú. Cocaine lords of his magnitude don't get where they are by being nice reasonable guys.'

Michael nodded. 'I know. But we don't have a choice. This is the only other lead open to us. Whatever happens, I have a feeling things are about to start moving pretty fast.'

After Michael and Danziger had left, Elias made his way quickly to the communications center. He picked up the phone and dialed the number connecting him to the Intel-Trace communications center through the satellite link.

He waited for the connection, listening to the first ring at the other end. The ring stopped and he knew that the short wait that followed was standard procedure while the line was checked for sterility.

Elias heard a double click, then a dial tone. His call had been rejected.

He repeated the process, waiting once again after the initial ring. The outcome was the same. He slammed the phone down in anger. The line was no longer sterile. Someone had tapped it since he'd last used it.

He stormed out of the communications center and all but ran the distance to Danziger's quarters.

Danziger answered the knock on his door, and was nearly thrown off his feet as Elias pushed his way into the room.

'What the hell . . .' Danziger began.

Elias's open-hand slam to the chest cut him off in mid-sentence as Danziger flew into the wall.

'Why did you put the tap on my line?' Elias growled, his voice filled with menace.

'Slow down a minute,' Danziger said, his arms raised to defend himself from further attack. 'I don't know what you're talking about. Start from the top and tell me what's on your mind.'

'You know goddamn well what's on my mind. You put a tap on my security line,' Elias snapped.

'Wrong. I'm on your side, remember?'

'Don't give me that. You're the only one with the authority around here.'

Danziger squinted in hurried thought. 'No, not the *only* one,' he said after a moment's deliberation. 'Delgado could do it.'

Elias stared hard at him. 'Delgado?'

'That's right. He's the security chief around here, remember? His people do whatever he says, without asking questions.'

'Why would Delgado . . .' Elias stopped in the middle of his question.

'Yeah, I'm asking myself the same thing,' Danziger said.

Elias backed out of attack mode to think. Michael's

assessment of the failed attempt on Building Two began playing back through his head. He had said there could have been inside help that never materialized when failure became evident. He also said that the only way out was up – with the aid of a helicopter. He had even suspected Skyco's helicopter. *Delgado's* helicopter. The same one that tried to blow away the last survivor, and would have finished the job if he hadn't done it himself.'

'The helicopter,' he said, almost talking to himself.

Danziger saw the implication immediately. 'Jesus, the helicopter,' he repeated with the same realization. 'A double-blind. They penetrated completely. They could know everything.'

'No, not everything. They know that we're on to Cantú and the trail, but they don't know that we're on to Delgado or the girl. They're just cleaning up their trail. They also don't know what Mike has in mind as regards retaliating against Cantú. We excluded Delgado early enough to ensure that much—' Elias stopped suddenly. 'Unless the rooms were bugged, too,' he said.

'We can't do anything about that now,' he said, concern written across his face.

'Then we go on as planned?'

'We don't have a choice. In the meantime I'll sweep *my* room for a bug. I'll also have to restore the integrity of my primary communications,' Elias said.

'I can guarantee that this time they'll be sterile,' Danziger said. 'I've got a setup that even Delgado doesn't know about. Let's go.'

Five minutes later they were passing through a hidden wall panel off the conference room.

'No one here knows about this except me and Asher Sky,' Danziger told Elias.

They entered the room and closed the door behind them. They were in complete privacy now.

'I can guarantee that this area is sterile. I use it to contact Sky. I check the sterility myself daily.'

'This ought to do it,' Elias said. 'I'll still have to go

through Bogotá to tap into the satellite network. The procedure is classified,' he said, looking back at Danziger.

'I understand. I'll be just outside the door,' Danziger said, then left the secret room.

Elias lifted the phone and dialed the number for the primary connection. This time a second ring followed the pause.

'Alpha security, may I help you?' the voice said.

'Yes, I'd like a direct link to Jack Tar. This is Triple Jack five-nine-three, clearance Alpha-Scramble.'

'Is your location sterile?' the voice asked.

'It is now,' Elias replied.

'Hold for verification,' the voice instructed.

Elias held his ear to the silence as a second, more highly sensitive scan was conducted.

'Access denied,' the voice returned. 'Class Four, ultrahigh frequency.'

The connection broke off.

Elias stood dumbfounded with the phone to his ear. *Access denied. Class Four, ultrahigh frequency*, his brain replayed.

He put the phone back in its cradle.

Class Four, ultrahigh frequency.

The method of tap had been identified, and it represented some highly sophisticated technology. So sophisticated, in fact, that the first scan had missed it. The UHF tap was an off-site tapping system that worked by signal interception. From everything he knew about Skyco's capabilities, they weren't capable of Class Four surveillance. That could mean that what was known about Skyco's capabilities was incomplete, or, worse yet, that someone else with that capability was involved.

Elias squinted hard at the phone, wondering who in God's hell it could be.

MOSCOW: A driving autumn wind raked the old Khodinka airfield, pushing early snow flurries harmlessly across the patrolled aerodrome. A howl from the kennels broke

115

the sound of the wind, followed by a quick chorus of ragged barks. The sounds faded and once again the wind reigned supreme as daybreak approached.

The aerodrome was surrounded on all sides by restricted buildings belonging to aviation firms, a rocket-construction firm, the Military Aviation Academy, and the Institute of Cosmic Biology. High walls and electrified barbed wire closed off access to the inner area except through one of the top-secret buildings or a single narrow lane leading to a ten-meter-high wall with a heavily guarded opening. But no car was permitted beyond this point into the inner area. It was perhaps the most closely guarded compound in all the Soviet Union, a small sign reading MILITARY DEPARTMENT 44388 the only clue to what lay within. But the clue held little meaning, for few people in the Soviet Union had ever heard of this department. Unknown as it was, no Soviet life went untouched by its presence. Behind the barriers of this almost sleepy compound lay the heart of Soviet military intelligence, the headquarters of the GRU.

The three most powerful elements of Russian rule – the Communist Party, the KGB, and the army – were in constant struggle with one another, with intense rivalries clearly in evidence. Each wished to destroy the others, but knew that it could not, for the others were needed. Like three jealous sisters, there were always two against one, with the relationship in constant flux. They spied on and infiltrated one another as readily as another country, often perpetrating well-calculated mayhem in the endless struggle for power.

Unit 44388 had been established by Lenin in 1918 as the Registered Directorate of the Workers' and Peasants' Red Army – an innocuous title. Today it was known as the Chief Intelligence Directorate of the General Staff of the Soviet Army. It was the eyes and ears of the army, the safeguard against its extinction.

There was no love lost between the KGB and the GRU – it was an enmity as fierce as any known in history. Each had fallen victim to ruthless purges at the hands of the other as ordered by Lenin, Stalin, and others since. Each watched the other with the eyes of wolves, ready to seize the bared throat if given the chance. Yet it was this very struggle that gave each its great strength, and in the end provided the reason for the unprecedented stability of the regime.

The day began early at Khodinka Field. All offices were manned well before sunrise in the nine-story headquarters building. Many of its staff members and their families lived within the compound in a large fifteen-story building situated within walking distance. Every inch of the compound was monitored by video camera, every movement watched and logged. Entry into the HQ was through multiple security checkpoints utilizing the very latest in electronic systems. No bags or cases were permitted in or out, no metallic items, from pens to cigarette lighters, could be carried in. All was provided, to the smallest item. There were no chances taken here, no familiar faces waved by, no exceptions to the strict security regulations. Everyone complied, from the GRU chief to the lowest janitor.

General Aleksandr Ivanovich Kozlov filled his cup with hot tea from the samovar in the corner of his office. He inhaled the aroma of the Russian tea and sipped a small amount to avoid burning his mouth.

Russian tea is the finest in all the world, he thought. But it couldn't replace the strong Turkish coffee he loved but could no longer drink, under doctor's orders. It just didn't seem fair. The chief of the Soviet GRU, with all his power and influence, was deprived of one of his simplest and greatest pleasures by the command of an underpaid, overworked army physician – and a woman to boot. Women as a class had made great strides in position and opportunity, and now most doctors in the Soviet Union were women. But that didn't make taking orders from a woman any easier.

Kozlov walked back to his desk and set down the cup. He pulled the folder containing the morning stack of 'gray' intelligence reports in front of him and flipped back the

117

cover. His eyes skipped with practiced speed over the words on the first sheets as his hands packed the well-worn briar pipe with Turkish long-cut tobacco – another forbidden pleasure, but one he refused to give up. There were limits to his deprivations, regardless of who gave the orders. Position was everything inside the Soviet Union, and with position went privilege. He had tried giving up the pipe once, and his resolve had lasted two days. He'd give the tea another week before loading the samovar with coffee.

It was standard practice within the Soviet Union for all intelligence heads, from chiefs to heads of directorates and directions, as well as first and second deputies, to review 'gray', or unanalyzed, unenhanced intelligence reports daily as their first official function. These reports were kept intentionally gray to allow each reader to form his own conclusions about their significance. Later in the morning they would be reviewed in committee. The most important issues would then be taken to the Kremlin, where Party, KGB, and army chiefs again reviewed the major issues, giving their own interpretations of what their respective intelligence services had come up with during the previous twenty-four hours. It was a daily contest of who could scoop whom on the really important issues. The tactics got downright cutthroat at times, to make the other fellow look bad in front of the bosses.

Kozlov turned another page and lit the pipe, reading through the eruptions of smoke. He lowered the pipe and studied the sheet before him in closer detail. His instincts perked up as he reread it slowly. The communication had been received from the Second Directorate intelligence office with responsibility for intelligence activities in North and South America.

On the surface it appeared to be a small matter – one easily passed over with the other 'noise'. It involved reports of unusual air activities in Colombia being conducted by the giant Skyco Corporation, based in the United States. Initial activity was centered on the area directly between Medellín and Bogotá, but then was expanded over a full 360-degree area. No official statements had been issued, in either the United States or Colombia, but special personnel had been brought in from the States either to assist or to take charge of the efforts.

Skyco had lost something, no doubt, by some officially unnoticed air disaster. This 'something' was as yet undetermined by the resident intelligence station, but efforts were continuing.

What caught Kozlov's interest most was the scale of the search, and how it had grown without ever coming to the attention of local authorities or the news media. Obviously, Skyco wanted this matter kept low-profile.

Medellín, Kozlov thought. Yes, Skyco has a research facility there, he recollected. He would need to know more about the nature of the work being conducted there. This was one worth following, he decided, separating it and starting a pile to the left of the folder. He'd return to the items in this pile after finishing his initial scanning of the reports. Then he'd get the proper procurement organs working to develop the background information in fuller detail. He'd also get an enhanced report prepared and on his desk by the following morning.

This was one item to watch closely yet avoid bringing up at his Kremlin review later in the day. The KGB's intelligence resources were a bit under par in Colombia as the result of a recent defection that had blown the section wide open. He doubted that the KGB's limited activities in the area would give weight to a seemingly small issue like this, especially since its immediate concern in that country was in covering its ass. If it turned out to be something of importance, he'd have scored a coup in making his KGB counterpart, General Petr Fedorovich Vladin, look bad. One point for his side, he thought with a smile, in a game where all points counted.

Vladin and Kozlov were open enemies. It was no secret that their intense dislike for one another would ultimately lead to the downfall of one of them. And the fall would be hard; that, too, was certain, for one did not fall from such heights with grace.

Kozlov went on with the gray reports, finishing them within the hour as the sunlight reached his window.

He rearranged the stack of important issues, then reached for the phone. He dialed the number of his second-in-command, Colonel-General Nikolai Mikhailovich Barchenkin, First Deputy Chief of the GRU.

'Barchenkin,' the voice answered.

'Good morning, Nikolai Mikhailovich,' Kozlov said. 'Have you finished the morning reports?'

'Yes, General Kozlov,' Barchenkin replied.

'Come to my office and bring the hot stack with you, please,' Kozlov instructed.

'Right away, General.'

It was perhaps two minutes until Barchenkin knocked on the closed door.

He entered, closing the door behind him.

Kozlov was standing by the samovar, filling a cup for his trusted second-in-command.

'It's going to be a pretty day,' Kozlov said in greeting, handing him the cup on a saucer. 'The snow has stopped. Just look at that sunshine.'

Barchenkin accepted the cup, looking down into the tea, relieved that it was not that horrible Turkish coffee.

'Thank you, General.'

Both men moved to a small conference table at the side of the office and sat.

'Let me see your reports,' Kozlov said.

He accepted them without further comment and went through them in silence. Barchenkin had a good mind. He also had a sense for what was important and what was not. Kozlov was not disappointed. He found the Colombian report.

Kozlov separated it from the others and handed it to Barchenkin.

'What do you make of this?' he asked.

Barchenkin checked it over quickly before responding.

'A quiet search,' he replied. 'Something of value. The operation is controlled out of the Medellín Research Institute. I can't yet speculate on what they're looking for, but it is something that we should know about. We've already begun monitoring all communications from the Institute.'

Kozlov smiled. He had hand-picked Barchenkin above other leading candidates when the position opened two years ago with the death of Barchenkin's predecessor from a sudden heart attack. It had been a good choice.

'Notify the Fifth and Tenth Directorates of this report. I want conclusive data gathered as quickly as possible on this matter,' Kozlov ordered. 'I want you to personally contact Zebochev in Archives, as well. I'd like expanded development on the Skyco Corporation, its chief owner and CEO Asher Sky, and the Medellín Research Institute. I feel, as you do, that this is something that we must know about. Everything low-level, so as not to alert our brothers in the KGB.'

Barchenkin nodded. 'This may take a few days to do quietly and in such detail. At the same time we can have efforts in Colombia intensified – also quietly.'

'Take whatever time you need. Say nothing of this report in our internal meetings over the next few days. Use only people that you trust.'

'Of course, General,' Barchenkin replied.

'Drink your tea, Nikolai,' Kozlov said, his hand lifting a napkin to uncover a small plate of tea cakes. 'Let's review the remainder of these reports.'

Kozlov selected one of the sweet cakes and bit into it. The GRU bakers were wonderful, and he enjoyed these little treats that they prepared for him. But this satisfaction was modest compared to what he sensed lay hidden in the Colombian report. It would, he was sure, provide a sweetness of its own, to be savored in a greater sense.

9

MEDELLÍN, COLOMBIA: It had been a miserable night for Bob Elias. News of the ultrahigh-frequency tap had put a serious crimp in his plans for sleep. The significance of the development could not be overstated. Someone with highly sophisticated capabilities had become interested in events of the past week. And the interest was new.

Elias knew this because he had used the Alpha satellite system daily since his arrival in Medellín. The security scans had not picked up the UHF interception until his last attempt to use it. He now had no secure way of communicating with Intel-Trace from Medellín. That meant he'd have to move operations out, most likely back to Bogotá. Once there, he could reestablish communication through the Alpha system, this time incorporating a scrambler device, which he did not have with him at the Institute.

Elias gave up on the idea of sleep. He sat up in his bed and turned on the table light. It was nearly three in the morning. Michael and Wadelaw should be in Bogotá already, he thought. That was another wrinkle he felt uncomfortable about. Michael was taking a grave risk in pursuing Hector Cantú. The mission could come apart in an instant, leaving Intel-Trace with Solis as their only lead – and not a very good one. Worse, it could leave Intel-Trace without a prime agent – and Elias without an agent he had come to appreciate a good deal. He didn't like the odds. The only comforting thought to lift his spirits came from knowing that his room had checked out clean during the security sweep earlier. At least the plans made there hadn't been compromised.

The development with Delgado was a surprise. He was a clever bastard, Elias had to give him that much. He had used the girl to set himself up as an innocent fool, with human frailty as his cover, when, in fact, he had done a good deal more for the other side than would have ever been known. He had singlehandedly engineered the failure of the attempt to take the strain, thereby setting up the successful theft of it by Gill. It was handled so smoothly that it would have never been learned if the plane hadn't been found.

Delgado!

Elias looked at his watch again. His team should have been here with him by now. Damn it! Why hadn't they notified him?

He got dressed quickly and left the room. Danziger was heading up the hallway toward him. His face had bad news written all over it.

'What is it?' Elias asked, thinking it must be dire news about Michael and Wadelaw.

'Delgado's dead,' Danziger announced.

'What? How?' Elias asked.

'Car bomb,' Danziger replied.

'Give me details.'

'Your team arrived at his house about two hours ago. Per your instructions, they tried not to arouse his suspicions, telling him that some major developments had come to our attention and that he was needed back at the Institute. When he insisted on taking his own car, they agreed, feeling that to prevent him might start him thinking,' Danziger explained.

'Didn't they check the car?'

'Yes. They anticipated that he'd want to use it, and checked it from engine to exhaust as quickly and as quietly as they could before approaching the house. They didn't check the radio. One of your team volunteered to ride with him to fill him in on some of the fictitious facts. The car following taped the entire conversation. Your man did a good job – until Delgado turned on the radio. They were halfway back when it happened. They were both killed instantly.'

'Damn!' Elias exploded.

'What about the authorities?' he pressed.

'No way to cover it. They're all over it,' Danziger replied.

'Then we wrap it up here fast. We'll pull everything out by morning and set up again in Bogotá. Everything covert from this point on. How much will they be able to develop?'

'We can hold them off for a few days. We can even set a cover, tying it to something dirty. Drugs are the easiest cover, with everything that's going on in Colombia these days.'

'All right, but leave that to my people. We'll want to keep Skyco as clean as possible,' Elias said.

'We'll plant Delgado's house and his office here at the Institute, to make it look like he was dealing big time. We can probably even tie in Cantú. That should slow up the investigation. They won't dig hard where he's involved.'

Danziger nodded his agreement.

'We'll plant the Comalinas apartment, too. That should put a neat little bow in the ribbon. Skyco will probably take a little flak over it,' Elias said.

'We can handle it. What about your man in the car with Delgado?'

'We'll set up a DEA cover for him. Build a file on Delgado and Comalinas – the works. It'll hold up. I've got friends with DEA.'

'Solis is going to be next,' Danziger said.

'You're right. The world won't miss the likes of him. We can let it go down and stay with whoever makes the hit. There wasn't much more to expect from his side of things, anyway.'

'It'll happen soon.'

'We'll be ready.'

Alexandra's departure was arranged early that morning, and she was on a helicopter out just before sunrise. She was not informed of Delgado's death. News of that would be filed with Danziger's next report from Bogottá after secure communications could be set up through Intel-Trace's Alpha system. Danziger's stay in Colombia would also change profile. He would be connected to the DEA investigation being created by Elias. The plane would be planted with some remnants of drugs as well, to give weight to the story. A minor drug scandal would offer satisfactory cover for his presence and leave the company relatively unscathed as far as political associations in Colombia. Rather sizable contributions to the proper Colombian agencies 'for the war against drugs' would assure the press and others that Skyco was properly concerned. They would also help keep the investigation away from Building Two long enough to prevent a damaging information leak about the real problem.

Within two hours of Alexandra's departure, Elias and all evidence of Intel-Trace's presence in Medellín were gone. There was nothing more to gain from the Institute. Repair efforts were begun immediately on Building Two, and the whole incident fell safely into a story of drug wars. It was a dirty cover, but it offered good insulation.

By midafternoon Michael had established a small base camp deep in the Chocó forests about two kilometers from Cantú's cocaine lab. After setting a series of simple mantraps and other nasty surprises around the perimeter of his camp, he settled in to prepare his equipment for the job ahead.

He had carried in special gear designed for observation, infiltration, and neutralization of his target. It was set out in the order of expected use.

For observation purposes he had requested highly sophisticated night-vision gear. This was a passive night surveillance system utilizing fiber-optic image intensifiers. In the old days these things were large, cumbersome affairs. Today's technology had reduced them in size and weight to the point that they could be worn like goggles to free the hands to carry weapons. It weighed a mere nineteen ounces and could be detached for hand-held use, if desired. The only adjustment needed was to turn it on or off. Brightness was controlled automatically to view images at constant levels, even with variations in background light intensity. Effective range was three hundred meters. With this capability, the night hid nothing.

He had a compact crossbow that could be used to shoot high-strength, ultralight lines for climbing, should observation need to be made from higher up in trees.

For infiltration, his gear was light and highly portable and consisted simply of wire-cutting and lock-picking tools, and wire leads to bypass electrical alarm systems. He carried the Glock 17 handgun and the Smith & Wesson Airweight as backup. Long-arm weaponry was a shortened version of the AAI Advanced Combat Rifle (ACR), featuring a light, injection-molded, glass-filled nylon stock, with the forearm shrouding the shortened, flash-suppressed barrel. The remarkable advance here was that the ACR featured use of caseless ammunition. Without the requirement of ejecting spent casings, the action was shortened and capable of incredibly high rates of fire, with extreme accuracy. It could be fired in semiautomatic, three-round bursts, or full automatic modes.

In the three-round-burst mode, the ACR could fire three rounds with a single pull of the trigger. The rate was so rapid – two thousand rounds per minute – that the three rounds would be off before the first hint of recoil could affect accuracy. An expert rifleman had a hit probability of one hundred per cent out to six hundred yards under conditions of combat stress. In the full-automatic mode, the rate of fire was six hundred rounds per minute with reduced recoil, enabling extreme accuracy not possible with other hand-held automatic weapons.

It was mounted with a 1x-to-3x variable night scope with infrared laser capabilities, to visually pinpoint hit location. He also carried his usual Ka-Bar combat knife and a self-locking garrote.

Neutralization was a matter of C4 plastic explosive with special adhesive strips for fast mounting. Detonation was controlled by radio signal. The radio controller was programmable to series-detonate up to thirty-two devices, or to individually select-detonate any or all of the same number.

The rest of the neutralization would be handled by Wadelaw, who would provide air support from an AH-1W Super Cobra attack helicopter – the big item on Michael's shopping list.

Michael had left nothing to question.

He carefully packed his surveillance gear and headed out with about two hours of daylight left, planning to use the first hour for a cautious approach, then position himself to observe the nighttime routine of the compound.

The lab wasn't difficult to locate. Well-used trails led straight to it, and the operations were anything but silent. There was the persistent sound of a diesel generator running within the compound, and Michael heard rock music blaring long before he had sighted the camp. The music and the heavy forest sparked memories of 'Nam. The 'untouchable' status enjoyed by Cantú clearly led to less than ideal security practices. The approach was made with ridiculous ease.

Michael used the daylight hours to observe from ground level, remaining well concealed in the heavy growth. His camouflage dress and skin paint made him all but invisible in the heavy forest cover.

As the sun lowered and dusk fell rapidly over the forest, he began a measured, silent movement around the perimeter of the compound. The entire camp was heavily fenced with double rows of chainlink, with about four feet between rows. It was easily wide enough for night-watch patrols and guard dogs to circle the camp without being exposed to silent attack from the forest. The double rows also meant more time would be needed to breach the perimeter, and that half of that time would be spent in clear view. At least he hadn't seen dogs. Finding the camp was one thing: getting into it was an entirely different matter.

The size of the camp surprised Michael. He had expected it to be much smaller and less permanent in its construction. Processing labs of this kind were usually small and highly portable; they were moved frequently to avoid detection by the authorities. This one, however, had many crude but well-built structures, further testimony to Cantú's powerful relationship with the authorities.

Michael found a good vantage point from which to assess the compound and began a head count. There were about thirty in all, including five women who appeared to be camp whores. Life was pretty complete.

The center of the camp was dominated by a watchtower high enough to give excellent vision in all directions. In was unmanned, and no patrols had been sent out as yet.

There was a large helipad marked just to the east of the tower. Men and supplies were lifted in on some kind of schedule. The helipad could be useful later, when it came time for Michael to be lifted out of the camp by Wadelaw.

The air was heavy with the usual chemical stink from the processes under way. Structures housing personnel had lighted interiors with few blackout precautions. The camp should be easy to spot from the air. The only building properly blacked out was the brothel. It was from that structure that the music originated. The camp wouldn't have lasted a week without the drug king's protection.

Michael sketched the compound, noting where the personnel were housed and the chemicals stored.

Lab operations ceased with the coming of night. The personnel settled into four different, relatively large structures. Michael noted carefully the numbers of men in each.

When darkness came, he used the crossbow to set a line high in a tree. He climbed slowly and silently to a position that provided a good vantage point, and put on the night-vision gear. He sat patiently for hours, watching the routine as the men were fed and settled in for the night.

Three guards were posted inside the double rows of fencing. They seemed more concerned with comfort than vigilance. He periodically removed the night-vision gear to jot notes on his observations, as he began to plan the locations and timing of the detonations.

He watched the changing of the guard and followed the movements of the relieved personnel as they returned their weapons to a small shed. This was obviously their arsenal. A single building housed most of their firepower. A few men wore sidearms, but most were unarmed, except, perhaps, for knives. There were no patrols dispatched outside the perimeter, and he had still seen no guard dogs within the compound. There was some sporadic traffic to and from the brothel hut. He'd have to be aware of this later.

When he had seen all he needed to see, Michael lowered himself from the tree in a silent rappel, then made his way back through the forest to his base camp.

He would spend the next day waiting for darkness to come. He knew better than to underestimate an adversary, even with the carelessness he had witnessed, and he would plan as though he expected a determined response. Life had been easy for these old boys, he thought. All that was about to change.

Angel Solis had wasted little time disappearing into the night. After killing the girl, he had stayed visible just long enough to return to his apartment and collect all the cash he could, and to arm himself. Then he was gone.

He moved cautiously through the underbelly of Medellín, the only thing keeping him in the city the fact that Ramón owed him a lot of money. But he had no intention of being stupid as well as greedy. He could hide quite well in the city while he arranged a meeting with Ramón to collect what was due him. It would be when and where *he* chose, to ensure his safety. He did not trust Ramón, especially now that his assignment was finished.

Solis hid most of the day in a shabby room in the worst part of the city. With the door securely locked, he sat by the window, peeking out from behind the stained curtain. He watched the street the entire day, the gun cradled nervously in his hands.

Fear played havoc with his mind. There were times when he swore he saw Ramón. He'd stare hard at the figure, the fingers tightening on the gun, only to see the face melt into unrecognition. He imagined disguises of every sort, trying to see a recognizable feature. Everyone looked like Ramón, then no one did. Then he couldn't remember what Ramón looked like, until he closed his eyes to shut out the faces. When he opened his eyes again he'd see him in a doorway, then on a corner, then in a window across the street. He trembled and he sweated, and he checked the gun again and again to be sure it was loaded. Fear and nerves were defeating him. At least in this room he was safe. Ramón could get to him only through that one locked door. And Solis would shoot anyone dead who tried to come through it.

Intel-Trace surveillance teams had locked in on the entire perimeter of Solis's hideout. They watched from a half-dozen hidden positions, photographing faces, eavesdropping on conversations with long-range audio devices. Anyone approaching the building was photographed and watched. Six teams were ready on the street to follow in relays, should Solis decide to leave the room. For all his caution, Solis had been watched from the moment he left Comalinas's apartment.

It wasn't until late afternoon that Solis left his room and went downstairs to the dingy lobby of the building, making his way nervously to a pay phone. He inserted change and dialed a number.

The phone on the other end was answered on the second ring.

'Yes,' said the answering voice. It was Ramón.

Solis licked his dry lips; his heart was pounding.

'It's done,' he said, waiting for his contact's reply.

'You've done well,' Ramón said. 'But then I knew you would. I had every confidence in you.'

'The money. I want it today,' Solis said in a low voice, his eyes darting around the lobby and to the parts of the street he could see.

'Of course. The final installment.'

'And the bonus. You promised a bonus.'

'Yes, I did,' Ramón confirmed. 'An additional twenty

130

thousand, in American dollars. Good pay for good work.'

The bonus was better than Solis had expected.

'When and where?' Ramón asked, leaving the choice to Solis.

Solis squinted. He had expected Ramón to try to call the place and time – a part of the setup. It confused him. He thought for a moment. Perhaps he had been wrong about the setup.

Solis bit his lip. No, he thought. He must remain cautious. A public place with lots of people.

'The San Diego Shopping Mall, near the Intercontinental Hotel. In one hour. You will come alone,' Solis said.

'One hour. That is satisfactory, my friend. The mall is large, there are many eyes.'

'Precisely,' Solis said. 'We'll meet in the main plaza. You will bring the money in a satchel and leave before me.'

'If you insist. But I must have your assurance that you, too, will be alone, and that you will leave Medellín within twenty-four hours,' Ramón said.

'Agreed.'

'I must also think of my own safety,' Ramón added. 'I will leave the money in plain view. You must not approach it until I have left the main plaza. It would be unwise for us to be seen together in public.'

'I warn you, Ramón. No tricks. The payment must be in full,' Solis said.

'You have my word,' Ramón replied.

'All right. In one hour, then.'

'In one hour.'

The line went dead.

Not having to come face-to-face with Ramón was even better than Solis had hoped for. He could watch Ramón leave, then retrieve the money and leave in the opposite direction. Ramón could never follow him without being seen. It was perfect.

Solis returned quickly to his room. He checked the gun one more time and tucked it securely under his belt; then grabbed the single bag he had packed and left the room.

He would get to the mall well ahead of time, and position himself where he could watch the main plaza carefully. If anything looked suspicious, he'd leave and abandon the final payment. It was a prospect he didn't relish, but getting out of Medellín alive was more important than any amount of money.

Intel-Trace's surveillance teams wasted no time staking out the San Diego Shopping Mall. Solis had made a critical blunder in using a phone so near his hiding place. The tap had taken only minutes to arrange after he had first settled in. Every word of the conversation had been heard.

All but two teams immediately broke off surveillance of Solis and rushed ahead to the mall. There was no secret now where Solis would be, and where the contact would be made. The agents were strategically deployed to cover every possible approach to the main plaza of the mall. Relay teams were set in place to follow Ramón once he was identified. The system was elaborate, with trackers and static watch personnel. No one person would stay in visual contact with him long enough to spark suspicion. Ramón was the new quarry, and his suspicions must not be triggered. To lose him would mean the loss of their only positive lead.

Solis arrived at the mall twenty minutes early, and made his way to the main plaza, stepping into a bookstore that permitted him a clear view of the drop location.

He stayed close to the large display window, pretending interest in the latest best-sellers, all the while watching for the first signs of Ramón. The wait was a short one.

Ramón, too, had arrived early. He did not make a direct approach to the drop point, however. He was cautious, alert to the possibilities of surveillance.

An attaché case hung from his left hand and with his right hand he clutched a small bag. He passed directly by the drop spot, then continued past it to the outer perimeter of the plaza. He looked in the window displays of several shops, turning occasionally to the right, then to the left, searching carefully for eyes that showed too much interest.

He circled the perimeter, spotting Solis in the bookstore, but continued on past. He would not approach the drop point until he was certain he was not being observed by anyone but Solis.

Solis fidgeted nervously with a book, pretending to read the dust jacket.

Ramón circled halfway around again before making the final scan for watchers. After a long assessment, he moved at a casual pace toward the center of the plaza. He stopped next to a waste disposal container and set the attaché case on the floor beside the receptacle. He reached into the small bag as the shutter snapped from long range. The second frame captured a close zoom as the hand removed a piece of chocolate-covered candy. The next caught him putting it into his mouth. By this time two cameras were on him.

Ramón finished the first piece of candy, then reached into the bag for a second. He popped it into his mouth, crumpled the bag, and tossed it into the trash receptacle. His eyes made a final scan and he walked away in the direction from which he had come.

In the next instant Solis was out of the bookstore, heading for the attaché case.

It was all that Intel-Trace's teams needed. Ramón had been made, and every effort was now concentrated on carefully tracking his movements without alerting him. Solis was no longer their concern.

Ramón didn't dally in the plaza, his obvious concern being to leave quickly at this point.

Solis moved just as quickly, and for the same reason. He needed to be away from that place, and from Ramón, as swiftly as possible. He made a straight approach for the case, picking it up without stopping.

The detonator trigger in the handle was silent, but the explosion was not. The blast shattered store windows and took heavy casualties among innocent shoppers. In one blazing instant, Solis became unrecognizable and the housecleaning in Medellín was complete.

The confusion and mayhem that followed made ideal cover for Ramón. He slipped into a quality men's clothing store and made his way directly to a street exit. Just that quickly, he was gone.

He walked briskly away from the mall for a block, crossed the street, then moved back in the direction of the explosion, now one of the curious moving toward the commotion. He continued onward into the confused mass of people, then through the crush of onlookers in the street. He hailed a cab and got in. The cab pulled away from the curb just ahead of the jammed street behind him. He looked back through the rear window and saw that no one was following. He wanted to smile, but didn't. Whatever was behind him was there to stay, he thought with smug satisfaction, paying no mind to the car in front of the cab, or to the eyes of the cab driver staring into the rearview mirror.

10

BOGOTÁ, COLOMBIA: The new control center in the capital city was modest by comparison to the one in Medellín, but it had everything Elias needed, most of all secure communications. He and Danziger stood in front of a large poster board to which had been attached the pictures taken earlier of Ramón. The photographic work was excellent. Ramón's features were captured in great close-up detail.

'This is Solis's contact?' Danziger asked.

'That's right, and for once we get a break. We know him.'

'I'm impressed,' Danziger commented. 'These pictures are hardly dry. What's the book on him?'

'He's a Basque terrorist, a killer and an expert in explosives. His real name is Juan Strassa. He's from the province of Euzkadi and is a former member of the ETA, a Basque separatist terrorist organization. It's a group patterned after the IRA, engaged in a 'revolutionary war' against the Spanish state.

'He's in his mid-forties; got his start early in 1968, killing Spanish policemen. He had a talent for it. About ten years later the ETA shifted its approach and began targeting military officers in an attempt to draw a military presence, to sort of Ulsterize the region. His big year was 1979, when he masterminded and took part in the killing of seven high-ranking military officers, including three general officers, two of whom were killed outside the province.

'It was at about that time his own people began to realize he was pathological and enjoyed his work a little too much. In 1980 we have him linked to two major assassinations in the province of Alava. The first was Major Jesús Velazco, the commander of the provincial police force, and then three months later to the killing of Eugenio Lazaro, Velazco's successor. The killings were in open defiance of the state's Home Rule Statute.'

'Why didn't the ETA get rid of him?' Danziger asked.

'Probably fear, at first. There was an attempt to curb his activities once, but the man responsible was blown to hell in his car, along with his whole family. It was never proved that Strassa did it, but no one tried very hard to make the case, either, if you get the point.'

'He pushed things too far, though, in 1982, right after the Spanish Security Forces made an impressive rescue of Julio Ingesias, a high-ranking Euzkadi official being held hostage in an ETA hideout. Strassa hit the people in his own group whom he believed to be responsible for this failure. There was no directive to do so. He acted strictly on his own. He was out after that. He left Euzkadi to stay alive. He was beyond salvage, and they'd have taken him out if he hadn't left.

'Since that time he's operated out of Europe on a contract basis. He's very good at what he does,' Elias concluded.

'Europe. That means he'll head back soon,' Danziger interjected.

'Yep. And when he does, we'll be right behind him. It's not likely that he'll be making any more contacts here in Colombia. He might not need to make any in Europe if he got paid up front. If he is still due money, it could be handled by deposit to a safe account somewhere. If that's the case, then we'll have to find a way to push him into a contact.'

Danziger shook his head. 'Whoever is behind this is one smart sonofabitch. He's planned every detail. There are no loose ends. He's like a shadow – always out of direct sight.'

'That's the way it looks. But everyone makes mistakes. His might just be in being *too* careful. Somewhere along the line it'll catch up to him. Then we'll be in a position to start making some of the rules.'

Night fell softly over the forests of the Chocó. The camp routine went much the same as Michael had observed the night before. He sat in the same tree, waiting patiently for the activity to cease. He used the time to visually trace a route of minimal exposure through the camp, once he was inside its perimeter.

Michael held his position until 2.00 a.m. and the changing of the sentries. They worked four-hour shifts, with this rotation being the one of least activity. The rest of the camp had settled in for the night and there was little activity, except at the brothel.

Michael rappelled to the forest floor. He pulled on the backpack containing the explosives, then drew back into the forest and began moving in a slow arc to reach his planned point of entry near the diesel generator. Its persistent sound would provide cover for any noise he might make getting through the double rows of fencing.

He emerged from the edge of the forest and patiently scanned the area before approaching the first row of fencing. He examined it carefully. It wasn't electrically charged, but it did have a secondary network of fine wires woven horizontally through the chain link at regular intervals. This secondary lattice was tied into some form of intruder-detection system, he was sure.

He removed from the backpack several sets of wire leads with alligator clips at both ends. These he attached to the finer wire network to provide a continuous circuit, then began snipping the chain link with the wire cutters. He cut the first charged wire and waited for a response. There was none. He cut the remaining wires, all the while listening for sounds above the noise of the diesel generator. So far, so good, he thought as he squeezed through the opening in the outer fence.

Light from the moon was almost nonexistent at this end of the compound, but that fact did little to dispel the moments of uneasiness that Michael felt while in the open between the rows of fencing. Without the friendly cover of the forest growth, the man who moved like a ghost through the forests was all to human – all too visible.

He took a moment to confirm that the inner row of fencing was uncharged and had no secondary wire woven through its links. He cut his way through quickly and glided silently to cover behind the lean-to structure housing the generator.

Michael used a moment to take his bearings within the camp, then looked for the sole sentry posted in this end of the compound. He spotted him, pulled the Ka-Bar combat knife, and crawled silently along the ground.

His progress slowed as he neared the unsuspecting sentry, advancing by inches without a breath of sound. He closed in, his eyes locked intently on the target. Slow, slow movement that an insect couldn't detect, pure silence.

The sentry was sitting with his back against a sapling, his mind a million miles away from the boring routine of uneventful nightwatch duty. He never heard the movement or sensed the face that appeared behind his left shoulder. Michael's hand darted out like a cobra, covering the mouth and nose of the sentry. The Ka-Bar flashed to the base of the skull with deadly precision. There was a grunt,

137

the sound muffled by Michael's hand, and a brief series of involuntary kicks.

Michael pulled the sentry's head close to his chest and gave the knife a final twist. Then all resistance stopped, replaced by the heavy limpness of death.

Michael froze and raised his eyes, white against his blackened, camouflaged face, and scanned the area to see if the faint sounds had alerted any of the camp personnel. After satisfying himself that the sounds had gone undetected, he raised the sentry's body back into a sitting position against the tree, laid the sentry's weapon across his lap, and moved cautiously into the compound.

He moved like a breeze past the soaking pits and made his way swiftly to the cover of the chemical shed. The air stank badly from the chemicals, and the smell of ether was strong. This alarmed Michael somewhat, for ether is highly explosive. Its heavier-than-air vapors tend to sink to ground level, where they are less detectable, and spread like a fluid seeking its own level, filling depressions in the ground. This makes them extremely dangerous. He had seen ether explosions before, where a spark fifty feet away could ignite a vapor fuse that traveled faster than the eye could see, straight back to the source of the leak. Ether explosions were powerful, and there was enough here to make this a party to remember. One accidental spark – even from a static electrical discharge – could put a sudden and rather unpleasant end to his day.

Michael took the first strip of C4 high explosive from his pack. He pulled the paper strip from the adhesive surface and pressed the plastic against one of the support columns of the shed. Then he inserted the first serial detonator and moved in silence across an open expanse to the armory shed, where he planted the second strip of plastic. With this accomplished, he scanned the compound once again for signs of movement.

Then the unexpected happened. A man stepped out of the armory shed, his legs just a few feet from Michael's face. Michael hugged dirt and froze. The man stood just outside the open door, inserted a clip into the automatic weapon in his hands, and slung the weapon over his shoulder.

Michael rolled very slowly to his side, putting himself as close to the base of the shed as possible. The man needed only to look down to his side to see him. It was the longest ten seconds of Michael's life before the man moved off.

Michael's heart pounded so wildly that he could feel it in his head and could hear the blood surging in his ears. He watched as the feet moved away. Perspiration rolled down his forehead and face, and the sweat burned in his eyes.

Michael raised his eyes against the stinging, and watched as the man climbed the ladder to the tower dominating the center of the compound. This sentry was unexpected. The tower had not been occupied the night before as he had watched and studied the compound routine. This was a very bad development.

The entire compound could be watched from that tower, making his maneuvers enormously more difficult. He still had the rest of his explosives to plant, and he was stuck in the center of the compound with open ground between his present position and the next available cover. He cursed the bad luck.

He had planned to eliminate only the single sentry nearest his point of entry. This new guard meant that a second would have to be taken, and at greater risk. Wadelaw could easily eliminate the tower, but the threat to Michael was immediate. His work had to be done before Wadelaw came in. He'd have to increase his risk and take the guard out himself.

He judged the distance too great to use the crossbow, even with the laser target-acquisition scope attached. He needed to be within thirty meters to guarantee a kill. He would have to risk movement within the compound to work himself into range, and this would take valuable time.

Michael watched the guard closely, waiting for him to turn his attention to the opposite side of the compound.

The moment he did, Michael sprinted across the first open expanse to the equipment shed. He crawled underneath it to safety, and planted his next strip of plastic.

He took a moment to check his diagram and the planned sequence of detonations. The personnel barracks were next on his list. They were closer to the tower, but provided no angle from which to take his shot at the tower guard. He looked back at the diagram. The best position would be from the brothel. It was a longer shot than he was comfortable with, but at least he'd have the major detonation points covered before he'd have to take it. He could always detonate the explosives if it didn't go smoothly, still gaining him his initial advantage of surprise.

The move to the first barracks was his greatest risk. The expanse was wide, and a bright band of moonlight cut across it. He moved to the side of the shed, raised himself upright, then stepped directly into the open. He walked slowly in a natural and casual gait, his pack of explosives over one shoulder and the ACR slung over the other. If he was spotted, he might be dismissed as simply one of the camp personnel moving to his quarters. He fought the urge to run, and to look up at the tower.

Every step was an eternity. His ears stayed keen to the slightest sound of alarm, a voice of challenge or the metallic clack of an arming bolt. But there was only the chug of the generator droning in the background, and the music from the brothel.

The ploy worked. He slid into the shadows behind the first barracks, then quickly crawled underneath it. He planted the charge, then crawled the short distance to the adjacent structure and planted his next charge. He repeated this until all four barracks were seeded with the deadly material.

He checked his diagram one last time, confirming his assessment of the shot possibilities from the brothel. He could also see the remaining two sentries, which meant that he could use the ACR to take them out when the time was right. He would also have easy access to the contraband storage area, which would provide cover when the show began. From that point inside the compound he could direct concentrated fire to most other parts of the camp.

He reslung the pack and the ACR and stepped into the open. He walked directly across the compound, moving toward the tower, again keeping a casual pace. This time he gave in to the urge to look up at the tower. The guard was looking straight down at him, his weapon hung over the edge of the tower, directed harmlessly away. Michael lowered his eyes nonchalantly and continued toward the brothel. He didn't look back as he moved away from the tower until he reached the brothel and turned the corner. The guard was no longer watching him.

Once out of sight, he dropped to his knees, pulled out the crossbow, and armed it, loading the metal arrow. He was about to switch on the laser scope when he heard a sound behind him. He spun on his knee and looked up. There was a rather large fat man standing directly behind him.

The crossbow hit the ground and the Ka-Bar flashed from the leg sheath. Michael was up on his feet and lunging before the startled man could react. Michael's left hand went to the man's mouth and the Ka-Bar struck the throat.

The man was big and strong, and his natural response was forceful. There was a hoarse grunt as the knife bit deeply, and Michael drove all of his weight into the man. They crashed into the side of the shed.

The man nearly pushed Michael off him, but Michael's superior balance saved him from disaster. He tore the knife through the man's throat, then pulled him with a rolling maneuver to the ground. The knife struck again and again, the left hand still managing to muffle the gurgling sounds of the struggling hulk on the ground beneath him. Michael suppressed the final writhing movements, praying for death to hurry. It was anything but silent, and it seemed like an eternity until stillness claimed the fat man.

The sounds of the brief struggle were too loud for Michael's liking. He froze in silence, listening for response to any alarm that the sounds may have signaled. There was none.

He breathed deeply for a few moments to get himself back under control, and wiped the blood from his hands. Then he returned to the crossbow.

He checked the tower. The guard stood facing to the left of Michael's position, unaware that he was the one being watched. Michael switched on the laser scope and readied the crossbow. He raised it and rested his arm against the side of the structure to help steady his aim. The tiny red dot found the guard's shoulder, then moved up to the side of the head. Michael's finger went to the trigger and began a controlled squeeze.

The twang of the bowstring was barely audible, followed instantly by a dull crack as the metal shaft smashed through the skull of the guard. He fell straight down to the floor of the tower stand like a sack of dirt, the gentle thump of his body going unnoticed.

Michael rapidly collapsed the crossbow and stowed it in the backpack.

He checked his watch and put the ultralight headpiece of his radio set on. He swung the mike arm into place and turned on the radio.

'Banshee, this is Desperado. Come back to me,' he said into the mouth-piece.

'Go ahead, Desperado. This is Banshee,' Wadelaw radioed from the attack helicopter waiting only minutes away.

'Get her up. It's time to rock and roll,' Michael instructed.

'Roger, Desperado. ETA in two minutes. I'll come in hot, give my blessings, and drop you the ladder in the center of the compound. Keep your head low when you see me, pal. I won't be able to tell you from the monkeys. Pull the green flare, wave me a sign, and move for the pickup point. I'll keep 'em praying for life after, and we'll blow out of there. Over.'

'Roger, Banshee. You'll see the party. Over and out.'

Michael unslung the ACR, turned on the infrared night

142

scope and moved to the edge of the baled stock of finished contraband. He set the ACR to the three-round-burst mode and readied the radio detonator controller. He checked his watch one more time, and set the countdown timer on the detonator controller. One minute and go. Automatic sequence.

He raised the ACR and focused on the first of the two remaining sentries to be sure the shot would be clean, then swung the weapon to the second sentry. Both were in easy range. He went back to the first and waited. And then what could go wrong did go wrong.

A high-pitched scream shattered the quiet of the compound. Michael's head snapped to the direction of the scream, which was now as continuous as an alarm. One of the camp prostitutes was standing over the blood-soaked body of the fat man.

Michael's response was automatic. The ACR barked a rapid three-shot burst that silenced the woman. He spun and drew the laser scope on to the first sentry, who was beginning to move toward the brothel. Another three-shot burst dropped him in midstride.

The last sentry had also begun moving in the direction of the frantic screams and had heard both bursts from the ACR. The second had given him a confirmed location of their origin and he managed to get off a single burst from his automatic weapon before the ACR delivered a tight grouping to his chest.

Reaction to the sudden outbreak of gunfire was immediate. Men began racing from the two nearest barracks.

Michael sprayed well-aimed bursts, taking five of the confused personnel in rapid succession before return fire erupted toward his position, sending him to cover. Not all of the weapons were in the armory shed as he had thought.

He inserted a fresh clip and changed his position, praying for the detonations to begin.

There were men moving in all directions now, most in a state of utter confusion and panic. The last two barracks doors flew open and more men began fighting one another

143

to get through the doorways. The odds were quickly changing as too many targets moved across too large an area. And most of them were armed with at least small arms.

Then the chemical shed blew, igniting in a tremendous orange ball of flame. The ear shattering and terrifying explosions continued at four-second intervals, adding to the confusion.

The first two barracks went up, taking more than half of their occupants with them. An undetermined number made it clear of the last two barracks before they, too, were destroyed.

The ACR began a rhythmic pattern of three-shot bursts, dropping one man after another. But the surprise had not been complete enough, and the determined response began.

Sudden and heavy gunfire concentrated on Michael's position. He fled and dodged with all of the speed he could summon, keeping himself just barely out of the fire being directed at him. Weapons were now discharging in all directions.

Michael reloaded the ACR on the fly, and switched the weapon to the automatic mode, cutting it loose at every moving figure and shadow he saw. It had now become an open firefight.

Wadelaw had little trouble spotting the camp as he sped toward the glowing mayhem. The modified AH-IW Super Cobra bore in like an angry wasp, all weapon systems at the ready, tied into the helmet-mounted interface controlling sighting. Wherever Wadelaw looked, the flex-guns aimed.

The sudden appearance of the Cobra added to the confusion as the flexies opened up, spewing death and terror from a new source.

Wadelaw dropped low over the compound, pivoting the Cobra on its rotor axis, firing the entire breadth of its arc.

Michael flattened himself into two dimensions as the flexies tore up everything standing.

Wadelaw had no way of spotting Michael in the confusion, and so he fired at everything that moved. He could hear the impact of gunfire against the armored body of his craft. He returned a murderous concentration of fire at flash sightings of the weapons in the compound.

Michael dropped the empty ACR and ignited the green flare.

Wadelaw spotted it immediately, cut a rocket at the tower that leveled it, then swung toward the helipad near the center of the compound, continuing to lay a fierce cover fire for his partner.

He dropped in and hovered over the helipad, straining through the hot glow for signs of Michael. Then he spotted him streaking toward the pickup point.

His eyes caught sight of more movement. The head turned, the flex-guns responding instantly in unison, blowing the figures to pieces.

Wadelaw released the dropline ladder for Michael, who was now breaking into the open center of the compound. Another figure was close behind him, but was too close for Wadelaw to direct fire against without endangering his partner.

Michael reached the ladder, grabbed it, and Wadelaw pulled up immediately, but not before the figure behind Michael could reach him.

The man grabbed Michael's legs as the Cobra lifted, pulling both men off of the ground.

Michael tried kicking his legs free, but they were too tightly grasped by the unwelcome and unexpected hanger-on.

The added weight of the second man made it impossible for Michael to let go of the ladder with one of his hands to fight the man off without losing his grip entirely. He hung on helplessly as the Cobra pulled straight up.

The man secured a grip on Michael's belt with one hand, let go with the other, and reached for his knife.

Michael could see it all without the ability to help himself.

He watched the knife blade flash, reflecting the blazing carnage below as it cleared the sheath.

He kicked frantically to dislodge the attacker. The knife drew back into a striking position at the same moment that the Cobra lurched forward and began acceleration. The dangling drop ladder crashed through the treetops as the craft picked up speed sharply.

The impact of the branches knocked both men from the ladder. The crashing descent through the trees seemed to take forever. Michael hit the ground with a thud and lay motionless, barely conscious and unable to breathe.

Wadelaw continued his steep climb and banked sharply away from the compound before noticing that Michael was no longer on the ladder. He spun the craft sharply, pitching the tail up to get a view down into the darkness. The wreckage of the lab burned fiercely, and the contrast made sighting into the dark trees impossible.

Wadelaw tried making voice contact over the radio, but Michael's radio had been torn away in the fall.

Michael rolled to his side, clutching his ribs. He forced himself to breathe through the pain. The branches that had battered him during his descent had also saved him by breaking his fall.

He struggled to his knees and scanned the surrounding area quickly for immediate signs of danger. The other man was nowhere to be seen.

The fall had taken him outside of the perimeter, near the spot from which he had made his earlier ground observations. He could see the helicopter above the trees, and had the presence of mind to activate the radio communicator in his watch.

'Drop-off point,' he gasped into it, barely able to speak. 'First sign of light,' he forced out.

'Roger, Desperado,' came the reply. The helicopter peeled off and disappeared into the night.

Michael rose slowly to his feet and looked back into the camp. There were no more sounds of ground fire, and only the scene of utter destruction remained. He could hear sounds of horrible pain and suffering emanating from the remains of the cocaine lab.

Michael limped a few steps, then turned away. Still dazed from the fall, he began as swift a retreat as possible. His head was clear enough, though, to recognize that luck had saved him today and that it was best not to press it any further. He set off into the safety of the darkness and the forest, leaving behind the results of his first offensive in what looked to be a long and costly battle.

For what it was worth, Michael Quinn had just played his first card against the drug lord Hector Contú.

11

BOGOTÁ, COLOMBIA: Michael Quinn stared with tired eyes out the window of the newly established command center. A brilliant dawn was breaking over the thriving capital city nestled against the Andes. There had been little time for sleep over the past two days, and Michael was feeling the effects of the fall to the forest floor. Everything hurt. He had been ragged with fatigue and pain when Wadelaw made the rendezvous at first light. But, as bad as he looked, he had never looked better to Wadelaw.

Michael turned away from the window as the door to the control room opened and Bob Elias entered, carrying a stack of file folders. The sound of the door closing woke Wadelaw from a light sleep. He raised one eyelid and focused on Elias and grunted wearily.

Elias breezed in, looking fresh and well rested. In reality he hadn't slept any more than they had, out of concern for them. He was glad to see them back safely.

'I just saw a satellite photo of your handiwork,' Elias said, then added with a smile, 'You guys are slipping. You left part of a building standing.'

'That was about all,' Wadelaw huffed. 'Your boy here is very thorough. There wasn't much left to shoot at when I got there,' he said.

'You guys did a masterful job. Cantú will have plenty to think about after last night.'

'That was the general idea,' Michael said.

'Where's Danziger?' he asked.

'He's back at the Institute, up to his ass in local authorities. There've been some developments since you left Medellín,' Elias began. 'Solis is dead, for starters.'

'How?' Wadelaw asked.

'Explosives. Right in the middle of a shopping mall. He was picking up his payoff and got more than he expected. Delgado is dead, too. Same medicine, in his car.'

'Delgado?' Michael said, surprised.

Elias nodded. 'He was involved from the start. We were in the process of bringing him in for protection when it happened. We lost one very good agent in the deal. We got a make on Solis's contact, though.'

'Anyone we know?' Michael asked.

'You bet. A mechanic by the name of Strassa. We have a good jacket on him and he won't go anywhere without us in his shadow. We expect him to head for safe cover soon. There could be another contact soon – a meaningful one. Strassa doesn't work cheap and operates through a tight network. Whoever hired him is going to be a significant figure. If we make that connection, we'll be much closer to the principal network behind all of this.

'The identities of the attack force at the Institute are insignificant compared to Strassa. Bunch of street kids trying to be heroes,' Elias told them.

'What's the next step with Cantú?' Wadelaw asked.

'He's been hurt,' Michael replied. 'And he'll want to find out who was behind the hit on the lab, and why. The next step is to play him along. If we're right about his trail, it was used to move the strain to the next transfer. If it was used as we suspect, then there's no doubt he was involved and was well paid for his services. You might be able to focus on that transaction, Bob.'

'We're working on it. DEA can assist us with Cantú's banks. Matching the cash movement won't be that easy in this case, however, because of the enormous amount of flow from his other operations. We may be able to get something of value by cross-referencing transactions based upon the timing of the payments. That will help us narrow the possibles to a few leads that we can pursue. It'll give us a starting point, and somewhere we'll get the right cross-reference, then we can move in.'

'So where's our next stop?' Wadelaw asked.

'Cartagena,' Elias answered.

'What's in Cartagena?'

'A major conduit into Cantú's network. His name is Raúl. He's Cantú's major dealer in the city. Handles just the big-time stuff. No small dealers. We approach like we want to deal, and get his attention. He'll report to Cantú, and if Cantú believes we're real, maybe we get to meet him.

'It ain't that easy, boss,' Wadelaw said. 'They don't just deal with any slick who shows up spouting big talk. You've got to have references or a reputation that they're familiar with. It could take weeks to build a cover they'll believe. And any time they think you're not legit or are DEA or something like that, you're a dead man. And a meeting with Cantú . . . I just don't think that'll happen.'

'It'll happen,' Michael said. 'And I won't even have to meet Raúl face-to-face to make it happen. I won't have to talk deals.'

Wadelaw stared at Michael, his brain ticking away, when it hit him. 'The lab. That's why you hit it. Shit, you'll be lucky to live through the night, much less meet with the big man himself.'

'I said before that he'll want to know who . . . and why. He'll talk to me, all right.'

'Yeah, he'll talk to you, then he'll cut your throat.'

'That's a chance I'll have to take. You just be there to back me up when I need you.'

MOSCOW: General Aleksandr Kozlov read carefully through the pages of the reports in front of him. His first deputy, Nikolai Barchenkin, turned idly through his copies of the same reports, familiar with every detail.

Kozlov finished and went back to the one folder of particular interest. It was the report on the Skyco Research Institute filed by the GRU Tenth Directorate, whose responsibility was close study of military economics worldwide, watching arms sales, studying production and technological developments, strategic resources, and vulnerable points in supply lines of those resources.

'It appears, Nikolai, that our instincts were correct,' Kozlov said. 'Our Tenth Directorate holds the Skyco Research Institute in very high regard. Look at these capabilities. I knew of its existence, but did not imagine it to be so large. The work conducted there goes into many aspects of petroleum recovery and use. Most interesting here are their capabilities in genetic engineering. Amazing.'

'Yes, General. Some of their most brilliant scientists work there. It appears obvious that their main intent in conducting this research in Colombia is to avoid the tight regulatory controls exercised in the United States. They shuttle scientists in and out regularly. The director of the Institute is Dr Vincent Stillings. His specialty is genetic research. He took the post as director about three years ago, and his move to Colombia is what triggered our close interest in activities there. Prior to that time, the research conducted in Medellín was concentrated on petroleum interests as they applied to Colombia's growing oil industry. Skyco has been a prime contributor to the impressive pipeline projects completed over the past eight years.'

Kozlov slid the folder to the side and pulled a second in front of him and opened it. This folder contained satellite photos of the Institute, taken and supplied by the

Directorate of Cosmic Intelligence, one of the most powerful directorates within the GRU structure. Kozlov himself sat as its sole authority. Its power was his power. Of the two thousand Soviet satellites in orbit, fully one-third belonged to this organ. The directorate had its own 'cosmodromes' (space-launch facilities), research institutes, computer centers, and vast resources. The majority of Soviet cosmonauts were GRU agents reporting to this directorate. Their satellites were exclusively GRU and were used for the purpose of collecting intelligence data.

'What do these photographs suggest, Nikolai?' Kozlov asked.

'Well, if we compare them with earlier photographs, we get a clear impression of major reconstruction work being done on one of the buildings,' Barchenkin replied.

'Which one?'

'Their designation is Building Two. This is where the genetic research is conducted. Close-ups clearly show damage to the exterior at one point near the rear of the building, close to the perimeter of the compound, which is fenced and under heavy security.'

'And the nature of the damage?' Kozlov asked.

'These photos, taken only two days ago from just outside the compound by the Resident Intelligence Station, show what looks to be damage inflicted by explosives and small-arms fire. Rather heavy concentrations of it, too,' Barchenkin said, spreading the photos in front of his boss. 'And these photographs indicate reconstruction efforts being made inside the building,' he said, pointing to more pictures in the satellite file. 'This suggests damage inside the building as well, judging from the materials being brought in.'

'Your conclusions?'

'An attack of some kind, directed at Building Two. Assuming usual investigation procedures, the attack probably occurred within the past week.'

'At about the same time that the air search was begun,' Kozlov added.

'That is correct, General.'

'So, an attack took place, and shortly afterward an air search was started,' Kozlov summed up, then thought quietly for a few moments.

'Were there signs of damage to the fenced perimeter of the compound?'

'No. And there were no signs of new fencing, so there were no recent repairs.'

'And the radius of the air search?'

'Perhaps two hundred fifty kilometers.'

'What is the status of the air search now?' Kozlov asked.

'Search patterns have continued, but are gradually lessening in intensity. This suggests that they may be giving up hope of finding what they are searching for . . . or that they have secretly found it.'

Kozlov smiled.

'Precisely,' he said. 'Continue the search activity as though the find had not been made, and move all aircraft out of the area. What else do we have?'

'Seven days ago, key Skyco personnel arrived in Colombia. Thomas Danziger, head of Skyco's intelligence, and Alexandra Sky, president of Skyco and daughter of Asher Sky, the chief executive officer. Later that same day, additional personnel were brought in – a rather large contingent from the United States, which we assume to be some kind of investigative staff. Three others arrived on the following day. Of these we have identified two.'

Barchenkin tapped a photograph of Bob Elias.

'Who is this man?' Kozlov asked.

'His name is Robert Elias. He is the director of an investigative firm called Intel-Trace.'

Kozlov knew of Intel-Trace. 'They've asked for help . . . very capable help. And the other two?' Kozlov asked, lifting pictures of Michael Quinn and Carlos Trevino. 'Which of these has been identified?'

'This one,' Barchenkin said, touching the end of his pencil to one of the pictures. 'His name is Michael Quinn.'

'This name is familiar,' Kozlov said. He shook his head after a few moments, unable to make the connection.

'Helsinki,' Barchenkin hinted. 'The Dieter-Tomarev incident.'

Kozlov's eyes widened in recognition. 'So he's the one who killed Tomarev.' Kozlov's lips tightened. Tomarev's death had been a harsh setback in a major investigation that could have seriously compromised Vladin's standing with the Central Committee. Kozlov had developed an airtight case against one of Vladin's top men. He had been only weeks away from dropping the hammer on him. The Helsinki incident had cost him that opportunity.

'He bears watching, General. He is a very capable individual. Dieter and Tomarev were both highly skilled. Quinn apparently had little difficulty with them,' Barchenkin said.

Kozlov nodded. 'They are very serious, Nikolai. They mean to have their property back. What about this third man?' he asked, holding up the last picture of Carlos.

'Unknown to us. We are working on the identity now.'

'Obviously another specialist of some kind,' Kozlov said. 'Please summarize the activity.'

'Two days ago, Alexandra Sky left Colombia and returned to the United States. One day later, Danziger and Elias left Medellín and returned to Bogotá. Danziger returned to Medellín today in early morning, Colombian time.'

'And the other two?'

'Unknown. They haven't been seen for three days. Also, two days ago a key employee of the Medellín Research Institute was murdered. His name was Ernesto Delgado. He was the head of security at the Medellín Research Institute. His car was blown up. There was a passenger with him. We don't know the identity.'

Kozlov thought for a moment. 'I want Robert Elias and Thomas Danziger watched carefully. When Quinn and the other man appear again, I want them watched as well. Stay close to them, but give strict orders not to engage them in any way.'

'Yes, General,' Barchenkin replied.

'Skyco has lost something of great value. They may already have found it, and possibly they have not. The fact that it may be of genetic nature makes it very important to us as well. We must learn what this is, and quickly. I want maximum effort in the United States to learn what we can through Skyco. Use our existing contacts and develop as many more as possible. Select your top agents and have them ready to go in immediately. Has Archives completed the file that I requested on Asher Sky?'

Barchenkin slid a thick file folder across the table to Kozlov.

'Thank you, Nikolai. Continue to keep all efforts in this matter secret. We are not yet ready to share this with anyone. Keep me informed of any developments.'

'Yes, General,' Barchenkin said. He collected his file folders and left Kozlov's office.

Kozlov pulled the Sky file in front of him and opened the folder. Some of this information he knew already, the rest he would learn.

He picked up the first sheet and began reading.

It was during the Great Famine of 1921 that the young Asher Sky first came to Russia. He was twenty years old and already a self-made millionaire. The historians of the world will forever debate what motivated the young industrialist to embark upon his journey to a land torn, exhausted, and starved by civil war. Some say he was driven by compassion for a land and its people forced to their knees by starvation and disease. And there is valid argument for this line of reasoning, for he came with a fortune in badly needed medical supplies to a nation blockaded by the powers of Europe in retaliation for their revolution and the brutal assassination of their royal family. Others say he had more guts than sense, and that what motivated him was his uncanny nose for profit. The truth is that Asher Sky, a consummate strategist, had not ventured to the land of his ancestors on wings of goodness. He had recognized quite correctly that a thirsty man would welcome a stranger bearing water. The medical supplies were the price of his admission, and made attractive tender.

He had come, against all advice, to a land that had crushed capitalism and eliminated its upper class. In achieving this great goal of the Revolution, the powers of this new system had destroyed their industrial and economic base. There were no means of recovery available to a land devoid of industrialists and economists. Sky's ingenious contribution was the capital and the know-how to ignite their economic recovery. It was a huge gamble on his part that they'd even accept his help. But he had not become a millionaire at the age of twenty by avoiding risk. Where there was venture, there was gain.

His journey was long and difficult. When he arrived he found cholera and typhus, mass starvation and death, the scope of which went beyond his imagination. Moscow seemed to him a vision of hell, windowless and bullet-pocked. Its people were in rags, their hands and feet wrapped in shreds of cloth, for there were no gloves or boots, except for those worn by Communist officials, who were well dressed in characteristic black leather coats and high boots. Despair could not have been more evident.

At first it appeared that his detractors were correct about his fool's mission. It seemed as though no one was willing to acknowledge his presence. He had been given quarters that made the worst prison look good. He sat and waited to be seen by officials who showed little or no interest in him. So he waited with patience as unrelenting as his determination, all the while studying the language with fierce diligence, confident that he would get his appointment, and determined to speak to them in their own language when he did. He waited for months, being slowly worn down by the feeling of helplessness. His supplies sat unused, still very much needed. He finally faced the reality that perhaps the warnings had been well founded and began to prepare for his return to the United

States when he received word of an appointment with the Foreign Trade Commission.

His persistence had been rewarded, and he received an invitation to join an inspection tour of selected areas of the country. He accepted immediately.

As an 'industrial adviser', Asher Sky traveled to formerly productive regions of the new Soviet Union. It was a nightmarish revelation. Starvation and disease were even worse in these areas than in Moscow. Even though some of the economic sanctions against Russia were beginning to be eased, he was shown huge stocks of valuable resources, from platinum to furs, that were next to useless to the Soviet Union. The problem was that, despite having these goods at their disposal, the Russians were unable to sell them rapidly enough to purchase badly needed food supplies for these industrial regions. In the United States there was a surplus of wheat, which had fallen in price to a dollar a bushel. Russia needed one million bushels to gain immediate relief until a new harvest season would permit self-help. Sky saw instantly the opportunity he had waited for. He had a million dollars, and made a contract on the spot to arrange for immediate shipment of the stockpiled American grain. In exchange for the wheat and his medical supplies, he would take furs and minerals in equal value and arrange for their sale in the United States. He offered to achieve what had been thought impossible.

Lenin himself approved the transaction by wire, ordering the Foreign Trade Monopoly Department to confirm the details, and to expedite the international transfer of goods.

The morning after the train returned to Moscow, Asher Sky received a personal invitation to meet with Lenin at his Kremlin office. Their historic meeting set the course of recovery for the struggling nation and formed the basis of a friendship and trust between the two men that would make Asher Sky a dominant figure in the Soviet Union.

Lenin was led by great curiosity to meet this exceptional American who had journeyed so far. They spoke for hours,

Lenin in excellent English and Sky in halting Russian. What impressed Sky was Lenin's awareness that he must use American capital, engineering know-how, and production techniques to get his country back on its feet. Secretly, he would have to detour from his theory of socialism and rely upon a system of private enterprise to get his country the things it needed for growth and survival. Sky had been absolutely correct in his assessment of the country's needs.

Lenin proposed a system of industrial and commercial concessions to foreigners who could help restore life to his nation. He offered major concessions to Sky, understanding that conditions must allow for good profits for concessionaires, otherwise there would be little capital invested.

Sky committed himself to rebuilding Soviet industry, about which he admittedly knew little. But Asher Sky was a young man of unlimited resourcefulness and complete self-confidence. What he didn't know he would learn, and he would get the best people to make it happen.

Lenin had seen something in the American boy capitalist that inspired belief. And he wasn't wrong, for Sky, together with his brother Nicholas and other key American figures, took on the massive task and rebuilt the industrial structure of a broken land, accepting one challenge after another without fear or thought of failure. And in the process he was well rewarded for his efforts and amassed a fortune beyond his wildest expectations from both concession profits and objects of art, which were everywhere in abundance for those with the eye to spot them and the relatively modest funds to acquire them.

The friendship between Sky and Lenin grew and continued until Lenin's death in 1924. It was a great personal loss to the young American, and the high regard in which Lenin had held Sky was carried over to Trotsky, Lenin's successor. He had formed a relationship that endured through all the succeeding years and changes in Soviet leadership. Sky touched every Soviet citizen in some way or another every day of their lives.

In 1935, Sky married. His wife was a young and beautiful Russian girl named Nadia Kurisheva, a talented Bolshoi ballerina. There had never been time for romance in the life of Asher Sky. But his first look at Nadia changed all that, and he pursued her with the same determination that guided his business successes, and with the same results. They were married in St Isaac's Cathedral, Leningrad's most prized jewel of its glorious past. The wedding was civil in nature, in keeping with Soviet policy, which did not embrace religious ceremony. Special permission had to be granted by the government for the wedding to take place in the cathedral. Sky's stature within the Soviet Union ensured easy acceptance by presiding officials.

Asher Sky's life seemed fulfilled in every way. His business ventures were immensely successful, and he came and went with unencumbered ease, his wife being granted permission to accompany him in and out of the country at will. By 1939, Sky had helped rebuild a good portion of Russia's industrial capabilities, having brought in the technologies for the manufacture of tractors and engines, aircraft, ball bearings, pencils, and fertilizers. He had also helped make the country competitive, worldwide, in its oil drilling and refining capabilities.

As the clouds of war darkened over Europe, Asher Sky decided to leave the Soviet Union and return to the United States, where the major interests of his growing empire lay. Permission was granted for Nadia to leave with her husband. Sky was also granted permission to take with him the bulk of his fortune, including the huge collection of art objects he had amassed with his brother's assistance. This concession was completely contrary to the Russian policy of keeping its art treasures within its borders, again the result of Sky's high standing with the Soviet government.

With the outbreak of war, Sky became deeply involved in America's industrial efforts to prepare for the country's inevitable entry into the conflict. Sky was highly influential in Roosevelt's decision to support the Soviet Union in its struggle for survival against the Nazis. The Soviet government was well aware of his instrumental role on their behalf.

In 1945, Sky returned to Russia at the request of Josef Stalin and undertook the exhausting task of once again helping to rebuild the industrial foundation of the torn country, especially the coal and oil sectors he had helped to establish in the 1920s and 1930s. He traveled tirelessly between the two countries and, despite the air of mutual distrust that hung over both powers, he was accepted once again as a full partner in the future of the Soviet Union.

Asher Sky, the American industrialist, was one of the most influential figures in modern Russian history. He had helped to restore this vast nation and propel it toward world leadership. In the process, Skyco had emerged as one of the world's largest corporations, spanning all the oceans and lands of the world.

Aleksandr Kozlov stared at the last page of notes on the American industrialist. This formidable capitalist had dedicated his life to building a corporate empire, yet his work had helped establish Russia and its communist system as a major world power. The contradiction was not lost on the GRU leader. Here was a man who could walk in two directions at once – and still reach his destination. His thoughts turned to the report of the search efforts around Medellín, and of Skyco's potential for genetic research. 'Two directions at once,' he mused. What was this entrepreneurial magician up to now?

12

CARTAGENA, COLOMBIA: As a child, Michael Quinn had loved tales of treasure-laden Spanish galleons and the pirates who hunted them. For centuries, the city of Cartagena had attracted those pirates and their elaborate sailing ships, and he thought how ironic it was that he was here now, on the trail of a twentieth-century pirate, one who was infinitely more sophisticated and dangerous than his nefarious predecessors.

Hector Cantú was a hard man to reach. Protected by a circle of agents, he preferred to remain aloof and safe until the final stages of any deal, and even then the buyer might not obtain a face-to-face meeting. Michael had been provided with a small but reliable list of places and names that should eventually lead to a contact with Raúl, one of Cantú's most trusted agents. Major deals with the drug king coming through Cartagena always went through Raúl before getting to Cantú.

Michael had spent the first two days in the city contacting the leads he had been given, making subtle but clear overtures of interest in talking to Raúl. It was almost dusk of the second day when the payoff for his efforts finally came.

It had taken little time for word of Michael's interest to reach Raúl. The Colombian was known to be cautious, and Michael wasn't sure exactly how the contact would be made. When he reached the door to his room in the Playa Hotel, part of his answer became immediately evident. He had left a tiny fold of paper between the door and the jamb on the hinge side, close to the floor, where it would not easily be seen dropping if the door was opened. It was on the floor. Someone had entered the room.

Michael inserted the key and opened the door just slightly, but did not step in immediately. The room was dark. He had left the curtains open. It was still light enough outside for there to be light in the room from the window, but there was none. The curtains had been drawn to close out the light.

He silently drew the Glock.

At any other time he'd have withdrawn, not risking his life, but he knew that his objective was to make contact. His heart began to pound wildly as he prepared to enter the room and face the uncertainty of what was inside.

He pushed the door open slowly and started in, the Glock cradled in both hands leading the way. He had barely passed through the opening when a hand grabbed the wrist of the gun hand. The grip was strong, and in an instant a powerful outward twist weakened his grip on the weapon and it was gone. He was pulled into the room. The door slammed shut, enveloping him in sudden darkness. His arm was pulled forcefully into a hammerlock, and a forearm came hard across his throat in a painful choke hold. He reacted instantly, pushing his body back into his attacker and reaching his free hand up over the top of his head to grab a handful of thick hair. He yanked on the fistful of hair, pulling the attacker's head forward, and threw a savage head butt straight back. At the same instant he jerked the captive arm free and spun, delivering a vicious blow to the throat of the assailant. There was a loud crash as the man slammed heavily into the wall, letting out a loud grunt. Michael crouched and slid quickly to his right. The backup Smith & Wesson Airweight was out and ready when the light snapped on.

There were two other men in the room. For an instant their eyes were locked in the direction of the crash, fully expecting Michael to be the one in distress. The sight of their own man on the floor was startling, but the recovery was immediate. In that split second Michael had moved almost all the way across the room. One of the other men was holding a gun, and swung it toward Michael's new location. But there was no exchange of gunfire. It was a standoff, as the man found Michael's gun trained squarely on his face. The third man was seated calmly in a chair by a small table near the window. Under any other circumstances the man with the gun would already be dead, but Michael's instincts told him that there would be no gunfire here.

'Hold,' the man in the chair said quickly, raising his hand with the command, his eyes locked rigidly on Michael.

There was a brief, fragile moment of tension when neither gun moved. Then the barrel of the other man's gun rose off line slowly and the man raised his free hand slightly, extending the palm of his hand.

Michael recognized the face of the man in the chair from the picture that Elias had given him. It was Raúl.

'You have an eccentric way of doing business,' Michael said in fluent Spanish.

'Don't get nervous, friend,' Raúl returned calmly. 'I've come to talk.'

Michael raised himself from his crouch, lowering his gun only after the gunman had lowered his. 'So talk. I'm listening,' he said, keeping his eyes on the gunman.

Raúl gestured with his head, signaling his men to leave the room. The man standing beside Raúl holstered his weapon and went to his friend and helped him to his feet. Michael's blow to the throat had been a disabling one, and the man had difficulty getting up.

There was silence in the room until the other two men had left.

'You're very alert,' Raúl complimented Michael.

'And you're careless,' Michael replied.

'Perhaps, but if I wanted you dead, I assure you that you would have been so long ago.'

Michael stared at Raúl without comment.

'You come to Cartagena to see Raúl, no?' the Colombian said, switching to English. 'So, now you see him. What is on your mind?'

'Business, sweet and simple.'

Raúl eyed Michael. 'That much is no secret. Now it is I who am listening.'

'My people want five hundred kilos a month, guaranteed delivery through Panama. We take it from there.'

162

That caught Raúl's attention quickly.

'Five hundred?' Raúl repeated. He squinted at Michael, assessing him carefully. 'You are talking very impressive numbers, my friend. Who are your principals?'

'Their money is good, all US. Why should it matter who I represent?'

'Because I don't know you,' Raúl replied coolly.

'Maybe that's not part of the deal,' Michael said.

'It is if you want to do business with me,' the Colombian said.

'We're interested in five hundred keys a month – for the first three months only, on a trial basis. Then it'll be eight hundred, like clockwork. The conditions are that we get a guaranteed price, and that we negotiate the price directly with Cantú,' Michael told the Colombian.

Raúl snorted. 'No one deals with Cantú directly. You work through me, or the deal doesn't happen.'

'Talk to him. Let *him* make that decision.' Michael said.

'Impossible. I can get you the five hundred keys, and the eight hundred later on. But you will not deal through Cantú.'

'That is a precondition to our doing business.'

Raúl thought hard about his cut in the kind of volume that was being discussed here. 'Perhaps I can speak to him. But I must have a name. There must be strong references . . . and you will be checked carefully. If you are not who you say you are, I will have the pleasure of killing you.'

A *name*, Michael thought. A *strong reference*.

'All right, I'll give you a name that will get his interest,' Michael said. 'Give him the name "Chocó",' he said. He walked to the dresser and took out a small box secured heavily with tape. He tossed it to the Colombian. 'Give him that. I think it will serve as ample introduction.'

It was two days before Michael heard from Raúl. He stayed close to his room the entire time, waiting for a phone call or a knock on his door. He did not risk carrying the replacement radio set Elias had issued him, because of

163

its size. Though small, it was still large enough to be mistaken for a recording device. Instead he relied upon the miniaturized system built into the watch he had been given. It was as fully functional a communication device as the radio, but didn't have quite the range, or clarity of reception. What it did have was the capability to receive visual data through its high-resolution screen. It could also send out a homing frequency for Elias or Wadelaw to follow, should the need arise.

Michael felt certain that any contact with Cantú would take place in an isolated area where complete control could be exercised by the drug king. It could be anywhere.

When Raúl finally made contact, it was by phone.

'Yes?' Michael said into the mouthpiece.

'You are in luck,' Raúl said. 'Cantú is interested in meeting you.'

'I'll bet he is,' Michael replied, knowing that Cantú would be, if for no other reasons than to learn why his lab had been destroyed and to watch the responsible party die. He hoped the *why* was the most driving force. He had based his whole gamble on it. If he was wrong he was a dead man.

'When and where?' Michael asked.

'Tonight at the old fortress of San Felipe. Eleven o'clock, at the base of the southernmost wall,' Raúl answered.

'Inside or outside?'

'Outside. You will come alone, of course.'

'I'll be there at eleven sharp.'

'Alone,' Raúl repeated.

'Alone. But my date will be real disappointed.'

'I hope your sense for business is better than your sense of humor.'

'Don't worry. I intend to be all business,' Michael said.

'See you at eleven, hotshot. Don't be late. Cantú won't wait if you are,' Raúl said, then hung up.

Michael placed the receiver back in its cradle. 'Did you get all of that?' he asked. The phone had been tapped and the conversation recorded.

'We did,' Elias's voice replied over the watch radio. 'I don't think they were being careless in contacting you by phone. They just don't give a damn,' he said.

'Think it's a setup?' Michael asked.

'Could be. I think the tip-off will be whether Cantú is there or not. If he is, he'll intend to kill you there. If he's not, and he really wants to see you, then you'll be taken to him. Either way, he means to do you harm, Mike. He'll try to get as much as he can out of you first. We'll give you close cover at the fortress, just in case he's there.'

Michael thought for a moment. 'I don't think that's wise, Bob. If your people are spotted, it will blow the only chance we'll have to come face-to-face with the man. We can't risk it.'

'What we can't risk is your safety, Mike. I'd rather come away empty than have to plant your cold ass in the ground. It's a long shot anyway. Save me the heartburn.'

'You'll never get inside the perimeter. They could be watching the area already,' Michael said.

'Wait a minute. I'm checking aerial photos here,' Elias said. There was a short delay. 'There's a big cathedral or something to the west of the fortress. We can give you rooftop coverage from outside the perimeter. Looks like about three hundred yards. No problem for a couple of good shooters. What do you say?'

Michael turned it over in his head. 'OK, I'll agree to that. But they don't shoot unless Cantú is there and they're certain it's going to go down, no matter what else happens. Is that clear?'

'Yeah, it's clear. I still don't know that I like it, but I'll do it your way. I'll trust your instincts, Mike. If you think for even one second that you're in danger of losing it, give a call. We'll take them out on the spot. Agreed?'

'Agreed.'

'OK. A team is on the way. They'll be in position well before you get there. We'll fill you in if it looks bad. Remember, Mike, don't try to do everything yourself.'

*

Michael arrived at the old fortress thirty minutes before the scheduled time. Elias's shooters were in position in a bell tower of the cathedral. The cathedral did not offer an ideal vantage point, however, as the ground near the old fortress sloped down and out of their vision. Moving only a few feet from the wall would take Michael out of the only field of fire they could establish to protect him. Michael was instructed by radio to stay as close to the wall as possible, and to avoid approaching the slope where they could not protect him.

Michael would be on his own during the meeting. The prearranged signal for help was a verbal one – 'Desperado' – a simple one not easily confused with anything he might say in the normal course of conversation. The decision to make the call was entirely his, and without the call the shooters would not go into action.

Michael had thought through his options carefully. The message he had sent back to Cantú with Raúl was clear. The objective of the action against the cocaine lab was to win a face-to-face meeting with the drug king. He had hurt him, and badly. Cantú would be angry, but he would also be cautious, and part of that caution would require obtaining information from Michael. Who had hit the lab? Why? Cantú would have to know the answers to these questions.

Elias's assessment of Cantú's intentions was correct, Michael knew. If Cantú showed up with Raúl, it would mean that he intended to learn those answers on the spot and take care of at least part of his problem right there. If he wasn't with his men, then Michael would be taken to him. And that was what he was counting on. He did not expect to be taken gently, and his resistance would be convincing, but token. His concern in that instance was that Elias's team would act too quickly in taking out Cantú's men. That would end any chance of a meeting with Cantú.

Eleven o'clock came, and not more than a minute had passed when headlights became visible to the east, moving across the lower slope toward him. The lights switched off as the car drew closer, only its parking lamps on now. Michael stood in plain view as the car approached.

'Remember, only on my command,' Michael said.

'Roger, Desperado.'

The car pulled to within fifty feet of Michael and stopped. The parking lights went off and all the doors opened at once. Michael watched as five men got out of the car and approached him. He could not see if anyone had remained in the car.

The group approached in silence. Michael could make out Raúl clearly, but didn't recognize any of the others. They looked like torpedoes out of a Mickey Spillane novel.

'Where's Cantú?' Michael asked as they drew nearer to him.

Raúl didn't answer the question. He continued toward Michael, stopping just short of him. The expression on his face was serious, his anger clearly behind the hard eyes.

'Search him,' Raúl ordered.

Two of the men flanked Michael and a third frisked him from behind. Michael did not break eye contact with Raúl during the shakedown.

'He has no weapons,' the man announced.

'I'll ask again. Where's Cantú?' Michael repeated.

Raúl answered him this time, but not with words. He threw a punch that caught Michael squarely in the face, knocking him back into the man who had frisked him. The others were on him in an instant, holding him as Raúl threw a series of blows that Michael could not defend against.

Michael struggled against the three men holding him as Raúl came in for another barrage. He could not break free from their combined strength, but did the next best thing and threw a vicious kick that caught Raúl in the solar plexus. The Colombian grunted and went down heavily. Michael then threw his head back as forcefully as he could, straight into the face of the man behind him, smashing the man's nose.

With only two men to contend with, he fared better, struggling sufficiently to free his left arm. He threw an eye strike at the man on his right, and then an immediate backhanded fist at the man on the left, catching him on the bridge of the nose.

The fifth man closed in rapidly. Michael prepared to throw a kick at him, but a hand caught him by the hair from behind. All leverage for the kick was lost as his head was jerked back, pulling him off balance. He turned to hit the man controlling his head as the fifth man slammed a club across the back of his shoulder. Michael crumpled to the ground from the force of the blow and tried rolling away, but the grip on the hair anchored him. The grip tightened and his head was jerked back farther. The fifth attacker delivered a kick to the stomach, followed by a second and a third. Michael writhed in pain, all of his wind taken by the savage blows.

He fought off a brief instant of panic that nearly prompted his call for help from the tower. But his instincts and discipline were stronger than his fear. If they had wanted him dead, it would have happened by now. They'd have thrown lead, not fists.

The grip loosened as he lay in defeat, gasping for air. His attackers stood over him, delivering no further punishment. They, too, were obviously disciplined, for their rage could have been spent further against him.

Michael grasped his sides and looked up, his eyes filled with involuntary tears, saliva and blood running from his mouth.

Raúl stood over him, clutching his own battered abdomen.

'I should kill you now, Yankee bastard,' he gasped. 'And I *will* kill you, let there be no mistake. Only one thing saves you now. Cantú wishes to see you. And when he is done, you will belong to me. You will be a long time dying, I promise you that.'

The fingers loosened on the triggers in the tower. They had come very close to acting without the command from

Michael. They followed the figures with their infrared rifle scopes as Michael was dragged roughly to the car and thrown in. They watched as the car turned slowly and went back the way it had come and disappeared from their view.

'Shepherd to Triple Jack,' one of the men called into his radio.

'Triple Jack. Go ahead,' Elias returned.

'They have him. It wasn't pretty. I have to hand it to him, he's one tough sonofabitch.'

Elias let out a sigh. 'Yeah, he's got his own style of doing things. I don't think "tough" describes him,' he said, then paused. 'We've got a clear signal on the beacon. We'll take it from here. Good job. Come on home.'

PARIS: The Hotel Louisiane, 60 Rue de Seine, in the heart of the St-Germain-des-Prés, haven for intellectuals and students, had once been the home of such notables as Jean-Paul Sartre and Juliette Greco. One did not find the typical sightseers on the narrow streets in this district of Paris. It was a part of the city where those who wanted atmosphere and an easy day of casual browsing through delightful little antique shops and quaint bookstalls along the Seine could find the quiet time to do so. It was also a place through which Rafael Sonterra could move with inconspicuous ease. He felt at home here on the Left Bank. The Hotel Louisiane wasn't a protected safe house like some he used, but he used it as often as any that were. This was his part of the city.

He left the hotel and walked the streets, stopping often to peer into a shop or to leaf through used books. Every stop was a check to be certain that he wasn't being followed. His eyes, staring through a window, were also studying the reflections in it like a mirror. His seemingly random pattern of movement was actually a carefully thought-out itinerary designed to expose even the best tail. No one could follow him for any length of time without his detecting it. A matching change of direction more than once, or a pair of eyes too slow to dart away a second time, many little clues that he picked up easily from the endless practice of looking for them. It took over an hour to cover just a few short blocks to Rue de Verneuil and another friendly little hotel, the Verneuil-St-Germain. Certain that he was not being followed, he entered and went to the small café, where he ordered a light breakfast, more to pass the time than to eat. This was the place for his next contact with Kammal.

As the time window drew near, he paid his bill and went to the small hotel lobby and approached the desk. He gave his name as Bisson and inquired whether any messages had been left for him. There were none. He tipped the man behind the desk and bought a paper, taking a seat within easy view of the desk. Ten minutes later the clerk with whom he had spoken raised a hand to get his attention. Sonterra folded the paper and approached the desk again. The clerk informed him that a call had come for him, and that it could be taken at the first phone booth just across the lobby.

A moment later, Kammal was on the other end.

'Bisson, is that you?' Kammal asked.

'This is Bisson,' Sonterra replied.

'At last, my friend, I have some good news. The details of the contract have been concluded. The product-liability waiver has been agreed to by all parties,' he said, indicating that the housecleaning he had recommended had been completed.

'That is very encouraging news, indeed,' Sonterra returned. 'It was fortunate that you could work through the negotiation difficulties you encountered earlier. Were any new concessions granted?' he asked, inquiring about the latest developments concerning Skyco's investigation efforts.

'Yes, there were. But unfortunately none that were advantageous to us,' Kammal replied, indicating that Skyco's progress was considerable.

'Explain,' Sonterra said, picking up the tension in the

other man's voice. The developments that had come about over the past week had obviously alarmed Kammal.

'The competition has brought in an outside agency,' Kammal reported.

Sonterra listened and waited. Kammal was having difficulty finding the words. He was either having trouble remembering the codes, or the developments were not covered by the prearranged word groupings. He needed to know what Kammal was trying to tell him.

'What terms are the competition offering?' Sonterra asked, trying to get Kammal to focus on the codes.

Kammal stammered. Then there was a long silence that disturbed Sonterra. Kammal was struggling.

Sonterra looked around the lobby once carefully to confirm that he was not being watched. 'Speak plainly, Kammal,' he said. He must have this information, even at the risk of dropping out of code.

'I was able to learn that Intel-Trace has been called in,' he said.

Intel-Trace! A sharp twinge of nervousness shot through Sonterra. *Damn it!* he thought. 'Go on,' he said.

'Specialists have been brought in. A man named Robert Elias is leading the investigation. He has brought in three others. One is a man named Michael Quinn, a rain forest specialist. Another is named Carlos Trevino, and he specializes in the area of aircraft recovery. The third is a pilot. His name is Wadelaw. This information was obtained from Delgado.'

'Continue,' Sonterra urged.

'They have located the landing site and identified Stillings. Gill's trail was discovered and tracked by Quinn and Trevino all the way to the rendezvous point. They continued past Cantú's trail, but recognized that the new trail was a false one and returned to the one used to transport the consignment. There they encountered one of Cantú's convoys. Trevino was killed by Cantú's men, but Quinn was not.'

'He escaped?' Sonterra asked.

'More than that. He engaged Cantú's men, five in all, and killed them.'

Sonterra was silent for a moment. 'One man against five. And he killed them?'

'Yes.'

'This man is more than a rain forest specialist,' Sonterra said.

'And there is more,' Kammal said. 'Two days later, Cantú's processing lab, located at the base of that same trail, was attacked and completely destroyed. The stories from the few survivors say that one man acting alone did the greatest part of the damage, and that he was lifted out by helicopter. The helicopter gave some support, but only after the severest damage had been done.'

'The same man?' Sonterra asked.

'It could be. A day later, Quinn arrived in Cartagena, trying to make contact with Cantú. They have somehow put facts together from very meager clues. It appears, however, that Cantú has put an end to the threat posed by Quinn. He was taken by Cantú's men. He'll never be seen again.'

'Are you certain that Cantú has him?' Sonterra questioned.

'Yes.'

'And the other man, Elias? Where is he?'

'I don't know. He left Medellín four days ago.'

Sonterra's brain was racing now. 'Was Gill's body found?'

'No. And it will not be. There would be little to learn from it if it could be,' Kammal replied.

'And Strassa?' Sonterra asked.

'His work is completed. He is in Bogotá now. He has been very careful. He was not followed.'

'Then what they know ends in Colombia,' Sonterra concluded.

'Yes.'

'When does Strassa leave Colombia?' Sonterra asked.

'Tomorrow.'

'And you?'

'Tomorrow also.'

'You will leave after Strassa. Be certain that he is not being followed. Then leave cleanly.'

'I can do that.'

'I will contact my sources concerning this man Elias, as well as the others. You've done well, my brother. Despite Intel-Trace's early gains, we have come away with our prize. Is the consignment in place?'

'Yes.'

'Then phase two begins immediately. Go safely, my brother.'

13

Michael sensed a slow, gentle rolling motion and felt a steady vibration, like the smooth idle of large engines. He fought off a heavy drowsiness and forced his eyes open while his brain wanted to sleep on. He looked around through blurry eyes for a few moments until his vision cleared.

He was in a small cabin of some kind. It didn't take him long to figure out that he was on a boat on a large body of water.

He tried to sit up, but the pain in his shoulder and ribcage stopped him momentarily. He lay back for a few seconds, letting things clear in his head. His hands went to the sore ribs. He was naked and cold.

Pain seemed to be the main signal his brain was receiving from every part of his body. His face hurt and his hands ached. Then he remembered the struggle at the old fortress and being dragged into the car. The struggle hadn't stopped there. He remembered the hypodermic needle and the war in the backseat of the limo as he tried to stop them from using it on him. It was some battle. He had lost, but not before doing enough damage to leave a permanent

173

impression. Everything closed in fast after the needle. He had no idea how long he had been out.

He forced himself to sit up through the pain, collected himself for a few moments, then rose to his feet. He looked down at his body and studied the bruises covering his chest and abdomen. He hadn't ached this badly since the first week of basic training at Parris Island.

He made his way to a small basin with a mirror over it, and looked at the bruised reflection. Shit, he thought. They must have dragged me here on my face.

He searched unsuccessfully for his clothes. Then he remembered the watch. It was gone too. So much for the homing signal.

He limped over to the small porthole and looked out. There was nothing but bright sunshine and water. His guess was that he was somewhere on the Caribbean, off of the Colombian coast.

Just then the door to the cabin opened and two men entered. Turning to face them, he recognized one of the men from the greeting committee at the old fortress. He didn't look a whole lot better than Michael. He figured out that this was why his hands hurt so badly.

'Cantú wants to see you,' the man with the bruised face said through cut and swollen lips. 'No tricks,' the man continued, leveling a handgun at Michael.

Michael left the cabin between the two escorts. A few moments later they had ascended a narrow stairway and were on the deck of a large yacht. Land was nowhere to be seen.

Michael estimated the yacht at about ninety feet. There had to be ten crewmen that he could see, all heavily armed. There was a tall, two-level conn. It was a luxurious craft with probably enough firepower to qualify it as a Colombian naval vessel.

The men led him to a spacious, well-furnished cabin. Cantú, a drink in his hand, was seated on a couch. His plump, dark face was expressionless and pensive. There was a long silence. Cantú assessed Michael

174

for a few moments, then a smile broke across his face.

There were two women in the cabin, both attractive and in bathing suits. Expensive playthings, no doubt. They giggled at Michael's nakedness, but he ignored them and didn't show any signs of embarrassment. He knew that Cantú was only trying to get inside his head a little by making him feel humiliated and small. It didn't work. The giggles stopped as the eyes saw more of the well-muscled physique. He was a handsome man by any standard, bruised as he was. It took Cantú just a few moments to realize that his idea wasn't going to work in his favor. The stares of the women had changed from amused to hungry just that fast.

'Get them out of here,' Cantú growled, waving a hand through the air.

The women were hustled out of the cabin, but not before getting a few last admiring glimpses of Michael at Cantú's expense. It was the Colombian who felt the discomfort intended for his guest. Without so much as a word, Michael had, in fact, become the intimidator.

The look on Cantú's face was angry now.

'Give him back his clothes,' the Colombian drug king ordered.

Michael's clothes were thrown at him. He caught them, the quick reflex action causing pain in the injured shoulder and ribs.

Michael felt through the pants as he put them on, searching for the watch. Without it, Wadelaw would have no idea where he was. And without Wadelaw he was as good as dead. It wasn't in the pants. He finished putting on his pants and slipped his shirt on very slowly, moving his left arm gingerly as he did so. He buttoned the shirt and tucked it into his pants.

'Short and to the point, shall we?' Cantú began in excellent English.

'As you wish,' Michael returned. 'It's your party.'

'Who are you?'

No doubt they had gone through his wallet, Michael

reasoned. There was no need for games now. 'Michael Quinn,' he responded.

'Whom do you work for?'

'I'm self-employed.'

Cantú evaluated the answer, knowing it was a lie.

'Do you work for your government? DEA, perhaps? Who sent you here?' the Colombian asked in quick succession.

'No to both of the first two questions,' Michael answered. 'I was sent here by someone who is really pissed off at you,' he replied to the third. 'You've taken something that doesn't belong to you.'

'It was you who destroyed my lab, no?'

'I'll take credit for that. And I won't stop at just your lab if I don't get back what you've taken.'

With that, Cantú broke into open laughter, but his anger was stronger than his amusement. 'You have great courage, I'll give you that much. But you're also naive. You're going to die. Do you know that?'

Michael stared at Cantú without replying.

'Three days before my lab was destroyed, five of my men were ambushed in the forests of the Chocó. They were killed and a valuable cargo was lost. It was spilled over the forest floor. This, too, was you?'

'You got my little present from Raúl?' Michael asked.

Cantú's eyes narrowed. He placed the small box that Michael had given to Raúl on the table between them. It contained five left ears.

'You said short and to the point,' Michael returned. 'That was me. But I wasn't there to do you or your men harm. I was after what was stolen. Your men killed my associate – my friend – and then tried to kill me.'

'And my lab?'

'That was my way of getting your attention, to tell you that you have something that belongs to my people, and that we want it back. It was purely business. I know you understand what I mean. Outside of that, I have no quarrel with you. Simply return what was taken, and I'll go my own way.'

'As simple as that?' the Colombian said, half laughing.

'It can be as simple as that or as hard as you make it,' Michael responded.

'You amaze me!' Cantú said, pointing a finger at Michael. 'You look certain death in the face and yet continue to dictate terms. You'll be shot in the head and dumped into the sea for the sharks to eat. Those are my terms,' he shouted.

'We're really not getting anywhere,' Michael said, sounding incredibly calm, though his insides were churning. 'Just tell me what you've done with the property I'm after, or return it if you still have it, and it will all end here.'

'I can assure you that it *will* end here,' Cantú said, assessing Michael for a long, hard moment. 'It's too bad that I have to kill you. I think I could like you. I admire courage, Mr Quinn. You face your death bravely. Most men would be pleading for their lives at this moment. But you continue to challenge. Despite what you have done and what you have cost me, I promise that your death will come swiftly.'

One of Cantú's men moved to the side of the couch, gun in hand. Michael looked at the gun – and saw his watch on the man's wrist. He wasn't out of hope after all. He needed to stall for as much time as he could get. If he could get Cantú to talk, he could buy that time, as well as send back some valuable information for Elias to use, should Wadelaw not arrive in time to save him. The radio was still on, and Elias was receiving every word of this confrontation.

'As long as I'm going to die anyway, perhaps you could tell me how you managed to steal the Luxus so efficiently?' Michael tried.

'I stole nothing,' Cantú began, with a bit of indignation. 'I am not a thief, Mr Quinn. I am a businessman. That pilot, Gill, was a thief. *He* stole your prize . . . what your people call the Luxus. I don't even know what this Luxus is. My contract was simply to *move* it, after obtaining it from Gill.'

'Is Gill still alive?' Michael asked.

177

Cantú shook his head. 'He was not so fortunate. One of my Guajiro Indians took a disliking to him.'

'Another part of your contract?' Michael asked.

'An option.'

'Is the Luxus still in your possession?'

'No. It was moved quickly through my distribution channels to Cartagena. It was out of Colombia within forty-eight hours,' Cantú replied, his tone easy and cooperative.

'Who did you move it for?' Michael pressed, playing for every second that he could buy and every fact that he could squeeze from his captor.

Cantú smiled. 'Again, you amaze me. You still haven't accepted your fate. You fight to the very end. All right, I'll tell you. Perhaps you have earned that much. I was contracted by Vigen Babayan. Do you know the name?'

'Babayan,' Michael repeated. He had heard it before. He paced a few steps, as though deep in thought. 'Let me think a moment,' he said to gain time to assess his chances against the odds in the cabin. There were three men, counting Cantú. Cantú wasn't armed. The other two were. Both with handguns.

He was about to turn to face Cantú when, through a window, he glimpsed a speck just above the horizon to the west. He focused on it a moment. It was a helicopter, far off yet, and he couldn't tell if it was approaching or just hovering at a safe distance.

He turned back to Cantú. 'Babayan the arms dealer?' he asked.

'Yes,' Cantu replied. 'The consignment should be safely in his hands by now.'

'You delivered it to him?'

'Not directly. It was he who made the arrangements and provided the payment in advance. I have had dealings with him in the past. We never deal directly. But he was to receive it. Of course, had I known what this simple contract would end up costing me, I would have charged him a great deal more.'

Michael glanced back out through the window. The

speck was larger. Wadelaw was on his way. And he was coming in fast.

'You're not through paying yet,' Michael said, the friendly tone gone completely from his voice. The tone was pure menace now.

Cantú's eyes narrowed. The easiness left his composure, and his face grew tight with anger. Michael's impertinence was beginning to lose its charm.

'Didn't you think for even one moment that we'd come for our property? Just as you want those responsible for destroying your lab, we want those responsible for taking what is ours,' Michael said. 'My action against your lab was just a warning from my people to you. It was also clear notice that we intend to get our property back, wherever it is. You took what was ours – we took what was yours.'

'That is very brave talk from a man who is about to die,' Cantú said.

'I assure you that if I die, everyone on this boat will die with me,' Michael replied.

Cantú laughed. 'You continue to amuse me.'

'Right at this moment your yacht is in the sights of a very sophisticated attack ship hovering to your port side. The same attack ship that helped destroy your lab. Look out the window if you don't believe me,' Michael said.

Cantú rose quickly and moved to the window. The Cobra was in plain view now, and it was a sight that could chill any man's heart.

Cantú's expression changed.

'Right now, I'm not your problem, Cantú,' Michael said. 'Either I get off this tub alive, or we all feed the fish. You're where *I* want *you*. It can be any way you want it to be. You decide.'

Cantú looked back at Michael. There was undisguised fear in his eyes now. He knew that this man meant business, and all of Cantú's power couldn't protect him from that helicopter now. It was *mano a mano*, one-on-one.

Cantú's man nearest Michael took full measure of the expression on his boss's face and gave in to the urge to see

179

for himself what had provoked the sudden change. He leaned toward the window and looked out. His eyes widened at the awesome vision of the gunship.

Michael used the brief instant of distraction to his advantage. He threw a vicious elbow into the back of the man's head, sending it crashing through the glass of the window. He twisted the arm holding the gun and yanked the weapon free.

The man at the other side of the cabin reacted, but couldn't get off a shot. Cantú had backed away to a spot between the gunman and Michael, cutting off his line of fire.

Michael swung the weapon as Cantú ducked in frightened response, and fired twice into the man across the room. Then he turned the gun on the man just pulling his bloodied face from the shattered window and fired a single, point-blank round into his head.

Cantú was on the floor looking up at Michael, his eyes wide with terror.

The cabin door was thrust open from the outside, and Michael fired three times in rapid succession, dropping the man in the opening.

Wadelaw heard the discharges plainly over the watch radio on the wrist of Cantú's dead bodyguard. The flexies opened up on the conn of the yacht, tearing it to pulp in methodical fashion.

'Don't kill me . . . don't kill me,' Cantú pleaded, his hands held up in front of his face.

'You had your chance to walk away from this,' Michael told him. 'One chance is all you get, you drug-pushing bastard.'

He fired the weapon. The bullet passed through Cantú's hand before entering his face just below the nose. A second shot entered the side of his head.

Michael moved quickly to retrieve his watch, then shouted a message into it.

'Bring it in, Banshee. Sink this tub of shit.'

The doorway filled with bodies again, looking more to

escape from Wadelaw's fire than to save Cantú. Michael emptied the clip into the men trying to get through the doorway. Then he raised and folded his arms across his face, sprinted across the cabin, and dove through the large window.

He hit the water and dove deep to escape the gunfire being directed after him from the lower deck of the yacht. He went deeper and turned in the water to look up. He could hear the ferocious firepower of the Cobra open up once again, and saw the bottom of the yacht, silhouetted against the surface, seem to jump and vibrate. Then there was a sudden flash and explosion above the water. The craft seemed to bob down momentarily from the force of the blast.

The concussion of the blast was intensified below the surface of the water. Michael's eardrums nearly blew from the blast, and he involuntarily took in salt water.

There was more vibration as the flexies pumped their destructive force into the doomed craft, then a final explosion, more severe than the first. Then there was silence.

Michael hung limp in the water like a stunned fish, nearly unconscious from the combined effects of the two explosions. He fought the panic from lack of air, and struggled to gain control of his limbs.

He kicked and clawed, fighting his way toward the surface. His lungs burned and felt as if they were going to explode. He spiraled up at an angle that took him gradually away from the debris of the once beautiful craft. He kicked and struggled to reach the air above.

He flailed through the surface, sucking in air in huge, desperate gasps. He felt the turbulence from the helicopter's rotors before he saw the craft as it descended from just behind him.

Michael looked up, dazed and in pain, and saw Wadelaw's concerned face staring down at him. Michael gave him a feeble thumbs-up, and Wadelaw dropped the ladder.

Michael struggled a few strokes to reach it and grabbed

the ladder. He hooked it securely with an arm, then looked back at the yacht. There wasn't much left but the scarred lower half of the hull, and it was burning fiercely. The entire superstructure was gone, and the surface of the water looked as though a garbage scow had just dumped its load.

Wadelaw started the winch, and Michael was pulled slowly out of the water.

'You keep up this shit, and you ain't gonna have too many friends,' Wadelaw said to him over the radio.

Michael heard the laugh that followed, and grinned.

'Come on, pilot. Pull me up and let's get out of here. I've had all the fun I can handle for one day.'

14

BOGOTÁ, COLOMBIA: Avianca Flight 313 to Frankfurt was late boarding, due to a lengthy repair to a faulty gyrocompass.

Juan Strassa sat in the gate area across from his own, using the delay to his advantage to study the faces in the adjoining gate areas. He did not expect anyone watching him to be close to his gate. Just as he sat opposite, a watcher could do the same, or sit a gate or two in either direction, and still see the Flight 313 boarding area with little difficulty. He had spent the better part of a lifetime watching faces, and saw nothing to cause undue alarm.

Elias had his very best teams on the job. There were twelve in all, with only one or two actively near the boarding area at any one time, never staying long enough to arouse suspicion.

When the boarding for Flight 313 was announced, Strassa changed his position, moving closer to the gate. He hung back until the boarding was nearly completed, primarily to make a final check, but also to get a better look at an extremely attractive woman standing at the check-in counter, trying to board as a standby passenger. Strassa loved the ladies, and this one was easy to appreciate. She wore tight jeans and a loose-fitting linen blouse with more than a few buttons left open.

When the flow of boarders fell below a trickle, he walked toward the gate, passing near enough to the counter to get a good look at the worried young woman. The view was great, and he was almost tempted to linger just a little longer, but didn't. He went on board and took his seat on the aisle in first class. The flight looked full except for the seat beside him. There had been several standbys at the gate, and he hoped with a wicked little smile that the seat beside him would go to the girl. The fates were with him. A few minutes later the girl walked through the door into the first-class cabin. He watched her eyes as they searched the seat numbers, stopping just above him.

Strassa rose from his seat to let her in and slid in after her, getting a good look down her blouse as she leaned over to shove her small carry-on bag below the seat in front of her. He had to force himself to take his eyes off her. She was exquisite. She sat back and closed her eyes, the top of her blouse open enough to provide a substantial view of her ample breasts. These were going to be the best twelve hours he had ever spent in the air, he was sure. With a little luck, and some of his Latin charm, it could turn out to be more fun than that. Go slow, plane. Very, very slow, he said to himself.

Flight 313 backed away from the gate in preparation for takeoff. The dark eyes of Kammal watched the plane through windows three gates away. He had spent the last ninety minutes watching the terminal. Strassa had not been tipped off because Kammal had stayed well out of range and had not really been watching *him*. Kammal had done basically the same thing that Strassa had, concentrating on the other people in the gate areas, looking for other watchers. But where Strassa had come away feeling certain that his departure was a clean one, Kammal had not.

It was Kammal's instincts, more than anything, that shouted warning. He hadn't *seen* anyone watching Strassa. Everything seemed perfectly normal. And that was what bothered him. With all that had happened, and with the progress that Intel-Trace had made, there should have been some routine activity in and around the airport, even if they hadn't pinpointed Strassa. They'd be looking for *something*.

Perhaps, he thought, Intel-Trace's efforts had truly run aground with Quinn being taken. Strassa's work on Solis had been wrapped up neatly. They had no other avenues to pursue beyond Cantú, and that should get them nowhere at all.

Maybe it was just his paranoia working overtime, he decided, still not taking the feeling lightly. Instincts were a big part of survival in this business, and they were sometimes all one had to go on. One learned to trust them as much as the eyes and ears.

Kammal checked his watch. His plane should be boarding within a few minutes, and it was a long walk to his gate. His eyes began the habitual scanning again, this time for his own benefit. He stopped on the way to post an airmail envelope to France, then proceeded to board his plane. Kammal had no beautiful woman sitting beside him to occupy his time or his fantasies. Ten minutes into the flight he got up and went into the lavatory. His shaking hands fumbled as he removed the top of the medicine bottle. The bottle toppled out of his hands and fell into the washbasin, the small pills and capsules rolling all about. Kammal tried to save them, but his reflexes were slow and his fingers not nimble enough. He managed to save just one – the wrong one.

He cursed and pounded the stainless steel basin in frustration. It was a long flight back to Europe, and the rest of his drugs were well hidden in his luggage. He had no more on him.

He looked at his flushed and trembling face in the mirror.

How could he go for more than ten hours without his drugs, he wondered. He'd have to, there was no choice. He looked at the one pill he had and knew that if he took it and followed it with a few drinks, it would make him sleep. He'd hold out for as long as his body would let him, then take the pill and some alcohol. At least for the time that he slept, there would be no pain. He'd make it up to himself when he reached Madrid. He deserved at least that much, he reasoned. His work in Colombia had been steady and flawless . . . except for the codes. Despite his failure to remember them completely and the need to abandon them earlier, he was sure that Sonterra was pleased with his performance so far. How could he not be? The plan had gone almost perfectly.

But *almost* was not a good word in this business. It was often the difference between winning and losing – or living and dying. It was a word that would have made Rafael Sonterra very, very nervous.

SAN ANTONIO, TEXAS: Tom Danziger was at the airport to meet Elias and Michael when they arrived. He greeted them warmly, glad to see Michael well, though badly bruised. He knew the great risks he had taken, which only served to fortify the strong impression Danziger had formed of him.

'Looks like you gave them hell,' Danziger said, staring at the purple welts covering Michael's face. 'Next time, don't lead so much with your face.'

'This is nothing. If you think my face looks bad, you should see their hands,' Michael replied, straightfaced. At least he still had his sense of humor.

Danziger chuckled and clapped him on the back of the left shoulder, which caused a wince on Michael's face.

'Jesus, I guess you didn't show them *any* mercy,' the Skyco security chief teased.

'Come on, let's get out of here before something falls off,' Elias said.

Danziger led them through the terminal to a lower-level

exit, where a car took them to a Skyco helicopter. Within minutes they were up and speeding north toward the hill country and Asher Sky's estate.

Michael had never been to San Antonio before. Like most first-timers, he was surprised to see how much green there was, having pictured almost all of Texas as sagebrush and desert. San Antonio was far from being desert.

The weather was almost perfect, with warm easterly winds and a brilliantly clear sky. The aerial view of the sprawling Sky estate was immediately impressive as the helicopter came from the east. Michael's eyes left the manicured wonders below and focused on a solitary figure standing beside the marked helipad, one hand raised to shade his eyes from the bright sunlight.

Michael saw the figure more clearly as the craft began its descent. It was Asher Sky himself, waiting to greet them. Michael had never met him, but had seen enough of him in media photos and news items to recognize him even from the air. A slight smile broke across Michael's face at the realization that he was about to meet one of the most influential people in the world, a man who had played an enormous part in the histories of two world powers, and in that of the rest of the world, for that matter.

The craft touched down and the engine cut to an idle momentarily before being killed. The three men exited and moved quickly away from the slowly swishing rotors.

Asher Sky extended his hand to Elias, who was the first to reach him.

'Welcome to San Antonio, Mr Elias,' Sky said, putting the proper name to the face.

'Thank you,' Elias replied.

'And you're Michael Quinn,' Sky continued, offering his greeting to Michael.

'It's a real pleasure to meet you, sir,' Michael replied, accepting the handshake. It was a firm handshake for a man of almost ninety, Michael thought. Asher Sky was not a tall man, was just a bit stocky, and didn't look anywhere

186

near his known age. His eyes were so full of energy that they were almost luminous.

'I trust that your flight was a good one?' Sky asked.

'Yes, it was. Thank you,' Elias answered.

'I'm sure you're both tired, and that the last thing you want to do is to start giving reports,' Sky said. 'I've made arrangements for quarters for you both in the guest cottages. You can freshen up and rest a bit before dinner.' He started off to show them to their accommodations.

'Thank you, that's very considerate,' Michael said politely.

'We dine at eight. I'll have a call placed to your rooms at seven-fifteen. That should give you sufficient time to dress. You'll find dinner jackets and everything you'll need in the cottages. I think we've got your sizes right.'

They were led to handsomely decorated cabins situated just off the Olympic-sized pool. Each had his own three-room cabin, with oversized, well-appointed furnishings. They were left on their own to settle in. Hanging in their respective closets were properly sized dinner jackets and slacks, plush bathrobes, bathing trunks, and a selection of casual wear for use while in San Antonio.

Elias found several pieces of mail in his room, mostly communications from Martin Trace that required his attention. There was a phone and a fax machine beside the desk for his use, should any of the matters need immediate response. Sky had seen to everything.

Michael spent part of the free time before dinner soaking in a hot tub, letting the air jets soothe his shoulder and other sore spots, then he showered and took a short nap. At seven-fifteen his phone rang, just as promised, to awaken him in plenty of time to dress for dinner.

At seven-fifty, Sky's majordomo knocked on their doors and led them to the house, where Sky, Alexandra, Danziger, and Dr de Roode were waiting in the study.

Sky was at the door to greet them.

'I hope you were able to make yourselves comfortable,' he said to his special guests.

187

'Yes, thank you,' Michael returned. 'Everything was just great. The clothes fit perfectly, and the hot tub was the best thing this body has felt in over a week.'

Michael stepped into the room. Alexandra was next to extend her welcome. She looked sensational in a long white evening dress with a low-cut back. Her almost blonde hair covered her shoulders. The clinging dress accentuated her figure very nicely. It was a good deal better than Michael remembered. The honey brown eyes were exactly as he remembered them, however, soft and friendly. He liked looking into them.

'Hi, Alex,' Michael said, taking her offered hand gently.

She looked at the battered face, feeling both sorry for him and impressed at the same time. Danziger had provided a short briefing of the events that had taken place after her departure from Colombia. 'I don't think I'll ask,' she said.

'I don't feel as bad as I look,' he replied with a short smile.

He was lying, she was sure. His movements were stiff, and he seemed to move his upper torso all in one piece, like someone suffering from neck or back pain.

Even as bad as he looked, she was glad to see him. She had become curious about him in Medellín. Something about this man had kept him in her thoughts: there was something almost electric about him. It made her feel good being near him. It made her want to be close to him and made her wonder what it would be like to be held by him . . . and kissed by him . . . and made love to . . .

'It's very good to see you again, Alexandra.'

Elias's hello almost startled her. She snapped quickly out of her brief fantasy and extended her welcome, then made introductions all around for the benefit of Dr de Roode.

Asher Sky stared with amused curiosity at his daughter. He had observed this little flare of chemistry and had seen quite clearly the look in her eyes when Michael walked into the room.

Before dinner, Sky offered them cocktails, which were accepted all around. Conversation was light, and the topic of Medellín was avoided. It was clear that the business at hand would come up soon enough, after Asher Sky had a little more time to gather impressions of the people sent in to help Skyco with its problem.

After a casual enjoyment of their drinks, the group went into the dining room and was seated for dinner. Conversation through dinner was mostly about San Antonio, Skyco, and Intel-Trace. The topic of Medellín wasn't even touched upon. Following dinner, the group retired to the study once again for after-dinner drinks.

Sky offered cigars to the men, but only he and de Roode took them.

Sky struck a match and coaxed the Rothschild gently to life, then blew out a gentle cloud of aromatic smoke. 'All right. Let's talk about Medellín,' he said with his characteristic directness. 'How bad is our situation?'

'I assume that Tom has briefed you?' Elias asked.

'Yes, to the extent that he was able, without full benefit of the latest facts,' Sky answered.

'Well, the situation isn't good,' Elias began, 'but we do have two valuable leads to follow. We still don't know who masterminded the plan to take the Luxus, but we have been successful in learning how it was obtained. The plan was carefully put together and executed. It was also well funded. We know that the Luxus is no longer in Colombia, and that an arms dealer named Vigen Babayan is involved.'

'Did he steal it?' Sky asked.

'No, Babayan is a dealer, not a thief. I believe he'll play some part in this before very long, but he's not the one behind the plan.'

'An arms dealer,' Sky repeated pensively. 'What does that suggest?'

'It could mean a number of things. Has there been any form of contact with Skyco regarding the Luxus?' Elias asked.

Sky shook his head. 'No, nothing.'

'Extortion is a possibility that must be considered. If this is the case, you'll receive a contact of some kind very soon. There's another possibility, and a stronger one, considering Babayan's involvement. That would be a sale.'

'To whom?' Sky asked.

'That depends on the strain and the ways that it can be used. It would be helpful at this point to learn more about it,' Elias replied.

Sky drew on his cigar, deep in thought. 'Tim, why don't you give our friends a thumbnail sketch?' he said at last.

The scientist adjusted his posture in the chair and thought for a few moments, searching for the clearest way to present what they had to hear. 'Think, if you will, gentlemen, of an orange that I have just cut in two and placed in your hands. Now, in your mind's eye, squeeze it mightily, collecting its juices in a glass. The remains of the orange are useless, so set them on the table beside the glass. Now think of the remains of the orange as being like a spent oil well.'

The scientist pointed toward Elias. 'If I were to give you these spent halves of the orange, how much more juice would you be able to squeeze from them?' he asked.

Elias shrugged. 'If I had done a good job the first time around, probably not more than a few drops.'

'And you?' de Roode asked Michael.

'I'd have to agree. Maybe a teaspoon or two.'

'Now picture a piece of dried fruit. A wedge of apple, perhaps. If I were to put this in your hand, how much could you squeeze from it?'

'Dried fruit? Nothing,' Elias answered.

Michael nodded his agreement.

'Think of that dried apple as coal. Finally, picture a piece of sedimentary rock. I put this in your hands like the others. How much water or oil might you be able to take from it?' de Roode questioned.

'These are trick questions, I know it,' Elias said. 'I'd have to say none.'

Again, Michael agreed. 'What does the rock represent?' he asked.

'Just what it is, sedimentary rock with no water and no oil,' the scientist responded.

'Now to my point. The juice from the orange contains water, sugars, essential oils, various aldehydes and acids, vitamins, and an assortment of other odd components that give it the flavor and nutritive value for which we prize it. Take, if you will, the spent halves of the orange from which we derived this juice. What might they contain? Well, besides the cellulose solids, they contain the same components contained in the juice. The only difference is that we can no longer get them out by the same methods we used to remove the juice. We *can* resort to more sophisticated means, using solvents and extraction processes, but these are relatively expensive compared to squeezing them with our hands, not to mention being much more time-consuming.

'Now imagine that I take these same spent halves and place them in a second glass. This time I sprinkle the surface very lightly with a weak suspension of a mystery component in water, then let it rest for a few hours. When I return, what might I find? I'll answer that for you. I'd find all of the same components contained in the juice separated from the cellulose, in a quantity equal to the juice, but much richer in concentration. So, with my mystery component I have taken a nearly useless waste product – I define "useless" as meaning without applying costly and highly technical extraction processes – and have benefited more than twofold from the same orange.

'I could do the same with the apple, except that the water content would be quite low. I would still extract all of the oils, acids, flavor components, vitamins, et cetera, that I could express from the whole apple, but again in greater quantity and higher concentration. As for the sedimentary rock, it may contain traces of water and oil, minute to be certain, but certainly there in some instances. The same mystery component would extract these, making them collectable and usable.

'Thus, from spent oil wells, coal, and even seemingly

useless rock, we can extract significant quantities of rich petroleum otherwise inaccessible to us by conventional means.

'This is the *potential* of the Luxus, gentlemen,' de Roode said. 'Have I made myself clear so far?'

There were nods all around the room.

'The Luxus is a genetically engineered strain of micro-organism capable of doing what I have described. But the work is not yet complete on it. At present, while this capability exists, so does a very negative property by which the organism digests the same oil that it releases, only at a much more highly accelerated rate than it can produce it. Now, here I must preface what follows with a statement that I will explain more fully in a few moments. There are *two* forms of the Luxus strain. The first, and the one in question here, is called the Alpha. The other is called the Beta. I will refer to them by those names to reduce any confusion.

'The Alpha, gentlemen, is what was on the plane with Dr Stillings. Its capabilities, both positive and negative, are controlled by enzymatic systems. Again, to prevent confusion, I will refer to these systems by simple names, for example, Alpha-negative, meaning the Alpha form of the Luxus is responsible for the negative action, or the destruction of the oil. Do you all follow me so far?'

The responses were all affirmative.

'Our objective in the continuing research with the Alpha is to find a way to block the action of the Alpha-negative enzyme system, thus allowing the Alpha-positive system – the system that *produces* oil – to function unimpeded, thereby making possible the efficient recovery of *vast* quantities of petroleum from sources thought useless or completely inaccessible by ordinary means. Obviously, these unfortunate events have occurred at a time when the Alpha represents a greater threat than a benefit to the world. In the wrong hands, the destructive potential of this strain could pose a catastrophic threat to the world's fossil fuel reserves.

'The Beta form of the Luxus is similar, but with a

ship akin to the head and tail of a coin. The Beta, however, produces *three* basic enzymes of importance to us here. The two primary enzymes, the Beta-negative and the Beta-positive, are similar in their relationship to those produced by the Alpha, except for one major difference. I must back up a step here to explain that in both forms of the strain the negative enzymes are produced more rapidly than the positive enzymes, which accounts for the speed of the destructive reaction when compared to the productive capability in the Alpha.

'Now, in regard to the difference that I mentioned: the Beta-negative enzyme, while destructive in nature, is not nearly so destructive to petroleum. It does *some* damage, but on a much smaller scale. Its primary destructive effect is to the *Beta-positive enzyme* – acting, if you will, like a suicide pill. It stops the positive system, as well as other enzymatic systems necessary for the life process of the Beta. It is so damaging that it extinguishes the Beta strain completely within hours.

'The important thing to note here, however, is that it also has a damaging effect on the Alpha-negative enzyme. And it does so at a greatly accelerated rate of reaction, due to the perfectly complementary structure of the Alpha-negative enzyme – the ideal lock-and-key fit. Their reaction is so fast and complete that the Alpha can be completely neutralized by a much smaller population of Beta. In short, what I'm saying is that the Beta-negative has a strong preference for the Alpha-negative.'

'If I understand what you're saying, and I believe I do, what I'm hearing is that there is a way to *stop* the Alpha,' Elias said.

'Potentially,' de Roode said. 'Remember that I said the Beta produces *three* basic enzymes of importance here. The third, which I'll call the Beta-supra, acts like a second-ary suicide enzyme to the Beta system, except that it *doesn't* react with the Alpha-negative enzyme, leaving its full effect directed against the Beta. This has been the greatest problem in regard to the Beta.

'The Beta would be very much closer to the ideal Luxus, except that it is so self-destructive it can't be propagated in sufficient quantity to work with on a practical basis. We can only propagate very low population levels, which must be desiccated quickly to ensure even a low level of survival. Upon reactivation it kills itself within hours.

'If the Beta-supra enzyme system could be eliminated, then we would have a countermeasure to the Alpha. But we have been unable to find the genetic key to turn off the Beta-supra production. The long-term prospect of finding a way to block the Alpha-negative enzyme is the better one right now, which is why our work has been centered around it. The Alpha does not self-destruct, and we can produce it in sufficient quantities for continued experimentation.'

'Let me ask a question,' Elias said. 'What would happen if the Beta alone were put into an oil reserve?'

'Nothing. Its damage to the reserve, as well as any beneficial effect, would be negligible. It would self-destruct too quickly,' the scientist replied.

'And the Alpha, in the same reserve?'

'It would totally destroy the reserve at incredible speed. The growth curve is not linear but logarithmic, as would be the rate of destruction of the reserve – until there was no more oil to feed upon. Therefore, the destruction is absolute and total. The organism would expire when its food source was gone.

'But – and this is very important – the target reserve would not be the only source of food for the Alpha. It can exist on even the tiniest traces of petroleum, such as exist in the sedimentary rock that I used in my description earlier. A small surviving population would act like a fuse, following those traces until it found a new reserve – or it might be moved along by underground rivers. Many large reserves have very complicated formations that often pass near, or actually network with, other reserves. *One* seeding of the Alpha could conceivably destroy a vast

194

number of individual reserve sites,' de Roode explained.

'Hypothetical question,' Michael interjected. 'What would happen if the Alpha were to be seeded in the Middle East? Say, in Saudi Arabia?'

'There would be, for all practical purposes, no more Middle East oil,' de Roode replied.

'You mean in Saudi Arabia,' Elias said.

'No, I mean that about seventy to seventy-five per cent of *all* Middle East oil would be totally destroyed in a very short time.'

'Years?' Elias asked.

'Months, and possibly even weeks, if the network is as interconnected as some theories suggest. This danger also exists where shale and coal deposits reside. So, gentlemen, you can see the enormous threat that exists with the Luxus out of our control.'

'And how much damage could be done with the missing twenty-four vials?' Elias asked.

'To put it into proper perspective, the nightmare just described in the Middle East could be achieved with just a small portion of a single vial. It would be very complicated to use so sparingly, though it could be done. In all likelihood, it would be used one vial at a time, considering the greater ease in using it that way. Assuming that *all* twenty-four vials could be ideally placed, I'd estimate that seventy to eighty per cent of the world's fuel reserves could be lost forever. However, along a more pragmatic line of thought, I'd say that the real – and I mean *very* real – possibility exists that forty per cent of world reserves could be totally destroyed with only four to six properly placed seedings.'

The room was filled with a stunned silence.

'And if the Alpha *was* seeded and then the Beta was seeded on top of it?' Michael asked.

'The Beta, as it's currently developed by our scientists, would have no effect whatsoever.'

'If you were successful in shutting down the Beta-supra enzyme, and this form of the Beta were introduced into the stricken reserve, what would happen?' Michael asked.

'*If* we could do this, and get to the reserve quickly enough – and speed here would be of vital importance – the Alpha could be stopped completely. Without the Beta-supra enzyme, the Beta is much faster than the Alpha. There would still be damage to the stricken reserve, the amount dependent upon how soon we could introduce the Beta after the initial seeding,' de Roode replied. 'If caught, say, within forty-eight to seventy-two hours, the reserve might suffer about five to ten per cent loss.'

'At what point would the Beta be incapable of catching up to the Alpha?' Michael asked.

'Their growth rates are different, and I'd have to create a computer model to answer that question accurately. Just guessing, and assuming a large reserve, I'd say that eight days is the point of projected total loss. The Beta would have a slowing effect, but the final outcome would ultimately be the same. The Beta just couldn't make up that much of a head start.'

'I hope that your work with the Beta is continuing,' Michael commented.

'Yes, it is. And with all possible haste. We are also working on a system to detect the presence of the Alpha. Again, we're keying on an enzyme system, a different one, but one that can be detected at exceedingly low levels. We're closer to the detection system than we are to a viable Beta, however,' de Roode explained.

'With that background information, Bob, whom do you see as a likely buyer of the strain, should it go up for sale?' Sky asked.

'The highest bidder,' Elias replied. 'There's no ceiling on the value of a weapon with that potential. And no end to the list of people who could use it. The limiting factor will be *affordability*. Fortunately, not everyone will be able to ante up the kind of cash that will be asked for it. I can see clearly how Babayan will figure into this now. Extortion probably isn't a factor here. The fact that he's involved suggests that whoever masterminded the entire plot intends to sell the Luxus. That makes Babayan *very* important to us.

'We have to get close to him, and *stay* close to him. Sooner or later the Luxus will surface for sale. That means, if we can't buy it back ourselves, it will have to be turned over to some other buyer. That point of transfer represents the best and possibly the *only* chance we'll get to *take* it back.'

'Can you get near Babayan?' Sky asked.

'That shouldn't be a problem. He's a very popular fellow,' Elias replied. 'He won't be hard to find.'

'Earlier this evening you mentioned *two* leads,' Sky began. 'What is this other lead?'

'A hit man. He was responsible for cleaning up loose ends in Colombia.' Elias looked at his watch. 'Right now he's back in Europe, trying to get to cover. We're tracking him, hoping that he'll lead us deeper into the network that staged this whole affair. He doesn't represent the better of our two leads, but we'll pursue it equally. There's always a chance it could develop into something positive.'

'Is there anything more that you need to learn from us?' Sky asked.

'Not at the moment. We know what we have to do from here. The rest is up to us,' Elias replied.

'Then I suggest we retire for the night. Please feel free to make yourselves comfortable, and ask for anything you may need. Until tomorrow, gentlemen,' Sky said, rising from his chair.

Everyone rose with Sky. Alexandra walked beside Michael as he left the study.

'I could arrange for a doctor to come out to the estate,' she said.

'Thank you, but that's not necessary,' he responded. 'All I need is a little time. I'll be fine.'

'I can arrange for a masseuse. A good rubdown would probably go a long way,' she offered.

'Don't tell me that you have one on staff here.'

'No,' she smiled. 'But I could arrange it quickly enough.'

'Thanks for the offer, but I think a little more time in that hot tub, and maybe a few easy laps in the pool, will be enough. I do appreciate your concern.'

'Well, the offer stands. If you change your mind, just pick up the phone and dial eight. That will ring my room. Enjoy the hot tub and your swim,' she said.

The night was invigorating. The heat of the hot tub made the cool air feel refreshing against his skin. A light mist was forming just above the heated water of the guest pool. It felt like bathwater when he hit it, the seventy-six-degree water a pleasant contrast to the chill.

Michael was a strong swimmer, as was evident from the long, easy strokes and effortless glide as he put in a few lazy laps. The gentle resistance of the water was just right for stretching out his aching muscles. The turns hurt. He took them with a flip, the forceful push off the wall making the abdominal muscles scream in protest, but each succeeding push hurt less and less.

He was just nearing the shallow end of the pool when he heard a splash to his immediate right and felt a strong ripple below him. He pulled up suddenly in the waist-high water, his hands coming into a defensive position.

The hands relaxed and the arms lowered back into the water when he saw the figure break the surface about eight feet away. It was Alexandra.

She straightened up, shook the water out of her hair, and looked directly at Michael.

'Hi,' she said. 'I hope you don't mind company?'

'No, I don't mind at all. You just took me by surprise,' he admitted. He'd have to be out of his senses to mind the company of a beautiful woman in a skimpy bathing suit, he thought.

'I didn't mean to startle you. I shouldn't have dived so close to you. I apologize,' she offered.

'It's not necessary to apologize, but if it will make you feel any better, I accept.'

'It's a wonderful night, isn't it?' Alexandra asked, wading in closer to Michael.

'Yes, it is. And I admit I don't usually go swimming at night in November,' Michael said.

198

'This is Texas. You can do a lot of things here you can't do in other places.'

'Sounds like Texas pride talking,' he said.

'We've got a lot to be proud of. You'll have to spend some more time here when this is over, to experience some of what Texas can offer.'

'That might be nice,' he returned.

'I could almost guarantee that,' she told him as she drew closer.

Alexandra stopped when she saw the bruises on his chest and abdomen. 'My God. Look what they did to you,' she said, her hand reaching out to touch his chest just below the left collarbone.

'I think you should see a doctor,' she told him, leaving her hand against his skin for a moment and drawing closer to his broad chest.

He shook his head. 'It's not necessary. I've had worse than this. I'll be all right in a few days.'

She slowly dropped her hand, but remained close, gazing into his eyes for a long moment and wondering what it was about this man that captivated her so completely. She almost felt lost in his magnificent eyes. 'Why?' she said, not meaning for the word to actually slip out.

Michael's expression grew a bit puzzled. 'Why what?' he asked.

Her mind raced to get back. 'Oh . . . why did you do it? I mean, why did you just let them take you like that?'

'I'm not certain it's in your best interests to know too many details beyond the general facts,' he told her. 'You want to avoid any complicity . . .'

'I want to know why you took such a grave risk,' she interrupted, the tone of her voice cutting quickly through the issues of protocol and legality.

Now it was Michael's turn to stare. 'There was no other way,' he said after a brief pause. 'We had to get to Cantú. He was the only lead that held promise. It was that, or come home empty-handed.'

'But you *knew* the risk,' she said.

199

'Yes, I knew the risk.'

She was awed by his courage. Her other hand went to his chest. 'And look what they've done,' she whispered.

She remembered the scars she had seen on his body the evening before she left Medellín. Her left hand moved slowly to his right shoulder and down his arm to the scar from the bullet wound he had suffered in some past adventure she knew nothing about. Then her hand moved lightly across his skin from the arm to his side to another scar. With her right hand she traced down his left arm and gently took his left hand. She raised the hand to her lips and kissed it. Her body moved closer, as though drawn to him by a power she couldn't control.

Michael's right hand came to her waist, and the touch of him started her trembling. Their faces came close together, and her breath seemed suspended. She looked up into his face – and those eyes.

'What do you see, Michael?' she said softly, their lips just inches apart.

'My eyes see a very beautiful woman. My brain sees the president of one of the world's largest corporations,' he replied, staring down into her honey-brown eyes. 'I see the daughter of Asher Sky.'

'Yes, I'm the daughter of Asher Sky, and I'm sure that to many people I'm exactly like my father in mind and spirit, Michael. But I can assure you that I have all of my mother's parts. And they work remarkably well,' she said, her final words a breathless whisper as their lips met.

Her arms went up and around his neck and he pulled her gently close to him. She felt like live current in his arms – hot, life-giving energy.

She surrendered to the kiss completely, her body going limp in his muscular embrace. She felt his strength envelop her and begin to take command of her senses. But with the same suddenness with which it had begun, the kiss ended, and Michael's hardened muscles flexed gently as he eased her away from him.

They stared into each other's faces, and the soft, glazed

look in her eyes evaporated. Confusion remained in its place.

'This is harder than you think,' Michael said to her softly. 'But . . .'

'But what?' she asked.

Michael let out a gentle breath. 'Believe me, it's not that I don't find you attractive,' he said. 'God, I'd have to be crazy not to. And I'm not close to being crazy.'

Her hands lowered from his shoulders to his forearms. 'I'm not in the habit of throwing myself at men, Michael,' Alexandra said.

'I know that.'

'Then what is it?'

'The problem isn't yours. It's mine. It . . . it just doesn't feel right,' he said.

'I don't know. It felt pretty good to me,' she returned, but saw in his face the hopelessness of continuing.

Michael thought for a second that perhaps he *was* crazy for saying what he had, and for letting the moment slip by. But he hurt, and he was tired . . . and he knew that this was one complication that Elias didn't need to have to deal with. As much as he wanted to continue, he knew that this was not the time or the place to give in to his biological urges.

Alex eased his hands away from her waist and fought back a brief flash of anger at his rejection. She stared at the battered face and the tired eyes.

'Please understand,' he said.

'Well, I don't,' she shot back, feeling immediately sorry for the unfair anger she displayed. She remained silent for a moment, then raised her hand to his face and brushed it gently with the back of her fingers.

'Well . . . maybe I do. Just a little. But I warn you, Michael, I'm like lightning. I don't strike twice in the same place – unless there's something there to attract me,' she said, the message clear.

'Another time, perhaps. And in another place,' Michael said.

Alex thought for a moment. 'Yes, a time when you're less distracted, perhaps. There's time, Michael. There's always time.'

Asher Sky stood by the upstairs bedroom window and watched as his daughter walked slowly back to the house and Michael returned to his quarters. He didn't move for a few moments. He wasn't sure what he was feeling, or what he should feel.

He had seen something in Alexandra that had been missing for a very long time. She had had two marriages. The first had failed when she picked up the fallen reins of the company after her brother Nelson had died in a plane crash. That first marriage hadn't been a good one, and was bound for failure at any rate. The second ended tragically after only six months, when a safety line broke, sending half of a climbing team to their deaths from the formidable west ridge of Mount Everest.

Alex had found true love for the first time in her life, only to have it taken from her cruelly and suddenly. It devastated her.

There were times when Sky thought he'd never see that look in her face again. She had dedicated herself to her job so entirely and for so long that romance had no place in her life. To see it now prompted conflicting emotions in him. One was guarded happiness, the other was apprehension over the possibility of losing her.

He picked up the phone and dialed a number.

'Danziger,' a tired voice responded.

'Tom, I want you to do me a little favor,' Sky said.

'Sure. What is it?'

'I want to know all there is to know about our young friend Michael Quinn.'

15

He didn't know how many times the phone had rung before he heard it. It had come like a relentless intruder into the back of his brain, and he had tried to shut it out. But it came back again and again until it defeated what remained of his first good sleep since leaving Colombia.

Michael opened his eyes and squinted at the table beside the bed. Damn, it wasn't a dream. The phone *was* ringing. He reached out and lifted the receiver from its cradle.

'Yeah,' he said wearily.

'Breakfast. Ten minutes, by the pool,' the voice of Alexandra Sky said. 'It's a beautiful morning, and you're wasting it. Let's go, sleepyhead. Out of bed.'

Michael smiled at the sound of her voice. He remembered the way she had looked in that bathing suit the night before, and how silken her body had felt against his when they kissed. He was almost sorry he had let his better judgment prevail.

'Well, are you awake, or what?' she asked.

'What time is it?' Michael asked.

'It's almost seven-thirty, and your breakfast is on its way out here right now. You'd better hurry, or it'll get cold,' she replied.

'I'll just be a few minutes,' he told her.

'See ya,' she said, then hung up.

Her call had shaken the sleep from his system, and he propelled himself out of bed. After one of the fastest showers on record, he selected a shirt, sweater, and pants from the casual wear provided for him by Sky, and was out of the room in just over five minutes.

The morning air was bracing and clear, and he filled his lungs with deep breaths as he approached the sumptuously prepared poolside table. Alexandra was already seated, a cordless phone at her side. She looked radiant.

'Good morning, Michael,' she said as he neared the table.

'It's a beautiful morning,' he said, smiling as he drew near.

'Yes, it is,' Alex returned, her eyes watching him every step of the way. He looked disarmingly handsome in the tan linen pants and patterned sweater. His dark wet hair was combed straight back and drawn tight into an intriguing short pony tail. 'You look well rested.'

'I am. I slept quite well last night,' he said as he pulled out a chair and sat at the table beside her.

'Well, things don't always turn out perfectly,' she said under her breath, but just loudly enough for the playful tease to be heard.

There was a brief moment of awkward silence between them before Michael spoke: 'I want to apologize for last night. It wasn't my intention to reject you.'

Alex placed her hand on his. 'You don't owe me any apologies, Michael. If there are any apologies due—'

'No, no, no,' Michael interrupted quickly. 'You don't need to apologize, either. I . . . what I mean is . . .'

'I know what you mean, Michael,' Alex said, her fingers still on his hand.

He closed his thumb over her fingers and gave a gentle squeeze, and nodded without speaking.

'I hope you were the least bit lonely last night,' Alex said after a short pause.

'I'll admit to that.'

'Well, you've just made my day a little brighter,' she told him.

'What's for breakfast?' Michael asked, following another awkward pause.

Alex poured two cups of steaming coffee. 'Black?' she said, remembering how he had taken it at dinner the night before. She lifted the silver plate covers from the eggs Benedict.

'That looks terrific,' Michael said.

'I can assure you it is. Gilbert is a marvelous chef. My father stole him from the Blue Fox in San Francisco almost ten years ago. The man is a culinary magician.'

Michael tasted the food and found it worthy of its billing.

'So, what does the president of Skyco do on a beautiful Saturday morning?' Michael asked.

'Anything she wants,' Alexandra replied. 'Usually I go into the office for a few hours to catch up on my reading and correspondence. But not today, unless you'd like to see Skyco Center.'

'I think I'd like that,' Michael returned. 'I'm not sure what Bob has in mind for today, but I imagine there should be enough time for a quick tour.'

'It would take an hour at the most.'

'Then let's plan on it,' Michael said.

Michael took another bite of his breakfast, then turned his head toward the expansive garden between the pool and the main house. 'Your father and Bob are coming,' he said.

Alexandra turned, but couldn't see them. A few moments later they rounded a bend in the path and came into view.

'How did you know they were coming?' she asked.

'I could hear them,' he replied.

'From that far away?'

He nodded.

'Good ears. So much for our quiet little breakfast,' she whispered.

Sky waved to them as he and Elias drew nearer.

'Good morning, Daddy, Bob. Would you like some breakfast brought out?' she asked.

'We've already eaten,' Sky replied as they came to the table. 'I'll have some of that coffee, though.'

Alexandra poured two more cups as they sat at the table.

'I was just telling Michael that I'd be happy to show him the Center if it can be worked into the schedule today. Would you like to come along, Bob?' she asked.

'I would, actually, but I have some rather important things to tend to today. It'll have to be another time,' Elias said.

'Is it something I can help you with?' Michael asked, willing to forgo the tour.

Elias shook his head. 'No. I can get it. You go ahead with your plans. There's a chance you may need to get back here in a hurry, though. I'll get to you over this,' he said, holding out a voice pager. Michael took it from him and clipped it to his belt.

'Babayan?' he asked.

'That's right. He's somewhere at sea, aboard his ocean-going yacht, on a presumed heading for Monte Carlo. He goes in annually right about this time for a few weeks of playtime and some serious gambling. He and a few regulars contract out one of the private parlors. It usually draws a lot of attention. Just to get into the room costs twenty grand, and it costs a whole lot more to stay. The big attraction is at a single table where Babayan and his pals play a no-limit game.'

'What do they play?' Alexandra asked.

'Poker. It's not uncommon for hundreds of thousands of dollars to change hands in those sessions,' Elias replied.

'For a few weeks, you say?' Sky repeated.

'Yes. He doesn't gamble the whole time, of course, but he does stay anchored in Port du Monaco.'

'So at least we'll know where he is.'

'That's right. We should be able to count on that much, if he stays true to habit,' Elias said.

'Do you think he has the Luxus with him?' Sky asked.

'It's possible, but I don't think so.'

'Would Monaco be a good place for him to make his sale?' Alexandra asked.

'It's possible, but, historically, Babayan leaves his business behind for this trip. That's not to say that a transaction couldn't take place. It could. I just don't think it will.

'I still feel that it will be offered to the highest bidder. That's how I see him fitting into the picture. He's not political or given to causes. He's strictly a merchandiser, selling anything to anyone with a need and the money to pay his price.'

'When is he expected to arrive in Monte Carlo?' Michael asked.

'That's the part we don't know yet. The game usually begins on the holiday of *Fête du Prince*. That's Thursday. So he should be getting there soon. We have to get there before him. That's why you're on call, Mike. We'll have to move fast when we learn his arrival date.'

'I understand.'

'We need to get as close to him as possible, and plant him with a tracking device of some kind if we can. Then we wait. When he moves, we move. And we stay with him until he's ready to deal the Luxus.'

'How do you plan on getting close to him?' Michael asked.

Elias smiled. 'How's your poker?'

'That depends on how much help you can arrange,' Michael returned.

'We might be able to manage something.'

'Planting him isn't going to be easy.'

'I'm working on a few possibilities. But you're right, it won't be easy. We'll need to break into his routine somehow.'

'Is there any way we can help you?' Alex asked.

'No, I don't think so. We'll handle all of the details.'

'What about this other fellow, Strassa?' Sky asked.

'He's in Berne, Switzerland. We're locked into his every move.'

'Then all you need is time,' Sky said.

'That's correct. Time and a little luck, which we can manufacture by constant surveillance and being ready to move in immediately when the deal begins,' Elias said. He was a firm believer that luck was no more than recognition and timing combined with the willingness to act. Somewhere along the way they'd get their chance. He had every intention of being ready for it.

The ride to Skyco Center was a short one, especially at the speeds Alexandra liked driving. She seemed to revel in her Porsche's speed and agility.

The impressive four-hundred acre complex was

impeccably landscaped, looking every bit the home of one of the world's mega corporations. Security at the Center complex was tight, with well-manned checkpoints. Even Alexandra had to provide proper identification in the form of an employee badge. Michael was signed in as a visitor and issued a badge similar to the one in Medellín.

They entered the massive headquarters building and passed through another security checkpoint. Beyond it was a huge reception area. A wide entrance foyer led to a registration desk. The walls of the foyer were covered with a spectacular exhibit of original art behind tall glass panels. These were museum-quality pieces worth a fortune that Michael couldn't even begin to estimate.

The center of the main reception lobby was open to the very top of the building, extending upward, almost cathedral-like, for a full eight stories. The perimeter of the reception lobby was more like an arboretum, with tall green trees surrounded by broad-leafed and flowering tropical plants. The lighting was mostly natural, coming from an enormous skylight that spanned the entire ceiling. There was such a feeling of space and size that Michael felt insignificant standing in the center of it. They signed in at an expansive reception desk.

'Is security always this tight? Or is it just since the incident in Medellín?' Michael asked.

'It's our corporate policy to maintain tight security at all of our locations,' Alex answered. 'My father made a fortune very early in his life, a part of that from getting into places he shouldn't have, and having good eyes and ears. He's a firm believer that one will always learn more with his eyes and ears than with his mouth.'

'I imagine there are a lot of interesting stories behind the building of your father's empire,' Michael commented.

'Daddy has more than a few, I can guarantee.'

'Has he ever put them down in an autobiography?'

'There have been several unauthorized biographies, but he feels strongly that the *real* biography of Asher Sky should not be written until after his death.'

'That seems like a strange request. I would think he'd want to supervise its writing,' Michael said.

'He does keep a very comprehensive set of journals that will be made exclusively available to the writer chosen for the job. He has always kept journals, from the time he was in his early teens. They fill a shelf in his private library,' Alex told him.

'They must encompass an entire history of the modern world, as seen through his eyes,' Michael mused aloud. 'I'd love to lock myself away with them over a long vacation sometime. Have you read any of them?'

'Yes, a very long time ago, when I was about thirteen. He caught me, and gave me hell for it, too. Daddy only has to give a person hell once to make a lasting impression,' she said. She remained silent for a moment, then a smile crept across her face. 'He felt terrible afterwards,' she laughed. 'He bought me a horse the next day.'

'He sounds like a real softy to me,' Michael kidded.

'He can be, at times.'

On the wall behind the reception desk were two large oil portraits, one of a handsome young man, whom Michael recognized to be Nelson Sky. Asher Sky had had one son, Michael recollected. But he had died in a plane crash some time back. It had been big news when it happened. The other portrait was of an older man who bore a strong resemblance to Asher Sky, but clearly was not the man himself.

Michael studied them for a moment before following Alexandra to the elevators.

A door opened silently in front of them and they stepped into the elevator. Alexandra pushed a button with the words EXECUTIVE OFFICES beside it, and the doors closed.

'That was a portrait of your brother, Nelson, wasn't it?' Michael asked.

'Yes,' Alex replied.

'Who was the other man?'

'My father's brother, Nicholas. He was five years older than Daddy. Uncle Nicky was Daddy's first and only partner. He died in 1955.'

'Nelson died in a plane crash, didn't he?'

'Yes, in 1980. He was on a small corporate jet that went down over the North Atlantic.'

'I remember the incident. It must have been a terrible blow to your father.'

'I don't think I could ever find the words to describe what Daddy went through after Nelson died. Nelson was so special to him. His life just seemed to suspend itself for some time after that.'

The elevator stopped and the doors slid open, revealing another large and beautifully appointed reception area. They stepped out of the elevator.

Alexandra stood in silence for a few moments, her eyes playing across the reception area. 'Everything that you see here was built for Nelson. It was all to be his one day, had he lived.' There was a sadness in her voice when she said it, one that hinted at exclusion, as if what was hers now was hers only by default.

Michael sensed her feelings, but remained silent.

'I loved Nelson,' she began, 'even though we weren't especially close as children. I think we were that way because we were so different. I was like my father, and he was more like my mother. He was very brilliant, that couldn't be denied. But he was a solitary person. As a child he had a closeness to my mother that Daddy always resented, I think. Nelson was distant and introspective. My mother was always very protective of him, much more so than she was with me. I think she could sense how much like my father I really was. I was a very independent child, and I lived for the time I could spend with my father.

'Nelson seemed to be afraid of Daddy. I believe that was because the relationship between my parents was strained. There was always tension when my mother and father were together. Nelson could see it and feel it, I'm sure, even as a young child. Then Daddy sent us off to private schools. I knew he did it to get us away from our mother, which created an even greater distance between him and Nelson . . . and between him and my mother.

'Then, when my mother died, Nelson withdrew into his own little world, of which Daddy wasn't a part. It wasn't until about ten years later that a relationship between them budded and grew. And in all that time my father longed for Nelson to embrace him, and to love him.

'I always felt I took second place to that relationship. Daddy didn't mean to be obvious about it, but I don't think he could help himself. Daughters are always special in some way to their fathers. But sons are their continuation, their immortality. When Nelson died, a part of my father died with him. I was there, and he came to me, more like my child than my father. I'm sure he had always loved me, but he had loved Nelson more.'

'Perhaps he felt that way once,' Michael said. 'But I can see in the way he looks at you how special you are to him.'

'It was a long time coming, Michael.'

'But he loves you, and you're his life.'

She leaned forward and gave Michael a light kiss on the lips. 'I didn't bring you here to tell you sad stories. Come on, I'll give you the VIP tour.'

Alexandra took him by the arm, pulling it gently against the side of her soft breast, and led him down the first long corridor. 'This is what we call Executive Row,' she began.

She led him through the entire complex, giving him a capsule but thorough description of how Skyco operated. She never once broke physical contact with him. Every minute with this man made her feel more and more comfortable about this strange attraction she felt for him. Just being with him and touching him filled her with an excitement she had never experienced before. Whatever it was that made her feel this way was real. It had to be. She had yet to be near him without being almost overcome by it.

Michael marveled at how Alex could change character so quickly, one moment sounding like a hurt little girl baring her innermost feelings to him, and the next being a polished corporate executive – who also happened to be a beautiful woman. He found her both interesting and pleasant to be with.

The tour took a little less than an hour and ended back on the executive floor, in Alex's immense, windowed office. This room and the office of her father were the heart of the giant corporation. There was a tangible air of power about the place; everything suggested it, from the curved mahogany desk to the patterned sofa and matching chairs and soft lighting.

'Well, what do you think?' Alexandra asked.

Michael smiled. 'I'm impressed. I don't think many people could imagine all of this. Even in their fantasies, I think they'd come up short.'

'Oh, I don't know. Some people have very active imaginations.'

'I can't disagree with that. We all have our fantasies. We need them, after all, don't we?'

'We do,' Alex replied, walking to the door of her office. She closed it.

'What do the rich and famous dream about?' Michael asked. 'It can't be about wealth and power . . . unless it's *more* wealth and power. There has to be something else.'

'We're a little more basic than that, I think,' she said, her fingers going to the buttons on her blouse. 'For instance, I've always had this one impossible fantasy about being here at the Center with a very attractive man. We're alone in my office and I just have this incredible urge to have him,' she went on, her fingers undoing the buttons one by one.

'Of course, it's impossible . . . I mean, for a thing like that to happen here, where I work. What would people think?' she said, coming close to him, her blouse now opened completely.

What had been delicious temptation beneath her bathing suit the night before was no longer a mystery. Michael's eyes locked on her beautiful breasts as she drew near to him. This was more than his biological system could take, and he couldn't stop the desire from building. He was no longer tired, and pain wasn't a factor.

She began to unbutton his sweater as they stood

face-to-face. Then her hands moved along his hard stomach to his belt, and she pulled him against her. She undid his belt and the snap on his trousers, and her fingers slid the zipper down.

'I mean, after all, what *would* people think?' she whispered, her lips brushing his as she spoke.

Michael's lips parted and covered hers as her hand went into his pants.

Beep . . . beep . . . beep!

The pager sounded loudly, startling both of them.

'Mike, we've got a contact. We need you back at the estate, stat.'

Elias was just leaving his cabin when Michael came into view by the guest pool. He raised a hand and gestured to Michael to join him.

'You made good time getting back,' Elias said to him as he approached. 'How was your tour of the Center?'

'Could have used about another hour. We were just getting to the best part when you called,' Michael replied. 'What's up?'

'We're all set on Babayan,' Elias began, leading Michael back into the cabin and closing the door behind them.

'He's in Monaco?'

'Not yet, but he's on his way there, just as we expected. He should be arriving there by yacht in about two days. That means we get you on a plane first thing in the morning to get you there ahead of him. Here,' Elias said, handing him a thick file folder, 'you'll have to read all of this before you leave in the morning.'

Michael took one look at the folder and knew immediately why he was needed 'stat'. He'd need all night just to read it. It was a poor substitute for what he could have been doing. Some sacrifices were harder than others.

Elias reached into the breast pocket of his jacket and removed an envelope. 'And here are your tickets. They'll take you directly into Nice – Côte d'Azur International Airport. I'll have a villa arranged for you with a complete

213

view of Port du Monaco. You should be able to keep his yacht under close surveillance from the villa.'

'What are we going to do about the DST? They'll be on me the minute I step off of the plane,' Michael asked, referring to the Direction de la Surveillance du Territoire, the counterespionage force of France, concerned generally with keeping track of undesirables entering or leaving France. Though Michael had never been formally connected to the killings of Dieter and the Russian in Helsinki, word had made its way through the network surely enough. Michael Quinn was classified as 'undesirable'.

'We'll just have to live with that,' Elias replied, showing only nominal concern. 'You're there for a holiday, Mike. And that's all it will appear to be. There will be plenty of backup to act as your eyes and ears, so you shouldn't have to make any unusual moves to pique their interest. Besides, unless you've been up to something I don't know about for the last nine months, you've been pretty well behaved as far as they're concerned. And you've been in France for seven of those nine months?' Elias asked, as if it were really a question. He knew exactly where Michael had been for the entire time.

Michael nodded. 'Right, seven months. All legitimate business, too.'

Elias nodded with a half-smile. 'Right. So you see why we're not worried. The chances of Babayan knowing you should be remote. It'll be important not to make yourself obvious from a distance. You'll have to get close to him, make him interested in you, so that your interest in him won't be a tip-off,' Elias explained.

'At the card table.'

'Exactly. But he won't be impressed by beating you. You'll have to beat him, and beat him badly. Losing a lot of money to you will get his interest level up in a hurry.'

'I'm not a gambler, Bob,' Michael said.

'You're more of a gambler than you think,' said Elias, with no trace of irony. 'And what you've got inside of you is enough to get you through any card game when it's only money at stake. Trust me. Just follow your instincts and you'll do fine. Intel-Trace will back all of your expenses, so play big. Remember, Intel-Trace is well established in Monaco. We're in a strong position to arrange some control of the game, if it becomes necessary.'

'How big is big?' Michael asked, wanting clarification on the stakes.

'Whatever it takes to stay in the game,' Elias replied. 'You'll get the drift of the game quick enough. Compared to the real stakes, anything passing across the table is small change. Any last questions?'

'Not concerning Babayan, for the moment. But I do have one question,' Michael said.

'What is it?'

'What can you tell me about Nelson Sky?'

'It's in the file I gave you. The whole background,' Elias replied, looking at Michael, a bit perplexed.

'All the factual information will be there, and the biographical details and the plane crash. But that's not what I mean,' Michael said.

'What exactly *do* you mean?'

'Well, when Alex and I were at Skyco Center, she gave me a bit of family background that isn't likely to be in the file. It's about the son and his father. Sky's got pictures of him all over the place. It was almost like being in some kind of a shrine. I guess what puzzled me was that, according to Alex, there was a curious relationship between the old man and the son, and next to none between Alex and her brother. I had to read a little between the lines, but I'm sure it was all there,' Michael explained.

Elias nodded slowly. 'I can give you that. But it won't have a damn thing to do with what's going on here.'

'No, but it'll give me a better feel of what the old man is really like – and what this company is really about.'

'*And* the girl?' Elias added.

Michael's face turned a light shade of red. 'And Alex,' he said with a slight nod.

Bob Elias had been through every word in the complete

file of Asher Sky, and, in fact, had studied it closely to help *him* form an impression of the man, as well. It was a critical requirement to know all there was to know about any major client in matters like these.

'What you read from her story was correct,' Elias began with a nod. 'Despite everything you see here, Sky's life isn't, and hasn't been, all happiness. In his mid-thirties he married a Russian woman. Her name was Nadia Kurisheva, and she was a rising star with the Bolshoi. From the pictures I've seen of her, she was stunning. He was enchanted by her the moment he saw her. She was a good deal younger than him – about fourteen years. They were married fifteen years before their first child was born. That was Alexandra, when Sky was forty-eight. Oddly enough, she was the first girl born to the Sky family line in about five generations. The family, by the way, was Russian in origin, the name back then being Skyuzov. It's a long and interesting story that I'll spare you, but the family was one of the elite in old Russia, having built its substantial wealth in trading. I'll just say that, as fortunes tend to do, they turned, and Sky's grandfather lost everything on a risky venture and was forced to leave the country in a hurry.

'Asher Sky worked his way up from nothing to become a millionaire at a very early age. You're probably aware of that part of his personal story from the dossier you were given.'

Michael nodded that he was.

'What Sky wanted more than anything else was a son to leave his empire to. He loved Alexandra, I'm sure, but she wasn't a son. His wish came true two years after Alexandra was born. He named the boy after his close friend Nelson Rockefeller.

'Sky's marriage changed dramatically after the children were born. The relationship between him and his wife fell apart quickly. With him being gone most of the time, it never improved. Despite the life of comfort that she lived, Nadia was very Russian in her ideals, and her constant influence over the children caused Sky a lot of frustration.

What hurt the most was that his son had formed a very close bond with the mother. In the late fifties, Sky tried to reduce her influence by sending the children away to private schools.

'This crushed Nadia. She wasn't a stupid woman, and she knew that her children were being taken away from her. What was left of the marriage disintegrated quickly after that. There was a separation and some rather nasty fighting over custody of the children – which Sky won. This only worsened the relationship between him and his son. The boy was young and needed his mother, and was deprived of her for reasons he couldn't understand. Alexandra, on the other hand, loved her father and preferred being with him. And although Sky loved her, his attention was somewhat one-sided toward Nelson.

'Over the next two years, Nadia waged a war of her own design against Sky. She was still a beautiful woman, and she began to get around in circles of both associates and adversaries alike, causing him deep pain and humiliation. What she couldn't do in the courts, she did in the beds of other men. And she was unmerciful.

'But Sky used his strength in the courts to retaliate, and did so decisively, completely depriving her of her children.

'The victory was total. The impact of the complete loss of her children, as well as the self-humiliation of her attempts at revenge, crushed her. She fell into deep depression, and on Thanksgiving Day of 1963, she took her life with a gunshot wound to the head.'

'Gunshot wound to the head?' Michael echoed.

Elias nodded. 'Right temple,' he said, tapping the spot with a finger.

Michael paced a few steps, then turned back to Elias. 'Beautiful women don't usually commit suicide in a way that messes them up, Bob. They take pills or something, but they don't blow their brains all over the room.'

'This one did.'

'What about the investigation? Was foul play ever suspected?'

Elias shook his head. 'I've seen the official reports. They called it a suicide – no hint of anything else.'

'Did she leave a letter?'

'No letter was found,' Elias replied.

'And that wasn't the worst of it,' Elias continued. 'It was her children and their governess who found her the next day.'

'Jesus,' Michael said, shaking his head.

'Nelson was twelve, Alexandra fourteen. The governess had always kept a secret loyalty to Sky's wife, and had brought the children to spend the day with her without Sky's knowledge.

'I don't have to tell you the effect it had, especially on the boy.'

'I can see her killing herself *after* the kids had left, Bob. Not before they arrived. I can't imagine her wanting *them* to find her like that,' Michael protested.

'That all depends upon how unstable she was,' Elias responded. 'And on how much she hated Sky. If you ask me, that's exactly what she wanted. It took from him the most valuable thing in his life: his son. Seeing his mother locked in that gruesome death pose crushed the boy. In his young mind, the cause of her death had been her sorrow. And the cause of that sorrow had been his father. There was no relationship after that.'

Elias went on to explain how at first Sky had thought it to be the effects of a child's grief and the inability of a young mind to cope with the loss of a parent. But the relationship had never improved. The boy remained distant and indifferent to his father. Nothing that Sky attempted could relieve it, and he resigned himself to the fact that time alone could cure that deep hurt.

The children remained in their private schools. Asher Sky kept busy traveling the world, making his deals, and building Skyco into the giant that it is today.

Nelson became a troubled young boy. He had difficulties in school, even though he had an extremely high IQ. He was largely unsuccessful in personal relationships. He became rebellious against his father and authority figures in general.

The relationship between father and son remained stormy over the following years, while that with Alexandra was a distant one. She wanted closeness, but it was not offered.

The rebellion in the son manifested itself still further when Nelson went away to college. He fell in with dissidents. The socialistic beliefs of his mother burned in his veins. He hated his father and everything he stood for. Nelson got into trouble repeatedly, but managed to finish his undergraduate education in good standing. Due to his father's influence, Harvard Law School followed. There Nelson once again became involved with radical dissidents and fell in love with a young Arab girl named Dahlia. Despite her politics, she was good for Nelson. He underwent an awakening, and with new purpose in his life he became a dedicated and brilliant student. He also began taking an interest in Skyco and what his father did. His reasons at first were purely to challenge Sky's beliefs with his own revolutionary doctrine. He argued for hour upon hour with his father, which, though it was frustrating for Sky, he viewed as an improvement. At least they were talking, and his son was coming home for holidays. There were times when they actually understood one another's positions, opposed as they were, and times when they smiled and talked of other things – school, the future, and Dahlia.

Then, in October 1973, the Yom Kippur War broke out. By November of that year the Egyptians and the Israelis had agreed to a truce, but the war between Syria and Israel continued.

Dahlia left her studies that Christmas break to return to the Middle East and join in the holy war against Israel. That February she was killed by Israeli commando forces in southern Lebanon. She had been a wonderful companion and a passionate lover, but she was a poor terrorist. Nelson Sky was completely devastated.

His father came to him and cried with him, abandoning all business interests to be with his son. It was then that the relationship between them changed. The love that had been held back for so long came forth out of their grieving together. It was, perhaps, the first time that Nelson could see how much his father really loved him. Asher Sky had his son back, and a renewed purpose for living.

Over time, Nelson recovered sufficiently to return to his studies. There seemed to be a new dedication in him. He no longer preached doctrines of revolution, and fell away from the questionable circle of friends. He graduated with high honors and willingly entered the family business. The Sky in him finally emerged from its cocoon, and he began meeting the expectations his father had always had for him. Nelson became a valuable addition to the Sky empire, sure to be the son that his father had hoped for – until the North Sea claimed him in that tragic plane crash.

The small corporate jet had left Reykjavik, Iceland, bound for Helsinki, Finland. It simply disappeared from radar and fell into the North Sea and was never found.

The search for the lost plane continued beyond all practical limits, with every Skyco plane and tanker in the region being diverted to assist in the recovery efforts. Sky himself sat in the copilot's seat of one of the aircraft. They ran endless patterns, crisscrossing the large sector of ocean where the plane was last recorded on radar. Efforts ceased only when Sky collapsed from exhaustion and the crushing realization of his loss.

Asher Sky, the dynamo, the tower of corporate strength, came to a full stop in his grief. He lost interest in everything, leaving his empire without a leader. But there was another Sky with every bit of the spirit and determination of her father. Alexandra responded quickly with the toughness of her family heritage. Her education had groomed her for the role: undergraduate studies at Oberlin, with an MBA from the University of Michigan. The rest was in the real world, with her father as professor.

For nearly a year she handled the business with the

intuitive genius of her father, astounding those around her who at first had harbored doubts. It didn't take long for her to earn the respect of associates and adversaries alike. Skyco continued, undaunted by the family disaster. Her devotion to the business cost Alexandra a marriage, but it saved Skyco.

Asher Sky never completely recovered from the loss of his son. But he recognized that his grief could not alter the fact of that loss, and he did come back with a fierce determination to build the Skyco empire into a lasting memorial to his son.

He had learned that all the power in the world could not protect him from fate. And he had learned that there was *another* Sky in the world, one who was strong and thoroughly capable and deserving of the love he had so long and so wrongfully withheld. There was, indeed, a Sky to carry on after him.

Michael stood for a long time digesting what he had been told, relating it to what Alexandra had explained to him earlier. Sky wasn't the only one who had paid the price of that relationship. Alexandra had, too. And in some ways she was still paying. He could finally understand the pain behind her words.

'That's some story,' Michael said at last. 'He built his empire in memory of his son, and now it's being threatened.'

And the threat was enormous. In the wrong hands, and used improperly, the Luxus could destroy Asher Sky and everything he had built.

Asher Sky walked into the sitting room of his luxurious mansion. Alexandra was already there, preparing a cocktail before dinner.

She turned away from the bar as her father walked toward her.

'Hi, Daddy. Can I make you one?' she asked cheerfully.

'Yes, I think I could use one,' he replied, sounding a bit serious.

'What'll it be tonight?'

'About three fingers of good Russian vodka,' he replied.

221

'My, we must be in a mood tonight,' she commented. 'Are you sure about the three fingers?'

He nodded.

Alex shrugged, opened the freezer, and took out the Stolichnaya. 'Ice?' she asked.

'Straight up,' he said.

She lowered the bottle to the bar and studied her father. 'I'm as worried as you are about the Luxus, but this isn't going to help matters, you know,' she said, pointing the bottle at him.

'You just pour, I'll worry about the headache.'

'It's your head,' she said, and opened the bottle. She poured his drink and handed it to him.

Elias and Michael would be arriving at the house shortly for dinner. This was probably as good a time to talk to her as any, Sky thought.

'You . . . have a certain glow about you tonight,' he began. 'There's something bright in your eyes that I haven't seen in a very long time.'

Alex didn't respond to the statement. She raised her glass and took a small sip of her drink, looking past the glass at her father.

'In fact, I first noticed it when you returned from Medellín,' he went on.

'Is it that obvious?' she said at last.

Sky nodded.

'I suppose there's no mystery involved,' she said.

'Not to me . . . and I'm sure not to Michael Quinn,' Sky replied.

'Somehow I have the feeling that you have a problem with that,' she said, her tone growing defensive.

'You don't know anything about the man, honey.'

'What's there to know?' she asked. 'I didn't go to Medellín looking for romance, you know. And nothing happened there . . . except that I met someone who made me stir inside. I really wasn't sure, myself, until he came to San Antonio.'

'It's called chemistry. There's nothing you can do about that.'

222

'But you *do* have a problem with it, don't you?'

'You know that I want nothing more than to see you happy,' Sky told her.

'Get to the point, will you?' Alexandra said a bit testily, her hands tightening on her drink.

'Honey, I don't want to tell what to do with your life, but you *really* don't know anything about this man.'

'I know that he's here to try to help us, and that he's taken some life-threatening risks on our behalf. He's not just some mercenary hired by Intel-Trace. He's a dedicated and courageous man.'

'I don't question the courage he's shown in doing the things he's had to do, or that he's a very good-looking man, and that you *are* drawn to him. But he—'

'But he *what*?'

'He kills people, Alex. He's from a dark world.'

'I don't think I want to hear this,' Alex said, shaking her head.

Alex stared hard into her father's eyes, her anger rising. 'He did what he *had* to do. His life was in danger. What would you have done?'

'I'm not trying to argue with you. I just want you to keep a clear head. He may very well be all the wonderful things you think he is, but that doesn't change the fact that part of him is capable of cold, remorseless brutality. He's a trained killer . . . and people try to kill him.'

'Mountains kill people, too. Everest killed Roy, and took a part of my life away. Or have you forgotten that? Cars kill people . . . and *planes* kill people, too.'

Sky's lips tightened. 'That's . . . not the same. Michael Quinn has been groomed to that other world. It's a part of him, and he's a part of it. Someday he'll go somewhere – you'll never know where or when – and he won't come back. And they won't send his body home wrapped in a flag. They'll stick him in some unmarked grave and he'll just cease to exist. I don't want that for you, Alex. You need someone from our world, not his.'

Tears began to fill her eyes. She stared through them at

her father, unable to speak. What he was telling her did not come as a revelation. She had suspected that there was a dark side to this man from the time she had seen the scars on his body at Medellín. They were bullet wounds. But then, as now, it didn't matter how they had gotten there.

'It's your life, Alex. You'll do what you want to, regardless of what I say or feel. You always have. I just don't want you hurt.'

'Well, I hurt *now*. I can't help the way I feel. Maybe deep inside, somewhere, I know the things you've just told me. I don't want to know them. I only want to enjoy what I'm feeling. It's been so long since I've felt alive inside. You can't know what it's been like for me all of these years. How could you not feel happy for me?'

'Alex . . .' he began, but did not continue.

'I'm not a little girl, and I resent being treated like one. I only want a chance at a little happiness. Is that too much to ask?' Her tone was almost scolding.

Alex looked up to the ceiling, tears beginning to run down her face. She had heard her father's words, but was also listening to her heart for the first time in so very long. She knew he was right . . . but so was she. She was no longer willing to let such an unexpected opportunity pass her by without at least reaching for it.

'When Roy died . . .' she began, then paused a moment to regain her composure. 'When he died, I thought that my world had ended forever. And then, as if by some miracle, I learned that I was pregnant with Roy's child. A child he never knew existed. That saved my sanity. And then, when . . . when I lost the baby . . .' She halted, momentarily losing her composure. It took a few moments for her grief to subside to the point that she could continue. 'Well,' she began, shaking her head and fighting back the tears, 'after that, I felt I had lost everything. But I survived, the same way you did when Nelson died. And what helped save me was Skyco . . . and my work. And from that time forward there was only Skyco and work in my life. I didn't let anything or anyone else in . . . perhaps for fear of losing it

224

again. But inside I remembered what it was like to be happy. I kept that memory. That . . . was so long ago. So long to be alone,' she said, raising her eyes to meet her father's once again. 'In all the time since, I've never seen or met another man who made me feel the way I feel now. Can you understand that?' she asked.

Sky nodded without speaking.

'All that time a part of me was dead with Roy . . . a part of my spirit was missing. I don't want to live that way anymore, Daddy. I shouldn't have to. And if Michael Quinn is less than perfect in the eyes of others, I don't care. I know how he makes me feel just to be with him. For once I want to accept something just for what it is, without breaking it down into a balance sheet of assets and liabilities. I just want to take it and run, and to run just as fast and far as I can . . . and to laugh . . . for a little while, at least. I deserve that much. I *need* that much,' she said, the tears again beginning to roll down her cheeks.

Asher Sky could not speak. He felt terrible for having made her cry, for telling her things he felt must be said. And he felt worse for not understanding that other part of her – the woman.

Sky lowered his head. 'I'm sorry, Alex. I never thought about . . .' He fell silent, then let out a short sigh and looked up. 'I know you're not a little girl, and that it's not my place to tell you what you can and can't do. I shouldn't have made it sound like that was what I was trying to do.

'You have your own life to live, I know that. And that means making your own decisions. But I'll always be your father and care about your happiness. So don't hate me for giving advice, even if it isn't very good at times. Just go slowly, for your own sake, honey, until you know what it is that you really want. I *know* what you went through when Roy died, and then when you had the miscarriage. I don't ever want to see you experience that kind of pain in your life again.'

Alex wiped the tears from her face and put her glass down on the bar. 'Please give my apologies to Michael and to Bob. I don't think I'd make very good company tonight,' she said.

Sky watched without comment as she left the sitting room. He stared down into his glass for a long time, then raised it and swallowed its entire contents in three large gulps, in true Russian fashion. He was distressed that he had caused such a painful reaction in his daughter, but he had seen and learned much in his almost ninety years. He had come in contact with many men like Michael Quinn, and as surely as he knew he must let Alex have her way in this matter, he knew the result would be disastrous. The problems of parenthood, it seemed, had no end.

He picked up the bottle of vodka and stared at it. 'Well, old friend, I'll probably hate you in the morning for the way I'll feel, but right now I could do with some of your comfort,' he said to it, and tipped it, pouring out another three fingers. At least tonight there would be no pain, and he'd take his chances with the morning.

16

BERN, SWITZERLAND: Juan Strassa had been back in Bern for two days, residing in a flat in the heart of the Old Town. This city, more than any other in Europe, suited him because it was quiet, conservative, and had somehow avoided most of the cosmopolitan influences arising from the international elements in any capital city. It was the ideal place in which to hide.

On the flight from Colombia, he had managed to engage the attractive woman seated beside him in a delightful conversation. She had turned out to be quite friendly and receptive to his charm.

She was from a well-to-do Colombian family, and was off

to Europe for a brief solo holiday before joining her father in Zurich.

They had spent twelve hours together on the flight, and Strassa had used the time well to weave his magic on her. She was bright and charming and seemed comfortable with him. When the time felt right, he had invited her to join him in Bern. She had refused, but the response wasn't immediate. There was some hesitancy, as if she were thinking over the proposition. Strassa had decided not to pressure her into changing her mind. He had used a very soft approach, and hadn't mentioned Bern again until shortly before landing in Frankfurt. By that time he had won her confidence a bit more, and she accepted.

His excitement had mounted with every passing hour. Not only was she beautiful, but from their conversations it was clear that she was rather liberal in her attitudes. His growing expectations were not disappointed. They made love to exhaustion their first night in his flat. It was a trip through paradise the rest of the time they were together.

He showed her Bern, with its arcaded walks, embellished fountains, and numerous towers in a way she would never be able to see them on her own, and she showed him things about sex that defied imagination.

He tried to persuade her to stay for a few more days beyond her plans, and she agreed to stay, but for just one more night. After that, she *had* to join her father in Zurich, or face disappointing him. And since her father supported her quite nicely, she wasn't inclined to press the limits of his patience and understanding.

Their last night together was to be special. She insisted on preparing him a meal in the small kitchen of his flat, and spending the entire night drinking wine and making love. That sounded perfect to Strassa. And the night progressed that way. They enjoyed the wine and ate a leisurely meal in soft candlelight, which they followed with a particularly energetic bout of passion. She told him how glad she was she had stayed the extra night, and how much the past few

227

days had meant to her. She poured two glasses of wine from a newly opened bottle, and made him promise to see her when he came to Colombia again. He smiled, said that he would, drank the wine – and passed dead out.

The Intel-Trace team was swift. They entered the apartment and set about quickly inserting a homing device in the right heel of every pair of shoes that he owned. They set one in the collar of his leather coat, and replaced the last round in all the clips of his handguns with dummy rounds also containing homing devices. They didn't expect to lose him, but they weren't taking any chances.

Inside the flat, they set highly sensitive audio monitors on the uppermost panes of every window. They would be out of view behind curtains and would permit audio monitoring of the flat by simply focusing directional microphones on the window of any room in question.

They went carefully through his wallet and searched the flat for any papers that could give clues to contacts, photographing anything that could have substance. When they were finished, they laid him in his bed, and the girl left a note telling him how wonderful her weekend with him had been. She left a fictitious address and telephone number of a Colombian residence, and reminded him of his promise to call when he was next there. Then the girl and the team left the flat. Strassa would awake in the morning with a wonderful memory and a rather bad headache. And Intel-Trace would have their man.

MONACO: The villa arranged by Elias was in La Condamine, overlooking the Port du Monaco, where Babayan was scheduled to anchor.

It was surprisingly spacious, and tastefully decorated in art deco fashion. It had a spectacular panoramic view of the harbor through expansive picture windows. The view in itself was worth the price of rental. There was even a telescope mounted on a tripod for more intimate inspection.

Michael made a minor adjustment to the tripod-mounted

telescope and aimed it toward the Port du Monaco and the gleaming yachts and pleasure boats anchored at their expensive moorings. The telescope was a powerful one, and permitted such close viewing that he felt almost intrusive. The fourth yacht he selected had a small party under way on the aft deck, with two topless women. This was better than cable TV, he thought as he panned to the foredeck, where another woman caught the last rays of the day in complete nudity. He whistled softly to himself as the woman sat up, adjusted the large towel she was lying on, and rolled over onto her stomach.

'I'm going to have to complain about these working conditions,' he said with a smirk.

He pulled his eye away from the telescope and stared out of the villa's window, his eyes not really seeing the harbor glowing in the setting sun. His mind flashed back to Alexandra in her office at Skyco Center, her blouse open, her hair down over her shoulders – and he felt a longing for her begin to burn inside of him.

There was no doubt in his mind that she had cracked his professional barrier. He closed his eyes and felt her press against him and imagined again the hot sensation that had burned through him when they kissed.

Then, right on cue, he heard that damned beeper of Elias's. He tried to imagine what would have happened if he hadn't worn it, or if Elias hadn't needed to contact him. He opened his eyes and almost ached to be with her again.

'It's been too long,' he said, shaking his head, and tried not to think about her. It didn't work. She was in his brain, and part of it just didn't want to let go.

She had achieved something that no other woman had done since the murder of his sister. She had broken through the hard crust of bitterness and hatred that had dominated his life. He had lived for one thing and one thing only – to find Dieter and kill him. And when it was done, the hatred had remained. A hatred for every Dieter and Cantú and their like who caused pain and terror in the world. He pulled back the cruel memory of his sister's body at the morgue when he had identified her, and he began to shake with anger at the painful memory of the way she had died. He clenched his fists so tightly that his knuckles cracked and his fingernails bit into the palms of his hands.

He turned away from the window, his head down, perspiration forming on his face. He unclenched his fists and breathed deeply, letting out loud exhalations through pursed lips. And then he remembered why he was there. He remembered Carlos's body held against the tree by the garrote that had killed him, and the scenes of the violence that had followed raced through his brain.

He took a few steps forward and sat in a soft chair that seemed to swallow him in comfort. He put his head back and raised his hands to his head, using his palms to massage his temples.

How he hated them, he thought. Every damned one of them. There was no place in the world for drug lords and pushers and terrorists.

He closed his eyes and tried to think of happier things. The only image that worked was Alexandra. First in his quarters in Medellín, then in the pool at the estate, and then in her office. The rest was all fantasy, and he let it carry him to sleep.

It was dark when he awoke. His clothes were damp from perspiration, and his eyes darted around the villa for a moment while his brain reestablished his surroundings.

Michael sat up in the chair and looked at his watch. It was midnight. He didn't even remember falling asleep.

He tried getting up and felt the pains in his body again. He hurt all over. He forced himself out of the chair and turned on the nearest light, then collected his bag and walked across the white-carpeted villa to the master bedroom. He unpacked his bag and began settling in, finding the clothes that Elias had arranged for him. The wardrobe was complete, with everything from formal wear to stylish

230

casual attire. He had to admit that Elias had good taste in clothes.

Michael took a long, hot shower, which helped to reduce the body aches, then turned in for the night. He felt thoroughly spent, and sleep came quickly.

He awoke the following morning just before sunrise, and eased out of bed, feeling less pain than he had expected. He went into the main room and walked to the windows overlooking the harbor. The sun was just beginning to rise, and there was barely enough light for the telescope to be useful. He tried using it to check out the port anyway.

Elias had estimated that Babayan would arrive that morning. The time was uncertain, and Michael didn't know exactly what to look for. There hadn't been time to get a picture of the yacht to him before his departure from San Antonio. Elias had told him that he would be advised. Still, Michael felt compelled to search the harbor anyway. He was filled with an urge to *see* the adversary.

The file on Babayan had contained several photographs of him. But pictures weren't the same as seeing the actual man. Michael could see very little in the low light. He gave up after a few additional minutes, thinking he would try again when the sun rose higher in the sky. He'd scope out the multitude of yachts with on-deck breakfasts and hope that he would make a lucky connection. If that didn't work, then he'd have to wait for the contact with Elias.

He went into the kitchen and poured himself a glass of juice and put on some coffee.

He spent the next hour going over a map of the principality of Monaco, marking key landmarks and major routes of travel to and around his points of interest. When the daylight was sufficient to use the telescope, he returned to the window and made a closer inspection of the routes he had mapped out. Then he tried scanning the port one more time.

The deck activity had picked up considerably. There

were a lot of faces and some prime flesh moving about on some of the yachts. Modesty didn't seem to be a concern at all. These women looked to be as casual about being naked as they would standing in their own bathrooms.

'Goddamn!' he whispered, feeling an almost unconscious rise of his manhood.

He fought back the urge to prolong his girl-watching and went back to scanning the faces of the men on the yachts. But there were too many boats and too many people. There was no way that he'd find Babayan without at least the name of the yacht. And he might not even be in port yet.

He finally gave up and ate a light breakfast of juice, fruit, and coffee, then showered. He dressed in some of the clothes that Elias had provided, then made a careful search of the villa for the weapons that were to have been supplied. They hadn't yet been delivered, but probably would be before the day was out. He decided to use the time to familiarize himself with the harbor and the Casino.

Michael left the villa, leaving the usual tiny fold of paper below the lower hinge of the door.

The route he took wasn't as random as it may have appeared to an observer. It was one he had carefully worked out from the window earlier. It took him down along Boulevard Albert to Avenue du John F. Kennedy, then up to the world-famous Casino Gardens. Then he visited the Casino itself to establish his line of credit, only to discover that it had already been attended to. The banks and the credit references were his – a precaution by Elias on the chance that the DST might do some checking. The entry fee to the private gaming parlor had also been prearranged. He spent about an hour wandering through the Casino to become familiar with its layout, then made his way up the stairs to the private parlor. It was locked.

He inquired when it would be open for play, and was informed that it was scheduled for a two o'clock opening in two days. That meant Babayan should be arriving very soon, and probably so would Elias.

He left the Casino and took the shortest route back to the villa. When he got there, he saw the small sliver of paper on the floor.

There was no reason to suspect trouble this early, but he used extreme caution just the same. He pushed the door open and looked inside.

The maid was in the main room, finishing her cleaning. He stepped in and said good morning to her in nearly perfect French. An unusual ability with languages was one of Michael's strong points, and one of the reasons for his success in the field.

She returned the greeting with a polite smile.

Michael eyed the room carefully as he walked farther into it. His attention was drawn back to the maid. She made very positive eye contact, then held up a folded book of matches for him to see clearly. She dropped the matches into a clean ashtray, then finished up a few final touches.

'I have left some extra towels for you and Madame, Monsieur,' the maid said to him in a soft voice. 'Is there anything special that you will need?'

'No. Thank you very much,' Michael returned, a bit puzzled by her assumption.

'I shall return in the morning,' the maid went on. 'You may leave your laundry here,' she said, pointing to a small basket in a corner near the entranceway. 'It will be returned later the same day.' Then she carefully laid a folded towel in the basket. She smiled and bowed her head, then left the room.

Michael walked straight to the basket and lifted the lid. The folded towel she had put in was clean. He reached into the basket and turned back the top fold. Inside were another Glock and two spare clips. This was a Glock 19, a shortened, more compact version of the Glock 17 he had carried in Colombia. It was smaller and easier to conceal, yet had the same seventeen-round capacity. Beneath the second fold was a compact holster designed to carry the gun in the armpit in a horizontal position for rapid draw.

233

He picked up the gun, the clips, and the holster, and remembered her obvious gesture with the matchbook. He walked directly to the table and took the matchbook from the ashtray and opened it. In neatly printed letters was the name *Eslabón*. That must be the name of Babayan's yacht, he reasoned. There was also a vague outline of the harbor with a small line on it.

Michael went immediately to the telescope, checked the diagram once again, then began to scan the port for a yacht in the area indicated and lying on a matching angle to the drawn line.

He found it.

'Jesus,' he said to himself. 'This man knows how to live.'

Nearly two hundred feet long, the *Eslabón* looked more like a ship than a boat. He panned to the bow just to double-check the name. It was clearly visible: ESLABÓN. He swung the telescope to the aft deck to see if he could spot Babayan. There were several of his crew, but the man himself wasn't there.

If Elias's information was accurate, and Michael knew that it would be, the big action would begin in the Casino on the first night. Babayan himself would gamble on five or six evenings, though the private parlor had been arranged for a full two weeks. The rest of the time the arms dealer would rest, take plenty of sun, and probably enjoy the pleasures of some female company. Then it was back to his usual nonstop pace of business. The days on which he gambled were never the same, except that he always played on the first day. According to Elias, Babayan always left the table a big winner, which was why beating people didn't impress him. He always beat people.

Michael set the matchbook on the table beside the telescope, leaving it open. He should have plenty of time to watch the yacht and observe Babayan.

Just then he heard the sound of the shower being turned on in the master suite. He turned his head in the direction of the partially open door and stared hard at it.

He picked up the gun and snapped back the slide to arm the weapon. The maid had said nothing about company. Then he remembered her odd statement about leaving extra towels for 'Madame'. He moved quickly to the master suite and the sound of the running shower.

He pushed the door open enough to slide in silently, and saw the open suitcase on the bed. It was filled with a woman's clothing.

'What the . . .' he began, and moved swiftly to the closed bathroom door.

He raised the Glock and opened the door, stepping in quickly with the gun raised in firing position.

His eyes locked on the glass shower stall and the naked figure inside.

'Jesus!' he said, lowering the weapon quickly. Alexandra stood wide-eyed, staring at him.

'Hi, sailor,' she said.

Michael grabbed a towed to conceal the gun.

'Alex, what are you doing here?' he asked, his shock at seeing her evident in his tone.

'Taking a shower,' she replied, her voice timid and elflike. She had seen the weapon and it had frightened her.

Michael placed the towel with the gun on the counter beside the basin.

'You scared me half to death,' he said.

'I didn't mean to,' she said softly, her eyes as wide as saucers.

They stood for an awkward moment staring at one another.

Michael let out a sigh of relief and for the first time let his eyes play down along her nude body, which she did nothing to conceal. She was more beautiful than he had imagined.

'Why are you here, Alex?' he asked softly.

'I needed someone to wash my back,' she replied.

'How did you find me?'

'Well, I knew you were in Monaco. That was no secret. I got the address of the villa from Tom.'

'You shouldn't be here. You *know* that.'

'I only know that, right now, I need to be wherever you are,' she said to him.

He wanted to be angry with her for taking the unnecessary risk of compromising Skyco. 'Damn, Alex . . .' he began, but stopped.

'Don't be angry, Michael,' she said, opening the shower door.

As much as he should have been, he couldn't be angry with her. In fact, he was awfully glad to see her. 'I'm not angry, Alex,' he said at last, then smiled. His face told the tale.

'Well, now that we have that behind us, are you just going to stand there, or what?' Alexandra asked with a pretty but naughty smile.

Michael stepped closer to the shower stall.

'I don't suppose you're wearing a beeper . . . or are you?' she said.

'No beeper,' Michael replied.

Alexandra grabbed him by the shirt and pulled him into the shower.

The hot water did little to put out the fire that was building inside him.

She opened his shirt and pulled his body close to hers, flesh against flesh, their lips meeting in the next instant.

He could feel her passion taking him over. And he didn't resist as it began to consume them both.

'No phone calls this time,' she whispered as she started tugging at his clothes.

'You're crazy,' he said, keeping her close to him.

'Shut up and get naked.'

It was the smell of coffee that woke her. Alex opened her eyes and stretched across the bed. She sat up and looked around the room for Michael. Of course, she thought, overcoming a moment of fear, he was making coffee.

It felt like morning, after a long night of lovemaking. It was, in fact, late afternoon, as evidenced by the long

236

shadows cast across the room by the sinking sun. She smiled like a cat. It had been better than any fantasy she had had since meeting him, and she had had some pretty elaborate ones.

Michael had been a very gentle and considerate lover. He was strong, yet had an easy touch; commanding, yet he gave up control to Alex when he felt she wanted it; and he was intuitive, knowing exactly how to please her and to take her to heights of pleasure she had only ever imagined. She had never had a lover like him.

She finally stumbled out of the bedroom, the smell of the hot coffee drawing her to its source. She saw Michael standing at the telescope, spying with easy patience.

'I hope she's beautiful,' Alex said, coming up behind him and wrapping her arms around him.

'Great tits,' he answered. 'And you don't even have to drop quarters into this thing.'

She smacked him on the behind. 'Leave those poor people alone,' she scolded playfully, then headed for the coffeepot.

He turned his head and watched her walk across the room. She was wearing his shirt and nothing else.

'I can guarantee that not a single one of them is poor, and that if they didn't want their tits seen, they wouldn't air-dry them the way they do,' he said, then put his eye back to the telescope.

He watched a launch approach the *Eslabón*. Accompanied by a uniformed operator, there were several beautiful, scantily clad women. He had a good idea what Babayan's plans were for the night. Having seen enough, he turned away from the telescope.

'Feel hungry?' he asked.

'I'm starving,' Alex called from the kitchen. 'Did you see all of the great things in this refrigerator?'

'Yes, I did. It was all there when I got here. Elias thinks of everything,' he replied.

'Well, not everything, exactly,' Alex said just as Michael walked into the kitchen. She looked at him sheepishly. 'He didn't plan on my showing up. I guess I'm a complication that you really don't need.'

Michael nodded his head slightly. 'But I'm not sorry you're here. Elias would chew my ass if he heard me say that to you, or if he knew what we just did. It has something to do with professionalism and never becoming personally involved with the client, and keeping the client as far removed from the matter as possible once it reaches a stage like this.'

'Are you having regrets?' Alex asked.

'The only regret I have is that I didn't take you into my cabin the first night we kissed. I was playing it by the book.'

'Sometimes you have to break the rules,' Alex said, happy that he wasn't having second thoughts.

'So, what do you feel like doing for dinner?' Michael asked after a short pause, leaving the previous topic behind them.

'What we have here is just fine. I think I'd like it to be just the two of us tonight. It feels nice and comfortable, and I don't want to change the mood right now.'

'That sounds good to me,' he said, and smiled. 'Why don't you let me pull something together. You go pick out a good bottle of wine from that rack in the living room and find some glasses.'

Alex smiled and gave him a short kiss, and then another, and another.

'Red or white?' she asked.

'White.'

She turned and walked out of the room.

Damn, he liked watching her. It was hard to imagine that both the polished business executive and the bomb-shell existed in the same body. And what a body.

Alex walked into the living room and found the wine rack. There wasn't any problem making a choice. Every bottle was first-rate.

She selected a bottle, found the corkscrew, and began to open it. She looked up and saw the telescope and walked over to it as she twisted in the corkscrew. A few seconds later the cork popped and she set the bottle down. She looked at the telescope again, and let her curiosity get the best of her. She put her eye to the instrument. It was still focused on the *Eslabón*.

She looked at the impressive craft, watching the women Michael had seen heading out to the boat scamper up the ladder to the deck. She saw a man step out of what looked like the main cabin and walk across the aft deck to greet them. He was of medium height, wearing a white sport coat and slacks with an open navy blue shirt. His longish, thinning hair moved in the breeze. He held a beautiful Siamese cat cradled in his arms.

He wasn't a bad-looking man, she thought. Certainly, the boat made him a lot better looking. But he did seem interesting at a glance.

She had begun to step away from the telescope to join Michael in the kitchen, when she saw the open matchbook. She picked it up and looked inside the cover. She read the name inside, and saw the diagram. She looked back into the telescope and checked the name on the enormous yacht. And her heart sank with the sudden realization that Michael hadn't been looking at the women at all. He had been watching this boat and this man. This could only be Vigen Babayan.

She looked back at Michael, her expression now totally serious. The reason for his being in Monaco came cruelly back into her mind. *No . . . no, no, no*, she thought, fighting the urge to scream it out loud.

Tears began to fill her eyes, but she fought them back. She looked again at the matchbook, and then out the window at the magnificent view of Port du Monaco. She remembered what her father had told her about Michael and about the dark world in which he lived. As the spirit and joy that had filled her evaporated, she had the sudden fear that she would never keep true happiness in her life again.

'Chow's on. This stuff looks great,' Michael said, coming

239

through the kitchen doorway, carrying a tray of food.

Alex put the matchbook back where she had found it. She forced a bright smile and turned, picked up the bottle of wine, then walked to the table to join him. But the food didn't look good any longer, and the wine wasn't tempting. She had suddenly lost all appetite.

Moscow: Nikolai Barchenkin, First Deputy Chief of the GRU, knocked on the door of his superior's office. It was early evening in Moscow, and he had put in a very long day. Barchenkin held a bundle of report folders in his arms, the fruits of his day's labor.

The door opened and Aleksandr Kozlov looked into the tired face of his second-in-command.

'You are right on time, Nikolai Mikhailovich. Come in,' he said, and turned to walk back to his cluttered desk. Large clouds of smoke erupted from the ever-present pipe and trailed in his wake as he trudged slowly back to his chair. He looked tired himself.

Barchenkin followed him, and took his accustomed seat directly in front of the desk.

'Would you like some tea, Nikolai?' Kozlov asked before sitting down.

'No, thank you, General,' Barchenkin replied.

Kozlov remained standing for a few moments as he quickly arranged the papers on his desk. What had looked from a distance to be a mass in utter disarray rapidly became neat stacks, ready for filing. The desk was now completely clear except for the tidy stack lying in the upper right corner.

He took notice of the folders in Barchenkin's arms as he sat down. 'I hope that is an indication of favorable progress in the Skyco matter?' he said, pointing to the files.

'Yes, General. I think you will be well pleased,' Barchenkin replied.

'It seems, at least for the present, that our knowledge of Skyco's difficulties is still exclusively ours,' Kozlov said. 'Our brothers in the KGB are still unaware of the developments in Colombia. It is vital, Nikolai, that we keep this to ourselves for as long as possible before bringing it to the attention of the Central Committee. We must hope to learn *what* was lost before we do so. Tell me, what have you learned?'

'Our efforts in the United States have not yet been productive. The affair is being kept very secret. No word of it has spread down through Skyco corporate ranks. When it does, we will hear of it.

'Our efforts in Colombia, however, have been more rewarding. We have been able to confirm that an attack did take place at the Medellín facility on the morning of October twenty-sixth. There were many casualties. Skyco has claimed the casualties to be the result of an explosion of a pressure chamber. All repair work is being done by special maintenance personnel flown in from the United States. Once that contingent returns home, information about the nature of the damage, and possibly the cause, will start to leak out.

'We have also confirmed that a fixed-wing aircraft *was* lost, and that Dr Vincent Stillings was on board.'

'You see, Nikolai, we were right!' Kozlov said with a smile of satisfaction. 'Were you able to learn what was on that plane with Stillings?'

'We don't know exactly what it was, but Operational Intelligence has learned that a cargo was on board that originated in Building Two, where the genetic experimentation is conducted,' Barchenkin answered.

'Excellent, Nikolai. Continue.'

'Operational Intelligence has also learned that two bodies were recovered and secured in the hospital facility in a temporary morgue.'

'Whose were they?' Kozlov asked.

'One is believed to be Stillings. Our theory on the other is that it was one of the special team brought in with Robert Elias,' Barchenkin said, handing Kozlov the picture of Carlos that was in the earlier file information. 'It fits. He was last seen three days after Elias's team arrived.'

'And what of Michael Quinn?' Kozlov asked.

'It is here that events become very interesting,' Barchenkin continued. 'Quinn left the Institute at the same time as the other specialist, the one we believe to be dead. It is not known where they went. That same day, the first body was returned to the Institute. This was Stillings. Three days later, Quinn returned with the second body.'

'Three days?' Kozlov repeated, then fell into a moment of silent thought.

'The aircraft was found on the first day, which explains Stillings's recovery. What did they do for the rest of that time?' he wondered out loud.

'Only *one* body was returned on the first day, General. Stillings was not a flier.'

'The *pilot*!' Kozlov said, pounding the table with his hand. 'They stayed behind to search for him.'

'Or to track him, General,' Barchenkin added.

'Yes, I see. To track the pilot *and* the missing cargo.'

'It would seem so, yes. Quinn left the Institute again on the day following his return. Our Second Directorate Intelligence field station reports that two days later a cocaine processing lab in the Chocó region of Colombia was attacked and completely destroyed, with extensive loss of life. The lab belonged to one Hector Cantú, an extremely powerful drug king.'

Kozlov looked puzzled. 'Quinn's disappearance is connected to this?'

'Yes, General. I am coming to that,' Barchenkin replied.

Kozlov nodded. 'Continue, please.'

'Quinn was by this time of great interest to us, and a standing order was issued to keep him under surveillance. He then turned up again, but this time in Bogotá, the day after the lab was destroyed. Elias was also in Bogotá at this time. Quinn then went to Cartagena, where he made discreet inquiries regarding Cantú. It is here that our information is regarded as highly reliable, as it was obtained from trusted street sources. Quinn then disappeared again after making these inquiries. The word on the street was that Quinn was connected to the destruction of the lab, and that Cantú took him.'

'Then he is dead,' Kozlov said as a statement of fact.

'Our intelligence station presumed as much, also. But they were *wrong*. He appeared in Bogotá again, late the following day,' Barchenkin said.

'Then Cantú had not taken him?'

Barchenkin leaned forward toward Kozlov's desk. 'Cantú *did* take him. But somehow – *somehow* – he survived. And Cantú has not been seen since. His yacht left the port in Cartegena the day after Quinn was taken. It never returned.'

By this time a frown had crossed Kozlov's face.

'Both Quinn and Elias then left Bogotá for the United States. They went to San Antonio, Texas, to the Sky residence. Two days later, Quinn left for Monaco, where he met a woman.'

'Another agent?'

'No. It was Alexandra Sky,' Barchenkin said.

Kozlov thought for a moment.

'And where is Elias?' he asked.

'He is still in San Antonio.'

Kozlov rubbed his chin. 'So, whatever they have lost, they believe will turn up in Monaco,' he surmised.

'That is the assumption. Now I will give you the background information that our Second Directorate has developed on Quinn.'

Kozlov leaned forward on his desk as Barchenkin opened the proper file folder.

'Michael Quinn was born in 1946 to a middle-class family. His father was killed in Korea in 1951. His mother remarried in 1954, to a wealthy businessman, and he grew up comfortably. He was educated in parochial school systems through high school, and attended De Paul University, where he graduated with a double degree in biology and literature. Intelligence is estimated in the very high superior range. He is also gifted with the ability to learn languages quickly. He joined the military upon graduation from the university, but, curiously, did not seek officer candidate training. He served three tours of duty in Vietnam, receiving many decorations, including three Purple Hearts. Served with the CIA for ten years: in Central and South America six years, and Western Europe four years. He is believed to have been with Intel-Trace for the past six years with wide-ranging activities.

'He fell out of favor with Intel-Trace following the Dieter incident in Helsinki. He killed Dieter for personal reasons.'

'What reasons?' Kozlov asked.

'Dieter is believed to have killed his sister. It seems that Quinn was involved in an operation against Dieter about one year earlier that cost Dieter a fortune in lost drugs and cash. The cash was never found.'

'Did he take it?' Kozlov asked.

'It was never proved. It does not seem consistent in his case. Quinn was left a considerable amount of money after the death of his mother. He could live quite independently for the rest of life.'

'But it may be consistent, Nikolai. Tomarev is known to have been carrying over two million American dollars. That, too, was never recovered.'

'That may also be part of the reason for his difficulties with his superiors after Helsinki,' Barchenkin said.

'This is a very interesting man, Nikolai,' Kozlov began. 'First, his education. Degrees in a science discipline *and* literature. He is a thinker. That makes him dangerous. Three tours of duty in Vietnam. That makes him capable, and I think he has demonstrated that sufficiently so far. Sixteen years in the field. That makes him experienced, and probably with many contacts. The most puzzling thing, Nikolai, is that he has personal wealth, and may be a thief. Why does a man with that kind of wealth do this type of work? Because he is a patriot. He *believes* in what he does, and that makes him the most difficult kind of adversary. If it were not for the trouble he caused me by killing Tomarev, I would like this man. He must not be underestimated.

'And what do you have on Elias, Nikolai?'

'Robert Elias also served in Southeast Asia. He was an intelligence expert, and his file is still classified. What is interesting here is that his term of service in Southeast Asia exactly corresponds to Quinn's final two tours of duty, and the time when he may have been on special assignment. The records do not indicate any association between the two in Vietnam, but records can be altered to hide many facts. Elias is the director of the New York office of Intel-Trace. The agency was founded in 1977 by Martin Trace and is funded quite heavily by private-sector sources. It is rumored that the most significant financial backers are really US intelligence agencies trying to work around limitations placed upon them by law.

'Intel-Trace employs very sophisticated surveillance systems, including satellites, and is an extremely large organization. Like an iceberg, only a small portion of it is visible.

'The agency is privately held. Its finances are not a matter of public record and are closely held. Details of its holdings and scope of activity are also jealously guarded secrets. It is also rumored that Intel-Trace has operated with unwritten carte blanche from the last three Presidents, and that the office of the Chief Executive of the United States is one of the principal customers of Intel-Trace.

'Intel-Trace is believed to have been the primary source of intelligence for the invasion of Panama, and possibly Granada as well. They are known to have accepted and executed secret sanctions against leading world terrorists. Joint actions with British, Israeli, West German, Canadian, Italian, and French governments are documented in classified files. They are rumored to have one of the foremost surveillance organizations in existence – second only to our own GRU.'

'You say that Elias is a director?' Kozlov asked.

'Yes, General.'

'Why, Nikolai, would he be *personally* involved?'

'Perhaps the importance of the client,' Barchenkin suggested.

'I think it is more, Nikolai. Somehow, it is much more than that,' Kozlov said. 'We must get someone very close to Quinn. Whom have you selected?'

'Gregor Tolvanin,' Barchenkin replied.

Kozlov raised an eyebrow. 'A very *interesting* choice,' he said with a half-smile. 'It is imperative that we get him to Monaco immediately. Whatever is going to happen next will happen there. They have obviously focused their attention in Monaco. Send sufficient teams to cover the entire principality and to give Tolvanin complete support. When they move, *we* must be prepared to move.

'Quinn must be watched closely. We must learn where his interest lies.'

'Tolvanin will need to be briefed in the field,' Barchenkin said. 'There is insufficient time to call him in to do so.'

Kozlov thought for a few seconds. 'Send in Brevig. He will serve as Tolvanin's control.'

'Brevig will have difficulties with Tolvanin. They do not like one another personally. Tolvanin is very independent, and has a reputation for being uncooperative with his control agents.'

'That is because he is an artist, Nikolai. He is creative, and quick – and too smart for his control agents. What keeps him in the field is that he is *successful*. He will need to be fast and resourceful, I feel, to deal with Quinn. He was a good choice, old friend.'

Kozlov sat well back in his chair and placed his hands on his head, then gave a tired stretch. He looked squarely into Barchenkin's face.

'Whatever it is that Skyco has lost, it is now in someone else's possession. They want it back. And to be sure, Nikolai, we want it just as badly.'

246

17

MONACO: It was the morning of 19 November, and Alexandra awoke to find Michael once again at the telescope. She wasn't in a very playful mood, even though this day marked the beginning of the *Fête du Prince* holiday celebration, one of the grandest attractions of the year in Monaco. She had managed to conceal the growing apprehension that had manifested after finding the matchbook cover with the name of the yacht on it. Every time Michael went near the telescope, she was reminded of his real purpose for being in Monaco and of the grave situation that Skyco was in. It all revolved around Vigen Babayan. By now she could tell when the device was trained on the yacht, just by its position. Michael was looking at it now.

Michael had spotted Babayan on the yacht just the day before. He was a little smaller than Michael had imagined him to be from the picture in the file provided by Elias. He also looked to be a bit older. According to the dossier, Babayan's age wasn't known for sure. There were many details of the man's early past that were vague, from a time when he was unknown and unimportant to the world. As the man grew, so did what was known about him, but the beginnings of Vigen Babayan were a mystery known mainly to him. The dossier conjectured an age of fifty years. The photo showed a man closer to his mid-forties, and was dated as being taken no longer than two years ago. Michael thought the age in the dossier was a fairly good estimate.

They ate a late breakfast, then went for a walk along the southern edge of the harbor on the Quai Antoine.

'Still have your headache?' Michael asked as they strolled slowly. This had been the excuse Alex offered for her quiet mood.

'No. It's gone,' she replied.

'You seem a bit low,' Michael said, putting an arm around her shoulders.

'It's nothing. Just my female hormones being a little overactive,' she lied.

'Are you sure?' he asked, knowing inside what the real reason was. Pregame jitters were a normal development.

She put both arms around his waist and squeezed. 'I'm sure. Stop being silly.'

They approached the edge of the harbor and stopped. Michael could see Babayan's yacht clearly.

'It's an impressive yacht,' Alex said.

'Yes, it is. One of the finest I've ever seen.'

'That's *his* yacht, isn't it?' Alex asked.

'Yes. The big man himself,' Michael answered and looked down into her eyes. 'He's right on schedule, just like Bob said he'd be.'

'So, what are we supposed to do next?' she asked, not remembering all of the details from Elias's briefing in San Antonio. She took his arm and started to guide him back up the Quai Antoine.

'We go to the Casino tonight,' he replied.

'To gamble?'

'That's the plan. And we hope we get lucky,' he said.

'That sounds like it could be fun. I feel like getting dressed up for tonight. I think the white dress.'

Michael gave her a squeeze. 'Don't overdo it, my sweet. I won't be held responsible for my actions if you insist upon looking too irresistible,' he teased. 'I have a weakness for ladies in white.'

'In that case, I definitely insist.'

Michael and Alex left the villa just at dusk. The Casino was impossible to miss – brilliantly lit, looking like a golden palace from a distance. The inside was truly a grandiose spectacle of exquisite marble, gilt mirrors, and crystal chandeliers. Everything about it was impressive.

Alex had wanted to be beautiful, and she was. Luminous in a full-length dress of white silk, she drew glances and stares from the moment she entered the fabled gaming establishment. Michael accompanied her with quiet pride, guiding her casually through the general salon, then up the stairs to the private room.

They signed in and were presented with large tokens bearing numbers. The numbers would be used to track their account activity as they played.

The salon was quite large. All the same types of games were here that were also downstairs, but on a smaller scale. There were also quite a few more people than Michael had expected. The place was almost full, in fact.

'Michael, these people are *serious* gamblers,' she whispered as she walked along with him. 'Have you set a limit on your credit with the house?' she asked.

'Everything has been taken care of,' he said, putting an arm around her and giving her a squeeze. 'The game plan was to play big, remember? We don't have to worry about limits.'

Alex's effect on men, as she moved through the room, was even more pronounced than it had been downstairs. She was stunning and could have taken an army of slaves if she had wanted to.

Another pair of eyes fixed upon Alex, at first drawn by her sheer beauty. But the recognition was almost immediate. The dark eyes squinted and stared from a distance, from along an outer edge of the room. But then they moved away from her and locked on to Michael. The sudden shock of seeing him came like a bolt of white-hot lightning.

Quinn! his brain screamed. His mind raced through the faces in the pictures he had received from Kammal just two days ago. It *was* him, he was sure of it.

Kammal had reported that Quinn had been taken by Cantú. He had been *certain* of that. Quinn should have been *dead*!

Rafael Sonterra moved in a wide arc along the outer perimeter of the room to get a better look at him. There was no mistake. It was Quinn, all right. The same man in the pictures sent by Kammal.

Sonterra felt shaken. Quinn was *here*! In Monaco, with

249

Babayan. And Alexandra Sky was here as well. *How much have they learned?* he wondered. It could not be coincidence. For the first time since the operation had started, he felt threatened.

There was a loud chorus of *oohs* and *ahs* from around Babayan's table as Michael and Alex approached it. Babayan had just won a large pot. Five men sat at the table, two of whom had seemingly had enough. One had been totally cleaned out of his table stakes, the other had but a few remaining chips. Both men folded from the game, leaving two unoccupied places.

'Two vacancies,' Babayan said in rather good but accented French. 'Are there any new players?'

There didn't seem to be too much interest. Babayan's run of luck was entertaining to watch, but few of the onlookers were willing to try to break it.

'It looks like the three of us will have to play on,' Babayan said to his tablemates.

Michael tossed his token on to the table in front of one of the empty chairs. 'I'll play,' he said.

Babayan looked up into the strange face for several moments, almost as though he were about to object. But he remained silent. He nodded his head and gestured to the chair with a hand.

Alex recognized him immediately as the man she had seen on board the *Eslabón*. Her heart raced at the sight of Babayan. This was the man they had come to Monaco for. Elias's plan was in action.

'Chips?' the dealer said, with a cold, impersonal stare.

Michael looked at what was on the table in front of the other players to get an idea of the kind of stakes they were playing for.

'Dollars or francs?' he asked.

'We play for dollars at this table,' Babayan replied quite cordially.

'American currency for an American game,' Michael said, staying in French. 'One hundred thousand,' he said.

Alex stepped forward and placed her hands on his

shoulders. She leaned well forward. 'You'd better be good at this,' she whispered in his ear. 'Good luck.' She kissed him softly on the cheek.

Babayan had been mesmerized by Alex from the moment she first touched Michael's shoulder. When she bent forward to kiss him, Babayan got a substantial view of her breasts, and all but fell in love on the spot.

Sonterra stayed at a distance along the wall off Michael's left shoulder. He had quickly overcome the shock of seeing Michael alive, and he now wanted to concentrate on observing him. He was almost amused at the direct approach he had made so effortlessly to Babayan. Babayan would have no way of knowing who Michael Quinn was, and obviously hadn't recognized the woman as Alexandra Sky, Sonterra reasoned correctly. It was probably better for him that he hadn't, too. An obvious reaction would be very harmful right now.

The game was seven-card stud. The dealer began. Michael watched him carefully for a few moments, wondering if *he* was Elias's way of controlling the game. He wondered if Elias really could do that. Normally, he would never doubt the man. But the circumstances weren't quite normal.

Babayan won the first hand.

These guys weren't kidding around, Michael thought. The hand cost him a quick twenty thousand dollars.

Michael won the second and got his twenty thousand back, plus a good bit more. Babayan won the next three, forcing Michael to buy more chips to continue.

Alex's nerves didn't show through her good looks, and her concern grew quickly when she saw how fast the chips went. She couldn't watch this, she decided.

She leaned forward again to Michael's ear and told him that she was going to freshen up a bit. Michael nodded without comment, and Babayan almost swallowed his tongue with the second good look at Alex's full cleavage as she bent forward.

Sonterra watched as Alex walked out of the parlor. He

sensed that Michael would stay in the game for some time, and decided to follow her at a safe distance.

Alex went straight to the bar downstairs and ordered a drink.

Sonterra hung back for a few minutes, then approached the bar, sitting a few seats away from Alex. He looked her over carefully and wondered why she had come to Monaco when Intel-Trace was involved.

Alex sipped her drink as she watched the other people in the Casino, trying to tell the gamblers from the tourists. There was a certain set to the face of the tourist-turned-gambler that differed from the genuine article. There was excitement in the face of the tourist, and a level of high energy – too much to last him long – whereas the real gambler had a lower, more sustained energy level that could take him or her through the night, and most often did. There were people who were truly gamblers, and people who only thought they were.

She finally turned away from the distractions, knowing that she had a decision to make. She finished her drink and ordered a second.

She was upset and wrestled with the way to handle her situation. Michael was in Monaco specifically to get near Babayan. She had come to Monaco on her own volition, prompted almost entirely by her desire to be with Michael, though she felt legitimate concern for Skyco's situation as well. She knew it was not in the best interests of Intel-Trace for her to be here, and this troubled her. She had a clear option to leave in the morning and head back to San Antonio. She also had a shaky option to stay with Michael – and to find some way to make herself useful. In the back of her mind was the warning that her father had tried to convey to her. But she had made up her mind that being with Michael was a chance she *had* to take, or she'd wonder for the rest of the days if she had made a mistake.

Michael was here for something that he felt he *must* do, and he would do it, whatever her choice. Her being doubtful and fearful wouldn't help him in any way, she knew.

And she wasn't sure she knew how to help him, or even if she could. However his involvement might escalate, it was for the good of Skyco that he was here. She knew that much. She also knew that Michael believed in Intel-Trace and the things it stood for. She and Skyco had used Intel-Trace's services often enough to know that it employed good men trying to do good things.

She stared down into her drink and knew that the answer could only be to help him, if she could find a way.

'Excuse me,' a low voice said from beside her.

She turned and looked into the handsome, dark features of the man sitting a few seats away.

'Have we not met before?' the man said, his French accented lightly with Spanish.

There was something about the way he said it that made Alex feel it wasn't just the standard come-on. She stared at his face, trying to remember it. There was something in the face, maybe the eyes. But she couldn't make a connection.

She looked at his face for a moment longer. 'I'm sorry, but I don't believe I've ever met you,' she said. 'Perhaps I remind you of someone else.'

'I don't think so. I have a very good memory for faces. Perhaps it was in Cannes . . . or St Tropez,' he persisted.

'I've been to both. It's possible that you've seen me there, but I would remember if we had ever met,' she replied politely in French.

'Please forgive me. I do not wish to make a nuisance of myself. I was just *so* sure. You are from the United States, yes?'

'Yes,' she said. 'Is my accent that obvious?'

'Yes, I'm afraid so,' he replied, and shook his head. 'I will remember, too late as usual. As I said, I have a good memory for faces, but unfortunately not a very good one for names or places,' he lied with an easy smile. 'What part of the United States are you from?'

'Texas,' Alex replied.

'When did you last come to France?' he asked.

'I was in Cannes for the Film Festival,' she answered.

'Ah,' the man said, as if he had seen a light in some dark corner of his memory. 'I was also in Cannes for the festival,' he lied again. 'I have been to the Film Festival for the past five years. I never miss it.'

'Well, you see it is possible that you may have seen me, then. I've gone the past three years myself,' Alex said.

'Have you? How interesting. Are you in the film industry?'

'No. I just appreciate the art form,' Alex responded. 'I know several people in the industry who have shown their films at the festival.'

'Yes, that may be the answer. I knew that I was not mistaken. My name is Francesco de Corella,' he said, extending his hand.

'I'm Alexandra Sky,' she replied, taking the offered hand.

'Well, it is a pleasure *finally* to meet you, then, Alexandra Sky. I hope that we shall meet again sometime, and this time we will both remember,' he said.

'Perhaps we shall,' Alex said, rising from her seat. 'I must be going now. I hope that you will enjoy your stay in France.'

'Thank you, I'm certain that it will be rewarding. Until we meet again.'

Alex gave him a pleasant smile and left the bar.

Sonterra followed her with his eyes. He would give her sufficient time to go back upstairs before returning himself. Then he would have to be careful to stay out of her sight for the rest of the evening.

Alex made her way back to the private parlor, not knowing what to expect when she got there.

She showed her token and entered the room. The crowd around the table had grown. It was obvious that something dramatic had happened since she left.

As she approached the table, she heard a new chorus of *oohs* and *ahs* arise. What she saw amazed her. Michael was pulling in a large mound of chips. She looked at the stacks in front of him. He was winning, and winning big.

Another player picked up his chips and left the game. That left only three players. The table stakes were now much too high for any new player to become interested.

Alex came up behind Michael and touched his shoulder to let him know she had returned.

She tried making a rough estimate of the chips in front of him. Her approximate tally came to $600,000.

The dealer began a new hand, the first two cards to each player down.

Babayan lifted the corners of his down cards. He had two kings, spades and clubs.

Michael had drawn a ten of hearts and a five of clubs.

The up cards came out. A jack of hearts to Michael, a ten of clubs to Babayan, and a three of hearts to the third player.

The bet was to Michael.

'Five thousand,' he said, sliding the chips forward.

Babayan saw the bet and raised it ten thousand more on the strength of his hidden kings. The third player saw both bets, and Michael saw Babayan's raise.

The second up card was dealt to each player. Michael drew a useless three of spades, Babayan a king of diamonds, giving him three kings. The third player drew an eight of hearts, for a possible flush. The third player peeked again at his hole cards, a six of diamonds and a nine of spades. He had a possible straight working.

The bet was to Babayan's king high. He bet $25,000. The third player studied his cards. He had three cards to draw yet. It was too early to give up on his hand. He had already lost considerable money at the table, and he agonized over the decision. He decided to go on for at least one more card. If it was strong, he'd play on. He saw the bet.

Michael saw the bet without hesitation, and raised it another fifteen thousand. The early betting told him that Babayan was going for an all-out attempt on this hand. Michael put his faith in Elias's hands.

The third open cards were dealt. Michael drew a queen

of hearts, showing weak possibilities for a straight flush. Babayan drew a ten of diamonds, giving him a pair of tens showing to go with the three kings. He was sitting with a strong full house. The third player drew a jack of clubs. The possible straight still existed, but the odds of drawing both of his needed cards were extremely low.

The bet went to the pair of tens showing. Babayan's face was characteristically cool and noncommittal. His bet was strong at a fat fifty thousand. The third player folded.

Michael studied Babayan's open cards, then saw the bet and raised another fifty thousand, which sent a murmur through the crowd.

Babayan squinted at Michael for a moment, then studied his cards and ran through the possibilities. The possible flush was not threatening; his full house would beat it. Otherwise, the most he could have was three of a kind or, more likely, two pair, jacks and queens. Even if he pulled another queen for the full house, Babayan's kings would beat him. Michael's possibilities seemed to be just that, possibilities. Babayan's full house was already in hand, with a chance for the fourth king still a possibility, as was a fourth queen for his opponent.

Babayan saw the raise.

The last open cards were dealt. Michael drew a nine of hearts, making the long shot at the straight flush still a possibility. Babayan drew the ace of hearts, and smiled ever so slightly. It was a card that Michael needed. There would be no royal flush. The most he could have was still three queens. The bet was still to the tens.

Babayan pushed out four stacks of chips, $100,000. The murmurs rose sharply.

Michael studied the cards carefully. Seventeen cards had been dealt, leaving thirty-five in the stack. He had a one-in-thirty-five chance of a clean draw of the king of hearts for the straight flush. The odds for pulling it off were very small. He already had $155,000 on the table, and was looking at another $100,000 without bumping it up.

Michael was here to play, and he did. He saw the

$100,000, and raised it another $100,000. There were groans from the crowd now.

Babayan's face grew tight. He went through the same recall exercise that Michael just had, and mentally reviewed the odds of the draw. He was sure he had lost one big hand to Michael earlier on a bluff. His face had been stone. It was stone again.

Babayan was sweating now. He thought for a moment, then slid the $100,000 to the center of the table, causing enough tension in the crowd to crack the air in the room.

The final down cards were dealt. The bet was still to the tens. Babayan peeked at the final hole card. It was a queen of diamonds. There would be no fourth queen for his opponent. The straight flush seemed an impossibility, with him holding the ace and the eight having come out earlier to the other player. Only the king would win it for him. Babayan had him, he was sure of it. He bet another $100,000.

Michael stared at the last down card without touching it. He didn't know what it was. Elias's word had either been true, and it was the winning card, or it was a loser. Either way, he intended to play it out. And he would do it with added pressure on Babayan.

Michael saw the bet, and toyed with the corner of the down card, then raised the bet $100,000.

Babayan couldn't believe that Michael had seen his bet and raised so quickly. He hadn't seen him look at the down card. He looked at Michael's open cards again, then straight into his face for an unnerving minute, trying to read behind the eyes.

But Michael offered nothing.

'I will see your raise, Monsieur,' Babayan said slowly. '*And* raise you another one hundred fifty thousand.'

Michael did not have the chips to cover. He looked to the dealer and waved a finger. 'Cover the bet,' he authorized. 'And one hundred fifty thousand more,' he said.

Babayan's face went ashen. Quick arithmetic told him

257

that he already had $705,000 sitting on the table. He looked across the table into the face, and in that one flash of a moment Michael let him see the uncertainty he had tried so hard to hide.

It *was* a bluff, Babayan knew in that instant. If it hadn't been, he would simply have seen the bet and called for a show of cards. The last raise was the giveaway.

Babayan did not have the chips to cover. He looked to the dealer. 'Cover the bet,' he said with certainty in his voice.

'Now we'll see the cards,' Babayan said. He turned over his hole cards, revealing the full house. Murmurs rose in the room, and heads began to shake.

Michael turned over the first two hole cards. Babayan saw the ten of hearts and the useless five of clubs. He felt sure Michael hadn't looked at the last hole card. *He had him!*

Michael looked into Babayan's eyes and reached down to the final hole card, still not looking at it. He prayed and turned it over.

There was an explosion of cheers, and he was immediately caught by Alex's embrace from behind and a dozen pats of congratulations from onlookers. He let his eyes slip down to the table and saw the king of hearts. He had pulled the straight flush.

Babayan's face went stark white, and he stood up at the table, staring at Michael.

There was a moment when Michael didn't know what Babayan was about to do.

Then the color returned slowly to the face of the arms dealer, and he leaned forward across the table, one hand resting on it, the other extended. 'That was the most exciting card game I have ever played in, or, for that matter, that I have ever seen,' he said quite calmly. 'Congratulations. It was worth the price to be a part of it.'

Michael rose to his feet and accepted the offered hand, his face as calm as if it were an everyday event to rake in over a million dollars in a single hand.

'Would you and your lovely companion have a drink with a much-humbled opponent?' Babayan asked.

'We'd be happy to,' Michael replied.

'My name is Vigen Babayan,' the arms dealer said.

'I'm Michael Quinn,' Michael returned, still staying entirely in French.

'And your lovely companion?' Babayan inquired.

'My name is Alex,' she said, not offering her last name.

They walked over to the small bar in the parlor and sat at a table. A woman came over and took their requests.

'I must compliment you, Monsieur Quinn. You are a very lucky man,' Babayan said, his eyes on Alex, his meaning double-edged.

'Thank you, Monsieur Babayan. You could be right,' Michael answered, placing a hand over Alex's.

Their drinks were brought to the table.

'You must answer one question,' Babayan began. 'I *must* know how you knew you had the king of hearts. You never looked at the card.'

Michael smiled without answering.

Babayan sat well back in his chair. 'So, it *was* intended as a bluff. But you drew the card by good fortune.'

'I'll only say that you never *saw* me look at the card,' Michael responded. He could see the uncertainty rise in Babayan's eyes.

'I guess it is best for posterity that I never *really* know the answer to that question. You must forgive me for asking.'

'No offense taken,' Michael returned.

'Tell me, will you be returning to the tables?' the arms dealer asked.

'Yes, but not for the next few days. Perhaps on Monday.'

'I will be here on Monday, then. I trust that you would honor me by sitting at my table again?'

Michael nodded. 'It would be my great pleasure.'

'I have never seen you in Monte Carlo before,' Babayan said.

'This is my first time,' Michael lied.

'What part of France are you from?'

'I'm from the United States, actually,' Michael replied.

'American?' Babayan repeated in surprise. 'Your French sounds perfect. The name, however, is American. These days, one can never tell.'

'I have always had an ability with languages,' Michael explained.

'And Alex – you, too, are American?'

'Yes, that's correct. I'm afraid my French isn't as perfect as that of some people I know,' she said, smiling at Michael.

'Nonetheless, you speak it quite well,' Babayan complimented her.

'You really must spend more time in Monte Carlo, Mr Quinn,' Babayan went on. 'With your luck you could become a very rich man.'

'I try not to push my luck too far,' Michael said.

'I would try, my friend. You never know how far it will take you while it is on your side. The thing is to recognize when it leaves. I wonder if you and Alex would honor me by accepting an invitation to dinner aboard my yacht one evening this week,' Babayan invited.

'Thank you very much. That would be nice. We'd be glad to accept,' Michael replied.

'If you will give me the telephone number where you are staying, I will call you later to firm up the arrangements. My yacht is in the Port du Monaco. She is called *El Eslabón*.'

Michael wrote the phone number of the villa on a matchbook and handed it to him.

An employee of the Casino approached the table. He informed Michael that the final tally of his winnings was ready, and that his signature was needed. Michael excused himself and left the table.

Babayan was glad for the opportunity to be alone with Alex.

'Forgive me, I do not wish to embarrass you, but I must tell you that you are a very attractive and elegant woman.'

'Thank you, Monsieur Babayan. I'm not embarrassed. Every woman likes hearing it said,' she returned.

'Do you think that you might join me aboard my yacht for breakfast or lunch one day very soon?' he asked quite directly. 'I would be most honored if you accepted. Perhaps you may help change my poor luck in the Casino.'

'Thank you,' Alex began, intending to decline the offer. But her brain saw in that one instant an unexpected opportunity. Babayan was their reason for being in Monte Carlo. She could sense his interest in her, and felt reasonably certain that she could manage to stay out of trouble with him. She decided to leave the possibility open. 'That would be quite interesting. I think I would like that,' she said, giving it a little eye language for fuel.

Babayan smiled with satisfaction. 'I will phone you, perhaps tomorrow or the day after.'

'I'll plan on it, then. Thank you,' Alex returned, opening up the charm still further.

Michael returned to the table as their conversation ended.

'Well, I'm afraid I must make my apologies,' Babayan began. 'It is getting late. It truly *has* been an enjoyable evening,' he said, looking at Alex. 'I don't often lose at the tables, but I do try to do so graciously on those rare occasions when it does happen. It is time to return to my yacht to lick my wounds. Perhaps I will somehow find a way to turn my luck.'

Michael and Alex wished him good night, and he left them.

'I still can't believe what happened tonight,' Alex began. 'It was incredible.'

'The only thing incredible about tonight is the way you look,' Michael told her.

She gave him a sultry smile.

'Come on, let's get out of here. You're making me crazy.'

18

MONACO: Rafael Sonterra waited patiently with the phone receiver to his ear. With the Colombian operation now ended, there were communication windows through which he could contact Kammal in Madrid. He had tried the previous evening, but Kammal had not made the window, which had concerned him because it was to be a primary contact. Phone delays were rare in Europe – unlike in Colombia – so a missed window could only mean that Kammal had not gotten to the prearranged location at the designated time.

The operator's voice returned to the line. She had his party.

'Hello?' queried Kammal's voice.

'Dr Bashir, my good friend, is that you?' Sonterra asked, though he had recognized Kammal's voice.

'This is Bashir,' Kammal answered. His voice sounded a bit shaky, as if he were frightened or ill.

'What is wrong?' Sonterra asked immediately.

'Nothing, my brother. I have not been well for the past few days. It is nothing of concern,' Kammal replied.

Sonterra squeezed the phone in frustration. Kammal had dropped out of code. The term 'my brother' was one they commonly used when speaking to one another while together, but never during coded communications.

'Do you require medical attention?' Sonterra asked.

'No. I am fine now.'

'You must have been very ill to miss my call yesterday. Are you sure you do not need a prescription, or some medication?'

'I did not miss the communication yesterday. Your call never came,' Kamal replied.

Sonterra held his silence for a brief moment. He had not missed the time window. In fact, he had hit it exactly. 'Where were you?' he asked.

Now Kammal was silent, his indignance felt across

262

the distance as surely as if it had been spoken.

'I was at the Hotel Compostela, on Muñoz Torero. Your call did not come,' Kammal said, his tone mildly defensive.

Sonterra let his disappointment out in a silent breath. 'You were to be at the Hotel Lisboa, on Ventura de la Vega,' he said.

Kammal was again silent, this time feeling confusion. 'I thought . . . no, I'm certain . . .'

'It is not important now,' Sonterra interrupted. 'Listen to me—'

'The Hotel Compostela, I'm certain . . .'

'Kammal!' Sonterra said sternly, dropping out of code. 'Forget yesterday. You must listen to me *now*.'

He could hear Kammal's breathing. It sounded labored.

'*Kammal?*' Sonterra repeated.

'Yes, I am listening,' Kammal answered, the voice almost trembling.

Sonterra considered breaking off the communication. With any other operative he would have done so in a moment, and never used him again.

'Listen to me, Kammal. There has been a serious development here,' he said, then remained silent to see if Kammal was receptive. Sonterra was sure he had been drinking again or, worse, using drugs.

'I am listening, my brother. Go on,' Kammal said, his voice sounding stronger.

'Quinn is in Monte Carlo,' Sonterra reported, staying out of code to prevent confusing Kammal further.

'*Quinn?*' Kammal's voice said fearfully. 'I *swear* that he was taken by Cantú. There was no mistake. He was taken at the old fortress of San Filipe.'

'I am not questioning that, Kammal. I am certain that your report was accurate. But he managed, somehow, to get away from Cantú. It does not matter how, he is here now. That is all that matters.'

'Monte Carlo! But how . . . ?'

'That does not matter. He is *here*. And he has made contact with Babayan.'

'That *can't* be,' Kammal said, his voice sounding near panic.

'He is also being followed,' Sonterra added.

'*Followed?* By whom? Are you certain?'

'I am certain. I watched as Quinn left the Casino last night. I saw a team follow him discreetly. I followed the team. Soviets. I am certain of it.'

'Is it KGB?' Kammal asked tensely.

'Possibly. It could be GRU.'

'But how could they know?' Kammal questioned.

'The GRU has a strong presence in Colombia. Too much has happened because our plan did not work cleanly. Intel-Trace learned too much when they should have learned *nothing*. The housecleaning was a necessity, but it drew attention. I am certain the Soviets do not know all that Intel-Trace knows, or they would have followed Babayan as well. It is possible that his yacht is being watched from land. In any event, they will soon learn that Intel-Trace's interest lies with Babayan. Then they will begin watching him. Our plan is well advanced, Kammal. In a few days it will not matter. We must now assume that Strassa is also being watched, at least by Intel-Trace, possibly by both,' Sonterra concluded.

'I watched Strassa leave Bogotá. I saw no surveillance,' Kammal insisted.

'And Quinn was also supposed to be dead.'

'I am not being followed. I *know* that. I was very cautious in Bogotá and after arriving in Madrid.'

'You are probably right,' Sonterra said, hoping that Kammal had been as cautious as he claimed.

'I shall warn Strassa,' Kammal said.

'No,' Sonterra returned. 'Say nothing to Strassa, and avoid contacting him under any circumstances. Strassa must be removed. He is a liability we cannot afford.'

'Removed?' Kammal repeated, shock in his voice. 'But he can be trusted. He did very well for us in Colombia, and we may need him again.'

'*Kammal!* You will *not* question my decisions,' Sonterra

said angrily. '*Remove him!* He is too close to the Dwarf, and the Dwarf is too close to you. If Strassa unwittingly leads them to the Dwarf, it may lead them to *you*, Kammal. *You* are in danger as long as Strassa lives. By removing Strassa we protect the Dwarf – and you, Kammal. It *must* be done.'

'Yes, you are right. It must be done,' Kammal repeated, a mild tremor in his voice.

Sonterra felt grave concern over Kammal's state of mind. He was beginning to come apart. Sonterra had sensed a decline with the last few communications. Kammal *must* hold together for a little while longer, he thought. Soon the plan would enter its advanced stages and Sonterra would be able to bring him in to safety.

'Just a little while longer, Kammal. Be strong and unafraid. I will protect you,' Sonterra said reassuringly.

'I will be strong, my brother. You can count on me as always. I will begin immediate plans to remove Strassa. With Intel-Trace and the Soviets all around you, you must be cautious. I can join you after the Strassa matter is taken care of,' Kammal said, his only thought now to help protect Sonterra. Kammal knew that he would be lost without Sonterra's strength to lead him.

'No, Kammal. I am safe. You must take care of Strassa, then go on as planned. Inform me when Strassa has been eliminated. If there are to be any changes, I will tell you then,' Sonterra told him.

'Yes . . . yes, I will do exactly as you say.'

'Go cautiously, little brother. *As-salaam alaikum*,' Sonterra said, then broke off the communication.

Sonterra made his way back to the small flat he was using that overlooked the southern end of the Port du Monaco, above the Quai Antoine. He went to the window and used high-powered binoculars to locate the villa he now knew Michael Quinn and Alexandra Sky were staying in. He could see lights on in the windows. He sat for a long time watching until the lights went out, knowing that for at least this night his danger was lessened.

He went to his bed and lay down and thought about Kammal . . . and about Greta, who was away in safety with their child growing in her womb. He wanted very much to be with her, to have her in his arms, to have Kammal near them, knowing that all danger was very far away. Soon, he knew. Soon his wish would become reality, and all that was ahead would be in the past.

He had come a very long way since that first day in Lebanon when he had met Kammal, who had been little more than a gangly teenager. How well he remembered it. It had been his beginning, his birth into this terrorist's world. It had been a bittersweet time of change, but a time that had brought him purpose and happiness. He closed his tired eyes and let his mind drift back long, long ago, into the comfort of those memories he held so dear.

LEBANON: He had expected a gray, clouded city of ghosts. Though racked by the constant ravages of human conflict since ancient times and its ever-raging civil war, Beirut rose from the steep rocky seaside cliffs like an uncovered jewel. It looked untouched from the air high above the blue Mediterranean, its high-rise buildings glowing white and tan and inviting. It had been the Paris of the Middle East in this once-gentle land. But the gentleness was gone now and only civil war remained.

13 April 1975, was the start of it. Pierre Gemayel, leader of the Phalangist Party in Lebanon, was attacked by Palestinians while attending services for the dedication of a new church in Beirut. He survived the attack, and only hours later a group of his loyal followers in the Phalangist militia stopped a bus carrying mostly Palestinians and executed twenty-seven of them in cold-blooded retaliation.

The potential for violence had been there since the late 1960s, when thousands of Palestinians fled to Lebanon from civil war in Jordan and the PLO established its headquarters in west Beirut. The city would feel the occasional wrath of Israel as it struck back at the PLO in retaliation for attacks made against it. The Lebanese army was unsuccessful in attempting to halt PLO raids against Israel, and Lebanon's political factions raised their own militias, some supporting the PLO, others opposing it. The violence of that April was the fuse that ignited Lebanon's civil war, which would leave the nation gravely wounded, perhaps so badly that it would never recover. Lebanon, not having a strong central army, lost control of its war, and the country became an arena for the battles of all. It became transformed into an anarchist's stewpot. Every day became a test of personal survival.

Lebanon, with its dazzling setting of sea and mountains and valleys through which had passed prophets and armies, had always been an inviting crossroads of history, learning resilience through the centuries beneath the trampling feet of the Roman legions, Christian Crusaders, Arabs, and Ottoman Turks.

The man with no name had first seen Kammal, a boy on the awkward edge of manhood, in a tiny, nameless refugee camp in southern Lebanon. The journey had been long and hot for this new man with no name. The boy liked him immediately and became his quick companion, showing him around the only home he had ever known. It was like so much of what this stranger had already seen on the journey to this place – poor beyond description, half knocked down to useless rubble by Israeli bombs. But life went on for these people, and he admired the simplicity of their lives, enduring and accepting of their fate.

It was not until the second day in this new home that he met Abu Hassan Nasir. He was an old man with great wisdom written across his lined and weathered face. The old man said nothing to him. They sat for what seemed an interminable time, Abu Hassan silently watching him. Then the old man rose and walked around him, still remaining silent, looking at him so intently that he felt his very soul was being scrutinized. Without a word, the old man walked out of the half-stone, half-sheet-metal hut. He heard words outside that he could not understand, then three young, strong men came in. And the questions began.

They questioned him for three days, almost without pause. They went over and over the information he had given them, picking a point here or there and probing it for every minute detail that his mind could reveal. Then they would start all over again, with the patience of ageless rock. They did not tell him their names and would not answer his questions. He learned quickly not to ask them.

He was left alone again when the interrogation ended. Completely alone. Even the boy Kammal was not to be seen. Then as the sun began to set over the tiny village, the old man came to him, holding a young dog in his arms. The old man entered the hut and sat beside the stranger, his hands gently stroking the soft fur of the dog.

'You have the virtue of patience. This is good,' the old man said at last in quite good English. 'You also know how to curb your emotions. That can save your life. But inside you, I think there is much anger. It is in your eyes. You must never be led by anger, for anger is a serpent with two heads, one to bite the hand at which it is aimed, the other to bite the hand that holds it. Always remember that. Let yourself be led first by your wisdom, and second by your passion.'

The stranger looked into the eyes of the old man, feeling by instinct that he was expected to listen and not to speak.

The old man stood beside him and placed his hand on his head. 'I shall call you Rafael,' he said, then handed him the young dog.

'Name it and care for it,' he said. 'It is like the men you will one day lead. It will follow you because you are its master. Whatever you are, it will know only what you become to it. It will love only you, and obey only you. Make it your companion. Teach it to listen to your every word, to obey your every command, and *only* your command. Be strict, be loving, and most of all, be patient'

'I will,' he replied.

The old man did not smile, but Rafael felt that a smile

was there, just below the leathery surface of his skin.

The old man left without another word. The dog did not try to follow. It lay at Rafael's side, looking up at him with eyes of infinite trust. Rafael smiled and stroked the dog softly. 'I'll name you Socrates,' he said, as the young animal began to bite at his hand playfully. 'We start tomorrow, Socks. Straight and narrow, and a lot of hard work. You heard what the man said, we're going to be pals.'

The hard work began for everyone the next morning before the sun had even risen.

'You will find the Palestinians an easy people to love,' the old man told him. 'For some, we are also an easy people to hate. They call us terrorists. Whether we are terrorists or not depends upon how one defines the word. It is all a matter of semantics. The same words used by two different people can mean two entirely different things. By *their* definition we *are* terrorists, perhaps. But why are we?

'We are terrorists because we resist dispossession from our homeland, because we continue to cry out for our right to what has always been ours. We are terrorists because we do not like our women and children killed by bombs from ships and planes and tanks of foreign armies. We are terrorists because no one will listen to our cries, and we must make them listen. We are terrorists because we are desperate and have no other way to turn. When no one will listen, and no one will act on our behalf, then *we* must do for ourselves. For this, for wanting our homes and our freedom, we are terrorists,' Abu Hassan told him.

'History recognized what England, Germany, and Russia did to Czechoslovakia as *wrong*. Did not England do the same thing to Palestine? Yet there were no tears for Palestine and its people.

'Please do not misunderstand me. You are not a Palestinian, and you are not being trained to become one. Only a Palestinian can be a Palestinian. You are being trained to carry the sword of truth for the many who are too weak to stand up against oppression. You are their justice, their voice, their mighty arm of retribution. You will do for all of those whom the world has forgotten and does not care about.' Abu Hassan's face held passion, but it was not anger. It looked more like pain.

'Your preparation will take place in three phases. The first is general training – that of a soldier to our cause. You will learn the ways of war and the ways of survival. Your war will not be on a battlefield, but in the cities and on the streets, or wherever you are. Your enemies are *all* those who will not listen, all those who wept for Poland and Ireland, but who could find no tears for the injustices done to us.

'The second phase will be very specific. You will have much to learn. You will become a great freedom fighter whom all the world will know. They will fear you and respect you – and they will try to kill you if they can. But you will be ready for them. This phase will take the longest, but it is the most important.

'The final phase is *change*. Physical change. We will alter your appearance to give you a time of invisibility from your enemies. This you must protect, for once they know the new face of Rafael, your dangers will be multiplied.

'We are a long time dead, my son. Use this short life well and to good purpose, so that all you do will live beyond you. Do this, and you will have done the world the greatest good.'

And so this Rafael stepped into the world at the side of his master, Abu Hassan Nasir. Month by month, his training progressed with patience and deliberate planning. He learned quickly and spent long hours perfecting the skills he was being given until he surpassed even the abilities of his many teachers.

When his instructors would finish each day, he would sit with Abu Hassan under a great spreading cedar, and his master would ask him what he had learned. The teacher would listen and nod with approval and talk to his pupil late into the night, sharing a lifetime of philosophy and experience. Rafael was in awe of the old man's understanding of human emotions and world events. Their discussions gave him great inner satisfaction, for he was being fed the very things he had hungered for his whole life. He was taking on purpose and form, where before there had been nothing but shallow existence.

And always at his side was his own student, Socrates, who was as good a learner, it seemed, as his young master. Socrates had grown into a fine young dog, smart and alert, and everything that Abu Hassan had asked that he be.

Abu Hassan took great pride in his student, whom he had come to love like a son. He had taught him much about the world in which he would someday live when the time came for him to leave. But there was one greater lesson yet to be learned, one that could not be imparted with words. It was a lesson for which the student must be his own master – the single most important lesson of all his training.

Abu Hassan summoned his student to him in the privacy of his quarters. Rafael walked in, tall, darkly tanned, strong and hardened from his training. Socrates was at his side like a shadow.

'Please sit,' Abu Hassan told him.

Rafael sat at the small table in the room, Socrates coming to his heel and lying beside him.

'You have done well, my son. There is but one more lesson and your first phase of training will be complete.'

Rafael sat attentive, waiting for the words he would drink in like life-giving water.

Abu Hassan looked at the dog and knelt beside it, stroking its head gently, much as he had on the day he had given it to Rafael, upon accepting him as his student.

'I once told you that this dog would be like the men you will someday lead. Do you remember?' the master asked the pupil.

'Yes, I remember.'

'You have taught it well.'

'Thank you,' Rafael replied.

'I know that it loves *you*. Do you love it?'

271

Rafael smiled and looked down at Socrates. 'Yes, I do.'

Abu Hassan rose to his feet. 'You will one day have to send men to their deaths. Men whom you know and trust . . . men whom you *love*. And they will go because you ask them to. Can you do that?'

Rafael was silent for a suspended moment. He looked up into the eyes of his teacher.

'You must *never* be uncertain of that answer! Your decisions must be made without hesitation. Hesitation *kills*. It kills your men, it kills you, and it kills your cause. Do you hear me?' Abu Hassan said sternly.

'Yes, I hear you,' Rafael replied, sensing what was coming, hoping against all hope that he was wrong.

'You *must* have strength, or you will not be worthy of the loyalty of those who follow you.' Abu Hassan placed a handgun on the table beside Rafael. 'This little dog loves you, and that which you love is the first test of that strength. The strength is within you, or it is not. You must show me *now* if it is there. You must prove to me and to yourself that you *can* make that decision, that you *will* make it.'

Rafael looked into the eyes of the old man. He couldn't believe what he was being asked to to.

'There is no place for weakness,' Abu Hassan said. 'The choice to do this is yours to make. You choose to go on, or to stop here. You must decide.'

Rafael looked away from the old man and down to the dog, whose tail began a soft *rap, rap, rap* on the floor. The eyes were innocent and loving, trusting and obedient.

Rafael felt his vision begin to blur with the tears welling in his eyes. He stood up, his head bowed low so as to conceal the tears from his master, and reached for the gun.

'Come, Socrates,' he said, his lips trembling.

He turned away from the master and walked toward the door, the tears now running down his cheeks. His hand tightened on the gun and he left the room.

Abu Hassan walked to the door and watched as Rafael made his way up the low ridge to the great spreading cedar under which they had sat for countless hours. Rafael stood there for a long moment, looking out over the horizon, Socrates at his side, seemingly doing the same.

Abu Hassan turned and walked away from the door. He stood facing the wall, not really looking at anything. His heart ached for his young student, but he could do no more for him.

The silence seemed unending.

And then the report of the single gunshot echoed across the hills.

Abu Hassan went to his student later that evening. Rafael was lying down, staring at the chipped ceiling of his quarters. The teacher sat beside his student, taking his hand in his own.

'You felt grief. That is good,' Abu Hassan began in a low voice. 'Grief is not a thing for which to feel shame. Causing the death of another living thing – any living thing – is worthy of our grief. Death is a part of the world in which we live. We will and must deal in death, for only death is heard the world over. But there is meaning to each and every life that must be shed. *Understand* why you must take that life, and honor that sacrifice to our cause.'

'That was such innocence,' Rafael said, meeting the gaze of his master.

'There is *no* innocence. There are only martyrs. Your cause is *their* cause. It is because of them that you exist. It is *for* them that you exist. You are their sword and their strength, fighting the war that they cannot. Every war – *every* war – will have its casualties.'

'I think I need a day off,' Rafael said.

Abu Hassan rose to his feet. 'There are no days off. Every day is real, every minute is live. You could be caught in a sickbed and shot dead.'

Rafael nodded. 'No days off,' he repeated in a low whisper.

'Phase one is complete. You are now ready for the second to begin,' Abu Hassan said as he walked to the door.

273

He held an arm extended out the door. There came the sound of feet moving rapidly, then skidding to a stop. A scrawny figure stepped into the doorway, Abu Hassan's arm going around his shoulders.

'This is *your* student,' he said to Rafael. 'Teach him well to be the most trusted at your side. He will never fail you. His name is Kammal. He is my last remaining child.'

Rafael rose to his feet. *My student*, he thought, *and the son of the master*.

Abu Hassan nodded and left.

Rafael regarded the scrawny youth and nodded, a short smile crossing his lips. He had never felt prouder at any time in his life than he did now as he stared at the boy. A tremendous honor had just been bestowed on him.

'Your training begins tomorrow, Kammal,' Rafael began. 'Straight and narrow, and a lot of hard work . . .'

The words made him think once again of the dog, and how close the training had brought them. And he wondered.

19

MONACO: Ivan Brevig held back the curtain just enough to let him see the street. The small flat from which he watched was situated above Boulevard Albert in the southern part of La Condamine, the residential area facing the Port du Monaco and its harbor of world-class yachts. He watched carefully as a cab stopped about thirty yards up the street. The passenger got out, paid the driver, and looked up and down the block before heading north in the direction from which Brevig was observing him. He was a day late.

Brevig felt his stomach knot at the sight of Gregor Tolvanin. He thoroughly disliked the man he had been assigned to control during this operation. Had Kozlov himself not personally approved Tolvanin, Brevig would have insisted upon another operative.

His dislike for Tolvanin was mostly personal. As an operational agent, Tolvanin was as good as they came, effective and possessing a solid record of performance – if one looked past the repeated file notations of insubordination, recklessness, and decidedly Western tendencies in his attitudes and demeanor. The Political Department of the Soviet GRU, which was responsible for the ideological monitoring of all GRU personnel, had even made several specific notations in his file that he was regarded as a liability for field work. They had even recommended recall to the Soviet Union, the implication being that he was a possible defector in the making. The Political Department, however, had no jurisdiction over foreign branches. Each foreign-posted resident director had personal responsibility for the ideological monitoring of his own field officers. In Tolvanin's case, Soviet ideology took a backseat to his success ratio.

The Personnel Directorate, on the other hand, staffed by officials who had worked abroad and who made such evaluations with more practical heads, considered him to be one of their best. To them, Tolvanin had all the characteristics and tendencies that marked an agent capable of handling the most troublesome assignments.

Brevig's dislike for Tolvanin stemmed from the fact that Tolvanin was everything Brevig had wanted to be, but couldn't. Tolvanin was like the handsome athlete who got all the glory, all the press, and all the women when the game was over. Brevig, on the other hand, was the short, stubby coach whom no one remembered, but who was responsible for the training and game plan.

Details were Brevig's strength, as were motivating and controlling his operational people. Tolvanin was the type who listened to the plan, agreed with how good it sounded, then went out and did it the way *he* wanted to anyway. Brevig had looked good because of it sometimes, but just as often he hadn't.

A knock sounded on the door to the flat. Brevig opened it slowly and looked up into the strong features of the man standing there.

Tolvanin looked down at Brevig, sensing the hostility immediately. Brevig was a short, squat man with close-cut hair and protruding ears. The smile dropped from Tolvanin's face and he shook his head almost imperceptibly.

'Monte Carlo. I thought this one would be fun. I can see that I was wrong,' Tolvanin remarked, then walked past Brevig into the room.

'What did you expect? A big-breasted woman and keys to a fast sports car? I am very sorry to disappoint you, but your superiors in Moscow had something else in mind for you. Perhaps on your next assignment. Come in, make yourself comfortable. You are *only* one day late,' Brevig said sarcastically.

Tolvanin went straight to the bar without comment, and poured himself a Jack Daniel's on the rocks.

The two men were complete opposites. Tolvanin looked more like an American. He dressed like one, talked like one, and drank like one. Brevig, on the other hand, looked like a Russian, dressed like a Russian, and drank like a Russian.

'You can pour me a vodka,' Brevig said.

Tolvanin already had the bottle open and was pouring out a healthy slug. 'Just the way you like it, Ivan, no ice and to the top. Of course, if you'd rather, you could just swig it from the bottle.'

Brevig frowned and took the glass from him.

'You were supposed to report yesterday. Why are you late?'

'My instructions were to break off my current assignment and report to Monte Carlo as soon as possible, to this address. I was in pretty deep and couldn't pull out with such short notice.'

'I hope she wasn't too disappointed,' Brevig remarked.

'Well, you know me, Ivan. I always like to leave them smiling.'

276

'Yes, I'm sure General Kozlov would be very pleased,' Brevig said, trying to get his serious attention.

'Kozlov?'

'It seems that we were his personal choices for this assignment. He has taken a particularly strong interest in this operation himself.'

The mention of Kozlov's name seemed to be of some help. Tolvanin raised his eyebrows and his drink in the same motion. 'To the boss,' he toasted.

Brevig did not return the toast. He waited in stony silence for the agent to finish having his fun.

'That's what I like about you, Ivan. You really know how to have a good time. OK, so what brings us to Monte Carlo?'

Brevig opened a file folder and handed three photographs to Tolvanin. 'These people bring us to Monte Carlo.'

Tolvanin accepted the photographs and looked at them. The first was a picture of Michael Quinn, the second of Robert Elias, both from the Colombian file prepared by Operational Intelligence. He studied them both carefully, then placed them on the table in front of him. The third he held for a longer inspection. It was a picture of Alexandra Sky, taken as she had arrived at the Casino the evening before. 'Perhaps I *could* have come a day earlier,' he said, more to himself than to Brevig. 'Who are they?'

'American agents.'

'CIA?'

'No, Intel-Trace. And they are not to be taken lightly.'

'And the reason for our interest in them?'

'A little over three weeks ago, the Skyco Research Institute in Medellín, Colombia, lost some very valuable property. We know only that it was of a genetic nature and of great value to Skyco. So great, in fact, that Skyco has enlisted the assistance of the Intel-Trace agency to get it back.'

Brevig went on to give him a detailed summary of the events as re-created by Operational Intelligence, describing the attack and air-search efforts known to have

277

taken place, and Michael Quinn's subsequent actions against Cantú and the cocaine lab, including his surprising escape from certain death at the hands of the powerful drug king.

Tolvanin listened attentively, his mood shifting to business as Brevig continued.

'Quinn showed up in Monte Carlo four days ago, with the Sky woman. Her interest in the incident is obvious, but we are not certain why she would be in Monte Carlo,' Brevig explained.

'And the other man?' Tolvanin asked.

'Robert Elias. We know him to be highly placed within Intel-Trace. He is in charge of the operation. He arrived in Monte Carlo this morning, but has not yet made contact with Quinn. Last night, Quinn and the Sky woman went to the Casino, where he was involved in a rather spectacular card game with Vigen Babayan. Quinn is a remarkable gambler. He won a staggering amount of money from Babayan.'

'Babayan is one of the world's richest arms dealers,' Tolvanin remarked, his brain already beginning to make a connection.

'Babayan is either a contact or their quarry,' Brevig added. 'We have begun surveillance of Babayan. He is aboard his yacht, the *Eslabón*, anchored in the Port du Monaco.'

Tolvanin thought for a few moments. 'He is not their contact, unless it is their plan to use him in some way as an agent to help reacquire this genetic material. More likely, they suspect, or have information, that he is involved in some way. This material must have some potential as a weapon. Babayan would not be involved otherwise.'

'We have also just received verification that several of Intel-Trace's personnel observed in Colombia are now in Bern, Switzerland. They are watching another individual, a known Basque terrorist named Juan Strassa, who may have had a part in the theft,' Brevig added.

'It would seem that they have developed good

information,' Tolvanin said. 'Babayan is obviously their strongest lead.'

Tolvanin held up Quinn's picture. 'This is the one to stay with. From what you have told me of him, and from what I expect to find in his dossier, he is their lead agent. He will never be far away from their most important lead. He will take us to this genetic prize. I am certain that they expect it to surface – either for an exchange or a sale. When he moves, we must be prepared to move also. We must stay very close to him. When he gets his chance, he will move quickly. We must be quicker.'

'This flat will be your base of operations while in Monte Carlo. You have a good view of the harbor and Babayan's yacht,' Brevig told him. He slid a piece of paper across the table to Tolvanin. It had a handwritten phone number on it. 'You can reach me here.'

Tolvanin looked at the number, memorized it quickly, then lit a match and ignited the paper. He used the gently flaming paper to light an American cigarette before dropping it into an ashtray.

'Study the Quinn dossier closely,' Brevig said. 'You must not underestimate him. He is a very dangerous adversary.'

This was a warning that Tolvanin did not need. He had not survived twelve years in the field by being careless.

'I assume that Quinn will be my responsibility,' he surmised correctly.

'Yes, but keep a safe distance from him. We do not want him aware of your interest in him. We have sufficient personnel available in Monte Carlo to keep him under close observation. You will receive daily reports of his movements and activities, as well as those of the woman, Elias, and Babayan. You are to avoid engaging any of these people directly until you are told to do so.'

'And if Babayan moves?' Tolvanin said.

'The decision will be made regarding whom to stay with. You will be informed.'

Brevig handed Tolvanin the dossiers that had been prepared in Moscow on Quinn and Elias.

'Are we to expect interference from the KGB?'

'At this time the operation is exclusively ours. But there is no guarantee it will stay that way. They probably know you are here, and are by now already trying to figure out why. If you are too obvious in your interest in Quinn, they may begin putting the facts together. We don't need their interference. We will also be observing *them*. As is often the case, they are to be considered equal adversaries.'

This situation was not new to GRU operations. The KGB and GRU often dealt harshly with one another when the stakes were high enough.

Brevig downed the remainder of his drink in several swallows, and placed the empty glass on the table beside the ashtray. 'You should have enough here to keep you entertained for several hours,' he said, gesturing to the dossiers. 'We'll keep you informed of developments both here and in Bern.'

Brevig walked to the door and looked back just once as he opened it. Tolvanin had already picked up the dossier folders. The briefing had gone smoothly, despite its poor start. His agent had accepted his assignment and the warnings, but that did little to ease Brevig's feeling that Gregor Tolvanin would find his own way of doing things.

The phone rang just as Michael eased the cork out of a bottle of fine Corsican rosé. He put the bottle down on the table and went to answer it, keeping the cork with him, sniffing it as he walked across the room.

'Hello?' he said as he lifted the receiver to his ear.

'Hi, Mike,' the voice at the other end said. It was Bob Elias.

'Hey, I was expecting to hear from you,' he said, turning to see if Alex was in earshot. She was in the kitchen, washing some fruit in the sink. 'What's new on the home front?'

'A few minor developments there, a major one or two here,' came the reply.

'Here? You're in France?' Michael asked, surprised.

'I'm about two minutes away. We need to talk.'

'Sure,' Michael replied, thinking quickly. 'I had better meet you,' he said, lowering his voice.

'I know she's there, Mike,' Elias said. 'That's one of the developments we need to address.'

Alex stepped into the doorway of the kitchen and watched Michael. He had turned away and was facing the windows, listening.

'Yeah, all right. You had better come right over, then. We have to have a plan on how to handle this,' he said into the phone.

'Tell him we've just opened a fresh bottle of wine, and all we need is a friend to share it with. I'll get another glass,' Alex said.

'I heard,' Elias said. He didn't sound overjoyed.

'See you in a couple of minutes,' Michael told him. He wasn't sure what he was hearing in Elias's voice, whether it was disappointment or resignation. In either case, he wasn't pleased.

He hung up the phone and squinted in her direction. She turned and went back into the kitchen. He followed her.

'How did you know that was Bob?'

'I knew his itinerary,' she answered.

'Did he know yours?' Michael asked.

She looked at him sheepishly. 'No, he didn't. Neither did my father. You knew that. But I'm here, and they'll both just have to live with that. Won't they?'

Michael was dealing with Alexandra Sky the executive now. 'I guess they will,' he replied dryly.

He turned and walked out of the kitchen. It was her turn to follow him.

'Michael,' she said, reaching out and touching his shoulder.

He turned to face her. There was no smile on his face.

'I came to Monte Carlo for *you*, not to put myself in the middle of this thing. I know there are things . . . things that you have to do. I won't get in the way, I promise you that. And I won't pull rank, because I don't think I have any in this matter.'

'Alex,' Michael began, holding up his hand to stop her. 'I'm glad you came. I mean that. But I don't know how Bob is going to feel about it. He could send you home, and if that's what he wants to do, you'll have to go. Your safety can't become an issue. And your involvement . . .'

'I'm already involved,' she interrupted.

'With me, yes. With my reason for being here, no,' he corrected her.

'And the Casino? And Babayan?'

'You helped provide some cover. It ends there. From this point on, you're out of it,' he said.

A knock sounded on the door before she could respond.

Michael silenced her with his eyes and went to the door and opened it.

'Don't ask,' Michael said, anticipating Elias's first words. When he turned to walk back into the main room, Alex was gone. She had returned to the kitchen.

Elias walked back into the main room with Michael.

'So, how is Asher Sky taking this latest development?' Michael asked. 'I suppose he's pretty pissed.'

Elias shook his head. 'He's not showing it, if he is,' he answered. 'She's her own woman. She can take care of herself.'

'So much for the feelings of the father. How about yours, boss?'

Elias shrugged. 'I'm not happy about it, professionally. It's an unnecessary complication to work around. But I'm in no position to control her any more than her father can. We've got a job to do, and that's my only concern. What goes on between the two of you is your business, as long as we accomplish what we came here to do. We'll just have to make the best of this situation and go on from here.'

Michael nodded. He felt bad, disappointing Elias as he had. He was torn between what he knew was, professionally, an unwise involvement with Alex and what was happening inside him, beyond his control.

'You implied more than one development here,' Michael said, getting back to professional form. 'What are we looking at?'

'You're being followed. We're *both* being followed. We have been since Colombia.'

'Terrific! Who is it?'

'Intelligence Central has made a few identities. It's the Soviets. GRU, to be exact,' Elias replied.

'Goddamn.'

'They put a UHF tap on our communications in Medellín. I didn't tell you about it because we didn't have any idea who it was at first. That's why we closed down operations in Medellín so quickly and took the act to Bogotá. I was able to scramble our communications from there.'

'How much do they know?'

'I can't really answer that. The fact that they know anything at all is too much, as far as I'm concerned. We haven't confirmed it yet, but they could be on to our operation in Bern, too.'

'Strassa?'

Elias nodded.

'Could they be behind the theft?' Michael asked.

'It's a possibility, I guess. But I don't think so. Strassa isn't one of theirs.'

'What about Babayan? Do you think they're on to him?'

'After your little show in the Casino last night, it's a good bet that they're checking him out. It's a major complication that we don't need.'

Alex peeked her head out of the kitchen. 'Hello, Bob. Is rosé wine OK?' she asked.

Elias smiled. 'Yes, that's fine. Thanks.'

'What are we standing here for? Let's go in where we can be comfortable,' Michael said, leading him the rest of the way into the main room.

Alex came out of the kitchen carrying a tray with the bottle of wine, three glasses, fruit, and some cheese.

Elias remained standing as she approached. 'I'm sorry to barge in on the two of you so unexpectedly,' he apologized.

'Apologies aren't necessary, Bob,' she said graciously. But her eyes revealed a frank expression that said, *You're not sorry. Not one little bit.*

'Please sit,' she continued.

Michael and Elias sat as she filled the glasses with wine. When she finished, she lifted one of the glasses, leaned forward, and kissed Michael on the forehead. 'I know that you have business, so I'll leave you two alone. We'll have time to talk later,' she said with all the poise of a corporate executive exiting a business meeting. She left them and went into the bedroom, closing the door behind her.

'How much does she know?' Elias asked when they were alone.

'She's very observant. She saw me watching Babayan's yacht through the telescope, and found the matchbook with the name of his boat. She must have checked out the yacht through the telescope, and probably saw Babayan on deck. She made the connection the minute she saw him at the table in the Casino. She put it all together from what she had heard at your briefing in San Antonio.'

'It won't hurt us,' Elias said. 'But they'll be watching her, too. We may want to get her out of Monaco as soon as possible.'

'I'm all for that. The sooner the better.'

'By the way, the report I got about that card game last night makes me wish I'd been there to see it,' Elias said.

'I don't know how you managed it. I assume it was the dealer?' Michael asked.

Elias nodded.

'He was incredible. I gave him a fat tip. I hope you don't mind. I left him a stack of chips and told him to find an honest job,' Michael joked.

'After last night, he'll probably have to,' Elias quipped.

'Has anyone made contact with Skyco concerning the Luxus?' Michael asked.

'No, not yet. I had Intelligence Central run a computer simulation of the theoretical reserve hits we talked about with de Roode. His estimates of projected damage were quite accurate. In the wrong hands the Luxus is a weapon of dreadful potential. I'm sure, now, that Babayan's role in this is to sell it.'

'They may want to demonstrate its potential first,' Michael suggested. 'That will get its value up fast.'

'I fear you're right. The advantage is all theirs right now. The only thing we can do is to stick with Babayan. I'm sure he'll move when the time comes to bring the cargo to market. And that brings me to my reason for being here. We think we've found a way to tag Babayan so that we can follow his movements.

'He's a cat lover. He has this remarkable Siamese cat that he takes everywhere with him. You may have seen it during your surveillance of his yacht.'

'I have,' Michael confirmed. 'He carries it around a lot of the time. It's always close to him. I haven't seen him take it off the boat, though.'

'No, but when he leaves the yacht to travel by any other means, he'll take it. He always does.'

Elias opened his attaché case and removed a picture of the cat. He handed it to Michael.

'That's the cat,' he confirmed.

Elias pulled out another picture, an extreme close-up. 'Notice the collar,' he said, handing the picture to Michael.

It showed a fabulous, diamond-studded collar.

'Jesus! There's enough ice there to make an awful lot of women very, very happy,' Michael remarked.

'That's how we'll do it,' Elias said, reaching back into the attaché case and removing an exact duplicate of the collar.

'Are these real?' Michael asked.

'They sure are, and I'm not going to tell you how much it cost to make this little prize. We've matched the stone weights exactly. Our little hook is in the clasp. We've built in a miniaturized homing device just like the one in your watch. We can activate it by radio signal and track it by satellite if we have to. Our problem will be to get it on the cat, and soon.'

The phone rang again, interrupting them. Before Michael could get up to answer it, the ringing stopped. Michael could just barely hear Alex's voice from the bedroom. She had answered it, and seemed to be carrying on a conversation with the caller.

The two men remained silent for a few moments, until it became obvious that the call was not for one of them.

'Babayan has invited Alex and me to have dinner with him aboard his yacht. That should give us the opportunity we'll need, but it's going to be difficult to change that collar without drawing attention. I'm going to have to think about it for a while.'

The naughty look on Elias's face told Michael that he was already a step behind. Then it hit him. Elias had already found an angle. *Alex would be there, too!*

Michael shook his head. 'You don't have to say it. I know what you're thinking, and the answer is no.'

'It could work, Mike. I'm sure you could draw his attention easily enough. There would be nothing unusual about her showing attention to the cat, holding it, petting it. It would only take a few seconds.'

'What if we're not alone with him?' Michael asked. 'He could invite any number of people, or have some security in the room with us. I don't like it.'

'It may be the best and only chance we'll get,' Elias said.

The bedroom door opened, and Alex walked out. 'Your friend has just invited me to breakfast tomorrow morning,' she announced.

'I thought he said dinner at the Casino?' Michael asked.

'Yes, he invited *us* to dinner, but he invited *me* to breakfast . . . alone.'

Elias's eyes went to Michael's. There was an almost urgent plea in them.

Alex stopped beside the low coffee table. She saw the pictures of the cat and recognized it immediately as the one she had seen in Babayan's arms. Then she saw the collar. Her eyes went back to the close-up of the cat . . . and to the collar in the picture.

'You make the call, Mike,' Elias said.

Alex picked up the magnificent collar and examined it, her brain putting the obvious facts together. She looked at Michael, then at Elias.

Michael rose to his feet. 'I don't like this,' he growled.

'I'm a big girl, Michael. I can handle Babayan and his overactive hormones. And if this means what I think it does,' she said, holding out the collar, 'I'm certain I can switch the collar on the cat . . . if you'll let me.'

Elias was impressed by her deductive powers. 'Remind me to offer you a job sometime,' he said, only half-kidding.

Alex went to Michael's side.

'Please, Michael. Let me help you, even in this small way.'

'This is not *small*, Alex. And it's not some kind of game. I want you out of this, as far away as you can get,' he told her.

'You don't think I can do it,' she said to him, her tone challenging.

'No, I think you *can*. But that will put you right in the middle of something that wasn't a part of your MBA training.'

'I'm a woman, and one whom Vigen Babayan finds very attractive. I don't need training for that. It comes naturally.'

'It'll put you right in the middle of things—'

'She's already in the middle, Mike. It doesn't matter what you or I or Alex wants. She was seen with you. It wasn't supposed to be this way, but it is. And we can't change that now,' Elias said, not having to repeat his message about Soviet surveillance.

'I don't want her involved or exposed to danger.'

'I know that, Mike,' Elias returned. 'I don't want her exposed to any unnecessary dangers, any more than you do.'

'They'll treat her no differently than they would me if she's caught.' Michael turned to Alex. 'These are arms dealers and possible terrorists, Alex. They play for keeps.'

'We'll give her the same cover we'd give you, Mike. I can equip her, and have a team ready to take the boat if we have to,' Elias assured him. 'This opportunity is just too good to let pass.'

'Then it's settled,' Alex said.

'Nothing is settled!' Michael snapped, his voice rising to the edge of anger.

'I'm not afraid,' Alex said calmly. 'I have faith in Bob and in you. You must have faith in me that I can do this.'

'I know you can.'

'And I promise you that if the danger looks to be too great, I won't even make an attempt.'

Michael looked into her face. He knew she meant what she said.

'I'll put teams right on the water, Mike,' Elias said, then turned to Alex. 'And you must make me a solemn promise to do exactly as I say. Is that clear?'

'Yes,' Alex answered. 'To the letter and without hesitation,' she added, trying to ease Michael's concern.

'You must stay on deck the entire time you're on that boat. If the cat's not on deck, then you forget that you even have the collar. I want you on deck for two reasons. If we can see you, we can protect you; and as long as you're on deck, you have a way of escape.'

'I understand,' she said.

'If there is any sign of trouble – and I mean *any* sign – you are to go over the side into the water. We'll neutralize anything that moves on the yacht after that. Our cover will be blown anyway, so there's nothing to lose. We'll monitor everything that's said between you and Babayan with long-range directional microphones. If *I* feel for even one second that something is wrong, you'll be alerted. You don't hesitate, you go over the side.'

Elias looked back to Michael. 'I'll blow that damn boat out of the water before I let them hurt her. I promise, Mike.'

Michael still had uncertainty written all over his face. He looked at Alex.

'I'll take no foolish chances,' she promised.

There was a long silence between them.

'I'll still leave it to you, Mike. We can look for another way,' Elias said.

'Are you certain you can protect her once she's in the water?' Michael asked.

'We'll drop everything that moves on the deck of that boat, Mike.'

'And you'll go over the side *without hesitation*,' Michael said to Alex. It was a statement of fact rather than a question.

She nodded. 'Without hesitation,' she confirmed, a sparkle of hope brightening in her eyes.

'I still don't like it,' Michael said, sounding less emphatic. Then he let out a long breath and nodded.

'I'll be back tonight with some special equipment for you,' Elias said to Alex. 'It'll be simple to use. You'll have to contact Babayan to tell him that you accept his invitation.'

Alex raised her glass and took a sip of her wine, a sly smile of satisfaction breaking across her lips. 'I've already told him I would. He's sending his launch to the quay to pick me up at eight.'

The morning was beautiful, the sky cloudless and blue. A gentle breeze moved lazily across the Port du Monaco as Alex stood on the quay watching the launch draw near. She was nervous, but not frightened.

Elias had returned the night before with the special equipment, and had carefully coached her in its use. He had given her a lovely watch with capabilities similar to Michael's. It had a radio-activated alarm that would serve as his way of signaling danger. If it sounded, she was to go over the side of the boat instantly. The watch would also be a backup to the long-range directional microphones that would be listening in the whole time. He had also given her a phosphorus flare pen to use in the event of extreme emergency. She was to discharge it straight down into the deck, then hit the water. It would burn through the deck in seconds and start a major blaze to capture the attention of Babayan and his crew. Elias's shooters would take over from there.

During the night, teams had been put in place on the water in smaller cabin craft anchored around Babayan's yacht, allowing ample coverage of all deck areas. The rest was up to Alex. She had only one task: to replace the collar on the cat with the duplicate.

Michael watched nervously through the telescope as the launch pulled up to the quay and Alex got in. He watched it take her out to the boat, and saw Babayan come to the ladder as she made her way up to the deck.

He could see that a table had already been set on the aft deck. Alex should be able to stay in view without difficulty.

True to form, Babayan was holding the cat in his arms when Alex reached the deck.

'You don't know how pleased I am that you could join me,' Babayan said in greeting.

'Thank you so very much for inviting me,' she replied, extending her hand.

Babayan gently took her hand, and then raised it to his lips and kissed it. He smiled broadly. 'I can feel my luck changing already,' he said, then gestured toward the aft deck.

Alex took a second to stroke the cat's head before turning and walking aft at Babayan's side. 'What a lovely animal. What is its name?' she asked.

'I call her Sasha,' he replied.

'Does she enjoy the water?' Alex asked her host.

'Yes, quite a lot, actually. She gets a bit nervous on the launch at times. But she is quite at home on my *Eslabón*, even with heavy seas.'

'Your yacht is a marvelous vessel,' Alex commented. 'It's no wonder that Sasha feels secure on these wide decks. It's almost like being on land.'

'Perhaps in port, or in calm seas. But the sea can make even the biggest of craft seem insignificant when out of land's sight. Have you ever cruised the Mediterranean?' Babayan asked.

'I have sailed a bit between Marseille and Nice. And I've been on several cruise ships, but not on the Mediterranean,' she replied.

'Well, I insist that you honor me someday by joining me on a cruise. Perhaps very soon. I'm sure you would find it an invigorating experience.'

'Thank you very much. I'm sure it would be enjoyable,' she returned, her eyes inviting the offer.

Babayan put his hand to her elbow to escort her to the waiting table. 'Yes, I think it must be very soon.'

The table was sumptuously set. There was a yellow long-stemmed rose across the plate at her setting.

'How nice. Thank you,' she said with a delicious smile.

Babayan returned the smile and extended an arm to the table. A steward dressed in spotless white pulled back her chair, and she sat. Babayan sat opposite her. He gave a small gesture with his hand, and a tray with hot beverages was brought to the table.

'Would you like coffee, tea, some hot cocoa, perhaps?' Babayan asked

'Coffee, thank you.'

The steward poured her coffee, and tea for Babayan.

'Your friend is very lucky at cards,' the arms dealer said. 'But I think his luck only begins there. How did you meet?'

'We met through a business arrangement, actually. I guess you could say that I chased him down after that. He was easy to catch,' she replied with a pretty smile.

'I don't find that too surprising,' Babayan said with a smile.

A silver platter was brought to the table, covered with a wide assortment of elegantly prepared pastries. A second tray followed shortly, with fruits set beautifully around a small ice sculpture of a swan. There was nothing second-class in the way Babayan did things.

'How wonderful,' Alex commented. 'Were these baked on board?'

'Yes, daily. I have a substantial weakness for pastries. Please help yourself,' her host invited.

Alex selected one of the pastries and some melon wedges. Babayan did the same, his left hand continuing to stroke the cat.

'Do you come to Monte Carlo often?' he asked.

'No, not very. But I do enjoy being here. My father used to bring me when I was young.'

'To me, Monte Carlo is one of the most relaxing places on earth,' Babayan began. 'My business schedule is rather hectic, and I have very little time for relaxation. At least while I'm here, I can leave it all behind. To unwind a bit, so to say. We all need to keep our edge, wouldn't you agree?'

'This certainly is a good way to go about it,' Alex said, letting her eyes play across the luxurious yacht.

'One of life's simpler pleasures,' he said, smiling contentedly.

'You seem to enjoy gambling a great deal,' she said, keeping her remarks open-ended to keep him talking as much as possible.

'Yes, I do. It is a wonderful test of one's self against chance and the courage of other men. And let there be no mistake, courage is an issue when the stakes are high on the gambling table. I enjoy winning – at everything I do,' he said.

When they finished their pastries, the main course was brought out. The artfully garnished presentation included thin slices of Ardennes ham, cheeses, and tempting omelets. Breads and croissants were set on the side in accompaniment.

Babayan picked sparingly at his food, his interest primarily in Alex. He fed small pieces of his omelet to the cat as they spoke.

'Tell me about Vigen Babayan,' Alex said, keeping the one-sided conversation away from herself. She had never identified herself as Alexandra Sky, and Babayan had never acknowledged making the connection. The simpler the conversation at this point, the better, in her opinion.

'There isn't much to tell, really,' he replied. 'I'm a simple merchant who enjoys the sea, the simple pleasures of life, a bit of gambling now and again. I also enjoy the company of a beautiful woman.' He didn't seem any more inclined to expose details about his personal life than she was.

Alex smiled pleasantly at his compliment. 'I doubt that there's anything simple about you,' Alex said.

'All of life is simple if one goes about it the right way.'

'You seem to do that very well.'

Babayan smiled. 'I make it a point to enjoy life these days. It wasn't always so easy to do,' he returned.

'Oh?' Alex responded, raising her eyebrows. 'It sounds like there's a very interesting story behind that remark.'

'There are some who would think so. A topic for another time, perhaps, when we have more time to get to know each other better.'

The cat pawed at the empty fork. Babayan responded with another bit of omelet.

'She certainly seems to enjoy life,' Alex said, thinking it was time to get closer to the animal.

'Yes. My Sasha is terribly spoiled.'

'Do you think she would let me hold her?'

'She does not often like women,' Babayan replied. 'She is a bit possessive, you see.'

'With good cause,' Alex flirted mildly. 'May I try?'

'She may scratch you,' he warned.

'I have been thrown by horses, kicked by bulls, and was once bitten on the behind by a dog. A small scratch won't bother me. Besides, I have some omelet left to tempt her with,' Alex told him. 'May I?'

'Perhaps the omelet will win her,' he said, and rose from his chair. He brought the cat around to the other side of the table and placed it in Alex's lap.

The purring stopped immediately and the cat sat stiffly, its head angled away from Alex, its neck muscles tense and rigid.

Alex's first offer of the omelet was refused, but the cat did not bolt from her lap. It looked up into her face, its eyes wide, its body tense. Babayan remained standing beside her, just in case it became necessary to take the cat away quickly.

The cat moved away a little, prompting Alex to pull back slightly. She was wearing a diamond pendant on a chain that sparkled in the bright sunlight. The cat's eyes went to it immediately. It stared at it as if in a trance.

Alex recognized the cat's interest and pushed the chain a bit with her forefinger. The cat reached up and poked at the pendant playfully a few times. Alex stroked the cat's back gently with her fingertips, then let her hand move up slowly toward the neck. Sasha didn't seem to object, so she continued stroking the animal gently, letting her hand move up toward the head. The cat pressed its neck into her fingers to accept the gentle caresses.

'Yes, pretty baby,' Alex whispered soothingly. 'You like that, don't you?'

Alex tried the omelet again with her free hand, and this time the cat took the bribe, the little motor in its throat starting a soft purring.

Babayan petted the cat and moved away slowly.

'I think it'll work,' he said, taking his seat once again.

The cat settled comfortably in Alex's lap, its interest now in the petting and the scraps of food on the plate. The purring grew louder.

'It seems I have a new friend,' Alex said softly.

'I'm impressed,' Babayan said. 'Sasha is a very good judge of character.'

'Animals often are. Even better than people.'

'A very good sign, I think,' Babayan said.

Elias's teams watched and listened carefully, ready to act in a moment. But their response wasn't needed.

The breakfast conversation went on in the same casual way, Babayan describing the many wonderful places to visit on the Mediterranean, hoping to improve his chances of her accepting his cruise offer. Both he and the cat grew more comfortable with their beautiful guest by the minute. A half hour passed before the steward cleared away the dishes. Babayan lit up a long cigar and talked some more about the many ports he had visited in the Mediterranean. Alex showed great interest, asking questions about the places she had never seen. She had him doing all of the talking now, and that was just fine.

The cat had by now grown quite used to her, and was nearly asleep in her lap.

Alex's fingers found the clasp to the collar. Elias had made her rehearse the operation of removing it over and over again in the villa the night before after returning with her special equipment. The replacement collar was in the loose, billowing sleeve of her blouse, held securely by the elastic cuff.

There were two other crew members on deck, but their interest was on minor chores, and not on her and Babayan. The steward was below decks, preparing fresh hot beverages.

'Would you have a shawl?' Alex asked. 'It's a bit cooler on the water than I had expected.'

'Certainly,' Babayan said, and turned to summon the steward, then remembered that he was below. 'Will you excuse me for just one moment?' he asked politely.

'Of course,' Alex replied.

Babayan rose from his chair and went into the main cabin.

Alex moved swiftly, her fingers performing the practiced task with quick ease. The collar was off in an instant. The substitute was out and on the cat only a moment later, so smoothly that even Elias's watchers couldn't recognize the movements. The original collar went into the sleeve easily and well before Babayan returned with the shawl.

He placed it around her shoulders, his mind not remotely on the cat or its collar.

Alex thanked him, and he returned to his chair.

'When will you be leaving port to continue your cruise?' she asked him.

'In one week. But first I hope to win back some of the money your friend won from me.'

'That won't be easy. Michael is a very lucky man in almost everything that he does.'

'You don't have to tell me, I can assure you. I was a

295

victim of his luck. But I think that perhaps it is you who brings him his luck. Will you be accompanying him to the Casino again?'

'Oh, yes. But probably just one more time. I plan to leave Monte Carlo in a few days to continue on to Corsica for a few weeks,' she said.

'What awaits you in Corsica?' Babayan asked, sensing opportunity on the horizon.

'Just a quiet time and relaxation,' she replied, knowing full well her destination would be elsewhere.

'And Michael will be joining you there?'

'No, he has business back in the United States.'

'It is such a pity that you cannot stay on in Monte Carlo for a while longer. I am certain my luck would change if you were to be at *my* side at the Casino. Can I not find some way to convince you?'

Alex smiled and looked down into her lap. She didn't say no.

'Perhaps afterward you could join me for a short cruise on the Mediterranean, instead of going on to Corsica. I'm certain it would be a great deal more . . . interesting. You don't have to say yes now,' he said quickly, before she could refuse him. 'Think about it for a few days, then decide. I would be only too glad to cut short my own stay in Monte Carlo to show you some of the wonderful places we have discussed. Would you consider that?'

She remained silent, as though contemplating the offer.

'Will you at least agree to think about it?' he asked hopefully.

'Thank you for your very generous offer. It does sound interesting. I promise to think it over very carefully,' she told him.

A smile of satisfaction broke across Babayan's face. 'Would you like a tour of the yacht? he asked anxiously, ready to jump up from his chair.

'Thank you, but I think I should be leaving now,' she replied, remembering Elias's instructions to stay on deck at all times. 'Perhaps another time . . . very soon.'

'This evening?' Babayan invited, trying not to sound overly anxious.

'I *do* wish that I could, but I have already made plans with Michael. They would be difficult to break.'

'I understand completely,' Babayan said, disappointment clearly evident in his voice.

'It will be soon, I promise,' Alex told him, a bit of teasing in her voice.

'I will keep myself available as your guide. May I call you tomorrow?' he asked.

'I'd like that,' she replied, baiting his interest, then looked at her watch. 'I'm afraid I really must go now,' she said, sounding sorry that their time together had ended so soon.

Babayan rose from his chair and went around to the other side of the table and guided her chair back as she got to her feet.

The cat stretched, and Babayan took it from her. As Alex began to remove the shawl, the collar fell to the deck. She looked down, and her heart almost stopped. Her hand went instinctively to her sleeve, only to find the real collar still in place. Her heart pounded in her chest.

Babayan bent down and picked up the collar. He examined it closely for a few moments, then reattached it to the cat's neck.

'That's very beautiful,' Alex said, her face flushed from the fright. 'I was afraid for a moment that it might fall overboard.'

'For a flash of an instant, I thought the same thing,' Babayan said. 'Yes, it is beautiful, and expensive. Naughty, Sasha,' he teased, caressing the cat. 'I love beautiful things,' he said, meeting her eyes squarely.

Alex once again began to remove the shawl.

'Please keep it. The launch ride to the quay will be cool. You can return it when you visit me again,' Babayan told her, confident that it would be soon.

'Then I will certainly have to come back,' she said, fueling his hopes.

297

Babayan took her by the arm to escort her to the stairway where the launch was already warming up. They stopped at the rail.

Alex pulled the arm away smoothly, fearing that he might feel the collar inside her sleeve.

'Thank you for a wonderfully delightful morning,' Alex said, turning to face him and putting some distance between him and the sleeve.

Babayan let his hand fall to her waist. 'Until later, then. I shall count the minutes.'

Alex put her hand on his shoulder and kissed him softly on the lips. It was a short kiss, her lips barely brushing his. 'Until later,' she teased. Then she started down the stairway.

She looked up at him as the launch pulled slowly away, her beautiful smile torturing him.

As Babayan watched the launch depart, he wasn't thinking about the money he had lost to Michael, or about the prospect of getting it back. If that was the price he had to pay for the chance to meet this lovely creature who had so completely captured him, then it was one he would gladly pay. He had a very confident feeling that she would be returning soon, and that the prize would be well worth the price.

20

She was the largest moving thing built by man. The *Skyco Hippalus* was a 1,250,000-ton Ultra-Large Crude Carrier (ULCC)-class tanker. The ULCC designation pertained to anything over 400,000 tons. The *Skyco Hippalus* was the first tanker of a new class that should more properly have been called a Mega-Class Crude Carrier (MCCC). But the terminology had never been formally adopted.

The first VLCCs (Very Large Crude Carriers) revolution-ized oil transport; they presented staggering potential, sur-passing even the greatest passenger liners in size. They established the belief that big was good, and embodied the concept that bigger was even better. Then, when the first ULCCs were launched, a new merchant marine era began that helped to feed the unprecedented world demand for oil. The demand never lessened, and ways were sought to move even greater quantities, resulting in bold experi-ments with Mega-Class Crude Carriers. If the ULCCs had dwarfed the great passenger liners of the sea, the MCCCs would make them seem insignificant. Man had finally built the colossus of his dreams to challenge the mighty forces of the sea, or at least so he thought. The *Skyco Hippalus* was so large that she provided a sense of conquest by size alone.

She had loaded full at Mina al-Ahmadi, at an offshore pipeline terminal. After being carefully maneuvered out by a harbor pilot, the *Skyco Hippalus* slipped past the Quoins at the Strait of Hormuz, the entrance to the Gulf, and around Ra's al Hadd, the cape at the southernmost coast of the Arabian peninsula. Ra's al Hadd was a sea corner, a natural divide of geography separating one exotic realm of sea environment from another. On the trip out, one passed from a region of sweaty, humid calm into a rolling, turbulent sea.

The *Skyco Hippalus* pushed on down the east coast of Africa, surfing along the backs of large waves with the northwestern monsoon at her back.

The precision of the monsoons is a phenomenon of nature. From April through September they blow from the southwest, then shift abruptly a full 180 degrees between October and March to blow from the northeast, providing swift passage for the wind-driven vessels of old. Today's great ships pass in either direction powered by mechanical means, regardless of the direction of these trade winds. There are, of course, great advantages of fuel savings and more rapid passage to be gained by sailing with them when-ever possible.

Today's super tankers are smartly appointed and luxurious compared to the small, austerely designed tankers of the pre-fifties era. This is largely because the new behemoths of the sea never put into port; they are too large and too deep-drafted. Too expensive to be kept idle for even short periods of time, they must be at sea for at least 340 days a year to remain profitable. To the ships and their crews, the seasons are merely different states of water – winter and summer seas, all in the same voyage. There are none of the shore memories that were once part of the glamor and attraction of merchant marine service in days gone by. Everything needed is provided on board, with supplies and mail flown out by helicopter or taken out by launch when the ships are close enough to land. The typical duty for crewmen is five to six months at sea without ever setting foot on land. The ship is everything to the crew – home, mother, and wife.

The deck and engineering officers of the *Skyco Hippalus* were British. The crew comprised a mixture of Pakistanis, Indians, and Chinese. Though American-owned, she was registered under the Liberian flag of convenience. This was because US regulations stated that ships of US registry must be built in the United States and manned by no less than three-quarters American crews. No construction site in the States was large enough to build her or deep enough to float her. She had been built in Japan. Without flags of convenience, the American merchant fleet would vanish because of costs and lack of deep-water ports. A full forty per cent of Liberian tonnage is US-owned, with even more being US-financed. Of the world tanker fleet, thirty-five per cent is owned by Big Oil, the rest chartered. It is good business to lease the mighty vessels and let independents move the oil, freeing capital, especially when slack times roll in and some tankers go unprofitably idle. Skyco alone owned or chartered five per cent of the world fleet. It was also a major leaser of ships, which required a keen instinct and a quick eye for opportunity. Tankers represent staggering profit potential, making supertankers one of the most remarkable investment opportunities in the history of world commerce.

As ships go, the *Skyco Hippalus* was an awe-inspiring specimen. She was 1,890 feet long and 282 feet wide, and drafted 104 feet when fully loaded. She had seven main tanks for oil and fourteen smaller tanks for ballast, which were adjusted to compensate for sea conditions.

One experiences a different perspective when viewing a supertanker as opposed to a giant liner. The liners climb high into the sky, most of the decks being above water level. The tanker is more like an iceberg, eighty per cent of it being submerged. Even with so much of the *Skyco Hippalus* hidden from sight, the greatest liner seems like a lifeboat when seen together with her.

Looking out from her bridge deck, one saw a great, seemingly endless acreage of red-painted steel with a raised catwalk amidships that disappeared into the distance over a quarter of a mile away toward her mighty bows.

The great tankers of today are built on what is called the Isherwood Longitudinal System, the reverse of the older, prewar vertical-strength concept. The ship is designed along horizontal lines, allowing long, flexible hulls capable of sitting deep in the water and holding great weight. They are, in theory, capable of riding through and beneath great waves, their design giving them excellent hydrodynamics, requiring less propulsion. The limiting strains of their fabric are constantly being put to the test against the forces of the sea in what amounts to battle without quarter – victory or death. They are wonders of technology, awesome tributes to man's achievement – and maybe his folly as well. Within their hulls they carry as much potential thermal energy as a large nuclear weapon, as well as the power to choke life from the very oceans they sail, should their cargoes be spilled, through misadventure or negligence, into the earth's greatest life-support system. A tanker the size of the *Skyco Hippalus* could spill in one place what all the rest of the world's tankers do in a normal year, a slick so large and menacing that it would challenge the imagination to estimate its impact on the ecology of the sea.

The *Skyco Hippalus* pushed southward along the African coast through strong seas crashing like thunder against her sides. She was a great vessel, but was subject to the flaws of economy, having but a single boiler system upon which the ship was totally dependent. She was quite literally at the mercy of her propulsion system, despite the ultrasophistication of her computerized control systems.

As tankers grew larger and their costs higher, economies were achieved by cutbacks in other areas – boilers, for instance. Today's ocean liners contain many boilers, with completely independent auxiliary systems in the event of boiler failure. It is an unwritten rule of ship design to build in backup systems, and then still more backup systems, and this is perhaps the single costliest part of building any ship. When ships the size of the supertankers came into being, cost relationships were bent as far out of proportion as the sizes of these new vessels. Cutbacks had to be made, and since *size* was the objective of the new class of tanker, savings had to come from somewhere else. So instead of many boilers with multiple backup systems, they put in single systems of new high-pressure design and *hoped* they would last the ten years of maximum-profit life expectancy before being sold off, after which the problem of boiler failure was someone else's concern.

To ease conscience a bit, they had included a single auxiliary diesel-driven boiler for emergencies. But the powering capabilities of these backup boilers were nearly a joke. At best, such a boiler was just strong enough to give the ship headway in fine weather. The only piece of equipment that would work, besides nominal computer navigational systems, was the steering wheel.

The way boiler systems were designed, complete shutdown followed almost any problem. When the ship's diagnostic systems detected trouble in the boiler system, they shut it down. This in turn tripped the main engine.

When the boiler tripped, the fires went out, so that there was no more steam generation. The remaining steam was used for alternators to give additional running time and electrical power – maybe twenty minutes' worth – then it was blackout time. And complete blackout was the worst thing that could happen to a tanker, even in calm seas. She would remain that way until the ship's engineers could find the trouble and repair it completely. Once repaired, the boiler could be 'flashed' back to life and the normal operations of the ship resumed.

The *Skyco Hippalus* experienced one such scare off the eastern coast of Africa, in the Mozambique Channel, when her boilers shut down due to seawater contamination of the highly pure fresh-water steam system. She was forced to limp for two days under her auxiliary diesel boiler system while the source of the contamination was located and repaired. Then her boilers were flashed and she was again on her way. The delay had put her slightly behind schedule. But, more important, it had put her on course for a confrontation with severe gales, which she might have missed otherwise.

She first met the edge of the storm at the Agulhas Plateau as she began rounding the tip of South Africa, heading for the Cape of Good Hope and the most treacherous waters on earth.

It was as she rounded the Cape, battling through fierce rollers, that she met the storm head-on. The fierce westerlies had conjured up angry seas well in excess of even the usual sixty-foot wave height.

The *Skyco Hippalus* had ridden rough seas before, and though a storm of this magnitude was reason for concern, there was no panic in her captain and bridge officers – until the sound of the boiler alarm pierced across the bridge.

The diagnostics systems indicated that the fans had stopped. The computerized fault-analysis system raced to find the cause, but without success. It could not detect that a tiny rubber diaphragm in a reducing valve had split, causing a brief dip in air pressure across the drafting fans.

The drop in pressure was significant enough to set off the automatic signal to the boiler that the fans had stopped, when in fact they hadn't. The emergency response was automatic. The boilers shut down and the fires went out before the engineers could physically check for the fault. The diesel kicked in automatically with the failure, but in the heavy seas its effect was inconsequential, providing the vessel with only nominal power.

The *Skyco Hippalus* became helpless on the water, relying upon her structural strength to hold against the battering effects of the angry sea. Her captain, with thirty years of experience, watched helplessly as the storm grew in fury, throwing nearly hundred-foot-high waves against her bows. Then a second alarm sounded. The diesel had suffered a fuel-line break and had been shut down by the same automatic systems that were making her a victim of the sea.

The great ship was being carried now only by the momentum of her size. But that, too, faded against the forces of the sea, and she fell still, totally at the mercy of the storm.

The remaining steam in her system kept the electrical power alive for perhaps thirty minutes. Her bridge crew watched as the digital electronic readouts flickered to zero, then went out. The radar screens went out one by one, their scanners receding to pinpoints of light, then complete darkness. It was like watching death claim the mighty vessel one piece at a time, from the outermost extremities first, until it stopped the brain . . . and then the heart.

The captain gripped the arms of his chair, his eyes locking on to an approaching wave of indescribable dimensions. The water below the forward half of the ship seemed to be sucked back into the wave, creating an enormous trough. The bow fell forward into the trough, and continued falling to almost thirty degrees. Then the wave smashed the mighty vessel amidships with all of its force. The *Skyco Hippalus* flexed and seemed to twist, a groan like a scream coming from her as she cracked.

The *hoot-hoot-hoot-hoot* of the ship's emergency alarm system was instantaneous. It was the last electrical system remaining in operation, besides the radio, both fed by reserve battery power. Then the starboard ballast tanks split, affecting her pliability.

A second wave of even greater dimensions mounted before her and drew an even deeper trough. The *Skyco Hippalus* dipped forward beyond thirty degrees to almost forty, as though baring her throat to a mighty predator. The wave pounded home, sending a wrenching shudder vibrating through the length of the tanker. The force of the mighty wave had gone beyond the ship's design parameters, far exceeding all limits of permissible stress. The fracture caused by the first wave widened with the impact of the second, and the *Skyco Hippalus* cracked nearly in two. She twisted in the ocean's fury like a jack-knifed truck trailer, her cargo tanks splitting.

The SOS signal went out, locked on automatic transmission, as the crew members who were not lost already scurried against the storm for the podlike enclosed lifeboats. The air filled with a horrible stench, nearly choking off all breathable air.

The ship reeled in the face of another wave and separated into two parts. On the bridge deck, her officers abandoned their stations at their captain's command. But the captain remained behind, playing the thin hope that the aft section of the ship would hold against the storm. Stranger things had happened at sea. Ships broken in two had even been brought into port and completed a voyage. The captain himself had even brought one in that had been cut in two by a collision. But the vision he saw through the thick plate windows told him that it would not be so on this occasion. A wave larger than any others approached, sucking a deadly chasm before it. Without the front half of the vessel to counterbalance its stern, the remaining half tipped forward to sixty degrees. The monstrous wave slammed down upon her, crushing the bridge deck like an empty aluminum can. And the *Skyco Hippalus* disappeared forever.

SAN ANTONIO, TEXAS: The air was electric in the hillcountry estate of Asher Sky. The Sunday morning news broadcasts were full of early reports of the sinking of the *Skyco Hippalus*. The phones had been ringing constantly, and reporters were everywhere trying to get into the estate for a statement on the disaster.

Sky walked swiftly into the private study just off his office, leaving an angry trail of cigar smoke in his wake. His hands were full of telegrams and fax reports, charts and maps of the South Atlantic, and a half-dozen front pages of leading newspapers.

Tom Danziger walked in just behind him, carrying more of the same. Dr de Roode was already in the study. More charts and maps had been spread out on the conference table.

'It's been confirmed, ' Sky announced. 'She was lost last night in a violent gale off the Cape of Good Hope.'

'My God!' de Roode exclaimed, and nearly fell back into the chair behind him. It was all he could say in the face of confirmation of the largest single disaster in maritime history.

'A Soviet tanker has picked up survivors,' Sky told them.

'How many?' de Roode asked.

'Ten. Three lifeboats were recovered. It must have been horrible for those poor men. Eight others were found dead in the boats. A fourth lifeboat was also found, but all aboard were dead.'

'Four lifeboats out of ten. Ten men out of a crew of thirty-nine. There were no others?' de Roode asked.

Sky shook his head.

'The Soviet ship made a gallant effort to rescue the crew. She crossed legal lane restrictions in the height of the storm to offer assistance. The wind was abating when she arrived, but they could locate no other traces of our ship, except the lifeboats,' Danziger added.

'The survivors are safely on board the Russian vessel now, getting medical attention. The Soviet ship is steaming toward Cape Town, where she will be met by South African helicopters to lift out those with no serious injuries,' Danziger explained.

'There is limited news from the crew. The first officer was one of the survivors. According to his report, the captain was last seen on the bridge just moments before the ship was crushed by a wave of demonic proportions. She was simply gone after that.'

Sky put his papers on the table. 'He reported that the tanker broke in two about five minutes before going down. She had lost all power due to boiler failure in the height of the storm. She never had a chance.

'The winds are down, and an air search has begun. The seas are still high, and there have been no further sightings of survivors. Some small traces of wreckage have been sighted.'

'How big is the slick?' de Roode asked, almost afraid of the reply.

Sky looked at his chief scientist with an expression of awful boding. 'There is no slick,' he answered, his words slow and deliberate.

'*No slick?*'

'None. Not a trace.'

'But you said the tanker had broken in two.'

'That's right. Clean in half.'

'A tanker of that size *can't* break in two without leaving a spill. A very, very large one,' de Roode said, clearing his throat.

Sky just stared at him.

'Is it possible that her tanks held intact when she broke?' de Roode asked, implying hopefully that her cargo had gone down with her.

'No. That's not a possibility,' Sky replied. 'Some of her tanks could have remained intact, taking their loads down with her. But at the very least, two of her tanks would have split wide open. More probably, four would have been breached.'

'The heavy seas could have dispersed the spill,' de Roode tried, offering a lame explanation.

'If she had broken amidships, half a million tons of crude would have spilled into the sea. No storm could disperse that much oil without a trace,' Sky said, dashing his hopes.

'The survivors' reports clearly indicate the ship had been severely battered and had cracked before being broken in two. She floundered afterward, taking additional damage. It's unlikely that only four of her tanks would have breached,' Danziger added. 'There were also reports of a terrible smell after the ship cracked open.'

The scientist rose slowly to his feet, his face suddenly pale and his expression tense. 'What kind of smell?' he asked.

'The reports were vague. They referred to a choking, putrid smell that made it hard to breathe.'

'Could it be?' de Roode asked, looking at Sky, his voice trembling on the edge of fear.

In that one moment the implication became clear.

'But how?' Sky asked.

'Never mind *how*!' the scientist said excitedly. 'Look at the facts. The largest tanker ever built by man flounders, is broken, and sinks. Yet there's not a trace of a spill. We're talking about the largest single spill ever known, possibly in excess of one million tons of crude. It would create a slick a hundred miles long, and miles wide. No storm could disperse a slick of those dimensions. And the *smell*. The smell of digestion. It *has* to be. There can be no other explanation.'

Danziger's face fell with another realization. 'And the Soviets right smack in the middle of it. It *would* have to be one of their ships involved in the rescue. You can bet *they're* wondering why there's no slick. And so will every other government in the world.'

'How many tankers do we have in the general area?' Sky asked.

Danziger dug into a pile of papers, leafing through them quickly.

'The two nearest are the *Skyco Argus* and the *Skyco Angelina*. The *Argus* is a five-hundred-seventy-five-thousand tonner, and the *Angelina* is a four-hundred-thousand tonner,' he replied.

Sky thought for a moment, wrestling with a painful decision.

'Get the *Argus* into the area and instruct her to release her cargo. We need a slick. A big one.'

'That's a violation of international law,' de Roode objected. 'How can we justify the environmental damage a slick of that magnitude will cause?'

'Survival!' Sky shouted, slamming his fist on the table. 'I don't like the thought of what that crude will do any more than you do, damn it! There's a great deal more at stake here than a moral issue. *We* are responsible for that organism. The damage it can do is far more frightening than a nasty slick. Every tanker in that area will use the *Hippalus* as cover to spill into the sea, every dirty tank will be cleaned at our expense, and all fingers will point to us as the cause.'

'We're not thinking clearly here,' de Roode said. 'We can't do this.'

'We can, and we *will*. Do you think for one minute the insurance companies involved are going to pay against a fully loaded tanker going down without leaving a slick the size of a football field? It stinks of insurance fraud, not to mention the real problem of the Luxus.'

'We're not going to fool anyone. We'll still have to explain the cargo aboard the *Argus*,' de Roode argued.

'Maybe we won't fool anyone, but we can buy time. And we *need* time. We *need* a slick. We have to try. Lay the slick,' Sky said with finality. 'I'd rather take the heat for a few damaged seagulls than know that I started a new world war.'

MOSCOW: General Aleksandr Kozlov had given up on the tea. The samovar was now filled with the strong Turkish coffee that he loved so much. He walked back to the conference table in his office, balancing the cup and saucer carefully so as not to spill a precious drop of the deep black brew.

'A giant tanker sinks, and there is no slick. Why, Nikolai?' Kozlov asked his First Deputy as he settled into his chair.

Barchenkin didn't answer.

'There is no doubt that the *Skyco Hippalus* broke apart. Her crew has confirmed that. They also tell of a terrible smell. What can it mean?' Kozlov went on, as though talking to himself.

He paused to relight his ever-present pipe, his brain pressing on the strange facts as clouds of smoke erupted into the air above him.

'This will be in every hot stack of intelligence reports in Moscow. We have lost our advantage. We must now use what is known so that we can move before the KGB can make up too much ground.'

'Do you believe that this is connected to events in Colombia?' Barchenkin asked.

'My instincts say yes, Nikolai.'

'In what way?'

'Review briefly what is known. The Skyco Research Institute in Colombia was attacked. A genetic strain of some kind was lost. Vigen Babayan, one of the world's largest arms dealers, a purveyor of sophisticated weapons, is discovered to be tied to it in some way. We may wonder, why is he involved? To *sell* what has been taken. Again, why? Because, Nikolai, it is a *weapon*. What kind of weapon?'

Kozlov thought in deep silence for a moment before going on.

'Perhaps the worst kind.'

'Are you suggesting that the missing organism is involved in the *Skyco Hippalus* incident?' Barchenkin questioned.

'That *smell*, Nikolai. And the fact that no trace of a slick can be found by even the closest satellite reconnaissance says that it just may be.'

'But why?'

'Perhaps to demonstrate its potential.'

'But the storm couldn't have been planned, General,' Barchenkin countered mildly.

'No, the storm could not. But the *Skyco Hippalus* was fully loaded at Mina al-Ahmadi, and was bound for Rotterdam. If the storm had not broken and sunk her, she would have arrived at her destination a victim of this missing weapon. An example for the world to see. A clear demonstration of its power – proof of its *value*.

'We have a very serious problem, Nikolai. If I am right, this weapon is a dreadful thing. It must not be allowed to get into the wrong hands, or the world as we know it may face a threat so great that it may not survive its use.

'I want the Science Directorate to perform a computer analysis projecting use of an organism capable of destroying oil reserves. Two scenarios are to be created. The first must postulate a major power using it as a direct threat against the Soviet Union; the second must show what would happen if a major terrorist organization were to use it against the world at large. The danger to us must be carefully analyzed.'

'I will start immediately, General,' Barchenkin returned.

'The Committee will ask questions. We must have answers.'

'This organism must work with incredible speed,' Barchenkin said. 'The *Skyco Hippalus* was loaded to capacity with over a million tons of crude just two and a half weeks ago.'

'*One million two hundred fifty thousand tons*, Nikolai. And not a drop left to float upon the sea.'

21

MONACO: Michael opened the door to the villa, half expecting Bob Elias to come flying in, from the way his voice had sounded over the phone. He wasn't far off. Elias rushed past him, his arms filled with maps and charts, a pencil stuck between his teeth, and a pocket calculator open in his hand.

'Jesus, what the hell is going on?' Michael asked as he closed the door behind him.

'One of Skyco's tankers was lost last night off the Cape of Good Hope,' Elias responded as he strode across the room to the table. 'We think it was a *hit*.' He dropped the load in his arms on the table and began opening one of the rolled charts.

'What do you mean, "a hit"?' Michael asked.

Elias looked up, then around the room. 'Where's Alex?'

'She just stepped into the shower. What's going on?'

'Last night the *Skyco Hippalus* was sunk in a violent storm. The ship broke up before she went down. She was a *big* tanker, Mike. A million-and-a-quarter tonner.'

'Was she full?'

'She was when she left Mina al-Ahmadi about two and a half weeks ago. She busted wide open, Mike, and she didn't leave a slick big enough to oil a bicycle chain.'

'The Luxus?' Michael asked, his voice rising in dreaded anticipation.

'That's the bet. The survivors have all described a vile smell that became overwhelming just after she broke open.'

'That would be about right,' Michael said, taking a seat opposite Elias, who by now was plotting a reverse course from the Cape back to the Gulf, and punching numbers into the calculator.

'Two and a half weeks,' Michael said to himself, his mind counting backwards in time. 'That would be about the time Wadelaw and I were leaving Medellín for

312

Bogotá. Cantú had said that the strain had been moved out of the country within forty-eight hours after he got his hands on it. It would be very close, but it could fit.'

'That's what all the numbers say, too,' Elias commented, beginning to plot the course from the site of the sinking to Rotterdam. 'The tanker was, at the most, three weeks out from her destination, assuming that she didn't experience any more boiler problems.'

'She had encountered boiler problems?'

'Yes, twice. Once in the Mozambique Channel, then again at the Cape, in the height of the storm. It was that last problem that killed her. The Skyco experts feel she would have made it through the storm, had she not lost power. She most likely would have sustained some damage, but she would have made it through. Intelligence Central has run a quick study on her designs, and concurs with their conclusions.'

'OK, let's assume she made it through with no more boiler problems. What was the object of the hit?'

'To set the table for the sale,' Elias replied. 'Proof that the Luxus was in their possession. A demonstration, perhaps, of its capabilities.'

'That means a communication of some kind would have to have been made at about the same time the tanker reached her destination,' Michael surmised.

'That should be correct.'

'The disaster will advance the schedule,' Michael reasoned. 'Babayan will move, and quickly, almost any time now.'

'*If* they decide to push the schedule up. They may not be prepared to move this quickly,' Elias cautioned. 'Babayan will be the key. It would be helpful if we could get some idea of his plans.'

'How do we manage that?'

'He may still invite you and Alex to dinner if he's not planning to leave within the next few days. You may be able to learn something.'

'And if he doesn't extend the invitation?' Michael asked.

Elias didn't answer right away. He had that look in his eye again.

'I'm sure Alex could get back on the yacht in a minute,' he said.

Michael's face grew taut.

'Babayan has even offered to take her on the cruise with him when he leaves Monaco.'

'*Very* bad idea. She's taken enough risks for us already,' Michael objected.

'I agree with you completely, Mike. And I don't like having to mention the possibility. But it might be all we'll get to work with. Anyway, it's not really our decision to make. Only she can do that.'

Michael shook his head slowly. 'You won't be able to protect her at sea. She'll be on her own. She's not a trained agent, Bob. The danger would be too great.'

Elias said nothing. He just looked at Michael, letting the facts carry his argument.

'We have the collar on the cat. We'll know his whereabouts,' Michael said to him.

'That's true – as long as he and the cat remain together. But it's not the same as having an agent on board with him.'

'Damn it! She's *not* an agent,' Michael shot back.

Just then the door to the bathroom opened and Alex took a step out with a towel around her neck – it was all that she had on. 'Oops! Sorry,' she said, backing up quickly, closing the door behind her.

A few seconds later the door opened again and she came out, with the towel wrapped around her this time. 'Hello, Bob. I didn't know you were here,' she said, her face pink from embarrassment.

She didn't wait for a reply, walking swiftly into the bedroom.

'I know it's not fair of me to ask, Mike,' Elias said. 'We just may not have anything better. Besides, he may not even ask her to join him.'

'I think he will,' Michael returned, his voice almost a whisper, his eyes on the bedroom door.

'We can't wait until he does to make our decision. *If* he asks, we must be prepared to take advantage of the opportunity – or to let it pass. Either way, we'll have to make our plans now. It's still your call,' Elias told him.

Michael felt his stomach tighten as he looked at Elias. He felt as if he were in a cage just large enough to hold him without any room to move. He knew that if he asked, she would say yes – and if he didn't, they'd lose a valuable opportunity. *This job would be easy if I had only myself to worry about*, he thought. But this time he would have to rely on luck.

Babayan called that evening. He explained that he was planning to take the yacht into the Mediterranean for a day of cruising, and asked if Alex would like to join him. Perhaps, he said, it would give her a small taste of cruising aboard the *Eslabón*. She could then think over his offer to join him on the cruise when he left port in eight days. He did not mention what his destination would be.

Elias was listening in on an extension. He nodded to Alex to accept the offer. Michael sat silently in a chair, watching.

'I think that would be very nice,' Alex said. 'What should I bring?'

'You need only bring yourself,' Babayan replied. 'The weather is supposed to be lovely and the seas calm. I have everything from bathing suits to suntan lotion. Just bring your lovely smile and a good appetite. You can plan on returning in the late afternoon. I will be going to the Casino in the evening.'

'What time will we be leaving?' she asked.

'The launch will come for you at eight. We can breakfast at sea,' Babayan replied.

'I'll be ready. Thank you so much.'

Alex hung up the phone. 'He plans on leaving port in eight days,' she said to Michael. 'He'll be returning to the Casino tomorrow evening.'

'Do I play again?' Michael asked Elias.

315

'Not tomorrow. He's too anxious to get his money back. Give him a few more days to stew over it. We still want to get that invitation to dinner. As long as you're holding his money, he'll have reason enough for wanting to see you,' Elias answered.

'Well, at least we have a better feeling for their timing,' Michael said, not quite so nervous now with the knowledge that Babayan wouldn't be leaving for another week. The danger to Alex would be greatly reduced.

'You must try to find out where he intends to go when he leaves Monaco,' Elias instructed Alex. 'The length of the cruise, the number and locations of the ports, that sort of information. As long as it appears that you are seriously contemplating joining him, it won't seem unnatural for you to ask. Try not to seem too obvious about it. I think he may even volunteer the information if he feels strongly enough that you'll join him.'

'Will you be able to hear our conversations?' Alex asked.

'Yes, your watch, set to the date mode, will act as a transmitter. From what he has planned, I doubt that you'll be in any danger. You may want to play up a bit. I think you can handle that.'

Alex smiled in a way that left little doubt of this.

'If he talks about the Casino, tell him that Mike is very anxious to play with him again. As for the rest of it, just enjoy the cruise. You'll never be far enough away that we can't get to you in a few minutes by helicopter. Any questions?'

There were none.

Elias looked to Michael and nodded confidently that he'd made the right decision. 'Wadelaw will be arriving tonight,' he said. 'Just for a little added insurance.'

Michael smiled and felt a little easier. But just a little.

The morning air was cool. Alex shivered and adjusted the shawl that Babayan had given her. The sky was slightly overcast, but the forecast was for an early-morning clearing followed by beautiful weather. She watched the launch as it approached, exactly on time.

She was assisted from the quay, and the launch headed for the boat.

Michael watched through the telescope. 'He's not on deck,' he said to Elias.

Elias walked over to the window, raised a pair of powerful binoculars, and swung them toward the stern of the yacht. The table was not set, either. It wasn't cause for alarm, however, as Babayan had specifically said they would breakfast at sea. As for his not being on deck, he would probably step out into the brief chill when the launch drew nearer. The signal from the cat's collar, when last checked only minutes before, had indicated that it was belowdecks at about amidships.

The launch pulled alongside the *Eslabón*. One of Babayan's crew descended the ladder to escort Alex to the main deck. She could feel a subtle vibration on the deck from the *Eslabón*'s engines as she stepped on to it. She looked about quickly for Babayan, but he was not in sight.

'This way, please,' said the steward who had served their breakfast the other morning. 'It will be a little warmer inside until the sun burns away the cloud cover.'

Alex followed him as they walked astern, then into the main cabin. She was almost stopped by the elegance and beauty of the decor. The main cabin was very large, thickly carpeted, its walls were covered with exquisite works of art. The ceiling was ornately painted, giving it a vaulted, spacious feeling.

'How very beautiful,' Alex said softly, almost reverently.

'Please,' the steward said, extending an arm toward an open door, in the right forward corner of the room, which led to a surprisingly wide hallway. 'I will show you to a cabin that you may use as you require to freshen up, or perhaps change clothing throughout our excursion.'

Alex smiled and nodded, then followed him.

Michael looked away from the telescope. 'Is that receiver working?' he asked Elias.

'Perfectly,' Elias said, his finger to the earpiece.

'He never did come up on deck. Was he in the main cabin?' Michael asked.

'No, he wasn't. Alex is being shown to a cabin that she'll have use of. He'll probably join her back in the main cabin when she returns,' Elias replied.

Alex followed the steward past a few closed doors. He stopped in front of one and opened it for her. 'You should find this quite comfortable,' he said as she walked in past him.

The cabin was the size of a large bedroom and elegantly furnished in dark woods and French blue fabrics.

Curled in the center of the bed was Sasha, who, upon seeing Alex, jumped from the bed and cantered quickly to her, purring softly and rubbing affectionately against her legs.

'You remember me, don't you?' Alex said, crouching to pet the animal. Her fingers brushed gently across the collar she had put in place.

Alex looked up and saw a bouquet of lovely long-stemmed roses lying across the pillows. Beside them was an envelope and a small, beautifully wrapped box.

She felt a gentle sensation of motion as the *Eslabón* began to move.

'Where is Monsieur Babayan?' she asked the steward in French.

But a smile was his only response as he closed the door behind him and backed out into the hallway to leave her in privacy. He was gone before she could rephrase the question in English.

Alex looked at the flowers on the bed again and smiled. Babayan did have a certain charm, she thought. She walked over to the bed and touched the flowers, then reached for the box. She unwrapped it, being careful not to destroy the ribbon or the paper, as if to do so would also undo the romantic gesture of her host. She opened the box and nearly gasped when she saw the magnificent platinum and diamond-laden Rolex watch it contained.

Alex picked up the envelope and opened it, sitting on the bed as she removed the single piece of folded paper. She unfolded it and read the brief message aloud.

My Dearest Alex,

Please accept this gift as a small token of my admiration . . . and apology for not being able to be with you at this very moment. I have a small matter of important business to attend to, which came up suddenly. Please make yourself comfortable until I can join you later, just a few days from now. Everything you need will be provided.

I know you will understand. I shall return to you as soon as I am able. Until later, I remain,

Yours, with deep affection,
Vigen

PS Take care of Sasha for me.

'*Christ!*' Elias said, removing the earpiece. 'Babayan is not on board the *Eslabón.*'

'*What?*'

'He got off somehow. He left a note for Alex, telling her he would be joining her in a few days.'

'A *few days!*' Michael said, racing the few steps to the telescope. 'The ship is leaving port!' he shouted urgently, looking hard at Elias.

'How could we have missed him?' Elias said in bewilderment.

'What about Alex?' Michael asked, his immediate concern for her safety far more important to him than Babayan's whereabouts.

'She'll be all right, Mike. I'll alert Wadelaw to be ready with the helicopter.'

'Jesus Christ, Bob. *Nothing* had better happen to her *Nothing!* Do you hear me?'

'I hear you, buddy. I'm sure she's not in immediate danger. I'll get a boat on the water in the *Eslabón's* wake. She'll be fine. Right now we've got a serious problem.

319

Babayan is out of our sight. He got off of that boat somehow during the night. He said in his note that a matter of important business had come up suddenly. He must be referring to the sinking of the *Skyco Hippalus*. They've moved the timetable up because of it. Damn it! How did he get off?'

'A boat that big probably has an opening below the surface for scuba diving. He must have used it in the night and swum to some point on the shoreline,' Michael offered as a possible explanation.

'Whatever he did, we've lost him. He could be a hundred miles from here. We're back at zero.'

'Not necessarily,' Michael replied. 'We knew he'd move when it came time to sell the Luxus. They'll make contact soon, I'm sure. We'll still have a chance at it, either to buy it back or to take it when it surfaces to exchange hands. We can be ready for that. *You* just stay ready to get Alex off that boat.'

MENTON, FRANCE: The *garçon* walked away from the table of the waterfront bistro, the empty tray tucked under his arm. He had just told two of his patrons a very entertaining tidbit of Menton legend that purported to explain why Menton lemons were the finest in all the world. It was not an idle claim, he had insisted. Though well known for its tropical setting, replete with palms, bananas, and citrus trees clinging to the amphitheater of hills, the town of Menton enjoyed an even more prestigious distinction as old as the history of man himself.

It seems, the waiter had told them, swearing every word to be the solemn truth, that the lemons of Menton were of such unequaled quality because they had been planted with seeds from the garden of Eden. Eve had secretly carried with her a fruit of a lemon tree, which she had taken as they fled the angry wrath of God. She and Adam had wandered aimlessly and in deep despair for a very long time, looking for a place like the paradise they had lost. They could find no such place, but had never stopped searching. Then one night, after a long and tiring descent from a range of mountains, they had come upon a place that offered comfort in the dark of a moonless night. Beneath their feet they could feel the comfort of a carpet of flowers, and in the air was the refreshing smell of the sea. The sound of the sea was hypnotic and soothing, and it lulled them gently to sleep. They slept long and peacefully for the first time since the horrible night they had been cast from their home in paradise.

When they awoke, they stared in wonderment at the place they had happened into during the night. To one side was the magnificent blue sea, to the other side were tall green hills, lush with life, and all around them was tropical beauty that paralleled that of paradise. The outcasts felt they had come home.

'Here we shall stay,' Eve had said to Adam. 'And I shall plant the seeds of the golden fruit of paradise.'

'It was Menton that they found, Messieurs, and the lemons have done well ever since,' the *garçon* had explained.

The table was drenched in sunshine, and all around in the distance the snow-capped peaks of the base of the Alps towered in beautiful majesty. Rafael Sonterra sipped from his glass of light Provençal wine, while Vigen Babayan stirred his espresso.

Menton was a city of particular interest to Sonterra. It was the last town at the extreme tip of the Riviera, with the Italian frontier only a few hundred yards away. It was only a few minutes' walk to the Italian border, where crossing on foot was uncomplicated, requiring only a passport and a visitor's visa. A few hundred yards to safety, should threat arise.

Babayan sipped the piping hot espresso, and lowered the cup.

'You are asking that the timetable be moved up by three whole weeks,' the arms dealer said, speaking in German.

'Is that a problem for you, my friend?' Sonterra asked, also in German.

'Only an inconvenience,' Babayan replied, thinking of his lost opportunity with Alex.

Sonterra cut a wedge of lemon from the plate of plump, ripe beauties the waiter had placed on the table for them, offering proof of his proud claim. He raised it to his mouth, biting gently into it. He held it away and looked at it, raising his eyebrows. 'This really is delicious. You should try some,' he said to Babayan, offering him the knife to cut himself a wedge.

'By inconvenience, do you refer to the money you lost, or to the woman?' Sonterra asked.

Babayan looked up in surprise.

Sonterra stared at him, waiting for a reply.

'The money is insignificant. The woman, however, is another matter.'

'She is on the *Eslabón*, yes?'

Babayan squinted at him, not entirely pleased that Sonterra had been watching him so closely. 'Yes, she is on the yacht,' he replied a bit warily.

'The yacht is at sea?'

'Yes. But I don't see—'

'She is their agent,' Sonterra said, raising the lemon to his lips once again.

Babayan went rigid.

'So is the man she was with.'

'Quinn?' Babayan gasped.

Sonterra nodded.

'But . . . how can that be?'

'Quinn was in Colombia just days after the strain was taken. It was he who found the plane. Nine days later he destroyed Cantú's largest processing lab. Five days after that, he was with Cantú.'

'Cantú?' Babayan repeated nervously, clearing his throat.

'Yes. And somehow he escaped Cantú with his life. A week later he showed up in Monte Carlo. I first spotted him at the Casino, the evening he played poker with you. I think the rest is obvious, no?'

Babayan looked away, shaken by what he had just been told. He had been neatly set up. Alex had played with his emotions, which wounded him personally. Quinn had played with him professionally and financially, and for that he felt outraged. 'What do we do?' he asked, licking his lips.

'You have already done the best thing. They no longer know where you are, and you are holding the woman,' Sonterra replied, not offering her identity at this point. 'She will provide us with one added advantage. An extra pawn on our side of the board. The unexpected sinking of the *Skyco Hippalus* does not hurt us. In fact, it may ultimately prove to be an advantage. Can you step up the timetable by three weeks?'

'Yes, I have no problem with that,' Babayan replied.

'Good. Then you will send these messages,' Sonterra directed him, handing the arms dealer a small stack of papers.

Babayan accepted them.

'From this point on, we move on a very strict schedule. There are to be no exceptions, no delays. We establish the rules, and they follow them. You will be firm. Any delay on their part will cost them dearly. Do you understand?'

Babayan nodded.

'That is very good, my friend,' Sonterra said, taking a bite of another wedge of lemon. 'You really must try some of this.'

SAN ANTONIO: Asher Sky had once again convened the Crisis Committee at his estate. There was a tense silence around the conference table as he addressed them. He appeared shaken and visibly older. The strain of the past weeks was beginning to take a heavy toll on him physically as well as emotionally.

'We have received a communication concerning the missing Luxus strain,' he informed them, his voice sounding frail. 'You were contacted and summoned here immediately upon its receipt. You already know what the

Luxus represents from our last meeting. We have some decisions to make, gentlemen.'

Sky looked to Tom Danziger to read them the communication.

Danziger opened a file folder and removed a single sheet of paper. 'This was received early this morning, gentlemen.' He began to read:

To all concerned:

By now you have irrefutable proof that the Luxus, as well as its potential, is in our possession. Our purpose is clear. The Luxus is to be offered for auction to the highest bidder. Similar communications are being sent to other prospective 'clients' as you read this.

You will be contacted soon with specific details concerning the rules of the auction. You are warned not to deviate from them in the slightest way. Any attempt to operate outside the established guidelines will result in unpleasant consequences. The Luxus will be used in retaliation against selected sites around the globe.

To demonstrate our serious intent, as well as the full potential of the Luxus, two additional demonstrations will become evident very shortly. You will be contacted.

'There was a PS attached to the communication,' Danziger went on. 'It reads: "Special to Robert Elias: We have your agent. Any attempt on your part to interfere with the sale of the Luxus will result in her immediate execution. Quinn is to be kept visible at all times. There will be no second warning!"'

'That concludes the communication. The agent referred to in the message to Elias is Alexandra,' he concluded.

There was a stunned silence in the room.

Asher Sky's face was stiff with tension.

Byron Moore, former member of the National Security Council, was the first to break the silence.

'Well, that tears it. What is your "intelligence estimate"

now?' he asked, directing his comment straight to Danziger.

Danziger let out a long breath before countering Moore's I-told-you-so innuendo. 'We decided early on not to take this to the White House because we felt confident we could handle the problem. But the situation has been complicated by the sinking of the *Skyco Hippalus*. We had no way of anticipating that something like that would happen.'

'Or that a Soviet ship would pick up the survivors,' Moore added sharply. 'So much for becoming news at Moscow Center, wouldn't you say?'

'Gentlemen, it would be best to avoid recrimination at this point,' Sky cut in. 'The problem is before us. We must devise a plan of action.'

'What do our friends at Intel-Trace have to offer?' Phillip Cleland asked.

'Their position remains unchanged,' Danziger replied. 'We knew that we had a serious problem when the Luxus was successfully taken out of Colombia. They have made substantial progress in identifying the people involved in the theft of the Luxus, and they will take immediate action the moment it surfaces. They know who will control it at the critical point of transfer, and are prepared to take it back, if necessary.'

'And in the meantime?' Moore asked.

'There is little difference between a kidnapping and what we are now facing. This is extortion, gentlemen. We play along for as long as possible, and move offensively when the time is advantageous,' Danziger replied.

'Your "problem" has become a threat to this country's security, Mr Danziger.' He turned to Sky and said, 'The President must be advised,' then added, 'Your daughter is at risk here, Asher, for Christ's sake. It's a different matter entirely with the Soviets involved now, Asher. I know that Intel-Trace is the best at what they do. But, with all due respect, the stakes have escalated beyond the point where you can hope to take care of this yourselves, despite the abilities of Intel-Trace.'

'According to Intel-Trace, the Soviets had been involved

in this for the past three weeks already,' Danziger said. 'I can assure you they've managed quite well to this point, despite that development. They still have my vote of confidence.'

Moore looked back at Sky. 'Call the President, Asher. That's a decision he'll have to make.'

'He already has, Clay,' Sky told him. 'I spoke with him this morning. Obviously he wasn't very happy about the situation, but he understands our position and has been made fully aware of Intel-Trace's progress to this point. He respects the opinions of the people in this room, and wants a report following our meeting today. So I'll leave it to you what he's to be told.'

'He has a lot of faith in Intel-Trace,' Phillip Cleland said. 'I say we stay with them a while longer. Involving other agencies at this point may only cause confusion and shift some advantage to the adversary.'

'I agree,' said Marcus Lent, the third outside member of the Crisis Committee. 'We need a highly focused effort with a short chain of command. Bringing in additional agencies would only slow us down.'

Moore didn't seem entirely happy about what he was hearing. 'I guess I'm just old-fashioned, gentlemen. I've always felt that the more minds one has attacking a problem, the better the chances of reaching a solution. This government employs a lot of experts who can offer valuable assistance. But I realize that Intel-Trace is highly capable. I just hope you're making the right decision. I'd hate to sit here a few weeks from now and say "I told you so".'

'If you're right and we're wrong, chances are none of us will be around in two weeks, anyway,' Danziger said.

'My point, precisely,' said Moore. 'But it seems I have lost this argument. Very well, if the decision is to go with Intel-Trace, then that's what I'll report to the President. And may God be with them, gentlemen. May God be with us all.'

Two days later the demonstrations manifested. Two minor reserves on opposite sides of the globe were 'hit'. The first was in Colombia, a remote but productive location not too far from the major oilfields of Orito, near the Ecuadoran border. The second was in the Soviet Union, in the Irkutsk region, also isolated and highly productive for its size. By the time the first traces of abnormality were detected, it was too late; both sites were hopelessly lost to the irreversible effects of the Alpha-negative strain of the Luxus.

There was no way of pinpointing when the seeding had taken place. It could only have been done after the strain had been taken, just four weeks earlier. Even assuming its immediate use, the rate of destruction was staggeringly swift.

The point was made eminently clear, by selection of a Soviet site, that *no-one* was safe from the potential of the Luxus. The fact that only minor sites had been selected was irrelevant. They could just as easily have been prime locations, with vast reserves at stake.

With great care, Asher Sky read the reports of the catastrophic developments, but especially troublesome was his daughter's abduction. Never had he felt so vulnerable, so responsible for the lives of so many people. Byron Moore's words echoed again and again in his mind with the awful realization of the evil now threatening the world – an evil spawned from the purest desire to give mankind a gift of hope for the future. A gift of hope . . . a gift of despair. 'God be with us all,' he whispered.

22

TULSA, OKLAHOMA: The strong, weathered hands of Culland Brice opened the pouch of Levi Garrett chewing tobacco. The fingers reached deep, kneaded a medium-sized quantity into a manageable ball, and withdrew it from the pouch.

Brice held out the pouch to Bob Elias, who had been called back to the United States for this meeting. 'Care for a chew, Mr Elias?' he asked, speaking with a country twang that was usually absent when he appeared in public or at official functions of state.

'No, thank you, Mr President,' Elias replied politely.

Brice stuck the wad of tobacco into his mouth and closed the pouch. He knew that neither Sky nor Danziger ever used the stuff.

Culland Brice was an imposing man in person. He looked even bigger, dressed as he was in jeans, sport shirt, and sheepskin coat, his worn cowboy boots adding an additional two inches to his height. The stained and weathered cowboy hat helped, too, making him seem gigantic beside the stocky, hunched figure of Asher Sky.

Brice was a cowboy at heart, having spent his childhood in Oklahoma, and he seized every opportunity to get back to the life he loved. The country was his escape from the incredible pressures of the presidency, a job that had suddenly been made a great deal more difficult by the shocking developments that had brought these men together at Brice's private ranch just outside Tulsa.

The trip to Tulsa had not been part of a planned vacation for the President. He had, in fact, canceled important appointments to make it. Developments over the past three days since the sinking of the *Skyco Hippalus* had brought international tensions to the crisis point. The moment word of the reserve hits in Colombia and the Soviet Union came to his attention, Brice had taken only enough time to make a single phone call. That was to Asher Sky. The message had been short: 'Get your buns to Tulsa, and bring answers.'

'How did this happen, Asher?' Brice asked as the four men walked on an oval track used for training the quarter horses bred at the ranch. Sky looked up at him, as if coming out of some deep thought. His face was dark and drawn. He seemed on the verge of collapse.

'Which part? The theft, the *Skyco Hippalus*, or the reserves?' Sky returned.

'I've read the reports about the theft, and the theories about the tanker. What I need to know is *how* an oil reserve inside the Soviet Union can be so easily compromised,' Brice said.

'It's not all that hard, Cully,' Sky explained. 'A capsule the size of a jelly bean could carry all the Luxus necessary to do the damage. Even Soviet security measures couldn't detect something that small without a great deal of luck. Once at the site, introduction could be made in any number of ways, from grout injections at new well sites, to simple back-pressure in a dormant pump station. There are dozens of ways to get it into the reserve itself. The technology isn't complicated; all it takes is having people in the right place. And obviously there *are* people in place to get it done. Most of the technology in the Soviet fields is ours. What it comes down to is a matter of sophisticated plumbing on a large scale.'

'I don't have to tell you that the Soviets are outraged,' Brice said. 'The Colombians are scared of total economic collapse, and so is every other oil-producing nation that's aware of the situation. How do we get out of it?' he asked, spitting a stream of tobacco juice with the accuracy of a hunting rifle.

'There's really only one way,' Elias answered. 'We have to recover the Luxus in its entirety.'

'Then let me ask the big question. Exactly what are our chances of doing that?'

'It depends on which option we take, Mr President. There are a number of them open to us. The surest but most expensive way is to outbid the competition. There's no telling how much that would cost us. We could *take* the strain back by whatever means possible, and we may get the chance. But this is the most dangerous option, because we would have to be successful on our first attempt. Failure could result in unimaginable consequences. We're dealing with people who *will* follow through on their threats.'

'Are we sure of that?'

'They've been ruthless to this point. I have no doubt they'd carry out their threat to use the Luxus,' Elias responded.

Brice shook his head, his jaws working the tobacco. 'That's all we'd need. We're in deep trouble already. The Soviets have pulled out of the summit meeting next month over this. They've got the usual rhetoric flying, holding us responsible for everything.'

'They're scared, Cully,' Sky said. 'Everyone is scared. And they should be. Our estimates are that thirty to forty per cent of the world's fossil-fuel reserves could be wiped out with only partial use of the Luxus if it gets into the right places. Maximum placement could destroy as much as seventy per cent of known major reserves.'

Brice stopped walking and looked hard at Sky. 'What in hell were you doing down there?' he asked.

'Just trying to make the world a better place, Cully. We were *that* close,' Sky said, holding his fingers an inch apart.

'Didn't you ever think about what was on the other side of that coin?'

'Of course we did. That's why we moved the research down to the Medellín Institute in the first place. The Pentagon would have commandeered the Luxus if they'd have known it existed,' Sky replied to his longtime friend.

'You're probably right,' Brice said, nodding. 'I can assure you they're plenty interested in it *now*. Everybody is going to want in on this, Asher. CIA, FBI, NSC, every branch of military intelligence. Everyone.'

'We can't allow that, Mr President,' Elias said. 'It would complicate matters terribly and diminish our chances of getting the Luxus back. We'd be fighting each other as well as the adversary holding the strain, not to mention the Soviets and potentially every other major intelligence community in the world. What we really need is a complete absence of interference. Anything less than that puts us at a great disadvantage.'

Brice let fly with another wad, and began walking

again. 'I don't see how I can guarantee that, Mr Elias,' he said. 'These people are like hunting dogs. The scent is in the air, and their instinct is to track the prey, no matter what stands in their way.

'You're the President of the United States, for Christ's sake, Cully,' Sky said, showing a bit of temper. 'These people work for you, or did you forget that? They'll do whatever the hell you tell them to.'

'You don't really believe that, do you, Asher?' Brice asked. He looked at Danziger and said, 'You need to have a good talk with your boss on how things *really* work under the covers.'

'You can at least delay them,' Elias said.

'Possibly, but not for long. The question is whether it's really to our advantage to stop them. Unless you can guarantee me that you have a reasonable chance of getting the Luxus back before it's used to cripple the world's economy, or before it gets into the hands of a potential enemy, I don't see that I have any other choice than to turn them loose.'

Elias thought for a second. 'There *will* be at least one good opportunity, Mr President, and that's when the strain is auctioned. We enter the bidding and stay in contention for as long as possible. If we can't win it outright, then we *take* it when it surfaces to change hands. At that one moment it will be vulnerable.'

'I'm sure everyone else will be thinking the same thing,' Brice countered. 'You'll have to take a number and wait in line for the chance.'

'Not if we're first in line. And I can guarantee that right now we're at least a few steps ahead of everyone else.'

'How soon do you expect this auction to take place?'

'I'd say within a week,' Elias replied.

Brice looked to Danziger. 'You used to be in this business, Tom. How long would it take for the Company to make up lost ground?' he asked.

'The operation was extremely well planned,' Danziger began. 'Going over old ground will take time, especially

331

with the way things were covered up. I'd say two, maybe three weeks at the earliest.'

'And the Soviets?'

'They're well ahead of that. But there's a lot they don't know. They're getting most of what they have by trailing us around. We only need to be one step ahead of them to pull it off.'

'And if they're not one step behind?'

'The most they can be is even. Then it comes down to speed and determination.'

The President weighed the options in silence. 'OK,' he said at last. 'I'll give an executive order to the other agencies to stay out of it. That won't stop them, but it will buy you some time – two weeks, maybe. Will that do?'

'It'll have to,' Elias replied.

'What about this agent of yours that they're holding?' Brice asked.

'It's not an agent, Cully. It's Alex,' Sky told him, tears nearly coming to his eyes. He looked so frail in that one moment that the President felt concern for his ability to hold up to the strain.

Brice's face became a hard frown. 'I'm truly sorry, Asher. I know what you must be going through. What's being done for her?' he asked Elias.

'We're maintaining a tight watch on Babayan's yacht. We'll plan a simultaneous operation to get her back when we go for the Luxus.'

'That operation should be top priority,' the President said.

'It will be, sir.'

'Cutting through all the bullshit, Mr Elias, what *are* our chances of getting back the Luxus without having to take it?'

'How big is your pocketbook, Mr President?'

'As big as you need it to be, Mr Elias. Do we have any other alternative?'

'I just need it to be big enough to keep our options open. Given that to work with, our chances are at least better than even.'

'Then see to it, Mr Elias. Get the Luxus back by whatever means necessary. You have two weeks. I'm not sure I can even guarantee you that much, but I'll give it a try.'

'Thank you, Mr President. I assure you that we'll make the most of any time you can give us.'

The President nodded, directing another stream of tobacco juice to the edge of the track. 'Two weeks, Mr Elias. Use it well.'

MOSCOW: Late-November snows came with an Arctic front, blanketing the Kremlin with a foot and a half of fresh powder. The icy blasts of frigid air whipping across the Kremlin compound had been a portent to Kozlov of what lay ahead within the Palace of Congresses. The Luxus communication from Vigen Babayan had been received just two days earlier, and news of the damaged Irkutsk reserve was hot in the hands of Party, KGB, and army chiefs.

Kozlov had acted swiftly following the pointed communication from Babayan. He had immediately made full reports available to his superiors in the army command, giving them as a group full advantage of the GRU's knowledge of the Skyco situation. The KGB had been caught completely off stride and unable to respond to the torrent of questions from Party chiefs. Kozlov's responses had been complete and well timed. His chief adversary, Petr Vladin, head of the KGB, had come away from the early meetings looking very bad in the eyes of the Party bosses, adding fuel to the bitter enmity between them. But even Kozlov could not escape the scathing criticism that had followed news of the stricken reserve in the oil-rich Irkutsk region of the Soviet Union. No one could have anticipated that development, nor could an explanation be offered as to how it had happened.

Kozlov had been summoned to meet privately with Mikhail Gorbachev after the security session adjourned.

Kozlov entered the richly impressive office of the Soviet leader, closing the door quietly behind him. Gorbachev

333

was standing at the window, staring out pensively, his right hand deep in his pocket.

He turned to face the GRU chief as he approached the massive, highly polished desk. The Soviet leader was a man of even temperament. There was no trace of anger in his face, though an expression of profound worry masked the otherwise pleasant demeanor. His authority was being challenged on all fronts. The last thing he needed was to have the security of the nation exposed to serious threat.

'Thank you for coming, General Kozlov,' the leader said softly.

'I am at your service, Mr Secretary,' Kozlov returned.

'Please sit and make yourself comfortable,' Gorbachev said to him.

Kozlov did as he was instructed, sitting directly in front of the desk. The Party Secretary took his seat behind the desk. There was a moment of silence before the Soviet leader began.

'I have read the reports from the Ministry of Science. They have concluded that the Irkutsk reserve will reach total destruction in less than a week. There is no way to save it, General Kozlov. No way to save even a portion of the oil. They can offer no explanation other than the obvious, that a microorganism capable of rapid oil digestion has somehow been introduced into the reserve. The KGB is without answers, and I have great difficulty believing that we are guilty of such gross incompetence and weakness as to let such a thing happen. You seem to be the only one with answers. What can you offer in the way of explanation?'

Kozlov sat forward in his chair and reached for one of the pencils in the holder on the Secretary's desk. 'May I?' he asked politely.

Gorbachev nodded.

'We are not incompetent, nor are we weak, Mr Secretary,' he said, snapping off the eraser end of the pencil. He held up the small eraser between his fingers. 'If I were secretly to select any citizen in Moscow and give him this small object and instruct him to conceal it carefully, how would you estimate the chances that our combined security forces could find it?' he asked.

'Without discovering the identity of the citizen you selected, I would say that they were almost nonexistent,' the Secretary replied.

'Would you judge from this inability that our security was weak?'

'No.'

'Now add to that the fact that our security forces were not even aware that they should be searching for it, and you have recreated the situation we faced in preventing this weapon from entering the Soviet Union. The Science Directorate has advised me that a vial no larger than this small eraser is all that was needed of this organism to start the reserve on the path to destruction.'

'In your reports two days ago and earlier today, you stated that the Skyco Research Institute in Medellín, Colombia, had been attacked and that a genetic consignment had been lost or stolen.'

'Yes, that is correct. But we could only speculate at first that the consignment was of a genetic nature. We obtained positive proof about two weeks later. The Science Directorate has also concluded that the organism in question had already been seeded into the reserve by the time this information was confirmed. Until the *Skyco Hippalus* incident, we had no clear indication as to what the nature of this organism was. It was already too late to save the reserve, Mr Secretary,' Kozlov explained.

'And the Colombian reserve, no doubt, was also already on the way to destruction,' Gorbachev concluded correctly, sitting well back in his chair.

'It would have to have been, yes.'

'Who is in possession of it?'

'We don't know who is holding it, Mr Secretary. We had correctly connected the international arms dealer Vigen Babayan to the eventual disposition of it by sale. But we have been unable to uncover the identity of the principal on whose behalf he is acting. State security is endeavoring to protect the knowledge of the loss of this reserve, but news of it is already out of our control outside the Soviet Union. It will be only a matter of time before that information makes its way back inside our borders. There could be some panic,' Kozlov said.

'The Ministry of Science reports that they have recovered some of this organism from the reserve site and are attempting to study it. They are having great difficulty sustaining its viability,' Gorbachev said.

'They will have to reduce it to a dormant state. Our tests so far show that it self-destructs rapidly when its food source is exhausted,' Kozlov told him.

'This missing consignment was obviously already in this state of dormancy?'

'Yes.'

'How much was taken?'

'Operational Intelligence has put it at twenty-four vials. This information was obtained from a highly regarded source within the United States. Bits of information are beginning to filter out of Skyco.'

'We must obtain the balance of this organism, General Kozlov. It is eminently clear that we are vulnerable to its use against us. The Soviet economy could be crippled beyond repair if we fail. We must be first in the race for this prize. We must be merciless in our efforts. I don't have to tell you, General Kozlov, how much uneasiness exists within the Soviet Union today, especially among the old Party leaders. A blow to our economy of this magnitude would create utter chaos and complete social breakdown. There would be only one option left to this office to restore order. That would be dictatorial rule, General. No other way would work. And all that I have worked for would be lost – *never* to be regained. Do you understand what I am telling you?'

'Yes, Mr Secretary. It has been given the highest priority.'

'There can be no room for failure,' Gorbachev said clearly.

'I understand, Mr Secretary,' Kozlov said, fully realizing

that Vladin's KGB efforts would be equally determined. The KGB would be no less an adversary than the Americans.

'I am placing formal responsibility for the acquisition of this weapon in your hands, General Kozlov. I have great confidence in you and your people. Do what you must. Your budget is unlimited. We must preserve the future of the State, Aleksandr Ivanovich. Do not disappoint your country,' Gorbachev said, rising from his chair. 'You are being given the opportunity to become a hero of the State.'

Kozlov rose to his feet with the leader of his nation, feeling fully the weight of the responsibility he had been given and realizing that the line between heroism and disgrace was a thin one. Whatever the outcome, he would have a place of immortality in a nation that honored its heroes above all else. He hoped his place would be one of glory.

23

MONACO: Bob Elias looked worn as he entered the villa. The two transatlantic crossings and the meetings in between had taken a physical toll on him. Sleep had been impossible on board the Concorde, where his mind had turned endlessly to the details of their dilemma. He had two weeks to solve their problem before outside agencies would be set loose. Two weeks to counter an as yet unidentified terrorist holding a briefcase of material that could stop the world.

Michael said nothing as Elias walked past him and into the main room. It had been five long and worrisome days since Alex sailed out of Port du Monaco on the *Eslabón*.

Michael had been kept busy during that time traveling a

circuitous route between Nice, Grenoble, Marseille, and Monte Carlo. Elias had kept him moving for two very good reasons. The first was to force the Soviet surveillance teams assigned to him into the open to establish the identities of their members. The second, and equally important, was to keep him from initiating some form of independent action against the *Eslabón* in an attempt to free Alex. Keeping him moving and visible also complied with the warning he had received in the communication to Skyco.

Elias had not shared the details of that communication with Michael for fear of the response it might trigger. And he was right. Michael's priorities would have changed with that knowledge, and he would have been difficult to stop.

Michael followed Elias into the room and watched as he sat heavily on the sofa. The silence continued before his patience abandoned him.

'Where is she, Bob?' he asked, the voice controlled but firm.

'The *Eslabón* is anchored off the coast of Corsica, just south of Ajaccio. She's doing fine, Mike. The communications have been continuous and well monitored. She's being cared for like royalty,' Elias replied in a tired voice.

'Is Babayan on the yacht?'

'No. We still don't know where he is. But he has made a direct communication to Skyco. We were right, the Luxus is to be auctioned to the highest bidder. We were right about the *Skyco Hippalus*, too. It was part of a demonstration to show its potential and to get the attention of interested parties. There have been two additional demonstrations just to drive home the point of the strain's full potential.'

'What kind of demonstrations?'

'Two reserves have been hit. One in Colombia, the other in the Soviet Union. Both were relatively small and isolated. They'll be history in a week or two.'

'Jesus Christ!' Michael said, running his hand through his hair. 'The Soviet Union?'

'They have a way of getting their point across,' Elias said. 'The message is clear. No one is safe. They can hit anywhere, anytime.'

'Everyone is going to be in on this now,' Michael said, pacing toward the windows. 'It's going to become a free-for-all.'

'Sky, Danziger, and I have met with the President. He's issued a firm executive order keeping US intelligence agencies out of it to prevent interference. Danziger estimates we'll get about two weeks out of it. After that, it's anybody's game,' Elias said.

'Two weeks,' Michael repeated to himself. 'Can we do it in such a short time?'

'Possibly. I expect the auction will take place within a week. If we get lucky, we can solve the whole problem with a lot of cash.'

'Who's going to pay the bill?' Michael asked.

'The President has given us a blank check.'

'Then Intel-Trace will handle the bidding?'

'That's the general plan,' Elias replied.

'What's the specific plan?' Michael asked.

'We don't have one yet. The objective is to get the Luxus back by any means possible. If our money doesn't buy it, we *take* it at the first opportunity.'

Michael thought for a long moment. 'We have to get Alex out, Bob. If we seize the Luxus, they'll kill her.'

'Wadelaw and a strike team are in Corsica now,' Elias told him. 'Our move on the *Eslabón* has to be properly timed with our seizure of the Luxus. We'll have one chance, Mike. Just one. We have to make it work.'

'I'm going to Corsica,' Michael said, his eyes staring out of the window to where the *Eslabón* had been anchored.

'I'm afraid not, buddy,' Elias returned, sitting forward on the sofa. 'You're carrying the bid when the time comes.'

Michael spun to face his boss, who said quickly, 'We

don't have a choice, Mike. I had you moving through France for a reason these past days. The Soviets are on to every step you take. If I send you to Corsica, they'll know exactly what we plan to do, and it will give away our timetable. Wadelaw is clean, and so is the strike team with him. I have to keep you visible to protect our chances of getting the Luxus back – and of keeping Alex safe.'

Elias let this logic sink in, then went on, 'The Soviets have their top operatives involved. We've identified Ivan Brevig in Monte Carlo. He'll be the GRU's case officer. We've identified another, Gregor Tolvanin, who has shadowed your movements to Nice, Grenoble, Marseille, and back to Monte Carlo. He's not watching you directly, but is staying close to your movements. We've also made most of their primary teams.'

'They're all GRU?' Michael asked.

'For now. We can expect KGB involvement, too, now that the situation has reached the Kremlin. They'll operate independently, possibly against one another, as well. The field has gotten crowded, and remember that the CIA and FBI aren't yet players – although they will be soon. And there can be others from the Mideast as well.'

'It's going to get messy,' Michael said.

'Exactly. And that's why we keep you away from Corsica and in the open. As long as they can see you, we can see them.'

'What about Strassa?' Michael asked.

'The situation is the same. We've put in secondary teams. When Strassa moves, the primary teams now in place will lead our Soviet friends in a different direction, leaving the secondary team in place to deal with Strassa. Right now Strassa is staying put. He could be out of it, for all we know. But we're going to stay with him.'

'So now we just sit and wait?' Michael asked, his voice tense with impatience.

'Yes. We sit and wait for the bidding to begin. We try to buy it back if we can, and take it if we can't.'

'And Alex?'

340

'An operation has already been planned to coincide with whatever opportunity is presented with the Luxus. We move swiftly and decisively on both fronts at the same time.'

'She has to be kept safe, Bob.'

'She will be. You have my word, Mike. Believe me, the old man has made the same point abundantly clear.'

Michael nodded and looked back out the window toward the port. 'Has Skyco made any progress on the Beta strain of the Luxus?' he asked after a long silence.

'I spoke with de Roode when I was back in the States. They're working frantically. They're making some progress with the probe prototype, but still aren't close on the Beta. At least they haven't admitted to any success with it.'

The phone rang, startling them. Michael answered it.

'It's for you,' he said, holding out the receiver.

Elias squinted in puzzlement, and went to the phone.

'Elias,' he said into it.

'Please hold,' the voice said. There was a short pause.

Elias looked at Michael and tossed a thumb in the direction of the kitchen, indicating that he needed privacy.

'Please state your identification code and clearance,' the voice said.

'I'm not alone,' Elias said.

'Mr Quinn has been given authorized clearance,' the voice returned.

'Triple Jack, five-nine-three. Clearance Alpha-Scramble,' he said into the mouthpiece.

'Hold, please,' the voice instructed.

There was a delay of perhaps twenty seconds.

'Good morning, Bob,' the voice of Martin Trace said.

'Good morning, Martin,' Elias returned. Making contact on such a high level with another operative in close proximity was a departure from usual security practices. The information that Trace was about to convey must be of a very urgent nature, Elias thought.

'A communication has been received regarding the

341

rules of procedure for the auction,' Trace began. 'It will commence the day after tomorrow and be conducted in two separate stages. The first will be handled directly by Skyco. The purpose of this first stage is to qualify the bidders, and to narrow the field to a final group of three. All bidding will be conducted using electronic deposits in specified accounts in Switzerland. Confirmation of deposits is required for a bid to be accepted. After completion of this stage, all but the three highest bidders will have their deposits returned.

'The three finalists will then convene at a time and place to be given later. One representative from each finalist will go in personally for the last stage, which will comprise two rounds of bidding only. No outside communication will be permitted. Delegates are to carry complete bid authority. Again, all bids are electronic, with confirmation required before acceptance. The highest bid at the conclusion of the second round will win. The two losers will be dropped off at a location to be made known only at the last moment, for security purposes. The winner will then be taken to an undisclosed location for transfer of the Luxus. The secrecy of the location is for the mutual security of the winner and the party now in possession of the strain.

'Quinn will carry the bid for our side. He will have full authority. If possible, we will monitor the proceedings closely. Units will be in place globally on alert to go into immediate action should we not win the bidding outright.

'Is your plan of action against the *Eslabón* complete and ready?' Trace asked.

'It's all set. All we need is the go,' Elias replied. 'We need the *Eslabón* to stay anchored, or it will be very difficult.'

'You should plan some contingency to ensure that,' Trace advised. 'Is Quinn aware of that situation?'

'To the extent that it is wise,' Elias replied.

'I understand. We can't afford for him to get out of control on us now.'

'Will we be able to trace the movement of the funds?' Elias asked.

'We are reasonably certain that we can. A great deal of money will be changing hands. The initial qualifying bids of the three finalists will not be returned; they will be considered an entry fee. There have been provisions outlined for the return of the losing bid amounts. But it is not our intention to lose. We must win it. Winning it will be easier than trying to take it from a third party.

'Whatever the outcome, we will want the Luxus *and* our money back, as well as the parties responsible. We won't rest until we have them.'

'I understand,' Elias said.

'I don't have to describe to you the terrible significance of losing the Luxus. We must recover it at all costs,' Trace concluded.

'We'll be ready.'

'You'll be advised when the second stage is to begin. Good luck.'

The line went dead.

Elias replaced the receiver in its cradle. Michael walked out of the kitchen when he saw Elias move back to the sofa.

'What's the word?' Michael asked.

'The table is set. It'll begin on Monday in two stages. Stage one, the qualifying round, will be handled by Skyco. You'll go in as our representative for stage two. You have unlimited authority. We've been instructed to win the bidding,' Elias said.

'And if we lose?'

'Then we take it however we can. You just do your best to win it, Mike.'

Michael thought for a long moment. 'What happens if we lose and the transfer takes place inside the Soviet Union?'

'I don't think it will. The party holding the Luxus now will want to guarantee their own well-being.'

'That could be part of the price. Or some of the strain could be held back as insurance,' Michael suggested.

'That's a possibility. If that happens, then we'll consider

343

risking every well-placed agent inside the Soviet Union. We'll risk the best we have to get it back – or to destroy it. If *we* can't have it, no one will.'

BERN, SWITZERLAND: The Soviets were the first to be spotted. There was something about them that made them stand out. Kammal had identified them easily by the second day. He had maintained a cautious, long-distance surveillance of Strassa from carefully chosen static positions over the first five days in the Swiss capital. It wasn't until the fifth day of establishing Strassa's routine that he recognized the more expert surveillance teams of Intel-Trace.

The presence of the Soviets didn't bother Kammal. Strassa, though a cautious man, was a known terrorist who was often under surveillance of one kind or another. But the Intel-Trace teams could be there for only one reason: because of events in Colombia. This *did* bother him. His instincts had been right in Colombia. Sonterra's decision to remove Strassa was turning out to be well founded after all.

The heavy surveillance centered on Strassa would make killing him difficult. Normally, Kammal's preference would be to get in close and take him with a down-loaded .22-caliber handgun, a favorite weapon of Israeli assassination teams. At close range the low-velocity .22 could do surprising damage. The reduced powder charge made for very little sound, and the lowered recoil enhanced accuracy to a great degree. But with the heavy surveillance, there could be no getting in close without a high level of risk and reduced chances of escape. He knew he would have to do it at long range. And long range meant getting a weapon.

It took a phone call to France and twenty-four hours to locate what he needed. It was expensive to deal in specialized weapons through the network. But anything could be obtained for the right amount of money.

It took the better part of the sixth day and three stops to

obtain the weapon, which was delivered in three separate components by three separate couriers. Kammal assembled the components in his room, tested the action, sighted make-believe targets, then broke the weapon down again for safe transport.

His patient observation of Strassa had paid off handsomely. For the most part, Strassa avoided strict daily routine. But there were two things that he *did* do with predictable regularity. Every Tuesday, Thursday, and Saturday he took a long late-morning walk through the Old Town, always stopping at the Zeitglocken Turm – the Clock Tower – Bern's colorful showpiece, with its mechanically operated puppet show marking each hour. Then he would continue on to the traffic-free Barenplatz, where he would visit the colorful and lively open-air market. He would shop there for a few provisions and walk at a casual pace back to his flat. His stops in the market were always at the same vendors. It was possible that one or more of these were a part of his communication network. In any event, he stopped at the same places at the same times on the same days.

Kammal formulated a plan around his observations, then concentrated his efforts on looking for a place that would permit a commanding view of the market from a fourth- or fifth-floor vantage point. It took him an entire day, but he found exactly what he was looking for when he spotted a young couple leaving their flat with five pieces of luggage. They were obviously off for some holiday adventure, which he hoped would carry through the upcoming weekend.

He returned an hour later and easily picked his way into the apartment. The view from the window was perfect, overlooking not just one, but two of the regular stops made by Strassa. As long as Strassa held to form, stopping every other day, excluding Sundays, Kammal would have a relatively easy shot of no more than sixty meters.

On the evening of the seventh day, Kammal again gained entry into the flat, where he assembled the weapon for the final time, loaded it, and made himself comfortable for the evening. The following morning, before the sun rose, he opened the window a few inches and set up a bench rest for the weapon using a low table and a stool. He took a pillow from the bedroom and set it on the stool, then placed the rifle across the pillow. He was set back three feet from the window. With the sunrise to the back of the building, he would be impossible to see from the street below. He trained the rifle through the opening in the window on to one of the two market stalls as the vendors set up. The line of fire was perfect. He needed only to wait now for Strassa to show up and make his stop. He checked his watch. He had two hours.

Kammal searched through the apartment, looking for something to drink. He settled on a bottle of schnapps, took a few pills to get himself up, and drank a bit too heavily, which was becoming a regular practice. The schnapps was too good, the wait too long. He fell asleep.

It was the sudden flapping of wings that woke him – a group of startled pigeons on the sill outside. Kammal came awake suddenly, his brain confused for an instant and heavy from the alcohol and drugs. He moved quickly to the weapon on the stool and looked out the window, only to see Strassa already moving away from the vendor's stall. Before he could raise the weapon, Strassa was already past the established zone of fire.

Kammal tried moving the table and stool to the left to reestablish an acceptable line of fire, but in his haste he knocked over the stool. The sound was not loud enough to be heard on the street below, but it was loud enough to scramble the remaining pigeons on the sill outside, further complicating his possibilities for making a successful shot. He panicked.

Kammal lifted the rifle and moved quickly to the window. But Strassa was passing out of sight behind a row of stall awnings. He raised the rifle and fired the silenced weapon out of desperation, hoping to hit Strassa through the awning.

346

The bullet sailed past Strassa, striking a woman just a few feet to his right in the face. Strassa crouched low in a frightened response, searching frantically to establish the line of fire. A second shot tore through the awning behind him to his right, hitting a table. It was enough for Strassa to determine the direction, and he bolted away, every step taking him farther from Kammal's capabilities.

Kammal worked the bolt action again and caught a glimpse of Strassa as he passed between stalls. He fired once again, hitting a vegetable scale immediately behind Strassa. The Basque was in full flight now.

Kammal's hand tugged frantically at the bolt action for a fourth time. The movement was jerky and rough, and the action would not function. By the time he finally drove the last round into the chamber, Strassa was gone.

There was panic on the street below, with people scurrying in all directions. Kammal moved to the window, pushed it open, and leaned out, hoping to get off one more round at his target. But Strassa was nowhere to be seen. The movement of the window caught the attention of eyes on the street. Kammal realized his mistake and dropped the weapon. He bolted from the flat, moving quickly through the building to a rear exit. He hit the street and ran.

Two members of an Intel-Trace team were up the stairs and into the room in seconds, weapons drawn, ready to drop anything that moved. They made a swift observation of the flat. In a matter of moments they, too, were gone. They had recovered the weapon, the stool, and the bottle, from which fingerprints could be obtained. But more valuable by far was one item obtained by a member of the second static team. It was a photograph that, when developed, would show the clear image of a man in the window with weapon in hand.

24

Phase one of the auction commenced on Monday, the last day of November, just as announced. All aspects of the bidding for the United States were handled by Skyco directly, with Tom Danziger acting as agent. The bidding proceeded in four steps. The first was a general collection of bids from all interested parties. Opening bids were received by Vigen Babayan, and electronically transmitted funds to the first numbered Swiss account were confirmed. All but the top ten were dropped and returned to accounts of origin. The remaining ten parties were then contacted by Babayan and informed of the highest bid. A second numbered account was identified and the process was repeated.

Following confirmation of receipt of the amended bids, the field of hopefuls was pared to six, the lowest bids again being returned to accounts of origin. The bidders were again advised of the highest bid, a third numbered account was provided, and all remaining bidders were advised that the next round of bids would be the final round in the first phase.

With all noncontenders out of the running, the bidding became serious.

The final bids were received and verified, and the announcement of the final three was made. They were the United States, the Soviet Union, and OPEC, which, in a surprise move, had bid the final round as a single entry, their combined financial capabilities posing a formidable threat. The remaining unsuccessful bids were returned. The accepted bids were acknowledged and retained as an ante to the final round.

The final phase of bidding would begin on Wednesday, 2 December. Skyco had successfully stayed in contention. The rest would be up to Intel-Trace.

MONACO: A smile of sly confidence crossed Bob Elias's face as he returned the phone to its cradle. He had just been

348

informed of the results of the first phase of the bidding.

'We're in,' he announced, great relief evident in his face.

'Now it's up to us,' Elias said. 'The final phase takes place tomorrow on board Babayan's private 747. You and the other two bidders will be picked up at Barajas International Airport in Madrid at oh-nine-hundred hours. You'll bid in secrecy, and the results of the bidding won't be made known until the two unsuccessful bidders are dropped off at a site to be made known only at the last possible moment.'

'Who are the other two bidders?' Michael asked.

'The Soviets and OPEC.'

'OPEC?' Michael echoed.

'A bit of a surprise, isn't it?'

'Very creative,' Michael said. 'What did it cost us to get in?'

'You don't want to know,' Elias replied. 'Those bid amounts did nothing but buy our way in. Phase two starts it all over again. The bids in phase one have no relevance. They've already been moved. From the tracking, it appears that Babayan got the lowest of the three as a fat commission. I think I'm in the wrong business.'

'So we start all over again. Where do I begin?' Michael asked. 'I need some guidelines.'

'The first bid won't be significant,' Elias began. 'It'll be a feeling-out process. You'll have only *one* chance after that.'

'I have to have an idea, Bob. I've got to know where to start.'

Elias thought for a long moment, turning the strategies over in his head. 'Start at two hundred million,' he said finally.

'And that's to *start* it?' Michael asked.

'It'll go higher, Mike. A lot higher. You'll be told what the highest bid is after the first round.'

Michael began toying with the strategies. The competition could deliberately underbid the first round. There would be no telling where they'd take their second bid. If his bid was the highest, his situation would be very difficult. He'd have no idea how much higher to take it.

'How high should I go? How high *can* I go?' he asked.

'High enough to win it,' Elias returned. 'It's something you'll have to try to sense once you're airborne.' But the answer offered no help. 'Look at it this way, Mike. It's not your money. Don't be afraid of overpaying. It's worth whatever it costs to get it back.'

' "Whatever it costs" could be the national debt,' Michael said, pacing nervously. 'I don't think the President had that in mind when he told you to go for it.'

'He didn't have losing in mind, either. You do what you have to do to get it back. Leave the rest to me,' Elias told him.

'And Alex?'

'She's still off the coast of Corsica. The *Eslabón* is anchored peacefully and she's still being treated well. We've been monitoring her situation constantly, and have a plan ready. Whatever happens, the plan goes into effect at precisely the right moment. If we win, we'll know it the moment the other two are let off. We'll start the operation the second you have the Luxus and are safely away. If you lose, we take the yacht the moment the strain changes hands. We also take the strain if we can set up quickly enough.'

'What if the *Eslabón* pulls anchor and leaves before the transfer?' Michael questioned.

Elias smiled. 'The *Eslabón* won't be going anywhere without her props. We disabled them last night. She's there to stay. The *Eslabón* is helpless and doesn't know it.'

'That's fine, as long as she doesn't try to pull anchor *before* the auction begins,' Michael countered.

'We're going to have to take that chance, but we're prepared to take Alex off at a moment's notice.

'There's been one more development, Mike,' Elias said.

Michael looked at him, waiting.

'There was an attempt on Strassa's life in Bern.'

'Is he dead?'

'No. The attempt failed. He bolted, but we managed to stay with him. The unexpected bonus was that we shook the Soviets in Bern. They weren't as prepared as we were, and their teams lost Strassa in the confusion. They keyed on our surveillance teams to pick him up again, but we were expecting that, and used the primary teams to lead them on a merry chase. Our secondary teams continued the tracking just long enough for previously unused teams to take it over, then they, too, ran a decoy. The Soviets don't have the slightest idea where Strassa is right now.'

'How does that help us?' Michael asked.

'It gives us another way to find out who's responsible for stealing the Luxus. Strassa is running scared. The people who contracted him have broken faith with him. It's a good bet he'll force a contact of some kind, which will take us a level higher into the network . . . if we can maintain the tail on him.

'We also got another break in the deal. We have a picture of the hitter and some good sets of prints.'

'Do we have an identity?'

'Not yet, but we will soon. The face in the picture was partially obscured, but we have several strong features to work with, mainly the eyes, most of the nose, and one ear. It's going through the computers now for enhancement.'

'What about the prints?' Michael asked.

'They've been altered surgically. But we recovered a weapon, a modified Mannlicher six-millimeter, and a stool the hitter used as a rest. The stool legs and the weapon have good palm prints, as well as full digit impressions. Even though the finger pads have been altered, there are usually some remnants of the original patterns. It's all in the computer now. Careful cross-matching can turn up a positive identification. It'll just take a little longer. That will give us a lead to follow.'

Elias picked up Michael's jacket and tossed it to him. 'Vacation's over, buddy. It's time to go to Madrid. Start thinking big numbers. You're going to need them.'

MADRID: A light rain fell over Barajas International Airport, giving the morning air a biting chill. Michael Quinn stood in the cold wetness, his jacket a bit too light for the unexpected chill. He was staring at the white, gold, and black jumbo jet of the arms dealer Vigen Babayan as it stood massive and silent near a remote hangar area on the airport grounds. His concentration was so deep that he didn't feel the penetrating cold. He could think only of Alex on board the *Eslabón*, and the auction about to take place at seven miles above the earth.

Bob Elias sat in the back of the limo, sipping a cup of hot coffee. He leaned over to the open door. 'Why don't you come in and warm up, Mike? At least get yourself out of the rain,' he said.

Michael shook his head, oblivious of the rain, not needing warmth.

It was interesting, he thought, how the three involved parties had arrived at almost the same time, a good deal ahead of the scheduled pickup. They had taken positions well apart from one another and sat patiently waiting, watching the plane – and one another.

He could feel the eyes on him, and knew that camera shutters were clicking away from distant points, just as Intel-Trace's cameras would be when the players came into the open. He couldn't see them, but he knew they were there. He thought they ought to just exchange pictures and dossiers; it would save time and film and make everyone's job a lot easier. Still, it was a serious business, and even making light of it couldn't relieve the quiet tension building inside him.

Elias climbed out of the car with two cups of steaming coffee in his hands. He handed one to Michael. 'Come on, take it,' he said.

Michael accepted it, sipping carefully.

'Give me your watch,' Elias said.

'Don't you want to listen in?' Michael asked.

'It won't be much use on that plane. You'll be out of range too quickly. He may have a sweeper on board, too,

352

which would detect the radio and make you very unpopular. Wear this instead,' Elias told him, handing him a new timepiece.

'Looks the same,' Michael said.

'It's not. It will deliver a very strong signal when you depress the button at the upper left. You're to use it if you lose the bidding. We have no idea where or when the losers will be dropped off. Your signal will alert us instantly, at which time we'll activate our contingency plans. We'll be tracking the course of Babayan's plane both by satellite and by an AWACS that the President has made available to us. The AWACS can track Babayan from a distance of greater than fifty miles. It will pick up your signal if it's needed, and alert us.

'Remember, Mike, that the first bid is just to test each other. The second bid is the one that counts because it's the last chance you'll get. Just do your best to win it. If you don't, we'll take over.'

'We don't have any idea where the exchange is going to take place. Are you sure you can get there in time to intercept it?' asked Michael.

'No, I'm not sure. But we have mobile teams in place at six different locations. They'll be airborne the moment you send the signal. We may get there in time. It depends on how long Babayan stays aloft and how soon we know where he chooses to put down again. But you can make our job a lot easier by just winning the bid.'

'Do you think the Luxus could be on board?' Michael asked.

'That would make things too easy. All we'd have to do is knock the plane from the sky. Then everybody's problems would be over. Everyone else is probably thinking the same thing, and I'm sure Babayan has figured that much out for himself. He'll be more cautious than that. It'll be interesting to see how he handles it. Let's hope we find out from a winner's perspective.'

Michael checked the time on the new watch. There was

one minute left. The pregame jitters began to build inside of him.

'You've left all weapons behind?' Elias asked.

Michael nodded and yawned. It was a nervous reaction, the need for oxygen.

'The OPEC representative is out of the car,' Elias said, raising a pair of binoculars to get a closer look.

'Anyone we know?' Michael asked.

Elias shook his head. 'I don't know him,' he responded. 'We'll put him through the computers at Intelligence Central. If he's important enough to be here, then he'll be in the files someplace.'

Both men watched as the OPEC man walked the distance in the rain to the plane. He was partway up the portable ladder when the Soviet representative stepped out of his car. He was flanked by a half-dozen security people.

Elias swung the binoculars in that direction. 'That's Tolvanin, your counterpart for the Soviets,' he said. 'It's still a GRU operation. But you can bet that the KGB isn't far away.'

Tolvanin walked slowly toward the plane. About halfway there he turned his head in the direction of the Intel-Trace cars and stopped for a moment. He appeared to be waiting for Michael to start for the plane.

'It's time, Mike. Good luck,' Elias said, patting him on the shoulder.

Michael looked into Elias's eyes. He felt uncomfortable on the concrete. He wished that the transactions were taking place in a rain forest somewhere. This wasn't his element.

'Take care of Alex, Bob. Get her off the yacht, no matter what happens on that plane. Get her out safely.'

'I'll take care of it.'

Michael turned and walked between the cars and out across the tarmac.

Tolvanin began to move once again when Michael appeared.

Michael walked the hundred yards to the plane, Tolvanin boarding ahead of him as he approached the ladder. Michael climbed the stairway slowly and stopped at the open doorway. He was searched for weapons, and a sweeping device was moved carefully around him to check for a wire.

'Step inside, please,' the man who had checked him said.

Michael stepped into the plane. It was a vision of luxury.

The three contestants stood in a close circle, eyeing one another cautiously. Babayan was nowhere to be seen. He was undoubtedly in a rear compartment.

'Please be seated, gentlemen,' the man who had searched them said. 'We will be taking off immediately. Be sure to fasten your seat belts. I will get some refreshments for you once we are airborne.'

Without words among them, the three men took seats in the luxurious sitting-room compartment and strapped themselves in.

The portable stairway was rolled away and the door secured. The engines started, warmed up a bit, and the luxury craft began a slow taxi.

Michael closed his eyes and put his head back. He thought about the $200-million opening bid and wondered how high he'd have to go to win it. The huge pot he had won from Babayan in Monte Carlo seemed like a child's allowance compared to what Babayan stood to make from this deal.

It was a short wait until the 747 taxied on to the runway. The engines surged with thunderous power and the plane began to roll. Within seconds it had attained airspeed and eased gently off the ground.

Elias watched the plane climb away and bank to the west. It had been thirty-eight days since the Luxus was stolen. It had now come down to this: a single part of a day in which to win or lose. If they won, the contest would be over. If they lost, it could be the start of their worst nightmare.

The jumbo jet set out on an initial south-southwest heading and continued a slow ascent to 38,000 feet. Refreshments were offered to the three contestants. Tolvanin was the only one of the three to partake. He swirled his drink, and the ice cubes tinkling against the sides of the glass was the only sound in the cabin besides the low din of the engines.

Tolvanin had been impressed by Quinn's file. What was most apparent was that he was a hard man to kill. He had used up the luck of ten men in his professional lifetime. There was no estimate to the number of men who hadn't shared his good fortune and had died in confronting him. He didn't look like a deadly individual, but Tolvanin knew that looks were the last thing by which to judge a person in this business. It was too bad, he thought, that this affair would end so soon before they could measure themselves against one another. It would have been a great challenge.

The door to the back of the sitting room opened and Vigen Babayan entered. The three men rose immediately to their feet. Babayan approached them, stopping first in front of the representative from OPEC.

'Greetings to you, Mr Sahm. It has been . . . five years?'

'Almost exactly,' the Saudi replied. 'Allah has been good to you, I can see. You look fit and well.'

'I am both, thank you,' Babayan returned.

The arms dealer moved a few steps to the Russian.

'Mr Tolvanin, isn't it?' he asked in very good Russian.

Tolvanin dipped his head in response and raised the glass in salute. 'At your service,' he said in excellent English, sounding almost like an American.

'It is *I* who am at *your* service today, sir,' Babayan returned, also nodding his head.

He turned to face Michael. 'And Mr Quinn. How good it is to see you again so soon,' he said, his eyes staring directly into Michael's. 'You are a man of many talents . . . so I've been told by mutual friends.'

'They're no friends of mine,' Michael said coldly.

'Yes, I got that impression. In any event, here we are. Here we all are.' He turned away from Michael and faced the others.

'As you are aware, gentlemen, I am the agent of sale for my principal, who shall remain nameless, and who is offering today a most valuable item for auction to the highest bidder. The rules are simple. The bidding shall consist of two rounds only. The bids will be entered electronically into a predetermined numbered account in Switzerland. You will enter your bids, separately and in complete privacy, through a special communications channel aboard this plane. When the transfer of funds has been confirmed, you will be advised of the single highest bid. We shall then commence the second and final round of bidding. When all funds have again been confirmed in place, we shall head for a destination known only to me. After our arrival, I shall announce the names of the two lowest bidders, who will disembark after the plane has been refueled. The plane will then continue on to a second secret location, where the item for sale will be turned over to the winner. I should point out that the Luxus is not aboard this plane, for obvious reasons. The plane will stay airborne for a sufficient length of time to allow the Luxus to be moved into position for safe transfer. The site of transfer is different for each possible winner. Are there any questions?'

'When will the bidding begin?' Tolvanin asked.

Babayan looked at his watch. 'In approximately one hour. In the meantime, gentlemen, I suggest that you partake of the wonderful breakfast I have had prepared for you. If you will,' Babayan said, extending an arm toward the back of the sitting room, 'please follow Jacques to the dining salon. Your breakfast awaits you.'

The three contestants fell in behind the steward and began moving from the room. Babayan walked beside Michael, who trailed behind the others. 'I wonder, Mr Quinn, if your luck will carry through this day as well as it has up to now,' he said.

'I think luck will have nothing to do with what happens today,' Michael returned, then walked on ahead.

'Yes, you could be right. We'll just have to wait and see,' Babayan said, falling in behind the tall American.

The breakfast looked wonderful, but no one was in the

mood to eat, except Babayan. Michael and Tolvanin drank coffee, Sahm chose tea. The only conversation during that hour was what amounted to a long monologue by Babayan, who talked casually about many things ranging from world politics to World Cup soccer.

The hour passed slowly, and Michael could feel the plane bank through several course changes, making it impossible to predict its position. Not that it mattered; the 747 was perhaps the most carefully tracked object in the sky on that day. There were many interested eyes watching its progress as the time passed.

At the conclusion of breakfast, the contestants were shown to the communications console over which the bids would be transmitted. They were instructed on how to use the transmitter. Each was given a code designation and told to transmit numbers only. No other communications were permitted.

One by one they entered the communications room and sent off their opening bids. When they were finished, they were instructed to return to the sitting room to await Babayan's announcement.

The confirmations were obtained quickly, but Babayan held back giving them the results as the plane continued through its course changes.

Finally the door at the back of the sitting room opened and Babayan appeared.

'The first round is complete, gentlemen. Everything went smoothly, and all funds have been confirmed. The leading bid amount is four hundred million.'

A hot flash of nervousness coursed through Michael. Twice his bid. Elias had been right. The numbers would go high.

He studied his two adversaries, trying to sense which one had made the high bid. Neither had shown strong reaction. Of the two, however, Sahm had showed the least. Michael's bet was on the Arab.

'The final bids will commence in thirty minutes,' Babayan announced. 'Let me remind you, gentlemen, of the potential of the Luxus. Certainly, you are aware that you will have *one* final opportunity. We are dealing here with an item of unlimited value. Quite frankly, these bids are very disappointing. My principal may well decide *not* to let his property go if the figures are not acceptable. I urge you to think carefully between now and the start of the final round,' he said, letting his eyes play from one to the other.

'You have thirty minutes, gentlemen,' Babayan concluded, and left the room.

Four hundred million, Michael thought. How high should he go? he wondered. He knew that losing the Luxus would make taking it back very difficult, not to mention the increased danger to Alex in the rescue operation that would follow. He *had* to win it outright. He figured that the bid could go to a billion. He decided to raise it to an odd amount. He chose $1,250,195,000. Let them choke on that one, he thought.

Gregor Tolvanin sat silently, watching Michael and Sahm. He too was not certain which of the two had placed the bid. The Arab had been calm when the announcement was made. Quinn's face had been stone, which only underscored the strength of his American adversary. He, too, knew the importance of winning the strain outright. He had not been sent here to lose. He decided to triple his bid. Losing could mean his recall to the Soviet Union, and no field operative wanted that. Life was good in the field, and being recalled would seriously curtail his lifestyle. Brevig would see to that.

Unlike the first period of waiting, this one went by quickly. Too quickly. The very real prospect of failure was at hand for two of these men. Each sat wondering whether he would be the one invited to stay for the second flight.

The door to the sitting room opened again.

'Gentlemen, it is time to take your place in history,' Babayan announced. 'Mr Sahm, you will go first.'

The last round took longer. Each man sat for some time before transmitting his figure, wrestling with the prospect of losing. Finally the process was completed.

It was nearly two hours before Babayan appeared again. Two *long* hours of nervous doubt and second thoughts in which each man alternated between the certainty that his bid would win and the fear that he had underestimated his adversaries.

'Congratulations on your improved competitive spirit, gentlemen,' Babayan said. 'There is a winner, and the principal has agreed to the offered purchase price. I will make the announcement shortly.'

The plane had begun a descent at about the same time that Babayan returned to the sitting room. They had no idea where the plane was setting down. It wasn't until the 747 descended to five thousand feet through cloud cover that Tolvanin recognized the Aegean Sea below, and the coastline of Greece. They were putting down in Athens.

After a smooth landing, the 747 taxied to the end of the runway and continued on to another remote hangar area. The three men sat nervously while the plane was refueled, each eyeing the others carefully, running through contingency plans should they be asked to leave the plane as losers.

The captain's voice announced over the intercom that the refueling had been completed. The engines were again started and the plane sat waiting for Babayan's command. A portable stairway was rolled into place and the door opened.

Babayan stood in the open doorway, breathing the fresh Aegean air. He turned to the three waiting men. 'It is time, gentlemen,' he said, his words ringing like a cathedral bell tolling at a funeral.

'When I call your name, please exit the plane. Remain on the tarmac until the plane has again taken off.'

Babayan took a few steps back into the sitting room, the tension building with each passing second.

'Mr Tolvanin . . . I'm sorry,' he said.

The Russian felt his stomach drop as a cold sweat broke out over his entire body.

'You will leave the plane,' the arms dealer said firmly.

Tolvanin rose stiffly, his face flushed. He walked to the door, stopping for a second in front of Babayan. There were no words between them, but Tolvanin's hostility was palpable.

Tolvanin stepped into the doorway and looked back at the remaining two for one embarrassing moment. This was not ended, he thought. Then he left the plane.

Babayan looked at the two men still seated in the room with him.

'The bidding was close, gentlemen. Unfortunately, only *one* can win.'

His eyes played back and forth in a vicious tease.

'Mr Quinn,' he said, extending his arm toward the open door. 'A bit of *bad* luck today, I'm afraid.'

25

SAN ANTONIO, TEXAS: Michael had activated the alert signal the moment he set foot on the ground in Athens. Minutes later, Elias's communication was en route to Danziger at the Sky estate.

'OPEC has won the bidding,' Danziger announced, then added, 'Intel-Trace has also identified the OPEC representative as a suspected Libyan agent.'

'Oh, Christ!' Asher Sky showed the first signs of true despair since the incident had started, a little over five weeks ago. The only thing worse than losing the strain was the potential danger that Alex faced. He slouched low in his chair.

'Intel-Trace sources say that all funds have already been moved out of the bid account in Switzerland. None of the losing bids was returned. They didn't waste a second,' Danziger said. 'They've also confirmed that the OPEC bid *wasn't* the highest, either. Our bid was, by almost a hundred million.'

'Then we never really had a chance of winning it,' de Roode said, outraged.

'That seems to be the case,' Danziger replied.

'Then it was that bastard Qaddafi behind it the whole while,' Sky said, his voice smoldering with anger.

'Not necessarily, but that *is* the way it looks right now.'

'What are our alternatives, Tom?' Sky asked.

'We're left with just one. We *take* it back.'

'Where is the plane?' Sky asked.

'It's over the Mediterranean right now, its destination still unknown. But it will put down wherever the strain is being moved for the transfer. It'll remain airborne for as long as it takes to get the Luxus safely into position. That could be anywhere in the Middle East.'

'How long can it stay in the air?' Sky asked.

Danziger thought for a moment. 'It's fully fueled. It could stay up for sixteen hours if it had to. It could go a long way in that time.'

'Or it could just circle until security has been established at a transfer site in Libya,' de Roode added.

'It could, yes,' Danziger confirmed.

'What's the worst-case scenario, Tom?' Sky asked.

'That's easy,' Danziger said. 'If Qaddafi *was* behind this, and does end up with it, the Luxus will be in the hands of dangerously unstable Middle East elements. It could, and probably will, be used in terrorist activities, which could be directed anywhere – possibly at the United States and our oil reserves, against Israel, or against neighboring Egypt. Qaddafi could use it to gain control of OPEC, which he has always felt it was his destiny to control. There are a hundred ways it could be used. If the right reserves were hit, it could send the value of Middle East oil right off the charts, or the world economy straight into the dumper.'

'The President will have to be advised,' said Sky. 'He's going to need to show plenty of muscle right now, and will probably point the Mediterranean Fleet at Libya in a hurry. He'll have no choice.'

'We'll need every agent in the Middle East alerted. The Luxus must be located,' Danziger said.

'Does Intel-Trace have the proper resources?' de Roode asked.

'Yes, but they'll need help because the Soviets have an inside track in Libya. They've been romancing Qaddafi lately with a good bit of success.'

'Assuming that the strain surfaces next in Libya, can Intel-Trace get it back?' de Roode asked.

'They'll have to, even if it means risking every agent and every network in the Middle East,' Danziger answered.

'And Alex?' Sky asked, his eyes dark with worry for her.

'There's no reason to wait any longer. The rescue mission will begin the moment the landing site is identified. To be honest, Asher, the operation will be dangerous, but we have no choice. There's no longer any advantage to them in holding her. The adversary will be no less ruthless now than they have been to this point.'

Sky lowered his head, feeling feverish, almost sickly from nervousness and concern. At last he rose to his feet, a look of grim resolve on his face. 'I'll have to call the President,' he said. 'He's expecting some news, though by this time he probably already knows.'

'I'm sure he was notified the second Quinn set foot on the runway in Athens,' Danziger commented.

'I know you're right, Tom. There's no point in putting it off any longer.'

Sky dropped his cigar into the ashtray beside his chair and excused himself from the others. He walked with difficulty into his office, adjacent to the study, and dialed the special security number that had been set up at the President's ranch.

The wait for clearances seemed eternal to Sky. He tried in his mind to find the proper words to deliver the message he had hoped he would not have to give his longtime friend. But his thoughts were really focused on his daughter's situation.

'This is the President,' the voice at the other end said.

The words he had prepared vanished like a mirage at the sound of the voice. He hesitated, cleared his throat, and began. 'I'm sorry, Cully. We've lost the Luxus.'

The 747 was on a southeasterly heading, toward the Sea of Crete. Babayan had sat with the elated OPEC representative during the takeoff, and had shared some refreshment with him for the first thirty minutes of flight. Then the arms dealer, feeling much relieved to have his part in this matter very nearly at an end, excused himself and left Sahm in his contentment.

Babayan moved aft, passing through a series of elegantly furnished compartments to the rearmost cabin at center level. These were his private sleeping quarters.

He entered the room, his eyes focusing on the dark figure seated comfortably in a plush sofa.

'Everything went *perfectly*,' Babayan said, raising his clenched fists in the air.

Rafael Sonterra looked at the ecstatic arms dealer without comment.

'Do you know how rich you are?' Babayan asked him. 'Have you *any* idea how much money you made today? You could buy a country! What a day! Never in my life will I have another like this,' he went on, contemplating the fortune he had just made in commission.

'That's a fact, my dear Babayan,' Sonterra said in his deep monotone. 'This is the most significant day in your entire life. You should celebrate it.'

'I will, I will . . . as soon as the last phase of your plan is finished,' he said, his hands caressing the metallic case at the foot of the bed. 'When do we land?' he asked.

'In about three hours,' Sonterra replied. 'Instruct your pilot to put the plane on a heading for Tripoli,' he said, revealing the final destination for the first time.

'Libya?' the arms dealer questioned.

'Can you think of a safer place to make delivery?'

Sonterra laughed gently. 'Sahm is a Libyan agent. We're just making his job easier.'

'You knew this all along?'

Sonterra's answer was a confident half-smile.

'I like doing business with you, Monsieur,' the arms dealer said.

'You should return forward to rejoin Sahm. It is best to keep him occupied. You may inform him of our destination at your leisure. I'm sure he will be pleased.'

'And after Libya, where shall I take you?'

'I will advise you later, after we are again airborne,' Sonterra replied.

'You are a very cautious man.'

'One has to be, in my line of work.'

Babayan turned and started toward the door, then stopped and turned back toward Sonterra. 'I have just one more question,' he said.

'Yes?'

'The woman. What do I do with her?'

'We shall put down in Tripoli at about nine o'clock. That will be eight o'clock, Corsica time. We have no more need for her. Radio the *Eslabón* when we make our final approach. Tell them to kill her.'

Babayan's mouth fell open. 'Kill . . . kill her?' he echoed in utter disbelief.

'She is their *agent*, Monsleur Babayan. Forget your plans for romance. Forget the *Eslabón*. Life for you will be very different from now on, my friend. They will not forget you. There will be other women, the most beautiful women money can buy. Besides, you've made a fortune to last ten lifetimes. I think you will find that you will need it. Be assured that you will need it, for they will come for you. Sooner or later, they will come.'

Babayan's elation turned quite suddenly to fear.

Sonterra could not resist a wicked smile.

In that one moment Babayan saw what a poor deal he had cut. He had been blinded by the prospect of the enormous commission, never fully considering the true price he would have to pay. He now realized he had made a fool's deal.

'What . . . what will I do?' he asked weakly, realizing that he was unprepared for the danger facing him.

Rafael Sonterra had regained his impassive, hardened expression. 'That, my friend, is *your* problem.'

MOSCOW: Nikolai Barchenkin looked into the troubled face of his superior as he finished the report in his hands.

Kozlov looked up, letting the papers fall to the desk in front of him. The GRU chief took the pipe from his mouth, placed it in the ashtray on his desk, and locked his hands together tightly. 'The heading is confirmed?' he asked.

'Yes, General. The plane is heading for Libya. It has already communicated with the control tower in Tripoli. It will land there within the hour,' Barchenkin verified.

Kozlov checked his watch. A special session of the Committee would meet in less than one hour, at about the same time the 747 landed in Tripoli. He did not relish the prospect of reporting his failure to obtain the Luxus at auction.

'The Committee will bare their teeth, Nikolai. Vladin will have backing now. He will be dangerous. The KGB will be dangerous. They will spare nothing to succeed in the shadow of our failure. Gorbachev will be unable to hold back his support. His own position has become too tenuous.'

'Our situation is strong in Libya,' Barchenkin said, offering hope.

'Yes, but is it strong enough? We must apply utmost leverage with Qaddafi. We must be prepared to offer anything – or threaten, if necessary – to obtain the Luxus. Or at least part of it.'

'Qaddafi fears no-one. He is a madman. The power that the Luxus will give him will make him impossible and very dangerous,' Barchenkin said. 'But he may respond to the *right* offer. Perhaps a change in our position to support him against Egypt and to install the secret missile sites. We can add even more, perhaps the promise of a *Siska*-class nuclear submarine and the surface patrol vessels he covets.

'Naval Intelligence reports that the US Mediterranean Fleet is headed for the coast of Libya. A strong, unsolicited show of support could help put his thinking right,' Barchenkin suggested.

Kozlov nodded. 'It will help. Alert our Libyan intelligence stations to go to full readiness and assemble the elite command units at points of debarkation. If that madman refuses our overtures, we must be ready to act with force, if necessary. We must obtain that strain, Nikolai. And we must get it before Vladin does. Our very existence may depend upon it.'

'And orders for Tolvanin?' Barchenkin asked.

'He is to go wherever Quinn goes. We must be cautious not to keep our eyes set so firmly on the KGB as to forget about the Americans. They will be no less desperate than we, and they will be just as determined. We must be prepared to deal with them as well.'

CORSICA: The *Eslabón* rocked gently in the calm waters to the south-west of Ajaccio, where it had been anchored for the past six days. Alex had the distinct feeling she was a prisoner, though her treatment had not even remotely suggested it. The crew had been courteous and responsive to her needs since she first came on board in Monte Carlo. She had been given complete freedom of the yacht. Her persistent inquiries regarding Babayan were smartly sidestepped. She could find out nothing about developments in the Luxus situation, though she knew Babayan's absence had something to do with it.

Having no way of knowing that the auction was under way, she had expected every day that Babayan would arrive. Though she had the communications capabilities through the watch on her wrist, she had received no word from Elias. Figuring that Elias would contact her if there was a problem, she had gone about passing time in the best ways possible. Babayan had a fairly extensive library on board, of which she had availed herself. But nothing could displace her growing concerns over the status of the Luxus – and Michael.

Alex began a slow, steady pacing around her cabin.

The cat raised its head, looked at her, then stretched out again across the bed. Sasha had become her constant companion in the absence of her master.

The night was dark, as dense cloud cover had rolled in with the dusk. The air was heavy and calm, though some rain and light winds were expected by morning.

Of the *Eslabón's* sixteen crew members and three officers, all but four were belowdecks. A nominal watch was stationed topside, with one officer and a first mate manning the bridge. As far as the crew was concerned, it was just another routine night aboard the luxury vessel.

The black rubber boats had come in silently in the blackness of the night. They had come in straight to the bow and made their way slowly along the side of the yacht to the stern.

The first member of the Intel-Trace team to board the *Eslabón* was Wadelaw. He climbed silently on to the aft platform, dressed entirely in black, nearly invisible in the darkness. He crouched low, staying below the aft rail as the night sentry made a routine pass.

The sentry stood at the rail, looking out over the water, unaware that directly below him were two boats carrying the rescue team. He needed only to look straight down and to his left to see them.

He stayed at the rail for a few moments before turning away. Wadelaw was up the second he turned, his hand cupping the face of the unsuspecting crewman. The knife went quickly to the throat and it was over for the sentry, swiftly and silently.

Wadelaw went over the rail and on to the deck, followed by two others, as the second raft began emptying to board the yacht. The team split and moved forward to take the rest of the deck crew.

The captain of the *Eslabón* was belowdecks in the communications cabin. He had been called there to receive a coded message from his boss. He accepted the transcribed message from the radio operator, and as he read it carefully, his face went white.

'Ask him to repeat the message,' he asked the radio operator, hoping there had been some mistake.

But the message came back the same. 'The sale is completed. Kill the woman. Proceed to Cyprus.'

The captain handed the communication to the steward. The steward read it and smiled. 'We'll dump the body at sea,' he said.

The steward pulled a stout automatic from a pit holster, snapped back the slide, locked the safety, and replaced the weapon. It would be over quickly – but not before he was through with the woman. There would be time for a little fun with her before completing his assignment.

He left the communications room and walked aft toward Alex's cabin. The thought of taking her forcibly gave him an erection. Until now, it had been just a pleasant fantasy.

Alex was fiddling with the magnificent Rolex that Babayan had left for her, when the watch Elias had given her emitted a short but distinct three-tone alarm. The suddenness of it startled her. She stared at the watch for a brief moment, then the alarm repeated. She clearly understood its significance and recalled Elias's specific instructions: 'If the alarm sounds, discharge the flare pen straight down into the deck and get off the boat immediately.' She turned, her eyes focusing on the bag on the dresser across the cabin. She started toward it.

Wadelaw's team moved in on the bridge after neutralizing the remainder of the night watch. The doors on both sides of the bridge burst open at once, catching the first officer and mate by surprise.

'Freeze! Touch nothing,' Wadelaw commanded, the weapons of his team bearing with menace on the two men.

The first officer looked quickly from side to side at the intruders, then his hand shot out and hit an alarm button. The wail of the alarm and the shots dropping the first officer sounded simultaneously throughout the yacht. All possibility of surprise was now past.

Alex was fumbling with her bag when the gunfire began. At the same instant, the door of her cabin burst open. The kindly steward stood in the open doorway, his hungry eyes showing anything but the pleasant manner he had shown previously.

The hostilities that had suddenly broken out on the yacht had ended the steward's prospects of pleasure with Alex. His visions of carnal pleasure with her vaporized as quickly as the stillness of the night. He became torn for a moment between his orders to take care of the woman and the defense of the *Eslabón*. He drew the weapon at the same time Alex pulled the flare pen from her bag.

He took a quick step toward her as she raised the pen, and swiped the gun at her hand, striking her wrist heavily. The pen flew from her hand and hit hard against the wall. The steward threw a vicious blow with his free hand that caught Alex on the side of the head, sending her into the same wall.

Alex came off the wall as the hand holding the weapon rose toward her. She threw a straight kick to the groin that crumpled the steward. He reeled backward and went down on one knee. Alex charged him, hitting him with her full force, and the two of them sprawled across the floor, the steward losing the gun.

Alex recovered before the partially disabled steward did, and lunged at him again, her hands going for his face, her nails digging into his eyes.

The steward let out a howl and threw a short but powerful jab to her ribs, knocking her away and to the floor. His hands went to his injured eyes and he moved away.

The blow to Alex's ribs had taken her breath, but not her instinct for survival. Her impromptu flight across the floor had put her close to the handgun, and she went for it.

The steward was on her in an instant, fighting her for control of the weapon. He hit her again, and then again, and the gun fell away once more.

Alex was strong, and fought surprisingly well. She jammed her fingers into his face once again, her nails tearing into his flesh. The steward reeled backwards, Alex driving into him with all of her weight. They crashed into a wall and the steward used the sudden stopping of her momentum to his advantage. He grabbed her by the shoulders, twisted, and threw her with all of his force across the cabin. She sprawled along the floor, coming to a stop near the flare pen.

The steward went for the gun as Alex reached for the pen. As the gun came up and swung toward her, she depressed the pen's trigger mechanism. There was a bright flash, and the steward's face went stark white as his solar plexus exploded into a brilliant, blinding white light. He let out a horrible scream and stumbled back against the wall.

There were two loud cracking sounds from the doorway, and the steward went down in a heap.

Alex looked frantically toward the door to see the tall figure of Christopher Wadelaw, his handgun still raised at the steward.

'Let's get the hell out of here,' Wadelaw shouted above the grotesque hissing of the phosphorus flare still consuming the body of the steward.

Alex got to her feet. Wadelaw threw an arm around her and practically carried her out of the cabin. They made their way swiftly to the deck, passing sprawled, lifeless bodies as they moved aft.

They got to the aft platform as one of the team members was being lowered to a boat. He had taken a bullet in the chest.

Wadelaw lowered Alex to waiting arms in the second boat, then climbed down into the same boat.

Small gas engines, which had not been used in the silent

approach, kicked to life and the rubber boats moved swiftly and steadily away from the *Eslabón*. Alex was looking back at the yacht about two hundred yards away, when it suddenly seemed to expand like a rapidly inflating balloon. There was a flash and a loud bang, and the *Eslabón* was gone in a hail of debris.

They ducked low in the boats as the debris crashed around them like spent shrapnel. The rafts sped away, keeping Elias's promise to Michael, and melted into the darkness and safety of the night.

Vigen Babayan cupped his hands around his eyes as he stared out into the darkness from one of the windows of the 747's plush sitting room. The plane was on its approach to Tripoli.

'We have just picked up a fighter escort,' Babayan said, looking back to Abdel Sahm.

Sahm rushed to a window and looked out. 'Yes . . . yes, they are Libyan,' he said happily, feeling truly safe for the first time since Quinn and Tolvanin had been dropped off in Athens. The sleek lines of the Soviet-built MiGs were the most welcome sight he could imagine.

'You return home a great hero,' Babayan said to him.

Sahm stared at the arms dealer, realizing for the first time that Babayan was aware he was a Libyan agent. 'Home?' he repeated cautiously. 'I am a Saudi,' he said.

Babayan smiled. 'If you wish. It makes no difference to me. Your money is good, and your politics are your business. In any event, in a few short minutes you will be safely on the ground in the company of friends. And whichever flag unfurls in your honor, you will be its hero.'

'When will you turn the Luxus over to me?' Sahm asked, realizing that he would be nobody's hero without the goods in hand.

'Before we dock.'

'*Before?* Do you mean that the Luxus was on the plane all along?'

'Yes,' Babayan replied.

'But we could have been blown from the sky and the Luxus destroyed. Everything would have been lost,' Sahm said excitedly.

'Like you, no-one knew that it was on board. They all believed it to be in a safe, unknown place where it could be used against anyone failing to adhere to the rules of sale. No-one would have dared take such a risk.'

'You *are* a gambler, Vigen Babayan,' Sahm said with a sly smile.

Babayan returned the smile. 'Yes, and a good one.'

The elevator stopped at galley level, one deck below the sitting room. The door opened and Rafael Sonterra stepped out.

There were two galley crewmen just completing the routine securing of equipment for the landing. They both stopped and looked at the slender stranger stepping out of the elevator.

'Who are you? You don't belong down here,' challenged the one closer to Sonterra.

Sonterra raised the silenced, small-caliber Beretta and fired twice in rapid succession at the first crewman, then twice more at the second. They died without a sound. He stood over them, putting a final round into the brain of each to guarantee his work, then returned to the elevator. He pushed the button for the deck level, and the elevator moved slowly upward.

When the door opened, the steward was standing there holding a tray with empty glasses and a half-bottle of vintage Dom Perignon, a look of utter surprise across his face. Sonterra reached out and grabbed the steward by his tunic and pulled him into the small elevator before a sound could leave his throat.

He jammed the Beretta into the sternum of the steward and pulled the trigger.

The steward stiffened with a violent jerk, the tray falling from his hands.

Sonterra yanked up on the steward's tunic to keep him from falling, and held him firmly against the wall, the horror-filled eyes of the steward staring straight into his own. He put the Beretta against the man's throat, raised it upward under his chin, and fired once again. The top of the steward's head exploded open like a ripe tomato. He released the tunic and let the body slide down the wall of the elevator, smears of blood tracing the line of his fall.

Sonterra removed the clip from the gun and inserted another, then stepped quietly from the elevator and began moving forward toward the sitting room.

As the seat-belt light snapped on, accompanied by an audible signal, Babayan and Sahm dutifully fastened their belts. They did not hear the cabin door open behind them.

'You will take official possession of the Luxus when the plane is on the ground,' Babayan said to Sahm. 'You may inspect it before we reach the gate area. The organism is in a dormant state, and will remain quite protected as long as—' Babayan's words cut off as he spotted unexpected movement at the edge of his peripheral vision.

He turned his head in time to see Sonterra step up behind Sahm, whose attention was still on the arms dealer.

The Beretta closed within inches of the back of Sahm's head.

The weapon made two coughlike sounds, and Sahm's head kicked forward. His body flopped forward, his chest almost to his knees, propped up by the seat belt. Blood began a slow trickle from his nose and mouth.

Babayan gaped in utter horror at what had just happened, his voice choked off by fear. Before he could say a word, Sonterra turned the weapon on him and fired twice into his chest.

Babayan kicked stiffly upright, his eyes locked in rigid disbelief.

Sonterra took a step closer and raised the gun once again, firing a third round into the brain of the arms dealer.

Lifeless, Babayan slumped to the left.

Sonterra pulled the partially emptied clip from the

weapon and inserted another full one, then began going through Babayan's pockets for the keys to the flight cabin.

A thousand eyes watched as the 747 jumbo jet descended slowly and touched down smoothly on the military runway, its fighter escort pulling up and away with a thunderous roar.

There was clapping and a small chorus of cheers from the entourage standing around Colonel Muammar Qaddafi, whose face was filled with a crazed satisfaction. He turned to his aide and let a small smile creep across his lips. 'Allah is good, Omar. He delivers into our hands the means to complete my destiny. All the world will tremble now before us. *All* the world.'

The plane braked and reversed the thrust of its powerful engines, slowing on the runway.

Rafael Sonterra inserted the key into the lock of the flight cabin door and pushed it open. The navigator looked up at the stranger standing in the doorway, and took two rounds square in the face.

The copilot spun in his seat.

Sonterra raised the gun. 'No radio! No radio!' he shouted. 'Off! Turn it off now!' he said, raising the gun with terrible menace.

The pilot turned and looked back over his shoulder. Sonterra aimed the gun right at his face. The pilot faced front quickly and turned off the radio as he had been instructed.

'Taxi to the end of the runway and stop,' Sonterra ordered.

'Easy! Easy with that thing,' the pilot said. 'We'll do anything you want. We've got plenty of fuel. We'll take you anywhere you want to go. Just don't let that thing go off again in here.'

'Taxi to the end of the runway and stop,' Sonterra repeated firmly.

'End of the runway and stop,' the pilot said, casting a worried glance at his copilot.

The plane taxied slowly to the end of the runway,

ignoring the tower's command to turn off, and came to a complete stop.

The pilot leaned forward slightly and turned to look back at the intruder in the cabin. 'Shall I pull it off the runway?' he asked calmly.

Sonterra looked out through the windows. 'No. Shut down your engines,' he commanded.

'The tower will be asking us to pull off the runway. This is not a safe place to stop,' the pilot said.

'Maybe you need a hole in your head to improve your hearing,' Sonterra replied.

'I can hear you very well,' the pilot said. 'Shutting all engines down.'

The tower repeated its orders to pull the plane from the runway, but there was no response. The plane sat for several long minutes.

'Cut all power. Now,' Sonterra ordered.

'Cutting all power,' the pilot repeated, complying with the command.

He turned back to Sonterra once again. 'Now what?' he asked.

Sonterra trained the gun on the pilot. 'Goodbye, gentlemen. You go to a better life,' he said, then squeezed the trigger.

The murmurs began in the tight entourage around Qaddafi. He stood alert yet motionless, perspiration beading on his forehead and upper lip.

An officer approached from the rear and leaned close to his leader's ear. 'The plane is not responding to the tower's commands to leave the runway,' he whispered.

Qaddafi did not turn. He continued staring out at the jumbo jet sitting immobile on the runway.

'The plane has cut its engines and all power,' the officer continued, then paused, awaiting further orders.

Perspiration was now running down the face of the Libyan leader. His face had grown tense and had begun to redden.

'I await your orders, Colonel,' the officer said softly.

Qaddafi turned his head very slightly to the side and looked at his aide. There was now anger in his eyes, and his lips grew tight.

'Surround the plane. If the tower cannot raise radio communication with the pilot, gain entry by force. Send in the commando teams,' he ordered.

His aide repeated the commands to the officer, and he was off at once.

Libyan troop vehicles sped on to the runway and surrounded the plane while the tower continued in vain to reestablish radio communication. There was a short wait, and then commando units commenced their assault on the plane.

They moved quickly into position, marked their watches, and waited for elements gaining entry from below, through the landing-gear accessways, to ready themselves. At a signal, the emergency doors, rear hatch, and belly entries were blown.

Within seconds the Libyan commando units were swarming through the plane's lavish compartments, uncovering the grisly scenes of death.

Qaddafi turned stiffly as the officer approached once again. 'What did you find?' the Libyan leader asked.

The officer stood nervously in front of his leader. 'Everyone on board is dead, General. They've all been killed.'

'And the Luxus?' Qaddafi asked, his voice rigid with tension.

'There is no trace of it. We have found the container in which it was kept. But it was empty,' the officer reported.

Qaddafi's face went livid with anger. 'Everybody on board is dead, and the container bearing the Luxus is empty!' he shouted. 'They did not all kill themselves, and the Luxus did not just disappear. *Someone* is on that plane. Search it, you fool! Tear every inch of it out if you have to. Do not stop until you have found who is responsible for this. Get out of my sight,' he hissed at the officer, thrusting an arm forcefully toward the plane. 'I am holding you responsible. Find him and bring him to me – *alive!*'

26

PARIS: Juan Strassa was no stranger to fear. What had happened in Bern was not the first time that someone had tried to take his life. He had been lucky, and he wasted no time celebrating his good fortune.

Strassa had gone into hiding for three days immediately following his escape from the attempt on his life at the market. He had not even returned to his flat for fear that he would become a target for a second time. Bern was his city, and hiding would have been relatively easy for him. But he also knew there were 'hunters' who knew the city every bit as well as he did. His best chance, he knew, would be to get out as quickly and unobtrusively as possible. And he had done just that after making a couple of stops to pick up hidden cash reserves and a few false passports. Men like Strassa are never really secure, and always plan for such contingencies.

Every instinct warned him to stay in deep hiding. But the suddenness of his departure had left him with relatively modest funds, which would not be sufficient to permit him to hide well for any length of time.

His first objective after leaving Bern was to get to a source of cash – a lot of cash. He would need substantial funds to reestablish himself securely and to start finding out who was after him and why. That information would make staying alive a lot easier. He knew that answers could be obtained from the right sources, and that it would take time and money to obtain them. To be sure, he had made many enemies in his lifetime, and any one of them could have been behind the attempt in Bern. But men like Strassa have a sixth sense, and his was telling him now that events in Colombia were tied to this in some way.

Strassa did not risk air travel. Airports were too easily watched, and planes too vulnerable. He rented a car in Bern, using one of his false passports, and drove north to

Basel, crossing the border there into St-Louis, and continuing straight into Paris on N19. The source of cash was there, and if he was right about Colombia, so was the answer to his first question.

Once in Paris, he found safe lodgings, then took to the streets to determine whether he was being followed. He hadn't detected any tail upon his arrival, but knew well that there was no guarantee in that. If there was a tail, this would be the time to find it. He moved about the streets at a casual pace, taking a long and complicated route, checking subtly for the telltale signs of surveillance. After almost two hours of this painstaking routine, he returned to his room, feeling secure – for the moment – that he was free to go about his business.

The Intel-Trace surveillance teams had kept a loose watch on him, having the benefit of the planted homing devices in his shoes and jacket. They limited their observation efforts to static agents and long-range positions, relying predominantly on the homing signals to track him when out of visual contact. They knew that he was searching for a tail, and allowed him to convince himself that he was unobserved.

Strassa spent the remainder of the first day in Paris in his room, making contingency plans for the various scenarios that might confront him.

The long drive to Paris and the time in the room had given him ample opportunity to think over his dilemma. The fear that had filled him in Bern left slowly in stages as his plans took form, replaced by a growing anger. The more he thought about Colombia, the more certain he became that he was right about the connection. He had eliminated loose ends to prevent any chance of comeback to the principal. Now someone was trying to do the same to him.

The Colombians he had killed were minor operators – amateurs trying to become heroes. They were all expendable, in his opinion, and it was common practice to remove fringe elements when the job was big enough.

That was his specialty. But he was also a high-level professional, and it was never part of the procedure to remove operatives at his level. It just wasn't done. There were unwritten rules that one did not violate within the system – rules of *faith*. Principals who tried to do so often ended up dead, especially when men like Strassa were involved. Things like that made him very angry, and when he got angry with people, someone usually ended up dead.

As Strassa saw it, he had two choices: he could run and hide once he got his hands on enough money, or he could get mad and fight back. In fact, he rather enjoyed the latter prospect. He was not one to run from a threat. He was also not eager to abandon the considerable fortune he had amassed in the accounts he had left behind. Removal of the threat facing him would free his access to those accounts. It would also notify the rest of the world that he was not to be made into fodder, whatever the cause. There was no choice at all, really. Strassa had one style. And running wasn't a part of it. It would be war. He was a fighter, and he would rather die confronting an adversary than spend his life running in fear.

Having made his choice, he set about solving his next biggest problem, which was obtaining the identity of the principal with whom he intended to do business.

His contact for the Colombian contract was a Frenchman known in the trade as the Dwarf. Strassa had done business with him many times in the past, and knew exactly how to find him. The Dwarf was also the source of the funds he'd need until he could settle accounts with the unknown principal. He would get the cash, then squeeze the Dwarf for the identity of the principal, if he knew it, or of the contact at the next level up if he didn't. Then he'd move up layer by layer until he confronted the principal himself and settled accounts in very certain fashion. Chances were that the principal would be no more than a few layers away, as the Dwarf was a major player who worked strictly big-time. Not just anyone could approach him, much less deal through him.

The Dwarf himself would be another matter. Strassa was bound by the same rules of faith within the brotherhood of his profession that he suspected of being broken in Bern. The remote possibility existed that the Dwarf had, in fact, sold him out. Ethically, he could not simply remove him without first proving his suspicion. No-one would contract him again if he broke faith. But he *could* teach the little slug a lesson about respect.

At nightfall, Strassa left the shabby rooming house to begin his search through the underbelly of Paris. The Dwarf was an underworld person, invisible by day, a creature of the night. The approach would have to be direct and unannounced, for word would get back to the Dwarf quickly that he was being sought. That word could be spread just as easily to the wrong ears. Strassa knew the Dwarf's habits well enough, however, to be reasonably certain that he could find him without making inquiries. It would just take time and patience.

The Dwarf was a mover, frequenting many places in a given night, making his contacts, working his deals, moving endlessly like a shark through his world of darkness. He was a careful creature who commanded a surprising level of respect from those he dealt with, despite the fact that he was a nasty, repulsive little man who had spent a lifetime overcoming the physical handicaps dealt him at birth, often to the point of overcompensation. He was living proof that a person did not have to be liked to be respected.

He was large as dwarfs went, being just under five feet tall, but exhibiting the distinct characteristics of stunted limbs and elongated facial features. Like most dwarfs, he was highly intelligent and quick-witted, and was often at least two steps ahead of his business associates. And he used his intelligence as a weapon of intimidation. Information was his business, and he had few equals when it came to obtaining it – information about anything and anyone, all of it locked permanently in a computerlike brain that remembered every face and every name. His memory was his livelihood and his protection.

His services were expensive but reliable, and available to anyone with the right amount of money. Payment for his services was routinely up front, and he always delivered exactly what was contracted for, guaranteeing the quality of his work and complete confidentiality. Few would dare to violate their agreements or break faith with him, though there were some who had tried and fared poorly for the attempt. He had many friends to whom he was very valuable and to whose advantage it was to offer him protection.

Strassa was well aware of the risks involved in trying to force information from the Dwarf. But as he saw it, the principal he sought had already broken faith and posed a greater threat to the Dwarf. Surely he would have to recognize this, for his own reputation stood to be damaged. Strassa was the Dwarf's client, too, and the line of betrayal would cross dangerously near to him, raising doubt in the minds of others who relied upon his integrity. Strassa's tactics would depend upon the Dwarf's perception of the problem. And Strassa was quite prepared to play by any rules to stay alive.

Strassa moved through the underworld of Paris, staking out several of the spots most often frequented by the Dwarf. The efforts of the first night were fruitless. He stayed hidden all the next day, and set out again with the night to resume his search. It was a Friday night, and his chances of finding him on this night would be better, he knew, for the Dwarf was a creature of some peculiar habits and was given to the enjoyment of perverse sexual pleasures.

The Dwarf, it seemed, was incapable of engaging in sex with a partner. It wasn't a physical thing, actually, for he was endowed with a male organ of average size and suffered no anatomical dysfunction. He had been with a woman once as a younger man, but had found the entire experience so frightening that it had been deeply traumatic. It wasn't that he didn't enyoy being with women, for he did, and he appreciated beauty as much as any man alive. But there was an awesome perfection in the beauty of a woman's body that intimidated him. While he was more than equal to most other men intellectually, his physical handicap made him inferior in his own mind. He hated the mortal shell in which he was imprisoned, and it became a barrier to the fulfillment of the desires that tormented him. Masturbation became his only release, as he imagined wild fantasies of sexual encounters. At first he had used pornographic pictures of women to feed the fantasy world of his sexuality, then had graduated to films with motion and texture, and had finally found his greatest pleasure in watching live sexual acts. But as his level of fulfillment grew, so did his appetite for sexual variation. The pleasures he derived from watching straight sex began to fade, and he sought out increasingly bizarre forms of sexual entertainment. And in Paris anything was available for the right price.

Strassa knew of many such places in Paris, but, more important, he knew of several that the Dwarf favored above all others. He found success on his second stop.

Entry to the small viewing room was expensive. He stepped into the narrow darkened room and spotted the Dwarf immediately. There were three rows of seats separated by a center aisle, with four seats to a row on each side of the aisle. The Dwarf was in the front row at the extreme right corner. There were two other spectators in the room, sitting as far apart as possible. Strassa took a seat in the last row, directly behind the Dwarf.

There was a large one-way mirror across the front of the stage through which to watch the show, which had just started, judging from the fact that the young girl blindfolded and tied in a chair onstage was still fully clothed. Three men were onstage with her, hovering around the chair, tormenting her verbally. The girl looked very frightened.

Strassa slouched well back in his chair to make himself

as inconspicuous as possible, and focused his attention on the Dwarf.

The show progressed in typical fashion, with the behavior of the men becoming more aggressive and somewhat brutal. As they began fondling her, she struggled against her bindings. One of the men struck her hard across the face and tore the top of her dress almost completely away, exposing her breasts. Then all three men closed in on her. The biggest of the men opened his pants and exposed his large, erect organ, bringing it close to her face. He touched it to her face and she jerked her head away instinctively. He grabbed her hair forcefully and struck her across the face and shouted at her.

The girl was crying now and trembling from fright.

The man pushed his penis into her face, and she tried to pull away once again, only to have her face pulled hard against him. He hit her again and screamed vile profanities at her, which could hardly be heard through the thick glass of the mirror. His left hand held firmly on to her hair as his right manipulated his penis toward her mouth. The girl struggled vainly against his strength as he forced his penis to her lips, plunging it into her mouth.

The girl gagged and almost retched from the sudden intrusion of the engorged organ. The man grabbed her head with both of his hands and began forcing her head in a back-and-forth motion, his pelvis pumping, driving his penis in and out of her mouth. The other men began tearing at the remains of her dress.

Her crying faded to whimpers as the man pumped away, his rhythm increasing as he began drawing nearer to his climax. He drove the huge organ over and over again, completely controlling her head. Then he stiffened and slowed the motion of her head to match the final spasms of his orgasm as it pulsed deeply in her throat.

When he finished, he removed his penis from her mouth, and the second man repeated the entire act. She was almost limp with the second oral rape, which was as brutal as the first.

Strassa watched as the Dwarf sat forward, close to the glass, his face almost touching it.

When the second man had finished his pleasure, the third lifted the girl by her hair to a standing position, the chair falling away. He pushed the girl forward, her body now almost completely naked and unresisting, until she flopped forward over a desk. He lowered his pants and held her forward over the desk, pushing his incredibly large penis against her from behind. He manipulated it until it was within her, and began driving at her so hard that the desk rocked up on two legs until he was well inside her.

The girl let out a painful cry, to the laughter of her captors, and whimpered weakly as the last attacker raped her with savage energy.

Strassa watched the Dwarf carefully, his body moving rhythmically in a matching cadence with the sexual act.

The first man wrapped a short length of cord around the neck of the girl as the rape progressed, and pulled hard. The girl kicked helplessly as the cord bit deep. The man behind her increased his tempo, reaching explosive culmination of the act as the struggling of the girl faded, then stopped.

The Dwarf's body jerked in climax at almost the same instant.

Strassa sat in silent revulsion, gritting his teeth tightly. If ever he wanted to take a life, it was now.

He watched as the men in the performance theater dressed in quick silence, oblivious of the limp form of the girl lying across the desk.

A red light flashed three times to signal the end of the session. Strassa remained low in his chair as the Dwarf closed his pants and rose from his seat, then filed out of the exit at the lower corner of the room.

The Basque sat in the room for a moment longer, weak from the horrible scene he had just witnessed. When he was sure that the Dwarf had cleared the exit sufficiently for him to follow without alerting him, he rose to leave.

He looked back at the window to the stage, outrage tearing at his insides, when he saw the girl raise herself from the table.

The first man who had assaulted her patted her on the behind and whispered something, a smile across his face. The girl draped an arm over his shoulder and kissed him. Then the team of actors left the lighted room through a door he hadn't even noticed.

Strassa shook his head in disgust and went through the door to follow after the Dwarf. What a sick world, he thought to himself. He no longer had any doubts as to what he had in store for the Dwarf. The world was about to be a better place by a factor of one.

Strassa hit the street about thirty yards behind the Dwarf, trailing him casually up the block. It was a very dark, cloudy night. The air was cold and a light drizzle fell, creating an atmosphere not unlike that of London. The Dwarf walked briskly, crossed one street, continued on for another block, then turned right and began heading down a narrow street.

Strassa saw the Dwarf turn, then turned himself, into a narrow alleyway running between two buildings. He picked up his pace considerably, nearly running toward the alley's opening on the next street over, to gain a position ahead of the Dwarf. When he reached the end of the alleyway, he turned left, and moved quickly to the street down which the Dwarf was traveling. He backed against the building, facing the same direction the Dwarf was moving, and looked down at the narrow sidewalk. Long shadows ran at gentle angles, cast from streetlamps. He'd be able to see the Dwarf's shadow before he crossed the mouth of the alley.

There were few sounds in the heavy air, and Strassa listened for the footsteps of his quarry. The wait was short. The sound of the Dwarf's shoes on the sidewalk came clearly, followed quickly by the long, bobbing shadow. Strassa readied himself.

'A moment of your time, friend,' Strassa said as the Dwarf pulled even with the alley.

The Dwarf jumped with a start, taking a sidestep toward the street as he turned toward the voice. He squinted and stared at the dark figure in the shadows.

Strassa took a step forward into the light, letting himself be seen. 'This is a lousy night for a walk,' he commented.

The Dwarf backed away another step, focusing his eyes on the face concealed by shadow. He knew the voice. As Strassa came into the light and his face became more visible, the Dwarf recognized him. 'Strassa,' he said, part question, part statement of fact.

'Yes. It is I.'

'Well, why didn't you say so? You nearly gave me a coronary,' he said, extending a hand. 'What brings you to Paris?'

'A bit of business, a bit of pleasure,' Strassa replied, accepting the hand.

'I trust all went well in Colombia?' the little Frenchman asked.

'Quite well, in fact.'

'And the second half of the payment was received?'

Strassa nodded. The Dwarf had not shown fear upon recognizing him. He did not act surprised to see him still breathing. Perhaps the Dwarf was not the one who had sold him out, after all.

'The amount was satisfactory, yes?' the Dwarf asked, trying to figure out why Strassa had come to him so unexpectedly and without following established procedure.

'Yes, except for the bonus,' Strassa replied.

The Dwarf looked at him, puzzled. 'In what way was it unsatisfactory?' he asked.

'My being killed was not a part of the accepted terms.'

The Dwarf looked up into Strassa's face with an expression of shock. 'What do you mean?' he asked.

'Someone tried to kill me five days ago in Bern,' the Basque told him, watching carefully for his reaction.

The Dwarf thought for a second. 'You have many enemies. What makes you think it was the principal?'

he asked, correctly assuming Strassa's line of logic.

'Just a feeling. A strong feeling.'

The Dwarf shook his head. 'It was not the principal,' he said, sure that Sonterra would not do such a thing to a man of Strassa's standing.

'And who might that be, little man?' Strassa asked, his tone suddenly not so friendly.

'You know I can't answer that question,' the Dwarf said firmly. 'I would no sooner give his name than I would yours.'

'I have wondered about that these past days,' Strassa said.

The Dwarf grew suddenly nervous. He knew Strassa's reputation well. No one crossed Strassa and lived. 'I assure you that I have never—'

Strassa's automatic came up into the face of the Dwarf, abruptly cutting off his words.

'I want the name of the principal,' Strassa demanded, his tone as menacing as the weapon.

The Dwarf held up a hand. 'Wait—'

'The principal,' Strassa repeated, his free hand grabbing the Dwarf's jacket. He backed the man up to the wall and shoved the gun straight into his face, pressing the barrel against his cheek. 'You will tell me now, or you will die,' he threatened.

The Dwarf's eyes grew wide with fear. 'He'll kill me if I reveal his name.'

'And I'll kill you if you don't.'

'It was *not* the principal,' the Dwarf repeated. 'I can assure you that if he wanted you dead, you would be by now.'

'I'm out of patience with you,' Strassa said, pressing his body close to the Dwarf, forcing him hard against the wall of the building.

'Wait! Wait! You can't do this,' the Dwarf blurted. 'You don't know who you're dealing with. If you kill me, he'll—'

'The name, you little pygmy – *now!*'

388

The Dwarf contemplated the barrel of the gun, now waving an inch from his left eye. He was looking at death and he knew it. Strassa was not one to bluff. It was death either way.

'The principal's name is Rafael Sonterra,' the Dwarf said, his face tightening to anger.

'Sonterra!' Strassa repeated, shocked. It was perhaps the only name that could strike fear in him.

Strassa backed off a half-step, the gun lowering just a few inches as the import of the Dwarf's words sank in.

That instant of reaction was all the Frenchman needed. His left hand grabbed Strassa's wrist, and with the speed of a cobra his right hand struck, jabbing the blade of a knife into the Basque's groin.

Strassa doubled over involuntarily, and the knife struck again. He tried to free the gun hand, but the Dwarf had surprising strength, fed by a rush of adrenaline.

Despite his diminutive size, the Dwarf was powerful, and he jabbed the knife into Strassa's solar plexus, just below the sternum, angling it upward and twisting it viciously.

Strassa let out an awful gasp.

The Dwarf pulled the gravely wounded Basque to the left and into the wall, and struck again and again with the blade.

The gun fell from Strassa's hand and he lurched forward, clutching at the smaller man. The Dwarf backed away as Strassa lunged, and the bigger man stumbled forward to his knees.

The knife struck again, to the side of the throat. Strassa's face went white and he let out a horrible gurgle, and flopped facedown to the ground.

The Dwarf stood over him, breathing heavily, his knife at the ready. But it would no longer be needed.

Strassa writhed on the ground for a moment, then let out a final gasp. As all movement stopped, the Dwarf's eyes closed completely, releasing the last of the pent-up energy from his body. The Dwarf calmly wiped the knife on Strassa's pantleg, then backed away and replaced the weapon in its spring-loaded forearm sheath. He wiped a trembling hand across his wet, flushed face, and turned.

Slowly, he told himself. *Walk away slowly.*

He stepped out of the alleyway and walked off into the rainy night.

27

Bob Elias waited patiently for the Alpha line connection to be completed from his headquarters in Paris. He had moved the control center there after the confounding double-cross in Libya. All hopes attached to Babayan had been suddenly and summarily dashed, leaving Strassa's line of contact their only lead.

All the attention that had previously been concentrated on Strassa's movements was now focused on the Dwarf. He had been picked up after his surprising despatch of the deadly Strassa, who had made the small mistake of letting his passion rule, while the Dwarf had maintained his composure. He had waited with admirable patience for the one opening to attack his superior adversary. The opportunity wasn't wasted.

'Good evening, Bob,' Martin Trace greeted Elias in his mellow voice.

'Good evening, Martin,' Elias replied.

'I understand there have been a few setbacks,' Trace began. 'Can you give me details?'

'The transfer in Libya was a complete double-cross. Babayan's jet set down, taxied to the end of the runway, and just sat there until the Libyans ran out of patience and stormed the plane. They found Babayan, their agent Sahm, and Babayan's entire crew dead.'

Trace listened in silence.

'There must have been somebody on the plane, but the Libyans found no-one. They found the Luxus transport case, but it was empty. For all their money and effort, they ended up with an empty suitcase. They're taking the plane apart piece by piece right now, but I don't think they'll find anything,' Elias said.

'How did the killer get off?' Trace asked.

'He simply walked off, as far as we can tell. We used a deep intelligence cell to monitor the whole affair. We photographed everything from long range. It was only when Intelligence Central began going back over the pictures that we figured out how the killer managed his escape.

'Intelligence Central advises that thirty-four Libyan commandos and intelligence specialists went into the plane in the first hour, before it was towed to one of the large hangars. They were precise in the count, photographing everyone that boarded and left the jumbo jet. The count leaving was thirty-*five*.'

'It seems our adversary had things well planned,' Trace commented. 'He used the confusion to his advantage to make his escape.'

'You're exactly right. He must have planned the whole thing in advance of the landing in Libya. There's enough evidence to bear this out. First, and most important, is the fact that the Libyan bid was not the winning one. It was almost a hundred million short of our own. That plane was destined for Libya, no matter what the results of the auction. Second is the fact that he got off so easily. He may have walked off in Libyan uniform, which means the guy has nerves of steel.

'But we've gained an advantage that he couldn't have anticipated: that's our photographic record of events. Somewhere in our collection is a picture of the killer. There are hundreds of pictures to study, however, and it'll take some time for Intelligence Central to single him out. The pictures were taken from a distance, and not all of them are as clear as we'd like. But he's there, all right, and we *will* make an identification. All we need is time,' Elias explained.

'So our setback is temporary, if I understand you correctly,' Trace said.

'Temporary only as regards the identity of the killer. He could be anywhere by now. Knowing who he is will help in finding him again, if we can manage that before he steps into another phase of his plan. His double-cross in Libya tells us that the sale of the Luxus was never his real objective. There's no telling what he intends to do with it now. That makes him immeasurably more dangerous, for now he has the Luxus *and* the money to facilitate using it in any way he chooses. The fact that he has gone to such extremes to cleanse his trail is a dangerous signal. He has violated the entire so-called code of ethics within his own circles. Killing your top agents is never done by those who plan to stay in the business, so the implication is that he's planning something of major proportions.'

'I don't like the sound of that,' Trace said. 'He obviously believes he can't be stopped.'

'Exactly. And he has the means to do great harm. We'll have to identify him, then stop him before he can use the Luxus to further his objectives. He's not leaving much to help us.'

'What about the back door?' Trace asked.

'It's opening a bit. The tail we had on Strassa has led to another identity. Every step we take on that side brings us closer to the principal behind the Luxus affair. We're getting up in the ranks. The newest identity on this side is Robert Crocq, a Frenchman known as the Dwarf. He's a high-level setup man. Strassa tried to force a contact with him after the attempt on his life in Bern. Strassa figured out that he had become expendable. He took matters into his own hands, but underestimated the Dwarf. The results were fatal. Now the Dwarf has to be thinking along the same lines, wondering how secure *his* future is. Our surveillance teams have him under close observation now.'

'Will he run?' Trace asked.

'No, he'll stay in Paris. But you can be certain that he'll be very nervous. The fact that the Colombian personnel were all so ruthlessly sanitized, and that an attempt was made on Strassa, will prey on his mind. He may suspect that he'll be next.'

'Do you think he would cooperate if we took him and offered him protection?'

'I don't know,' Elias said. 'His principal is obviously desperate, and powerful enough to risk removal of Strassa to prevent any comeback. Like Strassa, the Dwarf may try to make contact at the next level in order to save himself.'

'Or he may just stay in deep hiding.'

'He'll have to leave Paris to do that. He's too well known. If he runs, we'll know he wants to hide, and so we'll take him and make our offer. If he stays, he may attempt the contact. We may even be able to coax him in that direction,' Elias suggested.

'Explain.'

'We can engineer an attempt on his life. If we make it seem real enough to be convincing, he'll either bolt or make contact. Either way, it forces the back door open just a bit more. Perhaps even enough for us to get through.'

Trace liked the logic. 'Will you bring Quinn into Paris for the operation?' he asked.

'Yes, unless we develop a strong lead on the killer in Libya. We may be closer to our principal than we think. The fact that he was on the plane and close to Babayan suggests that our killer and the principal may be one and the same,' Elias said. 'We'll pull Wadelaw in to rejoin Quinn.'

'What is the status of Alexandra Sky?' Trace asked.

'The rescue operation was a complete success. She's safely in our keeping. We'll try to keep her out of it from this point forward. I feel it's safest to send her to the United States, and that would ease Quinn's concern for her. I'll advise Danziger that she'll be coming over.'

'We'll take care of those arrangements for you,' Trace told Elias. 'Get your operation on the Dwarf into motion as quickly as possible, and keep me advised. Hold back the details of your plan from Danziger and the Skyco people until it's fully developed. We shouldn't take any unnecessary risks of losing our slim advantage at this point.'

'That's a good suggestion. I'll start immediately, then contact you in a day or two in the usual way,' Elias told his superior.

'Good luck, Bob. Give our assurances to Quinn that Alex is safe and will be sent home.'

'I'll do that gladly. I'll be in touch.'

MOSCOW: A biting wind whipped through the Square of Cathedrals, the ancient center of the Kremlin. Nikolai Barchenkin walked briskly across the paved square framed by the three ancient Russian cathedrals of the Assumption, the Archangel, and the Annunciation. He had come in response to Kozlov's urgent phone call.

Barchenkin searched for the lumbering figure of his boss amid the groups of Soviet tourists huddled in the dim light of dusk and listening intently to their guides as they gave the historical backgrounds of the cathedrals and told fascinating tales of their rich heritage.

Kozlov had not elaborated over the phone his reasons for wanting Barchenkin to meet him. It was obvious to the First Deputy of the GRU that his chief was upset.

Barchenkin stopped at a point between the Cathedral of the Archangel and the Bell Tower of Ivan the Great, and scanned a full circle. He spotted Kozlov standing outside the square just to the south of the Tsar Bell, and headed in his direction.

Kozlov saw his second-in-command approaching, and raised a hand of recognition in the growing darkness.

'Thank you for coming so quickly, Nikolai,' Kozlov said as the First Deputy drew near. He placed an arm around the shoulders of his trusted adjutant, and started him walking toward the enormous bell standing on its stone pedestal.

'The Luxus situation is disintegrating rapidly,' Kozlov said in a low voice, just above a whisper. They took a few steps and stopped directly in front of the enormous bell.

'According to this morning's intelligence reports, Babayan's private jet landed in Libya and was boarded by Libyan commandos when it refused to respond to the control tower's commands to leave the runway. Babayan and his crew, as well as the Libyan agent Sahm, were all found dead. The container that was to carry the Luxus was found, but it was empty. The Libyans have found no trace of the killer or the strain.

'I have just left a special session with the Committee. There is a great deal of panic over these developments. Vladin is gaining support for the KGB, and they are making rapid progress in developing background information on everyone involved. Gorbachev can no longer keep them out of the affair.'

'We are pressing the Libyan networks, General,' Barchenkin assured Kozlov. 'We're expecting a breakthrough at any moment.'

'Continue to push them for results, Nikolai. The Committee is out of patience, and they are beginning to bare their teeth. We are under harsh criticism for not bringing our information concerning the Luxus forward sooner and sharing it with Vladin,' Kozlov said.

'There have been further developments, General,' said Barchenkin. 'As you know, we lost Strassa in Bern after the attempt on his life five days ago. We have just confirmed that he has turned up in Paris. Dead, I'm afraid.'

Kozlov frowned at Barchenkin's news. He dropped his head, shaking it slowly. 'We are completely without leads. We have lost all of our advantage to the KGB.'

'Not entirely, General,' Barchenkin said, causing Kozlov to look up suddenly with a tiny trace of hope.

'Go on, Nikolai.'

'Quinn is en route to Paris at this very moment, as are

Brevig and Tolvanin, who should arrive two hours behind him. We have alerted our agents to track Quinn as soon as he lands. He is obviously on his way to Paris for a reason. Intel-Trace may have developed useful information. Quinn is their lead agent, and he will be kept close to follow their possibilities. And we will be close to him.'

Kozlov was visibly pleased. 'You have done well, Nikolai. What has become of Alexandra Sky?' he asked.

'The *Eslabón* has been sunk off the coast of Corsica, undoubtedly an Intel-Trace rescue mission. Her whereabouts are unknown, however.'

'Perhaps Quinn will be our key to regaining momentum over the KGB. Stay with him. We need *one* development, Nikolai. One major break to beat Vladin to the prize. Without that break, our prospects are zero. I do not look forward to the endless nights of the Siberian winter, while Vladin soaks in Russian champagne and caviar. Nor, I am sure, do you.

'Push the networks relentlessly, both in Paris and in Libya. Vladin must not beat us, nor must the Americans. Somewhere there is a lead to follow. We *must* have it.'

TEL AVIV: The room was in darkness except for the halo of light cast over a table at its center. Three men sat around the table, columns of smoke rising from their cigarettes as they pored over the reports and photographs spread before them.

Moshe Simmerman sipped cold coffee from the stained mug, and drew hard on his cigarette.

'This material is brilliant, David. Your boys in Libya have outdone themselves,' he said, sitting back in his chair.

David Weitz was used to hearing such praise for his Libyan networks.

'I wish I could have been there to see the look on the face of that devil Qaddafi,' Simmerman said.

'It was a beautiful piece of work,' commented Karl Berstein, the third man in the room.

Israeli intelligence had monitored developments of the Luxus situation closely since the communication from Babayan inviting them to take part in the bidding for the strain. Their own bid attempts had failed in the first phase, but, like many other concerned parties, their interest had continued beyond the prospects of acquiring the strain through established procedures. The elaborate and costly trick on Qaddafi had delighted them, despite the threat to the security of the Israeli state that now faced them.

The Israelis wasted little time in alerting their deepest agents inside Libya after learning the destination of Babayan's 747. The reports and photographs covering the table detailed the findings of Libyan intelligence from the search of the plane.

Simmerman placed his mug back on the table and picked up a photo of a seemingly meaningless bit of evidence that had been recovered from Babayan's sleeping quarters. It showed a small paper matchstick that had been twisted in a tight spiral resembling a drill bit.

It was a small item, easily overlooked, except by those to whom it had meaning. To those who recognized it, it was as good as a signature.

'He has finally surfaced,' Simmerman said. 'How long has it been? Two years?' he asked.

'Yes, almost. One year and eleven months, to be exact . . . since Stockholm,' Berstein replied.

Rafael Sonterra had been one of the highest-ranking targets on Israeli hit lists for the past twelve years. Special assassination teams had been assigned over the years to hunt him down and remove him from the face of the earth. They had reported success in 1979, when he and three others of his close network were found in Holland. There was little doubt at the time that he had been killed. He had been observed in Gravenhage in September of that year. Two teams were assigned to ensure the kill. The flat that Sonterra and his associates were using was wired with explosives. They were observed as they entered the building, and were given time to reach the flat. Listening

397

devices confirmed their presence in the rooms, and a phone call was made to the flat to assure the fact. The moment it was answered, the detonation signal was sent by radio frequency. The force of the blast was so great that the bodies were impossible to recognize. Rafael Sonterra had died on that September day in 1979 – or so they had thought for the next three years, until he resurfaced with a surgically altered face. He immediately became number one on their new lists, and special teams had been hunting him ever since. But the resurrected Sonterra had remained invisible to the teams hunting him, and to information networks throughout Europe – impossible to find, impossible to stop.

The information networks responsible for locating him in Holland three years earlier had suffered harsh retribution at his hands, while the Israeli teams that had engineered the attempt fell, one member at a time – victims of his relentless revenge. There had been eight highly trained Israeli specialists involved on that September day. Seven had died, falling with terrible ease to the prey turned hunter. The last surviving member had been recalled to Israel before Sonterra could reach him. He had been given a new identity, and had lived in peaceful anonymity ever since.

Israeli intelligence had managed to turn up reliable leads two years before, through intercepted communications indicating that Sonterra would be in Stockholm at Christmas. They had responded to the lead, sending three top teams into the city. By Christmas, four Israeli agents had been transported to a better life and Sonterra had vanished yet again.

Simmerman stared at the picture of the twisted match for a long time, his mind turning over the known facts. They knew that the Luxus had been stolen from Skyco's Medellín Research Institute in Colombia, and that an elaborate housecleaning had taken place. They had been made fully aware of the potential of the Luxus by the awesome demonstrations orchestrated to prove its worth. And they had reliable information, which they had confirmed, that Intel-

Trace was the primary agent responsible for securing its return.

Simmerman drew hard on the short stub of his cigarette. 'Sonterra will have to be stopped this time,' he said. 'He is preparing his own personal Armageddon. He now has the means and the funds to destroy oil reserves anywhere in the world. He could singlehandedly plunge our global economy to a depth from which it would never recover. Nations and continents will wither and die if he succeeds, and there will be dreadful wars for control of the last remaining reserves of fuel.

'We have only two options. We can attempt to take Sonterra ourselves, with limited odds for success. Or we can share what we have discovered, and offer our assistance to the Americans. By pooling what we both know, and making a united attack, we may be able to stop Sonterra this time. There are, of course, benefits and risks associated with either option. If we act independently, we may well acquire the Luxus ourselves, but that might further alienate our relationship with our strongest ally. I don't have to remind you of the strain put upon that relationship over the past two years with the embarrassing disclosures of our intelligence operations in the United States. We cannot afford to weaken ties between our two governments. On the other hand, we have an opportunity to strengthen that relationship by showing our cooperation and by making our assistance available. We would also benefit by the elimination of Sonterra.'

'We will lose the possibility of obtaining the Luxus,' Weitz said.

'But we *will* benefit from it being returned to its rightful owner,' Simmerman countered. 'As long as it is secured with a strong ally it cannot be used against us.'

'We can't risk worsening our relationship with the United States,' Berstein said. 'We need their support. If we obtain the Luxus, they will expect its return. If we refuse, it will cause irreparable damage.'

'What does the Prime Minister have to say?' Weitz asked.

'We need the ally a great deal more than we need the weapon,' Simmerman replied.

'Then I recommend we approach Intel-Trace and reach an agreement of mutual assistance,' Berstein said. 'We will still benefit, even if we lose all opportunity to obtain the Luxus. Our interests will still be protected, we will strengthen our association, and we will get our best chance at Sonterra.'

Simmerman sat back in his chair again. 'David?' he said, looking to Weitz.

'There is no choice, really. How soon can we begin negotiations with Intel-Trace?'

'Immediately. Robert Elias is running the operation. He's a good friend of long standing with the Mossad. His lead operative is Michael Quinn, and I can't think of anyone better suited to deal with Sonterra on his own terms,' Simmerman replied.

'Quinn,' Weitz repeated, squinting pensively. 'Isn't he the one who was involved in the Dieter affair?'

Simmerman smiled. 'I see your memory hasn't failed you in your old age,' he joked. 'Yes, he is the one. The man is supremely capable, and it will be most interesting to pit him against Sonterra. We'll pull the most experienced people we have regarding Sonterra, build a joint team, and give all the support we can.'

'Do you think they will accept our offer of help?'

'I believe they will,' Simmerman replied. 'Elias is now in Paris. We'll arrange contact and make the proposition. We will offer to exchange all that we know, and provide full assistance. In return, we ask permission to assist in closing the account on Sonterra. Are there any questions?'

There were none.

'See to the details of assembling the team, Karl,' Simmerman said. 'We'll want to get them to Paris by tomorrow evening. Sonterra is already in deep hiding. There will be little time to waste.

'David, I want you to start contacting all of our sources in Europe. Sonterra will need help somewhere along the line. He has lost credibility among his fellow terrorists by eliminating Babayan, and that will work against him. Push hard and pay any fees required, whatever the amount. I sense that Sonterra is planning an unprecedented act of world terrorism. I sense that we'll have only one last chance at him. We must not fail this time.'

28

PARIS: Bob Elias stood at the base of the imposing stairway leading up to Sacre-Coeur. Its white mass stood dominant on a limestone hill, one of the highest spots in all of Paris. The lower stairway was actually a split set of stairs separated by about fifty feet of grassy knoll. Halfway up the knoll was a small terrace, and on the terrace were scattered a dozen or so chairs where people could sit and look out over the city. It was quite early, and the chairs were empty, except one.

Elias stared up at the tall, slim figure with glasses and thinning hair, and recognized him immediately. He headed up the stairs to the terrace, then walked along the terrace to the man, who was leaning forward in his chair and feeding a small group of aggressive pigeons that knew an easy mark when they saw one.

'Hello, Robert. Good of you to come,' the man said in a distinct Oxford accent. He didn't look up right away, but kept on feeding the birds.

'Hi, Pete,' Elias returned, stopping in front of him.

The man's name was Peter Streyer. He was a longtime friend of Elias, and a high-ranking contact in the Israeli Mossad.

'What brings you to Paris?' Elias asked, still standing.

Streyer took his attention away from the pigeons and sat back in his chair. 'A proposition that I think you chaps will not want to pass by,' he said with a confident grin.

'What's on your mind, Pete?'

'A little incident in Libya. It seems that our intelligence boys in Tripoli have come up with a bit of information that might be of value to you,' Streyer replied.

'What kind of information?'

'An identity.'

Elias stared down at the Israeli agent, then lowered himself on to a chair beside him. 'Go on,' he said.

'We've identified the man responsible for the killings of Vigen Babayan and all aboard his private plane the night before last. Are you interested?'

'I might be. What's it going to cost me?' Elias asked.

'A US-Israeli cooperative effort to hunt down this individual. Israel has a substantial interest in him. We want in on the kill.'

'What else?'

'A chance, shall we say, to wipe the slate clean between our two countries. There have been several unfortunate incidents over the past two years that have caused some hard feelings and a good bit of embarrassment to my people. Relations of late haven't been as open as they should be. There were mistakes made, we admit that. We just want to make things right and to put them sufficiently behind us. I believe our needs are mutual.'

Elias reflected for a moment. 'And the Luxus?'

'The Luxus is entirely your affair, as it should be. It would be to our benefit to have it back in its rightful place. We have no claims on it, nor shall we make any. Furthermore, if by some circumstance it should end up in our possession, it will be returned, intact, into your keeping. You have the word of my people on that.'

Elias gave a slight nod of approval. 'I can give you a yes on the first two parts. I can't speak for my government on the rest of it, but I think I can work things out with Brice.'

Streyer nodded. 'I know you're a man of your word. We

402

trust that the value of our information will show our sincere intent to your President. We'll take the chance with you.'

'Who's the player?' Elias asked.

'The man you want is Rafael Sonterra,' Streyer announced.

'*Sonterra?*' Elias repeated, nearly stunned. 'Are you sure?'

'Yes,' Streyer returned. He produced a photograph of the twisted matchstick. 'A genuine first article, found on board Babayan's 747. He might as well have spray-painted his name on the outside of the jet. There's no mistake; it's him.'

'I can see why you're so interested,' Elias said, taking the photograph and examining it. He knew how prominent Sonterra's name was on their most-hunted list.

Elias reached into the breast pocket of his coat and pulled out an enhanced close-up of the man in the window in Bern. 'We took this in Bern six days ago. Does it have any meaning to you?' he asked, handing the picture to the Israeli.

Streyer took the photograph and studied it for several seconds.

'Yes, it does. This man is Kammal Nasir, Sonterra's lieutenant. Sonterra trusts very few people. This man is his right arm. What else do you have?'

Elias gave Streyer a brief rundown on events concerning Strassa, including the facts surrounding his demise at the hands of the Dwarf.

'Yes, the Dwarf is Kammal's man,' Streyer said. 'Sonterra has used him in the past. The housecleaning all the way up to Strassa is very significant. Sonterra has dangerously isolated himself by his actions. This is *not* typical of him. He must have something monstrous planned, to take such risks. He is committing everything to his plan, even his possible existence.'

'Your information is very valuable, Pete. Our research has so far been unable to identify the principal behind the

Luxus affair. We had planned to play the Dwarf to lead us closer to him.'

'Yes. The Dwarf, if properly handled, will lead you to Kammal. Kammal, in turn, will lead to Sonterra. Sonterra will have to be killed to be stopped. As you know, he is perhaps the most dangerous and elusive man our agents have faced.'

'How do you want to proceed?' Elias asked.

'A meeting between you and my people to lay the plans and to form a lead team to hunt down Sonterra,' Streyer replied.

'When and where?' Elias asked.

'Tomorrow. Here in Paris. Is that agreeable?'

'We'll be there. Just name the place,' Elias returned.

Streyer's face broke with a smile of satisfaction. 'I'll contact you this evening with the details.'

Rafael Sonterra, Elias thought, his insides jumping with nervous excitement. At last they had the identity they'd been after.

SAN ANTONIO: Tom Danziger watched as the American Airlines plane pulled into gate 34 of San Antonio's Terminal 2. The aircraft came to a stop, and the enclosed boarding ramp pulled toward the plane. Danziger moved to a position with a direct view of the gate.

Intel-Trace's alternatives had been limited concerning Alex. Pulling her out of the Luxus affair had not been one of them. That much had been decided the second she was safely off the *Eslabón*. Her involvement was already dangerously deeper than they had ever intended. Concerned now for her complete safety, they chose to bring her as far as possible from the events now focusing in Europe. Bringing her to safety in the United States was their best option.

Danziger sharpened his attention as the flow of passengers began. He spotted Alex the second she came through the doorway, and stepped forward to meet her.

Alex stopped and studied him through large sunglasses.

She was sure he'd be upset with her for putting herself squarely in the middle of things.

Danziger could see traces of bruises on the side of her face and below the left eye, partially concealed by her sunglasses. He stared at her for a moment, wanting to be angry with her, but it was impossible. He was happy and relieved to see her back safely.

'Well, I suppose you and Daddy are angry with me for getting involved in this, right?' she asked. The look on her face said she was ready to defend her decision to the death.

Danziger shook his head. 'Worried, yes, but angry – no. We're just glad you're home in one piece. Looks to me like you've had a bit of excitement.'

'That would be an understatement,' she said, turning on a smile for appearances. 'But you should see the other guy. God, you'd have been proud of me.'

'I heard all about it,' Danziger said. 'Elias gave me a verbal report when he told us you were safe and coming back home. According to Wadelaw, you gave a pretty good accounting of yourself,' he told her.

'I *was* good,' she confirmed, neglecting to tell him that she had been so frightened that she had peed in her pants.

'He said that you kicked ass like a commando,' Danziger added.

Alex laughed. 'I've also retired from that line of work – permanently.'

'Everyone has been worried sick about you,' he said, putting an arm around her shoulders. 'Welcome home, Alex.'

She let out a heavy sigh. 'It's good to be home, Tom. I can really appreciate what Michael and his people are going through. I'm so worried about him,' she said. 'I don't suppose there's any secret to how I feel about him now. And I won't apologize for it.'

'There's no need to, Alex. And don't worry about Mike,' he comforted her. 'He can handle himself just fine.'

'How is Daddy holding up?' Alex asked.

Danziger's face straightened and grew serious. 'Not well, Alex. He had a mild heart attack this morning.'

'*Heart attack!*' she repeated, shocked.

Danziger held up his hand quickly. 'He's stable and not in danger. The doctor has recommended that we get him away from all this stress. Maybe to the clinic in Boulder.'

'Boulder . . .' she began, then hesitated.

The events of the past few weeks were enough to stress even the healthiest of constitutions. The last thing she wanted was to see her father drop dead from a massive coronary.

'That might be a good idea,' she said finally. 'I want to see him first, to reassure him that I'm OK.'

'He's home, waiting for you. But I suggest we get him ready to travel today. The clinic will be the best place for him. They can take care of him there.'

'Then let's get out of here,' Alex said, taking Danziger's arm and pushing him into motion. 'We can send for my things later.'

MÁLAGA, SPAIN: Rafael Sonterra inhaled deeply, filling his lungs with the fresh sea air blowing in off the Mediterranean. He sat on the large stone patio, listening to the gentle sounds of the waves in the darkness. He felt remarkably at ease as he looked out over the sea in the silver moonlight. His plan was progressing well, despite the complications, and he was enjoying a moment of satisfaction.

The only empty spot tonight was for Greta, whom he missed with an almost unbearable longing. He closed his eyes and tried to picture her, imagining how she would look with their son growing within her. He wanted very much to hold her and to feel the tiny kicks as they grew stronger and stronger.

That time would come, he knew. It would be only a month, perhaps two, before he could send for her. Then they could spend the rest of their days together. The rest of their days, he thought, wondering what it would be like, with no more running, no more hiding.

But men like Rafael Sonterra never know lasting peace. There was always one more thing to do, one more man to kill, one more time to run, one more place to hide.

The phone rang, breaking his train of thought.

He looked at his watch and noted with relief that Kammal's call was exactly on time. He went inside to answer the phone.

'Yes,' he said into the mouthpiece.

'Hello, my brother,' Kammal's voice said across the line.

'I trust that all has gone well?' Sonterra said. The codes had been set aside in Kammal's interests. The precision of the communications was too critical to risk at this point.

'The matter with the Basque has been resolved,' Kammal replied without detail. 'And all has gone well with you?'

'Like child's play,' Sonterra replied. 'Were there any unexpected complications on your end?' he asked.

There was a moment of silence over the phone.

'One minor detail,' Kammal replied.

'Please go on.'

'The Basque was more difficult than I imagined. I missed him in Bern. There was a delay of six days, but the contract is complete.'

'What happened?' Sonterra pressed, not pleased.

'The attempt in Bern failed, and the Basque went into hiding. I was able to learn that he went to Paris, and tried to force a contact with the Dwarf. My contacts say that the Dwarf took care of the matter himself. It was clean.'

'Six days! Are you sure it was clean?' Sonterra asked.

Kammal could tell from Sonterra's voice that he was distressed by the missed attempt.

'Yes, I'm quite certain. The Basque remained in hiding the entire time until he contacted the Dwarf. It was a single contact, and the deed was swift and sure. We have nothing to fear from the Basque.'

'How can you be certain?' Sonterra shot back. 'You were not there to confirm any of those statements.'

Kammal was silent again for a long moment.

'His contacting the Dwarf could compromise our position, Kammal,' Sonterra said at last, his displeasure evident. 'I don't have to remind you that the Dwarf is the last layer between you and the adversary. We can't risk Intel-Trace having spotted the contact. He will have to be removed.'

'Removed?' Kammal repeated incredulously. 'Certainly the Dwarf can be trusted. He has always been completely reliable, and he may still be useful.'

'We cannot take the chance. A single mistake at this level will put you in direct danger. We must remove all risk.'

'He would never betray us, my brother,' Kammal said, his voice nervous and strained. 'Surely you understand this. To remove him would be a serious breach of faith. It would be a mistake.'

'I understand only that we cannot fail, Kammal. Too much is at stake. *Everything* that we have worked for could be lost.'

'But . . . but he has never let us down in the past.'

'What you say is true, but the fact remains that the Basque was not taken swiftly. He could have been followed to the Dwarf. We can't be certain that he was not. *Your* life will be in danger if you are wrong, Kammal. He may try to contact you. And if he has been followed, the trail to you will be plain.'

Kammal's tension could be felt over the line.

'Yes, I realize the danger. But I feel that to remove the Dwarf would be going a step too far. We have already taken a very grave risk by removing the Basque. Our networks will deny us any assistance if we continue to remove all who help us. We must not break faith completely, or we will be beyond salvage, and our plan will never see completion. We still have a way to go, and it would be too difficult alone. We *cannot* do it alone.'

It was Sonterra's turn for silence. The words of his master, Abu Hassan Nasir, rang clear in his memory: *Be led first by your wisdom, and only second by your passion.*

You must leave your anger behind. Anger is a thief. It will rob you of your inner strength and cloud your wisdom. And you will need both to overcome your enemies.

'Perhaps you are right, Kammal,' Sonterra conceded. 'We will wait on the matter of the Dwarf. But you must make no further contact with him. I must insist on that.'

Kammal breathed a silent sigh of relief. 'There will be no further contact with him, my brother, unless you decide otherwise.'

'There is to be *no* contact with him under *any* circumstances,' Sonterra said for clarification. 'From this point forward, he represents a threat to us, and we must assume he is being followed. If he attempts to contact you for any reason, he must be eliminated without hesitation. Is that clear, Kammal?'

'Yes, I understand.'

'*Without hesitation*,' Sonterra repeated.

'I understand,' Kammal said.

'I have complete trust in you, Kammal. We are entering the final stage of our plan, and there is no room for error or weakness. Our contact schedule must be strictly maintained – every eight days, as planned, at the precise times and places. If they are missed for any reason, the plan will be affected. Every phase must now proceed exactly according to our timetable.'

'Our timetable is precisely on schedule,' Kammal said. 'The second seedings have been completed, and developments on the other side await only the manifestations.'

Sonterra smiled with satisfaction. 'You have done well, Kammal. But I knew you would. And how is Greta?' he asked.

'She is safe and well and sends her love. She is very anxious to join you.'

'We'll be together soon. Tell her that I am counting the days.'

'I will tell her.'

'Until eight days, then. Go safely, Kammal.'

Sonterra placed the receiver back in its cradle. He rose

to his feet and walked back to the darkened patio and looked out over the rolling sea. He felt suddenly troubled by developments concerning the Dwarf. His earlier confidence had evaporated. Their adversaries had made surprising gains since Colombia and Monaco. He could only assume that they had been just as effective with Strassa, which meant that the Dwarf was probably being watched at this very moment. And the Dwarf stood just one thin layer away from Kammal and the possible unraveling of his dream. It had to hold together just a while longer. He needed only three more weeks, and the design would be unstoppable.

Sonterra sat in his chair and leaned back, closing his eyes. He thought about Kammal's warning that they had gone too far in cleansing their trail. He *had* taken a grave risk in breaking faith with his own operatives, and he recognized this. He knew he had violated all the principles of his training. But he also knew he had waited his entire life for this moment of vengeance, and he was willing to violate any and all principles to achieve his goal. He was being led by his passion – his hatred – and he could not stop himself, despite the lessons of Abu Hassan.

He could not help feeling a small twinge of guilt as he thought back to the days of that training under his beloved master.

Abu Hassan had said that the second phase of training would be the longest and most difficult and he had spoken the truth. It was a rigorous and unending metamorphosis, in which every detail of his past and present life was replaced with what was to be. Rafael was like a piece of clay being transformed into some new shape that only Abu Hassan could envision.

There were many lessons to be learned, and what time was left over from the creation of this new form was spent at the side of Abu Hassan, beneath the cedar tree where so much of his education had taken place. The master taught Rafael the meaning of patience; of true courage and endurance; of unbreakable faith; of the real strength and power of wisdom.

'Your enemies will always be many and strong. But remember, size and might do not always go hand in hand; wisdom and might *do*. For wisdom *is* might.'

Abu Hassan was pleased with the progress of his prize student in all regards except one. For all that he had taught Rafael, and for all the transformation that had taken place, there was one thing this student could not set aside. His anger.

Anger was one of the first things he had seen in the young man. And unless he could drive it from him, much of what he had accomplished could be undone.

'Anger is a thief,' Abu Hassan told him. 'It is wasted energy that could be better channeled. It will rob you of your inner strength and cloud your wisdom. And you will need both to overcome your enemies. Remember the first lesson I taught you: always be led *first* by your wisdom, and only *second* by your passion. Anger is a fool's weapon, and a poor one. To act from anger is to invite failure. It is a confession of weakness both to your enemies and to those who will follow you. Your men will look to you for strength, for without your strength to lead them, they will be lost. And a leader is nothing without those who would follow.'

As the months passed and the transformation continued, the pieces of Rafael Sonterra were shaped one by one until the figure of a master terrorist began to take form. And always there was the patient review . . . from the beginning.

'What is your name?'

'I am Rafael Sonterra.'

'Where were you born?'

'I was born in Havana, Cuba.'

'What was the name of your father?'

'My father's name was Arturo Vasquez.'

'What was his occupation?'

'He was a baker, and a revolutionary.'

411

'When did he die?'

Hesitation, a painful expression with the 'memory'.

'He died on June sixth, 1967.'

'How did he die?'

'He was shot dead in his bakery.'

'By whom?'

'By assassins directed by Party adversaries.'

'Why?'

'Because he spoke out against them and their "revolutionary" doctrines. Because he saw their ideals change with power. Because they no longer represented the "people" for whom the revolution was fought.'

'What was the name of your mother?'

Real pain now, and anger.

'What was the name of your mother?' Abu Hassan repeated.

Silence for a moment, then the reply. 'Isabella Vasquez.'

'When did she die?'

The pain and the anger, and a memory that haunted him with cruel torment, like a memory seen through clear glass, vivid but untouchable.

'*When did she die?*'

'January thirty-first, 1968,' the reply came, drawing from new memory.

'How did she die?'

'She . . . was murdered.'

Abu Hassan's eyes narrowed with displeasure. The source of Rafael's anger was deep. An anger that had filled his life for almost as long as he could remember. Anger that had replaced the tears of a hurt child, leaving only hatred for those who had caused his pain.

'*How did she die?*' Abu Hassan asked again, sternly.

Rafael stared into the eyes of his master. *Let go of your hatred.* 'She died alone, from tetanus.'

'Why was she alone?'

'I was in prison.'

'Why?'

'For killing the man who had my father murdered.'

412

'How old were you?'

'Nineteen.'

Abu Hassan remained silent for a long time, reading his student. He was a long way from being satisfied. The anger must leave.

'Again, back to the beginning. What is your name?' the master asked.

'My name is Rafael Sonterra.'

'Where were you born?'

29

PARIS: It was in a small fifth-floor flat on Rue Soufflet, just a block from the Panthéon, that the seven came together.

Moshe Simmerman had answered the coded knock. He had never met the three Americans, but knew them well from their files and reputations.

'My name is Max,' he said, extending his hand first to Bob Elias, and then to Michael and Wadelaw in quick succession.

The three Americans stepped into the flat and walked down a short hallway to a larger open room. Simmerman made more introductions, keeping them brief.

The three Israelis with Simmerman looked like anything but a highly skilled team of assassins, but the Americans knew better than to judge competence by appearances.

The first was a woman introduced to them as Yelena. She was rather tall at five feet ten inches, slender, with close-cut hair. Her serious features had a hard quality that covered attractive possibilities. Her clothes were loose-fitting, giving little evidence as to what lay beneath them in the way of a figure or, more important, weapons.

The second was an older gentleman with thin gray hair

and a gentle face beneath spectacles that hung halfway down his nose. He was called 'Papa' Mier. A large pipe that billowed huge clouds of aromatic smoke was tightly clenched between the teeth of his square jaw. He looked like an old man whose days were more likely spent on quiet park benches feeding pigeons and playing chess with old cronies than in playing games of international intrigue. He wore a gray flannel shirt with large breast pockets stuffed with a notebook, loose slips of paper, an old mechanical pencil, and a pocket calculator. He was obviously the brains of the team.

The last man was small, standing no more than five feet four, with a mustache that dominated his face. He was called Abel and was perhaps in his mid-forties, and looked to be fairly well conditioned. He had the appearance of a thinker. The 'wire man', Elias thought as he released his firm but delicate hand. No doubt taps, bombs, and electronics were his specialty.

Elias looked the three over again. If he was right about the two men, that meant the woman was the lead 'trigger'. What a team, he mused. They looked like they couldn't kill a fly among them, much less track down and stop a world-class terrorist. But the fact that they were here in this room for a job of such significance told him otherwise. They were good, and he knew it. They had to be.

'We have some coffee – or tea, if you prefer,' Simmerman said, gesturing to a table with an electric brewer and a kettle and an assortment of mismatched cups.

There were no takers. The Americans sat in the three empty chairs, ready to get to the business at hand.

Simmerman took a sip of his cold coffee and set the cup on the table beside his chair. He struck a match, lit a cigarette, and waited for Elias to begin.

Elias wasted little time. He rose, took a few steps to the center of the room, and addressed the group.

'The five of you will lead the hunt for Rafael Sonterra,' he said, waving a finger at Michael, Wadelaw, and the three Israeli agents. 'It has been agreed that I will be your

414

case officer. My decisions will be considered final. Max will be available to assist the group in any way possible, using the resources of Israeli intelligence. There are many people in both of our countries watching with great interest, not only because of the threat posed by the missing Luxus, but also because of the terrorist known to be holding it. Rafael Sonterra is like no other terrorist. He is highly resourceful, elusive, and brutal in executing his goals. He is utterly ruthless, and will kill swiftly, without hesitation.'

Elias looked to Simmerman and nodded. 'I believe you have a developed background.'

Simmerman nodded and began.

'His real name is Rafael Vasquez. He was born in Havana, Cuba, in 1949. He made his first kill in 1968 at the age of nineteen. His victim was a not-so-straight official in the Castro government believed to have been responsible for the murder of his father. It was an impressive kill for an amateur. So impressive, in fact, that he was released from prison shortly after initial investigations were concluded by Cuban authorities. The release was authorized by the Cuban Secret Service. They didn't want to see such a natural talent go to waste.

'It is believed that it was really the KGB who spotted the potential in the young man. He worked for a brief time as a Cuban henchman, code-named Sonterra, until his worth was proven. Shortly afterward, he was sent to the Soviet Union for training and education.

'He attended Patrice Lumumba University in Moscow for two years. As you probably know, this is a selection center for promising Third World students. There he was instructed in the principles of revolution and terrorism. He studied Marcuse, Sartre, and others, as well as languages, for which he showed a particular ability. The KGB talent scouts had not been wrong about his potential.

'From there he went on to intensive training at Sakhodnaya, twenty miles from Moscow, where he was instructed in political propaganda and tactical weapons.

He continued to show an extremely high aptitude.

'He was next trained at Sanprobal, near Simferopol on the Black Sea. The subjects here were advanced explosives and bomb-making, with special instruction in chemical and biological warfare. So he is very familiar with microbiological weapons, a use to which the Luxus lends itself.

'It was at Sanprobal, however, that the Soviets began to have second thoughts about Sonterra. It was not that he didn't possess the necessary talents for their purposes, but rather that he seemed too enthusiastic to apply them. The psychological profiles of Sonterra pointed clearly to psychopathic tendencies. He also had a record of personal difficulties with fellow students at each of the training facilities. Then an incident occurred in Sanprobal that finalized their decision to dissociate themselves from him. This was the killing of a fellow student. It was well done – an icepick to the base of the skull – done so neatly that it was unsolvable. The fact that he had had difficulties with this individual made him a suspect. But it could never be proved.

'The Soviets decided that he was too great a risk, and his studies were terminated. His potential for undisciplined violence was too high.

'He did not return to Cuba, and to our knowledge he has not returned since. Instead, he went to Lebanon and undertook training with the PLO under Abu Hassan Nasir. He trained with Nasir for two years, and it is said that Nasir came to love him like a son.

'He worked for the PLO for a time after that, building an impressive record as a daring and imaginative assassin. But he was also known as a loner who did not work well in teams, did not believe in causes, and trusted no-one.

'He operated in Europe for three years, recording several spectacular kills, all unsolvable. His unconscious signature, and a clue left behind at every kill, was a twisted matchstick – just like the one found on Babayan's plane in Libya.

'Israeli intelligence took a great interest in this "phantom" assassin. He topped our list of targets to be sanctioned on sight. But our results with this individual were embarrassingly poor. He was elusive, impossible to locate. He would hit and vanish, then hit and vanish again with ease. He used no set network, varied his tactics and style, and left us with nothing to follow. Nasir had trained him well.

'We finally got an opportunity in 1979 in Gravenhage, when our sources learned that he had been recruited for a major PLO assassination plot. On this occasion he operated with a full PLO team. We succeeded in locating the team and got our first photographic records of him. An operation was set to sanction the PLO squad, and was successful. The entire PLO team was killed by explosives. No-one could have survived the explosion. The book on Rafael Sonterra was closed.'

Simmerman rose from his chair, drew hard on the short stub of his cigarette, then crushed it out. 'The book was closed for three years,' he said as he walked to a table near the windows of the main room. The table had several file folders and an assortment of photographs spread across its surface. He picked up one picture and handed it to Elias.

'This was the first clue that he had survived.'

Elias studied the photograph, but could see nothing conclusive in it. It showed a tall, fatigue-garbed man wearing the black and white checked kaffiyeh emblematic of the PLO. He stood with his back turned three-quarters away from the camera, his right arm raised and aiming an automatic pistol at the back of the head of a hooded man with his arms bound tightly behind him.

'This was taken by one of our agents in 1982. The man holding the gun is Rafael Sonterra. At the time, he was instructing a new crop of PLO terrorists. The hooded man was a PLO soldier who had disobeyed orders. He became a strong object lesson on the value of discipline.'

Elias continued to study additional details in the photograph. The left arm of the executioner hung straight down, the hand clutching a Soviet Kalashnikov rifle. The photo was rather clear, and Elias could see that the left hand was badly scarred, though not deformed.

'Did your records on Sonterra indicate the scarred left hand?' Elias asked.

'Not before this photograph,' Simmerman replied. 'Our agent reported that Sonterra was never seen without the kaffiyeh. His arms and legs were also always covered. Rumor had it that he was badly scarred from a nearly successful attempt on his life.'

'The bomb in Gravenhage?' Michael asked.

Simmerman nodded.

'But you said that no-one could have survived it.'

'No-one *should* have survived it,' the little man called Abel replied. 'The blast was so powerful that it demolished the entire side of the building. It was more than we intended, and there were innocent casualties. We did not stay to sweep the area as we normally would have.'

'*You* were there?' Michael asked.

'I set the explosives,' Abel replied.

'There is the remote possibility that he could have been positioned near an outside wall, or possibly a window, and was blown through it and somehow survived,' Simmerman offered. 'In any event, Rafael Sonterra was alive and back in business.

'We believe that he has undergone extensive reconstructive surgery, and now has an appearance totally unknown to us. Soon after we obtained this photograph of him, he disappeared again. But only for a short time.

'He began a ruthless campaign of retribution against those who had nearly killed him. You will find the details in the file we have provided.

'He has achieved many kills since then, all difficult to attribute to him, except for the matchstick he unconsciously leaves behind. True to his form of the past, he changes his style and identity, using many disguises, not that it would help us to see him without one, because we don't know what his new face looks like. He is not a pattern operator. He is well connected to loyal information sources, and is highly insulated. He seldom makes direct contacts, working instead through Kammal Nasir, the son of his teacher Abu Hassan Nasir. He is also known to use a woman, Greta Haas, an East German terrorist, who is believed to be a love interest. He usually remains well in the background, in deep cover, which is why you had such difficulty identifying him. Prior to the killings in Libya, his last known operation was two years ago in Stockholm, where he killed two OPEC ministers and four members of our lead team assigned to sanction him. He disappeared completely after that.'

'And there's no mistake that it was Sonterra involved in Libya?' Wadelaw asked.

'None,' Simmerman replied.

Elias opened a file folder that he had carried into the meeting with him, and removed several photographs. 'Here are your pictures of Rafael Sonterra,' he said, handing them to the Israeli intelligence chief. 'They're a bit fuzzy, but this is definitely the man who got off the plane in Libya.'

Simmerman accepted the pictures with great interest and studied them carefully, memorizing what little detail there was.

'How can you be sure this is Sonterra?' he asked.

'Pure deductive reasoning. We photographed everyone going on and coming off. When the counts didn't match, we began going back over everything. This is the only unmatched face,' Elias answered.

'The height and build are right, the dark features also. This is brilliant work,' Simmerman said, handing the pictures to his team.

The 'wire man' studied the pictures closely, his face growing stiff and pale, as though he were looking death squarely in the face.

'Abel?' Simmerman asked.

'This is him,' Abel replied, removing his wire-framed

419

glasses and wiping the sudden perspiration from his face. 'The face is different, but enough the same. This is the man.'

Yelena was next to study the photographs. She looked at them without comment, and passed them to Papa Mier, who studied them calmly.

'So, the phantom has a face,' Papa Mier said. 'We can work with this.'

'He'll remain in deep hiding for as long as possible,' Simmerman said. 'Kammal will run his contacts and take care of the general details of his scheme. It takes a great deal of money and help to stay so well hidden. He must get it from somewhere.'

'He's got plenty of cash now. But before the auction he didn't, and needed sources. We've tapped part of that network,' Elias told the Israeli. 'It's led us to the Dwarf. We tracked the network all the way from Colombia and through Juan Strassa, whom the Dwarf recently eliminated. Sonterra has cleaned house ruthlessly to this point. Help may not be so easily found.'

'He'll find it,' Simmerman returned. 'What assistance he doesn't get out of respect and loyalty, he'll get out of fear. We will tap into our information sources, many of them the same ones Sonterra will be forced to use, probably through Kammal. His having broken faith will provide us with a strong advantage. Strassa and Babayan had many friends. And so does the Dwarf, who must perceive himself to be in danger from Sonterra.'

'It's our hope that he'll feel endangered,' Elias added. 'We'll stay on the Dwarf, hoping for a possible contact with Kammal, or Sonterra himself. We may even be able to help force that along by applying a little pressure on the Dwarf to get his juices flowing.'

'Kammal will not be difficult to find,' Simmerman said. 'The trick will be in getting him to lead you to Sonterra. They have a special loyalty to one another. Sonterra would never break faith with him. He trusts him completely.'

'But Kammal *can* lead us to Greta Haas,' Michael said. 'If

you're right about her being a love interest, we can use her to draw him in.'

Simmerman nodded. 'Yes, that can work.'

'Sonterra will need safe houses,' Michael continued. 'Kammal will be arranging them. If we tap the network as you say we can, we can intercept him, or possibly maneuver the Dwarf to lead us to him. I have some additional sources that can possibly help us in France. If Kammal and Sonterra are in France, we'll learn of it. As you know, every major terrorist organization in the world has set up some kind of network in France.'

'There's an added complication,' Elias said. 'We've been under Soviet surveillance.'

'Yes, we are aware of this,' Simmerman replied, unperturbed. 'The GRU has been watching your movements closely. And the KGB has been watching the GRU. Whatever you learn, they will also eventually learn. They will be in your shadow constantly. We have identified Ivan Brevig and Gregor Tolvanin. Both are in Paris now.'

'I've met Tolvanin,' Michael said. 'He carried in the Soviet bid.'

'He is a highly respected and experienced agent,' Simmerman commented.

'We'll watch your backs,' Elias said to his team. 'You just concentrate on locating Kammal and Sonterra. We can handle the Russians when things heat up.'

'When do we get started?' Wadelaw asked Elias.

'Immediately. The team will split up to various parts of Europe to initiate contact with our information sources. I'll act as your communications control. As soon as meaningful information is obtained, you'll be notified as to when and where to regroup. Are there any questions?'

There were none.

'Then let's get moving,' Elias said to them. 'The sooner we break our first lead, the sooner we force Sonterra to surface – and to play by our rules.'

30

CLERMONT-FERRAND, FRANCE: It was late morning when the high-speed train from Paris pulled into the station. Michael stepped off into the pleasant December sunshine, a much-welcome contrast to the solid week of rain. Yelena followed and stretched stiff muscles. She had slept most of the way down, the first sleep she had enjoyed in nearly forty-eight hours since being called to Paris by Simmerman.

The team had split and headed in three separate directions to initiate their contacts with the various information sources from which they hoped to develop leads on Sonterra. Michael and Yelena had been teamed, and had come to Clermont-Ferrand to meet with the Vinzant brothers, former World War II Resistance fighters with the famed Group Alliance. Their help had been instrumental to him many times in the past. There were many old Resistance networks still in the information business, either out of patriotic interests or purely for profit. Michael had come today hoping that they could again provide useful information.

Wadelaw had been paired with Papa Mier. They would contact Paris sources before going on to Brussels and then Munich. Abel had left Paris for Amsterdam, with later scheduled destinations of Zurich and Madrid. Simmerman and Elias would work through more-official sources, tapping into the 'old boy network' with which they were well connected throughout Europe, utilizing fraternal law-enforcement contacts with eyes and ears everywhere. These combined efforts would tap them into the European information networks used by friend and foe alike, where loyalties were often determined by the amount of money being offered for information. The information was good, but the risks high, for it was often sold to more than one interested party.

Michael had called ahead to the Vinzants to tell them

that he was coming to see them. He had asked that they not tell anyone of his coming to Clermont-Ferrand, for news of his arrival would draw a lot of attention from former friends of Group Alliance. He wished to come and go as quietly as possible.

Michael and Yelena hired a rental car and drove out of the city into the peaceful countryside. There had been little conversation between them since leaving Paris.

The file provided by Elias offered Michael some insight into the attractive but hardened agent traveling with him. She was thirty-four years old and had been in the field for almost nine years, a long time for this kind of work. She had served four years with the Israeli army, followed by as unsuccessful marriage of three years before being recruited as a courier on European assignment because of her high proficiency in languages. It took little time for other potential abilities to become evident to her superiors. Within a year she had been assigned to an elite team of specialists operating in Europe, hunting down enemies of the Israeli state. She had proved to be a highly motivated and dependable agent. In Paris, within her first month, she scored a double kill, both at point-blank range in an elevator with the Israelis' favored Beretta .22 automatic. A month later she had made a third kill in Frankfurt, again with a small-caliber handgun, this time in the backseat of a taxi. Within yet another month she had recorded her fourth kill, a female terrorist, in a small restaurant in Rouen, with a knitting needle through the orbit of the eye. Thus she had quickly achieved superstar status among her superiors.

In 1983, in Cannes, she had eliminated the third-ranking target on the Israeli hit lists, by using poison administered through an alcoholic beverage. It wasn't until 1985 that she had marked up her sixth impressive kill, a particularly nasty German female terrorist who got her jollies out of blowing up women and children. The deed was done in Rotterdam, again at close range with a handgun. Her last recorded kill had been an especially bold one, claiming the second-ranking name on the hit lists. This was in Helsinki in 1986, in the left-luggage room of the Hotel Presidentii, with a tiny poisoned stickpin. Death was immediate and silent.

In a little under five years, the assassination team of which she was a part had eliminated four of the top ten names on the Israeli lists. In November of 1986 they had gone for the number-one name, Rafael Sonterra, in Stockholm. Their sources had uncovered a lead that an attempt would be made on a delegation of OPEC ministers. The outcome had been devastating. Sonterra had killed not only two OPEC ministers, but also four of the six members of the Israeli squad over a three-day period. Only Yelena and Papa Mier had escaped.

Two teams had made direct attempts on the life of Rafael Sonterra during the past twelve years. Eleven of the fourteen were dead. The surviving three had come again, relentless and out of hatred and fear and loyalty to their fallen comrades, to make yet another attempt on the life of this most elusive of terrorists. There was no mystery to Yelena's seriousness and her silent determination. A single goal motivated her like a force of nature, powered equally by the will to survive and the desire to kill. This time, Rafael Sonterra would not escape.

It was about noon when the rental car pulled up the long lane to the Vinzant farm. The narrow drive was bordered on both sides by low walls of piled rock that broke the land into neat parcels of pasture and grain fields brown and dormant with the winter. Michael had not been here in two years, yet with his memory for details, he knew nothing had changed. The two stone houses still stood, and the large barn still needed the same repairs. He could see the roof of the small wine cellar where so many plans had been laid for the Resistance effort, and where he and the Vinzants had conducted their business.

The car stopped near the larger of the two stone houses.

A stocky, rugged-looking man emerged from the house before the engine had been shut off.

'This is Jacques Vinzant,' Michael said to Yelena before opening the door to meet him.

'He looks like a fighter,' Yelena commented. 'I like him already.'

They got out of the car as Vinzant drew near. A broad smile broke across the Frenchman's face. He wrapped his big strong arms around the taller American, his hands pounding Michael's back with blows of affection.

'Michael, it has been too long,' Vinzant said, then backed away at arm's length, his rugged hands on the shoulders of the American. 'You are looking very good, yes? The years have not touched you.'

Michael smiled at his friend. 'Thank you for agreeing to see us.'

'No thanks are necessary. You are always welcome here.'

The Frenchman looked at Yelena and removed his hat with his left hand, revealing a completely bald head. A polite smile broke across his face.

'This is Yelena,' Michael said in introduction.

'Monsieur Vinzant, I am pleased to meet you,' she said, extending her hand.

Vinzant picked up on the accent quickly. 'Shalom,' he returned.

'You have a good ear,' Yelena said with a smile.

His alert blue eyes reflected his satisfaction. 'I am correct, yes?'

Yelena did not respond with words, but the answer was plain to him.

'Come, let's go into the wine cellar,' Vinzant said, taking both his guests by the arm. 'We will open a bottle and talk.'

'Where is Lucien?' Michael asked.

'My brother will be along shortly. He has a small matter to attend to.'

They walked to the wine cellar and descended the short flight of stairs into the cold dampness. Vinzant flicked on an overhead light hanging in the center of the room above a small table. 'Make yourselves comfortable,' he said, pointing to the table. He took several steps to a fully stocked wall rack and selected a bottle of his finest vintage, then took four glasses from a shelf. He returned to the table and sat with his guests and began opening the bottle.

Within moments the cork was out and he was filling the glasses. He set the bottle down and raised his glass. 'To friends,' he toasted.

Michael and Yelena raised their glasses. There was a moment of hesitation before drinking the salute, a moment of remembrance between the two men for the unspoken names of common friends lost in years past.

'How may we help you?' Jacques asked as he lowered his glass.

'We're looking for three people, Jacques. We must find them, and quickly. We know only that they will probably be in Europe, possibly in France. But even this is not certain. They're very dangerous and use highly insulated networks to obtain their information and to get assistance. They represent a grave threat that must be stopped.'

'What are their names?' Jacques asked.

'Greta Haas, Kammal Nasir, and Rafael Sonterra.'

'Sonterra?' the Frenchman repeated, rubbing his forehead with his hand. 'A very difficult problem, I'm afraid. Few people will be willing to deal, where he is concerned.'

'We'll pay any price to obtain this information,' Yelena said.

'To be sure, what little information that *can* be obtained will be *very* expensive. You said quickly. *How* quickly?'

'Days,' Michael replied.

Vinzant refilled the glasses. 'How much can you tell me?'

Michael glanced at Yelena, but she provided no clue. She was leaving this up to him. 'They have within their possession the means to cripple the economy of the entire world, possibly to destroy it completely. There is very little time, Jacques. Weeks at the most.'

The Frenchman sipped his wine, deep in thought.

'Sonterra has seriously broken faith with his most trusted networks,' Michael said. 'He's risking everything for this. That should have some value to us.'

The sharp eyes of Jacques Vinzant squinted and he gave an almost imperceptible nod.

Michael produced photographs from the inside pocket of his leather jacket and placed them on the table. 'This one is Sonterra,' he said, tapping the first photograph. 'The others are Kammal and the Haas woman.'

'How did you obtain this?' Vinzant asked, lifting the picture of Sonterra.

'It's a long story. But that's him. To our knowledge, this reflects his current appearance. Surely his desperate actions involving his close networks have made him some enemies,' Michael said.

'I'm sure you are correct in your assumption. But there will be very few, if any, with enough courage to risk his retribution.'

'Is there nothing you can do?' Yelena asked.

'With which networks has he broken faith?' the Frenchman questioned.

'He is responsible for the elimination of Juan Strassa and Vigen Babayan,' Michael answered.

Vinzant nodded. 'Both dead?'

'Yes.'

'There are many who will not mourn the passing of Strassa. But Babayan had many good friends. Are there any others?'

'Do you know a man called the Dwarf?'

'He is another with many friends. He is dead also?'

'Not yet. But he may be soon,' Michael replied.

'Sonterra has made a serious mistake. I will contact my most trusted sources. Do you have a pencil and a piece of paper?'

'Yes,' Michael replied, reaching into his jacket pocket. He handed them to the Frenchman.

Vinzant wrote a name and a phone number on the paper.

'Go to Perpignan and call this number. Ask for Polidor.'
He handed the pencil and paper back to Michael.

Michael looked at the name. 'Polidor,' he repeated.

'I will call ahead for you to make an introduction. But I must warn you, Polidor controls an extremely mercenary network. Their services are expensive and not without risk. They will sell information to anyone with enough money, possibly even to Sonterra himself. I'm sure he has used them in the past. Polidor and Babayan go back a long way together. Perhaps that association will provide the motivation to assist you.'

'I can't thank you enough, Jacques,' Michael said.

'Do not be so quick to thank me, Michael,' Vinzant replied with a serious expression. 'Polidor cannot be trusted. The information will be good, but in dealing with Polidor, you deal with the devil. Just be aware.'

The sound of the wine cellar door opening interrupted the meeting. Lucien Vinzant descended the stairs.

Michael rose immediately to his feet.

The younger Vinzant brother approached Michael and gave him a mighty hug. 'Two years! I can't believe it. You haven't changed a bit,' the second Frenchman said.

'Lucien. It's good to see you. You look well.'

'And I am well. How have you been?'

'Doing fine, thank you. Let me introduce a friend,' Michael said, extending an arm toward Yelena. 'This is Yelena.'

'You *are* doing well. She's beautiful,' Lucien whispered to him before taking her hand.

'I'm very pleased to meet you,' Yelena said.

'What did you learn?' Jacques asked, getting straight to business.

Lucien looked at Michael. 'You're being followed, as usual. But it is not the DST. These are Russians. Are you aware of that?'

Michael nodded.

'We can arrange a slight diversion, if you would like.'

'How slight?'

428

'No broken bones. Well, one maybe. It depends,' Lucien said with a smile.

'That would be helpful,' Michael replied.

'Consider it done.'

'You must leave quickly,' Jacques said, looking at his watch. 'You can still make the train to Perpignan, but you must not delay. From what you have told me, every minute is valuable to you. I will tell Lucien what has transpired in his absence. We will lose very little time in contacting our sources for you. After you have spoken with Polidor, call me. Perhaps we can use what you learn to help you further.'

'I will. Thank you, Jacques.'

'Polidor?' Lucien repeated with raised eyebrows.

'I'll explain later. We must not delay our friends,' Jacques told his brother. 'Go quickly and arrange your little diversion.'

'I am gone like the wind,' Lucien said. 'It was nice meeting you,' he said to Yelena, then turned to Michael. 'Watch yourself around Polidor. And don't wait another two years to come back. You are always welcome here.'

'I will, and I won't, in that order. Thank you, Lucien.'

Lucien turned and bounded up the stairs and was gone.

Michael, Yelena, and Jacques left the wine cellar at a more casual pace.

Yelena went ahead to the car. Jacques touched Michael's arm lightly to stop him.

'Whatever your reasons for wanting Sonterra, know that you have only to ask and you will have the full assistance of Group Alliance. We will never forget all that you have done to help us and our country in the past.'

'I appreciate your willingness to help,' Michael said.

The two men took a few slow steps towards the car.

'We were all very pained to hear of the death of your sister,' Jacques said, putting an arm around Michael's shoulder.

'Thank you, Jacques,' said Michael, his face suddenly dark with the memory.

'I know you were instrumental in providing information that helped me find Dieter. Elias told me about your assistance when it was over.'

'You may never know how much Elias did to help channel that information to you, Michael. He will probably never tell you himself.'

Michael looked into the Frenchman's face, surprised and yet not surprised. 'I didn't know,' he said.

'Be assured that he pressed all of his sources on your behalf, at some risk to himself. You are very special to him, Michael, but then *many* people feel that way toward you.'

Michael smiled in gratitude.

'And I'll never forget my friends, Jacques.'

Vinzant nodded. 'Well, at least that much is over,' the Frenchman said, clapping his large hand on Michael's shoulder. 'Send my regards to Elias when you see him next.'

'I'll do that. And thanks again, Jacques.'

'I hope that you will still thank me after you have met with Polidor.'

PARIS: Intel-Trace's close watch on the Dwarf indicated clearly that he had no plans to leave the city. This meant that either he didn't perceive himself to be in any danger from Sonterra or, if he did, that he felt confident his chances for survival were better on his home turf. With each passing day, Elias felt more certain of the latter, for although the Dwarf did not run, he also did not move about in his usual patterns. He was being very cautious.

Elias gave orders to maintain the surveillance, being careful not to spook the Dwarf this early. He still hoped for a contact of some kind.

They successfully tapped his phones and positioned teams with highly sophisticated listening devices to monitor his conversations from long range. The contact, if it was initiated by the Dwarf, would not likely be made over one of his many phones, but the precaution was taken anyway. A random phone would more than likely be selected and used, making a tap impossible. But the listening devices would at least let them hear his side of the conversation, or the entire content, should it be made face-to-face.

Elias also called in specialists to set up the 'nudge' he had discussed with Martin Trace. He would wait before deploying them until Michael had a chance to pursue his leads in France. If Michael's sources were productive, he would save the Dwarf as a backup. He'd wait a week, then decide. Elias doubted that Sonterra was good enough to move without leaving any traces. It was just a matter of time, he knew, before his team would uncover some vital clue. He just hoped it would be before the Luxus was employed in a major action.

CLERMONT-FERRAND, FRANCE: Michael and Yelena arrived at the train station about thirty minutes before the scheduled departure time to Perpignan. Michael used the time to contact Elias by phone and advised him of the results of the meeting with Jacques Vinzant and the lead that was provided to Polidor.

'Polidor was a personal friend of Babayan's, and for that reason he may choose to help us. Vinzant warned us, though, about dealing with Polidor. He felt that the information would be reliable, but that it might also be made available to others.'

'I'll get the computers working on Polidor, but his warning is probably worth heeding, Mike. You and Yelena just watch yourselves,' Elias advised.

'We will. I'll report back to you after we've made contact. Any progress on the Dwarf?' Michael asked.

'Not yet. He seems to be lying lower than usual, however. We're setting up right now to make the best use of him. I'll keep you informed.'

'How are the others doing?'

'Everything is going according to schedule. Wadelaw and Papa have made contact with their sources in Paris, and Abel has done the same in Amsterdam. He's on his way to Zurich now.'

'Good. With any luck, something should break within the week. Anything on Kammal and Greta Haas yet?'

'Not yet. But now that we know who we're looking for, I believe we'll find them quite soon.'

'All right. Good luck. I'll be in touch with you as soon as we have something to report. Yelena and I have to catch a train.'

'I'll put a support team in Perpignan, just in case you need them. Use the watch radio. They'll be monitoring the channel.'

'Right. I'll contact you soon.'

Michael hung up the phone and rejoined Yelena to board the train. He scanned the faces of the people on the crowded platform, wondering which belonged to the Soviets. He had not been able to single them out, and he wondered how Lucien had done it so quickly – and whether he had arranged his little diversion yet. It would be helpful to shake them, even for a little while.

Michael picked up his carrying case and placed a hand on Yelena's elbow to let her know it was time to board. They moved across the platform to the train. He took one last sweeping glance before stepping up into the train, and caught one overly interested set of eyes standing at the car behind theirs. The eyes darted away too quickly. He had just spotted the first Soviet, and burned the face into his memory.

The eyes returned to Michael and Yelena as they turned away and disappeared into the car. The Soviet looked farther up the platform, to the car ahead of the one Michael and Yelena had just boarded. Another inconspicuous figure leveled a short stare, then boarded the train as well. The first Soviet remained on the platform until the last possible moment to be sure that his subjects did not disembark. His foot left the platform just as the train began to move. He hung on the steps for a moment longer for confirmation, then stepped up to enter the car.

He waited for a moment behind the tall broad figure of a man standing in the doorway. The man did not move.

'Excuse me, please,' the Soviet said in passable French.

But instead of moving to the side to let him pass, the man turned straight toward him.

He was an enormous person. The Soviet's eyes stared straight into his chest. It took a moment for him to realize that the man was not giving way. It was when he looked up into the giant's face to repeat his request that he noticed the look of menace glaring back down at him.

Before he could speak or move, he felt the crushing blow to his testicles delivered by the man's knee.

He gasped in pain and reflexively crumpled forward.

The giant caught him under the armpits and drove the knee a second time with the same precise accuracy as the first.

The Soviet felt himself being lifted from the floor, and experienced the sudden sensation of flight. He coasted off the train, landed on his chest and face, then rolled twice from the force of the landing, ending up in almost a sitting position. He was hurt and dazed, but aware enough to see a second man sail off the moving train in much the same fashion that he had.

Lucien Vinzant and his colleagues had just made good on their word. There were no Soviets aboard the train to Perpignan.

A knock sounded on the compartment door, the call for tickets coming faintly through it. Yelena responded to the request, handing both rail passes to the official. Her eyes played past him and down the passageway as he checked and validated them. She accepted them back and closed the door.

A small slip of paper fluttered to the floor as she handed Michael's rail pass back to him. She picked it up and examined it.

'What is that?' Michael asked.

She read it and smiled. 'It's a note from your friends,' she replied, then read it aloud to him.

' "Temporarily free of tail. Depart train in Narbonne. A car will be waiting. Drive to Perpignan. Reasonable to assume that Soviets will have backup surveillance ready at Perpignan station. Good luck with Polidor." It's signed "Alliance".'

'Your friends are reliable,' Yelena said, the smile still on her face.

It was the first smile Michael had seen since they met. The hardness melted when she smiled, and her face was pretty.

'Yes, they are. I've learned to trust them completely,' he replied.

'How long a drive is it to Perpignan from Narbonne?' she inquired.

'I think it's about sixty kilometers. Motorway N9 runs direct.'

Yelena nodded, the smile faded, and she lit a cigarette. Michael noticed the slight trembling of her hands. He wondered how long she had been on the edge. She was as tight as a piano wire. The kind of life she lived was tough enough on anybody, even for short periods of time. The dossier had said nine years in the field. That was too long for anyone to live under the pressures that came with her kind of work. Agents had to be pulled in and rested. She was overdue.

She fell silent and took a seat near the window, staring out at the passing countryside.

Michael closed his eyes and laid his head back. The motion of the train was soothing, and the knowledge that there were Alliance members on board offered some comfort. He let his systems down and drifted gently to sleep.

The car was waiting in Narbonne, just as promised. They took a leisurely drive along the developed coastline of 'the poor man's Riviera', an undeserved term for this region of Languedoc-Rousillon increasingly popular as an alternative to the badly overcrowded Côte d'Azur.

They arrived in Perpignan at dusk, and found simple but charming accommodations in a rural farm cottage just outside the city. There was no phone, so, after settling in, Michael left and drove into the city, where he called the number provided by Jacques Vinzant. The entire conversation took less than thirty seconds. A meeting was set for the following afternoon at the abbey of St-Martin-de-Canigou, near Prades, about forty-five kilometers to the west of Perpignan. Jacques had called ahead as promised, and Michael's call was expected. He was to use the name St Thierry upon his arrival, wherupon he would be taken to Polidor.

Michael shopped for provisions before returning, picking up some Costieres-du-Gard wine – an excellent rosé – and an assortment of cheeses, breads, and *moules marinieres*. The delightful drive and the prospect of the meeting with Polidor had made him hungry.

He returned with his bundles and informed Yelena of their appointment with Polidor, then set about preparing their dinner.

They had eaten little throughout the day, and the quiet safety of their accommodations went a long way toward relaxing them both. The wine helped, too. Yelena had never had Costieres-du-Gard, and drank the first few glasses quickly, mellowing and reaching a level of relaxation she hadn't enjoyed in a long time.

They ate their dinner slowly, spoke casually of many things, and even laughed. It was a side of each other they hadn't seen, and they found each other's company pleasant.

'I'm stuffed,' Michael said finally, pushing himself away from the table.

'Thank you for a wonderful dinner. It was most enjoyable,' Yelena said to him.

'No thanks are necessary.'

She began clearing the table, leaving the wineglasses. 'I

435

meant what I said before. You have true friends in Group Alliance.'

'Yes, I know. They've helped me a great deal in the past.'

'They care for you. I could see it in their faces.'

'We go back to my first days in France. They were my eyes and ears when I needed them,' Michael replied, reaching for his glass.

Michael sipped his wine, watching her as she cleared away the plates. She didn't look anything like an assassin now in this comfortable setting.

'How long have you and Papa been together?' he asked.

'We met seven years ago,' she replied, finishing with the plates. She stacked them in the sink and walked back to the table. 'But it seems as if I've always known him. He's a good man, smart and quite reliable. He was always the heart of our team, the steadying force. They were all good. Now they're gone, except for Papa and me.'

'Stockholm?' Michael asked.

Yelena nodded. She sat at the table and picked up her glass, raised it to her lips, and drank.

'Are you afraid of him?' Michael asked, meaning Sonterra.

'Yes, a little, I think. But a little fear is good. It would be too easy to underestimate him if there were no fear. And he must never be underestimated. That was our mistake in Stockholm. We were the best team my country – or any country – could assemble. He was a name on a list. Oh, we knew he was dangerous. So were they all. But not like him. Not at all like him.'

'Tell me about Stockholm,' Michael said, hoping to gain some insight on Sonterra.

'There isn't much to tell, really. We got the lead from our sources that Sonterra was in Stockholm to assassinate certain members of an OPEC delegation meeting to discuss strategy to combat the falling oil prices. We moved in and set up surveillance on the OPEC ministers, hoping to spot him. We had descriptions of what he was supposed to look like, but had no picture to work with, as we do now. We couldn't identify him. The OPEC ministers never had a chance. We never had a chance.

'Word of the attempt reached the ministers, and they canceled their meeting schedule. Only that saved the others. He killed two of them as they were departing Stockholm. He must have spotted our team in his surveillance of the ministers, and stayed on after dealing with them. The very next morning, Victor was found dead in his car. The engine was still running when the police found him. He had been shot in the throat at point-blank range. The next day we found Ben dead in his room. He had been garroted so violently that he was nearly decapitated. The room was locked from the inside, and we could find no traces of his killer's exit. That same night Joseph was killed. He was in a phone booth talking to Max when it happened. He was shot from close range.

'The next morning Cerny was found dead in a park by a couple walking their dog. His face had been blown away. Within an hour Papa and I were ordered out of Stockholm. We wasted no time in leaving. We separated and were out of the country within two hours.

'We had worked closely together for five years without a casualty. We had shared so much,' she said, her eyes staring into nowhere. 'So much.'

'Papa and I were deactivated for almost six months after that. I returned to Israel, and Papa to Hamburg. We were assigned to new teams after that. I missed Papa very much. We weren't reunited again until Sonterra's involvement in Libya was discovered and we were called to Paris. Abel, of course, had been part of the team that nearly killed Sonterra in Gravenhage. Neither Papa nor I had worked with him before, but we knew of him. We were both surprised that he was reassigned to the field after so long. But his reasons for coming were the same as ours – to get Sonterra and to repay a long overdue debt.'

'You're very close to Papa, aren't you?' Michael asked, knowing the answer.

'Yes, I feel safe when we work together. There are no details left unattended.'

Michael poured them both some more wine.

Yelena emptied half of her glass in one long swallow, and lit a cigarette. The nervousness was back. The talk of Sonterra and the reliving of the horrible events in Stockholm had put her back on the edge.

'Things will be different this time,' Michael said reassuringly.

Yelena looked into Michael's eyes with some uncertainty in her own. 'Sonterra is a ghost, a devil who vanishes into thin air at will,' she said. 'I sometimes wonder if he *can* die. There was no way that he should have survived in Gravenhage. No way . . . but he did.'

'This isn't Gravenhage. And it won't be another Stockholm,' Michael assured her. 'He's flesh and blood just like everybody else. And he can't vanish into thin air.'

'No, this isn't Gravenhage. And it isn't Stockholm,' she repeated, as if from far away. 'But he does vanish.'

'This time it'll end differently,' Michael promised her.

Yelena didn't respond to Michael's final comment. She poured herself another glass of wine and stared across the room to a darkened window, her mind a million miles away.

PRADES, FRANCE: The abbey of St-Martin-de-Canigou stood high in the folds of the Pyrenees, lost to view in the austere beauty of its spectacular surroundings. Built in the eleventh century, it remained as isolated as it had been since its founding. Its walls breathed an austere, spiritual air, making it an ideal setting for retreats of both priests and laity.

Michael and Yelena had started in by car, but the solitary access road was at best passable by Jeep. They finished the steep approach on foot – a strenuous but invigorating walk.

'This Polidor character must be obsessed with seclusion,'

Michael said as they approached the large arched red door set at the base of the abbey's solitary tower.

He noted with a soldier's eye that the door provided the only access. The abbey wasn't built like a fortress, actually, for the tower was the only part of its structure to have a parapet. The rest of it, however, was impregnable to human passage, either in or out. It was a magnificent design that had doubtless discouraged invaders of ages past. With such a design, only one small point needed to be defended if it came to that, and it could probably be managed in a passive sort of way.

'This is not a place one can leave in a hurry,' Yelena noted. 'I hope we don't have to.'

For most people her statement would have been true. But for Michael its surroundings were like home. The steep ridges were densely covered with trees and heavy growth. He would need only to get into it to become invisible in its natural cover.

Michael rapped loudly on the thick wooden doors. There was a wait of almost a minute, and he was about to knock again when he heard a lock mechanism being released.

The door opened a little way, and a face peered out at them.

'May I help you?' a man in long brown clerical robes asked.

'Yes, my name is St Thierry,' Michael told the gentle-faced, soft-spoken man.

'Wait one moment, please,' the priest said, then closed the door.

After perhaps two minutes, the door opened once again. This time the figure staring out at them was not a priest but an imposing, serious-looking man with dark features and a face dominated by long, bushy eyebrows.

'St Thierry?' the man asked in a deep baritone.

'I am St Thierry,' Michael replied.

The man looked him over carefully, then shifted his eyes to Yelena.

'She is my associate,' Michael said before the man could speak.

The man regarded them both for a moment longer, then nodded and opened the heavy door to let them in.

'I've come to see Polidor,' Michael said as they stepped in. He noticed that the man was even larger than he had first thought – standing almost seven feet tall. He made Michael's six-foot-four-inch frame look small in comparison. Thick hair covered his hands and arms and stuck out above the collar of his shirt.

The man closed the door behind them and turned to face Michael.

'Please face the wall,' he instructed.

Michael turned as requested, glancing at Yelena from the corner of his eye.

Yelena backed off a step, her hand going into the pocket of her coat. The inside lining of the pocket had been removed, and the hand came to rest on the small-caliber Beretta.

The man watched her carefully as he frisked Michael thoroughly. He found Michael's Glock automatic and removed it. 'No weapons,' he said flatly. He finished the search down Michael's legs, not being too shy to check the crotch area. 'You may turn around,' he instructed.

'Your weapon will be returned before you leave,' the man said.

He turned next to Yelena, and motioned with his finger for her to turn to the wall as Michael had. She released the weapon and complied.

The man knew his business, and his hands said as much. Man or woman, it made no difference to him; he searched every inch of her body, knowing that a weapon could be concealed anywhere. He removed the Beretta and a long chain from around her neck.

'These will be returned,' he repeated.

'Follow me.'

Michael and Yelena fell in behind the giant figure and followed him down a long, dark corridor. They turned and ascended a small flight of stairs and made a few quick turns down short corridors. The man stopped at the mouth of a short dead-end hallway and pointed to a door at its end.

'I will be here,' he said in a voice that almost carried warning.

'Bigfoot lives,' Michael whispered to Yelena as they slipped past him and into the hallway.

They walked to the end of the corridor and stopped in front of the door. Michael recalled Yelena's words about this not being a place to leave in a hurry. She was right. There was no way out except past the human mountain at the end of the hallway. One thing was sure about Polidor, he knew how to control his space.

Michael gave the door three soft taps.

'Come in,' said a deep, hoarse voice from behind it.

Michael opened the door and looked in. The room was dark except for feeble rays of sunlight coming through a partially obstructed slit window less than a foot wide. He could see a table in the center of the room, and made out the shadow of an obese person behind it. A wine bottle and some glasses were on the table.

'Come in, come in. And close the door behind you,' the voice said.

They stepped in and closed the door.

'Please sit. There is another chair against the wall beside the door.'

Michael found the chair and brought it to the table. He and Yelena sat.

'Which of you is St Thierry?' the voice asked.

'I am,' Michael replied.

'And who might you be, my dear?'

'I am Yelena,' came the response in very good French.

'How can Polidor help you?'

Michael focused on the outline of the person across the table. His eyes had begun adjusting to the darkness. The hair was longer than a man's usually was, and the shoulders were more rounded. Polidor was a woman.

'We wish to obtain information,' he said.

'I know that much,' the hoarse, raspy voice returned. 'Whom or what are you looking for?'

'Rafael Sonterra.'

There was a moment of silence.

'Why do you come to me?' Polidor asked.

Michael recalled Jacques Vinzant's words that Polidor had been especially close to Babayan.

'You were highly recommended – and you were a friend of Vigen Babayan.'

By now Michael's eyes were well adjusted to the dim light, and he could see noticeable reaction on the face across from him. It looked like a cross between pain and anger.

Polidor raised her arms to the table and leaned forward slightly. Michael could see the fingers bent with arthritis, the knuckles swollen and deformed. The eyes behind the fat features squinted with interest.

Michael could sense that her connection to Babayan was more personal than business.

'What has one to do with the other?' Polidor asked, staring intensely at Michael's face.

'Sonterra broke faith with Babayan. He used him quite badly, then killed him when he was no longer useful to him. He also broke faith with Juan Strassa and had him killed in Paris. And there's more. He completely eliminated an entire network that he used in Colombia about four weeks ago. He has turned bad to his own, and he is holding stolen property that my people want back.'

Michael could see the effect of his words upon her. 'But more than the property, we want *him*,' he added.

'And if you find him?'

'I'll kill him,' Michael replied, and waited through a long silence.

'Rafael Sonterra is not an easy man to find. And as hard as he is to find, he will be more difficult to kill.'

'*You* can find him better than anyone. That's what I've been told. I'll worry about the rest of it *after* we've found him,' Michael told her.

Polidor did not reply. She slowly removed the last cigarette from a cellophane pack and lit it with a gold lighter. She let out a raspy cough, and drew again on the cigarette.

'It will be very expensive,' she said at last, lowering the cigarette in her bent and twisted fingers.

'We knew that coming in,' Michael returned.

Polidor dragged deeply on the strong-smelling cigarette. 'How do you know it was Sonterra who killed Babayan?'

'We have proof. A twisted matchstick that looks like a small drill bit, and a picture.'

'You have a picture of him?' Polidor asked, expressing both surprise and interest.

Michael reached into his jacket pocket and removed an envelope. He took out the pictures of the matchstick and of Sonterra taken as he left the plane in Libya, and handed them to her.

He watched as she accepted them and studied them carefully.

'Very few people know what he looks like. This is good. Very good. It will be helpful.'

'Then you'll help us?' Yelena asked.

Polidor looked at Yelena, then back at Michael. 'It will cost you five hundred thousand American dollars.'

'Agreed,' Michael said without hesitation.

'I don't care that Sonterra has broken faith with the others,' Polidor began. 'They can kill one another, it makes no difference to me. Their causes belong to them, and there will always be more paying customers to take their place – and yours, if you fail. Vigen Babayan was my . . . close friend. I care that *he* was killed. And if I help you, it will be for him.'

'Then we will help one another,' Michael said.

Polidor nodded slowly. 'Yes, if it can be done.'

Michael took out additional photographs of Kammal and Greta Haas, and offered them to her.

'We are also interested in these two friends of Sonterra. They are Kammal Nasir and Greta Haas.'

'Yes, I know them both.'

'Sonterra's last known location was Libya, five days ago,' Yelena said to her. 'The pictures of Kammal were taken eleven days ago in Bern, where he made an unsuccessful attempt on the life of Juan Strassa.'

'May I keep these pictures?' Polidor asked.

'Certainly,' Michael replied.

'I will need several days. Perhaps a week. I will give you a telephone number through which to contact me,' Polidor said.

She produced a pencil and with great difficulty wrote a number across the lower corner of the back of the picture of Greta Haas. Her bent fingers seemed not to want to obey the directions of her very deliberate mind. When she finished, she tore away the corner of the picture and handed it to Michael.

'Call this number daily, beginning two days from now. Use the name St Thierry, and ask for "Mother".'

Michael accepted the number from her.

'Be prepared to move quickly. He will not stay in one place long.'

'We'll be ready.'

'Be sure that you are. And for both our sakes, you had better be successful.'

Polidor raised the wine bottle, using both of her twisted hands, and poured out three glasses. She pushed two of them across the table to her clients.

'Remember, the fee will be five hundred thousand dollars.'

'To which we've agreed.'

'Then we'll drink to good fortune, and pray that it sits by your side.'

They raised their glasses, touching them gently.

Polidor looked at Michael with the eyes of a gypsy. 'Yes, to your good fortune. Drink deeply, my friend, for you will need it.'

444

31

PARIS: Bob Elias raised the Alpha phone to his ear. 'This is Triple Jack,' he said into it.

'We've met with Polidor, Bob,' Michael informed him. 'I think we'll get positive results from this contact.'

'Thank your friends in Alliance. They've come through again. What did you learn?'

'No facts, yet. But Polidor is willing to work with us. Jacques was right about the personal connection between Polidor and Babayan. Polidor, by the way, is a woman.'

'Yes, I know. Intelligence Central has discovered that the two were once lovers,' Elias said.

'Lovers? She looks a lot older than Babayan. I'd put her in her mid to late sixties.'

'Sixty-three, to be exact. Polidor's father was a Resistance fighter with the Maquis. She was just a teenager during the war, having only limited involvement. She acted as a courier mainly, and then only sparingly. After the war, however, her father made a lucrative business out of dealing in information, not to mention smuggling and the black market that thrived for years after the war. He kept on doing what he knew best, except this time it was for profit instead of patriotism. The information business was brisk, especially regarding war criminals and collaborators. It was also about the time the Soviets were making their big move in Eastern Europe. Everybody was watching everybody else, and wanted to know what the other guy was up to. No-one was going to let another world war happen without being ready for it this time.

'Polidor was firmly in the business by 1950. In 1955 she met Vigen Babayan. He was just getting his start in the arms business. She was young and, from what we can tell, a handsome woman. She and Babayan became lovers soon after they met, and remained so for about five years. Babayan's success stemmed directly from that relationship. Each grew tremendously after that, she in the

445

business of information and smuggling, and Babayan in arms dealing. They remained close through all the years,' Elias said.

'That explains her reaction, then,' Michael said. 'As soon as Babayan's name was mentioned, she became very interested in what we were after. Her former lover was dead, and we had the name of the man responsible. She seemed nervous about going against Sonterra, however. She's taking a great risk in committing herself to stop him. Her worry is understandable. If we fail to take him, he may come for her. Revenge is a way of life for Sonterra.'

'Her concern is a bad sign, Mike,' Elias said.

'Why do you feel that?' Michael asked.

'If you were in her position, what would you do?'

Michael thought for a moment. 'I'd try to improve my odds as best I could.'

'Exactly. She may peddle her information in every direction to ensure her own survival. The more people looking for Sonterra, the better her chances. But if too many people start searching, the more difficult it becomes for us to take him. He'll just go deeper into cover.'

'I see your point, but we don't have any choice other than to take the risks. We won't find him without help. Polidor wants five hundred thousand dollars for her services. I agreed to her demand, Bob. I didn't feel it was the time or the place to haggle.'

'You were right. We knew it would be expensive.'

'I'm supposed to make the first contact the day after tomorrow, then daily after that. I expect she'll want payment up front.'

'Agree to anything she wants. Let me know when and where to make payment, and I'll take care of it.'

'How are the other teams doing?' Michael asked.

'The Dwarf is under close surveillance but hasn't made a move yet. We're going to wait one more week to see if anything breaks from the information sources that have been contacted. If we don't get anything solid, we'll lure him out.'

'OK. I'll be in touch with you daily. If anything breaks, contact me over the watch radio. Yelena and I will head back north to Narbonne to avoid being picked up by the Soviets again. Our Alliance friends have given us a bit of a break. For a while, at least, we'll be unwatched. Jacques sends his regards, by the way.'

Elias smiled. 'I'll find a way to repay them. I have a feeling the Polidor contact will be fruitful. She's obviously motivated to strike back at Sonterra. Good luck to you and Yelena.'

'We'll make our own luck if we have to. I'll be in touch.'

Ivan Brevig closed the door behind him after entering the small flat in Paris. Tolvanin lowered the paper he was reading, and looked at the stocky control agent as he headed directly for the vodka.

'We've lost one of the teams,' Brevig said flatly as he opened the bottle and began filling a glass.

'Which one?' Tolvanin asked.

'Quinn and the Israeli girl.'

Tolvanin raised the paper again, not surprised, but also not concerned.

'We lost them in Clermont-Ferrand at the train station. They were believed to be headed for Perpignan, but they were not on the train when it arrived,' Brevig said, raising the glass.

'We shouldn't worry,' Tolvanin said nonchalantly. 'The other teams are under surveillance?'

'Yes, at least we have not bungled it with them.'

Tolvanin folded the paper and lit a cigarette. 'They will come together when the time is right.'

'I have just received word from Moscow that Rafael Sonterra has been connected to the affair in Libya,' Brevig announced. He drained the glass and poured another.

'Sonterra! This is getting very interesting,' Tolvanin replied. 'This has been confirmed?'

'Yes. There is no doubt. The Libyans would have missed it completely if we had not been there to go over their findings. They were not very cooperative at first.'

'Then they know this as well?'

'Yes.'

Tolvanin shook his head with disgust. 'We don't need their interference. The KGB will have that information by now, too. A week ago we had only the Americans to contend with. Now we have the Israelis, the Libyans, and the KGB. Kozlov must be pissing steam.'

'You have a talent for understatement,' Brevig said.

'Where are the other teams under surveillance?' Tolvanin asked.

'One is in Brussels, the other in Zurich.'

'And Elias?'

'He remains in Paris,' Brevig replied.

'They are making inquiries with their information sources.'

'To be sure, we are as well,' Brevig said. 'We no longer have to sit and wait for the Americans to lead us. We know whom to look for now.'

'Yes, but our best chance is still with them. The Israelis are good hunters, and the Americans have the most to lose,' Tolvanin reasoned. 'We must stay with them, especially Quinn. When they come together again, we will have him once more in our sight. Do try to do better this time, won't you? We must not lose him again. We need him – at least for a while longer.'

Brevig lowered his glass and stared at Tolvanin. He could not conceal his contempt for the man.

'Don't worry, Ivan. You won't lose your dacha on the Black Sea. I'll make you a hero . . . as usual.'

'Triple Jack,' Elias said, picking up the phone in Paris two days later.

'Bob, this is Tom Danziger.'

Elias looked at his watch. It had to be 5.00 a.m. in San Antonio.

'Good morning, Tom. What has you up so early?' Elias asked.

'Bad news, I'm afraid. Two more major reserves have been hit. Both in Colombia.'

'Colombia?' Elias repeated. 'What in hell is going on?' he asked.

'Major fields at Orito and Cúcuta have been hit. If the projections are correct, the reserves are doomed. Both are near Colombia's borders. Reserves in Ecuador and Venezuela could also be affected. This will ruin Colombia's oil economy, not to mention the possible losses in the other two countries. These are big-time hits, Bob. They could force Colombia into default and cripple one of South America's strongest economies. The effect will cause a tremendous ripple throughout the entire continent. This is no longer a "demonstration".'

'Orito was one of their two earlier hits. Is there any chance that these losses are an aftermath of the first demonstration?' Elias asked hopefully.

'Doubtful. The first hit was in a small, isolated reserve. There is some *remote* possibility that the reserves in Orito could be fallout effect, but it's unlikely. There's no way on the Cúcuta reserves,' Danziger replied.

'It's started, then. Can you determine when the seedings were made?' Elias asked.

'We can't tell exactly, but the computer simulation indicates it must have happened about two weeks ago.'

'That's when the other demonstrations manifested themselves. This adds fuel to the theory that Sonterra never planned to sell the Luxus.'

'There could be others that we don't know about yet, too,' Danziger added. 'But we won't have to wait long to find out.'

'Why is that?'

'Skyco's labs have been working nonstop on the probes that we told you about,' Danziger said.

'You mean the ones that can detect the presence of the Luxus?'

'Yes. De Roode has just announced that the work is complete. We now have two working prototypes, with more being made. The prototypes are being rushed to Colombia, and should be inserted in the stricken reserves within twenty-four hours. At least then we'll be able to monitor the effects of the Luxus.'

'But we can't stop it?'

'Not yet. But that's the rest of the news. Skyco has broken the genetic code on the Beta. Their researchers are searching for a way to eliminate the destructive enzyme, enabling the Beta to combat the effects of the Alpha form of the Luxus.'

'And that will stop it?'

'If they're successful, yes, and it will stop it completely.'

'How long will the research take?' Elias asked.

'There are a lot of genetic combinations to try. It all depends on how quickly they hit the right one. It could take weeks, or it could take years. There's no way of telling at this point.'

'How long to get more probes ready?' Elias asked.

'De Roode is saying that within two weeks he'll have enough to insert into every major reserve likely to be a target. It's not much, but at least we'll be able to determine where the Luxus has been used, and to assess the damage. Once the Beta is ready, it can be placed strategically around the globe and rushed to any site showing the presence of the Alpha. We can make the Beta seedings within twenty-four hours of detection, barring any interference from the governments involved. There will be some damage, but it can be kept at about five per cent if there are no delays,' Danziger explained. 'Brice has already begun high-level contacts to prepare foreign governments for this involvement.'

'How are you making out in the hunt for Sonterra?' Danziger asked. 'The President can't hold off the spooks much longer.'

'We're making progress, Tom, but still need more time. He *has* to hold them off just a little longer.'

'He's doing his best, but he's beginning to look rather foolish to his national security advisers. How much longer do you think you'll need?'

'I'd say a week, maybe two,' Elias answered.

'I can't guarantee you that much time, but we'll relay your information to the President. Keep at it, and good luck. I'll advise you of any developments on the probes and the work being done on the Beta. Oh, and tell Mike that Alex is safe and that she's recovered from the rescue mission on the yacht.'

'He'll be glad to hear it,' Elias said. 'Keep those scientists working, and keep me advised. A supply of Beta in our arsenal would be a powerful weapon.'

'Don't worry. Skyco's lab people are as concerned as we are to stop this thing. You just concentrate on getting that sonofabitch Sonterra.'

'We'll get him, all right. And we'll make him wish he'd never heard of Skyco or the Luxus or the word *oil*. Just buy us some time with Brice if you can.'

NARBONNE, FRANCE: Michael held the phone and waited for Polidor to pick up on the other end. It was four days after his meeting with Polidor. He had made his initial contact two days ago, as she had instructed. At that time Polidor had had nothing to report, and requested payment in advance, to which he had agreed. On the following day there were still no results, but Pollidor had confirmed receipt of the payment and told Michael to continue calling on a daily basis.

'Mother,' came the deep, scratchy voice at the other end.

'This is St Thierry,' Michael returned.

'I have some good news for you,' Polidor began.

'I'm listening,' Michael said, his senses on full alert.

'The man you are looking for was in Spain until yesterday. He journeyed through the Pyrenees, with the help of trusted Basque smugglers, across the border into France.'

'Where is he now?' Michael asked calmly, his hand tightening on the phone, his ear pressed hard against it.

'He is in the village of Sare, in the foothills of the Pyrenees, about fifteen kilometers from the Atlantic coast.'

'I know where it is. Go on.'

'A safe house has been arranged for him there.'

'How long will he be there?' Michael asked.

'Two days at the most.'

'Where in Sare?'

'I will have that information for you by tomorrow. You must be very careful, he has friends with him.'

'I thought he worked alone,' Michael said.

'He does, usually. But these are the people who took him through the Pyrenees. They have guaranteed his safety and will offer escort west along the Pyrenees to St-Jean-Pied-de-Port, two days from now. At that point their obligation ends – as might their lives, if he stays true to his recent form. You must act quickly to stop him.'

'Two days. Are you certain of that?'

'Do not question my information, St Thierry. You cannot begin to imagine the difficulty and risk involved in getting it. If you doubt what I tell you, you need not call again,' Polidor said acidly.

'I apologize,' Michael replied, angry with himself for expressing what seemed open doubt. 'I appreciate the personal danger you face by assisting our search.'

'Call me tomorrow at sunrise for the rest of your information,' Polidor said. 'Be swift and sure, Mr St Thierry, for if you miss him I will not be able to help you again.'

'I understand,' Michael told her. 'Thank you. I will call you tomorrow.'

The line went dead at the other end, and he placed the receiver back in its cradle. He looked at Yelena, whose eyes were electric with something more than excitement.

'We have him. Call in the team.'

SARE, FRANCE: Rafael Sonterra's safe house was a large and comfortable white dwelling with a red tile roof and red shutters – one of many such houses in the quiet village deep in the Basque region of France. The delicious aroma of *piperade*, a spicy omelet with pimientos and tomatoes, filled the lower rooms of the house and drifted temptingly to the upper floor. But the prospect of a robust, hot breakfast did not entice Sonterra. He was nervous. A sixth sense tapping away at his brain told him that there was something different about this day from the previous two he had spent here. He paced in his room, stopping at the window with each pass. Something was out of place.

He stopped at the window again on his next pass and stared out through the fine lace curtains, trying to recognize what had triggered the warning deep within his brain.

Today was the day he was to move on to St-Jean-Pied-de-Port, and he had risen before dawn just as on the preceding two days. The feeling had begun then. *But why?* he wondered. He continued to stare, his eyes searching to the right, then to the left – and then he found it. It was the cows. They were not in the pasture.

He moved closer to the window to get a wider field of vision.

For two days he had watched the daily routines of the village. He had watched each morning as the cows were led to the pasture after milking, just as the sun rose. But today there were none.

He left his room and walked across the hall to another bedroom and stopped at the window. He stared down to the back of a neighboring house, where he had watched the early-morning ritual of stuffing the geese to fatten their livers for the regional delicacy of *foie gras*, but the women were not there, either. He backed away slowly and stepped into the hallway and listened. He could hear the voices of the three Basques who had led him along the smugglers' trails through the Pyrenees. Their routine seemed quite normal; they obviously did not share his alarm.

He returned to his room, checked his handgun, and put it under his belt. He went to his bag and removed several articles until he found the kaffiyeh. He put it on and left the room.

The Basques had not heard his silent approach, and the

sudden vision of him standing there, tall, almost sinister, with the kaffiyeh wrapped around his face, forced them to immediate silence.

'Two of you go out and check the village,' he said, waving a finger at the nearest two. 'You stay with me,' he told the other.

'What is wrong?' one of the men asked.

'Just do as I say. We must leave immediately.'

'We aren't scheduled to leave for another twelve hours,' the man protested.

Sonterra glared at him until the man pushed his plate aside and rose to his feet. He motioned to the other man with his head, and the two of them were off without further comment or protest.

'Ready their things quickly,' Sonterra said to the one man who remained behind. 'And arm yourself.'

The man looked at him nervously and did as he was told.

Sonterra observed him closely as he left the room. They were about the same height and build. That would be useful before the morning was out.

'Two Basques leaving the house,' said the voice of Abel over the radio in Michael's hand.

Abel had made the observation from a well-concealed position behind a house diagonally across the narrow road from the safe house.

Michael's team had moved into place during the night, taking up positions across from, above, and below the safe house, from which they could cover all escape routes along the road. Abel had wired the car during the night with radio-controlled explosives tied to a depression trigger below the driver's seat. Any weight on the seat would activate the arming mechanism and require only Abel's signal to detonate it.

Michael and Yelena readied themselves in the lower position, while Wadelaw and Papa prepared in the upper one, across the street from the cathedral, the largest structure in the village. From their position Wadelaw and Papa could see all movement at the front of the house. Michael and Yelena could see only the side and rear, but could move quickly in a lateral direction to draw a line of fire across the front, if necessary. The road was the only avenue of escape in the car.

The team watched carefully as the two Basques walked out to the road and headed off in different directions. They had walked only a short way before realizing that the village routine had been broken for some reason. They stopped and turned at almost the same instant and walked quickly but nonchalantly back toward the house.

'They know someone's cleared the streets,' Wadelaw said into the radio.

'This is going to be it,' Michael said. 'Get ready,' he ordered, snapping back the arming bolt on his Ingram submachine gun.

Yelena did likewise on her Uzi.

'Let the car run about a hundred yards,' Michael advised Abel. This was to reduce the possibility of damage to surrounding structures and the chance of inflicting civilian casualties.

Sonterra had only to see the alarm in the two Basques' faces to know that his instincts were correct.

The third Basque returned to the kitchen with the belongings of the others.

'Leave everything behind,' Sonterra instructed.

He removed the kaffiyeh and handed it to the third man. 'Put this on,' he instructed.

The Basque took it from him, staring at the kaffiyeh with puzzlement. He didn't have the slightest idea how it should be done.

Realizing this, Sonterra took it back from the Basque and began putting it on him.

'There's movement on the other side of the cathedral,' Abel reported urgently. 'I see four men moving toward the

455

safe house. They're armed with Kalashnikovs. Soviets . . . KGB,' he reported.

'Jesus Christ!' Michael growled. 'They're going to blow this thing wide open.' There was no mystery in his mind how they had come to know Sonterra's whereabouts. Polidor was playing all angles. *I wonder how much* they *paid for the information*, he mused.

The Soviets moved into position with silent speed, splitting in different directions. The first three took positions giving them complete coverage of the front of the safe house, while the fourth cut off into a narrow stand of trees and continued to a vantage point that gave him a good line of fire across the rear of the house.

'More bad news, Mike,' Wadelaw's voice began. 'Two more are moving in from behind the cathedral, about seventy yards behind the others. And these aren't KGB.'

'What the hell is going on?' Michael blurted.

'Looks like more Russians to me, Mike. I've seen these guys before. They're GRU. We've got a real party developing here. All we need now is a troupe of dancing girls.'

Sonterra finished the final arrangement of the kaffiyeh.

'Get out immediately,' he said to the three Basques. 'Take the car and get out of Sare.'

'What about you?' the man wearing the kaffiyeh asked.

'I am no longer your problem. Get away quickly,' he said.

They didn't have to hear it twice. Once relieved of their responsibility, they were gone in an instant.

'Ready on the detonator,' Michael advised Abel.

Yelena readied the Uzi to begin raking the car the moment it came into firing range.

'All set,' Abel returned.

The Basques stepped out of the safe house and approached the car with long, rapid strides, weapons in hand, eyes searching everywhere.

The KGB opened up immediately, breaking the quiet of the morning with a thunderous volley of fire from their Kalashnikovs.

The Basque walking around to the driver's side of the car didn't have a chance. The opening volley shredded him like confetti, and he went down instantly. The remaining two Basques dove behind the car for cover.

'Sonterra's out in the open,' Abel shouted into his radio after seeing the kaffiyeh. He wished desperately that he had used a standard detonator. There was enough high explosive to end the matter with them huddled behind the car as they were. But the detonator would not arm until pressure was applied on the driver's seat.

Sonterra didn't lose a moment. The second the gunfire erupted, he headed for the back of the house. But he was too clever to leave immediately, recognizing that the back of the house would be covered as well. He crouched low, looking through the window for signs of movement behind the house. He didn't have to wait long.

The fourth KGB agent scooted up to get a position closer to the house. No sooner had he stopped than a second figure appeared some distance in back of him.

Sonterra watched in puzzlement as the second figure raised his weapon and put a slug through the back of the first man's head from twenty feet.

The GRU agent moved in closer to his victim to inspect his work. The second his attention was on the body of the KGB agent, Sonterra launched himself through the door, the handgun raised and ready.

The GRU agent looked up, and Sonterra dropped him cleanly with a single shot.

Sonterra bolted for the stand of trees behind the house, and was soon deep within their cover.

'One out the back,' Michael shouted into his radio. 'I'm going for him,' he said, and took off immediately. He

457

had been almost a hundred yards away and could not see clearly if the figure emerging from the house was Sonterra.

Yelena had already moved laterally to get a clean line of fire at the Basques behind the car. Abel moved in from his position to the right, closing in on the distracted KGB operatives.

The Israelis opened up simultaneously.

The Basques had no cover to protect them from Yelena's salvo. She had set her eyes squarely on the figure wearing the kaffiyeh, her heart pounding at the prospect of catching Sonterra so vulnerable and unable to defend himself. Her hail of bullets caught them against the car and they fell under the fierce concentration of her well-directed fire.

The KGB were likewise caught by Abel's well-concentrated volley, two of them falling to the accuracy of his fire. Abel spun to his right to direct a second burst at the remaining Russian, but the Russian was faster, and he cut loose a burst of his own, catching Abel squarely. The Israeli went down, the Russian continuing to pour fire into the fallen target.

Wadelaw saw Abel fall, but had no satisfactory line of fire at the concealed Soviet. He looked back to the other advancing Soviets, but they had disappeared behind the far side of the cathedral, and were moving in the same general direction as Michael. He broke from his position and sprinted across the road, circling behind the cathedral to flank the Russians.

The firefight in front of the safe house had narrowed to two participants. Yelena reached the safety of the side of the safe house, the KGB agent's fire ricocheting harmlessly off the wall. She could see the twisted, still body of Abel by the edge of the road, and she seethed with anger.

The Russian's clip emptied, and Yelena used the break in his fire to advance to the car. Using the vehicle as cover, she raked the Russian's position until her clip emptied, and ducked back behind the car to insert a fresh one.

Papa had also used the break in the Russian's fire to move down the road until he drew a clean line of fire at him. When the Soviet rose to direct his fire once again at Yelena, Papa opened up.

The Russian jerked violently from Papa's bullets, spinning out of Papa's line of fire, and moving right into Yelena's sights. She put him away swiftly. He crumpled heavily in the dust.

She turned and moved quickly to the inert body wearing the now bloody kaffiyeh. She trembled as she reached for the face covering and yanked it away. In that instant she realized that Sonterra had won yet again. With an anguished cry she rekindled all the anger she thought had been spent.

'The man wearing the kaffiyeh is not Sonterra,' she shouted into the radio. 'He has to be the one you're after, Michael.'

'Roger. I'm closing on him,' Michael replied as he moved swiftly through the stand of trees, no longer able to see Sonterra.

Sonterra emerged from the trees and sprinted along a high hedgerow, then continued on, moving parallel to a high wall toward the cathedral.

He came to the end of the wall and ran squarely into one of the KGB men Wadelaw had seen. He dropped the Russian with two quick shots, and sprinted toward the high wall surrounding the cathedral.

Tolvanin, having seen Sonterra's exit from the safe house, and Michael's pursuit of him, had taken a course parallel to Michael's. He sprinted along the opposite side of the wall that Sonterra had followed, while Michael traced Sonterra's route exactly. They were on opposing sides of the wall, moving in the same direction, Tolvanin trailing by perhaps fifteen yards.

Sonterra reached the wall of the cathedral, and was over it in an instant, landing almost on top of Tolvanin's man. Sonterra was the quicker to recover from the surprise, and the automatic in his hand spoke first.

Wadelaw heard the shots as he approached on the other side of the high wall. He readied himself to come up over the edge with a spray of gunfire, when he was caught in a stream of bullets directed at him from his right. It was another KGB agent.

Wadelaw hit the ground instead of the wall, miraculously escaping the barrage of gunfire. He could not see the Soviet who had fired at him.

Michael turned a sharp corner in the cathedral wall at the same time, coming right into the sights of the KGB agent. He eluded a short burst, then heard a second sharp tattoo of gunfire coming from behind him and from the left. He saw the KGB agent fall through the low hedge, and Michael looked back over his shoulder in the direction from which the gunfire had come. He saw Tolvanin lower his weapon.

Their eyes met for a brief moment, then Tolvanin was gone.

'Are you all right, Mike?' Wadelaw's voice asked from ten yards away.

'Yeah, I'm fine,' he answered, a bit confused by what had just happened. Tolvanin had saved his life, and he didn't understand why.

'Sonterra's on the other side of this wall,' Wadelaw shouted.

'Let's go,' Michael said, getting to his feet immediately.

Wadelaw followed, and they sprinted along the wall in the direction of the firefight with the KGB.

'Sonterra is inside the cathedral wall,' Michael shouted into his radio.

Papa was the closest to Sonterra's position, and crossed the road to the cathedral wall ahead of Michael and Wadelaw. He sprinted along the wall in the direction they were coming from.

Yelena had begun moving in the direction that Michael had taken, and intercepted him and Wadelaw just before a big bend in the wall. She fell in with them as they sprinted toward Papa's position.

Papa continued along the wall and reached a break in it. As he stopped and turned into it, he felt a sharp blow to his throat and dropped to his knees. He felt his throat fill with fluid, and saw blood spurting down his chest and arms. He looked up and saw Rafael Sonterra staring down at him, a knife clenched in his fist.

Sonterra had caught him in the throat as he came through the opening. The razor-sharp blade had done its damage so cleanly that there had been no realization of pain, except from the edge of Sonterra's fist as it impacted his neck. The knife had slit the Israeli's throat.

Papa stared up into the terrorist's face, immobilized by the realization that he was a dead man.

Sonterra kicked the gun from Papa's hands, turned, and sprinted away.

Michael, Wadelaw, and Yelena rounded the bend in the wall and came upon the opening. They found Papa as he slumped forward, pitching on to his face.

Michael looked up and caught a glimpse of Sonterra as he went over the wall and back onto the road. He let go a futile burst at the fleeing terrorist, but missed him entirely.

Michael sprinted off after him. He heard a car engine start on the other side of the wall, and the squeal of tires accelerating on the road. He leaped up to the edge of the wall and braced himself halfway with his elbows. He let go a volley at the car speeding away from him. But the aim was, at best, marginal.

Michael saw the car move away unharmed. Just as it reached a bend in the road, he saw two more figures appear. Both sent a fierce volley of automatic weapons fire at the fleeing car. He heard the hits on the vehicle, and saw it weave, then straighten out. Then it cleared the bend and was gone.

Michael looked back at the two men who had delivered the final volley. Tolvanin was one of them. The other was one of the Russian's men.

Once again Tolvanin exchanged glances with Michael. There was a brief moment of shared defeat between them, then the Russian turned away and was gone.

Michael dropped back off of the wall to the ground, and turned toward Yelena and Wadelaw. Yelena was bent over Papa, trying desperately to administer assistance.

Michael lowered his eyes to the ground and shook his head. They had missed their chance at Sonterra and had lost two of Israel's best agents in the attempt. If Polidor was right, they had just blown their *only* chance. Sonterra was gone now, and would be impossible to find again. But Michael didn't buy that completely.

The man had a certain survival magic about him – one that Michael understood well. And deep inside he felt that there would be another chance, somewhere and sometime soon. He wondered whose magic would be stronger in the end.

32

PARIS: Bob Elias finished reading the report on the Sare operation. His disappointment was no less profound than Michael's. He looked up at his top agent, who paced restlessly.

'I share your feelings completely, Mike,' Elias said as he let the report fall to the table. 'Things got out of our control. You couldn't help that.'

'I can't believe it was blown so badly,' Michael said. 'Sare isn't that big a town. We should have set a secondary perimeter. We were too intent on the target. We should have anticipated interference from the outside. We *knew* Polidor was nervous about the whole affair. We even expected her to improve her own chances of survival by taking her information elsewhere. *Damn it!* I can't believe we were so stupid.'

'It was a costly mistake that can't be changed. We can

462

only go forward from here,' Simmerman said from his chair, a short cigarette stub burning in one hand, the habitual cup of cooled coffee in the other.

'There's no going forward for Papa and Abel,' Michael returned, perhaps a bit unjustly.

There was a moment of heavy silence.

Simmerman felt again the anguish of losing Papa and Abel. They had been two of his longest-serving field agents. He thought of Yelena, who had been so shattered by the loss of Papa that she had secluded herself in her room. Simmerman had felt it best to let her skip the meeting.

'Yeah, well, there's also a pack of Russians that won't be going anywhere, either,' Wadelaw added.

'We've identified six of the Soviets as KGB, and two as GRU,' Simmerman said.

Michael thought for a moment. 'That explains it,' he muttered more to himself than for the benefit of the others.

'Explains what?' Elias asked.

'Tolvanin saved our lives. One of the KGB agents had us squarely in his sights, and Tolvanin shot him. I couldn't understand why he'd take out one of his own men.'

'That's taking the KGB-GRU animosity to extremes, but it just proves there's a lot at stake,' said Elias. 'Both groups are probably under extreme pressure to produce. And don't kid yourself, Mike, if that KGB agent had been CIA, he'd have dropped you and Wadelaw in a heartbeat, and for the same reason. It's the bottom line – Sonterra – that counts. And only the bottom line.'

'Where do we go from here?' Wadelaw asked. 'If Polidor was right about our getting only one chance at Sonterra, we may not get another try.'

'Sonterra will virtually disappear now. He'll trust no one, and we can't expect him to surface again. He may try for Polidor, however, so we'll set up a close surveillance just in case he does,' Elias answered.

Simmerman shook his head. 'He'll get to Polidor

eventually, I have no doubt of that. But first he will complete his objective. His plan is at risk, and he will not jeopardize his possibilities for success.'

'We still have the Dwarf,' Elias said, drawing their attention.

'Yes, the Dwarf,' Simmerman repeated. 'Proper handling of the Dwarf may lead us to Kammal.'

'Kammal is Sonterra's conduit to the outside sources he needs to execute his plan,' Elias continued. 'If we can make the Dwarf nervous enough, he may decide to make contact with Kammal.'

'Eliminating Kammal would force Sonterra to surface to make the necessary contacts himself, or abandon his plan,' Simmerman added.

'Can we do it?' Michael asked. 'Can we get the Dwarf to move toward Kammal?'

'If he thinks he's in enough danger, he will,' Elias replied. 'He's too clever and too aggressive to sit and let himself be picked off like everyone else who has helped Sonterra. I think we can count on his moving . . . and right now he's our *only* shot at Sonterra. We'll have to move immediately, too, because there have already been two more reserve hits in Colombia,' he announced.

'Two more?' Michael repeated, surprised.

'Yes, at Orito and Cúcuta. Skyco projects that the reserves will be totally lost.'

'Jesus!' Michael exclaimed. 'There's no telling how many more he could already have hit.'

'That's right,' Elias said. 'But Skyco has the means to determine that now.'

'The probes?' Michael inquired.

'Yes. They've already rushed two into Colombia to insert in the reserves. We'll have a damage report in a day or so. The plan is to manufacture more probes as quickly as possible and insert them into major reserves across the globe. They've also made progress on the Beta; they've worked out the genetic code that controls the destructive enzyme. If they're successful in shutting down that

464

enzyme system, they'll be able to combat the effects of the Luxus.'

'Does that mean we'll be able to stop it?' Wadelaw asked.

'Yes, *if* they can work out the mechanism quickly enough.'

'That's outstanding news,' Michael said. 'If we can do that, then we take the weapon out of Sonterra's hands.'

'That's what it means. But we're not there yet.'

'Then finding Kammal takes on much more importance,' Simmerman said. 'Sonterra has no way of knowing about the Beta. If we can reach Kammal and distract Sonterra long enough, we may buy sufficient time to make that possible.'

'*If* his loyalty to Kammal is strong enough to draw him in,' Michael added.

'I think it will be,' Simmerman said. 'Kammal and the Haas woman are very important to him. They're the only people besides his teacher, Abu Hassan Nasir, that he trusts . . . and loves.'

'And if we're wrong?' Michael asked. 'If it doesn't draw him in?'

'Then there's a good chance we won't stop him in time,' Elias answered for the Israeli. 'He has the means to sink the planet into a new dark age without power and oil.'

Michael watched as Simmerman crushed out the stub of another cigarette. 'OK, we find Kammal. And we pray that you're right.'

PARIS: Kammal's nerves were near the snapping point. Sonterra had missed his contact schedule by twenty-four hours, and there was still no word from him.

Kammal had stayed at the contact point for two hours longer than he should have, hoping Sonterra had simply run into telephone delays. But the call never came and he finally left.

He was certain that something had gone wrong. Sonterra *never* missed his contact schedules.

Kammal had spent the next twenty-four hours stewing about how to proceed, facing near-panic at the prospect that Sonterra might have been taken. He could not carry out the plan alone, not without the strength of his brother. The next contact was not scheduled for another seven days, each one of which would be an eternity to him.

Kammal checked the date on his watch for the hundredth time, then the date on his newspaper to be certain that it was correct. His shaking hands opened the notebook he carried, and he checked the schedule of contact times and places he was to have committed to memory. He had not made a mistake. Yesterday *was* the day, and he had been in the right place.

Feeling that he was about to explode from the pressure, Kammal opted for the single worst move he could make. He picked up his coat and left the room.

He rode the lift down to the lobby and walked unnoticed past the desk. He stepped out of the hotel and into the cold evening air, breathing it in deeply. He checked the street carefully, then walked away from the hotel.

The phone at the front desk rang.

'Havre-Tronchet. Good evening,' the operator answered.

'I would like to speak to Monsieur Aziz,' the voice at the other end said.

There was a wait while the phone in Kammal's room rang without answer.

'I'm sorry,' the operator began, returning to the line. 'There is no answer in his room.'

'Then I would like to leave a message,' Sonterra said. He was violating all of his own rules of contact. But he was left with no choice. His growing concern for Kammal's weakened state overrode the rules.

'Yes, please. How does it go?'

'St-Paul Métro station. Tomorrow at noon.'

The operator recorded the message. 'Is there anything else?' he asked.

'No, that will be sufficient. Please be sure that he receives it.'

'Certainly. Who shall I say has left the message?'

'His brother.'

'Thank you, Monsieur,' the operator returned, then the phone went dead.

The message was sent to the clerk, with the room number 417 clearly marked on it. He looked at it and folded it in half, holding it in his hand as he finished up details of a late registration. He could not take his eyes off the behinds of the two beautiful tourists as they walked away from the desk. He looked back briefly to the key boxes, then back to the two women holding his attention, and slid the message into a key box. But the message went to room 416, and he never looked back to check that it had been done correctly.

Kammal returned to the hotel two hours later, feeling bolstered by the assistance of the drugs he had purchased. He walked past the desk without stopping, and returned to his room.

MOSCOW: The GRU limo pulled slowly through the Kremlin gate at the Spassky Tower and accelerated gently through Red Square and past St Basil's Cathedral, the oldest structure on the square, its multicolored spires illuminated brilliantly against the night sky.

Kozlov puffed rhythmically on his pipe, his mind deep in troubled thought. He had just gone through one of the most unpleasant sessions with the Central Committee that he had ever experienced.

Nikolai Barchenkin watched his superior in respectful silence. He had not been in the session with Kozlov, but could hear small bits of the harangue through the closed doors. It had not gone well, and he knew it.

The tension between Kozlov and Vladin, his KGB counterpart, was so strained through the entire session that it seemed the two might come to blows. Neither was willing to accept blame for the failed operation in Sare, and each heaped blame in generous portions upon the other for his own salvation. Neither escaped unscathed.

Tolvanin's team had been the only Soviets to walk away from the disastrous encounter with Sonterra. Their account was, therefore, the only official one. They had formally reported the cause of failure as the unexpected presence and the ill-advised, premature action of the KGB. Parts of it were careful fabrication, of course, to save the GRU from blame. But failure for any reason was inexcusable to the Committee, and severe criticism flew, rightfully, in both directions.

The outcome was that Kozlov had orders to continue in his quest to stop Sonterra and to obtain the Luxus at any cost. Vladin had not been told to desist, but was made eminently aware that a second failure would not be tolerated.

Kozlov reread the secret report filed by Tolvanin, then folded it.

'Sonterra will be in deep hiding now. We will have little chance of finding him without informants,' he told Barchenkin, who nodded his agreement.

'We have little choice but to tighten our surveillance on Quinn and Intel-Trace. They clearly are ahead of us. Wherever this leads next, we will at least arrive together.

'But I'm afraid that may not be good enough, Nikolai,' Kozlov said. 'We are surrounded by adversaries. To beat them, we will have to arrive one step ahead. You are to direct all search efforts towards finding Kammal Nasir. When he is found, I want him taken alive. If we cannot find Sonterra, then we will lure him to us.'

'And the Americans?' Barchenkin asked.

'Continue close surveillance of Quinn. I'm certain the Americans will try the same approach. I also want Abu Hassan Nasir located. He trained Sonterra and knows him better than any man alive. Perhaps he will be willing to deal to save the life of his son.'

'I suspect he will not betray Sonterra, at any cost,' Barchenkin said.

'He is an old man, Nikolai. And Kammal is his last remaining son, the last piece of his immortality. He may surprise you.'

'And if he refuses?'

'Then there will be one less terrorist in this world to worry about. And I will send him the head of his son.'

PARIS: Yelena was on her feet immediately at the sound of the soft knock on her door.

'Who is it?' she demanded, moving quickly to the far side of the door.

Yelena lowered the automatic when she heard Michael's familiar voice and opened the door to let him in.

He stepped into the room.

'I've brought you something to eat,' he told her, offering a neatly wrapped paper bag.

'Thank you, but I'm not hungry,' Yelena replied.

She looked terrible. Her eyes were red and swollen from crying, and her hair hadn't been combed.

Michael went to her side and put an arm around her shoulder.

She turned her face into his neck and kissed him there, then kissed his cheek, his chin, and his lips.

'Please stay with me,' she said. 'Don't leave me tonight.'

Michael pulled her very close, feeling her need for him and understanding it.

'I'm here,' he whispered.

33

PARIS: Bob Elias directed the full resources of Intel-Trace against the Dwarf. Static tracking teams were set in place around his known location, and mobile teams in cars, on motor bikes, and on foot were set in concentric perimeters to cover movement in any direction. Across the street from the Dwarf's flat, Intel-Trace established photographic and sound surveillance units with highly sensitive directional microphones focused on the windows facing the street. They could pick up even the faintest sounds coming from inside the flat.

A penetration team was put in the building one floor above the Dwarf, with instructions to move in the moment he left his rooms. With the team was a demolitions expert who would perform the magic of pushing the Dwarf over the edge and into the hands of Intel-Trace.

Everything was in place, and the teams awaited only the chance to put the plan in motion.

The wait lasted through the night and all the next day, but their patience was rewarded when the Dwarf left his flat a few minutes before midnight.

They knew from almost two weeks of close surveillance that his business would be short, and that he would return to his flat in approximately one hour. He wasn't taking any chances. The less time he spent out of the safety of his flat, the less likely a target he would be.

The penetration team waited until static street teams reported that the Dwarf was outside of the first surveillance perimeter. Then they moved in quickly, gaining clean entry into his flat.

The team split into three pairs, the first setting an explosive device beneath the mattress of his bed. Like the car in Sare, it utilized a pressure-sensitive arming device that would activate the moment the Dwarf sat on the bed. It was a single-throw mechanism, meaning that it would arm with the first application of pressure and stay in the armed position even if the Dwarf got off of the bed. Detonation was radio-controlled. The explosive charge was large enough to kill anyone on the bed, but not sufficiently large to cause extensive structural damage to the rest of the building, outside of some broken windows and almost certain damage to the ceiling of the flat immediately below the Dwarf. There would be little danger to other residents of the building.

The other two teams set about installing highly sensitive motion detectors and microphones, to enable them to further track the movements and activities of the Dwarf after his return.

The demolitions expert carefully tested the arming mechanism before completing his connections. The first mechanism had to be replaced because it worked too well. It was completely silent. He selected a second, hooked it up quickly, then used a pair of long-nosed pliers to stress the tiny plunger shaft side to side a few times. He tested it again, and smiled. The action was less silent, emitting a faint click when depressed. It was exactly what he wanted. He reset the device and finished making the connections to the explosives.

Before they left the flat, they placed a micro-relay in the hinge of the door to the apartment, to signal each time the door was opened or closed.

The entire operation took less than thirty minutes. The team was well out of the building when the secondary perimeter surveillance teams reported that the Dwarf was returning to his building.

They marked his progress carefully as he returned to the building. A few moments later the relay indicated that the door to the flat had been opened. No lights shone in the windows. He was being cautious, choosing to stay in the darkness for his safety. The microphones and the motion detectors were closely monitored as the Dwarf moved about the flat.

He made some tea, smoked two cigarettes while he drank it, and went to the bathroom. He returned to the small kitchen, took a couple of stiff drinks to calm his nerves, and smoked two more cigarettes. It almost seemed as if he was prepared to stay up through the night.

Concealed surveillance teams reported two cars parking on opposite sides of the street about thirty yards to either side of the building. The occupants of the cars did not leave them, but appeared to settle in. A second surveillance of outside origin was being set up.

The team across the street observed the Dwarf through infrared binoculars as he made a rare appearance at his window. He looked deliberately at both cars and was seen to smile. The surveillance was his own, to watch his building. He was improving his odds.

The Dwarf took a final drag on his cigarette and let the curtain fall back into place. He felt safer now, with friends outside.

He crushed out the short stub of his cigarette and returned to the bathroom to wash up. He then went into the bedroom, removed a small automatic handgun from a belly holster, and laid it on the table beside the bed. At last he could rest, he thought.

He did not remove his clothing or shoes, just in case he had to move quickly. It was nearly two in the morning, and there was a heavy silence. He was nervous and could hear his heart pounding in his ears. He knew that a threat from Rafael Sonterra was not to be taken lightly. It was all probably foolishness on his part, he thought. Perhaps Strassa had been overreacting – but then again he may not have been. Only time would give that answer.

He stood motionless for a moment longer in the dark silence, then sat on the bed. The click was faint but distinct, and he froze.

It was not his imagination, he knew. He sat absolutely still as the sweat began to roll down his face. His body began to shake as the fear mounted swiftly inside him.

He had to make a very quick decision. The arming device was pressure-sensitive. He had supplied enough of them to know that it would work in one of two ways. Since it had not exploded when he sat on the bed, it would either detonate when he got up, or it would be radio-detonated. In the first case, he was safe as long as he remained on the bed. But in the second, he would have very little time to act. Either way, he had to do something, and quickly.

He reached out and took the handgun from the table, then knocked the lamp to the floor. The table was sturdy –

possibly heavy enough to keep the detonation device depressed by its weight alone.

He struggled as gently as he could with the table, dragging it closer to the bed. He tilted it and dragged it up on to the bed beside him.

The Dwarf closed his eyes for a moment and prayed, then eased himself off the bed. His clothes were soaked with perspiration, and he trembled like a man in an icewater bath.

His feet hit the floor and he stepped away from the bed. His gamble had worked. He dropped quickly to his knees and bent down to look under the bed, hoping his imagination was just playing havoc with his tired brain. But his eyes confirmed what his brain feared. He saw the explosives, neatly wired and secured to the heavy spring. It was all he needed to see. In the next instant he was off his knees and out of the room.

He bolted for the apartment door, his fingers working frantically at the locks. A moment later the door opened and he was in the hallway. He started first for the main stairway, then thought better of it. He turned and scurried down the hall for the back stairway that would take him to the rear exit.

The micro-relay in the apartment door hinge sent its message to the explosives man, who gave a count of ten.

The Dwarf reached the door to the back stairway just as the device went off. It was loud and the entire building seemed to shake for just an instant. The Dwarf never looked back, and he ran so fast his feet hardly touched a stair.

He broke out of the doorway into a dark alleyway. Caution was beyond him now, and he bolted through the alley without any thought that someone could be waiting there to take him out.

The first static team picked him up as he came out of the alley on to the street behind his building. He was in the open now and running flat out. The surveillance teams stayed with him through technique rather than speed. Every time he ducked out of sight, backup teams raced into positions that provided wide fields of vision down adjacent and parallel streets. By staying just one step ahead, they kept the surveillance intact.

When the clever Frenchman finally slowed his pace, he began making a series of contacts to put out subtle inquiries into the whereabouts of Kammal, whom he knew to be in the city. His efforts continued throughout the next day. He was using only his most trusted associates, and finally came to rest in the café of a friend, where he remained until his sources got back to him. It wasn't until late that evening that he retired to a back room of the café and dialed the number he had been given.

The ringing of the phone startled Kammal. He sat up stiffly in the bed and stared at the phone. There was no reason for a call to be placed to his room.

He let it ring, his brain racing with alarm at the possibilities. No-one knew where he was, not even Sonterra. When Sonterra had missed the contact, Kammal had moved smoothly into his backup plan, which called for a change of location. This was a precaution on the chance that Sonterra had been taken and forced to reveal the plan. With today's sophisticated use of drugs in interrogation, even Sonterra could possibly be made to give information. There were four days left until the next scheduled contact. If Sonterra had not been taken, he would not attempt contact in this way, Kammal was sure – or almost sure.

He stared at the phone as it continued to ring, wondering – and worrying. Maybe it *was* Sonterra, trying to inform him of some sudden and serious development. He did not put it past Sonterra's ability to find him if the reason was important enough. He fretted as the phone continued to ring. Perhaps it was Sonterra, after all, simply trying to reach him to assure him that everything was OK.

His worry finally overcame his fear and he reached for the phone.

'Yes?' he said into it, his ear pressed closely to the phone, listening for the sound of Sonterra's voice.

'You swine,' said the voice at the other end.

A wave of fear shot through him with the realization that the voice was not Sonterra's. It took him only a moment to recover and recognize his caller as the Dwarf.

'What is wrong with you, calling me like this?' he said angrily into the phone. It was a serious breach of their agreed procedure for the Dwarf to initiate contact with him without having received specific instructions to do so. 'And how did you find me?' he asked.

'Did you think you could kill me so easily?' the Dwarf said, his voice sharp with anger.

'What are you talking about?' Kammal demanded.

'Don't play games with me, you stupid maggot. You tried to kill me last night.'

Kammal listened in shocked silence, his brain replaying the Dwarf's words. 'What are you saying? I did no such thing,' he said at last.

'You have broken faith with the wrong person, Kammal. You will pay for this mistake,' the Dwarf spat.

'A lamb should never threaten a wolf,' Kammal shot back. 'Perhaps you had better slow down and tell me what has happened, and I will try to forget that you have threatened me.'

'As if you didn't know.'

'I don't know what you are talking about,' Kammal insisted. 'Tell me what has happened.'

'Your bomb nearly killed me last night.'

'What bomb?'

'I said no games.'

Kammal's brain began clicking with sudden clarity. Someone was playing the Dwarf. 'I can assure you that if I had wanted you dead, you would be by now,' he said.

'Oh, really?' the Dwarf said mockingly. 'Like you killed Strassa in Bern? Was it your plan for Strassa to kill me?'

Kammal sat in silence, thinking. The only other man who could have found him so easily in Paris was the Dwarf. He became more certain that his theory was right.

'Listen to me, you thick-skulled French pervert. I did not try to kill you last night, or through Strassa. Someone is using you to get to me. Your call is placing us both in a great deal of danger. Say no more over the phone. We must meet – tonight.'

'Do you think I am a fool?'

'I'm beginning to wonder. You are letting yourself be used,' Kammal replied. 'You should know that I would not do this thing.'

'That's what Strassa thought, too. And he's dead, thanks to me. You tried to kill him in Bern.'

'We cannot talk further over the phone,' Kammal repeated. 'We must meet immediately. Pick a place that you feel will guarantee your safety. I will come alone and unarmed. I swear that I mean you no harm.'

'You will come, all right. Alone and unarmed, or you will die on the spot.'

'Robert, I had nothing to do with the attempt on your life. You must believe me. Strassa *was* my doing in Bern. He had allowed himself to become a dangerous liability,' *Just as you are now, you little shit*, he finished in his mind. 'Pick your place. I will come.'

'Go to the bakery. In one hour. You will come alone. I will be watching you.'

'I will be there, Robert. In one hour. Trust me. I mean you no harm.'

'We shall see. In one hour, then. Remember, I will be watching.'

The phone went dead and Kammal replaced the receiver in its cradle.

He ran his hand across his forehead, wiping away the nervous sweat that had beaded there.

Someone *was* trying to play the Dwarf. No doubt, the Dwarf had many enemies. But he also had many friends. It could only be the other side. His thoughts went again to

Sonterra's missed contact. If he was lost, the plan was dead. He considered his choices.

He knew that the Dwarf could find him anywhere in Paris if he remained in the city. He could get out now and return only for the next scheduled contact. Or he could meet with the Dwarf and run the risk of being killed himself. If he left, the Dwarf would be convinced that he had made the attempt on his life. Yet if the Dwarf was being played, there was a strong possibility that he would be followed. That would place Kammal in direct danger. Either way, the Dwarf's call had created an awful complication. Thinking clearly for the first time in days, Kammal realized he had no choice. He *had* to meet with the Dwarf. Sonterra had been right – the Dwarf should have been removed earlier. Sonterra's wisdom always prevailed. He should never have questioned him.

The decision was made to meet with the Dwarf. And unlike what had happened in Bern, there would be no slipup this time.

It was nearly four in the morning when Kammal arrived at the bakery. He made a long and careful approach to be certain that he was not being watched. His eyes told him there was no danger, but his survival sense warned otherwise. Under any other circumstances he would have left the area immediately. Despite his uncomfortable feeling, he went in, knowing he had no other choice.

He entered the building, the heat from the ovens providing an unwelcome contrast to the cold night air outside. He kept his leather coat on as he moved silently through the bakery. There was no-one there, though the signs of a busy routine were everywhere. There had been people here until a very short time ago. The Dwarf had undoubtedly ordered everyone out.

Kammal moved cautiously past worktables covered with dough in various stages of preparation. There were racks of proofing dough destined for the heated ovens, and half-finished pastries. One mixer sat idle, its bowl still filled with partially mixed dough, another with a full load of unmixed flour, shortening, and water. He stopped and looked down into the bowl, and put his hand into it to feel the flour.

'Do not turn, you Palestinian pig,' said the Dwarf from behind him.

'I am not armed, Robert,' Kammal said to him without turning.

'I am,' the Dwarf returned. 'If you make any sudden move, I will kill you instantly.'

'I have come in good faith, Robert, just as I promised.'

'Good faith?' the Dwarf mocked. 'I hold the only faith you understand in my hand – cold, silenced steel. It is for you, Kammal,' the smaller man said as he moved around to the side of his target.

Kammal turned his head as the Dwarf came around him from his left, stopping on the other side of the mixer, the silenced automatic raised menacingly at his face.

Kammal held out his hands to show that he was unarmed.

'Easy, Robert.'

The Dwarf squinted at the taller Arab, his eyes hot with anger.

'Now go back to the beginning and tell me what has happened,' Kammal said to him, his right hand coming to rest on the mixer. 'Give me all of the details.'

'Talk will change nothing,' the Dwarf said.

'You must see that I mean you no harm,' Kammal persisted. 'Otherwise, do you think I would come to you so vulnerable?'

The Dwarf laughed. 'You don't for one minute think I'm going to trust you, do you?'

'*I* trusted *you*.'

'Then you are a fool, Kammal,' the Dwarf returned, moving a step closer.

'You are wrong, Robert,' Kammal insisted softly. He leaned casually toward the mixer, his hand coming to rest on the lever controlling the speed selection. 'Someone else tried to kill you last night, or made it look that way to get you to contact me,' he said, his hand making the silent shift to high speed. 'It is *me* that they want – not you.'

The Dwarf stared at Kammal with cold eyes, assessing his words.

'Listen to me,' Kammal began. 'Sonterra missed his contact with me three days ago. I have not heard from him since. That could only mean he is in grave danger – possibly that he has been killed.'

'What a shame,' the Dwarf said facetiously. 'Then that makes both of you—'

Kammal hit the power button, and the mixer kicked to life with an explosion of flour that caught the Dwarf squarely in the face, blinding him momentarily. The Frenchman's hand jerked upward and the gun went off harmlessly into the far wall.

Kammal grabbed a heavy dough hook attachment and swung it at the Dwarf, hitting him across the forehead.

The Dwarf reeled from the impact, still unable to see, or even to open his eyes. He fired twice more into the air before the dough hook crashed once again into his face. He fell back over a pallet of flour sacks on to his back.

Kammal was on him in a second, twisting the gun away with one hand and delivering another rapid series of blows with the dough hook in the other. He pounded the Dwarf over and over again until his struggling ceased. The little Frenchman lay nearly unconscious, moaning in pain, with blood spouting from the gashes caused by the heavy blade of the dough hook.

Kammal removed his belt and quickly rolled the Dwarf over on to his belly. He bound the little man's arms tightly behind him at the elbows, then picked up a work towel and stuffed it into the Dwarf's mouth to smother any further sounds. He then cut a piece of electrical cord from a second mixer and bound his legs tightly together.

Finally he went to the mixer that had saved his life and turned it off.

Kammal looked around to be certain there was no-one

else in the bakery, then returned to the helpless Dwarf.

Grasping the belt that bound the Dwarf's elbows, he lifted the Dwarf like a bundle of old rags, dragged him across the floor of the bakery toward one of the large brick hearth ovens, and dropped him hard on to his face. The Dwarf grunted, just beginning to regain consciousness.

Kammal knelt beside him and put his snarling face close to the Frenchman's. He yanked hard on his hair, pulling his face up to look him squarely in the eye. 'It was not I who tried to kill you last night, you little piece of garbage. I have *never* broken faith with you, and this is how you reward my loyalty. Well, it is *you* who have broken faith, and now it is you who will pay.'

Kammal opened the large door to the hearth oven and turned back to the Dwarf.

The Dwarf's eyes widened with terror and he began squirming wildly against his bonds.

Kammal delivered a savage kick to the Dwarf's face, sending him momentarily limp. Then he bent down and picked him up like a rolled-up carpet and carried him toward the oven. Though the Dwarf was not large, he was heavy, and Kammal struggled as he neared the oven door.

He gave a mighty heave, sending the head and shoulders of the Dwarf into the open oven.

The semiconscious state of the Dwarf cleared and he began screaming in horror, the sounds muffled by the towel stuffed into his mouth.

The Dwarf began kicking frantically as the flesh on his face and shoulders started to burn from contact with the hot oven surface, but the bindings rendered his efforts futile.

Kammal slid his grip farther down the torso to the waist and heaved the Frenchman still deeper into the oven, ignoring the gruesome cries and the grisly smell of burning flesh. He made one last adjustment to the legs, cramming them into the oven, then slammed the door shut. The screams became muffled to near silence as he threw the lever.

Kammal stood for a moment, looking at the door to the

oven, his breathing heavy, sweat rolling down the sides of his face.

He had to get out quickly, and somehow find a way to reach Sonterra. If he was alive, he had to be warned about developments with the Dwarf and the obvious involvement of the other side. He also had to flee the danger he was facing from this contact with the Dwarf. He left quickly by a back exit and disappeared into the darkness of Paris.

'We have him,' the voice of Surveillance One said into the radio, his eyes trained on the fast-moving Kammal through night-vision infrared binoculars. 'Surveillance Three, he's coming up on your position. Let's keep at a safe distance until we see where he roosts.'

The elusive back door to Rafael Sonterra had at last been opened.

34

Kammal was driven by fear and adrenaline. He knew that he was being watched now, and that his only hope of survival lay in swift, constant movement. As long as he moved, they would watch and follow.

He found a roving cab and hailed it, gave the driver instructions, and checked carefully to see if the cab was being followed. He saw nothing, but his instincts were alive with warning.

Daybreak was only an hour away, and life was already beginning to creep into the streets of the city. There was just enough traffic to make it difficult to tell whether he was still being followed. He knew that good professionals would be hard to detect. And everything about these people said they were very good at what they did.

He ordered the cab to drop him a few blocks from his hotel, and then he walked the remaining distance. Normally he would have followed a more elaborate route, but every second on the street was filled with danger. He went directly back to his hotel and headed straight to his room.

He remained in the room just long enough to collect the notebook containing his codes and contact schedule, as well as some additional sets of false identity documents and his stash of drugs. He changed quickly into fresh clothing and left the room immediately, leaving behind his luggage and most of his personal belongings, taking only what he would need later and could carry in his pockets. He was creating the appearance that he was leaving the room with all intentions of returning to it.

Kammal felt no obligation to remain where he was, and he was not waiting for trouble to come to him. The next scheduled contact with Sonterra was in four days. Between now and that time he would completely abandon all of his previous plans and leave the city, risking return only for the next contact. He knew that if Sonterra was safe, he *would* make contact according to plan. If he did not make that contact, then Kammal would assume that Sonterra had been lost, and he would do his best to complete the plan alone.

Alone.

He had never felt more fear in his life than he did at this moment. The prospect of Sonterra's loss was crushing him, and he felt paralyzed by the danger surrounding him. Sonterra had been a guiding presence, a constant source of strength. How could he go on without him? He forced that possibility from his mind and summoned his remaining strength. He walked through the small lobby without stopping at the desk, then out of the building and on to the street. He looked around carefully, then turned to his right and walked away at a casual pace.

The sudden reappearance of Kammal on the street was a surprise to the surveillance teams.

'He's on the street again, moving west,' came the report over the radio.

'Is he carrying luggage?' Michael asked.

'No,' came the reply.

Michael looked at Yelena. 'What do you make of that?' he asked.

'He plans to return to the room,' she said.

'Why would he leave?'

'Perhaps to report the Dwarf's death,' Yelena replied.

Michael thought for a moment. It had been their plan to take Kammal in his room. Perhaps in the end it would be to their advantage to take him away from the room. Should the attempt at the hotel not go smoothly, they could be forced to leave the site to avoid confrontation with the French authorities. If they were to take him on the street, they'd still be able to get a team into the room to search for documents related to Sonterra and the Luxus.

'Stay with him,' Michael said into the radio. 'Regroup the teams and give him plenty of distance. He may be attempting to contact Sonterra. Be alert for a dead drop. If he stops at a phone or engages in *any* conversation, cover him with directional microphones. I want a record of every word he says. Did you get a copy on that, Triple Jack?'

'Roger,' Elias replied.

'If we can take him on the street, it will give us plenty of time to search his room,' Michael said.

'Can you set up on such short notice?' Elias asked.

'One way or another, we'll get him on the street.'

'Go for it. I'll get a team from Intelligence Central into the room.'

Kammal continued walking at an easy pace, seemingly showing no regard for the fact that he might be under surveillance. He turned a corner about two blocks from his hotel and walked halfway up the block and stopped. He would try one maneuver he knew they wouldn't expect. He stood motionless on the sidewalk, looking in

483

both directions. His nerves were stinging within his body. He could feel the eyes and long-distance lenses on him. Every instinct said to bolt.

His eyes locked on to a cream-colored Mercedes 560 SL parked at the curb. He pulled a set of keys from his pocket and stepped up to the car, unlocked the door, and got in. He started the engine and pulled away from the curb.

'Jesus, he just got into a car,' a voice reported over the radio. The make of the car and its color and license number were reported.

'Get the mobile units on him. *Move! Move!*' Michael shouted into the radio.

Intel-Trace's teams went into action immediately.

'This is static position six. The Mercedes has just passed us heading east.'

'This is Mobile Two. We have him in sight. He has just turned north on to Rue de Clignancourt,' came the report from the first mobile unit to make contact.

The mobile surveillance units began a mad scramble into their pickup positions.

Kammal continued weaving north and toward the east, all the time under Intel-Trace's careful observation. He moved east on Rue Ordener to Rue d'Aubervilliers, which went north before bending east into Rue de Flandres. He doubled back to the west along Ney Boulevard to Rue de la Chapelle, then on to the access ramp to Boulevards Exterieurs, an express belt that ringed the entire city. He headed east on the beltway.

Michael breathed a short sigh of relief. Boulevards Exterieurs was a good development for his surveillance teams. They could easily set up checkpoints all along the way, in front of and behind him, as well as toward him from the opposite direction, to confirm his heading. Contact duration could be kept sufficiently short to prevent Kammal from making the connection that any one of them was a tail.

Michael reported the development to Elias, who gave the order for the penetration team to enter the room. If everything went according to plan, Kammal would not be returning to the room again.

Kammal circled the entire city on the beltway in the mounting traffic, his eyes unable to pick up signs of being followed. He circled the entire beltway a second time before heading off northeast toward Aubervilliers on roadway N2.

Three mobile teams raced ahead of Kammal to act as pickup teams. The surveillance chain was set. It would be routine procedure the rest of the way.

Michael, Yelena, and Wadelaw followed well behind and out of visual contact. They would move as directed by the position reports of the other surveillance teams until the time was right to close in. That precise moment would be determined either by Kammal himself the first time he stopped and left the car, or by the roadway if conditions allowed them to force Kammal to the side of the road.

Kammal continued on N2 past Le Bourget Airport to La Patte-d'Oie, where N2 forked off to the right. Mobile Six had closed to within several car lengths, but continued straight at the fork moving off along N17. Mobile One was already ahead of Kammal on N2. The Mercedes overtook and passed them at a good rate of speed. Mobile One increased speed, staying well behind Kammal, whose confidence was growing by the minute.

Kammal paid no mind to the flashy red Alfa-Romeo that overtook him and disappeared into the distance ahead of him. Mobile Five confirmed Kammal's heading after passing him, and continued at a high rate of speed, passing Mobile Three about a mile ahead of the Mercedes. The Alfa-Romeo sped on, gaining as much distance as possible. If Kammal did not head off to the north along A1, the open stretch on N2 just outside of Dammartin-en-Goele would be just what they were looking for. The team in Mobile Five would set up and wait.

Kammal continued on past A1, and the order was given to close the distance between all mobile units and the

Mercedes. Kammal was effectively covered front and back as he neared the waiting team of Mobile Five.

The Alfa-Romeo sat well off the road about two hundred yards ahead of the marksman. Mobile Three passed the spot and began coasting to a stop a hundred yards beyond the Alfa-Romeo. Kammal was not far behind.

The marksman lay in a prone position, low in the shrubs of the roadside and out of view. He spotted the Mercedes and raised the small-caliber, scoped rifle, bringing the crosshairs to focus on the rear tire of the car. He rested the rifle against his rolled-up jacket, steadied it, and took a short breath and held it. The finger squeezed gently.

Kammal never heard the shot. The tire exploded, causing a mild fishtail. Kammal corrected effectively, maintaining good control of the car. He braked gently, taking the car to the side of the road, passing the concealed marksman.

The car came to a stop. Kammal's heart was pounding from the sudden excitement of what he perceived to be a blowout. He sat for a moment to collect himself, then got out of the car to inspect the damage.

He walked around the car and looked down at the tire. He was not mechanically inclined. Beyond the disassembly and assembly of weapons and the building of bombs, even the simple dilemma of a flat tire in need of changing was a problem to him.

He looked up just in time to see a car with a man and a woman inside pass by. It slowed down after passing him and pulled to the side of the road.

The prospect of assistance lifted his spirits, and he began walking toward the car. The man and the woman got out of the car – and Kammal froze.

The man *and* the woman had gotten out. His senses cried a warning.

He backed away a few steps, then turned back toward his car. His weapon was in the glove box.

He took a few more steps, then saw two cars pulling to

the side of the road behind his Mercedes. The occupants of the cars were out of them immediately.

Kammal's heart sank when he saw the faces of Michael and Wadelaw. He recognized them instantly from the pictures taken in Colombia.

He turned to run away from the road, and stopped again. The marksman was standing no more than thirty feet away, the rifle in his hands pointing at him.

Kammal felt incredibly stupid. He was caught squarely in the open without the means to defend himself, or to even take his own life. He backed away from the marksman, toward the Mercedes. If he was going to die, he would fall trying for his weapon. He would take at least a few of the enemy with him.

He turned to reach for the door handle, heard a popping sound, and felt the sting of the sedative dart as it bit into his ribs. He looked up at the tall, dark figure of Michael Quinn holding the air gun. His arms and legs went suddenly numb and he staggered forward toward the car. His face went tingly and his legs collapsed beneath the weight of his body. He fell against the car and slid slowly to the right, unable to stop himself. Kammal crashed to the ground on his side. He could feel himself losing motor control of his eye muscles, and his vision began to close in swiftly into a ring of darkness. The last thing he saw was the cold, serious face of Michael Quinn.

COMPIÈGNE, IN THE PICARDY REGION: Kammal Nasir had been taken to a large farmhouse amid the rolling lands of Compiègne. He had been kept unconscious for twenty-four hours by the use of drugs, and then in a semi-conscious state for the next twenty-four. He was given plenty of fluids that had been laced with chemical agents intended to induce a raging thirst. This was to ensure his willingness to ingest additional drugs as deemed necessary by his captors during interrogation.

Simmerman had taken over this part of the operation, and as long as they had Kammal alive, they would attempt to extract every possible scrap of information from him.

The search of the room and Kammal's car had yielded generous results. They had found his notebook, numerous sets of false identification, and enough other evidence to put together a reliable record of his movements over the past three months. Intelligence Central could use this information to learn a great deal about events leading up to the actual attack at the institute in Medellín – possibly even the identities of earlier contacts used in the initial stages of their operation. But the one thing that held the most interest was the notebook. Simmerman had kept this back from the rest of the evidence turned over to Intelligence Central; it would be useful in his interrogation efforts.

Simmerman had spent the two days at the chateau in Compiègne methodically going through the notebook. Every entry bore a special significance, he knew. Kammal had committed a blatant violation of good operational procedure, and he was sure Sonterra would be unaware that Kammal had made such a damaging error.

It was plain to Simmerman that Kammal was coming dangerously close to losing all value to Sonterra. He had been using drugs and alcohol heavily, and the notebook had taken the place of what should have been memory. All of the contact dates and codes were clearly entered, even the time, place, and codes to be used in the next contact with Sonterra in two days. Simmerman was even able to learn some of the locations where Sonterra had stayed earlier in the operation. There were no indications, however, of where he would be any time in the future, as all of the later references were to Kammal's intended locations. It was also clear that all further contacts were to be initiated by Sonterra.

There were other entries that piqued Simmerman's interest as well. One was the code name 'January'. It was clearly meant to be a person, and from the earlier entries in the notebook the Israeli surmised that this person was an inside agent in the Skyco Corporation. It was also clear that January was not Delgado, the head of security at the Medellín Institute. This individual was in San Antonio. If Simmerman's interpretations were correct, January was playing a key role in the operation. One other notation made it clear that January was slated for 'housecleaning' in the not-too-distant future, which seemed consistent with Sonterra's form so far.

The other entries that held the most interest for Simmerman pertained to the code name 'Iris'. There were only three entries for this name. The first was very early in the book and seemed to refer to a meeting between Sonterra, Kammal, and this person. The second entry was just a little farther on and referred to Iris only. The final reference was in a special section of the notebook that contained contact codes. There were no indications of the expendability of this person. This was possibly, and probably, Greta Haas – their next objective in the plan to draw Sonterra in. It would be important to discover her whereabouts.

Simmerman shared these observations and interpretations with Michael so that they could be communicated to Elias. This would give Elias the chance to conduct further investigations in the hope of turning up additional leads of value to the team.

On the morning of the third day, the direct interrogation of Kammal began.

Kammal had been kept in a cold, dark room in the lowest level of the chateau. The room had been stripped bare except for a simple cot, and Kammal was without clothing. This was for two reasons: first, to deprive him of any means with which to take his own life, and second, to keep him as uncomfortable as possible.

Kammal looked up as the door to his cell was opened. He was still in a stupor from the drugs, his mind foggy, his vision unclear. He watched as Simmerman entered, carrying a stool and a paper cup with water.

The Israeli entered and closed the door behind himself.

The sounds of the lock being engaged from the outside followed.

Simmerman set the stool a few feet from the cot and walked up to the Arab. He held out the paper cup.

Kammal struggled to sit up. Simmerman lent him some assistance, then handed him the cup.

Kammal accepted it and drank its contents down thirstily in several long gulps.

'More water,' the Arab said. 'Please, please . . . more water.'

'Yes, there will be more water, and perhaps some food,' Simmerman replied. 'But first we will talk for a little while, yes?'

Kammal squinted at the Israeli. He crumpled the cup and threw it at him, forcing an expression of defiance on to his face.

'Perhaps there will be no water or food, after all,' Simmerman said calmly. 'We could just leave you here to die and rot away for the rest of time. No-one would know, and no-one would care. But that would seem very foolish, especially since the little adventure that you and Sonterra have dreamed up has ended so badly for both of you.'

Kammal's eyes strained to see the face of the Israeli clearly in the dim light. His heart pounded wildly from the realization of the words he had just heard. His brain was not so confused and fogged over that he could misinterpret what he had been told.

'We almost had him in Sare a week ago. Did you know that?' Simmerman asked, knowing from the notebook that a contact between Kammal and Sonterra had been scheduled for the day after the events in Sare. He had no way of knowing whether that contact had been made. He was playing on the assumption that it had.

'He had fortune on his side that day, and he managed to escape. But fortune, as it happens, swings both ways. We found him again two days later outside of Bordeaux. He did not survive the encounter,' Simmerman lied.

Kammal made a tight frown and his lower lip began to

quiver. His eyes seemed to stare right past the Israeli into nothingness, and they filled with tears.

'He was very brave, but in the end very unlucky,' Simmerman added.

What strength there was in Kammal drained from him quickly. The news he was hearing and the renewed effect of the drugs that had been in the water he had drunk defeated him totally. He broke down and wept.

Simmerman watched impassively as this weakened, wretched soul completely disintegrated. His strength and confidence had become so fragile that without the belief that Sonterra was there to rely upon, he simply could not carry on.

'We need some information from you, just to complete the records,' the Israeli told him, sitting on the stool in front of the cot. 'We need not hurry. We have plenty of time. Once you have given us these few details, you'll be taken to a proper and more comfortable confinement. We can begin whenever you feel ready.'

Kammal lay back down and buried his face in the thin mattress of the cot, his body heaving with grief.

The Israeli lit a cigarette and crossed his legs. 'We can begin with Iris . . .'

'We feel that we've gotten about all there is to get from Kammal, Bob,' Michael reported to Elias over the phone. 'Max has been at him for the better part of two days now. He's just not getting anything new.'

'How much have we been able to learn from him that will help us immediately?' Elias asked.

'The Haas woman is in Greece. She was not part of the operation, from what we can tell.'

'So we go to Greece to get her?'

'No, we won't have to do that. What we have is even better. A series of communication codes were set up between Sonterra, Kammal, and Greta Haas. There was a contingency phase of their plan in the event of an emergency that would send Haas to a predetermined destination. We need only to deliver that code to get her moving. Kammal has a scheduled contact with Sonterra tonight in Paris. It'll be by phone.'

'Let me interrupt for just a second, Mike. Where is Sonterra now?' Elias asked.

'We don't know. Sonterra kept those parts of his plan to himself. We believe he's still in France,' Michael replied.

'OK, go ahead.'

'We know where and when the contact is to be made. I suggest *we* keep that scheduled contact.'

'That won't fool Sonterra for a second,' Elias said.

'It doesn't have to. It only has to get the point across that we've taken Kammal and have his codes. The rest will take care of itself, according to Max.'

'I see it,' Elias said. 'If Sonterra realizes you have Kammal's codes, he'll know we can manipulate Greta through use of the codes.'

'That's right. And even if he tries to reach her, he'll be unable to. She'll already be moving toward the emergency contact point,' Michael explained. 'He'll either have to come in himself to try to save her, or let her walk straight into our hands.'

'Does Max think he'll come in to save her?'

'He feels sure of it.'

'When will this take place?'

'If we get the coded contact off to Haas today, she'll be in Malta in two days. That's Christmas Eve.'

'That would make a damn nice present to give to the President and to Asher Sky,' Elias said.

'That's right. But we may still have to contend with the Soviets. For lack of anything else to pursue themselves, they've got every one of us under surveillance. They'll trail us straight to Malta. We don't want another incident like the one in Sare.'

'You're right. But this time we'll expect their interference.'

'OK, let's set it up. I'll get some experts on Soviet faces to

Malta to incorporate into your teams. If they're going with their best, we'll at least know who they are.'

'There's one other thing, Bob,' Michael said, pausing to underscore its importance.

'What's that?'

'There's another agent working for Sonterra somewhere inside Skyco. We don't have an identification, just the code name "January". Kammal doesn't know the identity. Sonterra apparently arranged for this one on his own.'

'That's not a good development, Mike. Skyco has just announced that some of the improved Beta is ready. It, as well as a load of the probes, is being sent to strategic positions across the globe.'

'Then you'll have to work fast to identify him, Bob. January is an inside agent and is in the United States. We also know Sonterra has plans to houseclean him when he's no longer useful. That fact could be leverage if you can find out who he is.'

'I'll contact Danziger immediately with the information. It'll have to be someone pretty high up, or someone with access to the top. I'll get Intelligence Central right on it,' Elias responded.

'I have one last question for you, Bob.'

'Go ahead.'

'We're not going to get any more out of Kammal. What should we do with him?'

'I'll leave that entirely up to Max. He's earned that much and a great deal more.'

'All right, I'll tell him. We'll get the communication off to Greta Haas, and start back to Paris to keep the scheduled contact with Sonterra.'

'Start thinking about what you'll need for Malta, and give me a shopping list as soon as you can. Until then, good luck to everyone.'

The line went dead.

Michael placed the phone back in its cradle and looked at his watch. The contact with Sonterra would take place in just over three hours. He felt a twinge of excitement at the prospect of direct communications with Sonterra himself. He knew that Sonterra would not be fooled, but he also knew the revelation of Kammal's capture would be a stunning blow, forcing Sonterra to reevaluate his position.

For the first time since Colombia, Michael had the distinct feeling that the momentum was beginning to swing away from Sonterra. Intel-Trace was now in a position to make things happen.

35

PARIS: Dusk was setting in; the night would be cold. Michael stood at the nine corners formed by the many boulevards and streets that radiated out from the Place de la Bastille, on the corner of Rue de Lyon and Rue de Charenton, watching the typical French traffic as it whizzed into and around the square, circling the dominating figure of the July Column atop which stood the figure of Liberty. At the curb to his right was a cab, stopped at a taxi stand. Wadelaw was behind the wheel. To Michael's left was a public phone, not more than six feet away. He shoved his hands into the pockets of his jacket, hunched his shoulders against the cold, and waited.

Michael let his eyes play over the many windows of the buildings lining the square and the streets radiating out from it, wondering if Rafael Sonterra was standing in one of them now, watching. The call was late and he thought that, perhaps, it might not come at all if Sonterra was on to them. He looked at his watch. It was ten minutes past the scheduled contact time.

Wadelaw looked up at Michael, checked his watch too, and shrugged his shoulders.

Michael held up his hand, his five fingers extended to signal to his partner that they'd give it another five minutes. He figured that if Sonterra *was* watching them, the call wouldn't matter. Seeing them there would be enough to get the message across that they had taken Kammal and broken the codes. It would serve the same purpose.

Brrring!

Michael's head turned and his eyes locked on the phone. He moved to it quickly and let it ring again as he removed from his pocket a small microphone with a suction adaptor. He attached it to the receiver before lifting it on the third ring.

'*Oui*, Valmy,' he said into the phone, giving the correct recognition code, his voice low, the words spoken quickly.

There was a long pause at the other end. Michael didn't have to hear Sonterra's voice to know that he was there. He could *feel* him at the other end.

'Valmy? I think not,' the voice of Rafael Sonterra said at last. The voice was controlled and calm.

'This is Valmy,' Michael repeated in the same low voice he had used earlier, trying to play the bluff along further.

Sonterra responded with a short sentence in Arabic.

Michael's strong command of languages did not include Arabic. He hesitated a moment. '*Oui*,' he replied.

There was another long silence.

Michael waited patiently for Sonterra to speak again. It was clear to him that Sonterra knew it was not Kammal on the line. Michael thought quickly. He did not want Sonterra simply to break off the contact – at least not before he could make the message unmistakably clear that his innermost circle of security had been breached.

'I know that you're listening,' Michael said at last, casting all pretense aside. 'You may even be watching me at this very moment. But none of that matters,' he continued, then waited.

'This changes nothing,' Sonterra replied.

'You're very wrong if you believe that. It changes *everything*. Two can play at this game when the rules are clear.

You will do well to read the morning papers,' Michael told him, then hung up the phone.

Michael pulled the microphone from the receiver and walked to the cab. He opened the door and got it.

Wadelaw started up the engine. 'Was it him?' he asked.

Michael nodded his reply. 'He's here . . . and he's watching us. I can feel him.'

'Do you want the area staked out?'

Michael shook his head. 'No, I don't think so. He's too smart to let himself be spotted so easily. He'd be gone before we could even set up. I think we'll just proceed according to plan. He got the message, I'm sure of that. I told him to read the papers tomorrow. He will. The rest will take care of itself.'

'Do you think Max is right about him coming in for the girl?' Wadelaw asked.

'He'll come, all right. He'll realize we've broken the codes and that we know where she is. Then he'll try to contact her first. When he realizes that she's already gone, he'll have no choice – unless he's willing to let her fall into our hands. I don't think he'll do that.'

Michael picked up the radio on the seat between them as Wadelaw guided the car away from the curb and into the flow of traffic.

'This is Mobile One. The contact has been made. It went exactly as expected. Go to phase two.'

The Mercedes glided to a stop at the curb on Rue de Clery where it meets Boulevard Bonne Nouvelle near the Porte St-Denis, one of the many triumphal arches typifying Paris, this one in honor of the victories of Louis XIV in Germany.

The driver and the passenger in the backseat went to work quickly. Kammal Nasir sat in the front passenger seat, slouched against the locked door. He was unconscious and was dressed exactly as he had been the day he was taken.

The two Israelis moved Kammal across the front seat

496

toward the driver's seat, the driver getting out to make room for Kammal behind the wheel. The man in the backseat turned his attention to the explosive device on the seat beside him. He made a final connection, then eased the device over the back of the front seat, placing it in the lap of the Arab. Then he exited the car from the passenger's side.

The two men walked to the end of Rue de Clery, crossed Boulevard Bonne Nouvelle, and waited for just a few moments. Another car came to a stop at the curb. They entered and the car pulled away into the night.

Moshe Simmerman sat in the passenger seat of a small Renault not more than a hundred yards farther up Boulevard Bonne Nouvelle. Yelena sat in the driver's seat beside him, her eyes fixed intently on the rearview mirror.

'They're away,' she told her boss.

Simmerman picked up the hand radio. 'There must be one hundred per cent certainty. No pedestrians, no passing cars. There must be no innocent victims,' he reminded his positioned teams.

At this late hour there was little traffic. The vehicular movement along the adjacent streets was sporadic, but still too heavy for zero risk. There was no hurry. All positions watched their respective areas, reporting the presence of passing cars.

It took nearly twenty minutes before the conditions matched the established rules.

'Boulevard St-Denis and Rue de Clery are clear,' came the first report.

'Rue d'Aboukir is clear,' came the second.

'Wait . . . yes. Rue Beauregard is clear. One car is approaching slowly, but it is at a safe distance,' came the third.

Yelena made a final check along Boulevard Bonne Nouvelle. 'All clear,' she said.

Simmerman raised the radio detonator in his hand and pushed the button.

There was a loud *whomp*, a flash, and a bang that shook the Renault. A large ball of flame illuminated the night near the Porte St-Denis, and the Mercedes blew apart: its hood flew off, the roof peeled away from the disintegrated front windshield like a sardine-can top, and the passenger door tore away as if made of cardboard. The car lifted, the back wheels rising straight into the air, standing the car on end for a moment as though suspended from a wire, before it fell back on to all four tires. The sounds of shattering glass and the crashing of metallic debris reverberated off the buildings lining the street.

The Renault started and pulled away from the curb.

Moshe Simmerman put the small radio detonator into the breast pocket of his jacket as the car moved away from the scene of the explosion.

'And the world is a better place,' he said in a low voice. 'One down, two to go.'

MOSCOW: The sun had not yet risen over the Soviet capital, but the daily routine was already well under way at GRU headquarters. First Deputy Nikolai Barchenkin walked briskly past the desk of his boss's secretary, his arms loaded with the daily hot sheets from intelligence reports collected through the night. He did not usually hand-deliver these reports, but the report from Paris could not wait for the usual midmorning review.

He knocked on the frame of the open door and waited.

Kozlov was standing at a long credenza by the wide windows of his office, filling a tobacco pouch with his favorite long-cut Turkish pipe tobacco. He stopped and looked back over his shoulder.

'Good morning, Nikolai,' Kozlov said in greeting. He noticed the stack of intelligence reports in his arms. 'Come in, come in,' he bade him with a nod and a gesture of his hand.

Barchenkin stepped inside the doorway and closed the door behind him. 'There have been developments in Paris,' he announced.

Kozlov folded the pouch closed and replaced the top of the tobacco canister. He walked back toward his desk, Barchenkin falling in behind him.

Barchenkin handed Kozlov the two-page report and placed the stack of morning intelligence reports on the corner of his desk in the customary place.

Kozlov remained standing while he read the report, stopping once momentarily to light his pipe. He finished reading the report, then looked up at Barchenkin.

'There is no mistake? It was Kammal Nasir?' he asked.

'Yes, General. It was Nasir.'

Kozlov extended an arm. 'Sit, Nikolai,' he said, then sat in his old comfortable chair.

'After Nasir was captured by Intel-Trace four days ago, he was taken to Compiègne, most assuredly for interrogation. The car destroyed in the explosion was the same one used by Nasir when he was taken. He was seen and photographed being put in the car in Compiègne. Our surveillance teams never lost contact with the car until the explosion. Nasir did not leave it. Identification will take some time. There was little left for the French authorities to work with. Most of the skull and upper jaw were recovered. Identification through dental records should be possible, but it will not be a rapid process.

'As you can see from the transcript obtained by our surveillance teams using directional microphones, Quinn spoke with Sonterra on the phone. He even used the name Valmy, which must have been the recognition code pre-established between Nasir and Sonterra.

'The conversation was brief, intended to put Sonterra on the defensive. The part about the newspaper was clearly meant to draw Sonterra's attention to Nasir's death.'

Kozlov reread the dialogue between Quinn and Wadelaw that had also been picked up by the directional microphones focused on the window of the car before it drove off. 'They are going to use the Haas woman as bait to draw in Sonterra. But to where?' the GRU chief asked.

'The location was not mentioned in the dialogue. We need only to stay with Quinn and his team to learn this.'

'They were successful in breaking Nasir. They learned the Haas woman's whereabouts and the communication codes to start her moving. They have done remarkably well, Nikolai.'

'Yes, but we have not done so badly ourselves. We are not more than a step behind them. Very soon Sonterra, the Haas woman, and Intel-Trace will all come together.'

'But will Sonterra have the remaining vials of the Luxus with him?'

'It is doubtful,' Barchenkin replied.

'If he does not, then the danger to the Soviet Union will still exist. For as long as the Luxus is out of our control, it can still be used against us, Nikolai. It is a terrible weapon.'

'Yes, it is, General. But if he *does* have it, the danger can be put to rest. Even if Intel-Trace were to recover it, the immediate threat would be reduced.'

'Yes, the *immediate* danger would be reduced. But the Committee will not be satisfied. We must obtain the Luxus – or at least a part of it – to give the Soviet Union an equal potential, if for no other reason than to prevent its use against us. Despite the recent detente between our two countries, Nikolai, mutual threat is still the greatest deterrent.'

'I think it is unreasonable to expect Sonterra to have it with him,' Barchenkin said. 'He is far too clever for that.'

'Then the danger will exist until it is found.'

Kozlov drew on the pipe, sending clouds of smoke into the air.

'Brevig must make the approach to Abu Hassan Nasir at once. He may know details of the plan, or possibly even where the Luxus is being kept. Call Brevig off the operation in Paris. Tolvanin will take charge of the Quinn surveillance. Tolvanin must be poised and ready to take action instantly. We must beat the Americans to Sonterra and to the Luxus. Has Abu Hassan Nasir been located?'

'Yes, General. He is in Lebanon. Brevig can be in

Lebanon today and possibly with Abu Hassan Nasir within twenty-four hours.'

'See to it immediately, Nikolai. Every small piece of information will be valuable. We must not finish second again.'

PARIS: Rafael Sonterra sat at a small table near the window of the Café La Bohème on Place du Tertre in the Montmartre section of the city. He held the newspaper in his hands. His teeth clenched tightly as he reread the article describing the explosion on Rue de Clery. The article went on to explain the official theory that the detonation must have been accidental while the unknown terrorist was in the final stages of assembling the bomb, which appeared to be destined for either the Porte St-Denis or the Porte St-Martin, a short distance away.

Sonterra lowered the paper and let his hands rest against the table to stop the involuntary trembling caused by his grief over the loss of Kammal. He let the anger rise in his veins to help fight the tears that wanted to form in his eyes.

He could not help remembering Kammal as the gawky teenager he had first met almost ten years ago. And he thought about Abu Hassan Nasir, his teacher and 'father'. He felt a new and different kind of pain fill his heart with the thought of that old man being told of the death of his son, his last remaining child. He wanted very much to be able to be with him then, to help lessen that pain. But he knew it would not be possible, and it hurt him deeply to be unable to help him when the need would be so great.

Sonterra let the paper fall to the table, and his eyes looked outward toward the street, unseeing at first, until they focused on a young mother with her baby. It was an infant, not more than a few months old. Seeing the woman and child made him think of Greta, and about having to tell her of Kammal's death. The news would be crushing. He could just see her face, imagine her grief . . .

Her face! Valmy! The codes!

He suddenly recalled a part of the conversation with Quinn.

This changes nothing, he had said to the American.

You're very wrong if you believe that. It changes every-thing. Two can play at this game when the rules are clear, Quinn had replied.

Fear for the welfare of Greta sliced through him like a saber.

They had obtained the contact schedule and the recognition code from Kammal. *Could they have obtained* all *of Kammal's codes?* he wondered in sudden panic. If they had . . .

He got up from the table and left the Café La Bohème immediately. He had to reach Greta to warn her, to tell her of Kammal's death and of the compromise of the codes. She could be in grave danger.

Once on the street, he walked briskly until he found a cab. He hailed it and gave the driver instructions.

The ride was a blur. His mind was so filled with worry for Greta that he hardly noticed details of the ride until the cab stopped in front of his hotel. He paid the driver and raced inside to the registration desk.

He asked the clerk to get him a long-distance operator. A moment later the clerk directed him to the small bank of phones across the lobby.

Sonterra gave the long-distance number in Greece to the operator. And he waited for what seemed the longest moments of his life.

'Madame Hoffman, please,' he said when the connection was finally made.

He listened as the phone rang and rang and rang.

'I am sorry, sir, but Madame Hoffman does not answer,' the voice at the other end told him.

At least she is still there, he thought, feeling a little easier.

'I'd like to leave her a message, please,' he said.

'Yes, what is it?'

'Tell her—'

'Excuse me, sir,' the voice interrupted politely. 'I must apologize. I have just come on duty and did not realize this earlier. But Madame Hoffman checked out last night after my duty shift. She did not leave a forwarding address. I can still take the message if you would like, in case she should return or call for some possible reason.'

Gone!

His heart fell to his feet.

'Sir? Would you still like to leave a message?'

Sonterra hung up the phone. He felt the strength leave his body. Perspiration poured from him, and his legs and body shook. Quinn had used the codes to contact Greta. She was on her way to certain death . . . unless he could reach her. The only way, he knew, was to go to Malta.

They were entrapping him. He knew it, but could do nothing about it. The risk would be enormous, both to his plan and his life. He thought about Greta and their unborn child. His son. And he knew, as Michael Quinn knew, that he had no choice at all. He must go.

36

LEBANON: It was a small camp called Halrashayya, situated in the mountains about forty miles northeast of Beirut and just north of Basharri. It would not be found on any official map, for officially it didn't exist. At least the Lebanese government would never admit to it.

Ivan Brevig traveled to Halrashayya by car from Beirut, leaving behind its knots of snarled traffic and blowing horns to journey north along the inspiringly scenic Beirut-Tripoli road. He turned the Land Rover off to the east at a point where the road lay wedged between the sea and the shadows of purple mountains, and drove eastward, climbing steadily into the high mountains veined with flowing streams and waterfalls and valleys that would be lush and green when the spring returned. Brevig downshifted into a series of nightmare curves and rugged steep grades, until the road finally passed through a stand of snow-draped juniper and almond trees, then opened suddenly upon Halrashayya. The camp was an unexpected intrusion on the serenity of the surroundings, looking like a canker sore in contrast to the natural beauty.

Halrashayya was more like a shantytown than a village, filled with muddy paths and poorly constructed shelters with corrugated metal roofing. The gutters of the alleyways served as sewers and were filled with garbage, and lamb carcasses hung from doorways, preserved somewhat in the cold winter air.

Children ran about in rags, playing with sticks that they used like rifles. They were bravely killing imaginary enemies and dying with animated drama for the glory of the homeland they would one day win back for their fathers. Old men huddled around fires built in large metal cans, playing backgammon and drinking green tea and probably Turkish coffee, when there was some to be had. They talked and argued and passed time in the same way today as yesterday and all the days that had come before. Lebanon had always been a place of exiles, and nowhere was this better exemplified than in this pitiful little camp that existed on no map.

The absence of young adult males was what Brevig noticed first. But then it was winter, the season when young fighters left the mountains for the warmer lowlands, leaving behind their women and children, safe – they hoped – from the long reach of Israeli reprisals. In the spring they would return – those who still lived – bringing with them still more young commandos to rebuild their ranks. Here they would train and become very capable soldiers under the tutelage of their officers and the wisest of the elders, like Abu Hassan Nasir.

Abu Hassan Nasir had obtained almost legendary stature for the great freedom fighters he had trained. He was an old man now, too old to take an active part in the fighting. But he was still a teacher to be revered above all others, though nowadays he taught less and less due to failing health.

Brevig stopped the Land Rover. He approached a group of old men playing backgammon and inquired where he might find Abu Hassan Nasir. He offered them cigarettes and bundles of tea and much-welcomed Turkish coffee, which they accepted gladly with choruses of *Ilham'dilla* – 'Praise God'.

He approached a small stone hut with the typical metal roof. From the roof protruded a tin smokestack from which gentle wisps of smoke rose lazily. He knocked on the door.

Abu Hassan Nasir opened the door and stared at the face. He had grown very old since the last time Brevig had seen him. The dark eyes squinted suspiciously at the round face with reddened cheeks. It took a few moments before the eyes widened with recognition.

'Abu Hassan, how are you?' Brevig said in greeting.

Abu Hassan opened his arms and Brevig drew nearer to him. They embraced.

'This old fighter is well, Ivan,' the Arab replied.

'It makes my heart glad to see you,' Brevig returned, clapping the old man's shoulders gently.

'Come in out of the cold, my friend. I will make some tea.'

'Better yet, I have brought you some Turkish coffee,' Brevig told him, holding out a package.

Abu Hassan accepted the package.

'I have also brought you some tea, cigarettes, and the finest *kibbeh* in all of Beirut.'

'Then we will drink and eat and smoke together at my table,' Abu Hassan said to the Russian.

Brevig stepped into the austere one-room hut and closed the door behind him.

'I have brought you some newspapers. Do you still read Russian?'

'Of course. But with the help of glasses these days.'

The old Arab began to heat water for the coffee. He filled an old, dented brass pot with water and placed it on a wire triangle over a tin can that served him well as a stove. He poured out some of the ground coffee into his hand, looked into the pot at the quantity of water, and added a bit more coffee, then dropped it into the water. He turned back to the Russian, who had already started unpacking the other provisions he had brought.

Brevig looked up at the Arab, who looked very tired and very old. His color was not good, and the Russian had noticed the change in the voice. It was deeper now, and the words were spoken with a great deal of effort. He guessed that, perhaps, Abu Hassan was suffering from a cancer.

'Have you heard from your son?' Brevig asked casually.

'No, not for some months now,' Abu Hassan replied. 'How is General Kozlov getting on these days?'

'Very well. He sends his regards.'

The Arab nodded.

Brevig opened the package of *kibbeh*, a mixture of lamb and wheat that had been well mashed in a large mortar, kneaded, and seasoned. It was traditionally served uncooked, like steak tartare. The Russian also removed some Lebanese bread and set it on the paper in which the provisions had been wrapped. He shoved a pack of cigarettes, American, across the table to the Arab as he came to the table, then pulled out his pipe and began filling it.

Neither man spoke until Brevig had lit his pipe and Abu Hassan had lit a cigarette.

'You are looking well,' the Russian lied.

Abu Hassan looked right through him. 'You were always a good liar, Ivan. I know better, and *you* know better.'

'Have you had medical attention? I can get a doctor to the camp.'

'A doctor would be appreciated. For the others, however. He will do this old Arab no good. But the children and the women would benefit.'

'I will arrange the details immediately upon my return to

Beirut. I will also have some food supplies brought to Halrashayya, as well as general medicines. Why don't you let me take you to Tripoli for proper medical care?' Brevig asked with genuine concern.

Abu Hassan shook his head. 'I'm afraid I am beyond the help of medicine. I have seen my last spring, Ivan. How I would like to see just one more, to feel the warm sunshine on my face and smell the sweet fragrance of the budding jasmine.'

Brevig felt sadness for the old man, made deeper by the news that he carried and would have to tell him.

'I have the will to fight and to live a hundred years – but not the strength,' Abu Hassan told him. 'I am tired of war and sending the seeds of our future to die. I no longer have an appetite for it.'

'Every great conflict must have its casualties,' the Russian said.

'It must also have an end,' Abu Hassan said. 'My people are sad and tired. A man cannot be happy when all of his sons are away, and our sons have been gone too long. There is much tension here these days. The young do not have the patience of my generation. They are frustrated. Arab nationalism, which transcends borders and at other times does not exist at all, means little to them. It is abstract. They see Arab fighting against Arab and no longer feel that the unity of the Arab people will work for them in the regaining of their homeland. They are alone, and only their acts of desperation will bring the end to which they have dedicated themselves.'

Abu Hassan let out a racking cough, and nearly retched. Brevig watched as he swallowed with a great deal of pain.

The Arab crushed out the cigarette.

Brevig lowered his pipe to the table to let it go out.

Abu Hassan looked over his shoulder at the brass pot. 'The coffee will be ready soon,' he said, then looked back at the Russian. 'So what brings you to Halrashayya? I know with certainty it is not just to pay this old Palestinian a social call.'

Brevig's face became even more serious. 'I need your help,' he said.

'*You* need *my* help?' he said, raising his eyebrows. 'In what way?'

'I must find Rafael Sonterra,' Brevig told him.

Abu Hassan stared at the Russian without comment.

The Arab rose from his chair and went to the coffeepot. He poured its contents into two small cups and returned to the table, placing one in front of his visitor.

'I do not know where Rafael Sonterra is,' he said after retaking his seat.

'We had hoped you might.'

'We?'

'General Kozlov and myself.'

'And why must you find him?'

Brevig raised his cup and sipped the coffee, not taking his eyes off the worn face of Abu Hassan.

The Arab waited patiently for the answer to his question.

'He has a dangerous weapon that must be recovered.'

Abu Hassan squinted at Brevig. 'Has he used this weapon?'

'Yes. Against innocent people. And he will use it again to do great harm to the entire world if he is not stopped,' Brevig replied.

'There are no innocent people,' Abu Hassan returned.

'I don't wish to argue revolutionary doctrine with you, my friend. What he possesses can wreak irreparable damage to the entire world. It is to no-one's benefit to cripple the whole planet for the rest of time. Surely you can see this. He is not using it to achieve a political end. There is no purpose to his actions other than to destroy a global economy. By doing this, he will also destroy any chance at a future for the same children you wish to save. There can be no good in this.'

'What is this weapon?'

'It is microbiological. It can attack and destroy oil reserves, and it cannot be stopped.'

A deep frown crossed the face of Abu Hassan, and Brevig went on, 'It was never your teaching, I am sure, to destroy for the sake of destruction alone. And that is exactly what he is attempting to do.'

'What are his demands?'

'He has made none.'

Abu Hassan raised his hand to his chin. 'Perhaps he has yet to make them.'

'He will make no demands. He has even broken the deepest faith with all who have helped him.'

'Rafael Sonterra would not break faith with his own,' the Arab countered.

'He already has, in the most decisive way. He has killed everyone who has been a part of his plan. *Everyone*.'

'Exactly *who* is "everyone"?' queried the Arab, grave concern replacing the doubt on his face.

'He has killed Vigen Babayan, Juan Strassa, the Dwarf in Paris . . .'

Abu Hassan stared into the face of the Russian, waiting for him to go on.

'And he has killed Kammal,' Brevig said.

Abu Hassan's eyes seemed to roll up into his head.

'Kam . . . Kammal?' he stammered.

'Yes. In Paris,' the Russian lied.

'How . . . how did my son die?' he asked weakly.

'He was blown up. Sonterra used the same method in Colombia to kill at least three others. He has betrayed everyone solely for the purpose of protecting himself. He is no longer a soldier of the revolution. He has become a rogue killer bent on the destruction of the world. And he will stop at nothing to achieve this end. That is why we must stop him. And why you *must* help us. He has killed your son, Abu Hassan. He must kill no more.'

Abu Hassan's eyes reddened and filled with tears. His last remaining child had been killed.

The aging man rose from his chair and walked to a window at the far side of his hut. He lowered his head.

'Leave me,' he said after a long pause, his voice on the verge of breaking. 'I must pray to Allah.'

'Will you help us?' Brevig asked.

Abu Hassan did not reply.

Brevig waited a full minute before repeating his question.

'Will you help us, Abu Hassan?'

'I can only answer that I must pray to Allah for guidance,' the Arab replied.

Brevig rose from his chair. 'Then I will leave you to be alone with your God. I will wait. And I will understand . . . whatever the answer you give.'

MALTA: The capital city of Valletta at first looked quite unremarkable from high altitude. It wasn't until the plane had descended on its approach to Luqa Airport and passed close by the Grand Harbor that Michael got a better appreciation for the ancient city. It had looked drab and gray, almost dirty, when he first saw it from many miles out as the plane banked in its first approach turn. He could see now, however, that he had been mistaken. The city almost had the look of a massive fortress, built entirely of native limestone. It was not gray at all, but rather a light golden tan and white. Buildings were crunched together everywhere, as though every available space had been built upon.

Malta's limited commercial access made watching points of entry relatively easy for Intel-Trace's surveillance teams. All flights into the city's only airport were being monitored, as were those incoming from points of origin in Europe, Tunis, and Tripoli, as well as ferry crossings from Sicily, Reggio Calabria, and Catania. Even the cruise ships and pleasure craft anchored in the city's many sheltered harbors were watched.

A control center was immediately set up in Valletta in a small but adequate villa overlooking the Grand Harbor and Fort St Angelo on the Vittoriosa peninsula. Radio communications and land-line connections were set in place. Intel-Trace, with support from Israeli intelligence, had assembled a huge contingent of surveillance personnel. With Malta's dense population, both native and tourist, surveillance could become especially difficult. Not only was Greta Haas to be followed at all times after her arrival, but Rafael Sonterra had to be spotted, and the Soviets had to be identified and watched closely as well. It was a complex logistical puzzle, but Bob Elias thrived on such challenges and chose to supervise the operation from Paris, where he could coordinate efforts in Malta with those in the United States.

The villa looked like a war command center. Every bit of available wall was covered with detailed maps and charts of the sections of the city. Tables were covered with more maps and charts and telephones. There were telescopes and binoculars set at the windows looking out to parts of the harbor and city. Banks of electronic apparatus had also been set up for more sophisticated monitoring once the various quarry were located and put on watch.

The wait for Greta Haas was brief. She arrived on an Alitalia flight from Rome on the very first day. She was very punctual – and very pregnant.

'We hadn't counted on this,' Michael said, looking at the pictures taken at Luqa Airport. 'She's pretty far along in this pregnancy.'

'A serpent carrying eggs is no less poisonous,' Simmerman replied to immediately dispel any possible sentimentality. 'This in no way changes the objective.'

Michael nodded without comment, his eyes still on the photograph.

Simmerman dragged hard on his cigarette, then tapped it in an ashtray. 'If you are having doubts . . .'

Michael looked up at the Israeli. He had left sentimentality behind long ago, in Southeast Asia. He had seen the worst possible atrocities – and committed them himself out of necessity. He had left sentimentality behind at the coffin of his murdered sister, and again in the rain forests of Colombia, when he had held the body of his friend

511

Carlos Trevino in his arms. When it came to the forces of terrorism, there was no room for sentimentality.

'There are *no* doubts,' Michael replied evenly.

Simmerman nodded slowly, as though the matter were never in question.

'She has taken a small villa on the tip of the peninsula. Surveillance is in place. We will set up electronic monitoring when she leaves the villa for the first time. When she's on the street, she must be watched closely every moment. She may have intermediate contacts or dead-drop areas where she can leave or accept messages from Sonterra. He will be very cautious,' the Israeli said to the primary team.

'What are our chances of spotting him when he gets to the island?' Wadelaw asked.

'He will not come by common transport,' Yelena replied. 'No matter how closely Intel-Trace guards the ports of entry, Malta has hundreds of sheltered harbors and inlets in which to land a boat undetected. He could also make his initial landing on the islands of Gozo or Comino. A small boat could approach Malta quite easily from either of them.'

'He will attempt to warn her of the danger,' Simmerman added. 'He will know we are here, and will exercise the greatest caution. Physically coming in will be his last alternative. It will be our job to stay close enough to her to prevent her escape. Sonterra would then be forced out of hiding to come and save her.'

'*If* he comes,' Wadelaw said.

Simmerman smiled and drew again on his cigarette. 'He will come.'

Greta left the villa in the late afternoon, carrying a large shoulder bag. The moment she passed the immediate perimeter, the electronics team entered the villa and set up the usual listening and motion monitors, and made a careful search of her belongings, being sure to leave things exactly as they had been found.

A camera team followed her at close range, taking hundreds of photographs for later review by Simmerman. Their presence was masked by the throngs of pedestrian traffic enjoying *passeggiata*, the unique custom of the Maltese to take a stroll through the streets at sunset. Because this was two nights before Christmas, the *passeggiata* took on special significance. Hardly a citizen was indoors.

After two hours of playing tourist, Greta returned to her room with a small package of groceries. She prepared a light supper, and spent the remainder of the evening reading. Every sound was recorded for closer review.

Simmerman worked late into the night, going over the photographs, studying faces, marking the places she had stopped on the city maps, and establishing the route she had taken, to see if any of it was repeated on the following day. He also examined additional photographs taken at the ferry docks and Luqa Airport, as well as more from the streets in which Greta Haas was not the focus of the pictures. He tacked those that had special significance on a separate board.

In the morning he reviewed his findings with his team.

'Study these faces well,' he told the team gathered around the board. 'They are Soviets. All GRU operatives.'

It took Michael only a moment to find Tolvanin. The Soviets were here in force.

'They have set a loose perimeter around Greta's villa,' Simmerman explained. 'We will be monitoring their activities as closely as hers. We must be prepared for any sudden move on their part. Their objective will be the same as ours. Should Sonterra not take the bait and come in soon, they may attempt to take her instead. If they succeed, we will lose our opportunity. They will most certainly take her off the island and to a place easy for them to control. It will be much more difficult for us to operate under those conditions. At the moment the advantage is ours, and they will want to change that.'

'How long do you think they'll wait?' Wadelaw asked.

'Not long,' Simmerman replied. 'Three days, perhaps.'

'They'll risk blowing the whole operation if they try to take her,' Michael said.

'The risk will be only to *our* operation. If they succeed in taking her, they will deliver the same message to Sonterra that we did in Paris when you kept Kammal's contact. Control will shift from our hands to theirs if it is permitted to happen.'

'And we will not let that happen,' Yelena added. 'We lost Sonterra in Sare because of Soviet interference. Malta will be our last chance at this madman, and I won't permit them to ruin our mission again.'

'Another Sare could be messy in such a densely populated area,' Wadelaw said.

'We weren't prepared for their intervention in Sare,' Michael said to his partner. 'We will be this time.'

'We have the Soviets under close observation,' Simmerman added. 'Timing will be critical, but we will be looking for signs of their intentions.'

'And if they *do* move?' Wadelaw continued.

'Then we must take the Haas woman before they do.'

'We'll lose our opportunity on Malta.'

'Yes, but we will have the woman,' Simmerman returned.

'Sonterra will never negotiate,' Michael said.

'No, he won't. But there are still ways to bring him in. It will be difficult, but it can be done – as long as Greta Haas is in our possession. If the Soviets take her, then we have no hope.'

Michael read the determination in Yelena's eyes. The pain of Papa's loss in Sare still burned in her. The one night they had shared had been a powerful medicine for her. The morning after their encounter, the soldier in her was back, ready for battle. She was a Sabra, tough and determined to bring an end to Rafael Sonterra at all costs.

'Then we won't let that happen,' he said, repeating her commitment.

The sky over Malta was clear and bright on Christmas Eve morning. Greta Haas was out early, enjoying the sunshine and sixty-degree weather. For the surveillance teams, it was another day of intense work.

Greta boarded a bus for Paola, a ride of not more than five miles. Intel-Trace had two teams on the crowded bus, and another three following at intervals.

The bus carried primarily tourists bound for the Hypogeum, the most unusual place in all of Malta. The only known underground Copper Age temple in the world, the massive structure was a honeycomb of intricate chambers and tombs hewn out of solid rock, complete with an oracular shrine.

Michael and Yelena entered the Hypogeum with the large group of tourists. They walked hand in hand, like lovers on a romantic holiday. Their faces meant nothing to Greta Haas. The second team was also an inconspicuous part of the crowd. From Simmerman's photos Michael recognized two faces in the group as Soviets. They were not about to miss a thing, he thought.

The group moved slowly through the temple, following the guide, who explained the interesting history of the Hypogeum for their benefit.

'It was here that the worshipers heard the voice of the oracle,' the guide said.

Michael appeared to listen intently, keeping a casual eye on Greta Haas's movements.

'Quiet, please, and listen very carefully,' the guide told the group.

He went to the wall farthest from the huddled tourists, and spoke into an opening. His voice boomed out loudly from all around them. Its sound was magnified and rendered almost inhuman by the curved ceiling and the hidden passages behind the walls, sounding as though it came from another world.

'Imagine, if you will, the reaction of those ancient, simple people standing in the darkness or in the feeble reflections of light from just a small lamp, upon hearing the oracle speak to them.'

Michael observed Greta carefully during the distraction. She did not seem interested. Her eyes searched the chamber carefully.

Michael and Yelena drew in a little closer behind her as the guide went on to explain how the priestesses had slept here, their dreams inspired by the great deity that they served, finding the answers to worshipers' questions.

The guide turned and spoke once again into an opening in the chamber wall, the voice reverberating in that same inhuman tone. There was an instant at the end of his statement when there seemed to be a brief overlapping of voices.

Greta's head snapped around and her eyes narrowed. She tensed visibly.

Yelena's hand squeezed Michael's forearm.

'He's here!' she whispered urgently.

Michael looked into her face. 'Are you sure?'

Yelena's eyes moved frantically across the faces of the group.

'He spoke to her in Arabic,' she whispered. 'Didn't you hear it?'

'I heard something, but couldn't make it out,' Michael replied.

'He told her to leave at once,' Yelena said. She let go of Michael's arm and began moving through the crowd of tourists, her hand now deep in her coat pocket, resting on her handgun.

Yelena made eye contact with the second team, her message clear. They split up and began a similar movement through the crowd, looking for signs of identification. Sonterra could be among them in a disguise.

The guide led the group through the remaining chambers. Greta had moved in closer to the guide, and stayed almost at his side for her protection.

Michael and Yelena lagged behind the others and began inspecting the adjacent chambers, but if Sonterra was there, he wasn't visible.

The search became almost frantic as their efforts bore no fruit. They moved ahead quickly to rejoin the rest of the group, continuing to check additional chambers as they moved past them.

Greta stayed at the side of the guide as the tour concluded and the tourists left the temple. When she boarded the bus, she took the seat beside the guide. Her face was white as she searched the faces of the tourists reentering the bus.

Michael and the others stayed back in the temple and joined a second tourist group to help conceal an expanded search effort through the chambers for a second time. It was possible that Sonterra had evaded them and planned to exit with a following group. But they were no more successful than they had been on the previous search. Rafael Sonterra had simply vanished.

Michael stood on the small balcony of the control villa, looking out over the Grand Harbor. His mind swam with dark thoughts – in contrast to the fireworks and rockets shooting up from the far side of the harbor, illuminating the night sky with halos of silver and red and blue. The lights of the *dghajses* – elaborately crafted and painted rowing boats much like the gondolas of Venice – gleamed on the dark waters as they bobbed up and down.

He had witnessed nighttime visions like this before, but they had been scenes of war in Vietnam, and in place of joy there had been desperation and fear. The failed mission of Sare floated in his memory, too – how that quiet, peaceful village had been so suddenly turned into a zone of horror. He wondered if the same would happen here. Sonterra was near. He felt the man's presence with the same certainty he had felt in Paris.

His senses warned him that the universal peace and joy of this important holiday were about to shatter. He *knew* that Rafael Sonterra was out there somewhere in the darkness – perhaps watching him now – his instinct for self-preservation at war with the urge to protect his mate and unborn child. *If only the Soviets would stay out of it*, he thought. Sonterra was volatile enough without the added complication of a second attack force. *But if I were in their position, I'd do whatever I had to do to win. They'll move . . . I know it!*

Tomorrow was Christmas Day. It was also the third day, and Simmerman had guessed that the Soviets would wait only three days before making their move. Michael could smell and feel the tension, and he knew he could do nothing to keep it from igniting into something brutal and filled with death. How many Sares would there be, he wondered, before this would all come to an end?

Gregor Tolvanin finished reading the day's reports, then picked up the communication from Moscow regarding their situation in Lebanon. Abu Hassan Nasir had not yet spoken since learning of the death of his son. Brevig had felt certain that Abu Hassan believed his story about Rafael Sonterra being responsible for the death of Kammal. There was little Brevig could do but wait for the old man to break his silence, and hope that what he had to offer would be useful to them.

Tolvanin sat back in his chair and lit a cigarette. He considered the knowns against the unknowns, weighing the variables and alternatives like a chess master facing more than one opponent.

The one constant factor was Greta Haas. She was the center of the board. Every objective was directed toward gaining control of the center, with the knowledge that Rafael Sonterra would have to pass through it sooner or later for her sake. The fact that she carried his child only enhanced her value and increased the probability that he would come.

The great risk, of course, was that the Americans would beat them to her, or that they would take Sonterra when he appeared.

The Americans were well established on Malta – so well, in fact, that he had no real knowledge of their strength. He knew only that it was greater than his own. On top of that, Intel-Trace had the assistance of Israeli intelligence, whose interest in Sonterra was intense. Every day that passed allowed them to strengthen their situation, to draw in tighter and tighter.

He knew he could wait no longer. He must act quickly to take the Haas woman *before* Sonterra came for her, or he would certainly lose them both. She had to be moved to a place that offered the greatest possible advantage to the Soviet Union, while still being reachable by Sonterra.

Tolvanin reasoned that this operation was his complete responsibility. Its success or its failure would rest with his decisions. He weighed the alternatives one more time very carefully, then made his decision to act. He would take Greta Haas tonight.

37

Michael woke from a light, restless sleep and focused blurry eyes on the figure of Christopher Wadelaw as he made his way across the dimly lit room.

'It's going down, Mike,' Wadelaw told him in a low but urgent voice. 'The monitors in the Haas villa have all gone dead. One after the other, in rapid succession. She must have a detection device.'

'How long ago?' Michael asked, sitting up quickly.

'It just happened. The setup is busted. We have very little time, Mike. She'll be out of there in a hurry.'

Michael jumped to his feet and reached for his handgun. They had also been supplied with an assortment of Uzis. He grabbed one, and a fistful of clips.

'She must have gotten another warning. She had already settled in for the night,' Wadelaw said.

Yelena stuck her head through the doorway. 'The

Soviets are moving. Three mobile units are approaching the perimeter,' she said excitedly.

Michael was through the door in a blur. 'Come on, we can't lose a single second,' he said as the others fell in behind him.

The control center was only minutes away from the Haas villa, but the Soviets were moving in fast. Five Intel-Trace mobile units were engaged, with two already on the move, closing in on the perimeter from two different sides. Their unit and the remaining two would come in through the center.

Michael got behind the wheel, and the car squealed away from the curb of the narrow street, the other two mobile units close behind. In the deserted, early-morning hours of Christmas Day, they made good time up Kingsway, the main street of the peninsula.

They were approaching the villa from the southwest, where all the streets were closed to vehicular traffic. But there were many narrow pedestrian streets, barely as wide as a car, that radiated like ribs off Kingsway. Michael would simply use one.

'Which one do we go down?' he asked.

'Two more, then to the right,' Yelena replied from the backseat.

Michael reached the second right and turned down it, the other mobile units right on his tail.

The streets running to the east off Kingsway sloped down precipitously and were built with broad stairways – wide steps spanning the entire street to provide better footing for pedestrians. The cars thumped and bumped their way down at high speed, bottoming out and scraping against the walls of buildings that stood along the narrow passage. The villa was situated at the base of the street, near the edge of the harbor. Had it been midday, the street would have been filled with pedestrians, but at this hour, in the darkness, their crazed descent went unnoticed . . . except by the Soviets.

The Soviet units arrived ahead of the racing Intel-Trace

teams. The lead Soviet car continued a short distance past the villa and skidded to a halt, the driver expertly cutting the wheel to position the car so that no one else could pass. The last Soviet car stopped short of the villa, blocking the road in a similar fashion, closing off the back of the perimeter. The middle car stopped at the sidewalk even with the villa. Tolvanin and three of his team exited the car at a run and raced toward the villa's door. They kicked it in and raced up the long flight of stairs to the upper rooms, where Greta Haas was known to be staying.

The first man up the stairs hit the light, the others fanned out quickly, their weapons held ready to concentrate fire, if necessary.

Greta was taken completely by surprise.

She was standing in the far corner of the room, fully dressed, a large shoulder bag slung over her left shoulder.

'Make no move and you will be unhurt,' Tolvanin shouted in German. 'You will come with us immediately,' he commanded.

Michael had seen the first two Soviet cars pass the narrow opening at the end of the street. They were just a few seconds too late. It was going to be a fight, and he was ready.

He stomped on the brake pedal and skidded fully across the road intersecting the street he had come down. He cut the wheel, skidding the car to a stop behind the Soviet mobile unit at the curb of the wider street. The doors opened and the three agents exited the car and crouched beside it to protect themselves from the Soviet weapons.

The next two Intel-Trace units broke in opposite directions after reaching the wider road, and bore down on the Soviet units from inside the perimeter, just as the fourth and fifth units closed in from the outside. All cars screeched to a halt at about the same time, and sixteen more Intel-Trace agents hit the street, their weapons at the ready.

The Soviets who had not yet entered the building were caught flat in the open, outnumbered. Seeing that resistance was pointless, they lowered their weapons in capitulation.

Inside the villa, Tolvanin motioned to the stairway with his weapon. 'Move now,' he ordered the woman.

There was something about the look on her face that sent a flash of sudden uneasiness through him. There was no fear in her eyes, and it triggered an instinctive warning . . . but entirely too late.

The door behind and to the left of the Soviet team swung open slowly and without sound. Rafael Sonterra leveled his weapon and opened up with a murderous burst from the automatic Heckler & Koch MP5.

There wasn't time for the first two Soviets to turn before they were shredded by Sonterra's explosive close-range fire. Tolvanin turned to face the deafening sounds of the sudden discharge and caught two bullets in the chest. Their force knocked him backwards and down the flight of stairs.

The last Soviet caught a full volley and was knocked through the window behind him. He crashed through it and was gone from view.

From the street below, Michael watched as the Soviet came through the window in a spray of shattered glass and fell as if in slow motion. He landed on the hood of the Soviet car, his upper body smashing through the windshield.

Michael and Wadelaw crouched and sprinted for the villa. Yelena ducked back behind the Intel-Trace car and aimed her Uzi at the window to concentrate fire on anything that showed.

Michael and Wadelaw were through the splintered door in a second. Tolvanin was lying across the stairs, grimacing in pain. A bulletproof vest had saved his life.

The Russian pointed up the stairway. 'Sonterra,' he gasped.

'Let's go,' Michael said to Wadelaw, and sprinted up the stairs.

Michael came over the edge of the stairs at floor level

and sprayed a burst across the room from one side to the other. But the room was empty.

He came up the remainder of the way cautiously, Wadelaw close behind. They separated, ready for the first sign of movement, and swung through the villa, checking each room while providing cover for one another. The villa was empty.

'The roof,' Wadelaw said, pointing to a movable stairway that was still in the lowered position.

Michael went to the window facing the street and waved a hand before showing his face.

Yelena lowered the weapon, but kept it ready.

He signaled her with a thumbs-up. 'Roof!' he yelled, jerking the thumb upward.

She got the message and moved across the street to get a better vantage point.

Michael turned back into the room as Wadelaw began moving up the lowered stairway. He went to the base of the stairs to provide what cover he could in case Sonterra appeared from above.

Wadelaw moved up cautiously. He popped up, then down quickly. There was no fire. He began up again.

Just as his shoulders cleared the opening to the roof, there was a thunderous burst of gunfire. He fell back down the steps right on to Michael, both of them hitting the floor hard.

Michael rolled his partner over quickly and checked him. There was blood on his face and a gash in his cheek.

'I'm all right,' Wadelaw said, wincing with pain. 'It's just limestone from the ricochet. I'm not hit.'

Michael looked at the cuts and the bloody gash. 'You never were pretty, anyway,' he said. 'Come on, get on your feet.'

They got up, and Michael went to the stepway and began inching upward.

'Where'd the gunfire come from?' he asked.

'About ten o'clock. I never got a look at him.'

Tolvanin had made his way back up the stairs, one arm

across his hurting chest. 'I can provide additional cover,' he said as he approached them, his weapon ready in the other hand.

Michael looked back down at him and nodded.

He continued up the stepway, stopping just short of going over the top. He raised the Uzi, directed it at ten o'clock, and fired a blind volley. Then he fired a second, longer one, sweeping a ninety-degree arc, figuring that Sonterra may have moved his position. Then he started up.

Another volley cut loose at the opening from the ten o'clock position. Michael lowered himself quickly, raised the Uzi, and once again directed a clip-emptying volley in retaliation. He handed the emptied weapon down to Wadelaw, who handed Michael his own charged weapon.

Michael raised it once again and emptied the second clip.

Wadelaw had the first weapon reloaded and ready for Michael.

'I thought we had snipers on the rooftops. Where the hell are they?' Michael yelled.

'I don't know,' Wadelaw replied. 'Sonterra could have taken them out. Otherwise he'd have been spotted gaining entry to the villa. He sure as hell didn't get in from street level.'

'We're going up naked,' Michael said. I don't like it, but we're going. We don't have a choice.'

There had been no return fire at the last two volleys. Michael readied himself and went up, firing as he came partially through the opening.

There was no return fire. He scanned the rooftop quickly and saw Sonterra and Greta Haas moving across the roof of an adjoining building. He went all the way through the opening and sprinted for the cover of a high ledge.

Wadelaw followed him, with Tolvanin close behind.

Sonterra turned back and saw the three men on the roof of the villa. He took Greta by the hand and they hurried, moving parallel to the street in front of the villa.

Yelena spotted them from the street and fired a burst.

Sonterra and Greta ducked away from the flying debris kicked up by Yelena's well-placed shots. They moved low to stay out of her line of fire.

The three pursuers spread out and began a hot chase across the rooftops, moving more quickly than their quarry.

Sonterra stopped once to fire a short burst to slow them, and took Greta's hand once again, to make the most of the brief advantage. They continued moving across the uneven rooftops and came to a taller building. It was almost a dead end.

Sonterra looked back. The three men pursuing them had begun to move again. They were well spaced and could now provide effective cover for one another. He knew that he and Greta had to make the higher roof or they would die.

Sonterra fired another sweeping burst, sending his pursuers to cover once again. He slung his weapon and turned back to Greta.

'We have to get over the top of this ledge. I'll go first, then you. I'll help you over. Can you do it?' he asked, his breathing heavy.

Greta looked into his questioning eyes and nodded. 'Yes. Go. I will be right behind.'

The ledge was high. He would have to take a running start, hit the ledge of the lower roof, and power himself up. He unslung the weapon and handed it to her. 'Give me cover,' he said.

She took the weapon and turned and began firing short bursts across the rooftop at the men following them. The covering fire was effective in keeping them from advancing.

The second she began firing, Sonterra took off. He sprinted several powerful strides, hit the lower ledge perfectly, and was up. He hit the ledge at chest level, caught the edge with his arms, and pulled himself over.

Greta stopped firing and threw the weapon up to him.

Yelena moved swiftly along the far side of the street opposite the row of buildings. She saw Sonterra on the higher rooftop. Only his head and shoulders were visible. Then she saw Greta as she prepared to make her run for the leap.

Yelena raised the Uzi as Greta began her run, and fired.

A hail of bullets spattered against the wall as Greta reached it, catching her in the legs as she sprung for the higher wall.

She cried out and her leap was short. Sonterra lunged forward, barely catching her by the arms as she began to fall back. The weight of her almost pulled him back over, but he held on, bracing his thighs against the high ledge. Greta was dangling at arm's length, unable to use her wounded legs to help propel herself higher.

Sonterra strained to regain leverage, gritting his teeth and grunting. He managed to secure his hold on her, and took several deep breaths, like a weightlifter preparing for the mighty heave.

His eyes looked to the street below as Yelena took careful aim once again. As if through some terrible telescopic vision, he saw the Uzi steady and the eyes of the Israeli squint for clear sighting.

Sonterra grunted and heaved with all of his might as the Uzi unleashed a volley at the wall.

There was the sound of bullets hitting the limestone, and the dull thud of them hitting Greta. He saw the hair at the back of her head kick up and explode crimson, hot blood splattering across his face.

She let out a horrible cry and he lost his grip. One second she was there, and the next she was gone. He heard her hit the roof below, but couldn't see her buckle and pitch to her right, off the roof. She fell three stories to the street below. He heard the second thud of her impact – and in that sickening instant realized that she – and his unborn son – were gone forever.

He let out a demonic howl and raised the H&K at

Yelena. He expended the partial clip, but the burst missed its target. Yelena fired back, her shots showering him with cutting debris, as they exploded against the higher ledge.

Sonterra fell away from the ledge and sat stunned for a moment. He gritted his teeth in seething anger and the anguish of his helplessness to save Greta. There was no more he could do for her now, he knew. She was beyond the struggle and all pain. He forced himself to his feet and began to move away, fighting the urge to remain and hold his ground against her killers. He would never forget their faces. He would get away because he had to, though he wanted to stand and die. But he would not die on this day, he vowed. He would live . . . to bring death to the people who had taken those whom he loved. He would make each one of them suffer. Each one. And he ran.

Michael, Wadelaw, and Tolvanin reached the ledge of the higher rooftop behind the protection offered by Yelena from the street below. They went up and over, spreading to search for a ghost they knew would not be there. Once again, Sonterra had vanished.

They found his H&K lying on the rooftop. It was empty, which explained why their last movements had gone unchallenged.

Michael and Tolvanin stood side by side, their weapons lowered, looking out over the empty rooftops, breathing heavily from the chase.

For a brief moment they had ceased being adversaries. The necessity of stopping Rafael Sonterra had been the greater imperative. They looked at one another – not as enemies, not as friends, but as two men who had been beaten yet again by the elusive Rafael Sonterra.

The move to capture Greta Haas had lasted no more than eight minutes. When the authorities finally arrived, there was only wreckage and blood, but there were no bodies or witnesses to tell the tale of what had happened. It was clear from the physical evidence where it had all started, and where the action had moved as the drama unfolded.

The villa was in shambles, and the woman who had rented it had disappeared. It was assumed that she had been a victim and that the blood in the villa and on the street must be hers, but with no bodies the events of the morning remained a mystery.

The Soviets and the Intel-Trace teams had each dispersed after the last shots were fired. The Russians had taken away their casualties, and Intel-Trace had removed the body of Greta Haas. The bodies of Intel-Trace's two rooftop shooters had been found and recovered. Wadelaw had been correct in his assessment; Sonterra had taken them silently before gaining entry into the villa, explaining why they had not laid down a field of fire at the fugitives. It had been really quite remarkable that Intel-Trace and the Soviets had avoided direct armed confrontation. Both sides had been ready for it. Michael's desperate plunge through the center of the perimeter had permitted Intel-Trace's teams to engulf the Soviets and thus avoid further bloodshed. The Soviets had shown life-saving discretion by bowing immediately to Intel-Trace's superior forces.

Michael's dejection eased somewhat after he came down from the higher rooftop. Tolvanin had left immediately to see to his casualties. Wadelaw had also left to get some attention for his minor but painful facial wounds. Michael had stopped for a moment to inspect the bullet-riddled and blood-stained wall against which Yelena had concentrated her fire on Greta Haas. It was there, at the very edge of the roof where she had gone over to the street three stories below, that he found what turned an apparent defeat into resounding victory. He found the large shoulder bag that Greta Haas had carried with her everywhere she went since her arrival on Malta. It had not gone over the edge with her to the street.

He took a moment to open it before heading back down to the street. Inside he found a double inner cushion of foam, much the same as that used in a photographer's bag to protect lenses and cameras. When he separated the foam layers he found the shiny metal vials containing the missing Luxus. And an even greater mystery began, for when he counted them, he counted *twenty-six*. Only twenty-four had been reported missing.

'Give that to me once again,' Elias asked over the voice box in the control center, which had been moved in the night from Valletta to Floriana, less than a mile away.

'There are twenty-six vials. Twenty-four are coded in black, two in red,' Michael clarified. 'De Roode specifically said that twenty-four vials had been taken from the Medellín Institute.'

'Yes, he did,' Elias confirmed, puzzlement in his voice. 'He made no mention of different color codings, either. I don't know what to make of it.'

The mind of the scientist began to click inside Michael.

'We have a serious problem, Bob,' he said. 'The code numbers I have from Medellín match the vials coded in black. That means the Luxus consignment, as it left the institute, is intact. Right?'

'Right.'

'If it's intact, then Sonterra couldn't have been making the hits. Someone else has been arranging them – and they have a separate supply of the Luxus that isn't supposed to exist.'

'Of course,' breathed Elias. 'That would help explain the perfect timing of the *Skyco Hippalus* disaster and the hits in Colombia and the Soviet Union,' he said excitedly.

'Listen, Mike, we've also had another important development. Intelligence Central has found an overlay in Kammal's belongings. It took a while to figure out exactly what it was, but they've come up with the answer. Intelligence Central has succeeded in matching the overlay to a scaled global map by using the four known reserve hits as points of reference. The remaining markings line up perfectly with the world's largest reserve locations. They appear to be prospective target sites. There's even a key establishing the order of selection.'

'How many are there?'

'Seventy-four.'

'It's the insider at Skyco, Bob. He's controlling the reserve hits. Get Intelligence Central to match up the site markings on Kammal's overlay with the sites for the probe implantations planned by Skyco. If I'm right in my thinking, the two sets of locations will be identical. And I bet the schedule for each is the same, too.'

'I see what you're aiming at, and it's scary as hell.'

'We have to *stop* the implantations of the probes immediately. Those supposedly lifesaving probes are really the deadly Alpha strain of the Luxus. That's how the Skyco insider intends to hit the reserves. There isn't a second to lose,' Michael told him.

'It may already have started, Mike.'

'Then stop it! Now!'

'We can rush the Beta to any sites already implanted.'

'Check the Beta strains first, Bob. They may, in all probability, be Alpha.'

'I'll start immediately,' Elias said. 'What about Sonterra?'

'He's probably already off the island. I don't see him as our immediate threat just now. We've temporarily stalled him by recovering his part of the Luxus. It's his inside man who's the threat to us now. We have to identify that person. There aren't that many people who would have the necessary access or the ability to pull it off. Go right to the top. Check everyone, with special attention to de Roode. I think he's our man.'

'I'll be on my way back to the States within the hour. I'll get things started the second we're off the phone,' Elias said.

'We'll head back to San Antonio as soon as we close down here, Bob. We'll have the twenty-six vials with us, and I'll be very interested to see what's in the other two.'

'Bring them home, Mike. We'll be waiting.'

HALRASHAYYA, LEBANON: Abu Hassan Nasir stepped from his hut into the bright sunshine and cold air of the Lebanon Mountains. He stood for a moment, his eyes searching for

Ivan Brevig. He spotted him playing backgammon with a small boy three huts away.

Brevig looked up as Abu Hassan approached. It was the first time the old Arab had left the hut since learning of the death of his son.

Brevig turned his attention back to the boy and his own hopeless position on the board.

'I surrender,' he said, pushing a pack of cigarettes across the board in capitulation, making the stack in front of the smiling youth five high. 'You're too good for me,' he said, patting the boy on the head.

Brevig got to his feet and brushed off his pants.

'That one beats all the old men of the village,' Abu Hassan said with a smile. 'You never really had a chance, I'm afraid.'

'You could have told me that sooner. That was my last pack of American cigarettes. He would have taken my pipe next,' Brevig joked.

'Come, let's walk awhile,' Abu Hassan said to the Russian.

They walked without speaking and left the village, following a worn trail up a sharp incline and around a bend, then through a crevice no wider than a man. They came out on to a brief level plain upon which stood an ancient Roman ruin. It was a small structure, quite well preserved. A fourth-century marble pathway led to it from the crevice. The plain was quiet and protected from the wind and the elements, which explained why the structure had stood so well against time. Brevig felt that if he concentrated hard enough, he could be transported back in time by the magic of this preserved space.

They walked into the midst of the structure, its roof long since a memory, and sat on an intricately carved marble bench. They sat without speaking for several minutes, enjoying the shared silence between friends.

'You said when I first arrived that you knew I had not come just to renew old acquaintances,' Brevig at last began. 'I feel, Abu Hassan, that we have not come to this

531

place just to appreciate the virtues of Roman antiquity. It is time to speak of Rafael Sonterra, yes?'

Abu Hassan looked at his friend of many years. 'Yes, it is time to speak of Rafael Sonterra.'

'I am listening.'

'I loved Rafael Sonterra no less than my own children – now all martyred.' Abu Hassan's eyes reddened as thoughts of Kammal filled his mind.

Brevig waited patiently for the grief to subside.

Abu Hassan fought back the tears swelling in his eyes and blurring his vision. It took him a moment to regain his composure sufficiently to begin speaking once again.

'This man that you seek, whom I also loved like a son, is not the real Rafael Sonterra,' he began slowly. 'The real Rafael Sonterra *was* killed in Gravenhage by the Israelis, just as it was originally believed.'

Abu Hassan looked into the eyes of the Russian. 'But I resurrected him. Not in body, of course. The laws of nature are stronger than the wills of men. What I mean is that I re-created him.

'This man you seek came to me shortly after Sonterra's death. In him I saw much of Rafael Sonterra. We had never let it be known that Rafael had actually died. And in this man I saw the chance to give him life again. And to this I became committed.

'I trained him carefully for over two years, teaching him first all that Rafael had known. I gave him Rafael's past, his abilities, and his future. He was a good student, in many ways as good as Rafael himself. But he had one great flaw – his anger. The anger was deep and consuming, and it took great effort and patience to overcome it. But together we did this – or so I thought.

'When his training was complete, he was surgically altered to erase his real identity. He was "constructed" into Rafael Sonterra, right down to the scars of his wounds from Gravenhage. When the surgical alterations and the healing process were finished, the new Rafael Sonterra became the teacher of our cause. In this way he was reborn slowly into the world, and his existence re-affirmed.

'Then he went forth as a soldier, with my son Kammal as his student and brother. Kammal . . . loved him.'

Abu Hassan hesitated, a fresh sense of loss engulfing him. He collected himself after a few moments and continued.

'This man *became* Rafael Sonterra in spirit and body, igniting the flame of all who shared our cause. But his anger smoldered deep within him through the years until it grew into the consuming fire that now rules him. He is no longer Rafael Sonterra. And as you say, he must be stopped.'

'Who is this man, Abu Hassan? And how do we stop him?' Brevig asked.

'His anger will stop him. It will drive him to his death. He will go to all ends to satisfy it – to the point of his own destruction.'

'Who is he?' Brevig asked again. 'And what is this anger that burns inside him?'

Abu Hassan paused for a long moment before answering.

'His name is Nelson Sky . . . the son of Asher Sky. And his father is the flame of his hatred.'

38

SAN ANTONIO, TEXAS: Michael and the team were met at the San Antonio airport by Bob Elias and Tom Danziger, who congratulated them on their work in Malta. They were also informed by Danziger of the unexpected heart attack suffered by Asher Sky. He had been moved to a cardiac clinic in Boulder, for observation and treatment. He was currently listed as being in fair condition, in no present danger. It was estimated that his stay would be at least four weeks.

Simmerman, Yelena, and Wadelaw headed directly to the control center that had been established in a small industrial complex in the northeast section of the city. It would serve as their San Antonio base for as long as needed. Sky owned the complex, and Alex offered unlimited use of it, as well as any communications and electronic equipment that might be required.

Michael boarded a Skyco helicopter with Elias and Danziger, and headed for the hill-country estate of Asher Sky. It was a large helicopter with a plush passenger compartment separated from the crew cockpit.

'You and your team have done a fine job so far, Mike,' Danziger said after they had lifted off. 'I know how difficult it's been from the start.'

'Thanks,' Michael replied. 'There have been a lot of good people working on this with us. They all deserve to be commended. I don't know if we could have done it without the help of Max and his people. They're among the best I've ever worked with.'

Michael pulled the shoulder bag containing the recovered Luxus vials from his arm, and held it out to Elias. 'How soon can we get these checked?' he asked.

'Right away. I'm sure it will take a day or two to get definitive results.'

'Good. The sooner the better. I'm particularly interested in what's contained in the two red-coded vials.'

Michael turned to Danziger. 'Besides the three of us, who else knows about the recovered Luxus and the probe-implantation development?'

'I can't speak for Bob regarding the people in your organization, but within Skyco it's a very limited number. There are a few people on my staff whom I trust very highly and who were needed to conduct the investigations you requested. We've also had to involve a few personnel in Operations to get the implantation process halted. But they're mostly overseas, and no explanations were offered as to why they were told to do so. They were just told to terminate all procedures immediately. Alex and de Roode aren't even aware that the implantations have been stopped,' Danziger answered.

'I take it that the match-ups of Kammal's overlay and the implantation schedule were close?'

'They weren't only close, Mike,' Elias replied. 'They were exact. It looks like your hunch about de Roode was a good one. It all points straight to him. He devised the schedule himself.'

'How much *has* Alex been told?' Michael asked, turning again to Danziger.

'Only that the Luxus has been retrieved. There's been no mention of the number of vials. It's not that she's suspect in my mind, it's just that what doesn't need to be let out at this time shouldn't be. And what she has been told is being treated with the highest security. I don't believe she would even share it with her father at this point unless she was advised to. We certainly don't want to do or say anything that might cause a change in his condition. Even good news could do that, I suppose. We just aren't taking any chances.'

'And de Roode? How much does he know?' Michael asked.

'He doesn't know a thing. As far as he's aware, the implantations are proceeding as scheduled and the Luxus is still missing,' Danziger replied. 'We have a meeting with him in about an hour at the estate. He thinks he's being called in for an update, and to give a report on the implantation plan.'

'Not all of the news is good, Mike,' Elias cut in. 'As far as we can determine, all of the implantations scheduled at the time of cancellation have been held up. But two had already been made before the order went out.'

'Where?'

'One in Saudi Arabia, and the other inside the Soviet Union. Numbers one and two on the list. Both are the largest known reserve areas of those two countries and in the world. We aren't certain yet whether the probe itself was the actual vehicle to seed the Luxus, or whether, as you suggested, it was intended to be the organism we believed to be the corrected Beta. We've retrieved some probes and Beta for analysis. We'll have the results soon.'

'Assuming it is the probes, how long do we have to get good Beta into those reserves to save them?' Michael asked.

'The computers have said six days, with the count starting at midnight tonight.'

'How much will be lost?'

'At day six, assuming a healthy, activated Beta is used, the estimate is that eighty per cent can be saved. But, as I'm sure you know, the logarithmic growth possibilities of the Luxus make anything beyond day six doubtful. By day eight it will be unstoppable.'

'Do we have enough Beta available?'

'It's being collected and checked now. If it's healthy, we'll get it there in plenty of time. Possibly soon enough to save as much as ninety-five per cent of the stricken reserves. We're also rushing in clean probes to get an immediate read. We'll know within forty-eight hours if the reserves are in danger or not.'

'I sure don't want to be the one to have to inform the Soviets if they are,' Michael said, raising his eyebrows.

'That'll be my job,' Danziger said, the expression on his face requiring no further comment. The job had become his by default when Sky was incapacitated.

'Yeah, good luck,' Michael returned, shaking his head.

Danziger looked out the window at the hilly terrain below. 'We'll be landing soon. There's someone down there waiting very, very anxiously to see you. You'll have a few minutes to say hello. But keep it short,' Danziger advised. 'We don't want to keep de Roode waiting a minute longer than we have to. I've compiled a dossier that I'd like you to read prior to the meeting.'

'Fine,' said Michael, leaning over to look out the window. It had been five weeks since he had seen Alex.

He knew that she was safe and well. Wadelaw had filled him in with a few sketchy details of the ordeal she had been through, assuring him that she was fine. Wadelaw had saved her, and Michael knew that much. It was a debt he could never repay.

The helicopter swung in low over the estate, approaching the helipad from the east. Michael could see Alexandra waiting below.

'Have you provided her with protection?' Michael asked Danziger.

'Yes, but I don't want to tell you what I had to go through to get her to agree to it. She doesn't see the need,' Danziger replied.

'There've been no threats so far,' Elias said, 'but with Sonterra's plan derailed, there's no telling what he'll do next. This terrorist doesn't play by typical rules. Usually, with guys like Sonterra, when the plan gets busted, the operation is scrapped entirely. Our play on Babayan should have stopped him. So should the near miss in Sare. Perhaps our handling of Kammal and Greta Haas in such short order will drive him off for good, although I doubt it. There's just no way of knowing with Sonterra.'

'We're not through with him yet,' Michael said, as he watched the ground come up to meet them. 'We've hurt him, and badly. He'll hit back in some way – any way, just to get even. He doesn't behave like other terrorists because he's better than they are – and he's a rogue. The protection was a good move. I have a strong feeling we won't have to hunt for Sonterra any longer. He'll come to us in his own good time and fashion.' *We killed his woman*, Michael thought. *Now he'll try to kill mine.*

There was a chilling sense of resignation in Michael's words that Elias took in full measure. He knew that Michael and Sonterra were alike in some deep, dark way, and Elias had learned long ago to trust those instinctive feelings when they were offered. They had not heard the last from Rafael Sonterra. Just as Michael had hunted down Dieter, Sonterra would turn hunter as well. Michael would become his target, but only after sufficient pain had been inflicted to sweeten his revenge.

The helicopter touched down and the engines went to a lazy idle as the three occupants exited the craft and dashed out from beneath the powerfully swishing rotors. Danziger signaled back to the pilot to cut the engines, then followed Michael and Elias toward Alex.

Alex was so excited she could hardly keep her feet still, but the Sky in her wouldn't permit such a show of the real emotions inside – at least not in front of the others. That would come later. Right now, a constrained and polished executive stood erect and smiling, looking every bit the professional that she was.

Michael walked up to her and stopped. In her eyes, he could see what she was feeling, but he knew that the time and place were wrong to show anything but reserved behavior.

He set his bag down and placed his hands on her elbows.

'It's good to see you,' he said, squeezing her arms gently. '*Real* good,' he whispered.

'I was so worried about you,' she said. She let her hands go to his waist and gave him a quick hug, letting that be the limit of her expression to him in front of the others.

'I think I about drove Bob crazy the whole time you were on the *Eslabón*,' Michael said, bending to recover his bag.

'Crazy isn't the word for it,' Elias said, coming to his side. 'The man was obsessed.'

'Well, we're both here now, and all in one piece. The worry is behind us,' she said, turning and starting the group moving toward the house.

Michael knew that the worry was far from being over. But the less she knew of that for the present, the better it would be.

'How's your father?' he asked.

'Doing well, actually. This whole affair has put a tremendous strain on him. He seems to have aged twenty years in the past two months, and it has me worried. He's going to be eighty-eight years old in a couple of months, and I just don't think he has the strength to bounce back anymore,' she said.

'At least he's out of immediate danger,' Michael comforted her. 'He's in the best place he could be. They're prepared to treat any development.'

Alex nodded and forced a smile. 'I'm glad this is almost over,' she said.

Michael looked to his side at Elias, who raised his eyebrows slightly with an almost imperceptible shrug. She hadn't been given too many details to this point, and didn't know the full extent of the danger to the Saudi and Soviet reserves.

'Where's Christopher?' Alex asked.

'He's here in San Antonio, setting up the northeast command center. We'll use it to wrap up the final details,' he said. 'You'll get to see him a little later on.'

'At least there won't be any more danger,' she said, relief in her voice.

He smiled down at her, his eyes lending sincerity to the lie that came to his lips. 'No more danger,' he said. 'I have a debriefing session to attend right now. It'll last a little while.'

She smiled and nodded. 'Fine. Then we'll see each other at dinner, after you've had a chance to settle in.'

'I'm looking forward to it,' Michael said.

Elias and Danziger went ahead to the house. Michael gave Alex another warm hug and a kiss on the forehead. 'It's good to be back,' he told her again.

'You get that debriefing over with fast, and I'll show you just how good that can be,' she told him with a seductive smile.

Michael looked at her and raised his eyebrows. 'Maybe the debriefing can wait a few—'

She smiled. 'Come on, you have a meeting to go to,' she said, taking his arm and directing him toward the house. 'I'm not going anywhere.'

Michael kissed her again and headed after Elias and Danziger to join them at the house.

Tom Danziger handed Michael a file folder as he walked into the conference room. 'De Roode's dossier,' he said as Michael accepted it from him. 'In the first two pages you'll find a condensed summary. All the facts are there in greater detail in the pages that follow, if you need to refer to them.'

Michael opened the folder and began reading the summary sheets.

Dr Tunis (Tim) de Roode was born in Amsterdam in 1943, in the midst of the Nazi occupation. His father was a florist who had built a successful business that became one of the largest in the city after the war. The young de Roode grew up with all the benefits of wealth, and received a very fine education.

His parents were killed in a traffic accident while vacationing in Germany in 1962, when de Roode was nineteen years old. He was left the family business, but had no real talent for it, or any interest in running it in the successful fashion of his father. His interest lay not in flowers, but in science. He sold the business the following year, and used the substantial proceeds to come to the United States as a student at MIT.

De Roode graduated with high honors in 1967, and stayed on to continue graduate work that ultimately led to a master's degree and culminated with a Ph.D. in microbiology in 1972. His thesis work involved new and brilliant theories of genetic engineering. He accepted a staff position at Harvard, where he continued along a bold line of research well ahead of its time, his work supported by several sizable grants. Skyco was one of the major private-sector sponsors who supported his work.

While at Harvard, he met Nelson Sky in 1973. The acquaintance was made through a girlfriend of Nelson's, a beautiful young Arab girl named Dahlia Rashad. This was during the same period when Nelson was going through his rebellious stage and fell in with dissidents, Michael recalled from earlier Sky family background.

'Was de Roode a dissident in those days?' Michael asked Danziger.

'Our records don't show him in an active role, though a number of his friends were. Mostly harmless crap, long on rhetoric, short on action. A few common friendships were shared by de Roode and Nelson Sky,' the Skyco security chief answered.

Michael read on.

'According to this, he joined Skyco in 1977,' Michael said.

'Yes, he was recruited by Nelson personally. They became close friends after meeting through the Rashad girl. That friendship continued after Nelson concluded his studies.'

'From what I remember, Nelson went through a period of rebirth into the family fold, or something like that, didn't he?'

'Yes. Dahlia Rashad, who was his lover at the time, returned to her country during the Yom Kippur conflict. She stayed on after the hostilities officially ceased. In late February of '74 she was killed in south Lebanon by Israeli commandos. She had apparently gone into the terrorism business,' Danziger said.

'Nelson went to pieces after that. Asher devoted himself to helping his son through that traumatic episode in his life. Apparently, de Roode was in some way helpful during that time as well. Sky met him and liked him a great deal.

'Nelson came back strong after that. He became a dedicated student, completed his law studies, then joined the company in '75. Two years later, Skyco became involved in genetic research, and de Roode was recruited by Nelson. His judgment was apparently sound; Skyco's efforts were immediately successful.

'De Roode's record, as you can see from the rest of the dossier, is brilliant. In '79 he was made Vice-President of Research and Technology. He was very dedicated to

Nelson, right up to the time of Nelson's death in the plane crash the following year.'

'Did they ever find any signs of the wreckage?' Michael asked.

'No. The plane simply disappeared halfway between Iceland and Helsinki.'

'Aside from that dissident crowd de Roode was associated with, were there ever any other connections to radical groups? Friendships, contributions, anything like that?'

'Just some contributions to Greenpeace and a few other environmental groups. Nothing that could be interpreted as radical in any way,' Danziger replied.

'What about the girl, Dahlia Rashad? Have you run an in-depth book on her?'

'She was dead five years before I joined the company. To my knowledge, her file has never been expanded. I'd be willing to bet the FBI has one stuffed away in a dusty corner somewhere, though.'

'How strong are your contacts within the Bureau?' Elias asked.

'They're good. I can get the file opened.'

'Good. Then do that if you can. I don't know exactly what I expect to learn from it, but Nelson went bad somewhere. I'd like to find out where,' Michael said.

'I'll take care of it today,' Danziger responded. He looked at his watch. 'De Roode should be here by now. We shouldn't keep him waiting too long.'

'I have just one more question, Tom,' Michael said.

'Shoot.'

'After the initial news of the attack on the Medellín Institute, whose recommendation was it to move the Luxus?'

Danziger thought for a moment before answering. 'De Roode made the recommendation first, immediately after the news broke. In view of what was known, I supported his recommendation, as did Sky himself.'

'But his recommendation was made before all the facts were known, correct?'

'Yes, that's correct.'

'Your answer prompts one more question before we bring in de Roode,' Michael said.

Danziger nodded.

'Who actually prepared the transport case for shipment?'

'I believe that was Dr David Miller, acting on Dr Stillings's orders, which came directly from de Roode,' Danziger answered.

'Was he ever interviewed in Medellín?'

'Yes.'

'What did he say?'

'Exactly what's in the report. Twenty-four vials were shipped. In fact, when the original consignment was lost, it was he who prepared more to be sent back to the States.'

Michael looked at Elias. 'If anyone knows about the two extra vials, it will be Miller. Let's reach him to see what he knows. He may or may not be involved in this, though the fact that he's still living tells me that he's not. But we should proceed with him carefully in any case.'

'I'll take care of that, too,' Danziger said. 'Anything else?'

Michael shook his head. 'No, let's bring in de Roode.'

'How do we handle him?' Danziger asked.

'I'll establish the line of questioning,' Elias said. 'Stay with me, Mike. Pick it up anywhere you see an opening.'

Michael nodded.

'Tom, have you had the slides I requested loaded?'

'Sure thing. You can control the projections from the console at the head of the table.'

'OK. Let's have at him, then.'

Danziger rose from the table and went to the conference-room door. He stepped out for a moment, then reappeared almost immediately with de Roode closely behind, an attaché case and several rolled charts in his hands.

'Good afternoon, gentlemen,' said the tall, slender scientist.

He came into the room and took a place at the table.

543

'Good afternoon, Dr de Roode,' Elias began. 'It's good to see you again. I'm glad you could join us on such short notice.'

'I'm glad to be of assistance, Mr Elias.'

'And we appreciate your willingness. Thank you.'

Elias shuffled through a stack of papers in front of him, not really looking for anything in particular. He separated a few sheets from the rest and looked up at the scientist.

'I'd like to begin by reviewing a few of the facts, Dr de Roode. Just for clarification. You understand.'

'Of course.'

'I think we're all square on the events involving the attack on the Medellín Institute sixty-two days ago, and of what transpired in the days immediately following in regard to transportation of the Alpha strain of the Luxus. So we don't really need to go back over that information. There were, what was it, twenty-four vials in all?'

'That's correct. Twenty-four,' de Roode responded.

'Let's see . . . there have been four reserve hits in the time since.'

'Five, counting the *Skyco Hippalus*,' the scientist corrected immediately.

'Would it be safe to assume, then, that five of the vials have been used up to now?'

'Yes, although it is possible to use only portions of the vials to achieve the same results. Using them in such a way would be extremely difficult unless handled by someone expert in such matters. Also, the speed of the destruction of the reserves suggests very high concentrations of the organism, so I feel sure your assumption is correct. That leaves nineteen vials in question.'

'And these nineteen vials represent the total Luxus potential?' Elias probed.

'The total missing potential, yes. We were able to grow additional quantities after the consignment was lost from the remaining stock in Medellín. We stopped its destruction in time to get more produced for our use here to develop the probes and to conduct our work with the Beta form of the organism,' de Roode explained.

'But that's safely in our control.'

'Yes.'

'And, of course, we've been kept up to date by Tom on the successful progress of your work here in the States. You and your staff are to be commended on the speed and the competency of your work, Dr de Roode. I don't have to tell you how important that is, in the face of the situation facing us.'

'Thank you. The staff has worked nonstop on the problem.'

'I know that you have personally spent time running the computer simulations projecting various scenarios for possible use of the Luxus, and that you have formulated a plan of deployment for the insertion of probes to detect its use against the major reserves of the world.'

'Yes I have,' de Roode answered, reaching for a rolled chart. 'I have with me a diagram outlining that plan,' he said, starting to unroll it.

'I think I can help matters a bit,' Elias said, activating the viewing screen on the wall behind him. He hit the button to bring the appropriate slide into common view.

'Is this what you have?' he asked.

De Roode looked at the projection. It was a duplicate of his sheet, showing a global map with the world's reserve sites numbered in order of insertion sequence.

'Yes, that's it.'

'You've assigned a number to each site. I presume this indicates the relative importance or vulnerability of the sites?'

'Yes.'

'And you've based this upon the sizes of the reserves?'

'Yes.'

Michael rose to his feet and approached the screen. Elias sensed that he had found his opening, and held back any immediate questions.

'Is this kind of information available to the general public?' Michael asked.

'To a degree, yes. The relative location of known reserves, as well as projected quantities of fossil fuel, can be obtained by conducting detailed research through geological libraries.'

'I see. So it's possible that whoever is controlling the Luxus could be in possession of the same information you've generated here?' Michael went on.

'Yes and no,' de Roode replied. 'The relative locations of these reserves could be charted, but I've included certain interrelationships existing between these reserves that would not be available to general information sources.'

'I seem to remember hearing you explain that once already, but I don't think I'm quite clear on what you mean, exactly.'

'Well, it's a bit complicated, but in general I've taken into account the many ways in which these reserves interconnect with one another. This can be by underground streams, oil-soaked fissures, even rivers of raw petroleum. A reserve is generally thought of as a massive pool of oil, sitting in a static pocket. This isn't entirely true, though for the most part it is. In the more oil-predominant areas, there exist very intricate and complex passages, if you will. Some of these are like major arteries, others like tiny veins. But the networks exist. There are even finer, seemingly insignificant factors, like porous rock structures and sand deposits containing very low levels of fossil fuel that are insignificant to the reserve status in a more conventional sense. But to the Luxus, these would be as useful as a system of highways and country roads would be to someone in a car,' the scientist explained.

'Then what you're saying is that you've taken into account all of these factors to arrive at your chart, and that even a diligent researcher using information available through published sources wouldn't be able to match what you've prepared here?' Michael asked.

'I don't think that would be possible. Obviously we can't detect, or even predict, all of the possible ways in which these reserves interconnect. In some cases these inter-connections are theoretical, based upon our knowledge of subterranean geological structure. There are certainly some overestimates of these likely relationships. But in view of the situation, it is better to predict more inter-connections than fewer.'

'I think I understand this more clearly now,' Michael said, turning away from the screen and facing de Roode.

'Perhaps you could answer just one more simple question for me.'

'Surely,' de Roode responded.

'When did you first meet Rafael Sonterra?' he asked bluntly.

There was a deathly silence in the room as the color drained from de Roode's face.

Michael waited patiently for his reply.

'Excuse me?' de Roode said weakly, his face a mask of disbelief.

'I think the question is plain enough. When did you first meet Rafael Sonterra?' Michael repeated.

'I . . . have nev . . . never met him,' de Roode stammered, his composure completely gone.

'We know better, Tim,' Michael told him. 'Hit the over-lay, Bob,' he said.

Elias advanced the projection to the next slide, which showed de Roode's chart with Kammal's overlay super-imposed on it.

De Roode stared in disbelief at the slide.

'Do you know what you're looking at?' Michael asked the scientist.

De Roode did not respond.

'We caught up with Kammal Nasir in France, Tim. We recovered this from his effects. At first we didn't know what it was. But a little hard work and good thinking put it together quickly enough. He was carrying an overlay. I'd say it's a pretty good match, wouldn't you?' Michael said calmly.

De Roode's face had gone from white to light green. His hands clenched and fidgeted on the tabletop.

'You said yourself that no one could match your chart exactly. Yet here it is – exact to the smallest detail. A bit more than chance, I think.'

'That doesn't mean a thing,' de Roode said quickly, nervously.

'We think it does. We also caught up with Greta Haas – and what we found was even more significant. We found the Luxus, Tim. Twenty-four vials of Alpha – and two that we're not sure of. *Twenty-six* vials. You engineered the hits.'

'I don't know what you're talking about,' de Roode said, his voice all panic.

'What's in the other two vials, Tim?' Michael asked.

'I . . . don't know anything. I . . . I want a lawyer. I'm not going to say another word without a lawyer present.'

'You don't need a lawyer, Tim,' Michael told him. 'You need *us*. You need protection.'

De Roode's eyes shot nervously from Michael to Danziger, then to Elias.

'Kammal carried a notebook,' Elias began. 'In that notebook are details of Sonterra's plan. Details you aren't aware of. One of them concerns you.'

De Roode looked at him questioningly.

'I can give you other names in that section of the notebook, but they probably wouldn't mean anything to you – except that they're all dead. *All dead*, Tim. A neat little list of loose ends in need of trimming. Your name is on that list,' Elias told him. 'Code name January.'

'*No!*' de Roode shot out.

Elias nodded. 'Yes! *Your* name. You're nothing but a loose end to Sonterra. And, like the others, your fate was decided long ago. It's in the book, Tim. The same symbol beside it as beside the others – *all* dead now – by Sonterra's doing.'

'He wouldn't—'

'I assure you he would, and he *will* if you don't accept our protection,' Elias said.

De Roode let his head hang in defeat.

548

'We've stopped the insertion of the probes,' Michael picked up. 'It *is* the probes, isn't it?'

De Roode's lips started to tremble, and perspiration covered his face. He nodded slowly. 'It's too late,' he said in a whisper that was barely audible. 'I know that at least two probes have already been put in place. They can't be stopped.'

'What about the Beta?' Michael asked.

'It . . . it's useless,' de Roode responded weakly.

'You did complete the work with the Beta, didn't you?' Michael asked.

De Roode nodded again slowly. 'Yes, the work was completed. But I irradiated the vials before they were shipped,' he said, tears welling in his eyes.

Elias looked to Michael for an explanation.

Michael frowned and shook his head. 'The Beta is useless. He's destroyed it with radiation,' he said.

'We can't stop it?' Danziger asked, his voice near panic.

Michael squinted, his brain racing. 'The two vials,' he said suddenly. 'We recovered twenty-six vials, Tim. What's in the other two?'

De Roode looked up, a glimmer of hope in his eyes. 'They contain Beta – but in a very raw form. Our work on the Beta was more advanced than I let it be known. It's not refined . . . I'm not even sure it would work,' he said.

'Can it be tested?' Michael asked.

'Yes,' de Roode responded. 'We have Alpha to try it against.'

'How soon can we know?'

'Within forty-eight hours,' the scientist replied.

Elias looked at his watch. 'The vials are already on a plane headed back to our labs. I can turn it around and have the vials back here within an hour,' Elias said.

'Forty-eight hours,' Michael said, speaking more to himself than to the others. 'Another twenty-four to get it in place and inserted into the reserves. We can just make it. We can still save the reserves,' he said.

'I'll get the plane turned immediately,' Elias said. 'How

long will you need to prepare your testing procedures?' he asked de Roode.

'I can be ready by the time it arrives,' de Roode replied.

'It's the only chance we have,' Michael told the others. 'Put de Roode under protective custody. Sonterra is still alive and he knows we've recovered the twenty-six vials. He'll try to stop any chance that we have.'

'He'll come,' said de Roode. 'He knows about these things. And he . . . he'll come . . . for his father.'

'What do you mean, "he'll come for his *father*"?' Michael asked.

'It's not only the destruction of the reserves that Rafael Sonterra is after. That was only part of his plan.'

'What are you saying?'

De Roode looked up. 'He'll stop at nothing to destroy his father. That, more than anything else, is what drives him. He won't stop until he sees Asher Sky dead.'

'*Asher Sky?*' Michael asked.

De Roode nodded. 'Rafael Sonterra . . . is Nelson Sky.'

39

Bob Elias and Tom Danziger walked back into the conference room at the Sky estate, rejoining Michael.

'We've called the Intel-Trace Learjet,' Elias began. 'It's turned around and we'll have the Beta vials back in San Antonio in about an hour.'

'And de Roode is headed for Skyco Center right now to prepare for the necessary testing,' Danziger added. 'He's under tight security, and the Center has been put on double alert status.'

'I hope de Roode can be trusted,' Elias said to the others.

'I don't see that we have much choice, Bob,' Michael

replied. 'If the Beta isn't viable, or capable of stopping the Luxus, then it's over as far as the stricken reserves are concerned. We take the loss and consider ourselves lucky that the rest of the implants were stopped in time. If it *is* viable, then de Roode is our best chance of learning quickly whether it will stop the Luxus in time. We just don't have enough experience with the Beta to make that determination ourselves.'

'But can he be trusted to tell the truth?' Elias asked.

'I think he can,' Michael answered. 'He's frightened, and he wants to stay alive. He also knows it's up to us to keep him that way. That should guarantee his cooperation. He'll need round-the-clock protection until his work is completed and Sonterra can be stopped. We have to put him somewhere safe, and the estate may not be the best place to keep him.'

'We won't want to keep him at his place, either,' Elias added.

Danziger thought for a moment. 'There's a special VIP suite at the Hyatt in town. It was designed as a secure location for visiting presidents and dignitaries. The entire top floor can be closed off, with access only by use of special keys in the elevators and stairways. We can lock out selected elevators and control the whole floor. We can also monitor his movements throughout the suite with video security cameras.'

'Can we get the floor closed off on such short notice?' Michael asked.

'If Skyco wants the floor closed off, it gets closed off,' Danziger replied. 'We simply move any guests already on the floor to new rooms. We'll pay for any inconvenience.'

'Then let's make the arrangements,' Elias said. 'We'll get plenty of security on the floor and throughout the hotel. We'll control all access points and watch the entrances.'

'What about his work at the Center?' Michael asked.

'No problem,' Danziger replied. 'The Center is closed for an extended Christmas holiday and through the weekend. Security has already been doubled, and the technical wing can be closed off at the start of business on Monday. We'll keep it closed until his work is completed. We'll put him under heavy security while transporting him to and from the Center. We'll use one of Skyco's limos. They're bullet-proofed and armored to withstand conventional small arms attack, even explosives. When his job is done, we'll simply hold him under tight watch at the Hyatt until other arrangements can be made for him.'

'We'll get him out of San Antonio at the first opportunity,' Elias said. 'He can be made quite comfortable at the Intel-Trace Intelligence Central complex. We can also set him up for any additional lab work that might be necessary. We can move in the specialized equipment that he'll require.'

'That sounds good to me,' Michael said. 'In the meantime, I suggest we keep Alex at the estate for her own protection.'

'We had better put tight security around the estate. Sonterra grew up here and no doubt knows every inch of it,' Danziger advised.

'Can we really keep him out?' Michael asked.

'I don't know. But I'll make the arrangements to at least try,' Danziger said.

'When and why did Sonterra develop such hatred for his father?' Michael asked.

Danziger thought for a moment before trying to answer the question. 'There was never a normal relationship between them,' he began. 'It goes back to Nelson's early childhood and the difficulties between his parents. Sky forcibly separated the children from their mother because of these difficulties, and Nelson was devoted to his mother. He was only a young boy, but not too young to see the effect it had on her, and to feel his own deprivation. He watched her life being destroyed in stages by his father, without ever understanding the reasons behind it. He watched the power of Asher Sky crush out her spirit and her will to live, until she could no longer stand it. She killed herself. The children and the maid found her body.

She had shot herself in the head,' Danziger explained.

'Was there ever any question of foul play?' Michael asked, covering ground already gone over with Elias. Perhaps there was more to it.

'There were the usual investigations, but the final determination was suicide. The look on your face says you have problems with that.'

'I've seen pictures of her from the Sky family dossier. She was a very beautiful woman, even right up to the time of her death. Beautiful women seldom end their lives in a messy fashion – like a gunshot wound to the head. There are cleaner ways to die, like pills, or sitting in a car in a garage, with the engine running. They don't blow holes in their heads and leave half of their brains on the rug. Most beautiful women are vain about their looks, even at the end.'

'As I said, there were investigations, but the verdict was always suicide,' Danziger replied. 'But it still translated in the same way in the mind of a small boy. Whether she killed herself or was killed by someone else, Sky was the cause of it in young Nelson's mind. He had watched his mother being beaten down and destroyed. The hatred is understandable. He just never came to terms with it.

'The death of Dahlia Rashad must have triggered something inside his head. Sky was a strong supporter of Israel. Nelson could have attributed her death to him as well.'

'That's when he made his decision to destroy his father,' Elias surmised. 'He didn't know how – or when – just that someday he would find a way. So he fell back into the fold to get to know his father better so that he could find a way to get even. He killed a little bit of him first by making him think his son was dead. It wasn't enough to just do it quickly.'

'He wouldn't have been the first kid to take a gun and kill his father,' Michael said.

'That's true. But I think something inside wouldn't let him do that. The Sonterra identity provided the way. He became another man so that Nelson Sky wouldn't have to deal with it. He became a man who dealt in death. And he became that man entirely, killing without remorse or hesitation. Then, through de Roode, he found the way to destroy not only Sky, but his empire as well. And he wants Sky to *see* it die before facing death himself in payment for causing the death of Nelson's mother. I'm sure that in the twisted logic of that brain, blame for the deaths of Kammal and Greta Haas has also been attributed to Sky in some way.'

'We're going to have to stop him before he gets the chance,' Danziger said. 'Sky is one of the most important people in the world. His philanthropy has helped millions to find a better life, and his work isn't yet done.'

'Nelson never saw him in that light,' Michael said. 'He was too blinded by the pain and anger over his mother. And now he's driven by his passion. There's no worse enemy than one who has a cause he's willing to die for.'

Elias nodded his agreement. 'Then let's make it our job to stop him *before* he gets to Asher Sky.'

Michael lay awake in the darkness, unable to sleep. He looked at the clock on the table beside the bed. It was 4.30 a.m. and his meeting with Elias and Danziger wasn't for another hour. He rolled out of bed gently so as not to disturb Alex.

He stood beside the bed and looked down at her. How beautiful she was, he thought. It was good to be with her again, after all they had both been through. He knew how very much he cared for her.

He wondered about what must have gone through the mind of Sonterra when Greta Haas – along with their unborn child – was killed in Malta. Michael thought about how he had felt when his sister had been murdered. He remembered with crystalline clarity the pain and anger – and the determination that had filled him to take revenge against Dieter. He knew that Sonterra was feeling the same thing right now, and he knew how determined he would be. Michael couldn't help feeling *some* sympathy for him.

But the feeling left him quickly. There was no place for sympathy. Sonterra was a machine without sympathy or conscience, and the fact that he could feel pain made him no more human. His sole reason for existence now was to kill – to kill all those responsible in any way for his pain. And Michael was also responsible, they were all responsible.

He showered and dressed, then left the cottage. Elias was waiting for him in the darkness by the pool.

'Good morning, Mike,' Elias said.

'It's an early one, anyway,' Michael returned.

'I've just spoken with Danziger,' Elias began. 'He'll meet us up at the house. The first word from the Center is that the two vials of Beta are viable. De Roode is starting his tests this morning to determine its effectiveness against the Luxus. We'll know by midday tomorrow how effective it will be. Assuming the best, we can have the vials on their way in time to get them in place by day four of the countdown. We won't know how much of the reserves will be lost until de Roode finishes his tests.'

Michael nodded. 'Let's hope the news stays good.'

'Max has been setting up teams to put throughout the city, but I don't have to tell you the chances of their finding Sonterra are almost nonexistent.'

'I don't think we'll find him until he's ready to come to us,' Michael said. 'But we'll need the teams in position anyway. At least we'll be able to respond quickly to any part of the city.'

'Do you think he'll create a diversion?'

'Yes. He'll also raise a challenge to catch him if we can. He'll want us running all over the place, if he can manage it, if for no other reason than to spread us out. He wants revenge on us as well as on Sky. By spreading us out, he can deal with us one at a time. That's been his MO from what Max and Yelena have told us.'

'If we only knew when he would get here,' Elias said as they began walking toward the house.

555

'He's already here, Bob. I can't explain why, but I can *feel* when he's near. He's here. I know it.'

They spent the morning at Skyco Center watching de Roode set up his series of tests that would determine whether the Beta organism was capable of halting the destructive action of the Luxus.

They left Skyco Center and de Roode to his work and joined Moshe Simmerman at the control center set up in the northeast part of town. They reviewed Simmerman's plans and went over the handling of de Roode when he wasn't at the Center.

Simmerman was in agreement with Michael's belief that Sonterra would create some kind of diversion. Knowing Sonterra the way he did, he warned them that it would probably be something particularly nasty.

Day one of the six-day countdown ended uneventfully, but with the hope that de Roode's work with the Beta form of the Luxus would bear positive results and offer some way to save the stricken reserves.

Day two of the countdown began much the same as day one, with Michael, Elias, and Danziger arriving at Skyco Center early to get firsthand news of de Roode's progress.

It was almost noon when Michael joined the others in Danziger's office. The atmosphere was tense among the men waiting there for de Roode's report. Moshe Simmerman had arrived only a short time before, and was only vaguely aware of the details of what was going on at the Center.

'De Roode has just confirmed that it *will* work,' Danziger announced.

Michael slapped the table, letting out a loud whoop of victory.

Elias took Michael's hand and pumped it joyously. 'That's great, great news,' he said, breaking into a wide grin.

Simmerman sat back quietly, watching the celebrations.

'It's a bit sluggish,' Danziger began, 'but he feels confident that its metabolism can be speeded up considerably by enriching it for twenty-four hours at the reserve sites prior to its insertion. He feels that the time lost waiting for the enrichment process to be completed will be more than compensated for. The enrichment process will enable the Beta to achieve the accelerated growth phase in the logarithmic curve almost two days sooner than if the Beta were to be inserted as it is now.'

'Does this mean that the losses to the reserves will be reduced?' Elias asked.

'He'll be able to answer that more accurately after one final reading in the morning. Right now he estimates a loss no greater than twenty-one per cent if the insertion is made as late as day six, with as little as eleven per cent if it's made by day four. This isn't exactly the same organism, so the numbers are off from the original estimates by a little bit.'

'This is only day two,' Danziger said. 'When can we ship the vials?'

'As soon as his final readings are taken in the morning. Assuming the enrichment process can be started at each site immediately, we should be able to insert the Beta before the end of day four. Based upon what he learns tomorrow, he'll be able to give us a more accurate assessment of the final losses.'

'What if you weren't to wait the extra day for the enrichment?' Simmerman asked, finally connecting what the conversation was all about.

Danziger shook his head. 'We'd probably lose forty per cent at day four, and maybe lose it all at day six. The head start would be too great for the unenriched Beta to catch up.'

'Finding that consignment in Malta has just saved the world a huge part of its oil reserves,' Elias said. 'I have to congratulate everyone involved on a fine job again.'

'Now all that remains is to stop Sonterra,' Simmerman said.

The phone rang and Danziger answered it immediately. 'Danziger,' he said into it.

He looked up at Elias. 'Yeah, Steve, go ahead.

'Bureau contact,' he whispered to Elias, covering the mouthpiece.

Danziger listened for some time, writing notes in a quick, self-styled shorthand. He looked at Elias and gave him a short thumbs up.

'Yeah, that's good, Steve. It's enough. It's just what I needed. Thanks a million.' He hung up the phone.

'We know a lot of this already,' Danziger said. 'But we got something very valuable. The Rashad girl's real name was Dahlia Nasir. She was Kammal's sister.'

'Rafael Sonterra – *both* Rafael Sonterras – were trained by Abu Hassan Nasir, Kammal's father,' Simmerman told the others. 'Israeli intelligence has reported that Ivan Brevig of the Soviet GRU was seen in Lebanon. He went to the village of Halrashayya, possibly to see Abu Hassan Nasir.'

'When?' Elias asked.

'He arrived last Wednesday – after Kammal was killed in Paris. He left Halrashayya on Friday.'

Elias grunted. 'We don't need a crystal ball to know what he was doing there. The Soviets have learned the identity of this Rafael Sonterra. They're not stupid, either. They'll be here. We can count on that.'

'I don't see any threat from them at this point, Bob,' Michael said. 'We've already recovered the Luxus, so we don't face the danger of losing it to them. They'll just improve our odds of stopping Sonterra.'

'I agree with Mike's assessment,' Danziger told the group. 'They'll need the Beta to prevent total loss of their oil. We can't let the Russian reserve go down. It's our responsibility to save it.'

'You're right,' Elias said. 'I guess if they really want to get their hands on some Luxus strain, all they have to do is sip it out of their own reserve.'

'Not necessarily,' Danziger replied. 'They have yet to be

informed that the reserve is in jeopardy. We may be able to delay that news until the very last moment. Once the Beta has been seeded, any Luxus drawn out will also contain Beta. They'll end up with nothing – except a healthy reserve.'

'OK. We'll continue as originally planned, then. We'll have to alert all of our teams to the possibility of a Soviet presence and instruct them to avoid hostilities,' Elias said.

'Tolvanin will bring them in,' Simmerman said. 'There may be some advantage in contacting him. They may know things that we don't. If we can coordinate their teams with our own, we will surely better our own chances of success.'

'We'll have to *find* Tolvanin before we can contact him,' Elias pointed out.

Simmerman smiled his tired smile and lit a cigarette. 'You leave that part to me.'

The Skyco limo glided up to the brightly lit Hyatt entrance and stopped. Security personnel exited every door of the vehicle but the driver's, joining still more personnel already positioned outside the lobby entrance. All eyes sharpened, checking the windows and rooftops that were within view, as well as every face on the street. De Roode exited the car and was quickly flanked by security, who hurried him into the building.

Danziger followed the group in and gave a reassuring nod to Michael and Elias, who had arrived earlier and were standing farther back in the lobby area.

De Roode was led to the right, toward the bank of elevators. Only two of the cars were able to reach the top floor. The others had been locked out with the key switches. One was being held by Wadelaw. Danziger checked off with a wave to Wadelaw and moved to join Michael and Elias.

Three security personnel entered the elevator first, followed by de Roode. He was in turn followed by Wadelaw and another agent; both took positions in front of the scientist, facing the doors. Wadelaw inserted the key opening access to the top floor and pushed the button. The doors closed and the elevator began to move upward.

At almost that exact moment, there was a concussive explosion from somewhere outside the hotel, in the Riverwalk area – a brief shudder of intense vibration, then silence.

'What the hell was that?' Danziger asked.

'An explosion, outside of the building,' Michael said, pointing down to the Riverwalk level of the lobby, one floor below.

They could see heads turned to the right. People stood frozen in disbelief. Others turned away in horror at what their eyes had seen. Few, if any, moved in the direction of the blast.

Elias looked up to the elevator. Wadelaw had hit the emergency stop button and was staring down at him through the glass-sided elevator from two floors above. Elias jerked his thumb upward twice. De Roode had to be taken to the secured floor as rapidly as possible.

Wadelaw released the emergency stop and the elevator moved upward once more.

'How do we get down there?' Michael asked, pointing to the doors leading to the Riverwalk.

'Elevator,' Danziger replied, indicating an elevator to their left, near the Riverwalk side of the lobby. They headed for it immediately.

The elevator was at the upper lobby level when they reached it, its doors open and waiting. They got in quickly and pushed the button to go down the single floor to the lower lobby. The doors closed and the elevator began a painfully slow descent.

Michael was staring through the glass sides of the elevator, sure that what had happened was the work of Sonterra, when he felt suddenly very vulnerable. Here they were, the three of them, in a glass cage, moving at the speed of a garden slug, helpless to protect themselves if trouble arose. And then, with equal suddenness, he had a realization: *The explosion was a diversion.* For a very brief moment their attention had been drawn away from the only weakness in the security arrangements – the elevators. Just as they were helpless in this elevator, descending only a single floor, so were de Roode and the others now riding to the very top.

Michael looked up at the rapidly climbing elevator. He could barely make out Wadelaw's face looking back down. And then it exploded.

There were two explosions at the same time. Both elevators capable of climbing to the secured floor blew up at once. The one carrying de Roode shattered in a searing flash of light and a loud bang. Bodies and parts of bodies blew outward as the elevator car broke loose from its cables and plummeted straight down from the tenth floor. It crashed in an awful heap of screaming metal and flying debris. The fate of the second elevator was identical, but its free fall had been only six floors. The results were the same, however. There were no survivors from either one.

Michael winced and grasped the handrail of the elevator. 'Jesus God!' he said, his mind's eye seeing that last vision of Wadelaw looking back down at him. How much had they gone through together in the past two months? How many dangerous situations had they survived? And hadn't he saved both Michael and Alex? He gasped twice, deeply, at the shock and suddenness of Sonterra's first strike, and thought how easily it could have been all of them in that elevator with de Roode.

The blow delivered by Rafael Sonterra had been forceful. Michael Quinn felt like a stunned fighter who'd been knocked down on the seat of his pants.

The explosion outside the hotel had destroyed a river taxi fully loaded with tourists. It had blown up just outside the Bayous Oyster Bar, a short distance from the Hyatt. The explosive force was tremendous. Twenty-three people were killed and dozens of pedestrians on the crowded Riverwalk were wounded.

Inside the Hyatt, all six in de Roode's elevator had been killed, along with five hotel patrons in the second elevator. There were body parts all over the upper and lower lobbies, and in the decorative pools at the Riverwalk level.

True to established form, Rafael Sonterra had begun to even the score with his enemies, one by one, in methodical fashion. He had used the diversion to divide them and to take the first. His war of retribution had begun.

'How? How could he have known so quickly?' Michael asked himself out loud.

Michael, Elias, and Danziger were in the Skyco limousine, speeding back toward the hill-country estate.

Bob Elias had no answer to Michael's question. They were all still feeling the shock of what had just happened.

Danziger had been turning that same question over and over in his head since the explosions. 'There was only one way,' he said. 'The security systems at the Center. It was the only place he could have gotten the details. It was never committed to hard copy anywhere.'

'How?' Michael asked.

'The computer.'

'But how could he gain access?' Elias asked. 'He would have to get a clearance code, somehow. How could he?'

Danziger's brain was working. 'He could have gone through his father's terminal at the Center. Sky has access to *everything*. He could have used his father's clearance code. And from that CRT he could have gotten anything. He must have used it on Sunday night when the place was empty. There's a log. It can be checked.'

'How would he know Sky's clearance code?' Elias asked.

'You forget, Nelson Sky was once the president of Skyco. His father shared everything with him. For that matter, I don't know for certain that Nelson's clearance codes were ever stricken. He could have used his own to gain access. The log will tell us.'

'But Nelson disappeared over nine years ago! Haven't the codes been changed since then?' Elias asked.

'*Jesus!*' Michael breathed. 'We're sitting here arguing about clearance codes. Don't you see it? He's *been* to Skyco Center! The *Beta* is at the Center!'

Danziger directed the driver to speed them to Skyco Center. The shock of Sonterra's first strike had suddenly diminished in their minds – and with justification. For when they reached the secured location where the Beta vials had been placed, they found them missing. Sonterra had struck not once, but twice. Once with noise and violence, and once in hushed silence. And of the two, the quieter blow was the harder, for with it he had just taken their only means to save the world's largest known reserves.

40

It was the morning of day three and counting. Michael hadn't slept all night. He kept thinking about the explosion at the Hyatt, his mind replaying the whole grisly scene over and over again, starting with that last faint look at Wadelaw so high up. Then he'd see the flash and hear the earsplitting detonation, and watch yet again in slow motion as the elevator car plummeted downward.

And then he remembered Alex's face when he had told her. At first her expression had been blank, almost numb, as though she hadn't heard him at all. But it had dissolved into one of disbelief and pain with the terrible realization that it was true. And he remembered her eyes when she had realized in those terrible few moments that the danger hadn't ended at all – that it was here and real and more threatening than ever before.

*

The morning had begun with a bracing chill in the air, and the brilliant sunshine had turned to a dark, angry gray as a massive front moved in swiftly from the north. It was now midday, and the predicted heavy rains typical of Texas winter were imminently approaching.

Michael and Yelena made their way to the Riverwalk through the Palacio del Rio Hilton Hotel. This part of the Riverwalk showed no effects of Rafael Sonterra's attack just the evening before. The portion of the Riverwalk between the Hyatt and the Bayous Oyster Bar had been closed off, and the Hyatt itself had been shut down while official investigations were conducted. The FBI had been called in because of the obvious implications of terrorist activities.

Moshe Simmerman had wasted no time in making good on his word to find Tolvanin. By morning he had been located, and a meeting had been set up between Michael and the Russian. The rules of contact were simple. Neither Michael nor Tolvanin was to be armed, and the place was to be public and in open view. Each was allowed an armed second, for his protection in the unlikely event that Sonterra had not concluded his plans for mayhem on the Riverwalk. Yelena would act as Michael's second.

They moved slowly up the Riverwalk toward the Paloma del Rio Mexican restaurant, the mutually agreed-upon site. There were more people on the Riverwalk than might be expected after the horror show of the previous night. But this was a welcome development, as it would provide more natural cover against the possibility of observation.

Michael could see the Russian seated at one of the outside tables. He approached without speaking, pulled up a chair, and sat across the small round table from the Soviet. Yelena sat two tables away. The two seconds exchanged cold glances, then began an intense vigil, searching every moving face, scanning rooftops and windows for signs of the face they had burned into their memories.

'So, how do you like the city of San Antonio?' Michael asked, breaking the ice.

'Judging from last night's news and the morning papers, I'd say it's not a quiet little town,' Tolvanin responded in excellent English. He sounded almost like an American. 'But it's a very lovely city. Too lovely for this.' He tapped the headline story in the *San Antonio Light* newspaper on the table in front of him.

'So, our mutual friend is here,' he went on. 'He has made his presence known a bit sooner than I expected.'

'You know why he's here,' Michael said, more statement than question.

'Of course. A very surprising development, to say the least. Does Asher Sky know?'

'No, he hasn't been told. And he won't be, if there's any way to avoid it,' Michael responded, not offering details of Sky's whereabouts. It hadn't been publicized, and only a handful of people knew.

'That's probably best,' Tolvanin commented. 'It would serve no purpose in the end.'

The two men fell into an awkward silence. Tolvanin picked out a triangular corn chip from the basket between them, and dipped it into the bowl of *picante* sauce. He popped the chip into his mouth. His expression changed in a way that was almost comical after a few chews, but his pride wouldn't let him protest against the intense heat of the sauce. 'Very . . . interesting flavor,' he said, reaching for the water.

'The water will only make it worse,' Michael told him. 'Eat a few plain chips. That'll take away the heat.'

The Russian smiled and took a few chips, following the good advice.

A waitress approached the table to take their order.

Tolvanin looked over the brief menu, but was unfamiliar with the dishes. After a moment of helplessness, he looked up at Michael. 'What would you suggest?'

'Why don't you bring us a platter of fajitas,' he said to the waitress.

'Chicken or beef?' she asked.

Michael looked to the Russian for his preference. Tolvanin shrugged, leaving the choice up to Michael.

'Beef. And I'll have an iced tea.'

Tolvanin nodded to the waitress, and she left the table.

'What has Simmerman told you?' Michael asked.

'Just that it may be to our mutual advantage to meet. Perhaps you would care to elaborate,' Tolvanin returned.

'You're after Sonterra. We're after Sonterra. We might be able to make it a bit easier for each other if we don't tug at opposite ends of the rope,' Michael said, not sounding terribly convinced himself that cooperation was the best alternative.

Tolvanin smiled and almost chuckled. 'You seem to have some small difficulty with the idea of cooperating with someone who is ostensibly the enemy.'

Michael just stared at him.

'I think perhaps I'm right,' the Russian said. 'But I also think that you and I stopped being enemies some time ago,' he said, daring another try at a corn chip with the *picante* sauce. The second was easier than the first.

Tolvanin seemed completely at ease with the American. They could have done battle with one another in Sare, but had not. In Malta they had even worked for a very brief time together, though it had not been planned. Necessity had made them allies then. The need for their cooperation now was even greater.

They remained silent as the glasses of iced tea were brought to the table.

'By the way,' Tolvanin began after the waitress had left them, 'I wish to extend my condolences for the loss of your friend Wadelaw. He was a talented agent. It's never easy to lose a friend.'

'Thank you. We've both lost a few friends along the way.'

'Yes, too many. Abu Hassan trains his fighters well,' the Russian replied.

'How well can your teams cover the city?' Michael asked.

'Not well enough to find him. He knows this city too well. But by combining our resources we may have a chance – very small one, I'm sure. But that may be all we'll need against him. Sooner or later he'll have to come to us if he wants to get to Sky. I trust that Sky is being kept at the estate?'

'Yes,' Michael lied. 'Forcing him to come in may be the only chance we'll have at him. We haven't had much luck going to him.'

'But enough to recover the Luxus, yes?' Tolvanin said, certain of the answer.

Michael looked at Tolvanin, impressed. 'That's right,' he admitted.

'We realized too late that it had been within arm's reach in Malta. We were too preoccupied with licking our wounds. My superiors aren't very happy that we failed to obtain our primary objective, but at least they are breathing easier now with the biological threat ended. All that remains to be done is to stop Sonterra from killing Asher Sky.'

'I guess that job really belongs to us,' Michael said.

'*And* to us. Asher Sky is held in very high regard in my country. He is considered a great *citizen* of the Soviet Union.'

There was another long silence between them, in which Michael broke eye contact.

Tolvanin toyed with another chip. 'The threat *hasn't* ended, has it?'

Michael shook his head slowly. 'No, it hasn't ended. Sonterra managed to break into Skyco Center and retrieve two of the recovered vials.'

'I see,' the Russian said, his face suddenly very serious.

'No, you don't see,' Michael told him. 'These two vials have to be recovered within two days,' he said, feeding information that had been cleared by Elias to share with the Soviet.

'Why the urgency?'

'Because another reserve is in danger.'

'Where?'

'Saudi Arabia. The world's largest. But it's potentially much worse. It is theorized that many of the great reserves of the Middle East are interconnected. The destruction can spread unchecked. As much as a third of the world's oil can be lost.'

'*Can* be lost?' Tolvanin questioned, picking up quickly on the implication being offered. Michael had specified 'these' two vials. There was something different about them.

His brain raced ahead.

'What Sonterra has is in some way different from the Luxus, isn't it?' the Russian asked.

'It's a different form of the Luxus. One that we call the Beta. The form in the Saudi reserve is one we call the Alpha.'

'And their relationship to one another?'

'The Beta can stop the progress of the Alpha if – and *only* if – we can get it into the reserve in time.'

'Within two days?'

'Basically. It must be in our possession within two days to be used effectively.'

Tolvanin looked at Michael, suspicion growing in his eyes. 'Is there something else I should know?'

'That's all I can tell you for now. But I promise that you'll learn more when we've recovered the vials.'

Tolvanin squinted hard at Michael.

The waitress returned to the table carrying a sizzling platter of fajitas over a bed of browned onions. She set the platter on the table with accompaniments of *pico de gallo* and guacamole. The food smelled delicious.

Tolvanin followed Michael's lead as he put several strips of the marinated, charcoal-broiled flank strips across a warm flour tortilla and heaped generous amounts of onion and the trimmings on top, then rolled the tortilla.

'Sonterra needs only to have patience to put the reserve and much of the Middle Eastern oil into history,' Michael told him.

'But *will* he have patience?' Tolvanin asked.

'We're going to have to hope that he doesn't.'

Tolvanin fell into silent thought as he bit into his fajita.

'This is quite delicious,' the Russian said. 'We don't have anything like it in the Soviet Union.' But the small talk did little to soothe the feelings he had inside that a great deal more was at stake than just Middle East oil.

Michael smiled for the first time. 'Enjoy it. The lunch is on me.'

'Thank you. Perhaps one day, when we can sit as friends again, it will be *I* who can treat *you* to a good Russian lunch.'

The alliance was formed, and Tolvanin was comfortable with it. Whatever he needed to know would be made known to him in good time. Michael Quinn had said as much, and that was enough for Tolvanin. Any adversarial relationship that had existed between them before this moment was put in the past. From this time forward they were committed to achieving a common goal. He would take his chances on the integrity of this enemy he had come to respect.

The temperature plummeted fifteen degrees in the short time it took them to finish their lunch. The rain had not yet begun to fall, but the air was heavy and the dark clouds rolled low across the sky. They walked back along the Riverwalk toward the Palacio del Rio, Michael and Tolvanin side by side, with Yelena and the Soviet second just behind them.

'The cold is invigorating,' the Russian said. 'I find it very interesting how the weather changes so rapidly in this part of your country.'

'They call it a blue norther,' Michael explained as they began to climb the steps of an arching stairway passing over a man-made spur in the river that led off to the east toward the Convention Center. The tourist traffic had cleared considerably along the Riverwalk due to the sudden change in the weather.

'A "blue norther",' the Soviet repeated, trying to think how that would be translated into Russian.

They started down the steps to the Riverwalk, which continued on below the Market Street overpass. The metallic sound of the arming bolt was faint against the background noise of the city traffic. But it was just such sounds that Michael's ears were trained to hear.

His eyes snapped in the direction of the faint sound, which had come from the overpass above and in front of them.

Sonterra was standing at the top of a second stairway leading up to the overpass, an Ingram Model 10 submachine gun cradled in his hands.

Michael dove to his left, hitting Tolvanin with a vicious cross-body a split moment before Sonterra opened up at them. Michael's blow sent the two of them over the ledge of the archway. Sonterra's volley of gunfire splattered against the ledge, narrowly missing them as they fell to the water below, and out of his range of fire.

Yelena's weapon was out in a flash, her eyes locked on Sonterra. But the Ingram swung, still spitting its deadly discharge. Both she and the Russian second were caught in the shredding hail of bullets. Her gun discharged once harmlessly as she fell forward.

Sonterra continued the volley, the bullets tearing into them as they fell. His eyes burning with hatred, he pumped the last of the clip into Yelena as she rolled and flopped down the steps, the gunfire stopping only when the clip had been spent.

Sonterra changed the clip rapidly and sent one last burst into her motionless body to punctuate his act of vengeance before turning back toward the street behind him to make his escape.

He stepped into the street and turned back as a San Antonio police officer rounded the corner, gun in hand. Sonterra swept a burst at him, dropping him and a cab-driver standing beside his car parked at curbside on the corner.

He spun back toward the street, stepping out into the flow of traffic. Cars screeched and swerved to avoid him, one skidding to a stop just in front of him. He raised the gun and fired two rapid single shots through the windshield into the face of the young woman driver. He moved quickly to the driver's door and opened it. He shoved the woman's body across the seat and slid into the car. The tires squealed, leaving black strips of rubber as he darted into the intersection and cut the wheel hard right on to South Alamo. He sped past the front of the Palacio del Rio and away from the snarled intersection.

Michael and Tolvanin were out of the water the moment the gunfire stopped. They raced around the archway to the steps. Tolvanin started up the steps toward his man, but stopped partway up. The second was beyond his help. He turned back and hurried to the base of the steps, toward Yelena.

Michael was holding her limp, torn body in his arms, anguish in his eyes. She had dedicated her existence to the destruction of Rafael Sonterra. She had been the sole remaining member of the teams he had eliminated one by one in sure fashion. And now, with such terrible swiftness, she, too, was dead. Sonterra had beaten them yet again, and Michael wanted to cry out in rage.

'So much for his patience,' Tolvanin said.

He grabbed Michael by the collar of his jacket and pulled him, but Michael held tight to Yelena's body.

'Come quickly,' Tolvanin said to him. 'We can't help them any more. We have to get out of here before we're detained by the authorities.'

Michael looked up into the eyes of the Russian as the rain began to fall. There was a different, savage kind of anger on his face.

'Quickly,' Tolvanin repeated, tugging again on the jacket and hooking his arm to lift him away from Yelena.

Michael released her, letting her back to the ground gently.

'There is little time,' the Russian said with urgency.

Michael rose to his feet and backed away.

Tolvanin latched a tight grip on to the sleeve of

Michael's jacket and began leading him away toward the Convention Center as the skies opened up and the rain became a sudden downpour.

Michael looked back one more time as they moved away, a last good-bye to yet another friend left behind forever. It would stop here, he vowed. The next time Rafael Sonterra surfaced to take his vengeance, it would be his last.

41

The torrential rainfall continued through the night and into day four of the Beta countdown. Nearly ten inches of rainfall were recorded in San Antonio over the twenty-four-hour period. Flood warnings and travel advisories were issued over five counties, and low-water crossings everywhere were turned into raging rivers from the massive runoff. Movement across the city became nearly impossible, and another six inches of rain were predicted to fall before evening. It was one of the heaviest recorded rainfalls in San Antonio's history.

Tom Danziger walked into the conference room at the Sky estate. He looked like a drowned rat, and his appearance only amplified his mood.

'One of the teams found this at the northeast control center,' he said, tossing a tiny microphone on to the table.

Tolvanin picked up the miniature device and examined it. 'East German,' he said. 'It has exceptionally long range.'

'That explains how he knew about your meeting on the Riverwalk,' Danziger said. 'There's no magic in how he's managed to stay a step ahead of us. He's just plain smart. And he's prepared with a plan.'

'How would he have known about the location of the control center?' Michael asked.

'The same way he got hold of the details of de Roode's security arrangements – from the computer at Skyco Center.'

'He's thorough. We have to give him that much,' Elias said.

'He's intelligent and well trained,' Simmerman commented from the corner of the room. He had been very quiet since the death of Yelena. It had been a terrible blow to him. Her death, perhaps more than the others, weighed heavily upon him. 'He is everywhere that he is least expected. Mr Danziger is right. He *knows* what he wants to do. We can only react. We are at a serious disadvantage.'

'That's not entirely true,' Michael retorted, his tone mildly confident. 'He doesn't know that Sky isn't here. If we're right in our belief that he wants to do his father in, then he'll come. He still has to come to us, to get to him. That much won't change. He'll have to come in sooner or later. He might know when and how he wants to try it. But it has to be *here*. That's where control comes back to us.'

'I don't think he'll move in this weather,' Danziger said. 'The delay will cost us at least another day. A day we can't afford to lose.'

'If he sits back for the next two days, he'll put us right out of business,' Elias said, the frustration sounding in his voice.

'He could,' Michael replied, 'but every day that passes reduces his chances of getting to Sky. We know that, and so does he. The real question is whether he has the patience to wait.'

Simmerman sat pensively, listening to the conversation. He had his own opinions about Rafael Sonterra, but chose not to share them just now. There was no-one in the room who had a greater desire to stop Sonterra than Moshe Simmerman. There were too many good friends now lying in different parts of the world in unmarked graves, deprived of the honor they deserved for their gallant service to Israel. And it pained him deeply to know that Yelena was now a mere statistic, lying in a San Antonio morgue and destined for a similar fate. Her body would be unclaimed, and the identity of her false papers would be unconfirmed. He would possibly never know her final resting place. He could never stand at her grave to say his proper good-byes and to acknowledge his gratitude and profound respect for the supreme sacrifice she had made.

'You know, we're sitting here working on the assumption that he's aware of the time clock we're running against,' Danziger said. 'The fact is, he may not be aware of it at all. It was never discussed at the northeast control center, and it wasn't in the computer file at Skyco Center. Remember, it was *Kammal* who had the overlay, which means it's entirely possible that Sonterra wasn't aware of the exact schedule of probe insertions. And he may not know they've been stopped in time to prevent further damage.'

Tolvanin had been listening carefully, and he was also beginning to make his own connections. His eyes went back and forth quickly between Michael and Danziger as his brain assembled all of the facts known to him.

'So, it was the *probes*,' the Russian said, knowing full well that early probe insertions had been scheduled within the Soviet Union. The facts continued to fall into place in his quick mind, especially those concerning the bombing at the Hyatt in which de Roode was killed, and the tight security arrangements that had been set up around the scientist.

'Of course. De Roode,' he said in sudden realization. 'He was involved with Sonterra. The Saudi reserves are not our only concern, are they?' he asked pointedly.

Elias and Danziger looked at each other. There was no point in holding back the information any longer.

'No, the Saudi reserves are not our only concern,' Elias admitted. 'There's been a second reserve placed in jeopardy. It lies within the Soviet Union.'

Tolvanin nodded. 'I see,' he said with a deep frown of

concern. 'Has my government been informed?' he asked.

'No, not yet,' Danziger replied. 'It was our hope to introduce the Beta form of the Luxus in time to prevent appreciable loss to the reserve. But we didn't anticipate that Sonterra would manage to get the Beta back into his control. We didn't want to alarm your government, and therefore did not inform them.'

'Can the reserve be saved if the Beta is recovered?' the Russian asked.

'Yes, it can.'

'But *only* if the Beta is recovered – and within twenty-four hours?'

'That's correct,' Danziger answered.

'And if it is not recovered?'

There was a momentary silence before Danziger replied. 'If it is not recovered, both reserves will be lost.'

'Can more Beta be prepared?'

'No,' Michael responded. 'De Roode destroyed all of the active Beta supply by exposing it to radiation before we extracted his admission of complicity. We have no alternative but to recover the two vials if the reserves are to be saved. The Beta must be enriched for twenty-four hours prior to its insertion. Even if we were to recover the Beta within the twenty-four-hour deadline, there would still be damage to the reserves.'

'How extensive?' Tolvanin asked.

'The Soviet reserves have the advantage of wider distribution than the Middle Eastern reserves. Perhaps ten per cent will be lost if we get the Beta in time,' Danziger replied.

'And if we fail, what are your estimates of losses to the reserves within my country?'

'As high as thirty-five per cent of all known Soviet reserves. This is significantly lower than projections for the Middle East reserves, which could go as high as seventy--five per cent, or almost a third of the world's supply.'

'Thirty-five per cent would significantly damage the Soviet economy,' Tolvanin said.

'The entire world economy is in great danger of irreversible damage,' Elias added.

'And if the Luxus had not been recovered in Malta and the probe insertions stopped sooner than they were?' the Russian asked.

'We dare not think of that,' Simmerman said, breaking his silence for the second time.

'I thank you for your honesty,' Tolvanin said.

'It was always our intention from the very beginning to save *both* reserves,' Danziger assured the Russian.

'As would be ours, if the tables were turned. I think that goes without question,' Tolvanin replied.

The doors to the conference room opened and Alex walked in, accompanied by two armed agents. Everyone rose to their feet as she entered.

'Alex, I'd like to introduce Major Gregor Tolvanin of the Soviet GRU,' Danziger said.

Alex stepped up to the tall Russian, extended her hand, and said in excellent Russian, 'Major Tolvanin. It seems that we are all friends in this room today.'

'It is my greatest honor to meet you,' Tolvanin replied. He was genuinely excited to be meeting the daughter of one of the greatest men in Russian history, a man who had known the great Lenin and had called him friend.

'I've heard the reports of the attack on the Riverwalk,' Alex said, turning back to Danziger. 'I can't begin to express my shock . . . and sympathies,' she said, looking at Simmerman.

The Israeli nodded his silent gratitude.

Alex frowned with anguished sadness. 'And de Roode? This was also the work of Rafael Sonterra?'

'Yes, it was.'

Alex had not been informed of de Roode's complicity or the extent of it. But she was neither blind nor naive.

'I know I haven't been made aware of all of the facts,' she said, 'and I can appreciate your reasons. But it's time you told me more. Why was de Roode under protective custody?'

Danziger looked to Elias.

'De Roode was involved in the plot to destroy the major oil reserves of the world,' Elias replied.

'*With* Sonterra?' she asked, shocked.

'Yes.'

'I . . . I can't believe it.'

'It's true,' Danziger said. 'We obtained his confession.'

Alex thought for a long moment. 'Then that would help explain the precise selections of the reserve sites, as well as the excellent timing.'

'We recovered the Luxus in Malta,' Elias said. 'The consignment was intact.'

'All twenty-four vials?'

'Twenty-six, actually.'

Alex squinted. 'That means the reserve hits were made with a second supply of Alpha,' she theorized correctly.

'That's right. A second, unknown supply existed, which de Roode used to engineer the hits,' Elias explained.

'That also explains Sonterra's ability to hit the Soviet reserve five weeks ago. His resources were, in actuality, Skyco's resources,' she assessed accurately.

Elias nodded.

'Has this second source of the Luxus been found?'

'Yes. And it is now under our control. De Roode had planned to use the probes to introduce the Alpha form of the Luxus into reserves all across the globe. We were able to stop all of the insertions but two.'

'Then two more reserves are in danger?' Alex asked.

'Yes,' Elias replied. 'One in Saudi Arabia and another in the Soviet Union.'

Alex recollected the details of the insertion plan that de Roode had prepared. 'My God!' she said in disbelief. 'And the Beta?'

'It's useless. De Roode destroyed it before sending it out.'

'Then there is no hope,' she said.

'That's not exactly true,' Danziger said. 'The other two vials recovered in Malta were a crude form of the Beta. After de Roode acknowledged his complicity, he agreed to work with us to undo the damage he had helped plan. His work with the two vials showed that they were viable and capable of stopping the Alpha that had been seeded into the two reserves. But Sonterra managed to take them back from the Center just prior to killing de Roode. We have to get them back within twenty-four hours to save the reserves from total loss.'

'He has incredible persistence,' she said, shaking her head. 'And he came to San Antonio to recover the Luxus and the two vials of Beta that he lost in Malta?'

'Yes,' Elias answered. 'But the twenty-four vials of Luxus are still safely in our possession. He'll not be able to endanger any additional reserves.'

Alex thought for a moment, then said, 'Tell me, Bob, is it the Luxus he's come for? Or is it us?'

There was a long silence.

Danziger's radio crackled to life.

'Danziger. Go ahead,' he said into it.

'Alarms are going off everywhere at the Center,' an excited voice informed him. 'Everything's going crazy over here. There have been two explosions in the research wing, and some fires have started.'

'He's at the Center,' Danziger told the others.

He snapped the radio back up to his lips. 'I want the complex completely surrounded with every available man. *No-one* is to get out.'

He looked to Elias. 'We've got the sonofabitch now. He's probably trying to recover the Alpha.'

'He's finally made a mistake,' Elias said. 'The Alpha isn't even in San Antonio.'

'We've got to keep him trapped within the Center complex,' Danziger said.

'And we'll have to take him alive. He may not have the Beta with him,' Elias added.

'You won't take him alive,' Michael said.

'We don't have a choice,' Elias returned. 'He's the only one who knows where the Beta is. This is the last chance we'll have to save those reserves.'

'We're wasting precious time,' Danziger told them. 'We need to get all of the manpower we can over to Skyco Center immediately.'

Elias took a moment for thought. 'We'll pull half of the security from the estate. We'll draw what's left behind into a tight perimeter around the house. Every point of access will be watched.'

Michael turned to Alex. 'I'm afraid I must ask you to sit tight here and confine your movements throughout the house to as small an area as possible.'

'I understand,' Alex replied without hesitation, knowing that in her father's absence she could become the target.

'We've got to move out now,' Danziger said.

They began a quick procession out of the room.

Michael caught Tolvanin and then Elias by the arm.

'This could be a diversion to get us away from the estate,' he whispered to them. 'I think he's coming in, Bob.'

'He'd have to be crazy to try it in broad daylight,' Elias said to Michael.

'Either crazy or supremely smart,' Tolvanin said, agreeing with Michael's assessment. 'He's going to do what we'd least expect. And the storm will provide him with good cover.'

Elias looked from Tolvanin to Michael. 'You make the call, Mike. We can change our stance with Alex and take her with us. I'll go with your instincts.'

Michael thought hard for a long moment. He recognized that he could also be wrong, in which case he'd be sending Alex straight into the heart of the danger. He struggled with the decision. If she stayed behind, she'd still be protected by the security here, and he could double back to help protect her.

'We'll head out of here,' he said finally, making his decision. 'You pair up with Danziger. Gregor and I will double back after a few minutes, just in case he's watching us. I suggest we pull more than half of the security. The more the better. If he's here, he'll hesitate less to come in.'

'I don't know about pulling more of the security,' Elias said, expressing his doubts. 'Alex will be exposed to greater danger.'

'If we don't expose her, he may not come in,' Michael said, fighting every instinct inside him. 'If he wasn't in possession of the Beta, I'd agree. But if we're right about his ultimate motive – which is to get Alex as well – he *has* to come in, and it has to be *now*. We're running out of time.'

'We're taking an awful risk,' Elias said.

'The real risk to the world could be greater if we don't. If he's afraid to chance coming in, and takes a few days to rethink a plan, we lose. If we're wrong and he doesn't come in, we'll be no worse off. Then we take our chances with you and Tom at the Center. We have to cover both possibilities.'

Elias thought for a moment, then said, 'OK, we do it your way, Mike. The ultimate goal is to save the reserves. We'll have a fighting chance either way.'

Danziger stuck his head back into the room. 'The cars are ready.'

Elias, Michael, and Tolvanin moved out of the room to join Danziger in the hallway.

'Tom, I want all of the security pulled except for four men,' Elias said to the Skyco security chief.

Danziger looked at him dumbfounded. 'Pull the security? Are you sure?'

Simmerman was standing in the hallway within earshot. He looked back and forth between them without comment.

'This may be the *last* chance we'll get to stop him in time, and to get the Beta back. We can't blow it,' Elias said.

'If he hasn't already destroyed it.'

'That's a chance we'll have to take. If we miss him this time, the reserves are lost.'

Danziger hesitated a moment. 'OK,' he agreed reluctantly. 'We'll leave one of the Skyco armored limos for Alex at the rear entrance to the house just in case. And we leave four of the *best*, right?'

Elias nodded his agreement. 'It's not Alex that he wants, ̄om. We both know that. I don't think she'll be in any danger. We can't risk bringing her to the Center. All hell could break loose there. She'd be exposed to too much danger in an open firefight.'

Simmerman turned away and walked quickly toward the waiting cars.

'I don't think we should risk that, either,' Danziger agreed, concerned for her safety.

'All right, I don't want her under the same roof with that sonofabitch,' Danziger said.

'Agreed,' Elias nodded.

'Then let's roll,' Michael said.

Danziger took care of the arrangements to pull the security contingent, leaving only the four agreed upon, and notified Alexandra to follow the directions of the security team being left behind for her safety.

They filed out into the heavy rains and the waiting cars. Several of the vehicles had already loaded up and pulled away.

'We're all here,' Michael said, looking around. 'Where's Simmerman?'

Danziger looked around also. 'He must have left in one of the first cars.'

'OK, let's hit it,' Elias said. 'We'll regroup just inside the main gate at the Center.'

Elias and Danziger climbed into the nearest car. Michael and Tolvanin headed for the very last vehicle. Michael opened the driver's door and hesitated a brief moment before getting in. He stood motionless in the driving rain, like an animal on a scent.

He was right, and he knew it. Sonterra was near. Every fiber of his body could feel him. He fought back the strong urge to go back into the house to protect Alex. It tore at his insides to leave her there in the face of the danger he knew to exist.

It had all started for him exactly nine weeks ago. He thought back to the vision of Carlos strung to the tree in Colombia, and to Wadelaw's face in the elevator before it blew up, and he remembered Yelena lying dead in his arms on the Riverwalk. And in that one moment he knew that he would do whatever it took to end this thing here and now.

The caravan moved swiftly down the private lane to the highway, then headed south toward the 1604 loop. Michael eased off gradually on the accelerator, letting the car fall back from the rest of the caravan racing to Skyco Center. He continued on for a few miles until the other cars were barely visible through the pelting rain, then eased the car to the side of the road and made a 180-degree turn and headed back toward the Sky estate.

He pulled the car off to the side of the road about a quarter-mile short of the entrance, and guided it into the heavy evergreen Texas scrub to conceal it from view. He pulled a small radio out of his jacket pocket and handed it to Tolvanin.

'We can communicate with each other over this channel without the others being able to pick up our conversation,' he said to the Russian.

'This is only a single radio. Do you have another?' Tolvanin asked.

Michael tapped his watch.

'Very nice,' the Russian said.

'This part of the estate is rough hill country. We've got a hike of about a mile to the house. We'll have good cover until we reach the manicured grounds,' Michael began. 'We can circle around behind the tennis courts and approach under cover through the gardens to the rear of the house. We'll have to be very careful from that point on; the grounds and the house are well covered by video monitors.'

'It would be best to separate once we reach the house,' Tolvanin said.

'I agree. We'll use the radios to keep each other informed of developments,' Michael told him.

They both made quick checks of their weapons. Michael was carrying the Glock 19 handgun, while Tolvanin carried a lighter Mauser HSc.

The two men exited the car and crossed the road in the heavy rainfall. They quickly scaled the fence surrounding the estate and made their way into the cover of the thick Texas scrub. They moved without speaking, keeping a swift and steady pace, slowing only twice to cross narrow but forceful runoff streams. It took them about twenty minutes to come within sight of the house.

They moved with caution in a wide arc to the tennis courts, then crossed open areas one at a time, pausing behind whatever cover was at hand. They finally reached the garden, where they were once again able to move to a faster pace through the tall hedges and winter flower beds. They came to the edge of the garden at the back of the house and crouched low behind the last hedgerow.

The Skyco limo sat under a wide portico protected from the rain. Just beyond it was the rear entrance to the house. Michael squinted into the rain, looking for the security man who was supposed to be at the back of the house, but was not there. There was to be one more stationed at the front, with two inside the house in close proximity to Alex.

'This is where it gets tough,' Michael said to the Russian. 'We'll cross the open area to the house and work our way over to there,' he said, pointing. 'There's an entrance to a basement that houses the air-conditioning system. We can get to the house through it.'

'What about the security team?' Tolvanin asked.

'They won't fire on us if they see us, because they know we belong here. But to have an element of surprise against Sonterra, we'll have to gain entry undetected. Elias and the others will be busy enough pursuing the other possibility. I'd say that if we're right, we can expect one, maybe two hours before it's evident that Sonterra isn't at Skyco Center. They'll head straight back here after that.'

'If we're right about the diversion, Sonterra will move well within that time frame,' Tolvanin said.

'I think you're right,' Michael said. 'He'll want to get

583

it done as quickly as possible to improve his chances of escape. OK. Let's get into the house, then we'll separate and set up our welcome for him.'

'You cross the driveway to the portico first. I'll provide cover,' Tolvanin said.

Michael readied the Glock and sprinted from the cover of the garden. He reached the portico and continued to the foundation of the house, where he would be out of sight of the windows. He crouched low and, turning back toward Tolvanin, signaled with his hand. The Russian, moving with the speed of a conditioned athlete, came to Michael's side and crouched low beside him.

Michael turned and began moving toward the basement.

'Mike,' Tolvanin said in a loud whisper.

Michael stopped and dropped low to the ground. He looked around carefully for the reason of the Russian's alarm, but saw nothing. He turned his head back toward Tolvanin.

The Russian pointed to a spot partway between them, and began moving toward it. Michael moved back toward the spot, both men getting there at the same time.

Tolvanin pointed to the ground.

Michael's eyes fell to the spot indicated. He saw two feet, toes downward in the dirt behind a sculptured shrub. He moved closer and saw the security man lying face-down. There was a bullet hole in the back of his head.

'Your suspicions were right, it would seem,' Tolvanin said. 'Sonterra wasted little time.'

'And now he's in the house. Alex is in grave danger. And so is the rest of that security team. Let's move,' Michael said.

'One moment,' the Russian said. He worked his way back to the limo sitting under the portico, and opened the driver's door. He reached in and pulled the keys. He held them up for Michael to see, then put them into his pocket. Then the Russian closed the car door quickly and made his way back to Michael.

They sprinted in a low crouch along the side of the

house to the basement, and entered through the outer door. The basement was about thirty feet square and contained six twenty-ton airconditioning units, each controlling a separate zone of the massive house. There were wet footprints on the cement floor, indicating that Sonterra had used the same entrance to get into the house. They moved with silent speed up the stairs to the door leading into the house.

'I'll take the east wing, you take the west,' Michael said. 'The whole interior of the house can be monitored by video cameras, so move carefully.'

'Where are the monitor panels?' Tolvanin asked.

'In the security command center. It's located in the east wing. There's another set of monitors in a sitting room off Sky's bedroom on the second floor in the west wing. I don't have any idea where Sonterra will be, but he'll probably be near one set or the other before very long. It's possible that he hasn't gotten to either area yet. If you see him, take him immediately. We have to disable him without killing him, if that's possible. He may not have the Beta on him.'

'He'll never tell us where it is. And he'll never let himself be taken alive,' the Russian said.

'You're probably right. But if there's any chance at all of learning where the Beta is, we have to take it. He'll talk if I have to pump a gallon of Pentothal into his veins.'

'If he's at the monitors and he sees us, he'll kill Alex without delay.'

'He may. But that's the moment of satisfaction that he's lived for almost his whole life. I think he'll save that for last. He'll want us, too, and almost as badly. I think we can count on that. You and I are all that's left of Malta,' Michael said.

'Well, my friend, we must not keep him waiting, then,' Tolvanin said. 'We have work to do.'

'Keep the radio handy.'

Tolvanin nodded and gave a confident smile. 'It has been a pleasure working with you.'

'Yes, it has,' Michael said, returning the smile. 'Don't get yourself killed. You owe me a lunch.'

They moved to the door leading into the house.

'What about servants and house staff?' Tolvanin asked.

'Everyone but Alex and security are out of the house,' Michael replied. 'The staff should all be in their quarters behind the garages. I doubt they'd be out anywhere on the grounds in this kind of weather.'

Michael opened the door slowly and looked out. The door opened into a hallway just off the kitchen. He nodded his head, indicating that all was clear, and they stepped out into the hallway.

'If I can get to the monitors in the west wing, I'll be able to see the entire house from one place,' Tolvanin whispered.

'That's a good idea. It could work as well for us as for him. If you spot him, advise me of his location over the radio. You can also tell me where Alex is. I'll set up close by and wait. It'll be a lot safer waiting for him to come to us than vice versa.'

'I'll contact you the moment I reach the monitors,' the Russian confirmed.

Michael clapped Tolvanin gently on the shoulder and gave him a soft shove in the direction of the west wing, then turned and began moving toward the other side of the house.

He moved slowly and with great caution. Sonterra could be anywhere in the house. Seeing him first could be the only difference between living and dying.

He checked the kitchen first and found it clear, then moved along a wide service hallway that led to a back entrance into the dining room. The double doors were capable of swinging both ways. He pulled one of the doors partway in to permit him a view into the room. It, too, was empty.

He crouched low and moved along the side of the table, staying below it to conceal his movements as much as possible from the security video camera in the far corner of the room. He stopped for a moment and checked the camera. It was stationary. He moved quickly to the dining room doors, again opening one inward slightly to permit him an inspection of the massive foyer outside. It was clear also.

Michael moved into the foyer and began heading toward the living room situated across it. This was his most dangerous moment of exposure, and he moved across the highly polished marble floors with haste to limit the time of vulnerability.

He could see much of the room as he approached. He dropped low and poked his head and the readied Glock around the corner of the wide archway to get a look at the rest of the room. There was still no sign of Sonterra or Alex or the remainder of the security team. He crawled through the archway to get out of the open foyer and moved into the room, stopping beside a cushioned armchair. The next direction would take him to the business wing of the mansion. He could reach it by going through the living room and out through the back archway.

He had prepared to start across the room when the voice of Rafael Sonterra came to him over the intercom on the wall just above him.

'I knew you'd come,' the voice said.

Michael froze, his eyes scanning the room in near panic. It took him a moment to realize that the voice had come from the intercom. He looked up at it, then to the security monitor in the upper corner across the archway. It was pointed right at him, the tiny blue light below the lens glowing.

He rose slowly to his full height, the need for concealment gone. Sonterra was already at one of the monitor stations. Michael wondered which one it was.

'That makes both of us,' Michael replied, hoping to keep Sonterra's attention away from the other monitors and Tolvanin. He pushed the button on his watch that put the tiny radio on constant transmission.

'You can place the handgun on the coffee table in the center of the room,' Sonterra said.

'And if I don't?' Michael said in challenge.

'Then Alexandra Sky dies now, and I'll deal with you next.'

'You have Alex?'

'I do.'

'How do I know that?'

'You don't. But I can assure you I'm not bluffing.'

Michael heard a loud noise that sounded to him like a heavy slap, followed immediately by a muffled cry. It was followed by a second, then a third.

'Stop!' Michael said. 'I'm going to put the gun on the table. Just leave her alone.'

'Good. Put the gun down and follow my instructions,' Sonterra said.

Michael moved with exaggerated slowness toward the table, knowing Sonterra's eyes would be watching him and not the rest of the bank of monitors. He set the gun on the table and moved away from it, then turned to face the camera.

'OK, I've done as you told me. Now what?'

'Do you have any other weapons?'

'No.'

'Somehow I have the feeling that I shouldn't trust you,' Sonterra said. Michael could almost hear the smile.

'I said I don't have any other weapons.'

'For you, anything can be a weapon. Take off your clothes, one article at a time. Drop them to the floor and do it quickly,' Sonterra commanded.

Michael began to comply, starting with his soaked jacket. He peeled off his shirt next, followed by his mud-covered shoes and socks. Then he removed his wet pants.

'Take the belt off the pants,' Sonterra instructed him. 'Then hold them up where I can see them.'

Michael did as he was told; he dropped the belt to the ʼoor and then held up the pants.

'Turn the pockets out, then turn the pants inside out,' Sonterra told him.

Michael complied.

'Now put them back on without buttoning them closed.'

Michael again did as instructed. 'OK, it's done. Are you convinced that I'm unarmed?'

'As long as you have hands and feet, you're armed,' Sonterra answered.

'Well, I'm not taking *them* off. Now what do you want?'

'Come to the security control room. Do you know where it is?'

'Yes, the security control room,' he repeated for Tolvanin's benefit. Tolvanin was on the other side of the house, and he guessed Sonterra wasn't aware of it.

'I can watch your every step,' Sonterra warned. 'I'll have my gun at the woman's head the entire time, so don't try anything. If you do, I pull the trigger.'

Michael knew that Sonterra had that in mind anyway, but he would play for every second possible and hope that Tolvanin could close in on the control room undetected.

'I'm on my way. Just take it easy with that gun. I don't want any accidents,' Michael told him.

'I can assure you that if anything happens, it won't be an accident. Now join us, won't you?' Sonterra said in mock politeness.

Michael left the room and walked barefoot down the center of the hallway leading to the east wing. He turned right into a second hallway that led to the security control room. He saw a body on the floor near the closed door to the room. It was another one of the security detail. He was sure the other outside man had suffered a similar fate. The last man was probably in the control room.

Michael stopped outside the door. Before he could speak, he heard the buzz of the electronic lock, and he reached out and gave the door a gentle push. It swung open.

Michael looked in before stepping through. He could see Alex sitting on a stool in the center of the room. He hands were bound together in front of her with heavy strips of silver duct tape. Another strip went across her mouth. Her hair was mussed and her right eye was reddened and beginning to swell. A trickle of blood ran from her nose down over the duct-tape gag. He began to seethe with rage at the sight of what Sonterra had done to her.

Michael could see an arm on the floor behind a file cabinet, and the edge of a pool of blood that had footprints through it. The last security man, no doubt.

Michael looked into Alex's eyes. There was fear in them, but there was also anger. They were fixed to the left of the doorway. And he knew where Sonterra was.

He stepped through the doorway and was struck heavily across the back of the left shoulder.

Michael fell from the blow and rolled away quickly to avoid any kick that might follow. He quickly regained his feet and turned to face Sonterra.

Sonterra did not advance. He used the tip of his silenced Beretta to push the door closed again, then leveled it at Michael.

'Where's the Russian?' Sonterra demanded.

Michael knew that Sonterra had probably watched them get into the same car from a place of concealment somewhere on the estate grounds. He could only hope that he hadn't been watching them as they approached the house.

'He went on to Skyco Center with the others. I had him drop me off on the highway. I doubled back alone,' he lied.

Sonterra squinted at him, then swung the gun toward Alex.

'Point that thing anywhere you want, it won't change my answer. He went on to the Center. The others fell for your diversion. They're convinced they have you trapped inside the complex. It'll take them hours to learn they're wrong.'

'But *you* knew.'

'Yes, I knew.'

'And you did not tell the others?'

'We both knew it would come to this . . . to you and me. There was no need for the others,' Michael told him.

'Yes, we both knew. I knew it from the moment I saw you at the Casino in Monte Carlo that it would eventually be just the two of us. Your persistence and resilience are admirable.'

'Well, then. You're here . . . and I'm here. It's me you want the most, isn't it . . . after Malta? Why don't you just squeeze the trigger and get it over with?'

'Oh, I will. And I'll squeeze it more than once. You won't die quickly. You'll have time to remember Kammal . . . and Greta, who was carrying my child. And you'll have time to remember your friends as well. Time to remember . . . and feel more pain than your mind can possibly imagine. But somehow I don't feel very secure with the time estimate you say we'll have together before the others return. I wouldn't want them breaking in on our fun. So we won't be staying.'

Sonterra was succumbing completely to his hatred, Michael realized. That was a mistake. In the business of killing and escape, there was no place for lingering. If he had been in Sonterra's shoes, he'd have pulled the trigger the moment he had stepped into the room, and he'd be long gone by now.

'OK, so we're going somewhere. When, where, and how?' Michael asked.

'We go right now. We take the armored limo. And we go where I say. You'll drive. I'll have the gun pointed at her the whole time, so I'm sure you won't try anything foolish. Give me any reason – *any reason* – and she will die instantly before I turn to you. Is that clear?'

'I understand completely,' Michael replied.

Sonterra moved in a slow arc to Alex, and pulled her roughly from the stool. He took a firm hold of her collar and thrust the gun hard against the nape of her neck.

'You know the way through the house,' Sonterra said to Michael. 'Put your hands on your head and move slowly to the limo at the rear portico.'

Michael turned and walked through the door into the hallway. He was sure that Tolvanin had heard every word. But he wasn't sure how the Russian planned to act. He did not let his eyes betray the fact that he was expecting anything to happen. He walked ahead slowly, taking the most direct route toward the rear portico. With every step he expected to hear the eruption of gunfire, but it never came. Tolvanin was nowhere to be seen.

They stepped out of the house and descended the steps to the parked limo.

'The keys are inside,' Sonterra said to Michael. 'Get in and keep your hands on your head until we're in the car.'

Michael climbed in as directed. The leather of the seats felt cold against his skin, but his brain shut out his discomfort. He knew that once they were inside the car, Tolvanin would be unable to help him. The armor plating and bulletproof glass would make his weapon useless.

Sonterra shoved Alex in ahead of him, then slid in himself. He closed the door, and Michael's hopes plunged . . . until he saw the keys in the ignition. Tolvanin had made his way back to the car without being detected. But where was he?

'Lower your right hand and start the car. You will keep your left hand on your head at all times,' Sonterra ordered.

Michael started the car, shifted it into drive, then placed his right hand on the wheel. He looked into the rearview mirror and awaited further instructions.

'Pull away from the house,' Sonterra began. 'But do *not* drive toward the privacy lane. Instead, follow the path past the cottages and toward the stables.'

The car pulled out from the protection of the portico and into the heavy rain. It was falling in sheets, nearly defeating the car's high-speed wipers.

Michael moved the car forward slowly, straining to see the path closely. It was not much wider than the car itself, and every deviation from it resulted in a skid or a slide.

Michael continued driving until they reached the stables, then slowed the car to a stop. Once again he looked into the rearview mirror.

Sonterra pointed to the left with his gun. 'The golf course is out there. Continue on to it and go past the first tee. Stay on the cart path until it bends around the green at number two.'

Alex stared hard at Sonterra as she listened to him give directions describing the golf course.

Sonterra looked back at her and saw the eyes on him. He let go with a firm backhand to the side of her face.

Michael hit the brake, sending the car into a skid.

Sonterra swung the gun, pointing it at Michael's head. 'Keep moving!' he yelled.

'Leave her alone!' Michael shouted in rage, their words coming simultaneously.

'Go!' Sonterra shouted.

Michael turned in the seat. 'I said leave her alone!' He looked back at Alex, who had raised her bound hands to her injured cheek. She looked so terribly frightened . . . but also murderously angry. He was learning just how tough she could be.

'Just shut up and drive on to the cart path,' said Sonterra, smiling and swinging the gun back in Alex's direction.

Michael turned back to face the path and stepped on the accelerator. The tires spun in the wet grass, and the car fishtailed. There was a gentle thump that caught Sonterra's attention. He turned his head and looked out over the trunk of the car. His stare lingered a moment before he turned back to Michael.

'Carefully,' he said sternly. 'I don't want this car getting stuck in the mud. Keep it on the path. It's too heavy for the wet ground.'

'The path isn't wide enough,' Michael replied.

'Then keep it moving.'

Michael started out again, this time easing his foot down on the accelerator. The tires spun again, but he controlled the slight swerve of the rear end and got the car moving along the path.

The car continued along the first fairway, passing the

green. The second fairway ran off at a forty-five-degree angle, then doglegged back to the left.

The car rocked over a bump in the cart path, and the thumping sound was repeated. Once again Sonterra looked out over the trunk. He began dividing his attention between the front and the back of the car.

'Continue past the green. That's the fairway to number five,' he said, pointing out ahead and slightly to the right. 'Keep the car along the left side of the fairway. Pull around the green and stop the car at the number-six tee box,' he ordered.

'You have a good memory,' Michael said. 'I imagine it's been some time since you've played a round here.'

'Shut up!' Sonterra yelled, pointing the gun back at Michael.

'Sure. You're the boss . . . as long as you're holding the gun.'

Alex once again stared at Sonterra after the exchange, confusion in her eyes.

Sonterra looked at her for a brief second, then turned his eyes away to Michael.

The rain seemed to be falling even harder now, and Michael inched along, feeling the path more than seeing it through the dense water on the windshield.

Sonterra looked repeatedly out the back window with every sudden movement of the car. Tension was building in his face.

Michael reached the green at number five and continued around it as he had been directed. He saw the sign marking the sixth tee, but the tee was not visible. He stopped the car beside the sign.

It was only then that he noticed the tee boxes were at lower levels. A walkway made of railroad ties led down to them.

'Now slide across the seat with both hands on your head,' Sonterra ordered. 'Get out slowly on the right side, and move away from the car into the open, where I can see you.'

Michael stepped out into the cold rain and backed away from the car, remaining in plain sight.

Sonterra opened the right rear door and eased himself out of the car, then reached back in and dragged Alex out after him.

Alex flopped out into the mud. Sonterra kicked her in the buttocks and yelled at her to get to her feet.

Alex struggled to her feet and straightened up.

Sonterra motioned with the gun for Alex to move to Michael's side. She complied. Then Sonterra walked slowly to the back of the car and looked down at the trunk lid. It was partially open. It had caused the sounds he heard.

He crouched low beside the rear taillight and raised the gun at the trunk.

'You will throw out your weapon when I raise the trunk slightly,' he said. 'If you do not, I will lock it, and the woman and Quinn will die in the next second,' he warned.

He raised the trunk lid about two inches. 'Butt end of the weapon first,' he ordered.

The handle of the Mauser appeared through the opening, then slid out, falling from the bumper to the ground.

Sonterra stuck the end of the Beretta into the far side of the opening and fired a single shot, then flung the trunk open.

The bullet had ripped through Tolvanin's calf. He grimaced with pain as the lid flew up, his hands clutching at the painful wound.

Sonterra smiled. 'What a pleasant surprise. The party list is now complete,' he said.

'Naughty, naughty, Mr Quinn. If you're true to form, your friends are probably on their way back at this very moment. Pity for you that they'll not know where to look.'

Sonterra pointed the gun at Tolvanin. 'It seems that you have a knack for survival, too,' he said. 'Come out and join the others.'

He swung the gun quickly at Michael, who had taken a step to help Tolvanin. 'He will manage,' he said.

Michael froze and took a step back.

Tolvanin crawled out of the car and limped heavily toward the others. There was a look of apology in his eyes.

Sonterra pointed the gun at the stairway down to the tees. 'Down to the gold tee,' he ordered.

The three hostages moved slowly down the steps to the tee. It was about eight feet below the level of the car and out of view from the rest of the course.

The sixth was a short par three that looked down to a green about 150 yards away and sixty feet below. The blue, white, and red tee areas fanned off to the right. They were all on different levels, each one lower than the one before it by heights ranging to ten feet. Between the tees and the green was a violently rushing torrent of water, fed by a gushing waterfall to their right. Under normal conditions it was a serene setting, the fall scenic and gentle, with the stream narrow and deep at the base of the cliff upon which the tees were situated. But the heavy runoff was channeled to the waterfall, turning the stream into a deadly, raging wash that spilled over sharp, angry rocks into an even larger stream swollen to many times its usual width and depth.

Sonterra walked on to the tee with his hostages. He grabbed Alex and pulled her to the edge of the tee overlooking the rushing waters below.

'Why here?' Michael asked. 'Is there some special significance to this place? Why not just take care of business back at the house?'

'We will have more time together here,' Sonterra began in response. 'Out there is freedom,' he said next, pointing to the hill country beyond the limits of the course. 'They'll never find me out there in this storm.'

He pointed the gun next down to the raging waters below. 'And they'll never find you down there. Oh, they might find you someday, when some hunter stumbles across your bleached bones miles from here. Then again, they might never find you for the rest of time.'

'Have you told her yet?' Michael asked, looking at Alex. 'Have you told her who is behind the surgically altered face? Who knew how to gain entry into Skyco Center without detection, and tap into the security files of Skyco's computer?'

'Shut up!' Sonterra said. He wanted to break the news in his own way. A way he had planned a thousand times over the years. Michael was attempting to deprive him of that intense satisfaction.

'I had hoped to be holding Asher Sky here today,' Sonterra said. 'But she'll do nicely.'

'Have you told her how it is that you came to know every yard of this golf course? Have you told her who Rafael Sonterra really is?' Michael pushed, driving Sonterra's anger to the breaking point.

'I said shut up!' Sonterra screamed.

'Come on, tell her. Tell her how the corporate jet never went down in the North Atlantic . . . how it flew above the wave tops, below radar. Tell her how you've planned all these years for this one moment. Tell her!'

Sonterra raised the Beretta at Michael.

'Tell her why her brother wants to see her dead! Tell her, Nelson!'

Alex stared up into the face of her brother, her eyes wide and filled with tears. 'Why?' she asked, the word muffled by the tape, but still clear enough for the question to be heard.

Sonterra snarled and looked at his sister, the hatred of a lifetime filling the dark eyes.

'Why?' Alex implored with a pathetic sob, tears rushing to her eyes.

Sonterra grabbed Alexandra's collar and jammed the gun into her face. 'For my mother,' Sonterra hissed. 'Because *he* killed her as surely as I'm going to kill you. He broke her spirit and her will to live, and he drove her to that last act of desperation,' he yelled, his anger opened wide.

'I didn't kill her . . . Daddy didn't kill her,' Alex tried to protest against the gag.

Sonterra silenced her with a swipe of the gun across her mouth.

Alex staggered back and almost fell from the precipitous ledge, but managed to regain her balance.

'I wanted him to die as she did . . . a little at a time. To see the empire that he built crumble and crash in shame, just as her life crumbled into misery,' Sonterra said, shoving Alex away. His hand went into the pocket of his jacket and came out with the two shiny vials of Beta.

'It's here in my hand,' Sonterra shouted, punctuating his statement with the laughter of a madman. 'His empire in the palm of this hand, your life in the other,' he said, holding up the Beretta and advancing toward his sister. 'Isn't it perfect?' He laughed in her face.

'So simple, so very simple,' he hissed. 'Now I can take it all and know that he'll die in the worst possible misery.'

Alexandra's tear-filled eyes grew suddenly hard. She raised her bound hands to her face as if to hide behind them. But the hands crashed down suddenly and forcefully on to the vials, knocking them to the ground.

Sonterra swung the upheld Beretta wildly and fired once in the direction of his sister.

She stiffened and was knocked backwards, but did not fall from the elevated tee. She landed flat on the ground at its edge.

Sonterra froze for a moment, his eyes locked on the fallen body of his sister.

Michael and Tolvanin used the split second of hesitation to charge at him.

Sonterra swung the Beretta to the nearest target, Tolvanin, and fired. The bullet hit him in the chest, knocking him back off the tee box on to the railroad-tie steps. He swung quickly to draw a bead on Michael, but Michael was too fast. He hit Sonterra with a hard cross-body block, and both men disappeared over the edge of the tee box.

They landed on the blue tee area and sprawled in the thick grass, sliding out of control toward the edge. Michael was the first to rise, and he leaped at Sonterra. The weapon came up and fired, but without good aim. The bullet grazed Michael's side.

The minor wound didn't stop Michael, who was filled with an incredible surge of adrenaline. He bore in on Sonterra, and before Sonterra could straighten himself completely, Michael's left arm came down and locked around the forearm of the hand holding the gun.

He rammed his forearm up under Sonterra's elbow, locking the arm rigid, then threw a vicious blow, slamming his right palm into the point of Sonterra's nose. Sonterra's head slammed back to the sound of cracking bone.

His head snapped forward only to receive a second identical blow, which took Sonterra off his feet. He skidded along the wet grass, and came to a stop flat on his back.

He looked up, dazed, his vision all but gone, to see the blurred figure of Michael rushing at him.

Sonterra struggled to get to his feet. Michael hit him with a second vicious cross-body slam that sent them both sliding in the mud. The gun was lost over the edge.

Michael scrambled toward Sonterra as the terrorist rose to his feet. Their bodies slammed together and they became a tangle of arms and legs grappling desperately for control.

Michael managed to lock the right arm once again, and used his leverage to force Sonterra against the limestone wall below the gold tee above them. He threw an elbow to Sonterra's jaw that jarred his head back into the wall.

Sonterra's left hand shot from out of nowhere with a knife. As Sonterra raised his arm to strike, Michael instinctively lowered his right hand to stop the blow, but not before the knife penetrated partially into his side. Sonterra growled and drove the blade in with all of his strength, biting deeper into the wound. But Michael's arm strength was superior and he forced the knife out of his side and away from his body.

They were now eye to eye, grunting and hissing as they matched their strength against one another.

Michael used his lock on the right arm to force Sonterra closer toward him, then delivered a fierce butt with his head to his opponent's face. He followed with a knee to the groin that caused Sonterra to wobble and nearly lose his footing.

Michael slammed Sonterra's left arm against the jagged rocks of the wall, and the hand lost its grip on the knife.

Sonterra summoned a surge of strength against the pain of Michael's damaging blows, and flung him across his body and into the rock wall. He delivered a head-butt of his own at Michael's face, just inches away, gashing Michael's left eyebrow. He tore his arm from Michael's grip and delivered a punishing blow to Michael's throat, and they separated.

Michael lost his footing in the mud and slipped down to one knee, gagging from the punch to his trachea. Sonterra threw a short, powerful kick to the solar plexus that took Michael's wind, then closed in to press the sudden advantage. He charged at his injured foe.

Michael rolled back as Sonterra flung his body at him and threw a fist to the groin as he passed over him.

Sonterra cried out and sprawled past Michael, sliding across the wet grass of the manicured tee.

Both men rose slowly to their feet, gasping from the damage they had inflicted upon each other. They circled briefly before Sonterra made another rush, throwing a strike at Michael's eyes.

Michael jerked his head back, avoiding the strike, and delivered a powerful blow to Sonterra's rib cage. There was a crack and an awful gasp. Following through, Michael launched one straight kick into Sonterra's solar plexus, then another to the chest, and another, the last catching Sonterra in the collarbone as he went down.

Sonterra rolled and came to a stop in almost a sitting position, his left arm hanging grotesquely, a jagged end of collarbone protruding from the skin. He struggled to his knees and remained there, unable to rise to his feet. He looked up, blood streaming from his shattered nose, coughing and gasping for air.

'One piece at a time,' Michael said. 'Isn't that how it was going to be? Except this time I'm the one cutting the pieces. One piece for Carlos,' Michael said through gritted teeth as he threw a kick to the side of Sonterra's head.

Sonterra was jarred, and sprawled to the ground.

Michael pulled Sonterra up to his feet and drove his knee forcefully into his groin, yet again. 'And one piece for Wadelaw.'

Sonterra doubled over with a gasp, then tumbled backwards and rolled to his side. He groaned and lay motionless for a moment. Then he rustled and grunted, straining to right himself with his one good arm.

Slowly he inched upward, his face burning with pain and defiance. He was at the very edge of the precipice, the raging torrent of water behind him.

'And one for Yelena,' Michael said as he began to advance slowly.

There was a sudden *crack!* from behind and above them.

Sonterra's jaw tightened and went white where the bullet had struck him. His neck stiffened and he swayed.

Michael saw the small hole at the angle of the jaw, and a flash of white bone protruding. Then he watched as Sonterra pitched over the edge of the tee box to the raging water below.

Michael turned his head and looked up at the gold tee above him.

Moshe Simmerman was crouched there, Yelena's .22-caliber Beretta held at arm's length in the classic firing position.

The gun lowered slowly and Simmerman straightened to his full height. 'For Yelena . . . and the others,' he said.

He reached into his pocket and pulled out Yelena's radio, which had shared Michael's frequency on the watch radio.

Michael moved to the edge of the tee box and looked down into the rushing water. He caught just a glimpse of

Sonterra's leg as the current sucked him under and washed him away.

Michael turned back and looked up at Simmerman. The Israeli turned slowly and walked away from the edge of the tee box.

Michael's thoughts went immediately to Alex and Tolvanin, and he struggled back up the steps to the gold tee box.

Tolvanin was hunched over Alex, working to remove the tape from her mouth. Michael ran to the Russian's side and stared down at her, his heart pounding with the worst expectation.

His eyes saw the miracle his mind had prayed for. She was alive. He dropped to his knees beside her, taking her in his arms. She was half crying and half laughing, her joy at seeing him defeating the pain. There was blood on her left side, just below the rib cage.

'The wound is a minor one,' the Russian said with relief. 'It took flesh only, no bone or organ involvement.'

Michael's eyes thanked him and looked at the dark hole in the center of the Russian's chest. There was no blood. Then he remembered the vest that had saved his life in Malta. He placed his hand on Tolvanin's shoulder.

'I should have remembered that,' Michael said to him. 'You have more lives than a cat.'

The Russian sat back and winced. 'Perhaps. But I think my sternum is cracked.'

'Yeah, but at least you're here to complain about it,' Michael said, smiling weakly.

'Thanks to you, we all are,' the Russian replied.

'Don't try to get up,' Michael said to Alex. 'Help will be coming soon. I'm sure Bob heard it all through the watch radio. He should be getting here any second.'

She threw her arms around his neck and squeezed him with all her might. And the tears began.

He held her tenderly and kissed her neck and cheek, then her swollen, bloodied lips.

'Michael . . .' she began, but was unable to continue.

'Shhh . . . not now, Alex. Don't say anything. Everything is going to be all right,' he said softly.

Michael looked to the ground just beside Alex, and saw the vials lying in the wet grass. He leaned over to them, grunting from the pain of his injuries, and picked them up.

'Two little vials that saved the world,' he said, holding them in his open palm. He stared at them for a long moment.

'This is what you came after, Gregor,' he said, handing one of the shiny containers to the Soviet. 'You're not a hero until this reaches the place where it's most needed.'

Tolvanin looked at him, the gratitude clear in his eyes. 'I'm not the only hero here today,' he said.

Moshe Simmerman walked over to them. 'There were many heroes,' he said. He bent forward and lent a hand to help Tolvanin to his feet. The two men moved slowly away from the tee box toward the car above.

Michael cradled Alex, giving her shelter from the driving rain, letting his body offer warmth. His keen ears heard sounds above the rain. He stood up, lifting Alex in his arms, and carried her up the walk to where the car was parked. He focused his eyes in the direction of the sounds.

In the distance Michael could see the headlights of cars racing across the golf course to reach them. Like Simmerman, Elias had picked up the transmissions from Michael's watch radio.

Simmerman had never left the estate with the others. He had hidden on the grounds and followed the car on foot.

Michael gave Alex a mighty hug. He was so proud of her courage in the face of certain death. She was a Sky to the bone.

He felt a moment of deep pity for her. The realization of what her brother had become would haunt her for the rest of her days, he knew. But he also knew the tremendous strength within this woman. She would survive and be all the stronger for it.

Max was right when he said there were many heroes

This situation would have become the worst of all possible nightmares without their selfless efforts and their supreme sacrifices.

Heroism, Michael knew, was something they would all reluctantly share. He had fought enough battles in his lifetime to know that heroism was just another word for luck. They had won this battle because they had been lucky. And in winning, they had all lost a little. No, it was more than a little, he knew. They had lost good friends and comrades every step of the way. It was a road they had had no other choice but to travel. And they would travel it again, he knew, until their luck ran out, too, in some hot rainy jungle, or in a shattered elevator, or on some wet grassy knoll. There would always be wars to fight as long as there were Sonterras to start them. The question was, would there always be heroes?

THE END

THE WINDCHIME LEGACY
by A.W. Mykel

'A PAGE-TURNER THAT I COULD HARDLY WAIT TO
FINISH'
Washington Star

Meet SENTINEL, the world's most advanced computer,
possessing a capacity many million times greater than the
most developed human mind. But SENTINEL's supreme
control over the entire US defence network is threatened
. . . for one of its creators plans to sell to the Soviets the
blueprint needed to mastermind another SENTINEL.

When the KGB send their top spy, Centaur, to bring back
the scientist's information, SENTINEL's two most highly-
skilled agents are assigned to intercept him. But one of
them – Justin Chaple, codenamed 'Pilgrim' – soon discov-
ers that they are up against more than just the KGB . . . for a
secret plot to bring about Hitler's last dream – the Fourth
Reich – has already begun . . .

THE WINDCHIME LEGACY is no ordinary thriller. It's an
intricately-woven, brilliantly complicated novel, with as
many moves and countermoves as a championship chess
match, with break-neck action and intriguing plot twists
that will keep the reader thirsting to know more.

0 552 11850 8

THE SALAMANDRA GLASS
by A.W. Mykel

'FAST-MOVING, EXCITING AND CREDIBLE . . . A TWIST-
ING SPY THRILLER THAT WILL HOLD THE READER
UNTIL THE LAST PAGE.'
Library Journal

Michael Gladieux thought he'd finished with The Group, a
highly specialised unit he'd served with in Vietnam. Three
years of hunting and being hunted behind him . . . until he
learns that his father has been murdered . . . his body found
along with a note accusing him of Nazi collaboration during the war and a glass pendant anchored to his heart with
a shiny steel spike.

Who was Michael's father? Why has he been killed? And
why are Washington and The Group so interested?
Michael's search for answers leads him on a nonstop
journey from New York to Paris to the south of France . . .
back in time to a harrowing story of love and intrigue set
against the backdrop of the French Resistance. Michael's
purpose is to find his father's killer but what he finally
uncovers is far more deadly . . .

The suspense builds to a terrifying climax, as Michael
becomes the one man capable of stopping the twisted
legacy of THE SALAMANDRA GLASS.

0 552 12417 6

THE NEGOTIATOR
by Frederick Forsyth

The kidnapping of a young man on a country road in Oxfordshire is but the first brutal step in a ruthless campaign to force the President of the United States out of office. If it succeeds, he will be psychologically and emotionally destroyed. Only one man can stop it – Quinn, the world's foremost Negotiator, who must bargain for the life of an innocent man, unaware that ransom was never the kidnapper's real objective . . .

THE NEGOTIATOR unfolds with the spellbinding excitement, unceasing surprise and riveting detail that are the hallmarks of Frederick Forsyth, the master storyteller.

'Confirms Frederick Forsyth's position as one of the world's best thriller writers'
Wall Street Journal

'Intricately plotted, fast moving and full of surprises'
Evening Standard

0 552 13475 9

A SELECTION OF FINE THRILLERS
FROM CORGI BOOKS

THE PRICES SHOWN BELOW WERE CORRECT AT THE TIME OF GOING TO PRESS. HOWEVER TRANSWORLD PUBLISHERS RESERVE THE RIGHT TO SHOW NEW RETAIL PRICES ON COVERS WHICH MAY DIFFER FROM THOSE PREVIOUSLY ADVERTISED IN THE TEXT OR ELSEWHERE.

☐	12504 0	THE SMOKE	Tom Barling	£3.99
☐	13583 6	SMOKE DANCE	Tom Barling	£3.99
☐	13680 8	BAD BLOOD	Anthony Bruno	£3.99
☐	13719 7	BAD LUCK	Anthony Bruno	£3.99
☐	13808 8	BAD DESIRE	Gary Devon	£3.99
☐	13355 8	THAI HORSE	William Diehl	£3.99
☐	12550 4	LIE DOWN WITH LIONS	Ken Follett	£3.99
☐	12610 1	ON WINGS OF EAGLES	Ken Follett	£4.99
☐	12180 0	THE MAN FROM ST PETERSBURG	Ken Follett	£4.99
☐	11810 9	THE KEY TO REBECCA	Ken Follett	£3.99
☐	09121 9	THE DAY OF THE JACKAL	Frederick Forsyth	£4.99
☐	11500 2	THE DEVIL'S ALTERNATIVE	Frederick Forsyth	£4.99
☐	10050 1	THE DOGS OF WAR	Frederick Forsyth	£4.99
☐	12569 5	THE FOURTH PROTOCOL	Frederick Forsyth	£4.99
☐	13275 9	THE NEGOTIATOR	Frederick Forsyth	£4.99
☐	12140 1	NO COMEBACKS	Frederick Forsyth	£3.99
☐	09436 6	THE ODESSA FILE	Frederick Forsyth	£3.99
☐	10244 X	THE SHEPHERD	Frederick Forsyth	£3.99
☐	13281 0	IN PALE BATTALIONS	Robert Goddard	£4.99
☐	13561 5	INTO THE BLUE	Robert Goddard	£4.99
☐	13282 9	PAINTING THE DARKNESS	Robert Goddard	£4.99
☐	13144 X	PAST CARING	Robert Goddard	£4.99
☐	12160 6	RED DRAGON	Thomas Harris	£4.99

All Corgi/Bantam Books are available at your bookshop or newsagent, or can be ordered from the following address:

Corgi/Bantam Books,
Cash Sales Department
P.O. Box 11, Falmouth, Cornwall TR10 9EN

UK and B.F.P.O. customers please send a cheque or postal order (no currency) and allow £1.00 for postage and packing for the first book plus 50p for the second book and 30p for each additional book to a maximum charge of £3.00 (7 books plus).

Overseas customers, including Eire, please allow £2.00 for postage and packing for the first book, £1.00 for the second book, and 50p for each subsequent title ordered.

NAME (Block Letters) ....

ADDRESS ....

....